COUNTERATTACK

COUNTER-ATTACK

BOOK III OF *THE CORPS*

W. E. B. GRIFFIN

G. P. PUTNAM'S SONS   NEW YORK

G. P. Putnam's Sons
Publishers Since 1838
200 Madison Avenue
New York, NY 10016

Map illustration by Lisa Amoroso

The typescript of *The Corps* was written on a Sperry
PC/AT Computer System using Microsoft Word 5.0 software
and an AST Research Turbo Laser PS printer.

Library of Congress Cataloging-in-Publication Data

Griffin, W. E. B.
  Counterattack / W. E. B. Griffin.
    p.   cm.—(The Corps : bk. 3)
  ISBN 0-399-13493-X
    1. United States.   Marine Corps—Fiction.   I. Title.   II. Series:
Griffin, W. E. B.   Corps : bk. 3.
PS3557.R489137C68   1990   89-10772 CIP
813'.54—dc20

Printed in the United States of America
     4 5 6 7 8 9 10

The Corps *is respectfully dedicated to the memories of*
Second Lieutenant Drew James Barrett III, USMC
Company K, 3rd Battalion, 26th Marines
Born Denver, Colorado, 3 January 1945
Died Quang Nam Province, Republic of Vietnam, 27 February 1969;
and
Major Alfred Lee Butler III, USMC
Headquarters 22nd Marine Amphibious Unit
Born Washington, D.C., 4 September 1950
Died Beirut, Lebanon, 8 February 1984.

"Semper Fi!"

And to the memory of Donald L. Schomp
A Marine Fighter Pilot who became a legendary
U.S. Army Master Aviator
RIP 9 April 1989.

I

(ONE)

PEARL HARBOR

OAHU ISLAND, TERRITORY OF HAWAII

7 DECEMBER 1941

The Japanese Carrier Task Force charged with the destruction of the United States Pacific Fleet began launching aircraft approximately 305 nautical miles north of Pearl Harbor.

These aircraft proceeded in a single stream until they were about 125 miles from Pearl Harbor, where the stream split in two. Fifty miles from Oahu, the left column of the attacking force divided again into three more streams.

The first two streams of the left column turned right and headed for Pearl Harbor, across the island. The third stream continued on course until it had flown beyond the tip of Oahu, then turned toward the center of the island and made its approach to Pearl Harbor from the sea. It began its attack at 0755 hours.

Meanwhile, the right stream of Japanese aircraft had divided in two as it approached Oahu. One stream crossed the coastline and made for Pearl Harbor, on the other side of the island. The second continued on course past the island, and then turned back to attack Pearl Harbor from the open sea. Its attack began at 0900.

All of these attacks went off smoothly and as planned. And at 1030, the Task Force radioed a coded message to Imperial Japanese Naval Headquarters. The code was *"Tora, Tora, Tora."* It signified success.

Fortunately for the Americans, the Japanese success was not unqualified. The surprise attack had found all of the battleships of the United States Pacific Fleet at anchor, and had sunk or severely damaged most of them. But two U.S. aircraft carriers, seven cruisers, and their screening vessels were at sea, in three task forces, and were not harmed.

When the first Japanese bombs fell at Pearl Harbor, Staff Sergeant Joseph L. Howard, USMC, of Headquarters Company, 1st Marine Defense Battalion, was asleep. He shared a room with a mess sergeant, who was on duty, and who could be counted on to bring a thermos of coffee and some doughnuts back to their room when the mess had finished serving breakfast.

Staff Sergeant Howard was twenty-four, young for his rank. He was six feet one inches tall, weighed 185 pounds, and was broad-shouldered and slim-waisted. He had sharp features, intelligent eyes, and wore his light brown hair just long enough to part. At one time it had been seriously proposed that Staff Sergeant Howard be used as a model for the photographs in a new edition of the *Handbook for Marines.*

The *Handbook for Marines* was issued to every enlisted Marine; many officers—including most company-grade officers—also had copies. Among its many illustrations were photographs of a Marine modeling the various service uniforms. A Good Marine was supposed to look like that. Similarly, there were photographs showing the correct way to execute the manual of arms and the various movements in close-order drill.

Staff Sergeant Joe Howard, in one of his perfectly fitting uniforms, with his erect carriage and broad shoulders, looked *exactly* like the Perfect Marine.

Joe Howard had been a Marine for seven years and six months.

He had enlisted right out of high school, on what was called a "baby cruise," a term of enlistment which extended to his twenty-first birthday; the regular term of enlistment was four years. At that point (he turned twenty-one on August 14, 1937), he was given the choice of being transferred to the Fleet Reserve—in effect discharged—or shipping over for a regular, four-year enlistment.

For most of his "baby cruise," Howard served with the Marine detachment on board the battleship *Arizona,* and he won promotion to private first class at the recommendation of her captain, who had been impressed with his bearing and appearance when Howard had served as his orderly. After leaving *Arizona,* he was assigned to the Philadelphia Navy Yard.

At the Navy Yard, a salty old gunnery sergeant took a liking to him, had him assigned to the arms locker as an armorer, and taught him how to shoot. *Really* shoot. Not only well enough to qualify for the extra pay that went with the Expert Rifleman qualification badge, but well enough to shoot competitively. He almost made it onto the East Coast Rifle Team (one step down from the U.S. Marine Corps Rifle Team), and he was fairly confident that he could make it the next time around.

Gunny MacFarland also got him a job as an off-duty bartender in the officers' club, working Friday and Saturday nights and for the luncheon buffet on Sunday. That thirty cents an hour added enough to his

PFC's thirty dollars a month, supplemented by his five-dollar-a-month Expert Rifleman's pay, to permit him to buy a Ford Model A.

In August of 1937 he had to choose between getting out of the Corps and taking his chances on civvy street, where jobs were hard to come by, particularly if you didn't have a trade, or shipping over, which meant a dollar and a dime a day, plus uniforms, three square meals a day, and a place to sleep out of the rain. That's what Joe had told his mother.

But there was more to it than that. Not only were there other material advantages, like being paid to do something you liked to do— shooting, and the opportunities for travel that went with being a competitive rifle shooter, and things like that—but there was also the chance to make something of himself. And just *being* a Marine.

Gunny MacFarland told him that with his record, and providing he kept his nose clean, it was almost a sure thing that he would make corporal before his second hitch was up, maybe even sooner than that, say in two years.

Joe Howard knew that Gunny MacFarland was bullshitting him to get him to ship over. In two years he would be twenty-three. There were very few twenty-three-year-old corporals in the Marines. In 1937 the Corps had an authorized strength of only twenty-five thousand officers and men, which meant that nobody moved up in rank very fast. His chances of making corporal on his second hitch were almost nonexistent.

But it was more than a little flattering to have MacFarland bullshit him in order to get him to ship over and stay in the Corps. MacFarland was one hell of a Marine, and to know that MacFarland wanted him to stay in the Corps meant that MacFarland thought he had at least the potential to be a good Marine.

Besides, if Howard shipped over, there was nothing in it for Mac-Farland, either. He wasn't a recruiting sergeant. And nothing made MacFarland ask Joe over to his quarters for Sunday-night supper, sort of taking him into the family. Mrs. MacFarland even made him a birthday cake with candles when Joe turned twenty.

There really had not been much of a choice between going back to Birmingham, Alabama, and maybe getting lucky and getting a job in a steel mill, or shipping over in the Corps, even if MacFarland *was* bullshitting him about making corporal.

The same month he shipped over, PFC Howard met the Major General Commandant of the Marine Corps, Thomas Holcomb. More or less for the hell of it, thinking that it was at least practice, Joe Howard got into his civilian clothes one Sunday, drove his Model A across New Jersey to a place called Sea Girt, and entered a civilian rifle match run by the National Rifle Association on the New Jersey National Guard's rifle range.

You had to pay three dollars and fifty cents to enter, plus, he found out when he got there, another five dollars to join the NRA if you were competing as a civilian, as he was. So he was out eight-fifty, plus the cost of gas and wear and tear on the Model A, plus the loss of the dollar and a half he would have made working the Sunday brunch at the officers' club.

He'd just about decided that coming to Sea Girt was one of the dumber things he'd done lately, when he checked the scoreboard and saw that he was leading in the one-hundred- and three-hundred-yard matches. All that was left was the twenty-round timed fire at five hundred yards. If he took that, they'd give him a loving cup. He wasn't sure if it was silver, or just silver-plated, but he could probably get at least five dollars for it in a hockshop. And if it really was silver, he might even make a couple of bucks over his expenses.

When he fired the five-hundred-yard timed fire, Joe Howard tried very hard. It was some of the best shooting he had ever done, and luck was with him. The wind was light, and right down the range. He took the match by fifteen points, and he put eleven of the twenty rounds in the X-ring.

The only picture he had ever seen of Thomas Holcomb, Major General Commandant of the Marine Corps, was the photograph of the General in full uniform, medals and all, which hung at various places in every Marine Corps installation. He hadn't paid much attention to it.

So Joe did not recognize the civilian big shot who handed him the loving cup, a more or less chubby guy, sweating in his vested cord suit and flat-brimmed straw hat. For that matter, he didn't even look closely at the man until he made an odd remark:

"That was fine shooting, son. Congratulations. If you don't have any other plans, the Marine Corps always has a place for someone who can shoot like that."

The comment brought laughter from the other big shots.

The confusion on Joe Howard's face as Major General Commandant Holcomb shook his hand and simultaneously handed him the loving cup was evident. One of the big shots thought an explanation was in order.

"General Holcomb is Commandant of the Marine Corps, son. He was kind enough to come down here from Spring Lake to make the presentation of the awards."

For three years, Joe Howard, as a Pavlovian reflex, had come to attention when greeting any officer, from second lieutenant up. At that instant he popped to attention. Because the handle of the eighteen-inch-tall silver loving cup was in his left hand, however, this proved a little difficult.

His movement caught Commandant Holcomb's eye, and he turned to look at the young man.

"Sir," PFC Howard boomed in the manner he had been taught, "PFC Howard, Joseph L., Marine Barracks, Philadelphia."

"Carry on," General Holcomb said, and then added, with a smile, to the other big shots, "Why am I not surprised?"

He then walked off with the other big shots, but Joe Howard saw him say something behind his hand to a young man with him, who was also in civilian clothing. The young man nodded, took a notebook from his pocket, and wrote in it.

There was no doubt whatever in Joe's mind that his name had been taken down. He had had his name taken down before—always in connection with something he had done wrong, or for something he had omitted. So he decided that it was probably against some regulation for him to enter a civilian NRA match.

When he thought more about it, he decided his particular sin had been to go to the armory and take his rifle, a 1903 Springfield .30-06 with a Star Gauge barrel, and use it to compete in a civilian match.

Star Gauge Springfields were capable of extraordinary accuracy, far beyond that of standard-issue Springfields. They were so called because the Army's Frankford Arsenal, after checking their dimensions ("gauging them") and determining that they met a set of very strict standards, had stamped their barrels near the muzzle with a star.

With a sinking feeling in his stomach, Joe realized that if some other Marine came to his armory and asked to check out one of the Star Gauge Springfields so he could fire it in a civilian match, there was no way he would let him do it without written permission from some officer.

And he hadn't been caught using a Star Gauge Springfield in a civilian match by just some officer, but by the Major General Commandant of the Marine Corps!

On the way back to Philadelphia, Joe considered confessing his sins right off to Gunny MacFarland, but chickened out. The Gunny would really be pissed; the one thing he could not stand was stupidity. And it was also likely that the Gunny, being the Gunny, would try to accept the responsibility for his stupidity himself.

That wouldn't be right. Taking the Star Gauge Springfield had been his idea, Joe decided, and he would take whatever came his way because of it.

Nothing happened on Monday. Or on Tuesday, or Wednesday. And by Thursday Joe began to think that just maybe nothing would happen. Maybe he would get away with it, even though the officer in civvies had taken down his name.

On Friday, just before lunch, he was summoned by the Sergeant Major and told to report to the Commanding Officer.

"Sir, PFC Howard reporting as ordered to the commanding officer!"

"Stand at ease, Howard," said the Commanding Officer, a paunchy, middle-aged major, and then handed him a sheet of teletype machine paper.

HEADQUARTERS US MARINE CORPS WASH DC
27 AUGUST 1937

TO: COMMANDING OFFICER
    US MARINE BARRACKS
    US NAVY YARD PHILA PENNA
INFO: COMMANDING OFFICER
    US MARINE CORPS RECRUIT DEPOT
    PARRIS ISLAND SC

1. THE FOLLOWING IS TO BE RELAYED TO PFC JOSEPH L. HOWARD, AND SUITABLE NOTATION MADE IN HIS SERVICE RECORD: "REFERENCE YOUR WINNING 1937 NEW JERSEY STATE RIFLE MATCH. WELL DONE. THOMAS HOLCOMB MAJOR GENERAL COMMANDANT."

2. YOU ARE DIRECTED TO ISSUE NECESSARY ORDERS TRANSFERRING PFC HOWARD TO US MARINE CORPS RECRUIT DEPOT PARRIS ISLAND SC FOR DUTY AS RIFLE INSTRUCTOR. PFC HOWARD IS TO BE ENCOURAGED TO TRY OUT FOR USMC RIFLE TEAM.

BY DIRECTION OF THE MAJOR GENERAL COMMANDANT:

S. T. KRALIK, LT COL USMC

When he had graduated from Boot Camp at Parris Island, Joe Howard had devoutly hoped he would never again see the place. While he was willing to grant that he had come to Parris Island a candy-ass civilian and had left at least looking and thinking vaguely like a Marine, he had painful and bitter memories of the place and of his drill instructors.

It was different, of course, when he went back, but he still didn't like the place.

He ran into one of his drill sergeants at the gas station, and was surprisingly disappointed when the sergeant told him that he didn't remember him at all. And he was equally surprised to realize that not only did the drill sergeant not look as mean and salty as he had in his memory, but that he was in fact not nearly as sharp looking as some Marines Joe had come to know later. He was just an average Marine, doing his job.

Howard didn't get along too well, at least at first, with the other guys teaching basic marksmanship or the ones on the rifle team. He came to understand that was because he hadn't followed the established route to the Weapons Committee. They were supposed to select you; he had been thrust upon them by the Major General Commandant.

It got better after he qualified for the Marine Corps Rifle Team, and even better when he shot third overall at the National Matches at Camp Perry, Ohio, in the summer of 1938. And in September of 1938, he came out number three on the list for promotion to corporal. He had made it less than a year after shipping over, and a year before Gunny MacFarland had bullshitted him he might make it.

Almost as soon as he'd sewed his chevrons on, he started trying to think of some way to get out of Parris Island. He applied for transfer to the 4th Marines in China, and was turned down. He could, they said, enlist for the 4th Marines the next time he shipped over, but right now the Corps wanted him at Parris Island, teaching recruits how to shoot.

Then, out of the blue, he found himself at the U.S. Army Infantry Center at Fort Benning, Georgia. The Army Ordnance Corps had come up with a new rifle, the M-1, known as the Garand after the man who had invented it. It was self-loading, which meant that it was almost automatic. It used the forces of recoil to extract the fired cartridge from the chamber and then to load a fresh one from the magazine. The magazine held eight rounds. The Marines were invited to participate in the service test of the weapon, and they sent a provisional platoon to Fort Benning in charge of a master gunnery sergeant named Jack NMI (No Middle Initial) Stecker from the U.S. Marine Corps Schools base at Quantico.

A third of the platoon were taken from regular Marine units; a third came right out of boot camp; and the final third were people recognized to be outstanding marksmen. Corporal Joe Howard had been assigned to this last group.

Master Gunnery Sergeant Jack NMI Stecker had won the Medal of Honor in France in 1918, and was something of a legend in the Corps. Joe figured that probably had something to do with his being put in charge of the Fort Benning detail; it looked like a good detail, the sort of detail a man would be given who was entitled to wear the blue ribbon with the silver stars sprinkled on it.

When Corporal Joe Howard reported to Gunny Stecker, he was

surprised to see that Stecker was not wearing his Medal of Honor ribbon. The only things pinned to his blouse were his marksmanship medals. Not surprisingly, he was Expert in every small-arms weapon used by the Corps. Joe later found out, not from Stecker, that Stecker had taken High Overall at Camp Perry in 1933 and 1936; he was a world-class rifleman.

But Master Gunnery Sergeant Stecker was more than just impressive. Best of all, he got Corporal Howard out of Parris Island. A couple of days before they left Fort Benning, Stecker called him in and asked him what he thought of the M-1 Garand.

It was almost holy writ in the Corps that the finest, most accurate rifle ever made was the '03 Springfield. Even among the expert riflemen who had fired the Garand at Benning, the weapon was known as a Mickey Mouse piece the Army had dreamed up; it would never come close to being as good a rifle as the '03.

But Joe Howard had come to believe that the Garand was a fine weapon even off the shelf, and that with some fine-tuning by an armorer it would be capable of greater accuracy than the '03. He told Gunny Stecker just that.

"That makes it you and me against the Marine Corps, son," Gunny Stecker replied. "You happy at Parris Island?"

Joe told him the truth about that, too: he didn't like what was generally considered to be a great berth for a brand-new, very young corporal—as opposed, say, to being in a Marine detachment on a man-of-war, or in a line company in a regiment somewhere—and he had been trying to get out of it.

"Would you be interested in coming to Quantico and working on the Garand? The basic detail would be teaching riflery to kids in the Basic Officer Course, and college kids who come for training in the summer. But when you're not doing that, there would be time to work on the Garand."

"I'd love it, Gunny," Joe replied. "But they won't let me go from Parris Island."

"Why not?"

Joe told him about his getting sent there by the Major General Commandant.

"I'll see what I can do," Stecker said.

Two weeks after he reported back into Parris Island, Joe was put on orders to U.S. Marine Corps Schools, Quantico, Virginia.

The next year was good duty. Aside from maybe once a month catching Corporal of the Guard, and maybe once every other month catching Junior Charge of Quarters at Headquarters, Marine Corps Schools, Joe Howard was subject to no other details.

He was either teaching brand-new officers how to fire the '03, which he liked, or running people through the Annual Rifle Firing; but that didn't take all that much time. There was plenty of time to see what could be done with the Garand.

Putting several thousand rounds through M-1s taught him what was basically wrong with the weapon, and how to fix it. The primary problem was the barrel. When it was heated up by firing, it expanded and jammed into the stock. The result was that in rapid fire the later rounds through it (the twentieth, say) would strike a couple of inches— sometimes much more—from where the first round had struck.

The fix for that was to make the barrel free-floating. You had to carefully whittle wood away from the inside of the stock so that the barrel didn't get bent by the stock when it heated up.

The sights left a little to be desired, too. Joe learned to fix that by machining from scratch a new rear sight aperture, or "peep sight hole," that was smaller than the original, and by taking a couple of thousandths of an inch off the front sight. He also did some work on the gears that moved the rear sight horizontally and vertically, smoothing them out, making them more precise. And he tinkered with the trigger group, smoothing the sear so the let-off could be better controlled, and with the action itself, smoothing it to improve functioning. In the process, he learned where and how much lubricant was required. Finally, he mated barrels which had demonstrated unusual accuracy to his specially worked-over actions and trigger groups.

There were soon a half-dozen M-1s in the Arms Room just as accurate as any Star Gauge Springfield. One of these was informally reserved for Corporal Howard, and one other for Master Gunnery Sergeant Jack NMI Stecker.

Joe Howard made a nice little piece of change that year proving to visiting riflemen during informal sessions on the range that the M-1 Garand wasn't really the Mickey Mouse Army piece of shit everybody said it was.

And three times Gunny Stecker had handed him money—once ninety dollars—which the Gunny said was his fair share of what he had taken away from visiting master gunnery sergeants and sergeants major who also had an unfounded faith in the all-around superiority of the Springfield, and who were foolish enough to put their money where their mouths were. A Garand fine-tuned by Corporal Joe Howard, in the hands of a marksman like Gunny Stecker, was hard to beat.

In the late summer of 1940, after France had fallen to the Germans and Congress had authorized the first of what were to be many expansions of the Corps, there were a flock of promotions—promotions that came to many men long before they thought they had any chance of getting them. Joe Howard became a sergeant then. Six months later, a veteran ordnance sergeant assigned to the just-formed 1st Defense Battalion at the Navy Base at Pearl Harbor, Territory of Hawaii, became terminally ill. Soon afterward, someone in personnel remembered that Master Gunnery Sergeant Jack NMI Stecker at Quantico had a really bright and competent ordnance buck sergeant working for him.

That the kid had worked for Gunny Stecker for two years, and been promoted during that time, was all-around recommendation enough; people who didn't measure up to Gunny Stecker's high standards didn't get promoted, they got themselves shipped someplace else. On the same order that Headquarters U.S. Marine Corps ordered Sergeant Joseph L. Howard to the 1st Defense Battalion at Pearl, it promoted him to staff sergeant.

When the Japanese attack began, even as he listened to the sound of exploding bombs and the roar of low-flying aircraft, it was very difficult for Joe Howard to accept that what was happening *actually* was happening.

He had been conditioned to regard Pearl Harbor as America's mighty—and impregnable—fortress in the Pacific. In his view, if war came, the Japanese would probably attack Wake Island and Guam, and some of the other islands, and maybe even (Joe thought this highly unlikely) the Philippines. But Hawaii? Never. Not with Pearl Harbor and its row of dreadnought battleships, and its cruisers and aircraft carriers. And with the Army Air Corps fighters and bombers, not to mention the Navy and Marine Corps fighters and torpedo bombers afloat and ashore.

No goddamn way!

If the Japs were really stupid enough to try, say, invading Guam, Pearl would be the fortress from which the mightiest naval force the world had ever known would sail (carrying a Marine landing force aboard, of course) to bloody the Japs' noses and send the little bastards back to their rice paddies and raw fish with a lesson they wouldn't soon forget.

But, incredibly, when he looked out his barracks window, there was smoke rising from Battleship Row, and the sound of heavy explosions, and the same thing over at the seaplane base. And finally, when he saw a dozen Japanese aircraft in perfect formation—four three-plane vees—making low-level torpedo and strafing runs against Battleship Row, he realized that the impossible was indeed happening.

He couldn't do a goddamned thing to help the battleships, but he damned sure could do something at the seaplane hangars, where there were Marine-manned .50-caliber water-cooled Browning machine guns on antiaircraft mounts.

Because access to ammunition and the fully automatic weapons was limited to commissioned officers, he wasn't supposed to have a key to the arms locker, but he did; he was a good Marine Sergeant and knew which regulations should be violated. He went to the ammo locker and opened it up. By the time the first Marines came for ammo for the .50s, and to draw Browning Automatic Rifles and air-cooled .30-caliber Browning machine guns, and ammo for them, he was ready for them— long before the first officer showed up.

When an officer finally came and saw that most of the weapons and ammo had already been issued, he didn't ask any questions about how come the locker was open. Joe Howard didn't think that he would.

With nothing to do at the ammo locker, the officer went off to make himself useful somewhere else. That left Joe there alone with nothing to do either. After thinking about it a moment, he decided he couldn't just sit this goddamned attack out in an ammo bunker; so he took the last BAR and eight twenty-round magazines for it and ran outside.

A Ford ton-and-a-half truck came racing up with a buck sergeant driving and a PFC in the cab beside him.

"Have you got any belted fifty?" the buck sergeant demanded. "I can't get in our goddamned locker!"

"Come on!" Joe said, turning back toward the locker to show him where it was.

And then he looked over his shoulder to see if the sergeant was following him.

The sergeant was still sitting behind the wheel, but the top of his head was gone, and the windshield and the inside of the truck were smeared with a mass of blood and brain tissue.

Staff Sergeant Howard threw up.

Then he ran to the truck, grabbed the handle, pulled the door open, and dragged the buck sergeant's body out onto the ground. Blood spurted from somewhere and soaked Joe Howard's T-shirt and trousers.

After that he looked into the truck cab. The PFC was slumped in the seat, his head wedged back against the cushion, his eyes wide open but unseeing, his chest ripped open, blood streaming from the wound.

Joe Howard leaned against the truck fender and threw up again and again, until there was nothing in his stomach and all that came was a foul green bile.

And then he went back into the arms locker and huddled behind the counter, shaking, curled up, with his arms around his knees. He stayed there for he didn't know how long, except that when he finally came out, the attack was over, and the Ford ton-and-a-half had somehow caught on fire and burned, and the PFC inside was nothing but a charred lump of dead meat.

(TWO)

Technical Sergeant Charles M. Galloway, USMC, a good-looking, slim, deeply tanned, and brown-haired young man of twenty-five, lay naked on his back, his head propped up with pillows, in a somewhat battered but sturdy and comfortable bed in one of the two bedrooms of a hunting lodge in the mountains.

He had a Chesterfield cigarette in one hand. The other hand was wrapped around a large glass of pineapple juice, liberally laced with Gordon's London Dry Gin.

Ensign Mary Agnes O'Malley, Nurse Corps, USN, a slim, five-foot-four-inch, red-haired, pert-breasted woman, similarly undressed, knelt on the bed, about to begin another game of what she called "ice cream cone." This involved the dribbling of creme de cacao on certain portions of the body, and then removing it with the tongue. Until the previous day, Charley Galloway had never heard of—or even, in his sometimes wild fantasies, thought about—the kind of thing she was doing; but he was learning to like it.

The other bedroom of the hunting lodge, which was actually a simple, tin-roofed frame cabin, was occupied by Technical Sergeant Stefan "Big Steve" Oblensky, USMC, and Lieutenant Florence Kocharski, Nurse Corps, USN.

Big Steve, who was Polish and in his forties, was a great bull of a man. But Lieutenant Kocharski was big enough to be a match for him, which is to say that she was Valkyrie-like, in her late thirties, and also Polish. Several months before, she'd been attracted to Big Steve when she'd met him at the Naval Hospital at Pearl Harbor. He'd come in for his annual physical examination, and the examination had kind of expanded and become *more* physical.

And vice versa. So strongly that the two of them had chosen to ignore the cultural and, more important, the legal prohibition against socialization between commissioned and enlisted members of the Naval Service.

Florence Kocharski was a full lieutenant, about to make lieutenant commander; Big Steve expected to make master sergeant any day. Both of them had been around the service long enough to know about keeping indiscretions a hundred miles from the flagpole. A hundred miles was an impossibility on Oahu, but a hunting cabin in the hills was a reasonable approximation. (It was owned by an old pal of Big Steve's who had retired and gone to work for Dole.)

But to get to the cabin required an automobile. Lieutenant Florence Kocharski didn't have one, and Big Steve Oblensky was six months away from getting his driver's license back, after having been caught driving drunk. But not to worry: T/Sgt. Charley Galloway had a lovingly maintained yellow 1933 Ford V-8 convertible. Big Steve had been able to borrow Charley's car without any trouble the first time. He and Charley both knew that Big Steve would return the favor somewhere down the pike.

But the second weekend Big Steve asked to borrow the Ford, he had to tell Charley why he wanted it. And Charley Galloway asked if Big Steve's nurse had a friend.

"Jesus Christ, Charley! I can't ask her nothing like that! Be a pal."

"You ask her, she says no, then I'll be a pal. But you ask her."

To Big Steve's surprise, Flo Kocharski was neither outraged nor astonished when, with remarkable delicacy, Big Steve brought the subject up.

Ensign Mary Agnes O'Malley, Lieutenant Kocharski's roommate, had already noticed T/Sgt. Charles Galloway at the wheel of his yellow Ford convertible and asked her about him. She'd asked specifically about how he came to have pilot's wings. Ensign O'Malley had just recently entered the Navy and had not known that enlisted men could be pilots.

There was a small corps of enlisted pilots, Lieutenant Kocharski explained to her. These were officially called Naval Aviation Pilots, but more commonly "flying sergeants." T/Sgt. Charles Galloway was one of them. He was a fighter pilot of VMF-211, where her Stefan was the NCO in charge of Aircraft Maintenance.

"He's darling," Ensign O'Malley replied.

Lieutenant Kocharski didn't think "darling" was the right word, but Charley Galloway *was* a good-looking kid, and she was not surprised that Mary Agnes O'Malley found him attractive.

Lieutenant Kocharski ended the conversation on that particular note—to protect young Sergeant Galloway from Ensign O'Malley. Ensign O'Malley was not a bright-eyed innocent. She had entered the Navy late, at thirty-three, rather than right out of nursing school, which was usually the case. Florence, naturally curious, had in time wormed her history out of her.

Before she joined the Navy, Ensign Mary Agnes O'Malley had been a nun, a nursing sister of the Sisters of Mercy. She had become a postulant in the order at sixteen. And she had served faithfully and well for many years after that. First she became a registered nurse, and later she qualified as both an operating-room nurse and a nurse anesthesiologist. Later still, she was seduced by a married anesthesiologist, an M.D., while taking an advanced course at Massachusetts General Hospital.

She didn't blame the doctor, Mary Agnes told Florence. She had not been wearing her Sisters of Mercy habit at Mass General, and she had not told the doctor, ever, that she was a nun. But once she had tasted the forbidden fruit, she realized that she could no longer adhere to a vow of chastity, and petitioned the Vatican for release from her vows.

The Navy was then actively recruiting nurses, and she was highly qualified, so she signed on.

In the four months she had known her, Flo had come to understand that beneath Mary Agnes O'Malley's demure and modest façade, there lurked a predator with the morals of an alley cat. Mary Agnes frankly admitted, in confidence, that she was making up for lost time.

So when Big Steve came to her about Charley Galloway, Flo Kocharski felt a certain uneasiness about turning Mary Agnes loose on him. Charley was a really nice kid. On the other hand, if he hadn't leaned on Stefan to get himself fixed up as the price of borrowing his car, she wouldn't have had to.

What neither Flo nor Big Steve knew, or even remotely suspected, was that Charley Galloway was far less experienced in relations between the sexes than anyone who knew him would have suspected. During their first night together in the cabin, Mary Alice quickly and delightfully learned that Charley was the antithesis of jaded. Yet not even she suspected that the first time in his twenty-five years Charley had spent the whole night with a woman was that very same night.

Charley's sexual drives—and sometimes he thought he was cursed with an overgenerous issue of them—were flagrantly heterosexual. Neither was he troubled with any religious or moral restraints. His fantasies were about equally divided between the normal—meeting a well-stacked nymphomaniac whose father owned a liquor store—and meeting a nice, respectable girl and getting married.

He had encountered neither in his eight years in the Corps.

And there was something else: he didn't want to fuck up. The price would be too high. The most important thing in the world, during his first few years in the Corps, had been to work his way up to the point where the Corps would send him to Pensacola and teach him how to fly.

Catching a dose of the clap, or maybe just getting hauled in by the military police in one of their random raids on a whorehouse, would have kept him from getting promoted and getting sent to flight school. And once he'd made staff sergeant and won a berth at Pensacola and then his wings, just about the same restrictions had applied.

Naval Aviation Pilots were *non*commissioned officers, in other words, enlisted men. Since Aviation was set up with a general understanding that pilots would be commissioned officers and gentlemen, the

Marine Corps had never really figured out how to deal with noncom fliers.

Enlisted pilots had crept into the system back in the 1920s. The three originals had been aircraft mechanics who had learned how to fly on the job during the Marine intervention in Santo Domingo. The criterion for selection of pilots then, as Charley had heard it, and as he believed, was "anyone who was demonstrably unlikely to crash a nonreplaceable airplane."

The Marine commander in Santo Domingo had looked at his brand-new, fresh-from-flight-school commissioned pilots and then at his experienced sergeants, and had decided that the very, very nonreplaceable airplanes at his disposal were better off being flown by the sergeants, whether they were officially rated or not.

The second reason for the existence of "flying sergeants" was money. In the years between the wars, Congress had been parsimonious toward the armed services, and especially toward the Corps. Officer manning levels were cast in concrete. This meant that every enlisted Naval Aviation Pilot freed up an officer billet for use elsewhere. And, of course, flying sergeants were paid less than officers.

Charley Galloway had started out as an aviation mechanic, right out of Parris Island, when he was seventeen. Three years later, a space for an NAP had unexpectedly opened at Pensacola, and he was the only qualified body around to fill it. On the other hand, he was an enlisted man. Most Naval Aviators (Marine pilots were all Naval Aviators) were commissioned officers and gentlemen, and many of them were graduates of the United States Naval Academy at Annapolis.

There was an enormous social chasm between commissioned officers and gentlemen and noncommissioned officers, who were, under law, *men,* and not *gentlemen.* There was also resentment from the other direction toward flying sergeants from sergeants who didn't fly and who thus didn't get extra pay for what looked to them like a cushy berth.

Charley Galloway soon learned that about the only people who didn't think Naval Aviation Pilots were an all-around pain in the ass were fellow pilots, who judged NAPs by their flying ability. As a rule of thumb, NAPs were, if anything, slightly more proficient than their commissioned counterparts. In the first place, most of them were older and more experienced than Charley. And most of them had large blocks of bootleg time before they went to Pensacola to learn how to fly officially.

Charley had developed a good relationship with the pilots of VMF-211 (Marine Fighter Squadron 211), based on his reputation both as a pilot and a responsible noncom. That would go down the toilet in an instant if he came down with a dose of the clap, or got caught visiting a whorehouse or screwing somebody's willing wife. They would take his wings away and he wouldn't fly anymore. It looked to him like a choice between flying and fucking, and flying won hands down.

But since Friday night, when they'd picked up Big Steve's nurse and her roommate in Honolulu, there seemed to be convincing evidence that he could accomplish both.

"Ouch!" Technical Sergeant Charles M. Galloway yelped. "Jesus Christ!"

"Sorry," Ensign Mary Agnes O'Malley said contritely. "The last thing in the world I want to do is *hurt* it." She looked up at him and smiled. She kissed it. "All better!" she said.

She straddled him.

The door burst open.

Big Steve stood there in his skivvy shorts, a strange look on his face.

"Get the hell out of here!" Charley flared.

"Well, really! Don't people knock where you come from, for Christ's Sake?" Mary Agnes O'Malley snapped.

"The Japs are bombing Pearl Harbor," Big Steve said. "It just come over the radio."

"I heard the engines," Charley said. "I thought it was those Air Corps B-17s."

Charley Galloway sat up, and dislodged Mary Agnes.

How the hell am I going to fly? he thought. *I've been drinking all night.*

And then he had another thought.

I'll be a sonofabitch! I should have known that the first time I ever got to have a steady piece of ass, something would come along to fuck it up.

(THREE)

MARINE AIRFIELD
EWA, OAHU ISLAND, TERRITORY OF HAWAII
7 DECEMBER 1941

While everybody else on December 7 was running around Ewa—and for that matter, the Hawaiian Islands—like chickens with their heads cut off, Technical Sergeants Charley Galloway and Stefan "Big Steve" Oblensky had gone to Captain Leonard J. Martin, the ranking officer on the scene, and asked for permission to take a half-dozen men and try to salvage what they could from the carnage of the flight line and the mess in the hangars.

The reason they had to ask permission, rather than just doing what Captain Martin thought was the logical thing to do in the circumstances, was that some moron in CINCPAC (Commander-in-Chief, Pacific Fleet) at Pearl Harbor had issued an order that aviation units that had lost their aircraft would immediately re-form and prepare to fight as infantry.

Captain Martin had no doubt that the order applied to VMF-211. After the Japanese had bombed and strafed Ewa, VMF-211 had zero flyable aircraft. And it was possible, if not very likely, that the Japanese would invade Oahu, in which case every man who could carry a rifle would indeed be needed as an infantryman.

But it was unlikely, in Captain Martin's judgment, that infantrymen would be needed that afternoon. In the meantime, it just made good sense to salvage anything that could be salvaged. Captain Martin had been a Marine long enough to believe that replacement aircraft and spare parts—or, for that matter, replacement mess-kit spoons—would be issued to VMF-211 only after the Navy was sure that aircraft, spare parts, and mess-kit spoons were not needed anywhere else in the Navy.

It made much more sense to have Galloway and Big Steve try to salvage what they could than to have them forming as infantry. Even if he was absolutely wrong, and Japanese infantry were suddenly to appear, there was nothing Galloway and Oblensky could be taught about infantry in the next couple of days that they already didn't know. They were technical sergeants, the second-highest enlisted grade in the Corps, and you didn't get to be a tech sergeant in the Corps unless you knew all about small arms and small-unit infantry tactics.

And there was a question of morale, too. Big Steve, and especially Charley Galloway, felt guilty—more than guilty, ashamed—about what had happened to VMF-211. Their guilt was unreasonable, but Martin understood their feelings. For one thing, they hadn't been at Ewa when it happened. And by the time they got to Ewa, it was all over. *Really* all over; even the fires were out and the wounded evacuated.

Captain Martin knew, unofficially, where Big Steve and Galloway were when the Japanese struck. So he didn't have much trouble reading what was behind their eyes when they finally got back to Ewa, still accompanied by their nurse "friends," and saw the destroyed aircraft and the blanket-wrapped bodies of their buddies on the stretchers.

If we had been here, we could have done something!

Captain Martin agreed with them. And, he further reasoned, they had to do something that had meaning. Practicing to repel boarders as infantrymen would be pure bullshit to good, experienced Marine tech sergeants.

So Captain Martin told them to go ahead, and to take as many men as they could reasonably use. If they ran into any static, they were to shoot the problem up to him.

What Technical Sergeants Galloway and Oblensky had not told Captain Martin was that they had already examined the carnage and decided that they could make at least one flyable F4F-4 by salvaging the necessary parts from partially destroyed aircraft and mating them with other not completely destroyed machines.

It was a practical, professional judgment. T/Sgt. Big Steve Oblensky had been an aircraft mechanic as far back as Santo Domingo and Nicaragua, and T/Sgt. Charley Galloway had been a mechanic before he'd gone to flight school.

By sunset, Captain Martin saw that they had found tenting somewhere, erected a makeshift, reasonably lightproof work bay, and moved one of the least damaged F4F-4s into it. Over the next week they cannibalized parts from other wrecks. Then there was the sound of air compressors and the bright flame of welding torches; and finally the sound of the twelve hundred horses of a Pratt & Whitney R-1830 Twin Wasp being run up.

But Captain Martin was surprised to discover what Big Steve and Charley had salvaged. By December 15, the engine he had heard run up was attached to a patched-together but complete and flyable F4F-4 Wildcat fuselage.

"That doesn't exist, you know," Captain Martin said. "All the aircraft on the station have been surveyed and found to be destroyed."

"I want to take it out to the *Saratoga,*" Charley Galloway said.

"Sara's in 'Dago, Galloway," Captain Martin said. "What are you talking about?"

"Sara's in Pearl. Sometime today, she's going to put out to reinforce Wake. Sara, and the *Astoria* and the *Minneapolis* and the *San Francisco.* And the 4th Defense Battalion, on board the *Tangier.* They're calling it Task Force 14."

Martin hadn't heard about that, at least in such detail, but there was no doubt that Galloway and Oblensky knew what they were talking about. Old-time sergeants had their own channels of information.

"That airplane can't be flown until it's been surveyed again and taken through an inspection."

"Skipper, if we did that, the Navy would take it away from us," Oblensky argued. "The squadron is down to two planes on Wake. They need that airplane."

"If Sara is sailing today, there's just no time to get permission for something like that."

"So we do it without permission," Galloway said. "What are they going to do if I show up over her? Order me home?"

"And what if you can't find her?"

"I'll find her," Galloway said flatly.

"If you can't?" Martin repeated.

"If I have to sit her down in the ocean, the squadron's no worse off than it is now," Galloway said, with a quiet passion. "Captain, we've got to do something."

"I can't give you permission to do something like that," Martin said. "Christ, *I* would wind up in Portsmouth. It's crazy, and you know it."

"Yes, Sir," Oblensky said, and a moment later Galloway parroted him.

"But, just as a matter of general information," Captain Martin added, "I've got business at Pearl in the morning, and I won't be able to get back here before 0930 or so."

He had seen in their eyes that both had realized further argument was useless. And, more important, that they had just dismissed his objections as irrelevant. Charles Galloway was going to take that F4F-4 Wildcat off from Ewa in the morning, come hell or high water.

"Thank you, Sir."

"Good luck, Galloway," Captain Martin said, and walked away.

(FOUR)

ABOVE USS *SARATOGA* (CV.3)
TASK FORCE 14
0620 HOURS 16 DECEMBER 1941

A moment after Charley Galloway spotted the *Saratoga* five thousand feet below him, she began to turn into the wind. They had spotted the Wildcat, and her captain had issued the order, "Prepare to recover aircraft."

By that time Sara knew he was coming. Ten minutes after Galloway took off from Ewa, the Navy was informed he was on the way, and was asked to relay that information to the *Saratoga*. A Navy captain, reflecting that a week before, such idiocy, such blatant disregard for standing orders and flight safety, would have seen those involved thrown out of the service—most likely via the Navy prison at Portsmouth—decided that this wasn't a week ago, it was now, after the Pacific Fleet had suffered a disaster, and he ordered a coded message sent to the *Saratoga* to be on the lookout for a Marine F4F-4 believed attempting a rendezvous.

As the *Saratoga* turned, so did her screening force, the other ships of Task Force 14. They were the cruisers *Minneapolis, Astoria,* and *San*

Francisco; nine destroyers; the *Neches,* a fleet oiler; and the USS *Tangier,* a seaplane tender pressed into service as a transport. They had put out from Pearl Harbor at 1600 the previous day.

Charley retarded his throttle, banked slightly, and pushed the nose of the Wildcat down.

He thought, *That's a bunch of ships and a lot of people making all that effort to recover just one man and one airplane.*

He dropped his eyes to the fuel quantity gauge mounted on the left of the control panel and did the mental arithmetic. He had thirty-five minutes of fuel remaining, give or take a couple of minutes. It was now academic, of course, because he had found Task Force 14 on time and where he believed it would be, but he could not completely dismiss the thought that if he hadn't found it, thirty minutes from now, give or take a few, he would have been floating around on a rubber raft all alone on the wide Pacific. Presuming he could have set it down on the water without killing himself.

By the time he was down to fifteen hundred feet over the smooth, dark blue Pacific, and headed straight for the *Saratoga*'s bow, she had completed her turn into the wind. Galloway looked down at her deck and saw that she was indeed ready to receive him. He could see faces looking up at him, and he could see that the cables had been raised. And when he glanced at her stern, he could see the Landing Control Officer, his paddles already in hand, waiting to guide him aboard.

He started to lower his landing gear.

He did not do so in strict accordance with Paragraph 19.a.(1) of AN 01-190FB-1, which was the U.S. Navy Bureau of Aeronautics *Pilot's Handbook of Flight Operating Instructions for F4F-Series Aircraft.* Paragraph 19.a.(1), which Charley Galloway knew by heart, said, "Crank down the landing gear." Then came a CAUTION: "Be Sure the landing gear is fully down."

The landing gear on the Wildcat, the newest and hottest and most modern fighter aircraft in the Navy's (and thus the Marine Corps') arsenal, had to be cranked up and down by hand. There was a crank on the right side of the cockpit. It had to be turned no less than twenty-nine times either to release or retract the gear. The mechanical advantage was not great, and to turn it at all, the pilot had to take his right hand from the stick and fly with his left hand while he cranked hard, twenty-nine times, with his right hand.

Charley Galloway had learned early on—he had become a Naval Aviator three days after he turned twenty-one—that there wasn't room in the cockpit for anyone to come along and see how closely you followed regulations.

The records of VMF-211 indicated that Charles M. Galloway was currently qualified in F2A-3, F4F-4, R4D, and PBY-5 and PBY-5A aircraft.

The R4D was the Navy version of the Douglas DC-3, a twin-engined, twenty-one passenger transport, and the PBY-5 was the Consolidated Catalina, a twin-engined seaplane that had started out as sort of a bomber and was now primarily used as a long-range observation and antisubmarine aircraft. The PBY-5A was the amphibian version of the PBY-5; retractable gear had been fitted to it.

The Marine Corps had no R4D and PBY-5 aircraft assigned to it; Charley Galloway had learned to fly them when he and some other Marine pilots had been borrowed from the Corps to help the Navy test them, get them ready for service, and ferry them from the factories to their squadrons. He had picked up a lot of time in the R4D, even going through an Army Air Corps course on how to use it to drop parachutists.

He was therefore, in his judgment, a good and experienced aviator, with close to two thousand hours total time, ten times as much as some of the second lieutenants who had just joined VMF-211 as replacements. He was also, in his own somewhat immodest and so far untested opinion, one hell of a fighter pilot, who had figured out a way to get the goddamned gear down without cranking the goddamned handle until you were blue in the face.

It involved the physical principle that an object in motion tends to remain in motion, absent restricting forces.

Charley had learned that if he unlocked the landing gear, then put the Wildcat in a sharp turn, the gear would attempt to continue in the direction it had been going. Phrased simply, when he put the Wildcat in a sharp turn, the landing-gear crank would spin madly of its own volition, and when it was finished spinning, the gear would be down. All you had to do was lock it down. And, of course, remember to keep your hand and arm out of the way of the spinning crank.

He did so now. The crank spun, the gear went down, and he locked it in place.

Then, from memory, he went through the landing check-off list: he unlocked the tail wheel; he lowered and locked the arresting hook, which, if things went well, would catch one of several cables stretched across the deck of the *Saratoga* and bring him to a safe but abrupt halt.

He pulled his goggles down from where they had been resting on the leather helmet, and then slid open and locked the over-the-cockpit canopy.

He pushed the carburetor air control all the way in to the Direct position, retarded the throttle, and set the propeller governor for 2100 rpm. He set the mixture control into Auto Rich, opened the cowl flaps, and lowered the wing flaps.

All the time he was doing this, he was turning on his final approach, that is to say, lining himself up with the deck of the *Saratoga.*

The Landing Control Officer was ready for him. Using his paddles, he signaled to Charley Galloway that he was just a hair to the right of a desirable landing path. Then, at the last moment, he made his decision, and signaled Charley to bring it in and set it down.

Charley's arresting hook caught the first cable, and the Wildcat was jerked to a sudden halt with a force that was always astonishing. Whenever he made a carrier landing, Charley Galloway felt an enormous sense of relief, and then, despite a genuine effort to restrain it, a feeling of smug accomplishment. Ships and airplanes were different creatures. They were not intended to mate on the high seas. But he had just done exactly that. Again. This made Carrier Landing Number Two Hundred and Six.

And there weren't very many people in the whole wide world who could do that even once.

As the white hats rushed up to disengage the cable, he quickly went through the "Stopping the Engine" checklist, again from memory.

By the time the propeller stopped turning and he had shut off the ignition, battery, and fuel selector switches, a plane captain was there to help him get out of the cockpit. And he saw Major Verne J. McCaul, USMC, Commanding Officer of VMF-221, standing on the deck, smiling at him. VMF-221, equipped with fourteen F2A-3 Brewster Buffalos, was stationed aboard the *Saratoga.* Galloway had known him for some time, liked him, and was glad to see him.

Charley jumped off the wing root and walked to him.

"I am delighted," said Major McCaul, who was thirty-five and looked younger, "nay, *overjoyed* to see you."

Galloway looked at him suspiciously.

"The odds were four to one you'd never make it out here," McCaul said. "I took a hundred bucks' worth at those odds, twenty-five of them for you."

"You knew I was coming?"

"There was a radio from Pearl about an hour ago," McCaul said. *Apparently it didn't say "arrest on sight," or there would be a Marine with irons waiting for me.*

"Well, that certainly was very nice of you, Sir," Galloway said, not absolutely sure that McCaul wasn't pulling his leg. Proof that he was not came when McCaul handed him five twenty-dollar bills.

It then occurred to him that he had, literally, jumped from the frying pan into the fire. He had made it this far. But the next stop was Wake Island. The odds, bullshit aside, that Wake could be held against the Japanese seemed pretty remote. He had no good reason to presume that he would be any better a pilot, or any luckier, than the pilots of VFM-211 on Wake who had already been shot down.

Then he remembered what Big Steve Oblensky had once told him. The function of Marines was to stop bullets for civilians; that's what they were really paying you for.

"The Captain wants to see you after you're cleaned up," Major McCaul said. "In the meantime, I'm sorry to have to tell you, you're to consider yourself under arrest."

"Am I in trouble that deep, Major?"

"I'm afraid so, Charley. The Navy's really pissed," Major McCaul said. "I'll do what I can for you, but . . . they're *really* pissed."

"Oh, hell," Charley said. And then, not too convincingly, he smiled. "Well, what the hell, Major. What can they do to me? Send me to Wake Island?"

II

(ONE)

WASHINGTON, D.C.

19 DECEMBER 1941

As his taxi drove past the White House, Fleming Pickering, a tall, handsome, superbly tailored man in his early forties, noticed steel-helmeted soldiers, armed with rifles, bayonets fixed, guarding the gates.

He wondered if they were really necessary. Was there a real threat to the security of either the President or the building itself? Or were these guards being used for a little domestic propaganda, a symbol that the nation had been at war for not quite two weeks, and that the White House was now the headquarters of the Commander in Chief?

Certainly, he reasoned, even before what the President had so eloquently dubbed "a day that will live in infamy," the Secret Service and the White House police must have had contingency plans to protect the President in case of war. These would have called for more sophisticated measures than the posting of a corporal's guard of riflemen at the White House gates.

Fleming Pickering, Chairman of the Board of the Pacific & Far Eastern Shipping Corporation, was not an admirer of Franklin Delano Roosevelt, President of the United States. This was not to say that he did not respect him. Roosevelt was, he acknowledged, both a brilliant man and a consummate master of the art of molding public opinion.

Roosevelt had managed to garner public support for policies—Lend-Lease in particular—that were, in Pickering's judgment, not only disastrous and probably illegal, but which had, in the end, on the day of infamy, brought the United States into a war it probably could have stayed out of, and which it was pathetically ill-prepared to fight.

Fleming Pickering was considerably more aware than most Americans of what an absolute disaster Pearl Harbor had been. He and his wife had been in Honolulu when the Japanese struck. They had witnessed the burning and sinking battleships at the Navy Base, and the twisted, smoldering carnage at Hickam Field.

Despite his personal misgivings about Roosevelt, less than an hour after the last Japanese aircraft had left, as he watched the rescue and salvage operations, he had understood that the time to protest and oppose the President had passed, that it was clearly his—and everyone's—duty to rally around the Commander in Chief and make what contribution he could to the war effort.

Fleming Pickering had come to Washington to offer his services.

He had two additional thoughts as the taxi drove down Pennsylvania Avenue past the White House.

First, a feeling of sympathy for the soldiers standing there in the freezing cold in their steel helmets. A tin pot is a miserable sonofabitch to have to wear when it's cold and snowing and the wind is blowing. He knew that from experience. Corporal Fleming Pickering, USMC, had worn one in the trenches in France in 1918.

And second, that with a little bit of luck, when the American people learned the hard way what that sonofabitch in the White House had gotten them into, he could be voted out of office in 1944. If there was still something called the United States of America in 1944.

The taxi, a DeSoto sedan painted yellow, turned off Pennsylvania Avenue, made a sharp U-turn, and pulled to the curb before the marquee of the Foster Lafayette Hotel. A doorman in a heavy overcoat liberally adorned with golden cords trotted out from the protection of his glass-walled guard post and pulled open the door.

"Well, hello, Mr. Pickering," he said, with a genuine smile. "It's nice to see you, Sir."

"Hello, Ken," Pickering said, offering his hand. "What do you think of the weather?"

Once out of the cab, he turned and handed the driver several dollar bills, indicating with his hand that he didn't want any change, and then walked quickly into the hotel and across the lobby to the reception desk.

There was a line, and he took his place in it. Four people were ahead of him. Finally it was his turn.

"May I help you, Sir?" the desk clerk asked, making it immediately plain to Fleming Pickering that the clerk had no idea who he was.

"My name is Fleming Pickering," he said. "I need a place to stay for a couple of days, maybe a week."

"Have you a reservation, Sir?"

Pickering shook his head. The desk clerk raised his hands in a gesture of helplessness.

"Without a reservation, Sir . . ."

"Is Mr. Telford in the house?"

"Why, yes, Sir, I believe he is."

"I wonder if you could tell him I'm here, please?"

Max Telford, resident manager of the Foster Lafayette Hotel, a short, pudgy, balding man wearing a frock coat, striped trousers, and a wing collar, appeared a moment later.

"We didn't expect you, Mr. Pickering," he said, offering his hand. "But you're very welcome, nonetheless."

"How are you, Max?" Pickering said, smiling. "I gather the house is full."

"Yes, indeed."

"What am I to do?" Pickering said. "I need a place to stay. Is there some Democrat we can evict?"

Telford chuckled. "I don't think we'll have to go that far. There's always room for you here, Mr. Pickering."

"Is Mrs. Fowler in town?"

"No, Sir. I believe she's in Florida."

"Then why don't I impose on the Senator?"

"I'm sure the Senator would be delighted," Telford said. He turned and took a key from the rack of cubbyholes. "I'll take you up."

"I know how to find it. Come up in a while, and we'll have a little liquid cheer."

"Why don't I send up a tray of hors d'oeuvres?"

"That would be nice. Give me fifteen minutes to take a shower. Thank you, Max."

Pickering took the key and walked to the bank of elevators.

Max Telford turned to the desk clerk.

"I know you haven't been with us long, Mr. Denny, but you *do* know, don't you, who owns this inn?"

"Yes, Sir. Mr. Foster. Mr. Andrew Foster."

"And you know that there are forty-one other Foster Hotels?"

"Yes, Sir."

"Well, for your general information, as you begin what we both hope will be a long and happy career with Foster Hotels, I think I should tell you that Mr. Andrew Foster has one child, a daughter, and that she is married to the chairman of the board of the Pacific & Far Eastern Shipping Corporation."

"The gentleman to whom you just gave the key to Senator Fowler's suite?" Mr. Denny asked, but it was more of a pained realization than a question.

"Correct. Mr. Fleming Pickering. Mr. Pickering and Senator Fowler are very close."

"I'm sorry, Mr. Telford, I just didn't know."

"That's why I'm telling you. There is one more thing. Until last week, we had a young Marine officer, a second lieutenant, in the house. His name is Malcolm Pickering. If he should ever appear at the desk here, looking for a room, which is a good possibility, I suggest that it would behoove you to treat him with the same consideration with which you would treat Mr. Foster himself; he is Mr. Foster's grandson, his only grandchild, and the heir apparent to the throne."

"I take your point, Sir," Mr. Denny said.

"Don't look so stricken," Telford said. "They're all very nice people. The boy, they call him 'Pick,' worked two summers for me. Once as a sous-chef at the Foster Park in New York, and the other time as the bell captain at the Andrew Foster in San Francisco."

(TWO)

WASHINGTON, D.C.
1735 HOURS 19 DECEMBER 1941

When Senator Richardson S. Fowler walked in, Fleming Pickering was sitting on the wide, leather-upholstered sill of a window in the Senator's sitting room. A glass of whiskey was in Pickering's hand.

Senator Fowler's suite was six rooms on the corner of the eighth floor of the Foster Lafayette, overlooking the White House, which was almost directly across Pennsylvania Avenue from the hotel.

"I had them let me in," Fleming Pickering said. "I hope you don't mind. The house is full."

"Oh, don't be silly," Senator Fowler said automatically, and then, with real feeling, "Jesus, Flem, it's good to see you!"

Senator Fowler was more than a decade older than Fleming Pickering. He was getting portly, and his jowls were starting to grow rosy and to sag.

He looks more and more like a politician, Flem Pickering thought, aware that it was unkind. Years ago, as a very young man, Pickering had heard and immediately adopted as part of his personal philosophy an old and probably banal observation that to have friends, one must permit them to have one serious flaw. So far as Pickering was concerned, Richardson Fowler's flaw was that he was a politician, the Junior Senator from the Great State of California.

Flem Pickering had a habit of picking up trite and banal phrases and adopting them as his own, ofttimes verbatim, sometimes revising them. So far as he was concerned, Richardson Fowler was the exception to a phrase he had lifted from Will Rogers and altered. Will Rogers said he had never met a man he didn't like. Pickering's version was that—

Richardson Fowler excepted—he had never met a politician he had liked.

He had tried and failed to understand what drove Fowler to seek public office. It certainly wasn't that he needed the work. Richardson Fowler had inherited from his father the *San Francisco Courier-Herald*, nine smaller newspapers, and six radio stations. His wife and her brother owned, it was said, more or less accurately, two square blocks of downtown San Francisco, plus several million acres of timberland in Washington and Oregon.

If Fowler was consumed by some desire to do good, to lead people in this direction or that, it seemed to Pickering that the newspapers and the radio stations gave Fowler the means to accomplish it. He didn't have to run for office—with all that meant—for the privilege of coming east to the hot, muggy, provincial, small Southern town that was the nation's capital, to consort with a depressing collection of failed lawyers and other scoundrels.

But, oh, Flem Pickering, he thought, *what a hypocrite you are! Right now you are delighted to have access to a man with the political clout you pretend to scorn.*

Senator Fowler dropped his heavy, battered, well-filled briefcase at his feet and crossed the room to Pickering. They shook hands, and then the Senator put his arm around the younger man's shoulders and hugged him.

"I was worried about you, you bastard," he said. "You and Patricia. She here with you?"

"She's in San Francisco," Pickering said. "She's fine."

"And Pick?"

"He's at Pensacola, learning how to fly," Pickering said. "I thought you knew."

"I knew he was going down there," the Senator said. "I had dinner with him, oh, six days, a week ago. But he never came to say good-bye to me."

There was disappointment, perhaps even a little resentment, in his voice. Senator Fowler had known Pick Pickering from the day he was born.

"If you were a second lieutenant and they gave you two days off, would you spend them seeing an aging uncle-politician, or trying to get laid?" Pickering asked with a smile.

The Senator snorted a laugh. "Well, he could have tried to squeeze in fifteen minutes for me between jumps," he said. He turned and walked to an antique sideboard loaded with whiskey bottles. "I have been thinking about having one of these for the last two hours. You all right?"

Flem Pickering raised his nearly full glass to show that he was.

Senator Fowler half-filled a glass with Johnnie Walker Black Label Scotch, added one ice cube, and then sprayed soda into it from a wire-wrapped soda bottle.

"This stuff," the Senator said, raising his glass, "is already getting in short supply. God*damn* German submarines."

"I have four hundred and eleven cases," Fleming Pickering said. "If you treat me right, I might put a case or two aside for you."

Fowler, smiling, looked at him curiously.

"Off the *Princess,* the *Destiny,* and the *Enterprise,*" Pickering explained.

The *Pacific Princess,* 51,000 tons, a sleek, fast passenger liner, was the flagship of the Pacific & Far Eastern Shipping Corporation. The *Pacific Destiny* and the *Pacific Enterprise,* 44,500 tons each, were sister ships, slightly smaller and slower, but, some said, more luxurious.

"Is that why you're here?" Senator Fowler asked. "The Navy after them again? Flem . . ."

Pickering held up his hand to shut him off.

"I sold them," he said.

"When rape is inevitable, etcetera, etcetera?" Fowler asked.

"No," Pickering said. "I think I could have won that one in the courts. The Navy could have commandeered them, but they couldn't have forced me to sell them."

Senator Fowler did not agree, but he didn't say so.

"And it wasn't patriotism, either," Pickering said. "More like enlightened self-interest."

"Oh?"

"Or a vision of the future," Pickering said.

"Now you've lost me," Senator Fowler confessed.

"We came home from Hawaii via Seattle," Pickering said, pausing to sip at his drink. "On the *Destiny.* We averaged twenty-seven knots for the trip. It took us one hundred twenty hours—"

"Fast crossing," Fowler interrupted, doing some quick, rough arithmetic. "Five and a half days."

"Uh-huh," Pickering said, "testing the notion that a fast passenger liner can run away from submarines."

"Not proving the theory? You made it."

"The theory presumes that submarines are not sitting ahead of you, waiting for you to come into range," Pickering said. "And there may not have been any Japanese submarines around."

"OK," Senator Fowler agreed. *"Theory."*

"While we were in Seattle, I drove past the Boeing plant. Long lines of huge, four-engine airplanes, B-17s, capable of making it nonstop to Hawaii in eleven, twelve hours."

"Uh-huh," Fowler agreed. He had flown in the B-17 and was impressed with it. "That airplane may just get our chestnuts out of the fire in this war."

Pickering went off at a tangent.

"You heard, Dick, that some military moron had all the B-17s in Hawaii lined up in rows for the convenience of the Japanese?"

Fowler shook his head in disbelief or disgust or both. "There, and in the Philippines," he said. "Christ, they really caught us with our pants down."

"I talked to an Army Air Corps pilot in the bar of the hotel," Pickering said. "He said a flight of B-17s from the States arrived while the raid was going on. And with no ammunition for their machine guns."

"I heard that, too."

"Anyway," Pickering said, "looking at those B-17s in Seattle, it occurred to me that they could more or less easily be modified to carry passengers, and that, presuming we win this war, that's the way the public is going to want to cross oceans in the future. Twelve hours to Hawaii beats five or six days all to hell."

"Out of school—this is classified—Howard Hughes proposes to build an airplane—out of plywood, no less—that will carry four hundred soldiers across the Atlantic."

"Then you understand what I'm saying. The day of the passenger liner, I'm afraid, is over. And since the Navy was making a decent offer for my ships, I decided to take it."

"A decent offer?"

"They're spending the taxpayers' money, not their own. A *very* decent offer."

"All of them?"

"Just the liners. I'm keeping the cargo ships, and I will *not* sell them to the Navy. If the Navy tries to make me sell them, I'll take them to the Supreme Court, and win. Anyway, that's where I got all the Scotch. I can also make you a very good deal on some monogramed sterling silver flatware from the first-class dining rooms."

Fowler chuckled. "I'm surprised the Navy let you keep that."

"So am I," Pickering said.

"What are you going to do with all that money?" Fowler asked.

"Get rid of it, quickly, before that sonofabitch across the street thinks of some way to tax me out of it," Pickering said.

"You are speaking, Sir," Fowler said, mockingly sonorous, "of your President and the Commander in Chief."

"You bet I am," Pickering said. "I told my broker to buy into Boeing, Douglas, and whatever airlines he can find. I think I'd like to own an airline."

"And when Pick comes home from the war, he can run it?"

Pickering met his eyes. "Sure. Why not? I don't intend to dwell on the other possibility."

"I don't know why I feel awkward saying this," Senator Fowler said, "but I pray for him, Flem."

"Thank you," Pickering said. "So do I."

"So what are you doing in Washington?" Fowler said, to change the subject.

"You know a lawyer named Bill Donovan? Wall Street?"

"Sure."

"You know what he's doing these days?"

"Where did you think he's getting the money to do it?" He examined his now-empty glass. "I'm going to build another one of these. You want one?"

"Please, Dick."

"You think you'd make a good spy?" Senator Fowler asked.

"No."

"Then why are you going to see Donovan?"

"He called me. Once before December seventh, and twice since. Once when Patricia and I were still in Honolulu, and the second the day before yesterday, in Frisco. He got me the priority to fly in here."

"Do you know what he's doing?"

"I figured you would."

Fowler grunted as he refilled their glasses. He handed Pickering his drink, and then went on, "Right now, he's the Coordinator of Information. For a dollar a year. It was Franklin Roosevelt's idea."

"That sounds like a propaganda outfit."

"I think maybe it's supposed to. He's got Robert Sherwood, the playwright, and some other people like that, who will do propaganda. They've moved into the National Institutes of Health building. But there's another angle to it, an intelligence angle. He's gathered together a group of experts—he's got nine or ten, and he's shooting for a dozen, and this is probably what he has in mind for you—who are going to collect all the information generated by all the intelligence services, you know, the Army's G-2, the Office of Naval Intelligence, the FBI, the State Department, everybody, and try to make some overall, global sense out of it. For presentation to the President."

"I don't think I understand," Pickering confessed.

"Donovan makes the point, and I think he's right, that the service intelligence operations are too parochial, that they have blinders on them like a carriage horse. They see the war only from the viewpoint of the Navy or the Army or whatever."

The Senator looked at Pickering to see if he was getting through. Pickering made a "come on, tell me more" gesture with his hand.

"OK. Let's say the Navy finds out, as they did, that the Germans had established a weather station and aerial navigation facilities in Greenland. The Navy solution to the problem would be to send a battleship to blow it up—"

"Where would they get one? The Navy's fresh out of battleships. The Japanese used them for target practice."

"You want to hear this or not?"

"Sorry."

"You're going to have to learn to curb your lip, Flem, if you're going to go to work for Bill Donovan. Or anywhere else in the government."

"What happened to free speech?"

"It went out the same window with Franklin Roosevelt's pledge that our boys would never fight on foreign soil," the Senator said.

"I'm not working for him yet," Pickering said.

Smiling, Senator Fowler shook his head, and then went on, "As I was saying, if Navy Intelligence finds something, they propose a Navy solution. If the Army Air Corps had found out about the Germans on Greenland, they would have proposed sending bombers to eliminate them. Am I getting through to you?"

Pickering nodded.

"The idea is that Donovan's people—his 'twelve disciples,' as they're called—will get intelligence information from every source, evaluate it, and make a strategic recommendation. In other words, after the Navy found the Greenland Germans, Donovan's people might have recommended sending Army Air Corps bombers."

"That sounds like a good idea."

"It is, but I don't think it will work."

"Why not?"

"Interservice rivalry, primarily. And that now includes J. Edgar Hoover and the FBI. Until Bill Donovan showed up, Edgar thought that if war came, the FBI would be in charge of intelligence, period. Edgar is a very dangerous man if crossed."

"The story I got was that Donovan got Hoover his job, running the FBI."

"That was yesterday. In Washington, the question is, 'What have you done for me today, and what can you do for me tomorrow?' Anyway, the facts are that everybody has drawn their knives to cut Donovan's throat. I'm betting on Donovan, but I've been wrong before."

"Really?" Pickering teased.

"That's what you'd be getting into if you went to work for him, Flem. When do you see him?"

"He wanted me to have dinner with him tonight, but I wasn't in the mood. I told him I would come to his office in the morning."

"Boy, have you got a lot to learn!" Fowler said.

"Meaning I should have shown up, grateful for the privilege of a free meal from the great man?"

"Yeah. Exactly."

"Fuck him," Fleming Pickering said. "So far as I'm concerned, Bill Donovan is just one more overpaid ambulance chaser."

"You'd better hope he doesn't know you think that."

"He already does. I already told him."

"You did?" Senator Fowler asked, deciding as he spoke that it was probably true.

"He represented us before the International Maritime Court when a Pacific & Orient tanker rammed our *Hawaiian Trader.* You wouldn't believe the bill that sonofabitch sent me."

"I hope you paid it," Fowler said wryly.

"I did," Pickering said, "but not before I called him up and told him what I thought of it. And him."

"Oh, Christ, Flem, you're something!" Fowler said, laughing.

"I couldn't get near the club car, much less the dining car, on the train from New York," Pickering said. "All I've had to eat all day is a roll on the airplane and some hors d'oeuvres. I'm starving. You have any plans for dinner?"

Fowler shook his head no.

"Until you graced me with your presence, I was going to take my shoes off, collapse on the couch, and get something from room service."

There was a knock at the door. It was Max Telford.

"Come on in, Max," Pickering called. "The Senator was just extolling the virtues of your room service."

"I've got someone with me," Telford said, and a very large, very black man, in the traditional chef's uniform of starched white hat and jacket and striped gray trousers, pushed a rolling cart loaded with silver food warmers into the room.

"Hello, Jefferson," Pickering said, as he crossed the room to him and offered his hand. "How the hell are you? I thought you were in New York."

"No, Sir. I've been here about three months," the chef said. "I heard you were in the house, and thought maybe you'd like something more than crackers and cheese to munch on."

"Great, I'm starving. Do you know the Senator?"

"I know who the Senator is," Jefferson Dittler said.

"Dick, Jefferson Dittler. Jefferson succeeded where Patricia failed; he got Pick to wash dishes."

"Lots of dishes," Dittler laughed. "Then I taught him a little about cooking."

"Oh, I've heard about you," Senator Fowler said, shaking hands.

"You're the fellow who taught Pick how to make hollandaise in a Waring Blender."

"That was supposed to be a professional secret," Dittler said.

"Well, Pick betrayed your confidence," Fowler said. "He taught that trick to my wife."

"He's a nice boy," Dittler said.

Pickering turned from the array of bottles and handed Dittler a glass dark with whiskey. "That's that awful fermented corn you like, distilled in a moldy old barrel in some Kentucky holler."

"That's why it's so good," Dittler said. "The moldy old barrel's the secret." He raised his glass. "To Pick. May God be with him."

"Here, here," Senator Fowler said.

Fleming Pickering started lifting the silver food covers.

"Very nice," he said. "One more proof that someone of my superior intelligence knows how to raise children for fun and profit. Jefferson never did this sort of thing for me before Pick worked for him."

"He's a nice boy," Jefferson Dittler repeated, and then, his tone suggesting it was something he desperately wanted to believe, "Smart as a whip. He'll be all right in the Marines."

(THREE)
BUILDING "F"
ANACOSTIA NAVAL AIR STATION
WASHINGTON, D.C.
20 DECEMBER 1941

The interview between Mr. Fleming Pickering, Chairman of the Board of the Pacific & Far Eastern Shipping Corporation, and Colonel William J. Donovan, the Coordinator of Information to the President of the United States, did not go well.

For one thing, when Mr. Pickering was not in Colonel Donovan's outer office at the agreed-upon time, 9:45 A.M., Colonel Donovan went to his next appointment. This required Mr. Pickering, who arrived at 9:51 A.M., to cool his heels for more than an hour with an old copy of *Time* magazine. Mr. Pickering was not used to cooling his heels in anyone's office, and he was more than a little annoyed.

More importantly, Mr. Pickering quickly learned that Colonel Donovan did not intend for him to become one of the twelve disciples that Senator Fowler had mentioned, but rather that he would be an adviser to one of the disciples—should he "come aboard."

That disciple was named. Mr. Pickering knew him, both personally and professionally. He was a banker, and Pickering was willing to acknowledge that Donovan's man had a certain degree of expertise in international finance, which was certainly closely connected with international maritime commerce.

But the United States was not about to consider opening new and profitable shipping channels. Victory, in Fleming Pickering's judgment, was going to go to whichever of the warring powers could transport previously undreamed of tonnages of military equipment, damn the cost, to any number of obscure ports, under the most difficult conditions. In that connection there were two problems, as Pickering saw the situation.

First, there was the actual safe passage of the vessels—getting them past enemy surface and submersible warships. That was obviously going to be the Navy's problem. The second problem, equally important to the execution of a war, was cargo handling and refueling facilities at the destination ports. A ship's cargo was useless unless it could be unloaded. A ship itself was useless if its fuel bunkers were dry.

Carrying the war to the enemy, Pickering knew, meant the interdiction of the enemy's sea passages, and denying to him ports through which his land and air forces had to be supplied.

If the President was going to get evaluations of the maritime situation, it seemed perfectly clear to Fleming Pickering that it should come from someone expert in the nuts and bolts, someone who could make judgments based on his own experience with ships and ports, not someone whose experience was limited to the bottom line on a profit-and-loss statement, or whose sea experience was limited to crossing the Atlantic in a first-class cabin on the *Queen Mary* or some other luxury liner.

Someone like him, for example.

This was not overwhelmingly modest, he realized, but neither was it a manifestation of a runaway ego. When Fleming Pickering stepped aboard a P&FE ship—or, for that matter, ships of a dozen other lines—he was addressed as "Captain" and given the privilege of the bridge.

It was not simply a courtesy given to a wealthy shipowner. When Fleming Pickering had come home from France in 1918, he had almost immediately married. Then, to the horror of his new in-laws, he'd shipped out as an apprentice seaman aboard a P&FE freighter. As his father and grandfather had done before him, he had worked his way up in the deck department, ultimately sitting for his master's ticket, any tonnage, any ocean, a week before his twenty-sixth birthday.

He had been relief master on board the *Pacific Vagabond,* five days out of Auckland for Manila, when the radio operator had brought to the bridge the message that his father had suffered a coronary thrombosis and that in a special session of the stockholders (that is to say, his mother), he had been elected Chairman of the Board of the Pacific & Far Eastern Shipping Corporation.

Pickering tried to make this point to Colonel Donovan and failed. He was not particularly surprised when Donovan politely told him, in effect, to take the offer of a job as adviser to the disciple or go fuck himself. The disciple was one of Donovan's Wall Street cronies; Pickering would have been surprised if Donovan had accepted the wisdom of his arguments.

And, he was honest enough to admit, he would have been disappointed if he had. He didn't want to fight the war from behind a goddamned desk in Sodom on Potomac.

"General McInerney will see you now, Mr. Pickering," the impeccably shorn, shined, and erect Marine lieutenant said. "Will you come with me, please, Sir?

Brigadier General D. G. McInerney, USMC, got to his feet and came around from behind his desk as Fleming Pickering was shown into his office. He was a stocky, barrel-chested man wearing Naval Aviator's wings on the breast of his heavily beribboned uniform tunic.

"Why, Corporal Pickering," he said. "My, how you've aged!"

"Hello, you baldheaded old bastard," Pickering replied. "How the hell are you?"

General McInerney's intended handshake degenerated into an affectionate hug. The two men, who had become friends in their teens, beamed happily at each other.

"It's a little early, but what the hell," General McInerney said. "Charlie, get a bottle of the good booze and a couple of glasses."

"Aye, aye, Sir," his aide-de-camp replied. Although he was a little taken aback by the unaccustomed display of affection, and it was the first time he had ever heard anyone refer to General McInerney as a "baldheaded old bastard," he was not totally surprised. Until a week ago, General McInerney's "temporary junior aide" had been a second lieutenant fresh from Quantico, whom General McInerney had arranged to get in the flight-training program at Pensacola.

His name was Malcolm Pickering, and this was obviously his father. The General had told him that they had served together in France in the First World War.

"Pick's a nice boy, Flem," General McInerney said, as he waved Pickering into one end of a rather battered couch and sat down on the other end. "I was tempted to keep him."

"I'm grateful to you for all you did for him, Doc," Pickering said.

"Hell," McInerney said, depreciatingly, "the Corps needs pilots more than it needs club officers, and that's what those paper pushers in personnel were going to do with him."

"Well, I'm grateful nonetheless," Pickering said.

"I got one for you," McInerney said. "I called down there to make sure they weren't going to make him a club officer down there, and you know who his roommate is? Jack Stecker's boy. He just graduated from West Point."

Fleming Pickering had no idea what McInerney was talking about, and it showed on his face.

"Jack Stecker?" McInerney went on. "Buck sergeant? Got the Medal at Belleau Wood?"

The Medal was the Medal of Honor, often erroneously called the Congressional Medal of Honor, the nation's highest award for valor in action.

"Oh, yeah, the skinny guy. Pennsylvania Dutchman. No middle name," Pickering remembered.

"Right," McInerney chuckled, "Jack NMI Stecker."

"I always wondered what had happened to him," Pickering said. "He was one hard-nosed sonofabitch."

The description was a compliment.

The aide handed each of them a glass of whiskey.

"Mud in your eye," McInerney said, raising his glass and then draining it.

"Belleau Wood," Pickering said dryly, before he emptied his glass.

"Jack stayed in the Corps," McInerney went on. "They wanted to send him to Annapolis. Christ, he wasn't any older than we were, he could have graduated with a regular commission when he was twenty-three or twenty-four, but he wanted to get married, so he turned it down. Until last summer he was a master gunnery sergeant at Quantico."

"Was?"

"They made him a captain; he's at Diego."

"And now our kids are second lieutenants! Christ, we're getting old, Doc."

"Jack had two boys. The older one went to Annapolis. He was an ensign on the *Arizona*. He was KIA on December 7."

"Oh, Christ!"

The two men looked at each other a moment, eyes locked, and then McInerney shrugged and Pickering threw up his hands helplessly.

"So what brings you to Washington, Flem?" McInerney asked, changing the subject. "I thought you hated the place."

"I do. And with rare exceptions, everyone in it. I'm looking for a job."

"Oh?"

"I just saw Colonel William J. Donovan," Pickering said. "He sent for me."

"Then I guess you know what he's up to."

"I've got a pretty good idea."

"Out of school, he's giving the Commandant a fit."

"Oh? How so?"

"The scuttlebutt going around is that Roosevelt wants to commission Donovan a brigadier general in the Corps."

"But he was in the Army," Pickering protested.

"Yeah, I know. The President is very impressed, or so I hear, with the British commandos. You know, hit-and-run raids. He wants American commandos, and he thinks they belong in the Corps. I hope to hell it's not true."

"It sounds idiotic to me," Pickering said.

"Tell your important friends. Senator Fowler, for example."

"I will."

"Just don't quote me."

"Don't be silly, Doc."

"You were about to tell me, I think, what you're going to do for Donovan."

"Nothing. I decided I didn't want to work for him. Or maybe vice versa. Anyway, I'm not going to work for him."

"Won't you have enough to do running your company? Hell, transportation is going to win—or lose—this war."

"I sold the passenger ships, at least the larger ones, to the Navy," Pickering replied. "And the freighters and tankers will probably go on long-term charter to either the Navy or the Maritime Administration—the ones that aren't already, that is. There's not a hell of a lot for me to do."

"So what are you going to do?"

"Strange, *General*, that you should ask that question," Pickering said.

"What's on your mind, Flem?" McInerney asked, a hint of suspicion in his voice.

"How about 'Once a Marine, always a Marine'?"

McInerney looked at him with disbelief and uneasiness in his eyes.

"Flem, you're not talking about you coming back in the Corps, are you? Are you serious?"

"Yes, I am, and yes, I am," Pickering said. "Why is that so—to judge from the look in your eyes and your tone of voice—incredible?"

"Come on, Flem," McInerney said. "You've been out of the Corps since 1919—and then, forgive me, you were a corporal."

"There should be some job where I could be useful," Pickering said. "Christ, I've been running eighty-one ships. And their crews. And all the shore facilities."

"I'm sure the Navy would love to commission someone with your kind of experience. Or, for that matter, the Transportation Corps of the Army."

"I don't want to be a goddamn sailor."

"Think it through," McInerney said. "Flem, I'm telling you the way it is."

"So tell me. I'm apparently a little dense."

"Your experience, your shipping business experience, is in what I think of as Base Logistics. Moving large amounts of heavy cargo by sea from one place to another. The Navy does that for the Marine Corps."

"It occurred to me that I could be one hell of a division supply officer, division quartermaster, whatever they call it."

"That calls for a lieutenant colonel, maybe a full colonel. If there was strong resistance among the palace guard to commissioning people—Marines, like Jack Stecker, a master gunnery sergeant—as captains, what makes you think they'd commission a civilian, a former corporal, as a lieutenant colonel?"

"I'm willing to start at the bottom. I don't have to be a lieutenant colonel."

McInerney laughed. "I think you really believe that."

"Yes, I do."

"As a major? A captain? That your idea of starting at the bottom?"

"Why not?"

"Flem, when was the last time someone told you what to do, gave you an order?"

"Well, just for the sake of argument, I think I can still take orders, but I have the feeling that I'm just wasting my breath."

"You want the truth from me, old buddy, or bullshit from some paper pusher?"

"That would depend on what the bullshit was."

" 'Why, we would love to have you, Mr. Pickering,' followed by an assignment as, say, a major, and deputy assistant maintenance officer for mess-kit rehabilitation at Barstow, or some other supply depot. Where you would do a hell of a job rehabilitating mess kits, and be an all-around pain in the ass the rest of the time. You want to march off to war again, Flem, and that's just not going to happen. Unless, of course, you go to the Navy. They really would love to have you."

"Fuck the Navy," Fleming Pickering said.

He stood up. General McInerney eyed him warily.

"I suppose I've made a real fool of myself, haven't I, Doc?" Pickering said calmly.

"No, not at all. I'm just sorry things are . . . the way things are."

"Well, I've kept my master's ticket up. And I still own some ships. Taking a ship to sea is better than being . . . what did you say, 'a deputy assistant mess-kit-repair officer'?"

"Yes, of course it is. But I keep saying, and you keep ignoring, that the Navy would love to have you."

"And I keep saying, and you keep ignoring, 'Fuck the Navy.' "

McInerney laughed.

"Have it your way, Flem. But they *are* on our side in this war."

"Well, then, God help us. I was at Pearl Harbor."

"Is it fair to blame Pearl Harbor on the Navy?"

"On who, then?" Fleming Pickering said, and put out his hand. "Thank you for seeing me, Doc. And for doing what you did for Pick."

"If you were twenty-one, I'd get you in flight school, too. No thanks required. Keep in touch, Flem."

(FOUR)

THE FOSTER LAFAYETTE HOTEL

WASHINGTON, D.C.

20 DECEMBER 1941

"Thank you very much," Fleming Pickering said politely, then took the receiver from his ear and placed it, with elaborate care, in its base. It was one of two telephones on the coffee table in the sitting room of Senator Richardson Fowler's suite.

Then he said, quite clearly, "Well, I'll be a sonofabitch!"

Transcontinental and Western Airlines had just told him that even though he already had his ticket for a flight between New York and San Francisco, with intermediate stops at Chicago and Denver, he could not be boarded without a priority. He had explained to them that he had come from San Francisco with a priority and was simply trying to get home, and that he had presumed that the priority which had brought him to Washington also applied to his return trip. TWA had told him that was not the case; he would need another priority to do so.

Fleming Pickering considered his predicament and swore again. "That goddamned sonofabitch!"

He was referring to Colonel William J. Donovan, Coordinator of Information to the President of the United States. This was his fault. Donovan should have arranged for him to get home, gotten him a priority to do so. While he didn't think it was likely the ambulance-chasing sonofabitch was vindictive enough to have canceled his return-trip priority after their unpleasant encounter that morning, it *was* possible. And whether he had canceled the priority or simply neglected to arrange for one, what this meant for Fleming Pickering was that unless he wanted to spend four days crossing the country by train—and they probably passed out compartments on the train to people with priorities, which might well mean sitting up in a coach all the way across the country—he was going to have to call the bastard up and politely beg him to get him a priority to go home.

There was no question in Pickering's mind that Donovan would get him a priority, and no question either that Donovan would take the opportunity to remind Pickering that priorities were intended for people who were making a contribution to the war effort, not for people who placed their own desires and ambitions above the common good, by, for example, declining to serve with the Office of the Coordinator of Information.

Then Fleming Pickering had another thought: Richardson Fowler could probably get him a priority. Dick was a politician. Whatever law the politicians wrote, or whatever they authorized some agency of the government to implement—such as setting up an air-travel priority system—those bastards would take care of themselves first.

The thought passed through his mind, and was quickly dismissed, that perhaps he was being a horse's ass, that he was not working for the government and therefore had no right to a priority, and that getting one through Fowler's political influence would deprive of a seat some brave soldier en route to battle the Treacherous Jap. He was not going to California to lie on the beach. He still had a shipping company to run; coming here had taken him away from that.

There came a knock at the door. Pickering looked at it, and then at his watch. It was probably Dick Fowler. But why would Fowler knock?

"Come!"

It was Max Telford.

"Hello, Max, what's up?"

"I have a somewhat delicate matter I thought I should bring to your attention," Telford said.

"Will it wait until I pour us a drink? I've had a bad day and desperately need one."

"I could use a little taste myself," Telford said. "Thank you."

"Scotch?"

"Please."

When Pickering handed him his drink, Telford handed him a woman's red leather wallet.

"What's this?"

"It belongs to Miss Ernestine Sage," Telford said.

Ernestine "Ernie" Sage was the daughter of Patricia Pickering's college roommate.

"Where'd you get it?" Pickering asked.

"Miss Sage left it behind when she left the inn. The wallet and some other things."

"I don't quite follow you."

"She was not registered, Mr. Pickering," Telford said carefully.

"She was here with Pick?" Fleming Pickering's eyes lit up. He liked Ernie Sage, and there had been more than a tiny seed of hope in the jokes over the years, as Ernie and Pick had been growing up, that they could be paired off permanently. Still, it was a dumb thing for Pick to do. Ernest Sage, Ernie's father, was Chairman of the Board of American Personal Pharmaceuticals. And he routinely stayed in the Foster La-fayette. Pick should have known she would be recognized.

"With Pick's friend," Telford said. "Lieutenant McCoy."

"I know him," Pickering said, without thinking. "He's a nice kid."

Pick and McCoy had gone through the Officer Candidate School at the Marine base at Quantico together. They had nothing in common. McCoy had been a corporal in the peacetime Marine Corps, and what he had, he had earned himself. But Pickering had not been surprised when he'd met McCoy and seen the affection between him and his son. Doc McInerney and Flem Pickering had become lifelong friends in the Corps in France, despite a wide disparity in backgrounds.

"Then you know he was wounded," Telford said.

"No. I hadn't heard about that."

"I don't have all the details," Telford said. "I didn't want to pry, but McCoy is apparently some sort of officer courier. He was in the Pacific when the war started, and Pick got one of those 'missing and presumed dead' telegrams. He was pretty shook up about it. And then McCoy called from the West Coast and said he was back. Anyway, Pick came to me and said that McCoy was on his way to Washington, and if there was ever a time a Foster hotel should offer its very best, it was now, to McCoy. And his lady friend. And that all charges should be put on his account."

"And the lady friend turned out to be Ernestine Sage?"

"Yes, Sir. I recognized her immediately, but I don't know if she knows I knew who she is."

"And they were here for a while? Lots of room service?"

"Yes. That's a nice way to put it."

"Andrew Foster once told me that so far as he's concerned, he's prepared to offer accommodations to two female elephants in heat, plus a bull elephant, just as long as they pay the bill and don't soil the carpets," Pickering said. "So what's the problem?"

Telford laughed. "He told me a variant of that philosophy. It was two swans in heat, so long as they paid the bill and didn't flap their wings and lay eggs in the elevators."

Pickering chuckled, and then repeated, "So what's the problem? I'd rather my wife didn't hear about this, but so far as I'm concerned, whatever Ernie Page did in here with Lieutenant McCoy is their business and no one else's."

"The problem is how to return Miss Sage's property to her," Telford said. "The only address I have for either of them is the one on her driver's license. That's in Bernardsville, New Jersey. Her parents' home, I think."

"Telford, your discretion is in keeping with the highest traditions of the innkeeping trade," Pickering said, meaning it. "If Ernest Sage found out—or even suspected—that his only child, his precious little Ernie, was shacked up with a Marine officer in a hotel in Washington, there would be hell to pay. Let me think."

He did just that, as he took a deep pull at his drink.

"Ernie works for an advertising agency in New York," he said, after a moment. "J. Walter Thompson. It's on Madison Avenue. Check the phone book. Send it to her there, special delivery, and put Pick's address on it as the return address."

"All I have for that would be 'Pensacola, Florida.' "

"Add 'Student, Flight Training Program, U.S. Navy Air Station,' " Pickering said.

"I'm glad I brought this to your attention," Telford said.

"So am I. You about ready for another of these?"

"No, thank you."

The door opened and Senator Richardson Fowler walked in. There was someone with him, a stocky, well-dressed man in his sixties. He stopped inside the door, took gold-rimmed pince-nez from a vest pocket, polished them quickly with a handkerchief, and then put them on his nose.

"Good evening, Mr. Secretary," Telford said. "It's nice to see you, Sir."

"Hello, Telford, how are you?" said Secretary of the Navy Frank W. Knox.

"Fine, and on my out, Sir," Telford said. "Is there anything I can send up?"

"All we want right now is a drink, Max, thanks," Fowler said. He waited until Telford had left, closing the door behind him, and then went on, "Frank told me at lunch, to my surprise, that you two don't know each other."

"Only by reputation," Pickering said, crossing the room to Knox and giving him his hand.

COUNTERATTACK 51

"I was about to say just that," Knox said. "How do you do, Pickering?"

The two examined each other with unabashed curiosity.

"Scotch for you, Frank?" Senator Fowler asked, looking over his shoulder from the array of bottles.

"Please," Knox said absently, and then, "Dick tells me you're going to work for Bill Donovan."

"That didn't work out," Pickering said.

"I'm sorry to hear that," Knox said.

"Why should you be sorry?"

"It takes away an argument I was going to use on you."

"What argument was that?"

Senator Fowler knew Frank Knox almost as well as he knew Fleming Pickering. Sensing that their first meeting already showed signs of becoming confrontational, he hurried over with the drinks.

"You all right, Flem?"

"Oh, I think I might have another. You can't fly on six or seven wings, you know." He walked to the array of liquor.

"I gather your meeting with Bill Donovan was not entirely successful?" Fowler asked.

"No, it wasn't," Pickering replied.

"You want to tell me why?"

"Well, aside from the fact that we don't like each other, which is always a problem if you're going to work for somebody, you were wrong about his wanting to make me one of his twelve disciples. What he had in mind was my being a minor saint—Saint Fleming the Humble—to one of his Wall Street moneymen."

"You have been at the sauce, haven't you?"

"It is a blow to the masculine ego, especially in these times of near-hysterical patriotism, for an ex-Marine to be told, 'No, thanks, the Corps can't use you.' I have had a drink or five. Guilty, Your Senatorship."

"I don't think I understand you," Fowler said.

"After I saw Donovan, I tried to enlist, and was turned down."

"You were a Marine?" Knox asked.

"I was," Pickering said, "but, as the General reminded me, only a corporal."

"Both Napoleon and Hitler were only corporals," said Frank Knox. "I, on the other hand, was a sergeant."

Pickering looked at the dignified Secretary of the Navy, saw the twinkle in his eyes, and smiled.

"Were you really?"

"First United States Volunteer Cavalry, Sir," Knox said. "I charged up Kettle Hill with Lieutenant Colonel Theodore Roosevelt."

"The *good* cousin," Pickering said.

"Oh, I wouldn't put it quite that way," Knox said. "Franklin grows on you."

"I will refrain from saying, Mr. Secretary, how that man grows on me."

Knox chuckled. "The Marine Corps turned you down, did they?"

"Politely, but firmly."

"The Marine Corps is part of the Navy. I'm Secretary of the Navy. Are you a bartering man, Pickering?"

"I'll always listen to an offer."

Knox nodded, and paused thoughtfully before going on.

"The reason I was sorry to hear that you're not going to be working for Bill Donovan, Pickering, is that I came here with the intention of making this argument to you: Since you will be working for Donovan, you will not be able to run the Pacific & Far Eastern Shipping fleet, so you might as well sell it to the Navy."

"Since Fowler apparently has been doing a lot of talking about me," Pickering replied, not pleasantly, "I'm surprised he didn't tell you I told him I have no intention of selling any more of my ships. To the Navy, or anyone else."

"Oh, he told me that," Knox said. "I came here to try to get you to change your mind."

"Then I'm afraid you're on a wild-goose chase."

"You haven't even heard my arguments."

Pickering shrugged.

"We're desperate for shipping," Knox said.

"My ships will haul anything the Navy wants hauled, anywhere the Navy wants it hauled."

"There are those who believe the maritime unions may cause trouble when there are inevitable losses to submarines and surface raiders."

"My crews will sail my ships anywhere I tell them to sail them," Pickering said.

"There are those who believe the solution to that problem, which I consider more real than you do, is to send them to sea with Navy crews."

"Then they're fools," Pickering said.

"Indeed?" Knox asked icily.

"Pacific & Far Eastern doesn't have a third mate, or a second assistant engineer, who is not qualified to sail as master, or chief engineer," Pickering said. "Which is good for the country. My junior officers are going to be the masters and chief engineers of the ships—the vast fleets of cargo ships—we're going to have to build for this war, and my ordinary and able-bodied seamen and my engine room wipers are going to be the junior officers and assistant engineers. You can't teach real, as opposed to Navy, seamanship in ten or twelve weeks at the Great Lakes Naval Training Center. If somebody is telling you that you can, you had better get a new adviser."

"What's the difference between Navy seamanship, Flem, and 'real' seamanship?" Fowler asked.

"It takes three or four Navy sailors to do what one able-bodied seaman is expected to do on a merchantman," Pickering replied. "A merchant seaman does what he sees has to be done, based on a good deal of time at sea. A Navy sailor is trained not to blow his nose until someone tells him to. And then they send a chief petty officer to make sure he blows it in the prescribed manner."

"You don't seem to have a very high opinion of the U.S. Navy," Knox said sharply.

"Not if what happened at Pearl Harbor is any indication of the way they think. I was there, Mr. Knox."

Knox glowered at him; Fowler saw the Secretary's jowls working.

"There are those," Knox said after a long pause, "who advise me that the Navy should stop trying to reason with you and simply seize your vessels under the President's emergency powers."

"I'll take you to the Supreme Court and win. You can force me—not that you would have to—to have my ships carry what you want, wherever you want it carried, but you can *not* seize them."

"A couple of minutes ago, the thought entered my head that I might be able to resolve this difference reasonably by offering you a commission in the Marine Corps, say, as a colonel. That now seems rather silly, doesn't it?"

"I don't think *silly* is the word," Pickering said nastily. *"Insulting* would seem to fit. To both the Corps and me."

"Flem!" Senator Fowler protested.

"It's all right, Dick," Knox said, waving his hand to shut him off. "And I don't suppose saying to you, Pickering, that your country needs your vessels would have much effect on you, would it?"

"My ships are at my country's disposal," Pickering said evenly. "But what I am not going to do is turn them over to the Navy so the Navy can do to them what it did to the Pacific Fleet at Pearl Harbor."

"That's an insult," Knox said, "to the courageous men at Pearl Harbor, many of whom gave their lives."

"No, it's not," Pickering said. "I'm not talking about courage. I'm talking about stupidity. If I had your job, Mr. Secretary, I would fire every admiral who was anywhere near Pearl Harbor. Fire them, hell, stand them in front of a firing squad for gross dereliction of duty. Pearl Harbor should not have happened. That's a fact, and you can't hide it behind a chorus of patriotic outrage that someone would dare sink our fleet."

"I'm ultimately responsible for whatever happens to the Navy," Knox said.

"If you really believe that, then maybe you should consider resigning to set an example."

"Now goddamn it, Flem!" Senator Fowler exploded. "That's going too goddamned far. You owe Frank an apology!"

"Not if he really believes that, he doesn't," Knox said. He leaned over and set his glass on the coffee table. "Thank you for the drink, Dick. And for the chance to meet Mr. Pickering."

"Frank!"

"It's been very interesting," the Secretary of the Navy said. "If not very fruitful."

"Frank, Flem's had a couple too many," Senator Fowler said.

"He looks like the kind of man who can handle his liquor," Knox said. "Anyway, *in vino veritas.*" He walked to the door and opened it, and then half-turned around. "Mr. Pickering, I offered my resignation to the President on December seventh. He put it to me that his accepting it would not be in the best interests of the country, and he therefore declined to do so."

And then he went through the door and closed it after him.

Fleming Pickering and Richardson Fowler looked at each other. Pickering saw anger in his old friend's eyes.

There was a momentary urge to apologize, but then Fleming Pickering decided against it. He had, he realized, said nothing that he had not meant.

III

(ONE)
ON BOARD USS *TANGIER*
TASK FORCE 14
1820 HOURS 22 DECEMBER 1941

"**N**ow hear this," the loudspeakers throughout the ship blared, harshly and metallically. "The smoking lamp is out. The smoking lamp is out."

Staff Sergeant Joseph L. Howard, USMC, was on the bow of the *Tangier* when the announcement came. He was smoking a cigarette, looking out across the wide, gentle swells of the Pacific at the other ships of Task Force 14.

The USS *Tangier,* a seaplane tender pressed into duty as a troop transport, with the 4th Marine Defense Battalion on board, was in line behind the aircraft carrier USS *Saratoga,* which flew the flag of Rear Admiral Frank Fletcher, Commander of Task Force 14.

Behind the *Tangier* was the *Neches,* a fleet oiler, riding low in the water. The three ships considered most vulnerable to attack formed the center of Task Force 14. Sailing ahead of the *Saratoga* were the cruisers USS *Astoria* and USS *Minneapolis.* The cruiser USS *San Francisco* brought up the rear. The cruisers themselves were screened by nine destroyers.

Task Force 14 had put out from Pearl Harbor five days before, six days after the Japanese had attacked Pearl, under orders from Admiral Husband E. Kimmel, the U.S. Pacific Fleet Commander, to reinforce Wake Island.

Wake Island desperately needed reinforcement. Already there were what the Corps euphemistically referred to as "elements" of the 1st Marine Defense Battalion. These amounted to less than four hundred Marines, commanded by Major James P. S. Devereux. Devereux had two five-inch naval cannon, obsolete weapons removed from men-of-war; four three-inch antiaircraft cannon, only one of which had the necessary fire-control gear; twenty-four .50-caliber Browning machine guns; and maybe a hundred .30-caliber Brownings, mixed air- and water-cooled. That, plus individual small arms, was it.

Staff Sergeant Joe Howard knew what weaponry had been given to Major Devereux's "elements" because he'd talked to the battalion's ordnance sergeant. It had been decided, literally at the last minute, that the ordnance sergeant would be of more value to the Corps left behind at Pearl, doing what he could to get the newly formed 4th Defense Battalion's weaponry up and running.

And he knew what Task Force 14 was carrying to reinforce Wake Island. In addition to the 4th Defense Battalion, at near full strength, and the Brewster Buffalos of VMF-211 that would fly off *Saratoga* and join what was left of the dozen Wildcats already on Wake, there were, aboard *Tangier* and in the holds of other ships, nine thousand rounds of five-inch ammunition; twelve thousand rounds of three-inch shells for the antiaircraft cannon; and three million rounds of .50-caliber machine-gun ammunition.

After the devastating, humiliating whipping they had taken at Pearl on December 7, the Navy and the Marine Corps were finally coming out to fight.

Howard took a final, deep drag on his Camel, then flicked the glowing coal from its end with his thumbnail. He carefully tore the cigarette paper down its length and let the wind scatter the tobacco away. Then he crumbled the paper into a tiny ball between his thumb and index fingers and let the wind take that away, too.

Howard was "under arms." That is, he was wearing his steel helmet and a web belt from whose eyelets hung a canteen, a first-aid pouch, a magazine pouch for two pistol magazines, and a Model 1911A1 .45-caliber Colt pistol in a leather holster. The canteen was empty, as were the magazine pouch and the magazine in the .45. Ammunition had not been authorized for issue to the guard, much less to the troops, although there was a metal box in the guardroom with a couple of dozen five-round stripper clips of .30-06 ammunition for Springfield '03 rifles and a half-dozen loaded seven-round .45 magazines.

Joe Howard had seen the Officer of the Guard slip one of the loaded magazines into his .45 just before guard mount. The Officer of the Guard was a second lieutenant, a twenty-one-year-old, six months out of Annapolis. Joe had wondered whom he thought he was going to have to shoot.

He hadn't said anything, of course. Staff sergeants in the Marine Corps don't question anything officers do, even twenty-one-year-old second lieutenants, unless it is really stupid and likely to hurt somebody. If Lieutenant Ellsworth Gripley felt that it was necessary to carry a loaded pistol in the performance of his duties as officer of the guard, that was his business.

Howard set his steel helmet at the appropriately jaunty angle for a sergeant of the guard and set out to find the Officer of the Guard. He was a little worried about Second Lieutenant Ellsworth Gripley, USMC. It had finally sunk in on the young officer that this wasn't a maneuver; within forty-eight hours the 4th Defense Battalion would be ashore on Wake Island and engaging the Japanese, and he would be expected to perform like a Marine officer.

Lieutenant Gripley wasn't *afraid,* Joe Howard thought. More like nervous. That was understandable. And he saw it as his duty to do what he could to make Gripley feel a little more sure of himself.

The ships making up Task Force 14 were, of course, blacked out to avoid detection by the enemy. One of the functions of the guard detail—in S/Sgt. Joe Howard's opinion, the most important function— was to make sure that no one sneaked on deck after dark for a quick smoke. The glow of a cigarette coal was visible for incredibly long distances on a black night. Even so, there seemed to be a large number of people, including officers, who seemed unwilling, or unable, to believe that *their* cigarette was *really* going to put anyone in danger.

They seemed to think that maybe if three or four hundred people lined the ship's rails, merrily puffing away, a Japanese submarine skipper could see this through a submarine periscope, but one little ol' cigarette, carefully concealed in the hand? Not goddamned likely.

Because of his zealous enforcement of the no-smoking regulations, Howard had already earned a reputation among some of the officers as a rather insolent noncom. Marine officers are not accustomed to being firmly corrected by staff sergeants. Or to being threatened by them:

"Sir, if you don't put that out right now, I'll have to call the officer of the guard."

When he had said that, the cigarettes were immediately put out. But in half a dozen instances, the officer had asked for his name and billet. He didn't think the information had been requested so the officers could seek out the Headquarters Company commander to tell him what a fine job S/Sgt. Howard had been doing.

He had had less trouble with the enlisted men, although there were about ten times as many of them as there were officers. The lower-ranking Marines were either afraid of defying orders or of Japanese submarines—or probably of both. And Joe Howard was aware that most of the senior noncoms probably knew, as he did, just how far a cigarette coal could be seen at night and did not wish to end their war by drowning after being torpedoed.

And, besides, they would be in a shooting war soon enough. The word had leaked out of Officer's Country, via a PFC orderly whom Joe had known at Quantico, that at 1800 hours they were about 550 miles from Wake Island. The Task Force was making about fifteen knots, which translated to mean they were then thirty-six hours steaming time from Wake. In other words, they should be at Wake at daybreak the day after tomorrow.

The ships in the center of the Task Force, the *Saratoga,* the *Tangier,* and the oiler, had been making course changes regularly, zigzagging across the Pacific so as to present as difficult a target as possible for any enemy submarine that might be stalking the Task Force. The cruisers and destroyers had been making course changes that were more frequent and of greater magnitude than those of the carrier and the ships following in its wake. The destroyers had been weaving in and out between the larger ships like sheepdogs guarding their flock.

Joe Howard had grown used to changes in course—the slight tilting of the deck, the slight change in the dull rumble of the engine, the change in the pitching and rolling of the *Tangier*—to the point where he paid almost no conscious attention to them.

But now, as he made his way aft along the portside boat deck, looking for Lieutenant Gripley, he slowly came to realize that *this* course change was somehow different. He stopped, putting his hand on the damp inboard bulkhead to steady himself.

For one thing, he thought, *it's taking a lot longer than they normally do.*

And then he understood. The *Tangier,* and thus all of Task Force 14, was not changing course, but reversing course.

What the hell is that all about?

The *Tangier*'s public-address system, which never seemed to shut up, was now absolutely silent. If something was up, it certainly would have gone off, accompanied by harshly clanging bells, calling General Quarters.

He decided that nothing had happened, except that his imagination was running away with him.

He began moving aft again, telling himself that after he found Lieutenant Gripley, he would go to the guardroom and have a ham sandwich and a cup of coffee.

When he reached the rear of the boat deck, there was someone leaning on the railing beside the ladder to the main deck. At first he thought it was the guard posted there, and that he had deserted his post at least to the point of taking off his steel pot and assuming an unmilitary position. He was considering how badly to ream him when he saw the guard, steel pot in place, standing at parade rest.

Whoever was leaning on the rail was an officer—not Lieutenant Gripley, but somebody else.

When he got close, he saw that it was the Executive Officer of the 4th Defense Battalion. And when he heard Joe's footsteps, he first turned his head, and then stood erect.

"Sergeant Howard, Sir. Sergeant of the Guard."

"Yes," the Exec said absently. "How are you tonight, Sergeant?"

It was not the expected response.

"Just getting a little air, Sergeant," the Exec continued. "Stuffy in my cabin."

"Yes, Sir," Joe said.

"Trying to get my thoughts in order, actually," the Exec said.

"Sir?" Joe asked, now wholly confused.

The Exec straightened.

"Sergeant," he said. "At 2100 tonight, there was a radio from Pearl Harbor. Task Force 14 is to return to Pearl."

"Sir?"

"Task Force 14 is ordered to return to Pearl. We have already reversed course."

"But what about Wake Island?"

"It would appear, Sergeant," the Exec said throatily, huskily, speaking with difficulty, "that Major Devereux and his men are going to have to make do with what they have."

"Jesus Christ," S/Sgt. Howard blurted. He knew, perhaps as well as anyone, what few arms and how little ammunition, and how few Marines, were at Major James P. S. Devereux's command.

"Orders are orders, Sergeant," the Exec said, and pushed his way past Joe Howard. There was not much light, but there was enough for Joe to see that tears were running down the Exec's cheeks.

Goddamn them! Staff Sergeant Howard thought. *How the hell can they turn around, knowing that unless we can reinforce Wake, the Japs will take it, and all those guys will be either dead or prisoners? Who the hell could be responsible for such a chickenshit order?*

And then he thought: *Who the fuck are you kidding? If we'd gone to Wake, when the first shot was fired, you'd be hiding behind the nearest rock, curled up like a fucking baby, and crying, the way you behaved on December seventh.*

(TWO)

LAKEHURST NAVAL AIR STATION
LAKEHURST, NEW JERSEY
1605 HOURS 1 JANUARY 1942

PFC Stephen M. Koffler, USMC, heard his relief coming, the crunch of their field shoes on the crusty snow, the Corporal quietly counting cadence, long before he saw them. Koffler was eighteen years and two months old, weighed 145 pounds, and stood five feet seven inches tall.

The relief was marching across the front of the enormous airship hangar; and Koffler's post, Number Four, was a marching post, back and forth, along the side of the hangar.

Permission had been granted to the guard to carry their Springfield 1903 caliber .30-06 rifles at sling arms, muzzle down. The idea was to keep snow out of the muzzle.

PFC Koffler unslung his piece and brought it to port arms. The moment he saw the corporal turn the corner, he issued his challenge: "Halt, who goes there?"

He had learned how to do this and a number of other things peculiar to the profession of arms generally, and to the United States Marine Corps specifically, at the United States Marine Corps Recruit Depot, Parris Island, South Carolina, during the months of October and November and in the first weeks of December, but the first time he had done it for real was here in Lakehurst.

There were five rounds in the magazine of his rifle, and a total of forty more in the pockets of the "Belt, Web, Cartridge" he was wearing around his waist. His bayonet was fixed to the muzzle of his rifle. Sometimes, walking back and forth alongside the dirigible hangar, he had forgotten it was there and bumped into it with his lower leg.

"Corporal of the Guard," the corporal called.

"Advance, Corporal of the Guard, to be recognized."

The Corporal of the Guard ordered the guard detail to halt. When they had done that, he took another half-dozen steps toward PFC Koffler.

"Giblet," PFC Koffler challenged.

"Gravy," the Corporal of the Guard replied, giving the countersign.

When he had first been told the night's challenge and countersign, PFC Koffler had been more than a little surprised. Somebody around here apparently had a sense of humor. There had been none of that at Parris Island, not with something as important as guard duty.

Not that what he was doing here at Lakehurst wasn't serious. The hangar had been built to house dirigibles before PFC Stephen Koffler was born, back when the Navy had thought that enormous rigid airships were the wave of the future. It now held half a dozen Navy blimps, used to patrol the waters off New York harbor for German submarines. A blimp was a nonrigid airship, like a balloon. Last night in the guard-house, PFC Koffler had heard that the first Navy nonrigid airship had been called the "A-Limp," and the second model the "B-Limp." That's where the name had come from.

There were German submarines out there, and it was quite possible that German saboteurs would attempt to destroy the blimps in their hangar. There were a whole lot of Nazi sympathizers in New York's Yorktown district. Before the war, they used to hire Madison Square Garden for their meetings.

Guarding the dirigible hangar and its blimps was not like guarding the recruit barracks at Parris Island. PFC Koffler had taken his responsibilities seriously.

"PFC Koffler, Post Four, Corporal," Koffler said. "All is well."

They went through the formalized ritual of changing the guard. The first Marine in the line behind the corporal marched up and held his Springfield at port arms while Koffler recited his Special Orders, then the Corporal of the Guard barked "Post," and PFC Koffler marched away from his post and took up a position at the rear of the relief guard.

This was his last tour. He'd gone on duty, "stood guard mount," at 1600 yesterday afternoon, and been assigned to the First Relief. He'd gone on guard at 1600, walked his post for two hours, and been relieved at 1800. Four hours later, at 2200, he had gone on again and walked his post until midnight, which was New Year's. Then he'd had another four hours off, going back on at 0400 until 0600. Another four hours off until ten, then two hours more until noon, then four hours off, and then this, the final tour, two hours from 1400 to 1600.

It had not entered his mind to feel sorry for himself for having to walk around in below-zero weather on New Year's Day, any more than it had entered his mind on Monday, when he'd gotten off the Sea Coast Limited train that had carried him from Parris Island, South Carolina, to Newark, that if he got on the subway, he could be home in thirty minutes.

It had been instilled in him at Parris Island that he no longer had any personal life that the Corps did not elect to grant him. He was not a candy-ass civilian anymore, he was a Marine. He could go home only when, and if, the Corps told him he could. You were supposed to get a leave home when you graduated from Parris Island, but that hadn't happened. There was a war on.

Maybe he could get a leave, or at least a weekend liberty, while he

was going to school at Lakehurst. Or when he graduated. If he graduated. He wasn't holding his breath. For one thing, the sergeant major on
Mainside at Parris Island, where he'd been transferred after graduating
from Boot Camp, had really been pissed at him. They had gone through
the records looking for people with drafting experience, and they'd
found him and transferred him to Mainside to execute architectural
drawings for new barracks. He hadn't joined the Corps to be a draftsman. If he'd wanted to be a draftsman, he would have stayed with the
Public Service Corporation of New Jersey, where he had been a draftsman trainee in the Bus & Trolley Division.

There'd been an interesting notice on the bulletin board. Regulations said you had to read the bulletin board at least twice a day, so it
wasn't his fault he'd seen the notice. The notice had said that volunteers
were being accepted for parachute duty. And that those volunteers who
successfully completed the course of instruction at Lakehurst would
receive an extra fifty dollars a month in pay. That was a lot of money.
As a PFC, his total pay was forty-one dollars a month, thirty-six dollars
plus five dollars for having qualified as Expert on the firing range with
the Springfield.

So he had applied, which immediately pissed off the Sergeant
Major, who needed a draftsman. "Let some other asshole jump out of
goddamned airplanes," the Sergeant Major yelled at him. The Sergeant
Major was so pissed and he made so much noise that one of the officers
came out to see what was going on.

"Well, you'll have to let him apply, Sergeant Major," the officer
said, "if he wants to. Put on his application we need him here, but let
him apply."

Stephen Koffler felt sure that was the last he would ever hear of
parachute school, but three days later the Sergeant Major called him
into his office to tell him to pack his fucking gear and get his ass on the
train, and he personally hoped Koffler would break his fucking neck the
first time he jumped.

He never even left Pennsylvania Station when he got off the Sea
Coast Limited at Newark. He just went downstairs from the tracks to
ask Information about when the New Jersey Central train left for Lakehurst. They told him it would be another two and a half hours. While
he was waiting, he got asked three times for his orders, twice by sailors
wearing Shore Patrol brassards, and once even by fucking doggie MPs.
Steve Koffler was already Marine enough to be convinced that the
goddamned Army had no right to let their goddamned MPs ask a
Marine anything.

When he got to Lakehurst, a truck carried him out to the Naval Air
Station. And then the Charge of Quarters, a lean and mean-looking

sergeant, told him where he could find a bunk, but that he'd have to do without a mattress cover, a pillow, and sheets because the supply room was locked up. He might even have to wait until after New Year's.

In the morning, he had a brief encounter with the First Sergeant, who was lanky and mean-looking like the Charge of Quarters, just older. The First Sergeant said that he really hadn't expected him, and that he thought the new class would trickle in over the next couple of days, but now that he had reported in, he should get his gear shipshape and be ready to stand guard mount at 1600.

Koffler spent the day getting ready for guard, pressing his green blouse and trousers and a khaki shirt and necktie, which he now knew was not a necktie but a "field scarf." He restored the spit-shine on his better pair (of two pairs) of field shoes, and cleaned and lightly oiled his 1903 Springfield .30-06 rifle.

It had been pretty goddamned cold, walking up and down alongside the dirigible hangar, but there was hot coffee in the guardhouse when you'd done your two hours; and the Sergeant of the Guard had even come out twice with a thermos of coffee and fried-egg sandwiches, an act that really surprised Koffler, based on his previous experience with both sergeants and guard duty at Parris Island.

After the guard that was just relieved marched back to the guardhouse and turned in their ammunition, every round carefully counted and accounted for, Steve Koffler took a chance and asked the Sergeant of the Guard a question. He seemed like a pretty nice guy.

"What happens now? I mean, what am I supposed to do?"

"If I was you, kid, I'd make myself scarce around the billet. There's always some sonofabitch looking for a work detail."

"You mean we're not restricted to the barracks?"

"No. Why should you be? You just get out of Parris Island?"

"Yeah."

"It shows," the Sergeant said.

"Where should I go to get away from the barracks?"

"You can go anyplace you can afford to go. It's about an hour on the train to New York City, but you better be loaded, you want to go there."

"How about Newark?"

"Why the hell would you want to go to Newark?"

"I live just outside, a town called East Orange."

"You just came off Boot Camp leave, right?"

"No."

"What do you mean, 'No'?"

"I mean I didn't get any leave. When we graduated, they sent me to Mainside, and then they sent me here."

"No shit? You're supposed to get a leave, ten days at least."

"Well, I didn't get one."

"I find out you've been shitting me, kid," the Sergeant said, "I'll have your ass."

Then he picked up the telephone.

"I hope you're really hung over, you old sonofabitch," he said to whoever answered the phone.

There was a reply, and the Sergeant laughed.

"Hey, I just been talking to one of the kids who's reporting in. I don't know what happened, but they didn't give him a leave out of Parris Island. He lives in Newark, or near it. Would it be OK with you if I told the CQ to give him a seventy-two-hour pass?"

There was a pause.

"He already pulled guard. We just got off."

Something else was said that Koffler couldn't hear.

"OK, Top, thanks," the Sergeant of the Guard said, and hung up. "He was in a good mood. You get an *extended* seventy-two-hour pass."

"I don't know what that means," Steve Koffler confessed.

"Well, you get one pass that runs from 1700 today until 1700 Sunday. That's seventy-two hours. Then you tear that one up and throw it away, and go on the second one, which lasts until 0500 Monday. The First Sergeant says that nothing's going on around here until then, anyway."

"Jesus Christ!"

"Now for Christsake, don't do nothing like getting shitfaced and arrested."

"I won't."

An hour later, PFC Stephen Koffler passed through the Marine guard at the gate and started walking toward the Lakehurst train station. He hadn't gone more than a hundred yards when a Chrysler convertible pulled to the side of the road ahead of him, and the door swung open. The driver was a naval officer, a young one.

"I'm going into New York City if that would be any help, son," he said.

On the way to Newark, where the officer went out of his way to drive him into the city and drop him off at Pennsylvania Station, he told Koffler that he was a navigator on one of the blimps and had spent New Year's Eve freezing his tail ten miles off the Jersey coast, down by Cape May, at the mouth of the Delaware River.

Steve told him he had just arrived to go to the parachute school. And the officer replied that Steve had more balls than he did. There was no way anybody could get him to jump out of an airplane unless it was gloriously in flames.

Steve caught the Bloomfield Avenue trolley in the basement of Penn Station and rode it up to the Park Avenue stop by Branch Brook Park in Newark. Then he got off, walked up to street level, and caught the Number 21 Park Avenue bus and took it twenty blocks west across the city line into East Orange. He got off at Nineteenth Street, right across from his apartment building.

Steve's mother and her husband lived on the top floor of the four-story building, on the right side, in the apartment that overlooked the entranceway in the center of the U-shaped building. There were no lights on in the apartment, which meant they were out someplace; but there were lights on in the Marshall apartment, which was on the same side of the building, and a floor down.

He wondered if Bernice Marshall was home. He had known Bernice since the sixth grade, when his mother had married Ernie and they had moved into the apartment building at 121 Park Avenue. Bernice Marshall wasn't his girlfriend or anything like that. What she was was a girl with a big set of knockers and dark hair, and she was built like somebody who would probably get fat when she got older. But she was a girl. And as Steve looked up at her apartment now, his mind's eye was full of Bernice taking a sunbath on the roof of the building, with her boobs spilling out of her bathing suit.

Whenever the Marshall girls, Bernice and her sister Dianne, took sunbaths on the roof of the apartment, the males in the building usually found some excuse to go up there and smoke a cigarette and have a look. Dianne was a long-legged, long-haired blonde four years older than Bernice. She had run away to get married when she was a senior in East Orange High. And then she had had some kind of trouble and moved back home with her baby.

Dianne had gotten a job in the Ampere Branch of the Essex County Bank & Trust, right next door to where Mr. Marshall ran the Ampere One-Hour Martinizing Dry Cleaning & Laundry. Steve didn't know what Bernice was doing. She'd tried to go to college, at Upsala, in East Orange, but just before he had joined the Marines, Steve remembered now, he'd heard that hadn't worked out and that Bernice was going to try to get some kind of job.

It then occurred to him that he didn't have a key to get in. His keys and every other thing he had owned as a civilian had been put into a box and shipped home from Parris Island the very first morning he was there, right after they'd given him a haircut and a set of utilities and a pair of boots. Even before the Corps had issued him the rest of his gear.

Jesus Christ!

There was a door on either side of the lobby of 121 Park Avenue, which could be opened if you had a key, or if someone in one of the apartments pushed a button. Or if you gave the brass plate on it a swift kick. That's what Steve did next, giving him access to the first-floor foyer and stairwell.

He went up the stairs two at time. When he passed the third-floor landing, he could hear female laughter from the Marshall apartment, but couldn't tell if it was Bernice or Dianne, or maybe even Mrs. Marshall.

More or less for the hell of it, he tried the door to his apartment. It was locked, as he thought it would be. Then he went up to the roof. With a lot of effort he pushed the door open against the snow that had accumulated up there.

What they called "the deck"—the place where Bernice and Dianne took their sunbaths—was a platform of boards with inch-wide spaces between them. Now it was covered with ice and snow, and it was slippery under his feet as he made his way across it to the fire escape.

There was a ladder down from the roof to the top level of the fire escape, which was right outside his room. He climbed down it and tried his windows. They were locked.

Just beyond the railing of the fire escape was the bathroom window. If that was locked, he didn't know what the fuck he would do. He leaned over and pushed up on it, and it slid upward.

But to get through it meant you had to stand on the fire escape railing and support yourself on the bricks of the building, while you leaned far enough over until you could put your head and shoulders into the window without falling off. Then you gave a shove. After that, you could wiggle through and end up head-down in the bathtub.

Steve realized there was no way he could do that wearing his overcoat and brimmed cap and gloves. After he considered that, he decided he couldn't make it wearing his blouse either; so he took all of them off and laid them on the steel-strap floor of the fire escape.

Then he was so goddamned cold he started to shiver.

When he stood up on the railing of the fire escape, he thought there was a very good chance that he was not going to make it, and that when his mother and her husband came home, they would find him smashed and bloody on the concrete of the entranceway four floors down, dead.

Sixty seconds later, he was in the bathtub, head down.

He pushed out of the way his mother's underwear and stockings, hanging to dry over the tub, and found the light switch and flicked it on.

He saw himself in the mirror. He didn't look familiar. There was no fat on his face anymore, and his eyes looked like they had sunk inward. But the big difference, he realized, was the hair. Before he'd enlisted, he had had long hair, worn in a pompadour, with sideburns. What he had now was hair not half an inch long, and no sideburns.

He went into his bedroom, opened the window, and reclaimed the rest of his uniform from the fire escape. He opened his closet and put the cap on the shelf, then found a heavy hanger for the overcoat and hung that on the pipe. It really looked strange in there, he thought, beside his red and white Mustangs Athletic Club jacket.

His "rig" was on the shelf. He had been interested in amateur radio since he was a high school freshman and had joined the Radio Club. By the time he was a sophomore, he had learned Morse code and joined the American Amateur Radio Relay League. He had built his first receiver when he was still a sophomore, and his first really good receiver when he was a junior. He had passed the Federal Communications Commission examination for his ham ticket and had then gone on and gotten his second-class radio telephone license when he was a senior.

Getting the money to build his first transmitter and the antenna that it needed had meant giving up a lot of nights out with the Mustangs, but finally he had it up and running in the early spring of his senior year. That had lasted a week, until the neighbors in the building found out what was causing all the static when they tried to listen to "Lowell Thomas and the News" and Fred Allen and "The Kate Smith Hour." They'd bitched to the superintendent, and the super had made him take the antenna down from the roof.

His mother's husband had acted as if he had done something criminal. He'd even bitched at him for just *listening* to the traffic on the twenty-meter band, refusing to understand that receivers don't cause interference. The fights they had over that had been one of the reasons he had joined The Corps.

He took his Mustangs jacket off its hanger and slipped it on. It had a red velveteen body and white sleeves and red knit cuffs and collar. *Mustangs Athletic Club* was spelled out in flowing script on the back, and *Mustang AC* and *Steve* in smaller block letters on the front.

He closed the bedroom door to examine himself in the full-length, somewhat wavy mirror mounted on it. The Mustangs jacket didn't look right; either it had shrunk or he had grown. It was tight across his shoulders and chest, and the cuffs seemed to ride too high on his arms. He took it off and noticed something else. It looked cheap. It looked like a cheap piece of shit.

That made him feel disloyal and sad.

He hung the jacket back up and put on his uniform blouse, then looked at himself again in the mirror. He looked right, and the PFC stripe and the glistening silver marksman badges didn't look bad either. He had two, an Expert Medal with little medals reading RIFLE and

PISTOL hanging under it, and a Sharpshooter medal with BAR hanging under it. He hadn't made Expert with the Browning Automatic Rifle, but Sharpshooter was nothing to be ashamed of. He'd only made Marksman with the .30-caliber machine gun and mortar. They had a medal for that too, but he had elected not to wear it. Everybody who qualified—and you didn't get to graduate from Parris Island if you didn't qualify—was a Marksman, so why the fuck bother?

He went into the foyer, where the mystery of his missing mother and her husband was solved. There was a brochure on the table. *Three Days and Three Nights, Including New Year's Eve, at the Luxurious Beach Hotel, Asbury Park, N.J. Only $99.95 (Double Occupancy).*

That's where they were, not thirty miles from Lakehurst.

Christ, didn't they know there was a war on? That the Japs had taken Wake Island two days before Christmas? That the Japs had invaded the Philippine Islands? That while they were sipping their fucking Seven-and-Seven in the Beach Hotel, there were German submarines right offshore, waiting to put torpedoes into American ships?

(THREE)

121 PARK AVENUE

EAST ORANGE, NEW JERSEY

2105 HOURS 1 JANUARY 1942

What I'll do, thought PFC Stephen Koffler, USMC, *is get together with the guys, maybe get a couple of drinks.*

He went to the telephone mounted on the wall in the kitchen and dialed from memory the number of his best buddy.

Mrs. Danielli told him Vinny was out someplace, she didn't know where. She would tell him Steve had called, she said, and asked him to wish his mom and dad a happy New Year.

He started to call Toddy Feller, but remembered that his mother had written that Toddy had enlisted in the Navy right after Pearl Harbor Day.

He thought, unkindly, that at this very moment Toddy was probably on his hands and knees, his fat ass in the air, scrubbing a deck at the Great Lakes Naval Training Center with a toothbrush.

He went back into his bedroom, where he now remembered seeing the package from Parris Island, unopened, on the closet shelf. He took it down, tore the paper off, and dug through it. There was dirty underwear and dirty socks, and the pants and shirt and shoes and toilet kit (a brand-new one) he'd taken to the post office when he'd enlisted.

And his keys. To the lobby door, to the mailbox in the lobby, to the apartment door, and to his locker in East Orange High School. He'd kept that one for a souvenir, even though it meant paying the bastards two-fifty for a key you could have made in Woolworth's Five & Ten for a quarter.

He put the keys in his pocket and went out the front door and down the stairs to the Marshall apartment, on the floor below.

He heard conversation inside when the doorbell sounded, and then he heard someone who was probably Bernice say, "I wonder who that can be?" and then the door was opened.

Mr. Marshall looked at him a minute without recognition, until Steve spoke.

"Hello, Mr. Marshall, is Bernice around?"

"I'll be damned!" Mr. Marshall said. "I didn't recognize you. Hazel, you'll never guess who it is!"

"So tell me," Mrs. Hazel Marshall said.

"Come on in," Mr. Marshall said, taking Steve's arm, then putting his arm around his shoulder, as he led him into the living room.

"Recognize this United States Marine, anybody?" Mr. Marshall said.

"Why, my God, it's Stevie," Mrs. Marshall said. "Stevie, your mother and father are in Asbury Park!"

"Yeah, I know."

"Oh, she'll be heartbroken she missed you!" Mrs. Marshall said as she came to him and kissed him. Then she held him by both arms and looked at him intently. "You've changed."

"Hello, Stevie," Dianne Marshall said. "Remember me?"

"Yeah, sure. Hello, Dianne."

"And this is Leonard," Mrs. Marshall said. "Leonard Walters. He and Dianne are sort of keeping company."

Leonard Walters looked like a candy-ass, Steve decided. Dianne looked good. She didn't have big boobs like Bernice, but the ones she had pressed attractively against her sweater.

"I'm very pleased to meet you, I'm sure," Leonard said as he shook Steve's hand. "You're a Marine, huh?"

"That's right."

"How about a little something against the cold, Steve?" Mr. Marshall said.

"Charlie, he's only seventeen."

"Eighteen," Steve corrected her. "I was hoping Bernice would be home."

"She had a date," Dianne said. "She'll be sorry she missed you."

"No big deal," Steve said.

"Seven-and-Seven OK, Steve?"

Seven-and-Seven was Seagram's Seven Crown Blended Whiskey and 7-Up. Steve hated it.

"No, thank you," Steve said.

"See, I told you," Mrs. Marshall said.

"How about a little Scotch, then? That's what I'm having."

"Scotch would be fine," Steve said. He wasn't even sure what it was, only that he had never had any before.

"Water or soda?"

"Soda, please."

Dianne walked across the room to him.

"What are those things on your uniform, medals?"

"Marksmanship medals."

She stood close to him and bent over and examined them carefully. He could see her scalp where she parted her hair; and he could smell her; and he could see the outline of her brassiere strap.

"I'm impressed," she said, straightening, still so close he could feel the warmth of her breath and smell the Sen-Sen she had been chewing.

Mr. Marshall handed him a glass and Steve took a sip. It tasted like medicine.

"That's all right, son?"

"Just fine," Steve said.

Dianne walked away. He could see her rear end quiver; she was wearing calf-high boots. Steve thought that calf-high boots were highly erotic, ranking right up there with pictures he had seen in *The Police Gazette* in the barbershop, of women in brassieres and underpants and garter belts.

"So how do you like it in the Marines, Steve?" Mr. Marshall asked.

"I like it fine," Steve said. That wasn't the truth, the whole truth, and nothing but the truth, but he understood that he couldn't say anything else.

"What have they got you doing?"

"Monday I start parachute school," Steve said.

"I don't know what that means," Mr. Marshall said.

"The Corps is organizing parachute battalions," Steve explained. "I volunteered for it."

"You mean you'll be jumping out of airplanes?" Mrs. Marshall asked.

"Yes, Ma'am."

"Really?" Dianne asked. When he looked at her and nodded, she added, "I'll be damned."

"Dianne!" her mother said. "Try to remember you're a lady."

Steve sensed that Leonard wished he would leave, and while Steve thought Leonard was a candy-ass, fair was fair. If he had a date with some girl, he'd want to get her alone and away from her family and neighbors, too.

He refused Mr. Marshall's offer to freshen his drink, and then left.

He called the Danielli house again, thinking that maybe Vinny had come back; but Mrs. Danielli said she hadn't heard from him and didn't expect to, as late as it was. He apologized for calling so late and turned the radio on.

He quickly grew bored with that. From his living room window he could see the candy store on the corner of Eighteenth Street and Park Avenue but it was closed. So there was no place he could go without a car.

He had a damned good idea where Vinny was. He was up at The Lodge, on the mountain in West Orange, where you could get a drink even if you weren't twenty-one. But getting one around here was an impossibility. They all knew who you were and how old you were. And you needed a car to get to The Lodge.

But then he remembered hearing that if you were in uniform you could get a drink, period. The idea began to grow on him. There was a bar by the Ampere station. His mother and her husband never went there, so the people there wouldn't connect him with them.

It was worth a try. It was a shame to waste a seventy-two-hour pass sitting around listening to the radio all by yourself. If they wouldn't serve him, he'd just leave. He'd turn red in the face, too; but that wouldn't be too bad.

He put on his overcoat and his brimmed cap, turned the overcoat collar up against the cold wind, and walked to the bar by the Ampere station.

It was crowded and noisy. He pushed his cap back on his head, unbuttoned his overcoat, and found an empty seat at the bar.

"What'll it be?" the bartender asked.

"Scotch and soda," Steve said.

The bartender said, "You got it," and went to make it. Steve took a five-dollar bill from his wallet and laid it on the bar.

When the bartender delivered the drink, he pushed the five-dollar bill back across the bar. "On the house," he said.

Steve took a sip of the whiskey. It still tasted like medicine. Not as bad as the first one, but still bad. It was probably, he decided, another brand.

The bartender set another drink on the bar in front of Steve.

"From the lady and the gentleman at the end," the bartender said. Steve looked down the bar to where a middle-aged couple had their glasses raised to him.

"My privilege," the man called.

"God bless you!" the woman called.

Steve felt his face flush, and desperately hoped he wasn't blushing to the point where it could be seen.

"Thank you," he called.

It was the first time in his life that anyone had bought him a drink in a bar.

"You meeting somebody?" a male voice asked in his ear. He turned and saw that it was Leonard.

"No," Steve said. "I just came in for a drink."

"Whyn'tcha come sit with us?" Leonard asked, with a nod toward the wall. There was a wall-length padded seat there and tiny tables, eight or ten of them, in front of it. Dianne Marshall was sitting on the bench, smiling and waving at him.

"Wouldn't I be in the way?"

"Don't be silly," Leonard said. "If we knew you were coming here, you could have come with us."

Steve picked up his five-dollar bill and followed Leonard over. Dianne patted the seat next to her.

"You should have said something, Steve," Dianne said, "about coming here. You could have come with us. What did you do, walk?"

"Yeah."

"I guess you get a lot of that, walking, in the Marines, huh?" Leonard asked.

"Try a thirty-mile hike with full field equipment," Steve said.

"Thirty *miles?*" Dianne asked.

"Right. It toughens you up."

"I'll bet it does," Dianne said, and squeezed his leg over the knee.

She wasn't, he saw, looking for any reaction from him. She was looking at Leonard, smiling. She relaxed her fingers, but didn't take them from his leg.

She doesn't mean anything by that, he decided solemnly. *She has a boyfriend and I'm just the kid friend of her little sister. I mean, Jesus, she was* married, *and has a* kid!

He was not used to drinking liquor; he started to feel it.

"It's been a long day," he announced. "I'm going to tuck it in."

"You haven't even danced with me yet!" Dianne protested.

"To tell you the truth, I'm a lousy dancer," he said, getting up.

"Ah, I bet you're not," Dianne said.

"You better dance with her, kid, or she won't let you go," Leonard said.

"Don't call me 'kid,' " Steve said, nastily.

Jesus Christ, I am getting drunk. I better leave that fucking Scotch alone!

"Sorry, no offense," Leonard said.

"What's the matter with you, Lenny?" Dianne snapped. She got up and took Steve's hand. "I'll decide whether you're a lousy dancer."

She led him to the dance floor and turned around and opened her arms for him to hold her. And he danced with her. He was an awkward dancer, and he was wearing field shoes. And he got an erection.

"I think we better call this off," he said, aware that his face felt really flushed now, and that it was probably visible, even in the dim light.

"Yes, I think maybe we should."

He didn't sit down again with them, just claimed his overcoat and brimmed cap and put them on. After that he shook hands with Leonard and left.

It was a ten-minute walk back to the apartment. Snow had started again, but it was still cold enough for him to feel that he was sobering up. He told himself he had made a mistake leaving, that maybe Dianne *had* meant something when she didn't take her hand off his leg. And then came the really thrilling thought that she *had* felt his erection, and it hadn't made her mad.

By the time he got to the apartment, however, and was shaking the snow off his overcoat and wiping it off the leather brim of his cap, he had changed his mind again. Dianne was twenty-what? Twenty-two at least, probably twenty-three. She was an ex-married woman, for Christsake. She had a boyfriend. His imagination was running wild, more than likely because he had had all those medicine-tasting Scotch-and-sodas.

The telephone rang.

It had to be Vinny Danielli. The sonofabitch had finally come home, and his mother had told him he had called.

"Hello, asshole, how the hell are you, you guinea bastard?"

"Steve?"

"Jesus!"

"It's Dianne."

"I know. I thought it was somebody else."

"I sure hope so," she said.

"I'm sorry about that."

"What are you doing?"

"Nothing."

"We left right after you did. Leonard lives in Verona and was worried about getting home in the snow."

"Oh."

"Your parents get home?"

"They won't be home until tomorrow sometime."

"Mine are in bed," she said. "And so's Joey."

Joey, Steve now recalled, was her little boy.

There was a long, awkward pause.

"You want to come up?" he heard himself asking.

Oh, my God, what did I say?

"To tell you the God's honest truth, Steve, I'd love to," Dianne said. "But what if anybody found out?"

"Who would find out?"

"I wouldn't want Bernice to find out, for example. Not to mention my parents."

"She wouldn't get it from me," Steve said, firmly. "Nobody would."

"But, Jesus, if we got caught!" Dianne said, and then the phone clicked and went dead.

He felt his heart jump.

She wouldn't come up. She's had a couple of drinks, a couple of drinks too many, and it's a crazy idea. Once she actually went so far as calling up, she realized that, and hung up. She absolutely would not come up.

The doorbell rang.

He ran and opened it, and she pushed past him, closing the door behind her and leaning on it. She was wearing a chenille bathrobe and slippers that looked like rabbits. She had a bottle of Scotch in her hand.

"I saw that you liked this," she said, holding it up.

"Yeah," he said. "I'm glad you came."

"Can I trust you? If one word of this got out, oh, Jesus!"

"Sure," Steve said.

She leaned forward quickly and kissed him on the mouth.

"Leonard is a good man," she said.

"Huh?"

"Leonard is a good man. I mean that. He's really a good man, and he wants to marry me, and I probably will. But . . . can I tell you this?"

"Sure."

"He thinks you should wait until you're married," she said. "I mean, maybe that's all right if you're a virgin. But I was married, you know what I mean?"

"Sure."

"If I hadn't come up here, were you going to do it to yourself?"

"What?"

"You know what I mean," she said.

"Yeah, probably," he said. He had never confessed something like that to anyone before, not even to one of the guys.

"You didn't, did you?" she asked, and then decided to seek, with her fingers, the answer to her own question.

"I think I would have killed you if you had," she said a moment later, pleased with the firm proof she had found that he had not, at least recently, committed the sin of casting his seed upon the ground. "After I took a chance like this."

"You want to come in my room?"

"There, and in the living room, and in every other place we can think of." She pulled his head down to hers and kissed him again, and this time her tongue sought his.

It took him a moment to take her meaning. It excited him. He wondered if she would be able to tell, her having been married and all, that he was a virgin.

Jesus, I'm really going to get laid.

(FOUR)

121 PARK AVENUE

EAST ORANGE, NEW JERSEY

0830 HOURS 2 JANUARY 1942

Dianne Marshall Norman woke up sick with the memory of what had happened between her and the kid upstairs. She knew why she had done it, but that didn't excuse it, or make it right. She had done it because she was drunk. And she knew why she had gotten drunk; but that didn't excuse it, or make getting drunk right, either.

Maybe she really was a slut, she thought, lying there in her bed with her eyes closed, hung over. A whore. That's what Joe had called her when he'd caught her with Roddie Norman in the house at the shore. She'd been drunk then, too, and that had been the beginning of the end for her and Joe. He had moved out of their apartment two weeks later and gone to a lawyer about a divorce. And been a real sonofabitch about it, too.

His lawyer had told her father's lawyer that Joe would pay child support, but that was it. He would keep the car and all the furniture and everything else, and he wouldn't give her a dime. He would pay for her to go to Nevada for six weeks to get a divorce. If she didn't agree to that, he would take her to Essex County Court in Newark and charge her with adultery with Roddie Norman, and it would be all over the papers.

Dianne didn't think doing it with just one man (two, actually, but Joe didn't know about Ed Bitter) really made her a whore or a slut. And there was no question in her mind that Joe had been fooling around himself. She'd even caught him at the Christmas office party feeling up the peroxide blonde, Angie Palmeri, who worked in the office of his father's liquor store. And there had been a lot of times when he'd had to "work late" at the store and couldn't come home, and she had driven by and he hadn't been there.

What had happened with Roddie Norman wouldn't have happened if everybody hadn't been sitting around drinking Orange Blossoms all afternoon; it had been raining and they couldn't go to the beach. And the real truth of the matter, not that anybody cared, was that she had been mad with Joe because he had been making eyes at Esther Norman all day and looking down her dress.

And then, because Roddie was taking a nap on the couch and Joey was asleep, Joe and Esther had gone to get Chinese take-out at the Peking Palace in Belmar. God only knew what those two had been up to when they were gone, but that's when it had happened. Roddie had awakened and the phonograph had been playing and they'd started to dance, and the first thing she knew they had both been on the couch and he had her shorts off, and Joe had walked in.

Dianne sometimes thought that if Joe had been able to beat Roddie up, it wouldn't have gone so far as the divorce. What actually happened was that Roddie knocked Joe on his backside with a punch that bloodied Joe's nose. Getting beaten up by Roddie was the straw that broke the camel's back, so to speak.

So she'd gone to the Lazy Q Dude Ranch, twenty miles outside of Reno, Nevada, for the six weeks it took to establish legal residence. Then she'd gotten the divorce and moved back home, where her parents treated her as though she had an "A" for "Adultery" painted on her forehead.

And then her father brought Leonard Walters home. Leonard sold dry cleaner's supplies, everything from wire hangers and mothproof bags to the chemicals they used in the dry-cleaning process itself. She had seen him around, seen him looking at her, and knew that he was interested. That was really one way to get her life fixed up, she thought. But Leonard was the single most boring male human being Dianne had ever met.

Dianne's father brought him home to a potluck supper. That was so much bull you-know-what. They just *happened* to have a pot roast for supper, and Bernice just happened not to be there, and they ate at the dining room table off the good china and a tablecloth, all usually reserved for Sunday dinner, if then.

It had been carefully planned, including a little dialogue between her mother and her father to explain Dianne's situation. The story they fed Leonard used the phrase "Dianne's mistake" a lot. But "Dianne's mistake," the way they told it, was not getting caught letting Roddie Norman in her pants, but in "foolishly running off to get married."

In her parents' version, Joe Norman had stolen her out of her cradle. And then, once he got her to elope with him—in the process throwing away her plans for college and a career—he started to abuse her and drink and run around with a wild crowd who drank and gambled and did other things that could not be discussed around a family dining table.

Leonard Walters not only swallowed the tale whole, but embarked on what he called "our courtship." The courtship had not moved very rapidly, though. The reason was that Leonard's name had been Waldowski before his parents changed it when they were naturalized. The Waldowskis were Polish and Roman Catholic, and Leonard's mother was a large and formidable woman who did not believe Roman Catholics should marry outside The One True Faith. She knew that Dianne was a Methodist, but Leonard hadn't told her about Dianne's marriage, and she didn't know about Little Joey either.

It was not now the time to tell her about it, Leonard said. "Let her learn to know you and love you."

Leonard was pretty devout himself, and he did not believe in premarital or extramarital sex. In his view, the thing to do about sex and everything else was "wait until things straighten themselves out."

On the day that PFC Stephen Koffler, USMC, entered her life, Dianne and Leonard had dinner, served precisely at noon, at the Walters' house in Verona. It was a strain, relieved somewhat by several large glasses of wine.

Then they went to East Orange, where Dianne's mother had promptly dragged her into the bedroom to deliver a recitation about how badly Joey had behaved while she was gone. After that she demanded a play-by-play account of all that was said at the Walters' dinner. When Dianne explained that Leonard had not yet told his mother about Dianne and Joe, and, more important, about Joey, there followed a two-minute lecture about why Dianne should make him do that.

Once her mother let her go, Dianne went from the bedroom to the kitchen and made a fresh pot of coffee. She laced her cup with a hooker of gin. By the time Steve Koffler marched in, looking really good in his Marine Corps uniform, she was on her fourth cup.

At first he remained the way she always had remembered him— "the kid upstairs," a peer of Bernice's, one of the mob of dirty-minded little boys who always came up to the deck on the roof to smirk and snicker behind their hands whenever she and Bernice tried to take a sunbath.

It was difficult for her to believe that he was really a *Marine*. Marines were men. Stevie Koffler, she thought, probably still played with himself.

That risqué thought, which just popped into her mind out of the blue, was obviously the seed for everything else that happened. A seed, she realized after it was over, more than adequately fertilized by the gin in her coffee.

It was immediately followed by the thought—not original to the moment—that playing with himself was what good old Leonard must be doing. Either that or he just didn't care about women, another possibility that had occurred to her. She had tried to arouse Leonard more than once; and she'd worked at that as hard as she could without destroying his image of her as the innocent child bride snatched from her cradle by dirty old Joe Norman. But she'd had no luck with him at all.

Maybe Steve doesn't play with himself. Marines are supposed to have women falling all over them.

When Steve Koffler walked into the Ampere Lounge & Grill an hour after that, there was proof of that theory. Dianne saw several women—all of them older than she was—look with interest at the Marine who walked up to the bar in that good-looking uniform, his hat cocked arrogantly on the back of his head.

And then, if you wanted to look at it that way, Leonard himself was responsible for what had happened. If he hadn't gone to Steve at the bar and practically dragged him back to the table, Steve would have had a couple of drinks and gone home. Maybe with one of the women who had been looking at him.

But Leonard dragged him back to their table. And then she felt his leg. And it was all muscle. The couple of times she had squeezed Leonard's leg, playfully, of course, it had been soft and flabby. Steve Koffler's leg was muscular, even more muscular than Joe's, and Joe had played football.

And then, when she danced with him, and *that* happened to him, and she knew that he wanted her, too . . .

She tried to talk herself out of it. She even went so far as to put on her nightgown after Leonard took her home and gave her the standard we-can-wait-until-we're-married goodnight kiss. But then she decided to have a nightcap, so she could sleep. And when she stood in the kitchen drinking it, the telephone was right there, on the wall, in front of her nose.

Things, she told herself, always looked different in the morning. They did this morning. What they looked like this morning was that she'd gotten drunk and gone to bed with the kid upstairs. Marine or not, that's what he was, the kid upstairs.

Christ, he can't be any older than eighteen!

And what they'd done! What she'd done, right from the start, right after the first time, when it had been all over for him before she even got really started.

Joe had taught her that, and from the way Steve acted, she had taught him. That, and some other things she knew he had never done before.

Jesus, what if he starts telling people?

She had another unsettling thought: Sure as Christ made little apples, Steve Koffler is going to show up at my door.

She got out of bed and took a shower. When she came out, her father was in the kitchen.

"I promised Joe's mother that I would take Joey over there," she said. "Can I borrow the car?"

"Sure, honey," her father said. "But be back by five, huh?"

"Sure."

When she got back, a few minutes after five, she met Steve coming out of the apartment with his mother and his mother's husband.

Steve's mother didn't like her. Dianne supposed, correctly, that Steve's mother knew what had really happened with Joe Norman. So, as they passed each other, all Dianne got was a cold nod from Steve's mother, and a grunt from the husband.

Steve didn't know what to do. But then he turned around and ran back to her.

Dianne told him that she had to do things with her family that night and the next day. And she managed to avoid him the rest of the time he was home.

IV

(ONE)

The ten-story Pacific & Far Eastern Shipping Corporation Building had been completed in March of 1934, six months before the death of Captain Ezekiel Pickering, who was then Chairman of the Board. There were a number of reasons why Captain Pickering had two years before, in 1932, ordered its construction, including, of course, the irrefutable argument that the corporation needed the office space.

But it was also Captain Pickering's response to Black Tuesday, the stock market crash of October 1929, and the Depression that followed. Pacific & Far Eastern—which was to say Captain Pickering personally, for the corporation was privately held—was not hurt by the stock market crash. Captain Ezekiel Pickering was not in the market.

He had dabbled in stocks over the years, whenever there was cash he didn't know what else to do with for the moment. But in late 1928 he had gotten out, against the best advice of his broker. He had had a gut feeling that there was something wrong with the market when, for example, he heard elevator operators and newsstand operators solemnly discussing the killings they had made.

The *idea* of the stock market was a good one. In his mind it was sort of a grocery store where one could go to shop around for small pieces of all sorts of companies, or to offer for sale your small shares of companies. Companies that you knew—and you knew who ran them, too. But the market had stopped being that. In Ezekiel Pickering's mind, it had become a socially sanctioned crap game where the bettors put their money on companies they knew literally nothing about, except that the shares had gone up so many points in the last six months.

The people playing the market—and he thought "playing" was both an accurate description of what they were doing and symbolic—

often had no idea what the company they were buying into made, or how well they did so. And they didn't really understand that a thousand shares at thirty-three-and-a-quarter really meant thirty-three thousand two hundred fifty real dollars.

And it was worse than that: they weren't even really playing craps with real money, they were buying on the margin, putting up a small fraction of the thirty-three thousand two hundred fifty and borrowing the rest.

Ezekiel Pickering had nothing against gambling. When he had been twenty-nine and First Mate of the tanker *Pacific Courier,* he had once walked out of a gaming house in Hong Kong with fifty thousand pounds sterling when the cards had come up right at chemin de fer. But he had walked into the Fitzhugh Club with four thousand dollars American that was his, not borrowed, and that he was prepared—indeed, almost expected—to lose. To his way of looking at it, the vast difference between his playing chemin de fer with his own cash money at the Fitzhugh Club and the elevator man in the Andrew Foster Hotel playing the New York stock market with mostly borrowed Monopoly money was one more proof that most people were fools.

The stock market was a house of cards about to collapse, and he got out early. And he took with him his friend Andrew Foster. So that when Black Tuesday struck, and people were literally jumping out of hotel-room windows, both the Pacific & Far Eastern Shipping Corporation and Foster Hotels, Inc., remained solvent.

Of course, the Depression which followed the crash affected both corporations. Business was down. But retrenchment with cash in the bank is quite a different matter from retrenchment with a heavy debt service. Other shipping companies and hotels and hotel chains went into receivership and onto the auctioneer's block, which gave both Ezekiel Pickering and Andrew Foster the opportunity to buy desirable properties, ships and hotels, at a fraction of their real value.

There never had been any doubt in Ezekiel's mind that the domestic and international economies would in time recover. In fact, he agreed with President Franklin Delano Roosevelt's 1932 inaugural declaration that the nation had "nothing to fear but fear itself," and he said so publicly. Thus, when a suitable piece of real estate went on the auction block, he put his money where his mouth was and bought it.

The Pacific & Far Eastern Shipping Corporation Building was both a structural and an architectural marvel. It was designed not only to remain standing after what the engineers called a "hundred-year earthquake," but to reflect the dominant position of the corporation in Pacific Ocean shipping.

An oil portrait of Ezekiel Pickering, completed after his death, was hanging in the office of the current Chairman of the Board. It showed him standing with his hand resting on a five-foot globe of the earth. The globe in turn rested in a mahogany gimbal. There were the traditional four gold stripes of a ship's master around his jacket cuff, and a uniform cap with the gold-embroidered P&FE insignia was tucked under his arm.

His lips were curled in a small smile. In his widow's view, that smile caught her late husband's steely determination. But Fleming Pickering had a somewhat different take on it: while the artist had indeed captured a familiar smile of his father, based on Fleming's own personal experience with it, that smile meant, *Fuck you. I was right and you were wrong; now suffer the cost of your stupidity.*

He had once told this to his wife, Patricia, and it had made her absolutely furious. But when he had told the same thing to old Andrew Foster, the hotelman had laughingly agreed.

It was a quarter past two on a Friday afternoon, and Fleming Pickering was alone in his office. There was a glass of Old Grouse Scotch whiskey in his hand. He drank his Scotch with just a dash of water and one ice cube. His father had taught him that, too. Good whiskey has a distinct taste; it is stupidity to chill it with ice to the point where that taste is smothered.

While there was always whiskey available in the office—kept in a handsomely carved teak cabinet removed from the Master's cabin of the *Pacific Messenger* when she was retired from service and sent to the ship breakers—Fleming Pickering almost never drank alone. But the glass in his hand was the third today, and he was about to pour a fourth, when a light illuminated on one of the three telephones on the huge mahogany desk.

Since Pearl Harbor, Pacific & Far Eastern had lost nine of its fleet, eight to Japanese submarines and one, the tanker *Pacific Virtue,* at Pearl. It had been caught by Japanese bombers while it was unloading aviation gasoline. Three other P&FE ships were now overdue. Fleming Pickering thought it reasonable to presume that at least one of them would never make port.

He knew every officer on every crew, as well as a good many of the seamen, the black gang, and the stewards. He was not ashamed to have taken a couple of drinks.

Pickering reached over and picked up the handset of the telephone.

"Yes?"

"A Captain Haughton for you," said Mrs. Helen Florian, his secretary, adding: "A Navy captain."

I know what this sonofabitch is going to say, Pickering thought, as he punched the button that would put him on the line. *"I'm afraid I have some bad news to report, Mr. Pickering."*

"This is Fleming Pickering," he said to the telephone.

"Good afternoon, Sir. I'm Captain Haughton, of the Secretary's staff."

"How may I help you, Captain?"

"Sir, I'm calling for Secretary Knox. The Secretary is in San Francisco and wonders if you could spare him an hour or so of your time."

Well, no news is good news, I suppose.

"What does he want?"

I know goddamn well what he wants. He wants my ships. He's a tenacious bastard, I'll say that for him.

"I'm afraid the Secretary didn't confide that to me, Sir," Captain Haughton said. "At the moment, the Secretary is on the Navy Station at Treasure Island. From there he's going to the Alameda Naval Air Station to board his aircraft. Whichever would be most convenient for you, Sir."

"No," Fleming Pickering said.

"Excuse me, Sir?"

Obviously, Pickering thought, *Captain Haughton, wrapped in the prestige of the Secretary of the Navy, is not used to hearing "no" when he asks for something.*

"I said no. I'm afraid I don't have the time to go to either Treasure Island or Alameda."

"We'd be happy to send a car for you, Sir."

"I have a car. What I don't have is time. I can't leave my office. But you can tell Mr. Knox that I will be in the office for the next several hours."

"Mr. Pickering, you do understand that the Secretary is on a very tight schedule himself," Captain Haughton said, and then added something he instantly regretted. "Sir, we're talking about the Secretary of the Navy."

"I know who he is. That's why I'm willing to see him if he wants to come here. But you might save his time and mine, Captain, if you were to tell him that I have not changed my mind, and I will fight any attempt by the Navy to take over my ships."

"Yes, Sir," Captain Haughton said. "I will relay that to the Secretary. Good afternoon, Sir."

Pickering put the handset back in its cradle.

If I wasn't on my third drink, would I have been less difficult? Well, fuck him! I told him in plain English that if the Navy tries to seize my ships, I'll take it to the Supreme Court. He should have listened to me.

He stood up from behind his desk, walked to the liquor cabinet, and made himself another Old Grouse and water. Then he walked to an eight-by-twelve-foot map of the world that hung on an interior wall. Behind it was a sheet of light steel. Models of the ships of the P&FE fleet, each containing a small magnet, were placed on it so as to show their current positions.

After he checked the last known positions of the *Pacific Endeavor,* the *Pacific Volition,* and the *Pacific Venture,* he mentally plotted their probable courses. Then he wondered—for what might have been the seven hundredth time—whether it was an exercise in futility, whether he should move the three models down to the lower left-hand corner of the map to join the models of the P&FE ships he knew for sure were lost.

Almost exactly an hour later, the bulb on one of his telephones lit up. When he picked it up, Mrs. Florian said, "Mr. Frank Knox is here, Mr. Pickering. He says you expect him."

Well, I'll be goddamned. He really is a tenacious sonofabitch!

"Please show Mr. Knox in," Pickering Fleming said. He opened the upper right drawer of his desk, intending to put his Old Grouse and water out of sight.

Then he changed his mind. As the door opened, he stood up, holding the glass in his hand. The Hon. Frank Knox walked in, trailed by a slim, sharp-featured, intelligent-looking Navy officer with golden scrambled eggs on the brim of his uniform cap. He had to be Captain Haughton.

(TWO)

Before speaking, the Hon. Frank Knox, Secretary of the Navy, stared for a moment at Fleming Pickering, Chairman of the Board of Pacific & Far Eastern Shipping. There was no expression on his face, but Pickering saw that his Old Grouse and water had not gone unnoticed.

Christ, he'll think I'm a boozer; I was half in the bag the last time, too.

"Thank you for seeing me on such short notice," Knox said. "I know you're a busy man."

"I have three overdue ships," Pickering replied. "It's the reason I didn't come to meet you. I didn't want to get far from a telephone."

Knox nodded, as if he understood.

"Mr. Pickering, may I present Captain David Haughton, my administrative officer?"

The two shook hands. Pickering said, "We spoke on the telephone."

"I'd like to talk to Mr. Pickering alone, David, if you don't mind," Knox said.

"Yes, Sir."

"Mrs. Florian," Pickering said, "would you make the Captain comfortable? Start with a cup of coffee. Something stronger, if he'd like."

"Coffee will be fine," Haughton said, as he followed Mrs. Florian out of the office.

"May I offer you something?" Pickering asked.

"That looks good," Knox said, nodding at Pickering's glass. "Dick Fowler told me you had cornered the Scotch market."

Is he indulging me? Or does he really want a drink?

"It's Old Grouse," Pickering said, as he walked to the liquor cabinet to make Knox a drink. "And I'm glad you'll have one. I'm a little uneasy violating my own rule about drinking, especially alone, during office hours."

Knox ignored that. He waited until Pickering had handed him the glass, then he nodded his thanks and said, "Haughton doesn't like you."

"I'm sorry. I suppose I was a little abrupt on the telephone."

"He doesn't think you hold the Secretary of the Navy in what he considers to be the proper degree of awe."

"I meant no disrespect," Pickering said.

"But you aren't awed," Knox insisted. "And that's what I find attractive."

"I beg your pardon?"

"There was a movie—or was it a book?—about one of those people who runs a a motion-picture studio. He was surrounded by a staff whose primary function was to say 'Right, J.B.,' or 'You're absolutely right, J.B.,' whenever the great man paused for breath. After our interesting encounter in Dick Fowler's apartment, when I calmed down a little, I realized that sort of thing was happening to me."

"I don't think I quite follow you," Pickering said.

"This is good stuff," Knox said, looking down at his glass.

"I'll give you a case to take with you," Pickering said. "I have a room full of it downstairs."

"Because I'm the Secretary of the Navy?"

"Because I would like to make amends for my behavior in Fowler's apartment. I had no right to say what I said."

"The important thing, I realized, was that you said it," Knox said. "And you might have been feeling good, but you weren't drunk. I think you would have said what you said if you hadn't been near a bottle."

"Probably," Pickering said. "That doesn't excuse it, of course; but, as my wife frequently points out, when silence is called for, I too often say exactly the wrong thing."

"Are you withdrawing what you said?" Knox asked evenly.

"I'm apologizing for saying it," Pickering said. "I had no right to do so, and I'm sure that I embarrassed Richardson Fowler."

"But you believe what you said, right?"

"Yes, I'm afraid I do."

"You had me worried there for a moment," Knox said. "I was afraid I had misjudged you."

"It may be the Scotch, but I have no idea what we're talking about," Pickering said.

Knox chuckled.

"We're talking about you coming to work for me."

My God, he's serious!

"Doing what?"

"Let me explain the problem, and then you tell me if you think you could be helpful," Knox said. "I mentioned a moment before that David Haughton doesn't like you because you're not sufficiently awed by the Secretary of the Navy. That attitude—not only on Dave Haughton's part, but on the part of practically everybody else—keeps me from hearing what I should be hearing."

"You mean what's wrong with the Navy?"

"Precisely. Hell, I can't blame Haughton. From the moment he entered Annapolis, he's been taught as an article of faith that the Secretary of the Navy is two steps removed from God. The President sits at the right hand of God, and at his feet the Secretary of the Navy."

"I suppose that's so," Pickering said, chuckling.

"To Haughton's way of thinking, and to others like him, the Secretary of the Navy controls the very fate of the Navy. That being so, the information that is presented to him has to be carefully processed. And above all, the Navy must appear in the best possible light."

"I think I understand," Pickering said. "And I can see where that might be a problem."

Knox removed his pince-nez, took a handkerchief from the sleeve of his heavy woolen suit—now that he noticed it, Pickering was sure the suit was English—and polished the lenses. He put them back on his nose, stuffed the handkerchief back up his jacket cuff, and looked directly at Pickering.

"That might be an overstatement, but it's close," he said. "And to that problem is added what I think of as the Navy's institutional mindset. From the very beginning, from the first Secretary of the Navy, the men in blue have been certain that the major cross they have to bear is that the man with the authority is a political appointee who really doesn't know—is incapable of knowing—what the Navy is *really* all about."

"Huh," Pickering grunted.

"Their quite understandable desire is—and I suppose always has been—to attempt to manage the Secretary of the Navy. To see that he hears what they want him to hear, and that he does not hear—or at least is presented with in the best possible light—what they'd rather he didn't hear at all."

"One doesn't think of the Navy as an institution," Pickering said, "but of course that's what it is."

"On October 13, 1775, Congress voted to equip seven ships to support George Washington," Knox said. "Less than a month later, on November 10, 1775, the Congress authorized the Marine Corps. And before that, there were states' navies—Rhode Island's in particular. In July 1775, Washington sent a frigate of the Rhode Island navy to Bermuda to get gunpowder for the Continental Army. In 167 years, a certain institutional mind-set is bound to occur."

Pickering chuckled. There was something professorial in the way Knox had precisely recounted the origin of the Navy, and about the man himself, with his pince-nez and superbly tailored English suit. It was difficult to imagine him during the Spanish-American War, a Rough Rider sergeant charging up Kettle Hill with Lieutenant Colonel Teddy Roosevelt's 1st United States Volunteer Cavalry.

As it is difficult for me to accept that I once actually fixed a bayonet onto my '03 Springfield, and that when the whistle blew, I went over the top and into no-man's-land in Belleau Wood.

"They had an interesting tradition, early on," Pickering said. "Privateers. I don't suppose I could talk you out of a Letter of Marque, could I?"

Knox looked at him with annoyance, and then smiled. "You really think there's a place in this war for a pirate?"

"A pirate is an outlaw," Pickering said. "A privateer was authorized by his government—and our government issued a hell of a lot of Letters of Marque—to prey on the enemy's shipping. There's a substantial difference."

"You sound as if you're serious."

"Maybe I am," Pickering said.

Knox looked at him for a moment, his demeanor making it clear he was not amused that Pickering was proposing, even half-jokingly, an absurd idea. Then he went on, "I understand why you felt you couldn't work for Bill Donovan, but I think you'll have to grant that he has the right idea."

That was pretty stupid of me, Pickering thought. *He's going to think I'm a fool or a drunk. Or both.*

"Excuse me? What idea?"

"The country will be better off—if the Army and the Navy let him get away with it, which is open to some doubt—if, that is to say, intelligence from all sources *can* be filtered through Donovan's twelve disciples . . . and if they will use it as the basis for recommending to the President action that is in the best interests of the United States, as opposed to action recommended on the basis of the parochial mind-set of the Army or Navy."

"I agree," Pickering said. "I'm a little surprised—maybe 'disturbed' is the word—to hear you doubt the Army and Navy will 'let him get away with it.' "

"I try to see things as they are," Knox said. "And I'm fully aware that in addition to being at war with the Germans, the Italians, and the Japanese, the Army and Navy are at war with each other."

Pickering chuckled again.

"I laugh, too," Knox said. "Even knowing that it's not funny."

"Why do I think that the Navy is having a hard time managing you?" Pickering said.

"Well, they're trying," Knox said. "And the odds would seem to be in their favor. Franklin Roosevelt is partial to the Navy. He was once an Undersecretary, for one thing. For another, he has a lamentable habit of calling in Ernie King—"

"Admiral King?" Pickering interrupted.

Knox nodded. "King replaced Admiral Stark as Chief of Naval Operations on December 31. Stark was a good man, but after Pearl Harbor he had to go. Anyway, Roosevelt has already started giving Admiral King marching orders without asking or telling me about it. And he's about to throw Admiral Bill Leahy into the equation."

"*That* you'll have to explain," Pickering said.

"Leahy—and understand, Pickering, that I admire all the people I'm talking about—is functioning as sort of chief of military staff to Roosevelt, a position that does not exist in the law. They're about to organize a committee, comprised of the Chief of Staff of the Army, the head of the Army Air Corps, the Chief of Naval Operations, and the Commandant of the Marine Corps. They're going to call it the Joint Chiefs of Staff, or something like that. And Leahy will preside over that. Without any legal authority to do so, except a verbal one from Roosevelt."

"Huh," Pickering snorted, and added, "You seem to be outnumbered, Mr. Secretary. But I don't see what any of this could possibly have to do with me."

"My responsibility to the President, as I see it, is to present him with the most accurate picture that I can of the Navy's strengths . . . and, more importantly, its weaknesses. His decisions have to be based on the uncolored facts, not facts seen through parochial, rose-colored glasses. I cannot, in other words, let myself be managed by Ernie King, or Bill Leahy, or the Association of Annapolis Graduates."

Knox looked at Pickering, as if waiting for his reaction. When there was none, he went on, "I've come to the conclusion that I need some—more than that, several—people like Bill Donovan's disciples."

"And that's where I come in? As one of them?"

Knox nodded. "Interested?"

"I don't know what you're really asking of me."

"I want you to be my eyes and ears in the Pacific," Knox said. "You know as much about maritime affairs in the Pacific as anyone I know, including all of my admirals."

"I'm not sure that's true," Pickering said.

"I'm not talking about Naval *tactics,* about which I am prepared to defer to the admirals, but about *logistics,* by which I mean tonnages and harbors and stevedoring and time/distance factors. I don't want my admirals to bite off more than they can chew as they try to redeem themselves in the public—and their own—eye after Pearl Harbor. Logistics affects strategy, and advising the President on strategy is my business. I want the facts. I think you're the man who can get them for me."

"Yeah," Pickering said thoughtfully. "I could do that, all right."

"My original thought was to offer you an assistant secretaryship, but I don't think that would work."

Pickering looked at him curiously.

"You'd be political. *Both* the political appointees and the Navy would hate you and try to manage you. And they'd probably succeed. If you were in uniform, however, the political appointees would not see you as a threat. As a naval officer, as a captain on the staff of the Secretary of the Navy . . ."

"A Navy captain?"

"Yes."

"How's the Navy going to react to an instant captain?"

"We're commissioning a lot of 'instant captains.' Civil engineers, doctors, lawyers, all sorts of professionals. Even a few people who are already entitled to be called 'captain,' like yourself." Knox paused and smiled at Pickering. "Since you already know the front of the ship is the bow and the floor is the deck, you'll be way ahead of most of them."

Pickering chuckled.

"Does this interest you, Pickering?"

"You think I could do something worthwhile?"

"Yes, I do. I really do."

"Then I'm at your service, Mr. Knox," Pickering said.

Knox walked up to him and offered his hand. "I'd like to have you as soon as possible. When do you think . . . ?"

"Tomorrow morning be all right?" Pickering replied.

Now it was Knox's turn to chuckle.

"Things don't move quite that quickly, even for the Secretary of the Navy," he said. "Could you call Captain Haughton back in here, please?"

Pickering picked up one of the telephones.

"Would you ask Captain Haughton to come in here, please, Mrs. Florian?"

The slim Navy officer, his eyes wary, appeared a moment later.

"David, Mr. Pickering has kindly offered me a case of this excellent Scotch. Would you see that it gets on the plane?"

"Yes, of course, Mr. Secretary."

"And before we get on the plane, I want you to find out who handles officer procurement out here. Then call them and tell them I want a suitable officer assigned to walk Mr.—*Captain*—Pickering through the processing. Make it clear to them that this is important to me. As soon as we can get him sworn in, Captain Pickering will be joining my staff."

"Aye, aye, Sir," Haughton said. He looked at Pickering, briefly but intently. He was obviously surprised at what he had just heard.

"And stay on top of it when we get back to Washington," Knox ordered. "I don't want the process delayed by bureaucratic niceties. Tell them they are to assume that if any waivers are required, I will approve them. And while I'm thinking about it, tell the Office of Naval Intelligence that while we'll go through the normal security-clearance process with Captain Pickering, I have—based on my own knowledge of Captain Pickering, and on the unqualified recommendation of Senator Fowler—already granted him an interim top-secret clearance. Have that typed up. Make it official."

"Aye, aye, Sir."

Knox turned to Pickering. "That should get the ball rolling. Haughton will be in touch. Thank you, Pickering. Not only for the Scotch. And now I have to get out of here. They're waiting for me at Alameda."

"May I send someone for the Scotch, Captain Pickering?" Haughton asked.

"It won't take a minute to get it. You can take it with you."

"Whatever you say. I'll get the driver."

"It doesn't weigh all that much," Pickering said, without thinking. "I'll get it."

Haughton gave him a quick, dirty look.

Well, here you go, Fleming Pickering, not five minutes into your naval career, and you're already pissing people off.

"Let's get it now," Knox said. "Before he has a chance to change his mind."

Pickering led them to the storeroom on the ground floor that held the greater part of the whiskey removed from the sold Pacific passenger liners. He pulled a case of Old Grouse off a stack. When he started to carry it out, he saw that Haughton was uncomfortable, visibly unable to make up his mind whether he should volunteer to carry the case of whiskey himself—or to insist on it.

A sailor who had been leaning against the front fender of a 1941 Navy gray Chrysler quickly stood erect when he saw them coming out of the building. He opened the rear door, then quickly moved to take the case of whiskey from Pickering.

At least he *knows what he's doing,* Pickering thought.

Knox nodded to Pickering and got in the car. Houghton, at first hesitantly, and then enthusiastically, offered his hand to Pickering.

"Welcome aboard, Captain," he said.

"Thank you," Pickering said. He did not like the feel of Haughton's hand.

He watched the Chrysler move down Nob Hill, and then went back to his office.

He made himself another drink, and drank it looking out his window at San Francisco bay. Then he looked for a moment at his father's picture. He wondered what the Old Man would have said: *Hooray for you for enlisting!* or, *You damned fool!* Then he sat on the edge of his desk and called his home.

"Hi!" he said, when Patricia's cheerful voice came on the line.

"You've heard, haven't you?" Patricia Pickering said.

"What?" he replied, only afterwards remembering that she was talking about the overdue *Endeavor, Volition,* and *Venture.* They had, shaming him, slipped from his immediate attention.

"What's on your mind, Flem?" Patricia asked.

"Frank Knox, the Secretary of the Navy, was just in to see me."

"About the ships? Oh God, that sounds ominous!"

"He wants me to go into the Navy," Pickering said.

There was a pause before Patricia replied, "If you had turned him down, you would have said 'wanted.' "

"Yes, that's right."

He heard her inhale deeply; it was a moment before she spoke.

"When do you go? What are you going to do?"

"Soon. Work for him. He's arranging for me to be commissioned as a captain."

"Oh, goddamn him!"

"I suppose I should have discussed this with you," Pickering said.

"Why should you start now, after all these years?" It was a failed attempt at lightness; a genuine bitterness came through.

"I'm sorry, Pat," he said, meaning it.

"My father would say, 'Never be sorry for doing something you want to do.' And you do want to go, Flem, don't you?"

"Yes. I suppose I do."

"Don't come home now. I'd say things I would later regret."

"OK."

"Give me an hour. Make it an hour and a half. Then come."

He heard the click as she hung up.

(THREE)

BUILDING "F"

ANACOSTIA NAVAL AIR STATION

WASHINGTON, D.C.

30 JANUARY 1942

First Lieutenant Charles E. Orfutt, aide-de-camp to Brigadier General D. G. McInerney, stepped inside McInerney's office, closed the door quietly behind him, and waited until the General raised his eyes from the paperwork on his desk.

"Sergeant Galloway is outside, Sir."

That the news did not please General McInerney was evident on his face. He shrugged, exhaled audibly, and said, "Give me two minutes, Charlie, and then send him in."

"Aye, aye, Sir," Orfutt said, and quietly left the office.

Precisely two minutes later, there was a polite knock at McInerney's door.

"Come!"

Technical Sergeant Charles M. Galloway, USMC, in greens, marched into the office, stopped precisely eighteen inches from McInerney's desk, and came to attention. Then, gazing twelve inches over McInerney's head, he said, "Technical Sergeant Galloway reporting to the General as ordered, Sir."

General McInerney pushed himself backward in his chair, locked his fingers together, and stared at Galloway for a full thirty seconds before he spoke.

"Look at me," he said.

Oh, shit. Here it comes, Charley Galloway thought. He dropped his eyes to meet McInerney's.

"Do you have any idea how much goddamned trouble you've caused?"

"Yes, Sir. I think so."

"You don't look especially penitent, Sergeant."

"Sir, I'm sorry about the trouble I caused."

"But you think it was *really* caused by a bunch of chickenshit swabbies, and in your heart of hearts you don't think you did anything wrong, do you?"

The old bastard can read my mind.

Galloway's face went pale, but he didn't reply.

"You're thinking that you were almost a Marine Corps legend, is that it? That you'd be remembered as the guy who fixed up a shot-up fighter with his own hands, flew it without orders onto the *Saratoga*, and then on to Wake, and died gloriously in a battle that will live forever in the memory of man?"

Again, Galloway's face paled momentarily, but he didn't say anything.

That's not true. I wasn't trying to be a fucking hero. All I was trying to do was get that Wildcat to Wake, where it was needed.

"What the hell were you thinking, Galloway? Can you at least tell me that?"

"I was thinking they needed that Wildcat on Wake, Sir."

"Did it occur to you that in the shape that Wildcat was, you could have done some real damage, crashing it onto the deck of the *Saratoga?*

"Sir, the aircraft was in good shape," Galloway said.

"It had been surveyed, for Christ's sake, by skilled BUAIR engineering personnel and declared a total loss." He was referring to the U.S. Navy Bureau of Aeronautics.

"Sir, the aircraft was OK," Galloway insisted doggedly. "Sir, I made the landing."

General McInerney believed everything Galloway was telling him. He also believed that if he were a younger man, given the same circumstances, he would—he hoped—have done precisely what Galloway had done. That meant doing what you could to help your squadron mates, even if that meant putting your ass in a potentially lethal crack. It had taken a large set of balls to take off the way Galloway had. If he hadn't found Sara, he would have been shark food.

The general also found it hard to fault a young man who, fully aware of what he was going to find when he got there, had ridden—OK, *flown*—toward the sound of the guns. Purposely sailed, to put it poetically, into harm's way.

And he also believed that Galloway had actually come very close to becoming a Marine Corps legend. Professionally—as opposed to parochially, as a Marine—General McInerney believed that it had been a mistake to recall Task Force 14 before, at the very least, it had flown its aircraft off to reinforce the Wake Island garrison.

That move came as the result of a change of command. Things almost always got fucked up during a change of command, at least initially. How much Admiral Husband E. Kimmel, the former Commander in Chief, Pacific Fleet, was responsible for the disaster at Pearl Harbor was open to debate. But since he *was* CINCPAC, he *was* responsible for whatever happened to the ships of his command. And after the Japanese had wiped out Battleship Row, he had to go.

McInerney privately believed—from his admittedly parochial viewpoint as an aviator—that the loss of most of the battleship fleet was probably a blessing in disguise. There were two schools in the upper echelons of the Navy, the Battleship Admirals and the Carrier Admirals. There was no way that the Battleship Admirals could any longer maintain that their dreadnoughts were impregnable to airplanes; most of their battleships were on the bottom at Pearl.

Conversely, the Carrier Admirals could now argue that battleships were vulnerable to carrier-borne aircraft, using the same carnage on Battleship Row at Pearl Harbor as proof of their argument. That just might give command of the naval war in the Pacific to the Carrier Admirals.

McInerney knew that it wouldn't be an all-out victory for the Carrier Admirals over the Battleship Admirals. The battleships that could be repaired would be repaired and sent into action; those still under construction would be completed. But if it came to choosing between a new battleship and a new carrier, the Navy would get a new carrier. And the really senior Navy brass would no longer be able to push Carrier Admirals subtly aside in favor of Battleship Admirals.

No aircraft carriers had been sunk at Pearl. It might have been just dumb luck that they were all at sea, but the point was that *none* of them had been sunk. And since there were no longer sufficient battleships to do it, it would be the aircraft carriers that would have to carry the battle to the enemy. And when the discussions were held about *how* to take the battle to the enemy, the opinions of the Carrier Admirals would carry much more weight than they had on December 6, 1941.

Admiral Husband E. Kimmel had to go, and he knew it, and so did everybody else in CINCPAC Headquarters. From 1100 on December 7, Kimmel had had to consider himself only the caretaker of the Pacific Fleet, holding the authority of CINCPAC only until his replacement could get to Hawaii. As it actually turned out, he wasn't even given that. He was relieved, and an interim commander appointed, while Admiral King and the rest of the brass in Washington made up their minds who would replace him.

They had settled on Admiral Chester W. Nimitz. McInerney personally knew Nimitz slightly, and liked him. Professionally, he knew him better and admired him. But Nimitz hadn't even been chosen to be CINCPAC when the decision had been made to send three carrier groups to sea, two to make diversionary strikes, and the third, Task Force 14, to reinforce Wake.

The decision to recall it had come after the humiliated Kimmel had been relieved, and before Nimitz could get to Hawaii and raise his flag as CINCPAC.

McInerney believed the recall order did not take into consideration what a bloody nose the Americans on Wake had given the Japanese with the pitifully few men, weapons, and aircraft at their disposal. Commander Winfield Scott Cunningham, the overall commander on Wake, and the Marines under Majors Devereux and Putnam, had practically worked miracles with what they had.

The decision to recall Task Force 14 had obviously been made because it was not wise to risk Sara and the three cruisers. McInerney was willing to admit that probably made sense, given the overall strength of the battered Pacific Fleet; but there was no reason for not making a greater effort to reinforce Wake.

Another twelve hours' steaming would have put them within easy range to fly VFM-221's F2A-3 Buffalo fighters (and Galloway's lone F4F-4 Wildcat) off Sara onto Wake. It seemed likely to McInerney that risking the *Tangier,* with her Marine Defense Battalion and all that ammunition aboard, by sending her onto Wake would have been justified. Tangier could probably have been given air cover by VFM-221 and, for a while at least, as Sara steamed in the opposite direction, by Navy fighters aboard Sara.

Instead, *Tangier* had turned around with the others and gone back to Pearl Harbor . . . and at the moment she turned, she was almost at the point where the carriers could have launched aircraft to protect her.

McInerney was not willing to go so far as to assert that the presence of the additional aircraft (he was painfully aware of the inadequacies of the Buffalo) and the reinforcement Defense Battalion would have kept the Japanese from taking Wake, but there was no doubt in his mind that the planes and the men—and, more important, the five-inch shells— would have made it a very costly operation for them.

If that had happened, and if T/Sgt. Charley Galloway had managed to get his Wildcat onto Wake and into the battle, he *would* have become a Marine Corps legend.

But it hadn't happened. Sara and the rest of Task Force 14 had returned to Pearl with Galloway and his F4F-4 aboard.

There was a good deal of frustration aboard Sara when that happened. McInerney had learned that a number of senior officers had actually recommended to the Task Force Commander that he ignore the recall order from Pearl and go on with the original mission. In the end, of course, they had obeyed their orders.

Meanwhile, McInerney guessed—very sure he was close to the truth—that some chickenshit sonofabitch, probably a swabbie, had pointed out that what that damned Marine flying sergeant had done was in clear violation of any number of regulations.

Since that sort of thing couldn't be tolerated, charges were drawn up. And since people were looking for something, or someone, on whom to vent their frustration, Galloway had wound up being charged with everything but unlawful carnal knowledge.

General court-martial charges had actually been drawn up against him. But when it came to convening the court, they had found out that general court-martial authority was not vested in CINCPAC, but in the Commanding General of the 2nd Marine Aircraft Wing, back in San Diego, because VFM-211 was under its command.

So they had put T/Sgt. Galloway under arrest, on a transport bound for San Diego. And they'd air-mailed all the charges and specifications to the Commanding General, 2nd Marine Air Wing, "for appropriate action."

The Commanding General of the 2nd Marine Air Wing, realizing a hot potato had dropped in his lap, had quickly tossed it upstairs and into the lap of Major General D. G. McInerney, at Headquarters, USMC.

A court-martial was now out of the question, as a practical matter. It would be impossible to gather the witnesses necessary for a successful prosecution in Washington. They were all over the Pacific. And some of them were dead. There was, besides, the question of the press. It would look to the press—as it looked to McInerney—as though the Marine Corps was about to try to punish somebody for trying to fight for his country.

"But we have to do something, Mac," the Major General Commandant had said when McInerney reluctantly brought the matter to his attention. "Even Ernie King has heard about your Sergeant Galloway. Use your best judgment; I'll back you up, whatever you decide."

McInerney knew what would satisfy the Navy, short of a court-martial: a letter saying that Galloway had been relieved of flying duties and assigned elsewhere.

"I'm really furious with you, Galloway, about this," McInerney said. "You've cost me a fine fighter pilot and what I'm sure would have been a superior squadron commander."

"Sir?"

"You! You dumb sonofabitch!" McInerney said, with a fury that started out as an act, but became genuine as he realized that he was speaking the truth.

"I'm sorry, Sir, I don't understand."

"If you could have restrained your Alan Ladd–Errol Flynn–Ronald Reagan movie-star heroics for a couple of weeks, there would have been bars on your collar points and a squadron to command. You could more than likely have done some real damage to the enemy, a lot more than you could have caused even if you had managed to get that jury-rigged wreck to Wake. And probably taught some of these kids things that just might have kept them alive."

"I never even thought about a commission," Galloway replied, so surprised, McInerney noticed, that he did not append "Sir" to his reply.

"That's your goddamn trouble! You don't think!"

"Yes, Sir."

"The Corps spent a lot of time and money training you, Galloway, and now that's all going to be wasted."

"Sir?"

"It will be a cold day in hell, Galloway, before you get in a cockpit again."

"Yes, Sir," Galloway said.

McInerney saw in Galloway's eyes that that had gotten to him. The worst punishment that could be meted out to someone like Galloway was to take flying, any kind of flying, but especially flying a fighter plane, away from him.

I wonder why I said that? I don't mean it. For a number of reasons, including both that the Corps needs pilots like Galloway, and that I have no intention of punishing him for doing something I would have done myself.

"It has not been decided whether to proceed with your court-martial, Galloway. Until that decision has been made, you will report to MAG-11 at Quantico. You will work in maintenance. But you will not get in the cockpit of a Texan, or any other aircraft, to so much as taxi it down a taxiway."

"Aye, aye, Sir."

"That's all, Sergeant. You may go."

"Yes, Sir. Thank you, Sir," T/Sgt. Charley Galloway said. He did an about-face and marched out of General McInerney's office.

Lieutenant Orfutt came into General McInerney's office a moment later.

"Have a memo typed up to General Holcomb," McInerney said, "saying that I have temporarily assigned Sergeant Galloway to Quantico for duty as an aircraft maintenance supervisor. And then do a letter to CINCPAC saying that appropriate action in the case of Sergeant Galloway is being implemented."

"Aye, aye, Sir," Orfutt said. "Damned shame to lose his experience."

"You're not listening carefully, again, Charlie," McInerney said. "The operative word is *temporarily.*"

"Oh," Orfutt said, and smiled. "Yes, Sir."

"And I said something in the heat of anger that might make some sense. Get a teletype out to the 1st and 2nd Aircraft wings, telling them to review the records of the Naval Aviation Pilots and submit to me within seven days a list of those they can recommend for commissions. Put in there somewhere that the lack of a college degree is not to be considered disqualifying."

"Aye, aye, Sir."

"Is there anything else, Charlie?"

"Sir, you're having lunch at the Army-Navy Club with Admiral Ward."

"Oh, Christ! Can I get out of it?"

"This would be the third time you've canceled, Sir."

McInerney looked at his watch.

"Order up the car."

"I've done that, Sir. It's outside."

"Sometimes you're just too goddamn efficient, Charlie. With a little bit of luck, maybe it would have had an accident on the way here from the motor pool."

"Sorry, Sir," Orfutt said, and went to the clothes tree and took General McInerney's overcoat from it and held it up for him.

Fifteen minutes later, as the Marine-green 1941 Ford was moving down Pennsylvania Avenue near the White House, General McInerney suddenly sat up. He had been glancing casually out the side window, but now he stared intently, then turned and stared out the back.

"Stop the car!" he ordered.

"Sir?" the driver, a young corporal, asked, confused.

"That was English, son," McInerney snapped. "Pull to the curb and stop!"

"Aye, aye, Sir," the Corporal replied, and complied with his orders.

"There's a Navy officer coming up behind us on the sidewalk. Intercept him and tell him I would be grateful for a moment of his time," McInerney said. Then he slumped low in the seat.

The driver got quickly out of the car, found the Navy officer, and relayed General McInerney's desires to him. He walked just behind him to the car, then quickly stepped ahead of him to pull the door open.

The Navy officer, a captain, saluted.

"Good afternoon, General," he said.

"Get in," General McInerney ordered.

"Aye, aye, Sir," the Captain said.

The Captain complied with his orders.

General McInerney examined him carefully.

" 'Fuck the Navy!' Isn't that what I remember you saying, Captain?"

"Yes, Sir, I seem to recall having said something along those lines."

"And how long now have you been wearing Navy blue?"

"Three days, Sir. How do I look?"

"If people didn't know any better, they'd think you were a Navy captain. The look of confusion in your eyes, for example."

"Thank you, Sir."

"I've got a lunch date I can't get out of," General McInerney said. "But I can give you a ride. Where are you headed?"

"Just down the block, Sir."

"To the hotel your father-in-law owns?"

"Actually, General, to the White House. Secretary Knox wants me to meet the President. I've been invited to lunch."

"Oh, Flem, you sonofabitch! Why am I not surprised?"

(FOUR)

THE WHITE HOUSE
WASHINGTON, D.C.
30 JANUARY 1942

"My name is Pickering," Fleming Pickering said to the civilian guard at the White House gate. The civilian had come out of a small, presumably heated guardhouse at his approach. The two soldiers on guard, their ears and nose reddened by the cold, apparently were required to stay outside and freeze.

"Let me see your identification," the guard said curtly, even rudely.

Fleming produced his new Navy identification card. The guard examined it carefully, comparing the photograph on it to Pickering's face.

"Wait here," the guard said, and went back into the guardhouse. Pickering saw him pick up a telephone and speak with someone. He did not come back out of the guardhouse.

A minute later, a Marine sergeant in greens came down the driveway. He saluted.

"Would you come with me, please, Captain Pickering?" he said politely, crisply.

Pickering marched after him up the curving drive toward the White House. There was a crust of ice on the drive. It had been sanded, but the road was slippery.

The Marine led him to a side entrance, toward the building that had been built at the turn of the century to house the State, War, and Navy departments of the U.S. Government, and then up a rather ordinary staircase to the second floor.

Pickering found himself in a wide corridor. A clean-cut man in his early thirties sat at a small desk facing the wall, and two other men cut from the same bolt of cloth were standing nearby. Pickering was sure they were Secret Service agents.

"This is Captain Pickering," the Marine sergeant said. The man at the desk nodded, glanced at his wristwatch, and made a notation in a small, wire-bound ledger.

"This way, please, Captain," the Marine said, and led Pickering halfway down the corridor to a double door. He knocked. The door was opened by a very large, very black man in a starched white jacket.

"Captain Pickering," the Marine sergeant said.

The black man opened the door fully. "Please come in, Sir," he said. "The President's expecting you."

This was, Pickering realized, the President's private suite, the Presidential apartments, or whatever it was called. He was surprised. He had expected to be fed in some sort of official dining room.

A tall, well-built, bespectacled man in the uniform of a Marine captain came out of an inner room. In the moment, Pickering recognized him as one of Roosevelt's sons, he had no idea which one. The Captain said, "Good afternoon, Sir. Let me help you with your coat. Dad and Mr. Knox are right inside."

Pickering handed him his uniform cap and then took off his topcoat and handed that over. Captain Roosevelt handed both to the steward, then motioned Pickering ahead of him through a door.

The President of the United States, in a wheelchair, rolled across the room to him, his hand extended. Pickering knew, of course, that Franklin Delano Roosevelt had been crippled by polio, but the wheelchair surprised him. He was almost never photographed sitting in it.

"We've been talking about you, Captain," Roosevelt said as he shook Pickering's hand in a very firm grip. "Have your ears been burning?"

"Good afternoon, Mr. President," Pickering said.

He heard his father-in-law Andrew Foster's dry voice in his mind: "The sonofabitch is obviously a socialist, but giving the devil his due, he probably saved this country from going communist."

"Naval officers are forbidden to drink on duty," the President said, smiling warmly, "except, of course, when the Commander in Chief doesn't want to drink alone."

Another steward appeared at that moment with a glass of whiskey on a small silver tray.

"Thank you," Pickering said, and raised the glass. "Your health, Sir," he said, then took a sip. It was Scotch, good Scotch.

"That all right?" Roosevelt asked. "Frank said you're a Scotch drinker."

"This is fine, Sir."

"He also told me that you'd much rather be wearing a uniform like Jimmy's," the President went on, "but that he'd convinced you you would be of greater use in the Navy."

"I was a Marine, Sir," Pickering said. "Once a Marine, always a Marine."

Roosevelt laughed.

"Frank also told me to watch out for you—that if I let my guard down, you'd probably ask me for a Letter of Marque."

Pickering glanced at Frank Knox, who smiled and shook his head.

"May I have one, Sir?" Pickering said.

Roosevelt laughed heartily.

"No, you may not," he said. "I admire your spirit, Pickering, but I'm afraid you're going to have to fight this war like everybody else—including me—the way someone tells you to."

"Aye, aye, Sir," Pickering said, smiling.

I am being charmed. I wonder why.

"Why don't we go to the table and sit down?" Roosevelt said, gesturing toward a small table near windows overlooking the White House lawn. Pickering saw there were only four places set.

Stewards immediately began placing small plates of hors d'oeuvres before them.

Roosevelt began to talk about the British commandos. Pickering quickly saw that he was very impressed with them—as much for the public's perception of them as for any bona fide military capability.

"When Britain was reeling across Europe from the Nazi Blitzkrieg," Roosevelt announced, as if making a speech before a large audience, "when they were literally bloody and on their knees, and morale was completely collapsing, a few small commando operations, militarily insignificant in themselves, did wonders to restore civilian morale and faith in their government."

"I had really never thought of it in that context," Pickering said honestly. "But I can see your point."

Roosevelt, Pickering was perfectly willing to grant, was a genius at understanding—and molding—public opinion.

"A very few brave and resourceful men can change the path of history, Pickering," the President said sonorously. "And fortunately, right now we have two such men. You know Colonel Jim Doolittle, don't you?"

"If you mean, Mr. President, the Jim Doolittle who used to be vice-president of Shell Oil, yes, Sir. I know him."

"I thought you might," the President said. "Two of a kind, you know, you two. Not thinking of the cut in pay that putting on a uniform meant, but rather rushing to answer the call of the trumpet."

I really am being charmed, Fleming Pickering decided. *He wants something from me. I wonder what. Not the damned ships again!*

"Frank, have you told Captain Pickering what Jim Doolittle's up to?"

"It's top secret, Mr. President," Secretary Knox replied.

"Well, I think we can trust Captain Pickering. . . . Captain Pickering, would you be offended if I called you by your Christian name?"

"Not at all, Mr. President."

"Well, Frank, if Flem's going to be working for you, he'll find out soon enough anyway. Wouldn't you say?"

"Probably, Mr. President."

"Jim Doolittle, Flem, came to me with the idea that he can take B-25 Mitchell bombers off from the deck of an aircraft carrier."

"Sir?" Pickering asked, not understanding.

"The Japanese Emperor is sitting in his palace in Tokyo, convinced that he's absolutely safe from American bombing. Colonel Doolittle and his brave men are about to disabuse him of that notion," Roosevelt said, cocking his cigarette holder almost vertically in his mouth as he smiled with pleasure.

"The idea, Pickering," Secretary Knox said, "is that we will carry Doolittle on a carrier within striking distance of Tokyo; they will launch from the carrier, bomb Tokyo, and then fly on to China."

"Fascinating," Pickering said, and then blurted, "But can Doolittle do it? Can you fly airplanes that large from aircraft carriers?"

"Doolittle thinks so. They're down in Florida now, in the Panhandle, learning how," Knox said. "Yes, I think it can be done."

"Christ, that's good news!" Pickering said excitedly. "So far, all we've done is take a licking."

"And there will be other reverses in the near future, I am very much afraid," Roosevelt said.

"The Philippines, you mean?" Pickering asked.

"You don't believe that Douglas MacArthur will be able to hold the Philippines?" Roosevelt asked. He was still smiling, but there was a hint of coldness in his voice.

Jesus Christ, my mouth has run away with me again!

"Mr. President, I don't pretend to know anything about our forces in the Philippines, but I do know that they will require supplies. I do know something about shipping. I know that there are not enough bottoms to supply a large military force, and even if there were, there are not enough warships after Pearl Harbor to protect the sea lanes to the Philippines."

"Aren't you concerned, talking like that," Roosevelt asked, carefully, "that someone who doesn't know you might think you're a defeatist?"

"If I have spoken out of turn, Mr. President . . ."

Roosevelt looked at him thoughtfully for a long moment before he spoke again.

"I said, a while ago, we have two brave and resourceful men," he said. "Jimmy here is allied with the other one. And don't tell me this is top secret, too, Frank. I know."

"Yes, Mr. President," Knox replied.

"The commander of the Marine Guard at White Sulphur Springs a few years back," Roosevelt said, "was a man named Evans Carlson. You happen to know him?"

"No, Sir."

"Major Carlson is now out in San Diego, starting up a unit I think of as American Commandos. But I don't want it to appear as if we're slavishly copying our British cousins, so we're calling them Raiders. All volunteers, highly trained, who will hit the Japanese and then run."

"Sounds very interesting," Pickering said.

I wonder how he's going to move them around? It's thirty, forty miles from the English coast to the French. Distances in the Pacific are measured in multiple hundreds, multiple thousands, of miles.

"Frank had the Navy yards convert some old four-stacker destroyers to high-speed transports," Roosevelt said.

He's reading my mind, Pickering thought.

"The idea, Flem," Captain Roosevelt said, "is that by striking the Japanese where they don't expect it, in addition to what damage we do there, we will force the Japanese to put forces they could use elsewhere to work guarding all of their islands."

"I see," Pickering said.

"And, Flem," the President said passionately, "think of what it will do for morale! As you just said, all we've done so far in this war is take a licking and lick our wounds!"

"Yes, Sir. I understand."

"Well, I'm sorry to tell you that my enthusiasm is not shared by either the Navy *or* the Marine Corps," the President said.

"Now, Frank," Secretary Knox said, "that's not true."

"They are dancing with Evans Carlson with all the enthusiasm of a fourteen-year-old in dancing school paired off with a fat girl," Roosevelt said, and everyone laughed. "They have to do it, but they don't have to like it."

"Frank," Secretary Knox said, "if you really think that's the case, I'll send Captain Pickering out there to see what needs straightening out."

Roosevelt looked as if he had just heard a startlingly brilliant suggestion for the first time.

You fraudulent old sonofabitch, Pickering thought, *that's what this whole thing with your boy here for a private lunch is all about. Knox brought me here to let you know what he intended to do with me, and you'll let him, providing I take care of this Major Evans Carlson. Tit for tat. I haven't been here a week, and I'm already in politics.*

"That might not be a bad idea, Frank," Roosevelt said thoughtfully, and then added, "Now that I think about it, if you can spare Fleming, he's probably just the right man for the job. You *were* a Marine, Flem, after all."

"Yes, Sir, I was."

"I'll send him out there tomorrow, Mr. President," Knox said.

"Good idea, Frank!"

When they left the White House, Knox waited until they were in his limousine and then said, "I have a Commander Kramer who has all the background material on Major Carlson, the Raiders, and their target. An island called Makin. I'll have him bring it around to your hotel tomorrow. And then you get on the Monday-morning courier plane to San Diego. I'm not really sure how I feel about the whole idea. . . . I understand why people may be dragging their feet; they think it's both a waste of time and materiel and an idea that may go away. . . . But now I know that it's important to Roosevelt. Given that, it's important to you and me that you go out there and light a fire under people."

"I'm sympathetic to the notion that a victory, any kind of a victory, even a small one, is important right now."

"And it will be even more important when the Philippines fall," Knox said. "So it's important, for a number of reasons, that you go out there right away. We can get you an office and a secretary when you come back."

V

(ONE)
SECURITY INTELLIGENCE SECTION
U.S. NAVAL COMMUNICATIONS
WASHINGTON, D.C.
0730 HOURS 31 JANUARY 1942

When Mrs. Glen T. (Ellen) Feller passed through the security gate on her way to work, the civilian guard smiled at her and handed her a note. It read, "Ellen, please see me at 0800." It was initialed "AFK." Commander A. F. Kramer was the officer-in-charge.

Ellen Feller, who was tall and thirty, with pale skin and long, light brown hair which she normally wore in a bun, glanced at the note for a second. It sparked her curiosity, but it did not cause her any real concern. She often found essentially identical notes waiting for her as she came to work.

"Thank you," she said, smiling at the guard; then she entered the restricted area. She either nodded and smiled or said good morning to a dozen people as she made her way to her desk at the far end of the long and narrow room. People smiled back at her, some of them a little warily. Ellen was aware that her co-workers thought of her as devoutly religious. She had several times heard herself referred to as a "Christer."

Personnel records, and especially reports of what were known as Complete Background Investigations, are classified Confidential, the security classification a step below Secret. They were thus theoretically *really* confidential, and their contents were made available only to those with a "need to know," who had been granted the appropriate security clearances.

In practice, however, personnel records and reports, "interim" and "final," of Complete Background Investigations of new or potential employees were available to anyone who was curious—even secretaries. This was especially the case in the Security Intelligence Section, where even the clerk-typists held Top Secret security clearances. There the Confidential classification was considered something of a joke.

Before Mrs. Feller had reported for duty, some time ago, as an Oriental Languages Linguist, all the girls in the office knew that their new co-worker was married to the Reverend Glen T. Feller of the Christian & Missionary Alliance; that she had perfected her language skills in the Orient; and that until the previous May, she and her husband had operated a C&MA missionary school in China.

They also knew that the Fellers had no children and that Reverend Feller was off doing the Lord's work among the American Indians on a reservation in Arizona. Meanwhile, Mrs. Feller had noticed a classified advertisement placed by the U.S. Government seeking U.S. citizens with fluency in foreign languages, and she'd answered it.

Soon after that, the Navy offered her a job as an Oriental Languages Linguist. It wasn't known whether she accepted the job as a patriotic citizen; or because the Fellers needed the money; or because she didn't want to live in the Arizona desert. Her application for employment stated simply that she "wanted to serve."

In fact, although the job paid her more than she'd expected, she had taken it for the very simple reason that she really didn't want to go to Arizona. And that meant she had to find work.

The actual fact was that Ellen Feller had absolutely no interest in doing the Lord's work or, for that matter, in saving her immortal soul. And even more to the point, she loathed the Reverend Feller. She didn't want to live with him in Arizona or anywhere else.

Were it not for her father, who was rich and elderly—approaching the end of his time on earth—and a religious zealot, she would have divorced her husband. But a divorce would almost certainly inspire him to cut Ellen out of his will and leave all of his money to the Christian & Missionary Alliance. The way it stood now, he intended to leave half of his worldly goods to his daughter and her husband.

With that understanding, and of course after days of prayerful consideration, the Reverend Feller had announced to the hierarchy of his denomination that it was God's will for him to go alone to bring the Gospel of the Lord Jesus Christ to the Navajos. His beloved wife would meanwhile make what contribution she could to the war effort in Washington, D.C. This move would cause them both a huge personal sacrifice, but they had prayerfully and tearfully decided to endure it.

The Reverend Feller had been honestly unhappy to leave Ellen behind in Washington. Not because he particularly liked her, or even because he would be denied his connubial privileges, but because the old man was in a nursing home in Baltimore, forty miles from Washington. The Reverend was afraid that while he was off in Arizona, Ellen would attempt to poison her father against him with reports of his misbehavior, sexual and otherwise, in China.

In the end, he had acquiesced to the move solely because Ellen had threatened to go to the authorities, both governmental and ecclesiastical, and inform them of some of the lesser-known facts about her husband's activities in China. From the day they had entered that country, for example, he had been involved in the illegal export to the United States of Chinese archeological treasures looted from tombs.

The Reverend Feller had gone to great lengths to conceal what he called his "personal pension plan" from his wife. He had therefore been astonished to learn that she knew about it. He incorrectly suspected that one of the Chinese had told her. She had actually learned about it from an American Marine. As one of their last missions before being transferred to the Philippines, the 4th Marines had provided a guard detachment for the convoy of missionary vehicles as they left for home.

Ellen Feller had had a brief fling in those days with one of the young Marines. She now realized the affair had been both foolish and stupid; but at the time she had endured a long abstinence from men, the Marine himself was extraordinarily fascinating, and she'd imagined that the odds were very much against her ever seeing him again.

When she first saw him staring with interest at her body, she presumed he was a simple Marine in charge of the Marine trucks. It was only after they'd made the beast with two backs half a dozen times that she learned that Corporal Kenneth R. "Killer" McCoy, USMC, wasn't anything of the kind.

He was, in fact, on an intelligence-gathering mission for the 4th Marines. His mission was concerned both with the location of Japanese army units in the area he was passing through—and with reports that missionaries were smuggling out of China valuable Chinese artifacts: jade, pottery, and other items.

Until she was actually aboard the ship that brought her home, Ellen Feller managed to convince Ken McCoy that she was fonder of him than was the case. Largely because of that, she was reasonably assured that he did not report to his superiors that some of the shipping containers the Marines had obligingly transported for them to Tientsin contained material having nothing to do with the work of the Christian & Missionary Alliance.

But of course, she couldn't be sure.

Her concern diminished with time, and especially when she learned that the 4th Marines had indeed been transferred from China to the Philippines as scheduled. It was about that time that she entered the Navy's employ.

Just before Pearl Harbor, however, she was instructed to deliver to the office of the officer in charge, Commander A. F. Kramer, a packet of classified documents that were to be transported to the Far East by officer courier. The officer courier turned out to be Killer McCoy, now wearing the uniform of a Marine lieutenant.

Since McCoy was driven directly from the office to meet his airplane, there was no time then for Ellen Feller to do anything but make it plain to him that she was perfectly willing—even anxious—to resume their intimate relationship. There was enough time, nevertheless, for her to reassure herself that McCoy had still not informed anyone about the material her husband had illegally brought into the United States.

Not long after that, there was a cable reporting that Lieutenant McCoy was missing in action in the Philippines and presumed dead—news that for a few days flooded Ellen Feller with considerable relief. The matter was finally over and done with, she told herself.

But then McCoy dropped out of the blue alive and well, and that put her back on square one. Beyond that, McCoy showed no interest whatever in resuming their relationship. And soon after that, McCoy disappeared from Washington. There was a credible rumor (which she now thought of as "scuttlebutt") that McCoy was on a confidential, undercover mission in California.

Ellen Feller was nothing if not resourceful. A short time later—though after a good deal of thought—she came up with a reasonable plan in the event McCoy reported the crates. First of all, there was a good chance that he would not report them at all. If he did, the question would naturally arise as to why he hadn't made his report to the proper authorities in China; his failure to do so would constitute, almost by definition, dereliction of duty.

And even if he did report them, it would come down to his word against hers and the Reverend Feller's. Besides, Ellen Feller had so far been unable to locate the crates, although she'd tried very hard to find them. Her husband had obviously hidden them well. Under the present circumstances, she doubted that anyone in the government would spend a lot of time looking for them—or that they could find them if they did. Glen Feller might be a miserable sonofabitch, but he was not stupid.

And even if the crates did show up, she could profess to know nothing whatever about them; or alternatively, she could claim that she had reported the matter to McCoy. What was important, she concluded, was to earn the reputation of being a simple, loyal, hardworking employee, who was so devoutly religious that she could not possibly be involved in anything dishonest.

It was not difficult for her to play this role. In China she had successfully played the role of a pious, hardworking, good Christian woman for years.

Playing it in Washington turned out to be even easier. In fact, partially because of the mushrooming of the Intelligence staff, it produced unexpected benefits. Other linguists came aboard after she did, and many of them, like her, were former missionaries. Soon she was given greater responsibility: since there was neither time nor need to translate every Chinese or Japanese document that came into their hands, Ellen Feller became sort of an editor. She separated those documents that would be of interest to the Navy from the others, which were discarded, and then she assigned the job of translating the important ones to someone or other. She rarely made the actual translations herself. Because she had taken on greater responsibility, her official job description was changed, and this resulted in a promotion.

At precisely five minutes before eight, Ellen Feller rose from her desk and visited the ladies' room to inspect her hair and general appearance. She was generally pleased with what she saw in the mirror, yet she wished, as she almost always did, that she could wear lipstick without destroying the image she was forced to convey. Without it, she thought, she looked like a drab.

She checked very carefully to make sure that no part of her lingerie was visible. She took what she was perfectly willing to admit was a perverse pleasure in wearing black, lacy lingerie. It made her feel like a woman. But of course she didn't want anyone, especially Commander Kramer, to see it.

When she finished, she went to Commander Kramer's office, stood in the open doorway, and knocked on the jamb.

"Come in, Ellen," Commander Kramer said, smiling. "Good morning."

"Good morning, Sir," she said, and stepped inside.

There was a captain in the office, who rose as she entered.

"Ellen, this is Captain Haughton, of Secretary Knox's office. Captain, Mrs. Ellen Feller."

Haughton, Ellen saw, was examining her carefully. There was a moment's concern (*What does someone from the office of the Secretary of the Navy want with me?*) but it passed immediately. She sensed that Captain Haughton liked what he saw.

"Good morning, Sir," Ellen Feller said politely. "I'm very pleased to meet you."

(TWO)

THE FOSTER LAFAYETTE HOTEL
WASHINGTON, D.C.
31 JANUARY 1942

Captain Fleming Pickering, USNR, had been talking with his wife in San Francisco. Just after he put the telephone handset back in its cradle, the telephone rang again.

The ring disturbed him. During the last few minutes of his call he had said some unflattering things about the President of the United States, and he'd performed a rather credible mimicry of both the President's and Mrs. Eleanor Roosevelt's voices. As he did that, it occurred to him that his telephone might be tapped, and that Roosevelt would shortly hear what Fleming Pickering thought of him.

The possibility that his telephone might indeed be tapped was no longer a paranoid fantasy. Telephones *were* being tapped. The nation was at war. J. Edgar Hoover and the FBI had been given extraordinary authority. And so, certainly, had the counterintelligence services of the Army and Navy. The Constitution was now being selective in whose rights it protected.

The great proof of that was just then happening in Pickering's home state. A hysterical Army lieutenant general in California had decided that no one of Japanese ancestry could be trusted. And he had been joined in this hysteria by California's Attorney General, a Republican named Earl Warren. Warren was more than just an acquaintance of Fleming Pickering's. Pickering had played golf with him—and actually voted for him.

"To protect the nation," the Army lieutenant general and the California Attorney General had decided to scoop up all the West Coast Japanese, enemy alien and native-born American alike, and put them in "relocation camps."

Just the West Coast Japanese. Not Japanese elsewhere in the United States. Or, for that matter, Japanese in Hawaii. And not Germans or Italians either . . . even though it wasn't many months earlier that the German-American Bund was marching around Madison Square Garden in New York, wearing swastika-bedecked uniforms, singing *"Deutschland Über Alles,"* and saluting with the straight-armed Nazi salute.

It was governmental insanity, and it was frightening.

Pickering had already concluded that if he were J. Edgar Hoover— or one of his counterintelligence underlings (or for that matter, some captain in Naval Intelligence)—and had learned that Fleming Pickering, Esq., had appeared out of nowhere, been commissioned as a captain directly and personally by the Secretary of the Navy, and was obviously about to move around the upper echelons of the defense establishment with a Top Secret clearance, he would want to learn instantly as much as he could about Pickering and his thoughts and opinions. The easy way to do that was to tap his telephone.

Among the many opinions Pickering had broadcast over the phone moments earlier, he'd said that "the President of the United States is either the salvation of the nation, or he's quite as mad as Adolph Hitler, and I don't know which." And "if he goes ahead with this so-called relocation of the Japanese, especially the ones who are citizens, and isn't stopped, I can't see a hell of a lot of difference between him and Hitler. The law is going to be what he says it is."

Fortunately, he'd sensed that he was upsetting Patricia, so he'd switched to mimicking Roosevelt's and Eleanor's quirks of speech. He knew that always made her laugh.

Of course, he had not informed Patricia of the subjects discussed over lunch in the Presidential Apartments. Without giving it much solemn thought, he'd decided that anything the Commander in Chief had said to the Secretary of the Navy and a Navy Reserve captain was none of the captain's wife's business.

"Hello," he said, picking up the telephone.

"Captain Pickering, please."

"This is Captain Pickering."

"Sir, this is Commander Kramer. I'm in the lobby."

Oh, Christ. I should have answered the telephone in The Navy Manner. This isn't the Adams Suite in the Lafayette. This is the quarters of Captain F. Pickering, USNR, and I should have answered the phone by saying "Captain Pickering."

"Please come up, Commander."

"Aye, aye, Sir."

Pickering pushed himself out of the upholstered chair in the sitting room and went into the bedroom to put on his uniform. Commander Kramer had probably already decided he had been selected by ill fortune to baby-sit another goddamned civilian in uniform. Opening the door to him while wearing a Sulka's silk dressing robe would confirm that opinion beyond redemption.

The door chimes went off while Pickering was still tying his tie. He muttered, "Damn," then went to the door and pulled it open.

Commander Kramer, a tall, thin man with a pencil-line mustache, was not alone. He had with him a lieutenant junior grade and a woman. The JG was a muscular young man who was carrying a well-stuffed leather briefcase. Fleming would have given odds that he'd not only gone to Annapolis, but that he'd played football there.

The woman, smooth-skinned, wearing little or no makeup, was in her middle thirties. She was wearing a hat—a real hat, not a decorative one—against the snow and cold. She had unbuttoned her overcoat, and Fleming Pickering noticed, *en passant,* that she had long, shapely calves and a nice set of breastworks.

"I was just tying my tie," Pickering said. "Come in."

"Yes, Sir," Commander Kramer said, then thrust a small package at Pickering. "Sir, this is for you."

"Oh? What is it?"

"The Secretary asked me to get those for you, Sir. They're your ribbons. The Secretary said to tell you he noticed you weren't wearing any."

"Would you say, Commander, that that's in the order of a pointed suggestion?"

"Actually, Sir," Kramer said, "it's probably more in the nature of a regal command."

Pickering chuckled. At least Kramer wasn't afraid of him. Frank Knox had described Kramer as "the brightest of the lot," and Pickering had jumped to the conclusion that Knox meant Kramer was sort of an academic egghead. He obviously wasn't.

"Captain, may I introduce Mrs. Ellen Feller? And Mr. Satterly?"

"How do you do?"

Mrs. Feller gave him her hand. He found it to be soft and warm. Lieutenant Satterly's grip was conspicuously firm and masculine. Pickering suspected he would love to try a squeeze contest.

"Let me finish, and I'll be right with you," Pickering said, and started to the bedroom.

"Captain, may I have a word with you alone, Sir?" Kramer asked.

"Come along."

He held the door to the bedroom open for Kramer, and closed it after he'd followed him through it.

"Mrs. Feller is a candidate nominee, maybe, for your secretary, Captain," Kramer said.

"I wondered who she was."

"The Secretary said I should get you someone a little out of the ordinary," Kramer said. "I took that to mean I should not offer you one of the career civil-service ladies."

"How did you get stuck with me, Kramer?"

"I'm flattered that I did, Sir."

"Really?"

"It's always interesting to work with somebody who doesn't have to clear his decisions with three levels of command above him."

"So it is," Fleming said. "Tell me about Mrs. . . . . what did you say?"

"Feller, Captain. Ellen Feller. She's been with us about six months."

" 'Us' is who?" Pickering interrupted.

"Naval Intelligence, Sir."

"OK." He had figured as much.

"She and her husband were missionaries in China before the war. She speaks two brands of Chinese, plus some Japanese."

"Now that you think about it, she does sort of smell of missionary."

"She doesn't bring it to work, Sir. I can tell you that. She's been working for me."

"Why are you so willing to give her up?" Pickering challenged, looking directly at Kramer.

There was visible hesitation.

"The lady has character traits you forgot to mention? She likes her gin, maybe?"

"No, Sir. There's an answer, Captain. But it sounds a bit trite."

"Let's hear it."

"If I understand correctly what your role is going to be, you need her more than I do."

"Oh," Pickering replied. "That's very nice of you. I thought perhaps you might be giving her to me so she could tell you everything you wanted to know about me. And about what I'm doing."

"No, Sir," Kramer smiled. "That's not it."

"How do I know that?"

"Well, for one thing, Sir, I don't need her for that purpose. The back-line cables will be full of reports on you."

"What's a back-line cable?"

"Non-official messages. Personal messages. What the admirals send to each other when they want to find out, or report, what's really going on."

"OK," Fleming said. "You're a very interesting man, Commander."

"I don't know about that. But I like what I'm doing, and I'm smart enough to know that if I got caught spying on you—as opposed to getting my hands on back-line cables—I would spend this war at someplace like Great Lakes, giving inspirational talks to boots."

"Did you ever consider selling life insurance?" Pickering asked. "You're very convincing. People would trust you."

"Some people can. People I admire can trust me completely."

"How do I rate on your scale of admiration?"

"Way at the top."

"Is that what the Navy calls soft-soap?"

"I really admire the Secretary," Kramer said. "He admires you, or you wouldn't be here. Call it 'admiration by association.' And then there are these."

He walked to the dresser where Pickering had laid the small package Kramer had given him. He opened it and took out two rows of multicolored ribbons.

"These are very impressive, Captain. You didn't get these behind a desk."

Pickering went to him and took them, then looked at them with interest.

"I don't even know what they all are," he said.

"Turn them the other way around," Kramer said, chuckling. "They're upside down. And then, from the left, we have the Silver Star, the Navy and Marine Corps Medal, the Purple Heart with two oak leaf clusters. . . ."

"I never got a medal called the Purple Heart," Pickering interrupted.

"It's for wounds received in action," Kramer said. "It was originally a medal for valor conceived by General Washington himself in 1782. In 1932, on the two-hundredth anniversary of his birth, it was revived. It is now awarded, as I said, for wounds received in action."

"We had wound stripes," Pickering said softly, and pointed at his jacket cuff. "Embroidered pieces of cloth. Worn down here."

"Yes, Sir. I know. You had three. Now you have a Purple Heart with two oak leaf clusters. On the left of the lower row, Captain, is your World War I Victory Medal, and then your French medals, the Legion d'Honneur in the grade of Chevalier, and finally the Croix de Guerre. A very impressive display, Sir."

"Kramer, I was an eighteen-year-old kid. . . ."

"Yes, Sir. I know. But I suspect the Secretary feels, and I agree, that someone who has never heard a shot fired in anger—and we have many senior officers in that category, Sir—will not automatically categorize as a goddamn civilian in uniform a man who was wounded three times while earning three medals for valor."

Pickering met Kramer's eyes, but didn't respond.

"You've noticed, Sir, that the Secretary wears his Purple Heart ribbon in his buttonhole?"

"No, I didn't. I saw it. I didn't know what the hell it was."

"The Secretary got that, Sir, as a sergeant in the Rough Riders in Cuba in 1899."

"OK. You and the secretary have made your point. Now what about the young officer?"

"He's carrying the bag. I didn't know what you were interested in, so I brought everything you might be. It's a heavy bag. You pick out what you want, and he'll return the rest. Do you have a weapon, Sir?"

"I beg your pardon?"

"Are you armed? Do you have a gun?"

"As a matter of fact, I do. Am I going to need one?"

"Much of that material is top secret, Captain. It either has to be in a secure facility or charged to someone who has the appropriate security clearance and is armed."

"My pistol is stolen," Fleming Pickering said.

"Sir?"

"I brought it home from France in 1919," Pickering said. "It's stamped 'U.S. Property.' "

Kramer chuckled and smiled. "I'm sure the Statute of Limitations would apply, Sir. A Colt .45?"

"Yeah," Pickering said. He went to a chest of drawers, opened it, and held up a Colt Model 1911 pistol.

"Well, we'll get you another one, Captain. But that should do for the time being."

"Is there any reason I can't just read this stuff here and give it all back?"

"None that I can think of, Sir. May I make a suggestion?"

"Sure."

"Make a quick survey, select what you want, and then we'll send Mr. Satterly back to the office with the rest. For that matter, I could go with him. And then—presuming you find Mrs. Feller at least temporarily satisfactory—she could stay here until you're finished, then bring the rest back."

"What would Mrs. Feller do about a gun?" Pickering asked drily.

"She carries one in her purse, Sir."

"I'll be damned!"

Pickering put the Colt automatic back in the drawer and closed it. Then he examined his tie, straightened it, and shrugged into his uniform jacket.

"Let me help you with your ribbons," Kramer said.

He pinned them on for Pickering, then they went into the sitting room.

"Mrs. Feller," Pickering said, "Commander Kramer speaks very highly of you. If you think it's worth trying, I'd be grateful if you would come on board to help me."

"If you're not pleased with how I work out, Captain Pickering," she said, "I'll understand."

"Well, we'll give it our best shot," Pickering said. "Mr. Satterly, you want to hand me that briefcase?"

"Aye, aye, Sir," Lieutenant Satterly said. For the first time, Pickering saw that the briefcase was attached to Satterly's wrist with a length of stainless steel cable and a handcuff.

"Mrs. Feller," Pickering said, "why don't you call room service and order some coffee?"

"Just for the two of you," Kramer explained. "Ellen, you'll stay and see what Captain Pickering decides to send back with you to the office."

She nodded. As Pickering dipped into the briefcase, he heard her ask the operator for room service.

A moment or two later, he glanced around for Commander Kramer to ask him a question. Before he found Kramer, however, his eyes went up Ellen Feller's dress. Quite innocently, he was sure, she was sitting in such a way that he could see that her lingerie was lace and black.

I'll be damned, a missionary lady who wears black lace underwear and carries a gun in her purse.

"Commander, would you tell me what the hell this is, please?" he said, turning his attention to the business at hand.

(THREE)

HEADQUARTERS, 2ND JOINT TRAINING FORCE
CAMP ELLIOTT, CALIFORNIA
1005 HOURS 2 FEBRUARY 1942

Offices in Marine headquarters are usually well equipped with signs identifying the various functions performed therein. And often the signs identify the name of the functionary as well. That didn't seem to be true of Headquarters, 2nd Joint Training Force. There were sign brackets mounted over the doors, but no signs hung from them.

Second Joint Training Force, whatever the hell that was, was either moving in or moving out, Staff Sergeant Joe Howard decided. He was not surprised. The whole Corps seemed to be in a state of upheaval.

Though Staff Sergeant Joe Howard normally took a great deal of professional pride in his appearance, he looked slovenly now, and he knew it. He needed a shave, for one thing, and his greens were mussed and bore the stain of a spilled cup of coffee.

Howard had just flown into San Diego from Pearl Harbor on a Martin PBM-3R Mariner. The Mariner was a "flying boat," a seaplane. Most of the twin-engined, gull-winged aircraft had a crew of seven. They were armed with one .30- and five .50-caliber machine guns and had provision to carry and drop a ton of ordnance, either bombs or depth charges.

The one Howard had flown from Pearl Harbor, however, was the unarmed transport version, the "Dash-Three-R." But this one wasn't a standard Dash-Three-R. It had been fitted up inside for Navy brass. For admirals or better, Joe judged from the comfortable leather seats, the steward, and even an airborne crapper. There were sixteen passengers aboard, including a rear admiral, a half-dozen Navy captains, three Marine and one Army full colonels, and some lesser brass. And two enlisted men. The other one was a gold-stripe Navy Chief Radioman who had made it plain even before they were taken out to the airplane at Pearl that he was not interested in conversation.

Rank didn't get you on the Mariner, the priority on your orders did. They left a roomful of brass behind them at Pearl, including a highly pissed Marine lieutenant colonel who had strongly asserted that there was something seriously wrong with a system that made him give up his seat to a lowly staff sergeant.

It had been Joe Howard's first ride on an airplane of any kind. As a consequence, he had not been aware that aircraft have a tendency to make sudden rapid ascents and descents while proceeding in level flight. The price he paid to gain such an awareness was a nearly full cup of coffee spilled on his chest, soiling his shirt, field scarf, and blouse, and painfully scalding his skin. All this took place while the gold-stripe Chief Radioman watched him scornfully.

A heavyset, middle-aged master gunnery sergeant came down the deserted, signless corridor.

"Gunny, excuse me, I'm looking for Captain Stecker in Special Planning," Staff Sergeant Joe Howard said to him.

The Gunny examined him carefully, critically. There was no way he could miss the stubble on Howard's face or the brown stains on his field scarf and khaki shirt.

I am now going to get my ass eaten out, and this sonofabitch looks like he's had a lot of practice.

"You're Howard, right?" the Gunny said.

"That's right," Joe said, and then blurted, "They just flew me in from Pearl, Gunny. That's when I spilled coffee on me."

"Captain Stecker's the third door on the right, Howard," the Gunny said, turning and pointing. "You bring your records jacket with you?"

"Yeah," Howard said, surprised. An enlisted man's records were not ordinarily put into his hands when he was transferred. They either found some officer going to the same place and gave them to him, or they sent them by registered mail. But Howard had been handed his along with the set of orders transferring him to 2nd Joint Training Force.

"Good," the Gunny said, and walked down the corridor.

How the hell does he know about my records? Or my name?

Joe went to the third door on the right and knocked.

"Come!"

It was Jack NMI Stecker's familiar voice. But it was no longer Gunny Stecker, his friend from Benning and Quantico. It was now Captain Jack NMI Stecker.

Joe opened the door, marched in, and reported to Stecker as a Marine sergeant is supposed to report to a Marine captain.

"Jesus, you're a mess," Stecker said. It was an observation, not a criticism; and there was gentle laughter in his voice when Stecker added, "You may stand at ease, Sergeant."

Howard dropped his eyes to Stecker's, and saw that he was smiling at him.

"What did you spill on yourself, Joe?" Stecker asked.

"A whole goddamned cup of coffee," Joe said, and remembered to add, "Sir."

"Well, come on," Stecker said, "we'll get you cleaned up. You look like something the cat dragged in."

"I'm sorry," Joe said.

"You *look* sorry," Stecker chuckled.

He led him out of the building, opened the trunk of a 1939 Ford coupe, and motioned for him to put his bag in the back. At Quantico, Joe remembered, Stecker had driven an enormous black Packard Phaeton.

"I left Elly the Packard," Stecker said, as if reading his mind. Elly was his wife. "She went to Pennsylvania for a while. I bought this when I got here."

"How's she doing?" Howard asked uneasily. He knew that the Steckers' son, Ensign Jack NMI Stecker, Jr., USN, had been killed on the *Arizona*.

"All right," Stecker said evenly. "I suppose it's tougher on a mother than the father."

That's bullshit, Howard thought.

"How are you doing?" Joe asked.

"Well, I seem to be getting used to it," Stecker said. "At least I don't salute lieutenants anymore."

Joe chuckled, as he knew he was expected to. And he knew that Jack NMI Stecker had purposefully misunderstood him, in order to change the subject from the death of his son.

It doesn't matter, Howard thought. *I had to ask, and I asked, and he knows I'm sorry as hell about his kid. That's enough.*

"How was the flight? Aside from the coffee?" Stecker asked.

"It was a fancied-up Mariner. Real nice. They put a lieutenant colonel off it to put me on."

"Is that so?"

"What's going on?"

"That airplane used to belong to the Rear Admiral at Guantanamo," Stecker said. "They took it away from him to use it as a courier plane between here and Pearl."

"That's not what I was asking," Howard said.

"I know," Stecker chuckled. "Well, here we are. Home sweet home."

Howard saw that they were pulling into a dirt parking lot beside three newly built frame two-story buildings. There was a plywood sign reading, BACHELOR OFFICERS' QUARTERS.

It was the first time Joe Howard had ever been in Officers' Country for any purpose. For what he understood was good reason, these were off limits to enlisted men. If it had been anyone but Captain Jack NMI Stecker, he would have asked what he was doing here now.

Stecker's quarters inside were not fancy—the opposite, in fact. The studs in the wall were exposed. There were no doors on the closets, but just a piece of cloth hung on a wire. There was a bed, an upholstered chair, a folding metal chair, and a chest of drawers. In a small alcove there was a desk and another folding metal chair.

Only a few things in the room had not been issued. There were graduation pictures of Stecker's sons: one of Jack Junior in his brand-new ensign's uniform, taken at Annapolis; and another of Second Lieutenant Richard S. Stecker, USMC, his dress blue uniform making him stand out from his fellow graduates at the Military Academy at West Point. There was also a picture of Stecker and Elly and the boys when they were just kids. It was taken on a beach somewhere, and everybody was in bathing suits.

There was a radio, a hot plate with a coffeepot, and a small refrigerator. And that was it.

"You better take a shower," Stecker said. "You got a towel?"

"Yeah."

"And your other greens?" Stecker asked. "They going to be pressed?" He nodded toward Howard's bag.

"They should be all right," Joe said.

"I've got an iron if they're mussed."

Howard took his carefully folded greens from the bag. They would be all right, even up to Jack NMI Stecker's high standards.

"You going to tell me what's going on?" Howard asked.

"Take a shower and a shave," Stecker said. "Right now, you're probably the sloppiest sergeant on the base."

"In other words, you're not going to tell me."

"When you're shipshape," Stecker replied.

When Joe Howard came out of the shower, a tin-lined cubicle shared with the next BOQ room, Stecker was sitting slumped in the one upholstered chair, holding a beer in his hands.

Joe's eyebrows rose.

"You can have one later," Stecker said. "First let me tell you about Colonel Lewis T. Harris."

"Lucky Lew? He's here? I thought he was in Iceland."

"He's here. Scuttlebutt—I believe it—says he's about to make general. But right now he's Chief of Staff of the 2nd Joint Training Force."

"What's that got to do with me?"

"Well, among other things, he's the president of the Officer Selection Board for the West Coast."

"I don't even know what that is," Howard confessed.

"The Corps is pretty hard up for officers. We don't have enough right now, and the way they're building the Corps up, that situation will get worse."

"So?"

"When you're finished dressing—you better take a brush to your shoes, while you're at it—you're going to go up before him. We're desperately short of officers who know anything about small arms beyond what we taught them in Basic School at Quantico. I've recommended you for a direct commission as a first lieutenant."

"Jesus Christ!"

"You may not get it. You may have to settle for being a second lieutenant, but that's not so bad. Scuttlebutt has it again that from here on in, promotion will be automatic after six months."

How the hell can I be an officer? You can't be a Marine officer if you get hysterical and hide behind a counter when you see somebody get killed.

"I don't know what to say," Howard said.

"When you're in there with Colonel Harris, what you say is 'Yes, Sir,' 'No, Sir,' 'Thank you, Sir,' and 'Aye, aye, Sir.' "

"I meant about becoming an officer."

"Don't you, of all people, start handing me that crap," Stecker said.

"What crap?"

"Why do you think I had you brought here from Hawaii, for Christ's sake, so that you could go work in a battalion small-arms locker someplace? Goddamn you, don't you dare tell me, 'Thanks, but no thanks.' "

"A year ago, I was a corporal. I don't how to be an officer. Captain, I just don't think I could handle it."

"If I handed you a list with the names of every officer you know on it, you could go down it and say, 'This one is a good Marine officer,' and 'That one is a feather merchant.' Do what you've seen the good officers do."

"And what if I fuck up? What if I can't?"

"Then we'll give you your stripes back," Stecker said. "For Christ's sake, do you think I would have recommended you if I didn't think you could pass muster? And anyway, you'll be an ordnance officer; you won't have to worry about running a platoon."

"It just never entered my mind, is all. . . ." He stopped, then started to tell Stecker about what had happened at Pearl, but realized he couldn't. He added lamely, "I almost said 'Gunny.'"

"I get into something sometimes and answer the phone that way," Stecker said. "Usually with some real asshole calling." He laughed. "You know those indelible pens with the soft tip you use to write on celluloid overlays?"

Howard nodded.

"Harris came in my office when I first got here, told me to give him my hand, and when I did he wrote *C-A-P-T* on the palm. Then he said, 'Every time you answer your phone, *Captain* Stecker, read your hand before you speak.' He said he was getting tired of explaining to people that I was retarded."

"Really?"

"Yeah. Harris is one of the good guys. We were in France together. In Domingo, too. Nicaragua. We go back a long way. I had a hell of a time getting that stuff off my hand. It's *really* indelible."

"You sure you're doing this because you think I'd make a passable officer?"

"Or what?"

"Because we're friends."

"That pisses me off," Stecker snapped.

"Sorry, I didn't mean it that way. But, Jesus, this came right out of the goddamned blue!"

"You'll be able to handle it, Joe," Stecker said.

Maybe as an ordnance officer. Just maybe. Maybe they'll assign me here, or at Quantico. Someplace in the States, some rear area. I know weapons, at least. I could earn my keep that way.

"When is all this going to happen?"

"We'll go back to the office. You'll see Harris. If you don't fuck that up, you'll go into 'Diego to the Navy Hospital and take what they call a 'pre-commissioning physical.' That'll take the rest of the day. In the meantime, we'll get all the paperwork typed up, there's a lot of it. Jesus . . . you *do* have your records?"

"In the bag."

"OK. Come back to the office tomorrow morning, we'll get you discharged. And then you go over to the Officers' Sales Store and get your uniforms. Colonel Harris can swear you in after lunch."

"That quick?"

"That quick."

"Where will I be assigned?"

"Here. To work for me, stupid. Why do you think I went to all this trouble?"

"What will I be doing?"

"You ever hear of the Raiders?"

"No. What the hell is that?"

"American commandos. Long story. Nutty story. No time to tell you all about them now. But they've been authorized to arm themselves any way they want to. I need somebody to handle that for me, to get them whatever they want. You."

(FOUR)

HEADQUARTERS, 2ND JOINT TRAINING FORCE
CAMP ELLIOTT, CALIFORNIA
1205 HOURS 2 FEBRUARY 1942

One of the two telephones on Captain Jack NMI Stecker's desk rang, and he answered it on the second ring, and correctly:

"G-3 Special Planning, Captain Stecker speaking, Sir."

"Stecker, this is Captain Kelso."

There was a certain tone of superiority in Captain Kelso's voice. Stecker knew what was behind that. Although Captain Kelso was in fact outranked by Captain Stecker, by date of rank, he could not put out of his mind that Captain Stecker was a Mustang, an officer commissioned from the ranks. As an Annapolis man himself, Kelso considered that he was socially superior to a man who had served in the ranks. This opinion was buttressed by his duty assignment: he was aide-de-camp to the Commanding General, 2nd Joint Training Force.

What Captain Kelso did not know was that the Commanding General of the 2nd Joint Training Force had discussed him with Captain Stecker over a beer in the General's kitchen when Captain Stecker had first reported aboard.

"My aide may give you some trouble, Jack," the General had said. He and Stecker had been in Santo Domingo, Nicaragua, and France together. "He's an arrogant little prick, thinks he's salty as hell. Efficient as hell, too, to give the devil his due, which is why I keep him. But he's capable of being a flaming pain in the ass. If he does give you any trouble, let me know, and I'll walk all over him."

"General, I've had some experience with young captains who thought they were salty," Stecker had replied dryly, "going *way* back."

"Your commanding general, Captain, is sure you are not referring to anyone in this kitchen," the General replied, laughing.

"Don't be too sure, General," Stecker chuckled.

"I have never known a master gunnery sergeant who couldn't handle a captain," the General said. "I don't know why I brought that up."

"I appreciate it," Stecker said. "But don't worry about it."

"And how may I be of service to the General's aide-de-camp, Captain Kelso?" Stecker said, oozing enough sarcastically insincere charm to penetrate even Captain Kelso's self-assurance and cause him to become just a little wary. Kelso recalled at that moment that the General habitually addressed Captain Stecker by his first name.

"There's a Navy captain, from the Secretary of the Navy's office, on his way to see you . . ." He paused just perceptibly, and added, "Jack."

"Oh? Who is he? What's he want?"

"His name is Pickering, and I don't know what he wants. He just walked in out of the blue and asked for the General; and when I told him the General wasn't available, he asked for you. I've never seen a set of orders like his."

Now Stecker was curious.

"What about his orders?"

"They say that he is authorized to proceed, on a Four-A priority, wherever he deems necessary to travel in order to perform the mission assigned to him by the Secretary of the Navy, and that all questions concerning his duties will be referred to the office of the Secretary of the Navy."

"That's *goddamned* unusual," Jack Stecker thought aloud. "I wonder what the hell he wants with me?"

"I have no idea. But I'm sure the General would be interested in knowing, too."

"What did you say his name was?"

"Pickering."

Stecker's office door opened and his sergeant stuck his head inside.

"Sir, there's a Captain Pickering to see you, a *Navy* captain."

"He's here," Stecker said, and hung the telephone up. He got to his feet, checked the knot of his field scarf as an automatic reflex action, and then said, "Ask the Captain to come in, please."

Captain Fleming Pickering, USNR, walked into the office.

"Good afternoon, Sir," Stecker said. "Sir, I'm Captain Stecker, G-3 Special Planning."

Pickering looked at him, smiled, and then turned and closed the door in the Sergeant's face. Then he turned again and faced Stecker.

"Hello, Dutch," he said. "How the hell are you?"

"Sir, the Captain has the advantage on me."

"I always have had, Dutch. Smarter, better looking . . . You really don't recognize me, do you?" Pickering laughed.

"No, Sir."

"I would have recognized you. You're a little balder, and a little heavier, but I would known you. The name Pickering means nothing to you?"

"No, Sir."

"I'm crushed," Pickering said. "Try Belleau Wood."

After a moment, Stecker said, "I'll be damned. Flem Pickering, right? California? Corporal? You took two eight-millimeter rounds, one in each leg, and all they did was scratch you?"

"I don't think 'scratch' is the right word," Pickering protested. "I spent two weeks in the hospital when that happened."

"You went into the Navy? Back to college, and then into the Navy? Is that what happened?"

"I just came into the Navy," Pickering said.

"Am I allowed to ask what's going on? You awed the general's aide with your orders, but they didn't explain much."

Pickering reached into his uniform jacket pocket and handed Stecker a copy of his orders.

"*I'm* awed, too," Stecker said, after he read them.

"You don't have to be awed, but I thought I should show them to you."

"What do you want with me?" Stecker asked, as he handed the orders back. "You didn't come from Washington to see me?"

"To tell you the truth, it wasn't until that self-important young man told me that General Davies was not available that I remembered that Doc McInerney told me you were out here someplace."

"You've seen Doc?"

"Sure have. And I got another interesting bit of information from him. Our boys are roommates at Pensacola."

"I'll be damned!" Stecker said. "How about that?"

"It would seem, Dutch, that we're getting to be a pair of old men, old enough to have kids who rate salutes."

"I don't know about you, Captain," Stecker said dryly, "but *I* still feel pretty spry. Too spry to be sitting behind a desk."

"They don't want us for anything else, Dutch," Pickering said. "Mac made that painfully clear to me. We're relics from another time, another war."

"How'd you wind up in the Navy? Or is that one of those questions I'm not supposed to ask?"

"I tried to come back in the Corps. I went to see Mac. He made it pretty plain that I would be of no use to the Corps. Then Frank Knox offered me a job working for him, as sort of a glorified gofer, and I took it. I jumped at it."

"*Frank* Knox? The one I think of nearly reverently as *Secretary* Knox?"

"You'd like him, Dutch. He was a sergeant in the Rough Riders. Good man."

"And you're out here for him?"

"Yeah. I'll tell you about it over lunch. Let's go over to the Coronado Beach Hotel. They generally have nice lunches."

"They generally have *great* lunches, and everybody knows about them, and you need a reservation. I don't think we could get in. We could eat at the club here."

"Indulge me, Dutch," Pickering said. "It isn't only the food I'm thinking of."

"You want to see somebody else?"

"I'm about to appoint you—I'd really rather have gotten into all this over lunch—the Secretary of the Navy's Special Representative to See that Carlson's Raiders Get What They Want. You know about the Raiders?"

"I'm already the General's man who does that," Stecker said. "Is that why you're here?"

Pickering nodded. "So much the better, then. The Navy brass are as curious as a bunch of old maids about what I'm doing here. It will get back to them that I had lunch in the Coronado with you. It might come in handy for them to remember you have friends in very high places when you're asking for something outrageous for the Raiders."

Stecker looked at Pickering for a moment, until he concluded that Pickering was both serious and right.

"OK. But first we have to get from here to the hotel, and my car may not start. Bad battery, I think. I had to push it off this morning."

"The Admiral's aide met my plane and graciously gave me the use of the Admiral's car for as long as I need it," Pickering said.

"And *then* we have to get in the dining room."

"I think I can handle that," Pickering said. "Can I have your sergeant make a call for me?"

"Sure," Stecker said, and called the sergeant into the office.

"Yes, Sir?"

"Sergeant," Pickering said, "would you call the dining room at the Coronado Beach for me, please? Tell the maitre d' that Captain Stecker and myself are on the way over there, and that I would like a private table overlooking the pool. My name is Fleming Pickering."

"Aye, aye, Sir," the sergeant said. "A *private* table, Sir?"

"They'll know what I mean, Sergeant," Pickering said. "They'll move other tables away from mine, so that other people won't be able to hear what Captain Stecker and I are talking about."

"Why is this making me nervous?" Stecker asked.

"I have no idea," Pickering said. "Maybe because you're getting old, Dutch."

"If there are any calls for me, Sergeant, tell them that I went off with Captain Pickering of Secretary Knox's office, and you have no idea where I went or when I'll be back."

Pickering chuckled. "You're a quick learner, Dutch, aren't you?"

"For an old man," Stecker said.

(FIVE)

UNITED STATES NAVAL HOSPITAL
SAN DIEGO, CALIFORNIA
1515 HOURS 2 FEBRUARY 1942

"Tell me, Sergeant," the Navy doctor, a full commander, said to Staff Sergeant Joseph L. Howard, "do you suffer from syphilis?"

"No, Sir."

"How about gonorrhea?" Commander Nettleton asked.

"No, Sir."

Commander K. J. Nettleton, MC, USN, was a career naval officer. In his fifteen years of service, he had discussed venereal disease with maybe fifteen thousand Navy and Marine Corps enlisted men. In his experience, it was seldom possible to judge from an enlisted man's appearance whether he had been diving the salami into seas of spiro-chetes or not.

He had treated angelic-looking boys who—as their advanced state of social disease clearly proved—had been sowing their seed in any cavity that could be induced to hold still for twenty seconds. And he'd treated leather-skinned chief bosun's mates and mastery gunnery ser-geants who had not strayed from the marital bed in twenty years, yet were hysterically convinced that a little urethral drip was God finally making them pay for a single indiscretion two decades ago in Gitmo or Shanghai or Newport.

But it was also Dr. Nettleton's experience that when regular sailors and Marines—sergeants and petty officers on their second or third or fourth hitch—contracted a venereal disease somewhere along the line, they tried to get their hands on their medical records so they could remove and destroy that portion dealing with their venereal history. They had learned how the services subtly and cruelly treated men with social diseases.

His experience told him that's what he had at hand, in the person of Staff Sergeant Joseph Howard, USMC. Sergeant Howard was taking a pre-commissioning physical. That meant he had applied for a commission. An Officer Selection Board was likely to turn down an applicant who had a history of VD, even one who was obviously a good Marine. You didn't get to wear staff sergeant's chevrons as young as this kid was without being one hell of a Marine—and one who looked like he belonged on a recruiting poster.

"Sergeant," he said, "if anyone was to hear what I am about to say, I would deny it."

"Sir?" Howard asked, confused.

"There are ways to handle difficult *situations,*" Commander Nettleton said. "But destroying your records is not one of them. Now, what did you have, and when did you have it?"

"Sir, if you mean syphilis or the clap, I never did."

Nettleton fixed Howard with an icy glare.

You dumb sonofabitch, I just told you I'd fix it!

"Never?"

"No, Sir," Howard replied, both confused and righteously indignant.

I'll be damned, I think he's telling the truth!

"Then how do you explain the absence of the results of your Wassermann test in this otherwise complete stack of reports?"

Staff Sergeant Howard did not reply.

"Well?"

"Sir, I don't know what—what did you say, Wasser Test?—is."

"Wassermann," Doctor Nettleton corrected him idly. "It's an integral part of your physical."

"Sir, I don't know. I went everywhere they sent me."

Commander Nettleton looked at him intently, and decided he didn't really know if he was looking at Innocence Personified or a skilled liar.

He reached for the telephone, found the number he was looking for on a typewritten sheet of paper under the glass on his desk, and dialed it quickly.

"Venereal, Lieutenant Gower."

"This is Commander Nettleton, Gower. How are you?"

"No complaints, Sir. How about you?"

"You don't want to hear them, Lieutenant. I need a favor. How are you fixed for favors?"

"If I've got it, Commander, you've got it."

"You got somebody around there who can draw blood for a Wassermann for me? And then do it in a hurry?"

"Yes, Sir. I'll take it to the lab myself. They owe me a couple of favors up there."

"It has to be official. I need the form and an MD to sign off on it."

"No problem."

"I'm sending a Staff Sergeant Howard to see you. Make him wait. If it comes back negative, send him and the report back to me. If it's positive, put him in a bathrobe and find something unpleasant for him to do. Call me and I'll see that he's admitted."

"Aye, aye, Sir," Lieutenant Gower said.

"Appreciate it, Gower," Commander Nettleton said, hung up, and turned to Staff Sergeant Howard. "You heard that, Sergeant. The Venereal Disease Ward is on the third floor. Report to Lieutenant Gower."

"Aye, aye, Sir," Staff Sergeant Howard said.

Like Commander Nettleton, Lieutenant Gower was a career naval officer, with nearly as much commissioned service as he had. She had entered the Naval Service immediately upon graduation from Nursing School, and, in the fourteen years since, had served at naval hospitals in Philadelphia; Cavite (in the Philippines); Pearl Harbor; and San Diego. She had just learned that she was to be promoted to lieutenant commander, Nurse Corps, USN.

While on the one hand Lieutenant Hazel Gower did not consider herself above the mundane routine of the VD ward, of which she was Nurse-in-Charge, on the other hand, Rank Did Have Its Privileges.

She rapped on the plate-glass window surrounding the Nurse's Station with her Saint Anthony's High School graduation ring, and caught the attention of Ensign Barbara T. Cotter, NC, USNR. Ensign Cotter had just reported aboard, fresh from the Nurse's Orientation Course at Philadelphia.

Lieutenant Gower gestured to Ensign Cotter to come into the nurses' station.

"Yes?" Ensign Cotter asked.

"The way we do that in the Navy, Miss Cotter," Lieutenant Gower said, "is 'Yes, Ma'am?' "

"Yes, Ma'am," Ensign Cotter said, her face tightening.

"This is not the University of Pennsylvania, you know."

"Yes, Ma'am," Ensign Cotter said, just a little bitchily.

That remark made reference to Ensign Cotter's nursing education. Ensign Cotter, unlike most of her peers, had a college degree. She had graduated with a bachelor of science degree in psychology from the University of Pennsylvania Medical School, and had earned, from the same institution, the right to append "RN" to her name. She'd been trained as a psychiatric nurse. And she had been lied to by the recruiter, who told her the Navy really had need of her special skills. In fact, the Navy used medical doctors with psychiatric training and large male medical corpsmen to deal with its mentally ill.

When Ensign Cotter reported aboard Naval Hospital, San Diego, the Chief of Nursing Services told her that since they had no need for a female psychiatric nurse, she wondered how she would feel about working in obstetrics. An unpleasant scene followed, during which it was pointed out to Ensign Cotter that she was now in the Navy, and that the Navy decided where its people could make the greatest contribution. Following that, Lieutenant Gower in Venereal received a telephone call from the Chief of Nursing Services, a longtime friend, telling her she was getting a new ensign who was an uppity little bitch who thought her college degree made her better than other people. The little bitch needed to be put in her place.

"There's a syphilitic Marine sergeant on his way up here," Lieutenant Gower said to Ensign Cotter. "Draw some blood for a Wassermann."

"He's not on the ward?"

"I'm getting tired of telling you this, Cotter. When you speak to a superior female officer, you use 'ma'am.' "

Ensign Cotter exhaled audibly.

"He's not on the ward, *Ma'am?*"

"No."

"Then how, *Ma'am,* do we know he's syphilitic?"

"The Wassermann will tell us that, won't it, Miss Cotter?"

"Only if he *is* syphilitic, *Ma'am,*" Ensign Cotter said.

"Commander Nettleton wouldn't have sent him up here unless he was," Lieutenant Gower flared. And then she remembered that Nettleton had said to send the sergeant back if the Wassermann was negative. She was going to look like a horse's ass in front of this uppity little bitch if it did come back negative.

"Just do what you're ordered to do, Miss Cotter," she said icily.

"Yes, *Ma'am.*"

Barbara Cotter saw Staff Sergeant Joseph L. Howard the moment she walked out of the glass-walled nurses' station, and she reacted to him precisely the same way most other men and women did when they first saw him. *God, that fellow looks like what a Marine should look like!*

"Excuse me, Ma'am," Joe Howard said, "I'm looking for Lieutenant Gower."

"You're here for a Wassermann, Sergeant?" Barbara asked, telling herself that she had sounded professionally distant.

This beautiful man has syphilis?

"Yes, Ma'am. I was told to report to Lieutenant Gower."

"I'll take care of you, Sergeant. Come with me, please."

"Yes, Ma'am."

She led him to an examination room.

"Take off your jacket, please, and roll up your shirt sleeve."

When he took his uniform jacket off, Barbara saw that his shirt was tailored; it fit his body like a thin glove, which allowed her to clearly make out the firm muscles of his chest and upper arms inside it.

What's going on with me? He's not only an enlisted man—and there is a regulation against involvement between officers and enlisted men—but he's syphilitic!

She wrapped a length of red rubber tubing around his upper arm, drew it tight, and told him to pump his hand open and closed. He winced when she slipped the needle into his vein.

"Have you had any symptoms?" she heard herself asking, as his blood began to fill the chamber.

"Ma'am?"

"Lesions . . . sores? Anything like that."

"No, Ma'am."

"Then what makes you think you've contracted . . . ?"

"I don't think I've contracted anything," Joe Howard said, unable to take his eyes from Ensign Cotter's white brassiere, which had come into view when she had leaned over his arm to stick him with the needle.

"Then why are we giving you a Wassermann?" Barbara blurted, looking up at him and noticing that he quickly averted his eyes. *God, he's been looking down my dress!* "You know what a Wassermann is for, don't you?"

"For syphilis," he said. "I just figured that out."

"Why has somebody ordered the test?" she asked. "If you don't think you've—"

"They put me in for a commission," Joe said. "Some asshole—oh, shit! Sorry, Ma'am."

He's going to be an officer? Is that what he means?

"Some asshole *what,* Sergeant?" Barbara said.

"Somebody forgot to send me for the test," Joe said. "And now that Commander . . . he thinks I've got it."

"And you don't?"

"I *know* I don't," Joe said.

Barbara pulled the needle from his vein, dabbed at the puncture with an alcohol swab, and told him to bend his arm.

"Well, we'll soon know for sure, won't we?" she said.

It will come back negative, she thought. *I* know *it will come back negative. Up yours, Lieutenant Gower, Ma'am!*

(SIX)

OFFICERS' SALES STORE
U.S. NAVAL BASE
SAN DIEGO, CALIFORNIA
1100 HOURS 3 FEBRUARY 1942

To Joe Howard, the Officers' Sales Store looked like a cross between a supply room and a civilian clothing store. There were glass-topped counters, and shelves loaded with shirts and skivvies, and racks containing jackets and trousers. There were even mannequins showing what the well-dressed Naval or Marine Corps officer should wear. Even two mannequins of Navy nurses, one wearing blues and the other summer whites.

He had a semi-erotic thought: Here there were no female mannequins in underwear, as there were in civilian department stores. That was just as well; those always made him feel a little uncomfortable. It didn't take him long to guess why that thought popped into his mind: the nurse at the hospital yesterday. It would be a long time before the image of her brassiere and the soft, swelling flesh above it faded from his mind.

Jesus, she was a looker!

"Can I help you, Sergeant?"

It was a plump and middle-aged Storekeeper First Class, obviously the man in charge. He looked ridiculous in his bell-bottomed pants and blouse, Joe thought. The Navy's enlisted men's uniform was worn by everybody but chief petty officers. It didn't look bad on young guys. But on middle-aged guys like this one, with a paunch and damned little hair, it looked silly.

"I need some uniforms," Joe said, and handed the Storekeeper First a copy of his brand-new orders.

Paragraph One said that Staff Sergeant Joseph L. Howard, USMC, was honorably discharged from the Naval Service for the convenience of the government.

Paragraph Two said that First Lieutenant Joseph L. Howard, USMCR, was ordered to active duty, for the duration of the war plus six months, with duty station 2nd Joint Training Command, San Diego, Cal.

"Well, you came to the right place," the Storekeeper First said. "It's going to cost you."

"I figured," Joe said.

He had a lot of money in his pocket, so it didn't matter. They had brought his pay up to date for his discharge. And they had returned to him the savings money they had been taking out of his pay every month; the government had been paying him three percent on it. He had been saving money since he'd come in the Corps, redepositing it when he shipped over. Now it had all been returned to him. Officers were expected to manage their own money, not have their hands held by the Corps to encourage them to put a little aside.

There was even more. He had been paid for his unused accrued leave, and for what it would have cost him to go to his Home of Record. And Captain Stecker had told him that when he drew his first pay as an officer, he would be paid for what it took to come from Birmingham out here. And finally, there was a one-time payment of three hundred dollars for uniforms.

The Storekeeper First was far more helpful than Joe had expected him to be. And in a remarkably short time, one of the glass counters was stacked high with the uniforms Joe would need as an officer.

The three-hundred-dollar uniform allowance didn't come close to covering the cost of the uniforms. The officer's brimmed cap alone, for example, with just one cover—and he needed four more covers—came to $19.65. The covers were expensive, because Marine officers' covers—unlike Army and Navy officers' covers—had woven loops sewn to their tops. These were now purely decorative, but they went back to the days of sailing ships, Joe remembered hearing somewhere. Marine sharp-shooters in the rigging could distinguish their officers on deck below because of woven line loops sewn on top of their caps.

Aside from the Sam Browne leather belt ($24.35), there wasn't much outward difference between officers' and enlisted men's greens. Officers' trousers had hip pockets, and enlisted men's trousers did not. The quality of the material was better.

The only alteration Joe required was the hemming of the trousers. The chubby little Storekeeper First said he would have a seamstress hem one pair immediately, and Joe could pick up the rest the next afternoon. Joe suspected he was getting a little better service than most people. The Storekeeper First was probably one of the enlisted men who was pleased when a peer became an officer. A lot of people resented Mustangs.

When the Storekeeper First helped Joe into his blouse, expertly buttoning the epaulet over the crosspiece of the Sam Browne belt, the reason why he was being so obliging came out.

"I can offer you a little something for your enlisted stuff," he said. "Not much, because it's nowhere near new, but as much as you'd get hocking it off the base."

Joe had not considered getting rid of his old uniforms; still, all of them were in a duffel bag in the trunk of Captain Stecker's Ford, which he had borrowed.

"Make me an offer," he said. "I've got a duffel bag full."

"Here?"

"Outside. In the trunk of a car."

"Let's go look at it, maybe we can do a little business."

"I'm not sure I'm allowed to wear this yet," Joe said, staring at the image of First Lieutenant Joseph Howard, USMCR, in a three-way mirror. He found what he saw very pleasing—yet unreal enough to make him feel uncomfortable.

"Why not?"

"I don't get sworn in until half past two."

"You're supposed to get sworn in in uniform," the Storekeeper First said, *"Officer's* uniform. Nobody's going to say anything."

"You're sure?"

"You aren't the first Mustang to come through here."

"OK," Joe said. "When they throw me in the brig, I can quote you, right?"

"Absolutely," the Storekeeper First said. "Pay for this, and then we'll go see what you've got in the car."

The price the Storekeeper First offered for all of Joe's enlisted men's uniforms was insulting. He was being raped, but he could think of nothing to do about it. He could, of course, tell him to go fuck himself, in which case when he returned to The Officers' Sales Store for the rest of his new uniforms tomorrow, they wouldn't be ready. Or worse.

He managed to get the total price up to $52.50, but beyond that the Storekeeper First not only wouldn't budge, he showed signs of getting nasty.

"Sold to the man in the bell-bottom pants," Joe said, forcing a smile.

"A pleasure doing business with you, Lieutenant," the Storekeeper First said as he hoisted Joe's duffel bag onto his shoulder.

"Don't forget my fifty-two-fifty," Joe said.

"I'll have it for you tomorrow."

"You can have the stuff tomorrow, then," Joe said.

"You don't trust me?"

"Not as far as I could throw you," Joe said. "I show up there tomorrow and you're not there, then what would I do?"

The Storekeeper First heaved the duffel bag back into the trunk, and then shrugged. He dipped his hand behind the thirteen-button fly of his bell-bottoms and came out with two twenties and a ten.

"That's all I got," he said. "I'll have to owe you the two-fifty."

"Either look in your sock or somewhere, or put two of the wool shirts back."

The Storekeeper First looked carefully at Howard, then shrugged and dipped into his thirteen-button fly again. He came out with a wad of singles and counted off three of them. Joe put them in his pocket and gave the man two quarters in change. They exchanged dry little smiles, and the Storekeeper First, grunting, hoisted the duffel bag to his shoulder again and marched off.

That fat old sonofabitch has got a nice little racket going, he thought. *He paid me less than half of what that stuff is worth in any hockshop. And there's probably one or two guys like me going through there every day. Christ, not only Marines! The Navy must be commissioning Mustangs too.*

"I'll be a sonofabitch," he said aloud, more out of admiration than anger, as he considered that the Storekeeper First must be taking in probably as much as a hundred fifty dollars a day.

"I'm almost afraid to ask what all that was about," a voice, a female voice, said behind him. Surprised, he turned quickly to see who it was. It was an officer, a female officer, a Navy nurse, and specifically the one who had drawn his blood for the Wassermann test the day before.

Joe saluted crisply, without thinking about it, a Pavlovian reflex: an officer had spoken to him; therefore he saluted.

"I think I was supposed to do that," the nurse said. She was carrying a paper sack from the Commissary.

"Excuse me?" Joe said.

"Those are silver bars you're wearing? Mine, you'll notice, are gold. I think I was supposed to salute first."

"Jesus Christ!" Joe said.

She smiled. "What *was* going on?"

"I sold him my old uniforms," Joe said.

"You look very nice in your new one," Barbara Cotter said, smiling. "Are congratulations in order?"

"I haven't been sworn in yet," he said.

"But you did pass the Wassermann," Barbara said. She had suspected this Adonis could blush when she had told him he looked nice in his uniform; now there was inarguable proof. His face was flushed.

This isn't the first time, she thought. *He blushed when I caught him looking down my whites. Adonis is actually shy!*

"Yeah, I did that, all right," Joe said. And then he took the chance: "Can I offer you a ride? I've got a borrowed car."

Ensign Barbara Cotter hesitated, not about taking the ride, but because she had her own car.

I don't want to start off lying to this man. Isn't that strange?

"I've got a car," she said. "I'm on my way to lunch. Have you eaten?"

"No."

"Follow me over to the hospital, then," she said. "The food's not bad."

Joe looked at his watch. There was time.

"Sure," he said.

"The blue Plymouth coupe," she said, and pointed down the line of cars.

With a little bit of luck, Lieutenant Hazel Gower, USN, will be having her lunch when I walk into the officer's section of the hospital mess with this Wassermann-negative Adonis. Is that why I went up to him in the parking lot? To get at dear old Hazel?

As she put her key in the ignition of her Plymouth, she understood that while zinging Lieutenant Gower might be nice, it was *not* the reason her heart had jumped when she saw Joe Howard standing by the open trunk of the Ford.

"Oh, *God!*" she muttered, as she pushed the starter button. "What is this?"

(SEVEN)

OFFICE OF THE CHIEF OF STAFF
HEADQUARTERS, 2ND JOINT TRAINING FORCE
SAN DIEGO, CALIFORNIA
1445 HOURS 3 FEBRUARY 1942

"Congratulations, Lieutenant Howard," Colonel Lewis T. "Lucky Lew" Harris said, offering his hand to Joe Howard. "You are now a Marine officer. I have every confidence that you will bring credit to the uniform you're wearing, and to the Corps. Good luck to you!"

"Thank you, Sir," Joe said.

"Will you wait outside a moment, please?" Harris said. "I'd like a word with Captain Stecker."

"Yes, Sir," Joe said, and did an about-face and marched out of Harris's office.

"That one, I think, will do all right," Harris said to Stecker. "But, frankly, I'm a little uncomfortable about not sending him to Quantico for Basic School."

"Sir, he's not going to get a platoon, or even go to the Division—"

"Not today, anyway," Harris said, dryly. "I've already read today's teletypes from Washington reassigning our officers. But what about tomorrow?"

"Until he appears on a list of officers who have completed Basic School, he's not eligible for assignment with troops," Stecker said. "And as long as we 'forget' to request a space for him at Quantico, he won't be ordered there. In the meantime, we can put him to work."

"And if some zealous paper pusher sends a TWX asking why we haven't requested a Basic School slot for Lieutenant Howard, what do we say?

"When all else fails, tell the truth," Stecker said. "We tell them that Howard, a small-arms expert, has been charged with getting the 2nd Raider Battalion the weaponry they want. And, that since this is a matter of the highest priority, according not only to the Commandant, but to the Secretary of the Navy as well, we thought this assignment was more in the best interests of the Corps than sending him to Quantico."

Lucky Lew Harris still looked doubtful.

"Colonel," Stecker said, "I talked to Captain Pickering about him. He said if anybody gave us any trouble, to call him. He made it pretty plain to me that what the Secretary of the Navy wants is to give the Raider Battalions what the President wants them to have . . . which is anything they want."

"Just between you and me, Jack, I don't like the whole idea of these so-called Raider Battalions a damn bit."

"I don't really know how I feel," Stecker said. "Evans Carlson is a hell of a Marine."

"He *used* to be, anyway," Harris said. "But it's a moot point, Jack, isn't it?"

"Yes, Sir, it is."

"And your pal Captain Pickering makes me nervous, frankly. Can he be trusted?"

There was a moment's hesitation before Stecker answered. "He can be trusted to do what the Secretary tells him to do. And beyond that, I think he still thinks like a Marine."

"What did he tell you about me? About the General?" Harris asked.

"Sir?"

"I suppose what I'm asking is whether he wants reports from you directly."

"Sir, he told me to feel free to call him if I saw any problems coming up. But I wouldn't do that without checking with you."

"No, of course you wouldn't," Harris said. "No offense intended. Christ, Jack, why do things get so complicated?"

"It wouldn't be the Corps, Sir, if there wasn't some moron putting his two cents in and getting in the way of simple riflemen trying to do their job," Stecker said.

Harris chuckled.

"Keep Carlson happy, Jack," he said. "Let me know if I can help."

"Yes, Sir. Thank you, Sir."

Lieutenant Joe Howard was sitting on a battered, chrome-framed, plastic-upholstered couch in Colonel Harris's outer office, thumbing through a copy of *Collier's*. He got to his feet when Stecker came out of Harris's office.

"What we'll do now, *Lieutenant,*" Stecker said, "is take you out to the 2nd Raider Battalion and introduce you to Colonel Carlson, his S-4, and Captain Roosevelt. Then we'll get you settled in a BOQ. And then, I thought, tonight we'll celebrate your bar, wash it down, and maybe get a steak, at the officers' club."

Howard looked a little uncomfortable.

"Something wrong with that?"

"Sir, I've got sort of a date tonight."

"Oh?"

"I met a nurse at the hospital," Joe said. "I asked her to supper."

"Well, hell, I wouldn't want to interfere with that," Stecker said. Then he smiled, dug in his pocket, and came out with a key. "Here," he said, handing it to Howard.

"What is this, Captain?" Joe asked, confused. Stecker had handed him a hotel key from the Coronado Beach Hotel.

"We Mustangs have to stick together," Stecker said, as they walked down the corridor toward the front door. "Captain Fleming Pickering, USNR, gave that to me. We served together in France in the first war. I was a buck sergeant, and he was a corporal. He just came in the Navy, as a captain."

Howard was visibly confused.

"Between wars, Pickering is in the shipping business. Specifically, Pacific & Far Eastern Shipping. He owns it. And they keep a suite at the Coronado Beach Hotel, permanently, to put up their officers who are in port. If you want to impress the nurse, take her out there. Just show that key to the maitre d', and he'll give you a table. Without a reservation, I mean."

"And I can use it?"

"I think Captain Pickering would be delighted to have you use it, under the circumstances," Stecker said. "And who knows, Joe, you might get lucky. The suite has four bedrooms. Odds are, one of them ought to be empty."

"She's not that kind of a girl," Joe Howard said.

"The one thing I've learned about women, Joe, over the years," Stecker laughed, "is that you never can tell about women."

"I said she's a nice girl," Joe Howard said sharply. "From Philadelphia. She's even got a college degree."

"I'm sure she is," Stecker said.

(EIGHT)

THE CORONADO BEACH HOTEL
SAN DIEGO, CALIFORNIA
1930 HOURS 3 FEBRUARY 1942

There was a long line of people waiting to get into the main dining room. The line overflowed the bank of upholstered benches intended for those waiting for a table.

"We're never going to get in here," Ensign Barbara Cotter said to Lieutenant Joe Howard.

"Trust me," Joe said, with far more confidence than he felt. He put his hand on her arm and marched her past the sitting and standing people waiting to get in. Some of them, senior officers, many with their wives, looked at them either curiously or unpleasantly.

The maitre d', in his good time, raised his eyes from his list of reservations.

"Your name, Sir?"

Joe showed him the hotel key.

The maitre d's eyebrows rose.

"Certainly, Sir, will you come with me, please?"

The enormous, old fashioned, high-ceilinged dining room was almost full, but here and there there were empty tables with Reserved signs mounted on brass stands. The maitre d' led them to a table by a wide window overlooking the water. The window was now covered by a heavy black curtain.

"Your waiter will be here shortly, Sir," the maitre d' said, as he held Barbara's chair for her. "Enjoy your meal."

"What did you show him?" Barbara asked.

He handed her the key.

"I don't know what you think I am, or who you are—" Barbara flared, and started to get to her feet. She saw the horrified look on his face, and stopped.

"Captain Stecker loaned me that," Joe said. "He said to show it to the headwaiter, and it would get us a table."

"Who is Captain Stecker?" Barbara asked, partially mollified.

Why am I so furious? So far, he hasn't even looked directly at me, much less tried to put his hands on me.

"He's my boss, the one that got me the commission," Joe said, and then blurted, "I'm not trying to get you into a hotel room or anything like that."

"I certainly hope not," she said.

"All the key is for is so we could get a table," Joe said.

"You said that," she said. "He lives here, or something?"

"No. The key . . . this is an involved story. . . ."

"I'm fascinated," she said.

He told her what Stecker had told him. Their eyes met, and in them she saw that he was telling the truth.

And now that's over, she sighed inwardly. *The key has been explained, and I believe he did not get himself a room here, confident that I would jump in bed with him. So why do I feel a little let down? He almost sounds as if he doesn't want to go to bed with me. My God, this is an insane situation!*

"I'm sorry," he concluded.

"Why should you be sorry?"

"Because you thought—"

"Let's just let it drop, OK?"

"OK," he said, with enormous relief. "What would you like to drink? I mean, do you drink?"

"Scotch," she said.

"Scotch?" he asked, in disbelief.

"Something wrong with Scotch?"

"I didn't think girls drank Scotch."

"Girls drink gin fizzes and brandy Alexanders, right? Things like that? And then they get sick to their stomachs. Well, this girl learned that in college, and this girl drinks Scotch. If that's all right with you."

My God, why did I snap at him like that? What the hell is wrong with me?

"Sorry," he said.

"Stop saying you're sorry!"

"Good evening," a waiter said. "May I get you something from the bar?"

"Scotch," Joe said. "Scotch and soda. Two of them."

"I'm very sorry, Sir, we're out of Scotch."

Barbara looked at Joe, and she saw that he was looking at her, and that his lips and his eyes were curled in laughter he was afraid to let out.

"That figures," Barbara said, and then she laughed; then, without thinking about it, she reached out and touched his hand with hers. But instantly withdrew it.

"What now?" Joe asked.

"Do you have any rye whiskey?" Barbara asked the waiter.

"Yes, Ma'am."

"Rye and ginger ale, please," Barbara said.

"Two, please," Joe said.

He handed them menus and left.

They read the menu. Joe was astonished at the prices; Barbara was horrified.

He's only a first lieutenant. He can't afford this. I wonder how he would react if I suggested we go Dutch treat?

"I'm not really very hungry," she said. "I think I'll just have a salad."

"I know what you're thinking," he said.

"I certainly hope not," she said. "What am I thinking?"

"You're thinking the prices are crazy."

"They are," she said.

"Two big things have happened in my life in the last forty-eight hours. And I happen to have a lot of money. Let me splurge. Please."

"What two big things?"

"Look at my shoulders," Joe said. "A year ago, I was a buck sergeant."

"Being an officer is important to you, isn't it?"

"I'm not sure I'll be able to hack it," he said.

"Why not?"

He shrugged. "I'm just not sure, is all."

As if with a mind of its own, her hand touched his again, and was again instantly withdrawn.

"What was the other thing?" she asked, idly curious.

"You," he said.

Her eyes moved to his, and then away.

My God, he means that. And I'm blushing!

"I wish you hadn't said that," she said.

"Why?"

"It makes me uncomfortable."

"Sorry."

"Stop saying you're sorry!"

The waiter appeared with a silver ice bucket on a stand. There was a towel-wrapped bottle in the cooler.

"We didn't order any wine," Joe said.

The waiter disappeared without a word.

"What's that all about?" Barbara asked.

Joe shrugged.

The waiter reappeared, this time carrying a silver ice bucket, tongs, two glasses, and a soda-water siphon.

"What's all this?" Barbara demanded.

"I wasn't aware before, Sir, that you're Pacific & Far Eastern," the waiter said, almost in a whisper. "The cooler contains Scotch, Sir. From the P&FE cellar. You won't mind mixing your own? And please keep the towel in place. Because of the other guests."

And he disappeared again.

"Do you understand what he said?" Barbara asked.

Joe shook his head, then took the bottle from the cooler. He unwrapped the towel, then closed it again.

"Scotch," he said. "Something called Old Grouse."

"Let me see," Barbara said, and he handed her the towel-wrapped bottle.

"It's Scotch, all right," she said. *"Good* Scotch."

"Where did it come from?" Joe asked.

"You ever hear the expression 'Don't look a gift horse in the mouth'?"

He took the bottle from her, and made a drink for her. It was, to judge by the color, far stronger than Barbara would have preferred, but she didn't want to make a fuss.

After the first couple of sips, I'll dilute it with more soda.

She waited until he had fixed his own drink, then touched her glass to his.

"Congratulations on your promotion," she said.

"To you and me," he said.

She met his eyes for a moment, then echoed him.

"To you and me," she said.

The waiter took his sweet time coming back for their order. She had just about finished her second drink by the time he did. She had really only wanted one, and that to be sociable. The second drink was as dark as the first, but it didn't seem to taste as strong.

She indulged him and gave up the idea of having just a salad, telling herself that she would make it up to him somehow. She ordered a shrimp cocktail, a New York strip, and asparagus.

"And for a wine, may I suggest a very nice Cabernet Sauvignon? It's Mr. and Mrs. Pickering's favorite, I might add."

"Well, if it's good enough for them . . ."

"I think you'll like it, Sir. It's made right here in California."

I will have just one sip of the wine. The last thing I can afford to do is get tight.

She looked down at her glass and saw that he had refilled it.

I don't need that. I just won't drink it.

"What's a New York strip?" Joe asked. "I don't think I've ever had one."

The admission took Barbara by surprise.

He really doesn't know, which is not surprising. Since the day before yesterday he was a Marine sergeant, a prewar Marine sergeant, someone my father would claim was in the Marines because he couldn't find a job, and because the Marines offered three square meals a day and a place to sleep. Regular Marine enlisted men have few of what my father would call the social graces. And no social graces came to Joe miraculously when he put on that officer's uniform. Ordinarily, God forgive me, I am uncomfortable around the enlisted men. Why is it different with this man?

"You know a T-bone?" she asked, and he nodded. "The big piece. They cut the bone out of T-bone. The little piece is a filet mignon, and the big piece is a New York strip."

"I came in the Corps when I was seventeen," Joe said, and she took his meaning: that she had a social background and he didn't; and that was why he didn't know what a New York strip was. New York strip was not common fare for Marine enlisted men.

My God, is he reading my mind?

She felt a wave of compassion for him as her mind's eye filled with a picture of Joe Howard at seventeen, looking like the kids she saw in the Marine Recruit Depot here. Frightened little boys in uniform.

That's all he is now. The only difference is that he's twenty-four or twenty-five and wearing an officer's uniform. But he's still alone and more than a little frightened.

She finished her drink before the meal was served. And she had three glasses of the Cabernet Sauvignon with the steak. The steak was delicious. While they ate, a band started to play. When they were finished eating, he asked her to dance.

She could smell his after-shave when they were close, and she remembered the firm muscles of his chest and arms.

What I'm going to do now, when we finish dancing, is go back to the table and have a cup of coffee, and then I'm going to tell him I have an early day tomorrow and have to go home.

He spun her about, and her eyes moved across the people at the tables around the dance floor.

And fell on Lieutenant Hazel Gower, NC, USN, who was staring at her. She was with another nurse, the skinny little old bitch who had sent her to the Venereal Diseases Ward after Barbara told her she didn't want to work in Obstetrics.

"Let's quit," Barbara said to Joe. "I'm a little dizzy."

When they returned to the table, the wine was gone, and so was the Scotch in the wine cooler. These had been replaced by a tray of cheese and two brandy snifters.

I don't want that, either. But it's his party and I don't want to appear bitchy.

"Did you order that?" she asked.

He shook his head.

"If you don't want it, don't drink it," he said.

"It would be a shame to waste it," she said.

A short time later, Joe said, "I don't think I've ever had a better time in my life. I hate for it to end."

"It has to. I've got a busy day tomorrow."

"Sure. I understand. I didn't mean . . ."

Her hand reached for his again, and touched it, and this time she did not immediately withdraw it.

"I've had a fine time, too. Really. I'm glad we came here."

His hand closed on hers, and they held hands for a moment, and then he pulled his away.

"I'll get the check," he said, and started looking for the waiter. It took him some time to find him. After the waiter noticed Joe waving and started moving toward their table, she caught Joe glancing at her, and then averting his eyes.

"Will there be something else, Sir? A pastry, perhaps?"

"You want a piece of cake?" Joe asked, and she shook her head. "Just the check, please."

"Excuse me, Sir?"

"Can I have the check, please?"

"Sir, that'll go on the Pacific & Far East house ledger."

"I'd like to pay for it," Joe said.

"Sir, that would be . . . difficult."

"Let it go, Joe," Barbara said. "Don't look a gift horse in the mouth."

"OK," he said, hesitantly. "Thank you."

"I hope you enjoyed your meal, Sir."

He took her arm again as he led her from the room. They walked within ten feet of Lieutenant Gower and her friend. When Barbara smiled at her, Gower stared right through her.

In the lobby just outside the dining room entrance, Barbara stopped.

"Where's the room the key goes to?"

"I don't know. It says 418."

"Then it would seem reasonable to assume it is on the fourth floor, wouldn't you say?"

"I suppose."

"And I think it would also be reasonable to assume that it would have a bathroom, wouldn't you say?"

"Sure. I'm sure it would."

"Nature calls," she said. "And there, lucky me, are the elevators."

"Would you like me to wait here?"

"No."

She walked ahead of him and got on the elevator.

"Four, please," she said to the elevator operator.

She didn't look at him on the way up. He followed her into the corridor.

She stopped and turned to him, and looked into his eyes.

"If you don't kiss me right now, I'm going to lose my nerve," she said.

He didn't move. He looked paralyzed.

"Didn't anybody ever tell you not to look a gift horse in the mouth?" Barbara said.

He kissed her.

And then they walked, arms around each other, down the corridor until they found suite 418. He had a little trouble fitting the key to the lock, but once they were inside, and after he kissed her again, everything went off without a hitch.

VI

(ONE)

BUILDING "F"

ANACOSTIA NAVAL AIR STATION

WASHINGTON, D.C.

0845 HOURS 13 FEBRUARY 1942

"General McInerney," Brigadier General D. G. McInerney answered his telephone, not taking his eyes off the thick stack of paper before him.

"Colonel Hershberger, Sir."

"Hello, Bobby, how are you? What can I do for you?"

Colonel Robert T. Hershberger was Chief of Staff, 1st Marine Air Wing, Quantico, Virginia.

"General, the General is gone. He's at New River. I'm minding the store."

The General was Brigadier General Roy S. Geiger, Commanding, 1st Marine Air Wing.

"Got something you can't handle, Bobby?"

"General, I can handle this. What I would like is your advice on *how* to handle it."

"Shoot. Advice is cheap."

"I have a requirement to send one R4D, rigged for parachutists, to Lakehurst, to arrive NLT 0600, 14 February. That's tomorrow."

"I know. I laid that requirement on you."

"And your Major made it pretty plain that this is a must-do."

"It is."

"And thirty minutes ago, I got a call from the Director of Public Relations, just checking to see that the aircraft was scheduled, and asking me if I could take particular care to see that the crew was 'photogenic.'"

"The sonofabitch called me just a few minutes ago," General McInerney said. "He told me that the Commandant had 'expressed enthusiastic interest in the project.' You know what it is?"

147

"*Life* magazine is sending a photographer. Photographers. Plural. To watch the parachute trainees jump out of the airplane."

"Right. The idea, apparently, is that when the red-blooded youth of our nation see these heroic daredevils, they will rush to the nearest recruiting office to join up," General McInerney said dryly.

"That being the case, I figured there was no way I could get out of sending my only R4D up there," Colonel Hershberger said.

"If that's why you called, Bobby, save your breath. I don't know if General Holcomb really knows about whatever this public-relations operation is, but that requirement came down here from the Throne Room."

"There are four people here qualified in the R4D," Hershberger said.

"That's all?" McInerney asked, surprised.

"General, you may not have noticed, but people have been sending my pilots overseas."

"I can do without the sarcasm, thank you very much, Bobby," McInerney said. "And you may not have noticed, but there's a war on."

Colonel Hershberger did not reply.

"What's the problem, Bobby?" McInerney said, more cordially. "It only takes two pilots to fly one of those things, doesn't it?"

"Two of the four pilots don't look old enough to vote; and they have just finished the checkout. The check pilot, aware of the pilot shortage, was not as critical as he should have been."

"How do you know that?" McInerney snapped.

"I was the check pilot," Hershberger said. "Primarily because I am the only R4D Instructor Pilot here."

"You said four pilots."

"Well, *he* has two hundred–odd hours in the aircraft, and he went through the parachute-dropping course at Fort Benning."

"Well, then, what the hell is the problem? Send him. And send the two kids with him to see how it's done."

"Aye, aye, Sir. I hoped the General would say that. The name of the only fully qualified pilot for this mission is Technical Sergeant Charles Galloway."

General McInerney exhaled audibly.

"Oh, you sonofabitch, Bobby," he said. "You sandbagged me."

"The options, General, as I see them, are to send the two kids and pray they don't dump the airplane, or drop the parachutists in the Atlantic or over Central Park, while *Life*'s cameras are clicking. Or fly it myself. I've never dropped parachutists. I can probably find Lakehurst all right, but it occurred to me that it would look a little odd to have a full bird colonel flying a mission like this. Or send Charley Galloway."

"I told you about Galloway."

"Yes, Sir, I know that he embarrassed the U.S. Navy by getting repaired an airplane that BUAIR said was beyond repair. And then he further embarrassed the U.S. Navy's security procedures by finding out where a Task Force was, and then flying the unrepairable airplane out to it. And I know the only excuse he offered for this outrageous behavior was that he thought Marines were supposed to fight the enemy."

"It's a damned good thing we've been friends for twenty-odd years, Bobby," McInerney said. "Otherwise, I'd have your ass for talking to me that way."

"Doc, for God's sake, I'm bleeding for pilots. Not only for this stupid public-relations nonsense, but all over. It makes absolutely no sense to have a pilot like Galloway sitting on the goddamned ground with a wrench in his hand when he could be, for example, teaching the kids how to fly the goddamned R4D."

McInerney didn't reply.

"And if we hadn't been friends for twenty years, Doc, and somebody else was sitting at your desk, I would have just sent him without asking, and said, 'Fuck you, court-martial me,' if anybody said anything about it."

There was a long silence.

Finally, McInerney said, "Got your mouth under control now, Bobby?"

"Yes, Sir. Sorry, Sir."

"Colonel Hershberger, you have my permission to restore Sergeant Galloway to flight status. You have my permission to have Sergeant Galloway fly this public-relations mission to Lakehurst. And you may utilize Sergeant Galloway in such other flying roles as you deem appropriate for someone of his skill and experience, except that he will not leave the Quantico local area without my express permission."

"Aye, aye, Sir. Thank you, Sir."

"And you tell that sonofabitch, Bobby, that if he so much as farts and embarrasses you, me, or Marine Aviation in any way, I personally guarantee that he will spend the rest of this war as a private in a rifle company."

"Aye, aye, Sir."

General McInerney slammed the handset into its cradle and returned his attention to the thick stack of papers on his desk.

(TWO)

LAKEHURST NAVAL AIR STATION
LAKEHURST, NEW JERSEY
14 FEBRUARY 1942

Lieutenant Colonel Franklin G. Neville, USMC, who was thirty-seven years old, balding, barrel-chested, and carried 212 pounds on a six-foot-two-inch body, had seen the future and it was Vertical Envelopment.

In 1937, as a very senior (and nearly overage-in-grade) captain, Neville was appointed Assistant Naval Attaché, United States Embassy, Helsinki, Finland. His previous assignment had been as an infantry company commander.

When he was not selected to attend the U.S. Army Command and General Staff College at Fort Leavenworth, Kansas, and was then asked if he would accept the Helsinki embassy assignment, Neville understood that his Marine Corps career was drawing to a close.

If he was lucky, he might be promoted major while on the four-year embassy assignment. But promoted or not, he knew—in fact, he'd been unofficially informed—that in the spring of 1941, when his Helsinki tour was over, he would be retired.

He'd also been told—and he believed—that he himself was in no way personally responsible for his coming retirement. He had, in other words, not been found wanting. He was a good officer who performed his assigned duties well. There was no record, official or whispered, that he was too fond of the bottle or of the ladies, or of any other sport inappropriate for a Marine officer.

The bottom line was that there were only so many billets available for majors in the peacetime Marine Corps, either in the serving Corps or in the professional schools. And others competing for these spots were *better* qualified than he was. The rule was "up or out"—meaning that if an officer was not selected for promotion, he was either separated from the Corps or retired. Retirement was the fate of officers like Captain Neville, who had enough years of service to qualify for it.

He'd understood the rules of the game when he'd accepted a regular Marine commission in 1919; and he had no complaints now—although, naturally, he was disappointed.

Franklin G. Neville had entered the Marine Corps as a second lieutenant in June of 1916, on his graduation from Purdue University. He had come home from France a wounded, decorated captain, who had taken over command of his company when its commander had been killed at Belleau Wood.

The Corps, and the war, had changed him. He no longer wanted to become a lawyer specializing in banking law, like his father. He now knew that any personal satisfaction he might find in the practice of law could not compare with the satisfaction he had known leading men in battle.

His father never understood that. Worse, he shared with most of his peers the notion that a man served in the peacetime military only if he could do nothing else. And he was simply incapable of understanding why anyone would want to settle for the pittance paid regular officers when a financially rewarding career right there in St. Louis was available.

Available, hell, it's being handed to you on a silver platter, you damned fool!

Estelle Wachenberg Neville, whom he had married five days before shipping out to France, *had* understood. And she had also brought into the marriage a substantial trust fund established for her by her maternal grandfather, who had been one of the original investors in the Greater St. Louis Electric Power Generation & Street Railway Company.

So money was never a problem, except in the perverse sense that he and Estelle had had to be very careful not to let their relative affluence offend anyone. In fact, this did not turn out to be much of a drawback. Franklin didn't think that a young lawyer in Saint Louis could drive a Harmon or a Pierce Arrow, or even a Cadillac, without offending someone senior to him. Not many in that hierarchy had a quarterly check from a trust fund.

By the time the Helsinki assignment—his "tailgate" assignment—came along, there was no longer a requirement to be "discreet" about their affluence. So he and Estelle decided to go out in style. They left the boys behind in the States, at Phillips-Exeter, to join them in the summers. And in Finland, Estelle found a furnished villa in Helsinki's most aristocratic section, Vartio Island, about five miles from the embassy.

The waters of Kallahden Bay were solidly frozen from February to April, permitting the Neville's Packard 280 sedan (Estelle's) and Auto-Union roadster (Franklin's) to drive directly from the mainland to the front door. In the warmer months, a varnished speedboat carried them back and forth from the island to the shore.

His Excellency the Ambassador was a political appointee, a deserving St. Louis Democrat who professed a closer friendship with both Estelle's and Franklin's parents at home than was the case. In point of fact, a letter from Estelle's father indicated that so far as he was concerned, the Ambassador was a traitor to his class for supporting that socialist sonofabitch in the White House.

Nevertheless, the polite fiction served both to keep the Naval and

Army attachés off Franklin's back and to open social doors that permitted Estelle to enjoy a role as hostess that she had been denied all those years.

Between Franklin's social contacts within the diplomatic-military community and Estelle's with the diplomatic people and their neighbors on Vartio Island, it was a rare evening indeed when their butler served dinner to them alone at home.

When the boys arrived in the summer (they spent the Christmas holidays with their grandparents in St. Louis), they were, as Estelle wrote home, "received by the best young people in Finland." They fished and sailed, and they danced and kept close company with a number of splendidly beautiful and astonishingly blond Finnish girls. In due course, Franklin found it necessary to have a serious man-to-man talk with them about how they would embarrass not just their mother but the United States of America if one of the young ladies should find herself in the family way. He then counseled them on the absolute necessity of faithful use of rubber contraceptives.

In October of 1939, Captain Franklin G. Neville was promoted major. The promotion came as a surprise. He could not imagine that his immediate superior, Lieutenant Commander H. Raymond Fawcett, USN, the Naval Attaché, had been writing glowing efficiency reports on him. Fawcett's disapproval (and/or jealousy) of the Nevilles' lifestyle was nearly visible. But still, it would be nice, when they went back to St. Louis, to be able to call themselves "Major and Mrs. Neville."

In November of 1939, the Union of Soviet Socialist Republics attacked Finland across the southeastern province of Karelia. Before the 1917 Revolution, Finland had been part of Tsarist Russia; specifically, it was a Grand Duchy thereof. When Finland declared its independence, the military forces of the Soviet Union were in no position to do anything about it.

Now they were. They regarded Finland as part of Russia, and they wanted it back.

Major Franklin Neville immediately went to the war zone as an observer. It was clearly his duty, perhaps the most important duty a military attaché can perform, to observe the combatants at war, to report on their relative efficiency and capabilities, and to learn what he could.

Neville, along with an officer from the Finnish High Command and Lieutenant Colonel Graf Friedrich von Kallenberg-Mattau, an assistant military attaché at the German Embassy with whom Neville played golf and tennis in the summer and hunted and skied in the winter, drove to Karelia in Freddy von K's Mercedes. Freddy argued that the Mercedes had a better heater and more luggage space than either Neville's

Auto-Union roadster or the official, smaller Mercedes sedan the Finnish General Staff officer had been given.

As they drove off, there was little question in Franklin Neville's mind that soon, perhaps within the day, he would be in the hands of the Russians. They outnumbered the Finns by a factor of better than twenty to one. As courageous as the Finns might prove to be, that sort of a disbalance of opposing forces could result in only one end: the Finns would be overrun and wiped out.

He wondered if the Russians would honor his diplomatic status, or whether he would be shot out of hand, or whether he would perhaps simply disappear.

It didn't matter. It was his duty to go; and without any false heroics whatever, he could no more not have gone than he could have flapped his wings and flown.

What he found in Karelia Province was not in any way what he expected.

He could not believe that the military forces of a major, contemporary world power would be committed to combat with such poor planning, or with such an absolute ignorance of the kind of warfare they would have to wage.

Though the wintertime temperature in Karelia regularly dropped to below minus forty degrees Fahrenheit, eighty or ninety percent of the attacking Russian forces were not clothed or otherwise equipped to fight in such conditions.

The apparent Russian plan to penetrate and overrun the Finns swiftly, through sheer numbers and massive artillery barrages, was an absolute disaster. The Russian artillery, for instance, was almost useless in the bitter cold. And when the pieces could be coaxed into firing, most of the projectiles simply buried themselves deep in the snow before exploding. Rarely did they do any real harm.

The Finns, on the other hand, were not only superbly equipped to deal with the weather (they even had stoves and facilities to build "warming areas" where troops were routinely returned to be fed and warmed), but were able to wage war effectively in it. Their infantry was equipped with skis and snowshoes, permitting rapid movement over deep snow. They had snow-colored parkas, glasses to prevent snow blindness, and even white sleeves to place over their rifles to camouflage them.

And they were superbly led and disciplined.

The result was that the Finns were able to cause severe personnel and materiel losses to Russian forces at little cost to themselves. Finnish forces would suddenly appear when and where the Russians did not expect them. When the Russians marshaled forces sufficient to repel the

Finnish attackers, the Finns simply disappeared in the vast snowy terrain, where the Russians were unable to pursue them.

Any other army but the Red Army, Neville cabled Washington, would have called off the offensive after suffering such terrible losses. Yet even their apparent total willingness to disregard personnel losses was not going to permit them to accomplish their objective of a quick and decisive victory.

But the Russians did have one military capability that deeply impressed Major Neville, even if they used it improperly—they literally threw it away. The Russians had massed a large fleet of transport aircraft, from which they parachuted infantry, plus some supplies, to the ground.

In practice, the Russians generally dropped their parachute troops in the wrong places, where Finnish forces quickly wiped them out; and Russian planning made little or no provision for reinforcing or resupplying the parachutists once they were on the ground, which meant that they ended up, in effect, dying on the vine. In Neville's professional opinion, however, these failings did not detract in any way from the obvious fact that the use of parachute troops—the Theory of Vertical Envelopment—was an idea whose time had come.

This theory was not new. Neville recalled that in the notoriety surrounding his court-martial for insubordination, it was often forgotten that U.S. Army Air Corps Brigadier General "Billy" Mitchell had written as long ago as the World War that parachute troops would play an important—perhaps a dominant—role on the battlefields of the future.

As for poor little Finland, in the end, of course, Goliath prevailed against David. Courage, discipline, and skill in the techniques of warfare cannot stand up forever against an enemy who possesses both overwhelming logistical superiority and manpower, and who is not responsible to his people for the loss of their sons in battlefield slaughter. The Finns sued for armistice in early 1940.

In February 1940, shortly after the armistice was put into effect, Major Franklin G. Neville was ordered home—but *not* to retire, as he had anticipated. Instead, he was ordered to Headquarters, USMC, in Washington. There he was given a desk in a crowded office and asked to expand on the reports he had cabled from Helsinki of the Russo-Finnish conflict. He was to make such observations and recommendations as he thought would be of value for planning for possible Marine Corps operations in the future.

It was temporary duty, and government quarters were not authorized in Washington. He was, however, paid a per diem allowance. Quarters at his next duty station, USMC Schools, Quantico, Virginia, *were* authorized; but Estelle had no intention of going to Quantico alone and hibernating there while her husband was in Washington. And he had no quarrel with her on that.

So the Nevilles moved into a suite at the Wardman Park Hotel. After Helsinki, Estelle argued, she was not about to return to that idiotic business of living as if they didn't know where their next nickel was coming from.

It was generally agreed among those who counted that Major Neville's reports on the Russo-Finnish conflict were outstanding. Indeed, his paper on Finnish command relationships and discipline earned him a "well done" on a buck slip from the Major General Commandant himself.

But Major Franklin G. Neville was now a *much* changed man. Retirement from the Corps no longer loomed before him. No more did he have to face a suitable job arranged by his family in Saint Louis, with lunch at the Athletic Club and drinks at the Country Club. Instead, he could now look forward to further service as a Marine officer.

There was a new war coming, he felt sure of it. And he—prophetically—had a vision of a new cutting edge for the Marine Sword. He saw properly trained and equipped and properly utilized Marine parachutists changing the face of Marine warfare.

No longer would Marines assault an enemy beach from the sea, he wrote in a paper he titled "Hostile Shore Assault by Vertical Envelopment." They would no longer be left vulnerable to murderous fire from shore batteries as their landing barges brought them to the beach. Aerial reconnaissance would show where the enemy was *not*. And in *that* place a fleet of transports would drop, by parachute, companies, battalions, and possibly even full regiments. Initially, these forces would be resupplied from the air, until, attacking from the rear, they could secure the beach.

And, of course, he saw Franklin G. Neville, appropriately promoted, leading this invulnerable force of elite Marine parachutists. He had led men in combat well as a young captain. It was not arrogant to presume he could do so even better as a colonel. Or as a brigadier general.

After completing his Headquarters assignment, Major Neville asked for and was granted a thirty-day leave. He went to Fort Benning, Georgia, where he met like-minded Army parachute enthusiasts. They received him cordially; not only had he seen the light, but he had actually witnessed vertical assaults in combat. He gave several little seminars on Russian parachute operations and techniques, pointing out in these talks his perceptions of Russian strengths and weaknesses.

The Army obligingly arranged for him to go through their experimental parachute-jumping program. He made nine jumps, and, in a quasi-official ceremony at the Benning Officers' Club, was given a set of silver Army parachutist's wings and named an Honorary U.S. Army Paratrooper.

When Major Neville reported to Quantico, he was assigned to the G-2 Section, where his duties were to examine French, English, and German military publications, extracting therefrom material he believed should be made available to the Corps.

He did not find this difficult. He was fluent in German, primarily because of his long friendship and association in Helsinki with Lieutenant Colonel Graf Friedrich von Kallenberg-Mattau; and he had no trouble reading the German material made available to him. Equally important, he had two sergeants of foreign extraction who could make the actual translations into English.

Major Neville therefore had the time to gather all his thoughts, distill them, and express them clearly. The result of this was, "Vertical Envelopment in the U.S. Marine Corps: A Study of the Potential Uses of Parachute Troops in Future Warfare, by Major Franklin G. Neville, USMC, based on his observations during the Russo-Finnish War," which he submitted for publication in *The Marine Corps Gazette.*

It was duly decided that Neville's article was "not appropriate" for publication, and it was returned to him with the thanks of the editors.

But it wasn't long before the article took on a life of its own—especially after scuttlebutt had it that the piece had been killed by someone far superior to the Major who edited the *Gazette.* Copies of it were run off on mimeograph machines and made their way around the Marine Corps.

Despite the resulting wide distribution, Major Neville's concept of the Theory of Vertical Envelopment as it could apply to the Marine Corps met a mixed to negative reception. There were those who genuinely believed Major Neville was just one more of those harmless Marine Corps characters who were doomed to play the game of life with less than a full deck:

Marines going into combat by jumping out of airplanes? Jesus H. Christ! Do you remember that loony who actually proposed building troop-carrying submarines, so we could sneak *up to the enemy's beach?*

And there were those who read Neville's arguments with a more open mind and decided that whatever merits the theory might contain, for the time being at least, it was an idea whose time had not come.

Parachute warfare would require large numbers of large airplanes, but these were not available, nor were they likely to be. And even if an aircraft fleet were miraculously to materialize, it would require an enormous logistical tail, which the Navy certainly would not want to provide:

You could do the arithmetic for that in your head. There are roughly two hundred men in a company. With, say, twenty men per airplane, that would mean ten airplanes to drop one company. There aren't that many R4-Ds, the only airplane that will carry that many people, in the whole Marine Corps. Using the rule of thumb of 1.5 pilots per cockpit seat, ten airplanes would require thirty pilots per parachute company, plus a like number of mechanics and crew chiefs.

And Neville makes the doubtless valid point that the reason the Russian parachute troops couldn't get the job done was that the Russians made no provision to resupply them. So, since a reasonable ball-park figure for resupply of ammunition and food is a couple of hundred pounds per man, and since a couple of hundred pounds is what a man weighs, that means you would need ten airplanes to drop the infantry, and another ten airplanes to resupply them.

That's twenty airplanes, sixty pilots, sixty mechanics, and twenty crew chiefs for one company. Not to mention things like people driving the gas trucks, and extra cooks to feed the pilots and mechanics and truckdrivers.

And what good could one lousy company do? You'd need a battalion. A battalion is five companies. Multiply the above by five, and you get one hundred airplanes, and three hundred pilots. . . .

Major Neville, the poor bastard, obviously got carried away with the romance of it all. As a practical matter, there's just no way the Corps could do it. No wonder the brass killed his article.

But, as a result of Major Franklin G. Neville's rejected *Marine Corps Gazette* article, there were those in the senior hierarchy of the Marine Corps who were forced to consider, for the first time, that the U.S. Army was indeed going ahead with Vertical Envelopment. If the Army was successful in fielding a regimental-size airborne force—and there was already scuttlebutt that the Army intended to redesignate the 82nd Infantry Division as the 82nd *Airborne* Division—this would constitute a threat to the Marine Corps' perception of itself, and, more important, to the Congress's perception of the Marine Corps, as the assault element of United States military forces.

The Marine Corps believed—as, for that matter, did many soldiers and sailors—that the function of the Marine Corps was to storm enemy beaches, holding them only long enough for the Army to follow up with its heavy artillery and logistical elements.

If the Army developed its own capability to land regiments or divisions on hostile shores—in other words, if they could field an airborne division—the question would naturally be raised, "So why do we need the Marines?"

On the other hand, if the Marine Corps had—in place—its own

experts in Vertical Envelopment, or possibly even its own small force of parachutists, say a battalion, together with plans to apply their techniques to larger forces, up to a division, then the Marine Corps could reasonably argue that the Army was treading on its turf and should back off.

While no one really thought that the Army's parachutists posed a deadly threat to the very existence of the Marine Corps, neither was any senior Marine officer prepared to state that they posed no threat at all.

And money, as 1941 passed, became less and less an issue than it had been in previous years. There was little doubt in Congress's mind that war was on the horizon and that the American military establishment was ill-prepared to wage it. And Congress devoutly believes the solution to any problem is to throw money at it.

The Marine solution to the problem posed by the Army's parachutists proved to be simple. In a supplemental appropriation, Congress provided funds for USMC Schools, Quantico, to conduct such tests as the Major General Commandant of the Marine Corps thought pertinent regarding the use of parachute forces in future Marine Corps operations.

Marine Corps Headquarters delegated overall responsibility for Marine Parachutists to Marine Aviation, following the German practice of subordinating their *Falschirmjaeger* to the Luftwaffe rather than to the Wehrmacht. And they decreed that Major Franklin G. Neville would be action officer for the program.

In August 1941, Major Neville submitted a report to Headquarters, USMC, of the original tests at Quantico, together with a list of recommendations. Surprising no one, he reported that the tests proved beyond any doubt that Vertical Envelopment offered great advantages to the Marine Corps. He recommended also:

(1) That a provisional battalion of parachute troops be formed, and that a suitably experienced officer be named as its commander. Neville listed desirable qualifications for such an officer. These surprised no one: With the exception that the recommended commanding officer should be a lieutenant colonel, these qualifications matched those of Major Franklin G. Neville and no one else anyone could think of in the Marine Corps.

(2) That Marine parachutists should be removed from subordination to Marine Aviation.

(3) That the Marine Corps establish a formal parachutist's school, preferably at some location other than Quantico, whose training facilities were already overloaded.

The report was submitted through Marine Aviation channels to Headquarters, USMC. The endorsement stated that the Director of

Marine Aviation did not feel qualified either to recommend or recommend against the incorporation of parachutists into the Marine Corps. But, clearly, parachutists were now a practical matter.

If, however, it was decided to establish Marine parachutists, Marine Aviation was in complete agreement with Major Neville's recommendations that such a force be withdrawn from subordination to Marine Aviation. And Marine Aviation strongly endorsed the recommendation that any further Marine parachutist training be conducted elsewhere than Quantico. For example, the U.S. Naval Lighter Than Air Station at Lakehurst, New Jersey, which was currently underutilized, might well prove to be a suitable location.

There were those who regarded the Marine Aviation endorsement as another example that there was really no intraservice rivalry between the air and ground components of the Marine Corps. But cynics maintained that Marine Aviation actually wanted to distance itself as far as possible from paratroops generally and from Major Franklin G. Neville specifically. That Neville was now known popularly as "Fearless Frank" was not taken as an auspicious omen for the future development of Marine Vertical Envelopment. Almost to a man, Marine Aviation personnel believed that anyone who willingly jumped out of a perfectly functioning aircraft was, kindly, a little strange.

Action on the Neville report and its recommendations came unusually quickly, within a month. All the recommendations were approved:

Marine Aviation was relieved of responsibility for airborne forces.

A Provisional Parachute Battalion was authorized, to be subordinate to Fleet Marine Force, Atlantic.

The Director, Marine Corps Parachute Forces, was authorized to seek volunteers for parachute duty from Marine units within the continental limits of the United States.

Marine Corps Schools, Quantico, was ordered to establish a subordinate facility to train parachutists at Naval Lighter Than Air Station, Lakehurst, New Jersey.

Major Franklin G. Neville was appointed Director of Marine Corps Parachute Forces.

Franklin G. Neville was promoted lieutenant colonel the day he first visited Lakehurst to determine how its facilities (which is to say those not needed to support the Navy's blimps) could be quickly adapted to train parachutists.

With the exception of not being named Commanding Officer of the Parachute Battalion (and it could be argued that there was no point in naming a commanding officer of a battalion that did not yet exist), Neville had gotten everything he'd asked for.

He understood, however, that the greatest test was yet before him: turning the theory into reality. And he had a plan for that, too. And high on the plan was getting rid of every last damned one of the Marine Aviation people. Especially the enlisted men. The only Marine Aviation people he wanted to see in the future would be the ones flying the aircraft.

Based both upon his experience as a company commander in France, and on what he had observed in the Russo-Finnish War, Colonel Neville knew that the keys to military success were esprit de corps and impeccable discipline. The two went hand in hand. The former, Neville believed, was a result of the latter.

In his early planning phases, he had been foolish enough to believe that because he was starting with Marines, he would have a leg up. All Marines, in his opinion, had the kind of esprit de corps and impeccable discipline that the Finns he so admired in combat had possessed. The only thing he had to worry about, then, was how to actually instruct them in the skill of parachuting.

His experience at Quantico with Marine Aviation, and especially with the enlisted men there, quickly showed him how wrong he was about that. Not only were the enlisted men a long-haired, slovenly bunch, who slouched around with their ties pulled down and their blouses unbuttoned, but their officers let them get away with it.

At the officers' club in Quantico, he actually came as close to losing his temper in public as he ever had as a Marine. He sought out a Marine Aviation major to have a word with him, out of school, about a situation he found intolerable. He had come across a Marine lieutenant, an aviator, a staff sergeant, some sort of aircraft mechanic, and a PFC, whose function he did not really know, leaning on the wall of hangar, laughing and joking together as if they were civilians in a pool hall.

When he relayed what he had seen to the Major, telling him that while he didn't want to bring charges, he felt sure the Major would agree that sort of behavior was intolerable and had to be nipped in the bud, the Major actually said to him, "You have to understand, Neville, that Aviation is different."

"We are all Marines," Neville argued.

"Yeah, of course we are," the Major replied. "But that doesn't mean everybody has to walk around as if he has a broomstick shoved up his ass like you do."

"I can't believe I'm hearing what I'm hearing," Major Neville said indignantly.

The Aviation Major beckoned Major Neville closer with a wiggle of his index finger. Then he whispered in Neville's ear, "Go fuck yourself, Fearless. Leave my people alone." Then he leaned back on his barstool, grinned cordially, and asked, "Do we understand each other, Fearless?"

Neville realized at the time that reporting the incident to Colonel Hershberger, the Marine Aviation Major's immediate superior, would have been fruitless. Those goddamned aviators stuck together. And, furthermore, it would have been necessary to report that "Fearless" business, too, a matter he didn't want to get into.

The solution to the problem was to get rid of the Marine Aviation people. He went from Lakehurst (now that he was Director of Marine Corps Parachute Forces, he no longer had to justify official travel) to Quantico, where he asked for volunteers. One of them he knew: a handsome, charming lieutenant named R. B. Macklin, who shared his enthusiasm for Vertical Envelopment. Macklin had served with the 4th Marines in China and, for reasons Neville did not understand, had been wasting his talents as a mess officer at Marine Corps Schools. He also recruited six second lieutenants from a group about to graduate from Officer's Basic Course.

He actually had eleven volunteer second lieutenants. But some sonofabitch from the 1st Division, to which the young officers were supposed to be assigned on graduation, complained to Personnel that the 1st Division had a more critical need for them than Neville did. And after a rather bitter discussion, he was allowed to take only six.

From Quantico he went to Parris Island and recruited from boots about to be graduated and from the cadre of drill instructors. He argued to them that if making Marines out of civilians was important, making Para-Marines out of ordinary Marines was even more so. And besides, once they became parachutists, it would increase their pay by fifty dollars a month. Over protests from both the 1st Division and Parris Island itself, he was allowed to take nine drill instructors and no more than three volunteers from each graduating platoon of recruits, up to a maximum of 1,200 men.

He then went to Fort Benning, Georgia, where he received permission for the nine ex–drill instructors and forty-one others (to be named when they became available) to go through the Army's Jump School en route to the Marine Parachute Training School at Lakehurst.

As the drill instructors reported aboard Lakehurst from Fort Benning, the Marine Aviation parachutists would be returned, on a one-to-one basis, to Marine Aviation. He couldn't get rid of all of them, of course; he had to keep some around—parachute riggers, for example. But by the first of the year, Major Neville's broom would otherwise have swept a new and clean path through Lakehurst.

PFC Steven M. Koffler, USMC, of course knew nothing about any of this. All he knew was that he was being carried as AWOL when he returned from the "extended" three-day pass the Sergeant of the Guard had arranged with the First Sergeant for him to have when he had first reported aboard Lakehurst.

There is legally no such thing as an "extended" three-day pass. Absences of less than seventy-two hours are not chargeable as leave. Absences over seventy-two hours are. Consequently, someone who is absent over seventy-two hours and is not on leave orders (which will charge the time against his accrued leave) is absent without leave, or AWOL.

Steve Koffler, who did not understand this technicality, told his First Sergeant what had happened. The First Sergeant, who had had a number of "extended" three-day passes himself over the years, decided to buck the problem up to the Company Commander. So Steve Koffler repeated his story to the Company Commander, First Lieutenant R. B. Macklin.

Lieutenant Macklin, who was a graduate of the United States Naval Academy at Annapolis, was very concerned with his professional reputation. He was a very senior lieutenant whose promotion to captain was long overdue.

Before the war, he had been stationed in Shanghai, China, with the 4th Marines. There, for reasons he had never been able to fathom fully, he had earned the dislike of the Regimental Intelligence Officer, a captain named Banning. Banning, for still more reasons Macklin simply couldn't understand, was held in the high regard of the Regimental Commander, even though, in Macklin's professional judgment, Banning's performance of duty left a good deal to be desired, and his off-duty conduct was inexcusable.

Among other things, Banning maintained a White Russian mistress, and didn't particularly care who knew it. If that wasn't conduct unbecoming an officer and a gentleman, Ed Macklin couldn't imagine what would be.

Banning had entered the Corps from the Citadel, a civilian trade school, which of course was not the same thing as coming out of Annapolis. That probably explained some of the trouble such people had. It was well known that men from places like the Citadel, Norwich, and VMI were not only jealous of Annapolis graduates, but went out of their way to get them, whenever and however they could.

What happened in Shanghai was that Banning, demonstrating a clear lack of good judgment, had assigned a corporal—a corporal!—to gather intelligence data on Japanese troop dispositions, while he was ostensibly serving as a truckdriver in a motor convoy under Macklin's command.

Predictably, even though Macklin tried to help him, the Corporal was unable to perform his mission in the best interests of the command.

Not only that, but he managed to touch off a confrontation with Chinese bandits that saw more than twenty Chinese killed.

Macklin wrote a report about the failure of the intelligence-gathering mission and the causes of the shooting incident. The report made clear that the whole thing could have been avoided if a low-ranking enlisted man had not been placed in a position he could not be expected to handle. Instead of accepting the report for what it was, namely constructive criticism, Banning wrote a wildly imaginative, wholly dishonest reply in which he placed on Macklin the blame for both the failure of the mission and the shooting incident.

It was difficult to believe, but the Colonel (who had gone into the Corps from Princeton, of all places!) took Banning's side. And an efficiency report was placed in Macklin's personnel file that questioned his judgment, his honesty, and his potential for command.

At the time, Macklin was so upset by this gross injustice that he did not demand, as was his right, a court-martial to determine the truth of the accusations against him. It was his intention to just leave the Corps. After the way he had been treated, he no longer could serve in good conscience.

But with war on the horizon, resignations were no longer being accepted. He was consequently assigned to the Marine Corps Base at Quantico, Virginia, as a mess officer at Marine Corps Schools. He was prepared, of course, to carry out to the best of his ability that and any other assigned duty.

Several months later, he was shocked but not especially surprised, when he later thought about it, to see Banning's corporal from Shanghai enrolled as a candidate for a commission as an officer. The man had no education beyond high school, and was, literally, a murderer.

Corporal Kenneth R. "Killer" McCoy was so called because he had stabbed three Italian Marines to death on the streets of Shanghai. And here he was, about to become a Marine officer!

While he realized that he had no proof of any allegations he could make about McCoy, he was sure it was his obligation to the Corps to see that a man like that never became an officer. Macklin therefore had had a quiet word with several of the noncommissioned officers in the school. If McCoy could be terminated from the school for failure to meet its high standards, that would be the end of the matter. He would be no worse off than he had been; he would be assigned as a corporal.

It was then that Macklin learned just how much the Corps was infiltrated and corrupted by secret alliances, and how much power they had. Corporal McCoy must have gotten the word out that he was in trouble; for the next thing Macklin knew, a master gunnery sergeant named Stecker (he was the senior enlisted man at Quantico, and presumably had more important things to do) was nosing around the rifle range. And the day after that, Ed Macklin was standing in front of his Colonel, accused of improper interference with the officer candidate class.

"Find yourself a new home, Macklin," the Colonel told him then. "Or I'll find one for you!"

It was at that point that Macklin volunteered for and was accepted in the Marine Corps parachute program.

He and Lieutenant Colonel Franklin G. Neville saw eye-to-eye from the first. And after a period of time, he was able to tell Neville how unfairly he had been treated in Shanghai and at Quantico. Neville understood and was instantly sympathetic.

"You do a good job with my parachute school," Neville said, "and I'll write you an efficiency report that will take care of any problems you had in Shanghai. You should be a captain, and if you do a good job for me, you will be."

Macklin knew all about "extended" three-day passes: he considered them an affront to his perception of good order and discipline. So armed, he concluded he had in PFC Koffler a fine opportunity to make his position on "extended" three-day passes known to his new command.

He announced to Koffler that he didn't believe a word of his story; that no Marine NCO worthy of the name would tell a PFC not to worry about the seventy-two-hour limitation. He went on to explain that absence without leave was nearly as heinous an offense as cowardice in the face of the enemy, and that he really deserved to be brought before a court-martial.

But since the former First Sergeant and the Sergeant of the Guard had been transferred to Quantico, and since it would be inconvenient to bring them all the way back to Lakehurst to testify, and since Koffler was new to the Corps and probably didn't realize the seriousness of his offense, Macklin told Koffler he would graciously give him a second chance.

He would thus be permitted to begin parachute training. But the first time he stepped half an inch out of line would prove he was unworthy of a second chance. In that event, the whole business would be brought up again, and he could expect a court-martial and confinement at the Portsmouth Naval Prison.

If he managed to get through the course, there would be a clean slate.

And, of course, it went without saying that he could forget any liberty or other privileges while he was in parachute training. He would, in fact, consider himself confined to barracks when off-duty.

(THREE)

First Lieutenant James G. Ward, USMCR, and First Lieutenant David F. Schneider, USMC, marched into the office of Colonel Robert T. Hershberger and came to attention before his desk.

"Sir," Lieutenant Ward barked, "Lieutenants Ward and Schneider reporting as ordered."

Lieutenant Ward, a tall, brown-haired, loose-framed twenty-two-year-old, had come into Marine Aviation via Princeton, Officer Candidate School at Quantico, and Pensacola. Lieutenant Schneider, who was stocky, broad-shouldered, and wore his blond hair in a closely cropped crewcut, was also twenty-two, and had received his commission upon graduation from the U.S. Naval Academy at Annapolis.

With war on the horizon, and because he had the necessary credit hours, Lieutenant Ward had been permitted to graduate from Princeton (B.A., with a major in history) halfway through his senior year. He was graduated from Officer Candidate School at Quantico and commissioned five days before Lieutenant Schneider got to throw his midshipman's cap into the air at Annapolis. He had similarly been promoted to first lieutenant five days before Schneider was given that promotion.

Although he was personally fond of Lieutenant Ward, Lieutenant Schneider regarded himself as a member of the professional officer corps of the Naval Service of the United States; he did not like being outranked by a goddamned reservist from Princeton.

There was an enlisted man sitting in Colonel Hershberger's office. He stood up when the two lieutenants marched in. Colonel Hershberger promptly introduced him.

"This is Sergeant Galloway."

Sergeant Galloway was wearing utilities. Both Ward and Schneider had seen him on the flight line, working as a mechanic. They had also heard scuttlebutt that the sergeant had stolen an airplane somewhere and taken it for a joy ride, and had been sent to Quantico to await court-martial.

Schneider nodded uncomfortably at the Sergeant. Because Lieutenant Ward was a reservist and couldn't be expected to know the subtleties of dealing with an enlisted man over his ass in trouble, he graciously offered Galloway his hand.

"You will be taking our R4D to Lakehurst tomorrow," Colonel Hershberger said to them. "Headquarters USMC has arranged for *Life* magazine to do a story on the Marine parachutists being trained there. This operation, I am reliably informed, has the approval of the highest authority within the Marine Corps. In other words, if you screw up, you will embarrass not only yourselves, but me, Brigadier General McInerney, Marine Aviation, and the Corps itself as well. I want you to understand that very clearly."

"Yes, Sir," they parroted.

"Sergeant Galloway has kindly offered to go along on this little jaunt," Colonel Hershberger said, smiling wryly, "And I have accepted his offer."

Both young officers looked between the Colonel and the Sergeant with mingled curiosity and surprise.

"Sergeant Galloway will function as pilot-in-command," Hershberger said, startling them, "And the reason I called you all in here is to make sure you know what that means."

"Sir," Lieutenant Schneider said, "I'm a little confused."

"I thought you might be, Mr. Schneider," Hershberger said. "So I will explain it to you. What it means is that senior authority—in this case, me—has reviewed the qualifications of the pilots available to fly this mission and has chosen the best-qualified pilot—in this case, Sergeant Galloway—to serve as pilot-in-command. And *that* means just what it says. He is in command of the aircraft and is responsible for the accomplishment of the mission. So long as it has to do with the airplane and the mission, he speaks with my authority. Clear?"

"Yes, Sir," Lieutenant Schneider replied.

Colonel Hershberger looked at Lieutenant Ward until it occurred to Ward that a response was expected from him.

"Yes, of course," he said.

Hershberger went on, apparently not concerned that Ward had not appended the expected "Sir" to his answer, "If, in Sergeant Galloway's judgment, there is time and opportunity on this mission, he can give you instruction in the operation of the aircraft and on dropping parachutists from it. Galloway is both an R4D IP and a graduate of the Army Air Corps course on parachutist dropping. He has also been flying since you two were in high school. Any questions so far?"

"No, Sir."

"On the other hand, we all of course are in the Marine Corps, and are therefore subject to all the rules and the customs of the Service. Sergeant Galloway is required to treat you with the military courtesy to which your rank entitles you. The flip side of the coin is that as officers you are as responsible for Sergeant Galloway's well-being—his rations and quarters, so to speak—and his conduct, as you would be for any enlisted man you found yourselves associated with on a mission. In other words, if it should come to my attention that Sergeant Galloway got drunk and punched out a shore patrolman while you are all off doing this public-relations nonsense, it will be your ass as well as his. Questions?"

"No, Sir," Lieutenants Ward and Schneider said in unison.

"Charley?"

"Colonel, what I've been thinking of doing is shooting some touch-and-goes here—I haven't flown one of these for a while—and then fueling up and going up there this afternoon."

"Sure, why not? Just don't bend the goddamned bird."

"Sirs," Sergeant Galloway said, looking at Lieutenants Ward and Schneider, "would it be possible for you to pack your gear and meet me at Base Ops in an hour?"

"Certainly," Lieutenant Schneider said.

"Yes, Sir," Lieutenant Ward said, which earned him a look of amazed disgust from Lieutenant Schneider and a chuckle from Colonel Hershberger.

"Charley," Colonel Hershberger said, "am I going to have to remind you that you're on thin ice?"

"No, Sir, you don't," Sergeant Galloway said.

"That will be all, gentlemen, thank you," Colonel Hershberger said, dismissing them.

While they packed their bags in the bachelor officers' quarters, and as they drove to Base Operations, Lieutenants Ward and Schneider discussed Sergeant Galloway and the situation they found themselves in.

Lieutenant Schneider could not restrain himself from reminding Lieutenant Ward that officers should not say "Yes, Sir" to sergeants. After that, they considered all the possibilities of the scuttlebutt concerning Sergeant Galloway, the significance of Colonel Hershberger's remarks about Sergeant Galloway being on thin ice, and the Colonel's pronouncement that if Sergeant Galloway got drunk and punched out a shore patrolman, they would be held responsible.

Once they arrived at Base Operations, however, Sergeant Galloway's behavior and appearance made them a little less nervous. He was wearing green trousers and a fur-collared leather flight jacket when they joined him. There were golden, somewhat wear-faded, Naval Aviator's wings just like their own stamped on a leather patch on the breast of the flight jacket; and the real thing was pinned to the breast of his uniform blouse, which he carried on a hanger. The hash marks on the blouse cuff, signifying eight years of Marine service, were also reassuring.

And there was something about his calm competency as he laid out the flight plan, went through the weather briefing, and dealt with the crew chief and the preflight inspection of the aircraft that reminded them of their IPs at Pensacola. Since flight instructors, like drill sergeants, are always remembered by their former students as individuals of vast knowledge and awesome competence, both Ward and Schneider were able to tell themselves that whatever else Sergeant Galloway was, he was an extraordinarily qualified aviator. And this too was reassuring.

They even found his little joke with the crew chief, himself a technical sergeant, somehow comforting: "Well, let's wind up the rubber bands and see if we can get this thing in the air."

Galloway climbed up the door ladder and walked through the fuselage to the cockpit. Then he turned and found Lieutenant Ward behind him. He pointed to the copilot's seat.

"Why don't you crawl in there, Lieutenant?" he suggested. But it was an order, and both lieutenants knew it. Sergeant Galloway was now functioning as pilot-in-command.

Lieutenant Schneider stood between the seats and watched critically as Galloway went through the checklist and fired up the engines. He could find nothing to fault, even when he was summarily ordered to the cabin: "You can go strap yourself in now, Lieutenant."

That was simply following established safety regulations, Schneider told himself, actually a little chagrined that he had to be told by a sergeant to do something he knew he should do, and hadn't done.

Galloway then took the R4D off, got in the pattern, and shot four touch-and-go landings. All of them, Schneider was forced to admit, were as smooth as glass. Then he shot another five. The first of these was pretty rough and sloppy, Schneider was pleased to judge—until it occurred to him that *Ward*, not Sergeant Galloway, was now at the controls.

And then Ward came into the cabin, sat down beside Schneider, and said, "Your turn."

When Schneider went to the cockpit, Galloway was in the copilot's seat and obviously functioning as an IP. Schneider made five touch-and-goes, more than a little annoyed that not only was his performance being judged by this damned sergeant, but that he had found it wanting.

"Go around again," Galloway ordered, shoving the throttles forward. "Try to set up your approach so that you touch down closer to the threshold."

Dave Schneider's next landing was better, but still apparently not up to Sergeant Galloway's standard. He told him to go around again.

They refueled then, rechecked the weather, and got back into the

R4D. This time Galloway told Dave Schneider to get into the copilot's seat. Schneider, chagrined, correctly interpreted this to mean that Galloway thought he required more of his instructional attention than Ward did.

While they were climbing to their ten-thousand-foot cruising altitude, Galloway summoned Ward from the cabin and installed him on the jump seat in the cockpit. When Ward had his headset on, Galloway explained that they were going to fly the airways, first to the east of Washington, about twenty-five miles from Quantico, and then over Baltimore, and then Wilmington, Delaware, 120 miles and forty-five minutes from their departure point.

Galloway didn't touch the controls, letting Schneider fly and make the en route radio calls. When nothing was happening, he delivered, conversationally, what Lieutenant Ward genuinely believed was a truly learned discourse on the peculiarities of R4D aircraft and instrument flight techniques generally.

The sun had come out, and the day was clear, and the flight very pleasant.

And then Sergeant Galloway's voice came over the earphones.

"There's a little roughness in the port engine," he announced.

Neither Ward nor Schneider had detected any roughness in the port engine. Both quickly scanned the instrument panel for any signs of mechanical irregularity, but found none. Lieutenant Ward was perfectly willing to defer to Sergeant Galloway's expert judgment, but Lieutenant Schneider was not.

"Sergeant," Lieutenant Schneider said, "I don't hear anything in either of the engines."

"You really don't have all that much time in one of these things, do you, Lieutenant?" Galloway asked tolerantly.

Schneider's face flushed.

"I think we better sit down and have a look at it," Galloway went on. He picked up the microphone: "Philadelphia, this is Marine Two-Six-Two. I am diverting to Willow Grove at this time. Estimate Willow Grove in five minutes. Please close me out to Willow Grove."

The Willow Grove Naval Air Station, just north of Philadelphia, was not far from Lieutenant Ward's home in Jenkintown, Pennsylvania, an affluent Philadelphia suburb. He looked out the cockpit window and saw that they were approaching South Philadelphia. He could see the Navy Yard.

"Marine Two-Six-Two, Philadelphia," the Philadelphia controller replied, "understand diverting to Willow Grove at this time, ETA five minutes."

"Roger, Philadelphia, thank you," Galloway said, and then

switched to the Willow Grove tower's radio frequency: "Willow Grove, Marine Two-Six-Two, an R4D aircraft, fifteen miles south of your station. Approach and landing, please."

Curiosity overwhelmed Lieutenant Dave Schneider.

"What's going on?"

"I told you. The port engine sounds a little rough. I'm going to sit down and have a look at it."

"I don't hear anything wrong with the engine," Schneider said.

"I could be wrong, of course," Sergeant Galloway said. "But you can never be too careful, can you?"

"Willow Grove clears Marine Two-Six-Two as number one to land on Runway One-Niner. The winds are from the north at five miles. Visibility and ceiling unlimited. The time is ten past the hour."

"Roger, Willow Grove, we have the field in sight," Galloway said, and then added, to Schneider, "I've got it, Lieutenant."

Schneider took his hands and feet off the controls, turning control over to Galloway, who began to make the descent.

"We probably could have made it into Lakehurst," Schneider said. "It's only forty miles, maybe not that far."

"That's very good, Lieutenant," Galloway said dryly. "A copilot should always be prepared to give the pilot their location, and the location of an alternative airfield."

Schneider had the feeling Galloway was making a fool of him, but he couldn't figure out exactly how.

"I really would like to know why are we landing here," Lieutenant Schneider said.

"Lieutenant, do you know what they have at Lakehurst in February?" Galloway asked. "One of the world's biggest buildings, maybe a dozen blimps, and a lot of snow. Period." Then he picked up the microphone and said, "Willow Grove, Marine Two-Six-Two turning on final," and began to line the airplane up with the runway.

Lieutenant Schneider was now sure what Sergeant Galloway was up to. It fit in with everything he had heard. There was nothing wrong with the engine. Galloway did not want to go to Lakehurst because there was nothing, in his own words, at Lakehurst in February but one of the world's largest buildings, a dozen blimps, and a lot of snow. Period.

What was outside of Willow Grove Naval Air Station was the city of Philadelphia. And in Philadelphia there were a lot of bars where Galloway could get drunk and punch out a shore patrolman, for which, Colonel Hershberger had made it absolutely clear, they would be held responsible.

Schneider motioned to Ward to come close, covered his mouth with his hand, and said, "We have to talk."

Galloway greased the R4D onto the runway, then reached for the microphone again.

"Willow Grove, Two-Six-Two. We'll need some gas, and I'd like a mechanic to check out one of my engines, please."

"Two-Six-Two, take taxiway C, and taxi to the transient area by the tower. A fuel truck and a maintenance crew will meet you there."

"Thank you very much, Willow Grove."

"We flew right over my house," Lieutenant Ward said.

"We did?" Galloway said.

"I live in Jenkintown," Lieutenant Ward said.

"Well, I guess that means you can go home for supper, huh?" Galloway said.

"Sergeant Galloway," Lieutenant Schneider said, with what he hoped was the appropriate combination of courtesy and firmness, "if the engine checks out all right, I think we should go on to Lakehurst."

"Jesus, Dave, why?" Lieutenant Ward said. "I don't live fifteen minutes from here."

Schneider gave him a look of mingled disgust and fury.

"In fact, Sergeant," Schneider said, "I'm afraid I must insist that we do so."

"You don't have the right to insist on anything, Dave," Lieutenant Ward said furiously. "You heard what Colonel Hershberger said. So far as the airplane and the mission are concerned, Sergeant Galloway's in charge."

"Goddamn it! Can't you see what's going on?" Schneider flared. "He doesn't want to go to Lakehurst! You heard what he said about Lakehurst! What he wants is a night on the town. That's why he landed here. There's nothing wrong with that engine."

"Let's hope not," Sergeant Galloway said innocently.

"Then we're going to fly on to Lakehurst?" Schneider snapped.

"If we could, and I say *if*, then Lieutenant Ward wouldn't get to go home," Galloway said reasonably.

"So what?" Schneider snapped.

"That engine sounded a little rough to me, too," Lieutenant Ward said solemnly. "I think we better have it checked out pretty carefully."

The two Navy mechanics who came out to the R4D were accompanied by a gold-stripe Chief Naval Aviation Pilot. He saluted Lieutenants Ward and Schneider and shook hands cordially with Sergeant Galloway.

"What seems to be the trouble?"

"The port engine sounded a little rough," Galloway said. "I thought it best to sit down and have an expert look at it."

"Good thinking!" the Chief said. "I'll have a look at it myself."

That sonofabitch did everything but wink at Galloway, Dave

Schneider thought furiously. *He knows exactly what's going on! Two goddamn birds of a feather flocking together!*

The mechanics backed their pickup truck under the wing and started to remove nacelle panels.

Schneider took Ward's arm and led him out of hearing.

"You know damned well what's going on here, Jim," he said. "Galloway wants a night on the town. There's nothing wrong with that engine."

"I'd like to go home," Ward said.

"And let him go out on the town? You heard Hershberger. We're responsible for his conduct."

"We can take him with us," Ward said.

"What do you mean?"

"We all go to my house. We have dinner, a couple of drinks, and then we all come back here together. I'd like to see my girl. And I'm sure she has a friend."

"We can't go out in public with him. To a restaurant or a bar, you know that. Officers cannot socialize with enlisted men."

"So we don't go to a restaurant or a bar," Ward said. "We go to my house. I repeat, we don't let him out of our sight."

Dave Schneider grunted.

The Chief Aviation Pilot, surprising Lieutenant Dave Schneider not at all, returned from his mechanic's initial inspection of the port engine to report that they could find nothing wrong with it, but that in the interests of safety, he thought it would be a good idea if they drained the engine oil and had a look at it. That way they would know for sure. That would take an hour or an hour and a half; so why didn't they just RON here and take off first thing in the morning? The initials were short for "remain overnight."

The Chief said he could put Sergeant Galloway up in the Chief's quarters, and there was room in the transient BOQ for the officers.

"That's very kind of you, Chief," Lieutenant Schneider said, "but Lieutenant Ward lives near here, and we'll just go to his house. We'll leave you the number, and when you find out about the engine, you call me. All right?"

The Chief Aviation Pilot shrugged and said, "Aye, aye, Sir."

Tough luck, Chief! You did your best for Sergeant Galloway, but I outsmarted you.

Thirty minutes later, a wooden-sided Mercury station wagon with a VISITOR placard stuck against the dashboard pulled up in front of Base Operations.

"That your mother?" Dave Schneider asked.

Ward looked.

"No. It's my Aunt Caroline," he said, and pushed open the door.

Caroline Ward McNamara, who was thirty-two, blond, long-haired, long-legged, and three months divorced, kissed her nephew and shook hands with Lieutenant Schneider and Sergeant Galloway. Charley Galloway thought that Mrs. McNamara was as beautiful and elegant as a movie star. Like Greer Garson, except with long blond hair.

"I was at the house," she said. "Your mother wanted to go to the Acme to get steaks, so I volunteered to come get you."

Any woman that beautiful has to be married. Or engaged. And even if she wasn't, she's a lady. She wouldn't want to have anything to do with a Marine Sergeant.

Lieutenant Schneider and Sergeant Galloway got in the backseat of the Mercury, and Jim Ward got in front beside his aunt.

"Which airplane is yours?" she asked.

"The third one," Jim Ward said. "The one with 'Marines' painted on the fuselage."

"I'm impressed," Aunt Caroline said. "I didn't know you were flying something that large."

"I'm just learning how, to tell you the truth," Jim Ward said.

"And you're the teacher, Lieutenant Schneider? Is that it? Is Jim a good student?"

"Actually, Caroline," Jim Ward said, "Sergeant Galloway is the IP. Instructor Pilot."

Aunt Caroline shifted her head so that she could see Sergeant Galloway in the rearview mirror.

Their eyes met. Charley Galloway felt his heart jump.

"Isn't that a little unusual?" she asked.

"No, Ma'am," Charley Galloway said.

The hell it isn't, Aunt Caroline thought. *And that isn't all that's interesting about that young man!*

"Have you been flying airplanes like that long, Sergeant?"

"No, Ma'am," Charley Galloway said.

"What do you ordinarily fly? And stop calling me 'Ma'am,' it makes me feel ancient."

"Until recently, I was a fighter pilot," Charley Galloway said. "I usually fly Wildcats."

"I didn't know that, Charley," Jim Ward said, impressed. Aunt Caroline picked up on that, too.

"Why aren't you flying them now? And for that matter, what's a Wildcat?"

"The hottest fighter in the world," Jim Ward said firmly, almost with awe.

"We lost all of our planes on December seventh," Charley Galloway said. "At Pearl."

"You were at Pearl Harbor?"

"Yes, Ma'am."

"If we're going to be friends, Charley," Aunt Caroline said, "you're
really going to have to stop calling me 'Ma'am.' "

How the hell could we possibly get to be friends?

Charley saw, in the rearview mirror, that Aunt Caroline was smiling at him. He had a momentary, insane thought: *She's smiling at me
the same way Ensign Mary Agnes O'Malley smiled at me just before she
grabbed my joint in the Ford on the way up to the cabin in the mountains.*

Immediately, he had more sensible thoughts:

*Jesus Christ, I'm letting my imagination run wild. Lieutenant
Ward's Aunt Caroline is a lady, for Christ's sake! Probably a married
one. Not a slut in a Navy uniform. Ward's Aunt Caroline is not about
to grab the joint of a Marine sergeant! And you better watch your
fucking step, pal. You're out of your depth around these people.
Schneider, that starchy little prick, would love to tell Hershberger I got
out of line here. And Hershberger told me what General McInerney said
would happen to me if I so much as farted and embarrassed Marine
Aviation. You know the rules. It's always been the same choice, fucking
or flying. They're giving you a second chance to fly. Don't fuck it up!*

Charley Galloway smiled politely at Ward's Aunt Caroline's reflection in the rearview mirror.

"Yes, Ma'am," he said.

Lieutenant Ward laughed.

Charley took the chance. He winked at her reflection in the mirror.

Aunt Caroline stuck her tongue out at Charley's reflection in the
rearview mirror. Charley's heart jumped again.

(FOUR)

2307 WATTERSON AVENUE
JENKINTOWN, PENNSYLVANIA
2140 HOURS 13 FEBRUARY 1942

Because Lieutenant Jim Ward's mother and dad really went out of
their way to make Sergeant Charley Galloway feel welcome and comfortable, they severely undermined his determination to stay off the
sauce in the process. Mr. Ward, who'd been in the Army in World War
I, made a pitcher of martinis soon after they came in the house. Charley

didn't like martinis, but he had two—the first to be polite and the second because he saw that Lieutenant Schneider didn't like to see him drinking at all.

There was red wine during dinner to go with the steaks; and cognac after dinner, when they went down to the basement game room. Mr. Ward poured generously, and whenever Charley lowered the level in his glass a quarter-inch, he "topped it off."

Jim Ward's girlfriend and a friend of hers for Lieutenant Schneider were both good looking, but Charley thought that neither of them was as classy or as good looking as Aunt Caroline. Wearing a soft, pale blue cashmere sweater and a pleated skirt, she was even more beautiful than he had thought the first moment he saw her. With absolute innocence, they had been sort of paired off, as the only unattached people who would make up a couple.

They sat beside each other at dinner, and several times their knees brushed under the table. Charley didn't think it was his fault. He didn't have much room for his knees, squeezed as he was between Ward's mother and Aunt Caroline.

Aunt Caroline was wearing a perfume he had never smelled before. He had a wild fantasy of burying his face between Aunt Caroline's breasts and inhaling to his heart's content.

He smelled the perfume again in the basement game room when Aunt Caroline bent over, at Mr. Ward's order, to "touch off" his cognac snifter.

"No more for me, please, Ma'am," Charley said.

"I don't think you're having a very good time, Charley Galloway," Aunt Caroline said.

"I'm having a fine time, thank you," Charley said.

"Why don't you dance with Sergeant Galloway, Caroline?" Lieutenant Ward's mother said.

"Would you like to dance with me, Charley?" Aunt Caroline asked.

I'd cut off my left nut for the chance to put my arms around you.

"I'm not a very good dancer," he said.

He saw Lieutenant Schneider looking at him uneasily.

He's afraid I'm going to grab her on the ass, or say something dirty in her ear.

Aunt Caroline spread her arms for him, and Charley stood up.

He put his arms around her and felt the warmth of her back, and then the soft pressure of her breasts against his chest; and the smell of her filled his nostrils; and the primary indicator of his gender popped to attention the moment that Aunt Caroline elected to move a little closer to him.

She was startled; but he was literally immobilized with humiliation.

They stopped dancing. When he glanced nervously around to see if anyone was watching, he saw that they were alone in a small corner of the game room. He wondered how they had gotten here.

"I'm sorry," Charley said.

"I'm not," Aunt Caroline said matter-of-factly, not withdrawing her midsection at all. "I was beginning to think you were a faggot."

"Do I look like a faggot?" Charley asked, shocked, after a moment.

"Not at all, but neither did my husband, and he was—is—as queer as a three-dollar bill," Aunt Caroline said.

"Your husband's queer?"

"My *ex*-husband is," she said.

Her hand had been brushing his neck. She dropped it, caught his hand, and led him back to the main area of the game room. She let go of his hand.

"Charley's too polite to say so," Aunt Caroline said. "But he's bushed and wants to go back to the base."

Very quickly, Lieutenant Schneider said, "Galloway, we'll all be leaving shortly. We can leave together."

"Oh, I know how Charley feels," Aunt Caroline said. "Four's company and five is a crowd, right, Charley?"

"Something like that," Charley said.

"And I've got a busy day tomorrow, too," Aunt Caroline said. "And I drive right past Willow Grove, so I'll take Charley back to the base."

"That's very good of you, Caroline," Charley's dad said. "Then I'll take the boys back later."

"Oh, I can drive them, Mr. Ward," Jim Ward's girlfriend said. "You won't have to."

They were almost at the gate to Willow Grove before Aunt Caroline spoke.

"I'm sorry you didn't have a good time tonight."

"I had a good time."

"You were uncomfortable," she argued. "Because Jim and his friends are officers, and you're not?"

"That didn't bother me," Charley said.

"Then it was me," she said. It was not a question. "You don't have to be afraid of me, Charley."

He didn't reply.

"How old are you, Charley?"

"Twenty-five."

"I'm thirty-three," she said. "Is that what's been bothering you? God, that never happened to me before, the older woman."

"I don't give a damn how old you are," Charley blurted. "You're the most beautiful woman I've ever seen."

Startling him, she pulled the station wagon to the curb and slammed on the brakes. She switched the interior lights on and looked at him intently, into his eyes. After a long moment, her hand came up and lightly stroked his face.

Then she turned from him, switched off the interior lights, and pulled away from the curb. When they reached the gate to the Willow Grove Naval Air Station, she drove right past.

(FIVE)

WILLOW GROVE NAVAL AIR STATION

PHILADELPHIA, PENNSYLVANIA

0205 HOURS 14 FEBRUARY 1942

When Lieutenant Schneider and Ward and their dates returned to Willow Grove Naval Air Station, Dave Schneider asked the MP at the gate how to find the Chief Petty Officer's Quarters. He had the girls drop them off there.

But then he wanted to be absolutely sure that Sergeant Galloway was there and not drunk in some saloon, about to punch out a shore patrolman. After Colonel Hershberger's little speech, Lieutenant Schneider regarded the likelihood of that happenstance as probable.

Technical Sergeant Galloway was not in the Chief Petty Officer's quarters. A chief petty officer, visibly annoyed to be wakened by a pair of damned jarhead lieutenants, gave Schneider directions to the transient enlisted quarters. Technical Sergeant Galloway was not there, either.

The crew chief was. He reported that he had not seen Sergeant Galloway since he had "driven off with you and that knockout blond lady," and that he had no idea where he might be.

"He'll show up," Lieutenant Jim Ward said, without much real conviction. Sergeant Galloway had left the Ward home with Aunt Caroline Ward McNamara at about ten minutes to ten.

"He goddamed well better!" Dave Schneider replied angrily. "I knew damned well we shouldn't have left him out of our sight!"

When Sergeant Galloway did not appear by half past three, Schneider began preparing to make the flight to Lakehurst without Technical Sergeant Galloway. He checked the aircraft books. The redline "engine roughness" comment had been written off: "Sparkplug replaced. Running smoothly."

They made up the flight plan, which was pretty simple. Direct, VFR, off the airways. It was about forty miles from Willow Grove to

Lakehurst. They got a weather briefing, and made sure that the aircraft had been fueled and that a ground auxiliary power unit and a fire extinguisher would be in place. And then they waited.

"Absence without leave," Lieutenant David Schneider declared five minutes later, "is defined as 'failure to repair at the properly appointed time at the proper place in the properly appointed uniform.' If Galloway's absence does not meet those criteria, I'd like to know why not."

"Come on, Dave," Jim Ward said uncomfortably. "What's the 'properly appointed time'? Did you tell him to be here at any specific time? *I* didn't."

"I think," Dave Schneider said, "that the courts will hold that 'the properly appointed time' in this case would be when Sergeant Galloway knew he had to be here in time to fly to Lakehurst, in order to arrive there at the scheduled time. In other words, 0600, less the time to prepare to fly there, and make the flight. Zero four-thirty hours. I'm going to give him until 0430, and then we're going, Jim, without him; and I will report him AWOL when we get there. It might also be called 'missing a scheduled military movement.' The Judge Advocate will have to decide that."

There was no reply from Jim Ward. And Dave Schneider, who was nearly as annoyed with Jim Ward as he was with Sergeant Galloway, looked at him angrily.

"Here he comes, I think," Jim Ward said, pointing out the door.

A wooden-sided Mercury station wagon was pulling into the Base Operations parking lot. Technical Sergeant Galloway was driving. It looked to Dave Schneider as if he was driving with his arm around Aunt Caroline, but he couldn't be absolutely sure.

But he *was* sure that they walked from the station wagon almost to the door of Base Operations with their arms around each other.

And then Sergeant Charley Galloway came through the door, touched his hand to his forehead in a gesture that might just barely be considered a salute, smiled brightly, and said, "Good morning, gentlemen."

"Where have you been, Galloway?" Dave Schneider demanded.

"With me," Aunt Caroline said. "Good morning. Jim, I wanted to talk to you about that."

"About what?"

"Well, on the way here from your house last night, it occurred to me that it was pretty late. And then I got to thinking about all the empty bedrooms in my house, just a few minutes away from here; and then that it hardly made sense for Charley—Sergeant Galloway—to go through the bother of checking into a hotel, or whatever you call it, here on the base. So we went to my house."

"Oh," Jim Ward said lamely.

"So we sat around there for a while, and had a cup of coffee and whatever, and then Charley got a couple of hours' sleep in one of the bedrooms."

"Oh," Jim Ward repeated.

"But then it occurred to me that maybe your mother wouldn't understand," Aunt Caroline went on. "So maybe it would be better if you didn't mention it to her. OK?"

"Sure," Jim Ward said.

While Lieutenant Dave Schneider, in all modesty, did not regard himself as an infallible expert in sexual matters, he did have enough experience to recognize the signs on the female of having just had her bones jumped upon—almost certainly more than once; and the signs of sexual satiation, plus a hickey on the neck, on the male.

Either Jim Ward is too stupid to realize what happened, or he knows that this goddamned sergeant has been screwing his Aunt Caroline and doesn't give a damn.

He realized that whatever he said would be likely to exacerbate the situation, so he said nothing. But at that moment, his fondness for the reserve and enlisted components of the U.S. Marine Corps was at a low ebb.

The crew chief appeared.

"They changed a plug on number-five cylinder," he reported to Galloway, "and she's fueled."

"We filed a flight plan," Jim Ward said, "and weather says nothing significant until tonight, if then."

"Let me see the flight plan," Galloway said, and Schneider handed it to him, aware that by so doing, Galloway had again put on the mantle and authority of pilot-in-command.

Galloway read it carefully.

"OK," he said finally, handing it back to Schneider. "Then let's go. You want to drive, Lieutenant Ward?"

"Yes . . ." Ward replied, thrilled—stopping himself, it was clear to everyone, a split second before adding, "Sir."

"OK. Then you do the preflight," Galloway said. He turned to Aunt Caroline. "Thanks for all the hospitality," he said.

"Oh, don't be silly," she said. "It was my pleasure."

I'll bet it was, Dave Schneider thought bitterly. His sexual status was exactly the opposite of Charley Galloway's. Jim Ward's girlfriend's girlfriend had roused him to exquisite heights of sexual anticipation, allowing him, among other things, to explore the soft wonders of her naked bosom. She had then made it clear that she was not the sort of girl who did *that* on the first date.

His attitude was improved not at all when he noticed that Aunt

Caroline was running her fingers between Charley Galloway's legs while she kissed him chastely on the cheek.

"Jimmy," she then said, "if I drove over to Lakehurst, could I watch you drop the paratroopers?"

"I don't know," Jim Ward said. "What about it, Charley?"

"Why not?" Galloway replied. "Just tell the guard at the gate that you're there to meet the plane from Quantico."

He set that up, too, Dave Schneider realized furiously. *What has that sonofabitch got planned for tonight?*

As they were climbing out of Willow Grove, on a due-east course for Lakehurst, the crew chief, who was wearing a headset, got out of his seat and leaned over Dave Schneider.

"He wants you up forward, Sir," he said.

Schneider walked through the cabin into the cockpit. Jim Ward was in the pilot's seat. Galloway mimed for Dave to put on a headset.

"You still plugged in back there, Nesbit?"

"Yes, Sir."

"OK. Now, since the weather isn't going to be a problem, we will discuss what is going to probably be the problem at Lakehurst. His name is Neville. He's a lieutenant colonel. Just made it. Starchy sonofabitch."

Dave Schneider was about to speak, to point out to Galloway that, aircraft commander or not, he was a sergeant, and sergeants did not refer to a Marine Corps lieutenant colonel as a "starchy sonofabitch." But then Galloway went on, "Colonel Hershberger warned me about him and gave me the game plan. If he proposes something idiotic for us to do—this is a public-relations job, and there's no telling what nutty ideas they'll come up with—I will take the heat for refusing to do it. All you have to say to him is that Hershberger told you I'm the aircraft commander, and the only person who can change that is Hershberger himself. Clear?"

"What makes you so sure, Sergeant Galloway," Schneider asked icily, "that Colonel Neville will propose something . . . idiotic, as you put it?"

"Well, for one thing, they call him 'Fearless,' " Galloway said. "What does that tell you? And for another, Colonel Hershberger wouldn't have given me the game plan if he didn't think it would be necessary. He's dealt with this sonofabitch before."

"I am deeply offended, Galloway, by your repeated references to a senior officer as a sonofabitch!" Dave Schneider said icily.

"Oh, for Christ's sake, Dave!" Jim Ward said, turning to look at Schneider in disgust.

Galloway met Schneider's eyes.

"Lieutenant," he said politely, "you want to go back in the cabin now and strap yourself in? It's getting a little turbulent, and I wouldn't want you to bang your head on a bulkhead or anything."

"This conversation is not over, Sergeant," Dave Schneider said before he took off the headset and went back in the cabin.

VII

(ONE)
LAKEHURST NAVAL AIR STATION
LAKEHURST, NEW JERSEY
0515 HOURS 14 FEBRUARY 1942

L ieutenant Colonel Franklin G. Neville had driven up from Washington in his Auto-Union roadster the day before. He would have preferred to take the train, which was quicker and more comfortable, but he might need the car at Lakehurst because of the press people. It even entered his mind that the press people might want a photograph of him in his Auto-Union. Fast sports cars and parachutists, that sort of thing.

Actually he had hoped to travel to Lakehurst in the R4D from Quantico; it had even occurred to him that he might arrive at Lakehurst by jumping from the R4D just before it landed, to give the press people a sample of what they could expect. But when he'd asked Hershberger whether the R4D could pick him up at Anacostia, Hershberger told him it was already en route to Lakehurst.

When he got to Lakehurst, of course, the airplane wasn't there. And it was only after frantic telephone calls to Colonel Hershberger and Willow Grove that he was able to put his worries about that to rest. Hershberger told him the plane had made a precautionary landing at Willow Grove. And then Willow Grove told him there was nothing wrong with the airplane, and that it was on The Board for an 0430 takeoff.

It was vital for the R4D to arrive. It *had* to be a *Marine* airplane doing the dropping for the press people's cameras—*not* a Navy airplane. Neville would not lie about it, but he had no intention of *volunteering* the information to the press people that Navy pilots, flying Navy R4Ds, actually had done all the dropping of Marine parachutists at Lakehurst so far.

Colonel Neville was convinced that if things went well today, their future would be secure—presuming, of course, that it all resulted in

183

Life magazine doing one of their spreads on Marine parachutists, and that the spread showed Marine parachutists in a good light. On the other hand, if things did not go well, it could be a fatal blow to Vertical Envelopment within the Marine Corps.

Consequently, a lot of thought and planning and effort had gone into preparing everything and everybody for the visit of the *Life* photojournalists to Lakehurst. The public-relations people at Marine Corps headquarters had been enthusiastic and cooperative, which was more than could be said for some other people in the head shed.

The Deputy Chief of Public Relations, Headquarters USMC, a full colonel named Lenihan, had told him that he had assigned the task of publicizing the demonstration jump to Major Jake Dillon, who would head a team of nine public-relations specialists.

"You've heard of Dillon, of course, haven't you, Neville?" Colonel Lenihan asked.

Neville searched his mind, but could come up with no recollection of a major or a captain named Dillon.

"No, Sir, I don't think so."

"Metro-Magnum Pictures," Colonel Lenihan said, significantly.

Metro-Magnum Pictures was a major Hollywood studio.

"Sir?"

"Dillon was Chief of Publicity for Metro-Magnum," Colonel Lenihan said. "He just came on active duty. Amazing fellow. Knows all the movie stars. He introduced me to Bette Davis at the Willard Hotel last night."

"Is that so?" Neville replied. He wondered if this Major Dillon could arrange for a movie star to be present at Lakehurst. Bringing somebody like Bette Davis there, or even Lana Turner or Betty Grable, would get his Para-Marines in the newsreels.

Major Dillon's public relations team had come to Lakehurst two days before. The team had two staff cars, two station wagons, and a jeep. The tiny vehicle, officially called a "Truck, ¼ Ton 4X4," had just entered the service. Neville had seen one in the newsreels—it was actually flying through the air—but this was the first one he had ever seen in person. The team also included four photographers, two still and two motion-picture.

When Colonel Neville mentioned his notion of asking some beauty like Lana Turner to the demonstration, Major Dillon, a stocky, crewcut man in his middle thirties, explained that he didn't think that publicizing the Marine parachutists was the sort of job that required teats and thighs to get good coverage.

"I really don't want to sound as if I'm trying to tell you your job—" Colonel Neville began, convinced that the presence of a gorgeous star would insure a public-relations coup.

"Then don't," Dillon interrupted.

"I'm not sure I like your tone of voice, Major."

"Colonel, I think you're going to have to trust me to do my job. If you don't like the way I'm doing things, you get on the horn and tell Colonel Lenihan. He's the only one I take orders from."

Franklin G. Neville considered the situation quickly, and forced a smile.

"No offense, Major. I was just trying to be helpful."

Later, Major Dillon explained to Neville that the still photographers would back up the *Life* photographers; they'd make the pictures they took available to the magazine in case it missed something. After a seven-day "embargo," the pictures *Life* didn't want would be made available to the press generally.

The motion-picture film would be taken to Washington, processed, reviewed, and after the same seven-day embargo to preserve *Life*'s exclusivity, it would be made available to the various newsreel companies.

Dillon brought with him three Marine "correspondents," two corporals and a sergeant, supervised by a lieutenant. They had prepared a "press background packet," which included a history of parachuting generally, and of Marine parachuting in some detail. There were short biographies of Lieutenant Colonel Neville and Lieutenant Macklin, together with eight-by-ten-inch official glossy photographs of them.

All of this served to impress Colonel Neville with Major Dillon's expertise. It even caused Neville to realize that he would best forget the little flare-up he'd had with the Major over inviting a Hollywood star to the demonstration.

Besides, Colonel Neville was feeling pretty pleased with himself in general. Everything was going well. And everything at the school itself was shipshape. In a remarkably short time, the ex–Parris Island drill instructors had done marvels in establishing standards of discipline and dress that were appropriate for the men Neville considered "the elite of the elite." In Neville's view, if Marines were by definition disciplined military men, Marine parachutists had to strive to reach even higher standards.

The Major, of course, wanted to go a bit further in helping the press than Major Dillon was prepared to go; and the Major had to caution him that in his experience, it was possible to "direct" the attention of the press, especially high-class places like *Life*, only so far.

"If they begin to feel they're getting a snow job," Major Dillon said, "they start looking for what's hidden under the rocks. The best way to deal with them is to make yourself useful but not pushy, and to somehow convince them that what you want publicized is something they discovered themselves."

Major Dillon, his lieutenant, and Lieutenant Macklin were going to meet the press people at the Lakehurst gate when they drove over from New York City. Colonel Neville decided that it would be beneath his dignity as Director of Marine Corps Parachuting to be at the gate himself.

The press people would then be taken to his office, where coffee and doughnuts would be served. Following that, Lieutenant Macklin would brief them. Neville attended a rehearsal briefing, made a few small suggestions, and then approved it.

The press would then be taken on a tour of the school's facilities. The tour would demonstrate how the school was turning Marines into Para-Marines. Neville intended to use that term, even though he had specific directions not to do so. He thought it was honestly descriptive and had a certain flair to it—and he was convinced that once it had appeared in *Life,* it would become part of the language.

Then there would be luncheon in the enlisted men's mess. Neville would have preferred to feed the press people in the officers' club, but Major Jake Dillon argued that the press liked to eat with the troops. In the event, that really posed no problems. Lieutenant Macklin directed the mess sergeant to move up the stuffed-pork chop, mashed-potato, and apple-cobbler supper to the noon meal. The troops could eat the bologna sandwiches originally scheduled for the noon meal at supper, after the press people had gone.

At 1245 hours, the press would be taken to the far side of the airfield to witness their first parachute drop. Chairs, a table, and a coffee thermos would be set up for their convenience. The Marine R4D from Quantico would have been dropping parachutists, four times, during the morning. It would probably have been better to show the press people a jump before they toured the school facilities, so that then they'd know the object of the whole thing; but Neville had insisted on scheduling the demonstration drop for 1245, so that the R4D crew would have a chance to practice.

The drop was all-important. If that didn't go well, nothing else would matter.

Actually, there was to be more than one drop for the press. At 1245, the first drop would show them how it was done. Then the R4D would land, taxi up to the press people, and take on another load of parachutists there. That would give the press people the opportunity to see how quickly and efficiently that was done.

Then the plane would take off, wait for the press people to move over to the actual drop zone, and then drop the second load of parachutists. This would give the press people a chance to see the parachutists landing.

Neville had earlier persuaded the Commanding Officer of Willow

Grove Naval Air Station to let him have a pair of SJ6 Texans, which were low-winged, single-engined, two-seat trainers. While the R4D landed to take on still another load of parachutists, one of the two Texans would have taxied to where it could take aboard a *Life* photographer. The second Texan, carrying a Marine photographer equipped with a motion-picture camera, would by then already be in the air.

He would capture on film the Para-Marines exiting the door of the R4D. Individual prints made from that motion-picture film would be offered to *Life,* if they wanted them. After that the film would be made available to the newsreel companies.

So far as Lieutenant Colonel Neville could see, he and Lieutenant Macklin had covered all the bases.

When, as he asked them to, the Lakehurst Control Tower telephoned to report that a Marine R4D out of Willow Grove had just requested landing permission, he felt the situation was well in hand.

And then things, of course, promptly began to go wrong.

He went out to watch the R4D land. He liked the sight of it, gleaming in the sun of the crisp winter day, with MARINES lettered along the fuselage. He wondered, for the future—it was too late to do anything about it now, of course—if he could arrange to have an aircraft lettered PARA-MARINES. But then, as the aircraft turned off the runway and started to taxi toward the dirigible hangar, he saw that the port engine nacelle and the wing behind it were filthy. Absolutely filthy!

He started walking toward the spot where Lieutenant Macklin had marked out the parking space for the aircraft. He reached it moments after the airplane arrived, and he waited while the pilot turned it around. In order to do that, the pilot had to gun the starboard engine; when he did so, the prop blast caught some snow in its path and blew it all over Neville.

It wasn't clean snow; it was mixed with dirt and parking-area debris, and it soiled Lieutenant Colonel Neville's fresh green uniform. He was not in a very good mood when he stood by the door of the aircraft, waiting for the door to open.

A sergeant in coveralls looked at him curiously, and then dropped a ladder from holes in the bottom of the doorframe. Only then did he finally remember rudimentary military courtesy. Still not wearing suitable headgear, he saluted and said, "Good morning, Colonel."

"Inform the pilot that I would like to see him. I'm Colonel Neville."

"Aye, aye, Sir," the crew chief said, and disappeared inside the aircraft.

In a moment, a good-looking young man appeared; he was wearing a fur-collared jacket with Naval Aviator's wings. Hatless. But he at least looked like a Marine, Neville thought, and acted like one.

"Good morning, Sir," he said, saluting crisply; he held it until Neville returned it. Only then did he start climbing down the ladder. "Are you Colonel Neville, Sir?" Neville nodded. "I was told to report to you, Sir."

"Your airplane is dirty," Colonel Neville said.

"Sir?"

"The port engine nacelle and wing. They're filthy!"

The pilot looked surprised and went to look.

"Don't you have a uniform cap?" Neville called after him.

"Yes, Sir. Sorry, Sir," the pilot said. He took a fore-and-aft cap from the pocket of his leather jacket and put it on.

An enlisted man's cap! That goddamned Hershberger knows how important a mission this is to me and to the Para-Marines, and he's sent me a goddamned Flying Sergeant!

Neville walked to the wing.

"Sir, they drained the oil at Willow Grove. I guess they spilled a little, and it picked up crud from the taxiway and runway," Charley Galloway said.

"Well, have it cleaned up," Neville said. "We don't want *Life*'s readers to think the Marine Corps tolerates filthy aircraft, do we?"

"Aye, aye, Sir."

"Tell me, Sergeant, does Colonel Hershberger routinely send non-coms on missions of this importance?"

"I don't think, Sir, that the Colonel had any qualified officer pilots to send."

That's so much bullshit and we both know it. Goddamn *Hershberger!*

"Colonel, I have two lieutenants on board," Galloway said, adding, "Pilots, I mean."

"Then where are they? I told your crew chief I wanted to speak to the pilot."

"Sir, I'm pilot-in-command."

"How can that be, Sergeant?" Neville said, making what he recognized to be a valiant effort not to jump all over the sergeant. He was a sergeant; he was just doing what he was told. "With officer pilots, how can you be in command?"

"Colonel Hershberger set it up that way, Sir."

"Would you tell the officers I would like a word with them, Sergeant, please?"

"Aye, aye, Sir."

Lieutenants Ward and Schneider were standing on the ground beside the rear door when Charley Galloway went to fetch them.

"Colonel Neville would like to see you, gentlemen," he said loudly, and added softly, "Watch yourselves. He's got his balls in an uproar about something."

Lieutenant Schneider gave Galloway a withering look, and then saluted Colonel Neville as he appeared.

"Which of you is senior?" Neville asked.

"I believe I am, Sir," Jim Ward said.

"Jack," Galloway said to the crew chief, "will you get the crud off the port nacelle and wing?"

"What the hell for?" the crew chief replied. "The minute we start to taxi through this shit, it'll get dirty again."

"Do me a favor, Jack," Galloway said, nodding his head toward Neville. "Do what you can to clean it up."

Neville felt his temper rise. An order had been given. Instead of carrying it out, the recipient had replied "What the hell for?" And instead of immediately correcting the man on the spot, the response was "Do me a favor." And all of this with two commissioned officers watching and doing or saying nothing.

These people, none of them, are Marines. They're goddamned civilians wearing Marine uniforms!

"Then, Lieutenant, may I presume you're in charge of this aircraft?"

"No, Sir."

"'No, Sir'?" Neville echoed incredulously. "Are you qualified to fly this aircraft or not?"

"I'm checked out in the R4D, Sir. Yes, Sir."

"Then, according to the Customs of the Service, since you are the senior officer present," Neville pursued icily, "doesn't it then follow that you are in charge of this aircraft?"

"Sir, Colonel Hershberger, the Chief of Staff, 1st Marine Air Wing—"

"I know who Colonel Hershberger is, Mr. Ward," Neville interrupted him.

"Sir, Colonel Hershberger appointed Sergeant Galloway as pilot-in-command," Ward said uncomfortably.

"I never heard of such a thing!" Neville exploded.

"Sir," Galloway said, "I've got more experience in the R4D than either of these officers. I believe, considering the importance of this mission, that that's what Colonel Hershberger had in mind."

"Are you in the habit of offering your opinions before they're solicited, Sergeant?" Neville flared.

"No, Sir, sorry, Sir."

There was sound of aircraft engines. Charley Galloway's eyes rose involuntarily toward the sky and confirmed what his ears had told him: *Pratt & Whitney Wasp, probably the six-hundred-horse R1340-49. More than one.*

There were two North American Texans in the landing pattern.

"There are my other aircraft," Colonel Neville announced. "Mr. Ward, will you give my compliments to their pilots, and ask them to join me in my office as soon as possible? And bring this officer and the sergeant with you."

(TWO)

The shit, thought Technical Sergeant Charles Galloway, *is about to hit the fan.*

He rose, very reluctantly, to his feet.

"You have a question, Sergeant?" Lieutenant Richard B. Macklin asked. He had just finished explaining, with the help of a blackboard and a pointer, where the Texans would fly relative to the R4D, so that the still and motion-picture photographers could capture the Para-Marines jumping from the R4D's door.

"Sir, that would be dangerous," Charley said.

"Would it, now?" Macklin asked, smiling but sarcastic.

"Sir, one aircraft flying close to the R4D is dangerous enough. Two are too dangerous."

"Would you care to explain your position?"

"Yes, Sir. I'll be flying the R4D—"

"That hasn't been decided yet," Lieutenant Colonel Neville said.

"Sir, *whoever* is flying the R4D will have enough trouble keeping his eye on one Texan. It would impossible to keep an eye on both of them, if they were flying close enough to take pictures."

"And?" Macklin asked, now clearly sarcastic. "Are you suggesting that they would fly into you, Sergeant?" He looked at the two Texan pilots, both lieutenants junior grade, and smiled at them. "I'm sure these officers are skilled enough not to do that."

"I'm more concerned about dropping the paratroops—"

"Para-*Marines,*" Colonel Neville said.

"—into the flight path of one of the Texans," Charley finished.

"That's our concern, Sergeant, isn't it?"

"No, Sir, with respect, it's mine," Charley said.

"Galloway," one of the Naval Aviators said, "believe me, I intend to stay as far away from you as I can."

Galloway smiled at him, but didn't reply.

"I presume your concerns have been put to rest, Sergeant?" Lieutenant Macklin said.

"No, Sir," Charley said. "With respect, they haven't."

"What exactly are you saying, Sergeant?" Colonel Neville asked.

"Sir . . . Sir, if you put two Texans near my aircraft at the same time, I won't drop your paratroops."

"Then we won't burden you with that responsibility, Sergeant. Lieutenant Schneider will pilot the R4D. I can see no necessity for you even to be aboard."

"Sir, Lieutenant Schneider is not qualified to drop parachutists. I won't authorize him to do so."

"Well, we'll just see about that, Sergeant," Neville flared. "We'll see who's authorized to give—or refuse—orders around here. Will you all wait outside, please? Macklin, get Colonel Hershberger on the telephone. Make it a priority call."

Four minutes later, Lieutenant Macklin appeared in the door to Lieutenant Colonel Neville's office and beckoned for Galloway to come inside.

"Colonel Hershberger wishes to speak with you, Sergeant," he said.

Galloway picked up the telephone that was lying on its side on Neville's desk. As he did so, he saw Neville pick up an extension and cover the mouthpiece with his hand.

"Sergeant Galloway, Sir."

"You didn't waste any time stirring things up, did you, Charley?"

"I'm sorry about this, Sir."

"Tell me about the filthy airplane."

"They drained the oil from the port engine at Willow Grove, Sir. They spilled some. It got on the nacelle and wing and picked up crud when I moved the aircraft."

"Tell me about Willow Grove," Hershberger said. "Was that necessary?"

"I was attempting to avoid a storm I had reason to think might be in the Lakehurst area, Sir," Charley said. He stole a quick look at Neville, and saw that he hadn't picked up on that.

"OK," Colonel Hershberger said, after a barely perceptible pause which told Charley that Hershberger had correctly interpreted his reply. "So tell me about the Texans."

"I don't want two of them off my tail when I'm dropping parachutists, Colonel."

"Neville says you refused to fly with *any* Texans around you."

"No, Sir. I can keep my eye on one of them. Two are too dangerous."

"Anything else you want to say?"

"No, Sir."

"Get Colonel Neville back on the line, please, Charley."

"Sir," Charley heard his mouth run away with him, "the Colonel has been on an extension all the time."

"Hang your phone up, then, Charley," Colonel Hershberger said, pleasantly enough, after a moment. "I want a private word with Colonel Neville."

Charley put the telephone back in its cradle and started to leave the office. But Lieutenant Macklin hissed at him that he had not been dismissed. So Charley assumed the at-ease position facing Lieutenant Colonel Neville's desk, and was thus witness to the conversation between Hershberger and Neville. Both sides were audible, because Colonel Hershberger seemed to be talking considerably louder to Colonel Neville than he had to Charley.

Both Lieutenant Macklin and Sergeant Galloway pretended, however, not to hear what Colonel Hershberger said. They both knew that it was an embarrassment for a senior officer to be referred to as a "pompous asshole" by an even more senior officer in the hearing of his subordinates. And it got worse: Colonel Hershberger went on to say— actually shout—that Neville was not only unfit to wear a lieutenant colonel's silver leaf, but the Marine uniform, period. Any officer who calculatedly lied in order to get in trouble a good Marine sergeant who was just obeying his orders was worse than contemptible.

Lieutenant Colonel Neville's replies to Colonel Hershberger were a number of brief and muted "Yes, Sirs."

When Lieutenant Colonel Neville finally hung up, Charley shifted from "at ease" to "parade rest" (head erect, eyes looking six inches above Colonel Neville, hands folded smartly together in the small of the back), and stayed that way for a very long sixty seconds.

Finally, Lieutenant Colonel Neville said, "That will be all, Sergeant. Thank you."

Charley Galloway popped to attention, did a smart about-face, and marched out of Neville's office.

(THREE)

PFC Stephen M. Koffler, USMC, participated in three parachute jumps on the day everybody involved was to remember for a very long time as "the day it happened."

They were his eighth, ninth, and tenth parachute jumps. His first five jumps had been performed as a student. Four of these had been during daylight, and the fifth at night, all onto what Lieutenant Colonel Franklin G. Neville had named Drop Zone Wake, in memory of the heroic Marine defense of Wake Island.

Drop Zone Wake was in fact an area between the runways in the center of the Lakehurst airfield. It was marked out with white tape and little flags on stakes.

According to what he had been told when he began the course, he would be rated as a Marine Parachutist after he had successfully completed his fifth jump, a night drop. That hadn't happened. Lieutenant R. B. Macklin, who was the Deputy Commandant of the Marine Parachute School, had announced that Colonel Neville had decided to postpone the ceremony during which Parachutists' wings would be awarded until 14 February. On that day, a team of civilian (from *Life* magazine) and Marine Corps journalists would be at Lakehurst, Lieutenant Macklin told them; Colonel Neville thought the journalists might want to photograph the ceremony.

Meanwhile, PFC Steve Koffler had changed his mind about wanting to be a Para-Marine. He was now convinced that volunteering for parachute duty was about the dumbest thing he had ever done in his life. *Really* dumb: there was a very good chance that he was going to get killed long before he got near a Japanese soldier.

He had begun to form that opinion long before he made his first jump. For starters, the physical training the trainees had gone through made the physical training at Parris Island look like a walk through a park.

Beginning right after reveille, the trainees had been led on a run around the airfield fence. Somebody said that the distance was 5.2 miles, and he believed it. And they made you run until you literally dropped. As often as Steve Koffler had run around the fence, he had never made it all the way without collapsing, and usually throwing up, too.

The running, he had been told, was to develop the muscles of the lower body. The muscles of the upper body were developed in several ways, primarily by doing push-ups. Steve Koffler had come out of Parris Island proud that he could do forty push-ups. During parachute training, he had once made it to eighty-six before his arms gave out and he collapsed on his face onto the frozen ground.

But there were other upper-body conditioning exercises. Ten trainees at once picked up a log, about ten inches in diameter, and performed various exercises with it. Most of these involved holding the log at arm's length above the head. And there was a device that consisted of pipes inserted through large pieces of wood, sort of a ladder mounted parallel to the ground. One moved along this like Tarzan, swinging by hand from one end to the other. The difference being that all Tarzan wore was sort of a little skirt over sort of a jockstrap; but the Para-Marine trainees wore all their field gear, including helmets, full canteens, and Springfield rifles.

There had also been a lot of classroom work. Steve and the others had a good deal of trouble staying awake in classes. Not only were they pretty worn out from all the upper- and lower-body-developing exercises, but the lesson material was pretty dull, too.

When you fell asleep, the penalty was for one of the sergeants to kick the folding chair out from under you; then you had to run around the building with your Springfield held at arm's length over your head and shout at the top of your lungs, "I will not sleep in class." You did that until the sergeant finally decided you had enough—or you crashed to the frozen earth, unconscious or nauseated.

Steve Loffler would thus remember for the rest of his life a large amount of esoteric military data. For example, he now knew that his parachutes were manufactured by the Switlick Company of the finest silk that money could buy; that his main 'chute was thirty-five feet in diameter and had twenty-eight panels (each of which was made up of a number of smaller pieces, so that if a rip developed, it would spread no farther than the piece where it started); and that his main 'chute would cause him to fall through the air at a speed of approximately twenty feet per second. This meant he would strike the ground at approximately 13.5 miles per hour.

The main 'chute was worn on the back. It was opened upon exiting the airplane by a static line connected to the airplane. This pulled the canopy from its container, and then ripped free. The canopy would then fill with air, with the parachutist suspended beneath it.

If something happened, and the main 'chute did not deploy, there was a second parachute, worn on the chest. This 'chute, which had twenty-four panels of the best silk money could buy, was approximately twenty-four feet in diameter. It would slow the descent of a falling body to approximately twenty-five feet per second, which worked out to approximately seventeen miles per hour. This emergency chute was deployed by pulling a D-ring on the front of the emergency 'chute pack.

If both 'chutes failed, the sergeants told them, there was no problem. Just bring them to the supply sergeant, and he would exchange them for new 'chutes.

Since the human body was not designed to encounter the earth in a sudden stop at thirteen and a half miles per hour (or seventeen, if the emergency 'chute was utilized), the Marine Corps, ever mindful of the welfare of its men, had developed special techniques which permitted the human body to survive under such circumstances.

These were demonstrated; and then, until the correct procedures were automatic, the trainees were permitted to practice them: first they jumped from the back of a moving truck, and later from tall towers, from which they were permitted to leap wearing a parachute harness connected to a cable.

A parachutist's troubles didn't stop once he touched the ground.

Once he touched down, he might encounter another hazard. The parachute canopy, which had safely floated him onto the earth at 13.5— or seventeen—miles per hour, had an unhappy tendency to fill up again if a sudden gust of wind took hold of it. The 'chute would then drag the parachutist along the ground, often on his face, until the gust died down—or the parachutist encountered an immovable object, such as a truck, or possibly a tree.

Because of that hazard, the techniques of "spilling the air from the canopy" had been demonstrated to the trainees, who were then permitted to practice them. This was accomplished by placing the trainee on his back behind the engine of a Navy R4D aircraft. He was strapped into a parachute harness with the parachute canopy stretched out on the ground behind him. The engine of the R4D was then revved up so that prop blast could fill the canopy (held up by an obliging sergeant to facilitate filling). The prop blast dragged the canopy and the Para-Marine trainee across the ground, until he managed to spill the air from it by pulling on the "risers" that connected the harness to the canopy.

Inasmuch as every Para-Marine trainee was a volunteer, it was theoretically possible to un-volunteer—to quit. But PFC Steve Koffler believed that option had been taken away from him as a result of the "extended three-day pass" that had already gotten him in so much trouble with Lieutenant Macklin. If he quit, he would be brought before a court-martial and sentenced to the Naval Prison at Portsmouth.

Several times during his training, he'd actually wondered if Portsmouth—as bad as everybody said it was—could really be worse than Jump School. In fact, on several occasions he'd come close to standing up and screaming at one instructor or another, "Fuck it! I quit! Send me to Portsmouth!"

But for several reasons he had not done that: he believed, for instance, all the horrible things he'd heard about Portsmouth. It was logical that Portsmouth had to be worse than Parris Island and the Jump School; otherwise it would be full of refugees from both places.

The most important reason, however, was Mrs. Dianne Marshall Norman. He went to bed every night thinking of Dianne and all they had done to each other in his bed and on the living room couch, and even on the kitchen table. And he woke up thinking of very much the same thing.

He even called her to mind in the R4D just before he made his first jump. He credited thinking about Dianne not only with keeping him from getting sick to his stomach but from quitting the Para-Marines right there.

He was in love with Dianne. He could not bear the thought of having her learn that he was a craven coward who had not only quit Jump School but had been sentenced to the Naval Prison at Portsmouth. He would rather die—say, from a "cigarette roll." That was what they called it when your 'chute canopy failed to fill with air, and instead twisted around itself until it looked like a cigarette instead of a big mushroom. When that happened, the parachute hardly slowed you down at all, and you went down like a rock, ultimately hitting the ground at something like 125 miles per hour.

And furthermore, once he had won his wings as a Para-Marine, that AWOL business would be forgotten (if he could believe Lieutenant Macklin), and he would have a clean slate. When that happened, he would be eligible for another pass—and maybe even the leave he never got when he graduated from Parris Island. And he could go and be with her.

He had managed to establish communication with her only once since he had started Jump School. On his fourth attempt to call her, he'd gotten her on the phone. The first three times, Bernice or her mother had answered the phone, and he'd just hung up. Dianne seemed glad enough to hear from him, but she told him that her parents and Bernice would not understand his calling her—her having her Leonard and being older and everything—so it would be better if he waited until he got home again, and then maybe they could get together and talk or something, if it could be arranged without making anybody suspicious.

He didn't want to say it on the telephone, but in addition to all those things that went through his mind the last thing at night and the first thing in the morning, he did want to just talk to her. He would tell her that he wasn't just an ordinary PFC anymore but a Para-Marine, which meant that with his jump pay he was making almost twice as much money as a regular PFC. And it also meant that he stood a better chance of making corporal, and maybe even sergeant. And then there was an allowance, called an allotment or something, that he could get if he was married. And he intended to tell her that he would be honored to raise little Joey just as if he was really his kid.

So a great deal hinged on his getting through Jump School, and having his slate wiped clean, and getting at least a pass so that he could go see her.

But then they didn't hold the graduation ceremony because of the people coming from *Life* magazine. And when he went to the First Sergeant and reminded him about what Lieutenant Macklin had said about getting the slate wiped clean if he kept his nose clean and got through Jump School, the First Sergeant told him that so far as he was concerned, his slate was wiped clean. But when Steve asked about a pass, the First Sergeant said that would have to wait until the *Life* magazine people had come and gone. In the meantime there would be no free time.

Over the days before they arrived, there were several pre-inspections; and then the last inspection itself, conducted by Lieutenant Macklin, to make sure everything would be shipshape.

On the morning of 14 February, they were marched out to a Marine R4D. It was the first one Steve had ever seen; he didn't even know the Marines had R4Ds. Then they 'chuted up and took off just as usual. But this time, instead of just making a swing around the field and then dropping the parachutists, the pilot flew the airplane out to the ocean, and then over the beach from Asbury Park down to Point Pleasant, and then back and forth several times, until he apparently got the word on the radio and flew back to Lakehurst. Then they jumped.

That was Jump Six.

The Marine R4D landed while Steve was still folding up his parachute; and he watched it take on another load of Para-Marines while he was walking back to the staging area after the truck had come and taken up the 'chutes.

As he and the others were 'chuting up again, he saw that stick of Para-Marines jump. The R4D landed immediately, and they loaded aboard and jumped almost immediately.

Steve decided that what they were doing was showing the people from *Life* magazine how it was done.

That was Jump Seven. It was just like Jump Six, except that the guy leading the stick, a corporal, sprained his ankle because he landed on the concrete runway instead of on the grassy area. So he was not going to be able to jump again for a while.

That made Steve lead man in the stick for Jump Eight. He wasn't sure if he would have the balls to jump first. If you were anywhere but lead man in the stick, it was automatic, and you didn't have to think about it. But in the end he decided that if he hesitated, the jumpmaster would just shove him out the door.

Another trainee was added to the stick at the end. He would jump last.

And then, after the pilot had already restarted the left-hand engine on the R4D, something very unusual happened. A face in a helmet appeared at the door and ordered the crew chief to put the ladder down. And then Lieutenant Colonel Franklin G. Neville himself climbed into the airplane, wearing a set of coveralls. And his parachutes. And all of his field gear—except that he had a Thompson submachine gun instead of a Springfield rifle.

And then they took off.

Colonel Neville pulled Steve's head close to him and shouted in his ear.

"I'm going to jump with you," he said. "You just carry on as usual."

"Aye, aye, Sir!" Steve shouted back.

This time, instead of just circling the field and jumping the Para-Marines, the R4D flew south. From where Steve was sitting, he couldn't see much, but he became aware that there was a little airplane out there, too, flying close to the R4D.

During one of the brief glimpses he got of it, he saw that there was a man in the backseat with a camera.

Colonel Neville apparently knew all about it. He was standing in the door, hanging onto the jamb, making what looked like "come closer" signs to the pilot.

And then they were making their approach to Landing Zone Wake.

The commands now came quickly.

"Stand up."

"Hook up."

"Check your equipment."

"Stand in the door."

There were two little lights mounted on the aircraft bulkhead by the door. One was red and the other was green. The red one came on when you started getting ready to jump. The green one came on when the pilot told the jumpmaster to start the jumping.

Steve stood by the door, watching the red light.

"One minute!" the jumpmaster shouted in his ear.

Steve nodded his understanding.

He thought of Dianne Marshall Norman's breasts, and how their nipples stood up.

The light turned green.

Somebody pushed him out of the way and dove out the door. Steve saw that the little airplane was really close, and that the man in the backseat had what looked like a movie camera in his hands. The jumpmaster shouted "Go!" in his ear and pushed him out the door.

It all happened pretty quickly, maybe in two seconds, no more. As Steve went out the door he saw that something was bent around what he thought of as "the little wing on the back" of the R4D.

And then, as he fell beneath it to the end of the static line and he could hear the main 'chute slither out, and as he steeled himself for the opening shock, he realized that what he had seen wrapped around the little wing on the back of the R4D was a man. And then, as his canopy filled and the harness knocked the breath out of him, he realized that the man must be Lieutenant Colonel Neville.

And then he looked below him.

And saw a man's body falling, just falling, toward the earth. There was no main 'chute, and no emergency chest 'chute. The body just fell to the ground and seemed to bounce a little, and then just lay there.

PFC Stephen M. Koffler, USMC, lost control of his bowels.

And then the ground was there, and he prepared to land as he had been taught; and he landed, and rolled as he had been taught. And then he got to his feet. He was immediately knocked onto his face as the canopy filled with a gust of wind and dragged him across the hard, snow-encrusted earth.

He had been taught how to deal with the situation, and dealt with it. He spilled the air from the canopy by manipulating the risers, and then he slipped out of the harness.

He stood up and rather numbly began to gather the parachute to him. He knew the truck would appear to pick it up.

And then he saw the body of Lieutenant Colonel Franklin G. Neville, not fifteen feet away. It looked distorted, like a half-melted wax doll.

He was drawn to it. Still clutching his parachute harness to his chest, he walked over to it and looked down at it.

A photographer, one of the civilians, came running up, and a flashbulb went off.

Oh, shit! PFC Steve Koffler thought. *What are they going to do to me when they find out I've shit my pants?*

Another flashbulb went off, and Steve gave the photographer a dirty look. It didn't seem to bother him.

"What's your name, Kid?" he asked.

"Fuck you," Steve said.

"That's PFC Koffler, Stephen M.," a familiar voice said. Steve turned his head and saw that it was Lieutenant Macklin. "He is, understandably I think, a little upset."

"I wonder why," the photographer said, and took Steve's picture again.

(FOUR)

LAKEHURST NAVAL AIR STATION
LAKEHURST, NEW JERSEY
1425 HOURS 14 FEBRUARY 1942

Major Jake Dillon had returned to active duty with the U.S. Marine Corps sixty days previously. The last time he had worn a Marine uniform was in Shanghai, China, with the 4th Marines in 1934. Major Dillon had then been a sergeant.

In 1933, while watching an adapted-from-a-novel adventure motion picture in Shanghai, it had occurred to Sergeant Dillon that it was a bullshit story and that he could easily write a better one. Blissfully unaware of the difficulties facing a first-time novelist, he set out to do so. It was a melodrama; its hero, a Marine sergeant, rescued a lovely Chinese maiden from a fate worse than death in a Shanghai brothel. Dillon had no trouble calling forth from memory the description of that establishment.

Next, Dillon's hero slaughtered Chinese evildoers left and right; there was a chase sequence on horseback; and the book ended with the sergeant turning the girl back over to her grateful family and then returning to his Marine duties. Dillon wrote the novel at night on the company clerk's typewriter. It took him two months. He mailed it off, and was not at all surprised two months after that when a contract, offering an advance of five hundred dollars, arrived in Shanghai.

The book was published, and it sold less than two thousand copies. But it was optioned, and then purchased, by a major motion-picture studio in Los Angeles. The studio saw in it a vehicle for a very handsome but none-too-bright actor they had under contract. With all the fight and chase scenes, plus a lot attention devoted to the Chinese girl having her clothing ripped off, it was believed they could get the handsome actor through the production without him appearing to be as dull-witted as he was.

It was necessary to find a suitable vehicle for the handsome young man because he was a very close friend of a very successful producer. More precisely, he was sharing the producer's bed in an antebellum-style mansion in Holmby Hills.

Sergeant Dillon was paid five thousand dollars for the motion-picture rights to his novel, an enormous sum in 1934. And he had, he thought, discovered the goose that laid the golden eggs. If he could write one novel in two months, he could write six novels a year. And at $5,500 per, that was as much money as the Major General Commandant of the Marine Corps made.

He did not ship over when his enlistment ran out. Instead, he was returned to the United States aboard the naval transport USS *Chaumont*, and honorably discharged in San Diego.

Since he was so close to Los Angeles, and his film was in production there, he went to Hollywood.

When he visited the set, the Handsome Young Actor greeted him warmly, expressed great admiration for his literary talent, and invited him for dinner at his little place in Malibu.

That night, in the beachfront cottage, as Dillon was wondering if he could gracefully reject the pansy's advances (and if he could not, how that might affect his literary career), the Producer appeared.

Words were exchanged between the Producer and the Handsome Young Actor, primarily allegations of infidelity. The exchange quickly accelerated out of control, ending when the Producer slapped the Handsome Young Actor and the Handsome Young Actor shoved the Producer through a plate-glass door opening on a balcony over the beach.

A shard of heavy plate glass fell from the top of the doorframe, severely cutting the Producer's right arm. Dillon noted with horror the pulsing flow of arterial blood. And then he saw the Handsome Young Actor, his face contorted with rage, advancing on the fallen, bleeding Producer with a fireplace poker in his hand, showing every intention of finishing him off with it.

Without really thinking about it, Dillon took the Handsome Young Actor out of action, by kicking him repeatedly in the testicles. (The story, when it later, inevitably, made the rounds in Hollywood, was that ex-Marine Dillon had floored him with a single, well-placed blow of his fist.) Then he put a tourniquet on the Producer's arm and announced that they needed an ambulance.

The Producer told him they couldn't do that. The police would become involved. The story would get out. He would lose his job.

Dillon was even then not unaccustomed to developing credible story lines to explain awkward or even illegal circumstances on short notice, prior to the imminent arrival of the authorities.

"We were fixing the door. It was out of the track, and it slipped," he said.

"But what was I doing here, *with him?*" the Producer asked somewhat hysterically, obviously more concerned with his public image than with losing his arm, or even his life.

"You brought me out here to introduce me to the star of my movie," Dillon replied, reaching for the telephone. "Where do I tell the cops we are?"

Two days later, at the Producer's request, Dillon called upon him at Cedars of Lebanon Hospital.

The Producer was no longer hysterical. And he was grateful. His doctor had told him that if Dillon hadn't applied the tourniquet when he did, he would almost certainly have bled to death before the police arrived.

"I am very grateful to you, Mr. Dillon," the Producer said.

"Call me Jake," Dillon said. "That's my middle name. Jacob."

"Jake, then. And I want to repay you in some small way . . ."

"Forget it."

"Please hear me out."

"Shoot."

"What are your plans, now that you've left the Marine Corps? Do you mind my asking?"

"Well, I thought I'd do another couple of quick novels, put a little money in the bank for a rainy day . . ."

"And if you can't sell your next novel?"

The Producer had had a copy of *Malloy and the Maiden* by H. J. Dillon, sent to his hospital room. It was arguably the worst novel he had ever read; and as a major film producer, he had more experience with really bad novels than most people. He couldn't imagine why a publisher had ever acquired it, except possibly that it had been bought by an editor who knew he was about to be fired and wanted to stick it to his employers.

Dillon had not considered that possibility. But looking at the Producer now, he saw that it was not just possible but probable.

"I don't know."

"Are you open to suggestion?"

"Shoot."

"You obviously have a way with words, and you have proven your ability to deal with potentially awkward situations. In my mind, that adds up to public relations."

"Excuse me?"

"Public relations," the Producer explained. "Making the studio, and our actors, and our films, look as good to the public as they possibly can."

"Oh."

"The man who runs our studio public relations is a friend of mine. I'm sure that he would be interested in having someone of your demonstrated talents."

Dillon thought it over for a moment.

"How much would something like that pay?"

"About five hundred to start, I'd say. And there would be time, I'm sure, for you to continue with your writing."

"Everything seems so expensive here. After China, I mean. Can you make do around here on five hundred a month?"

"You can, but I'm talking about five hundred a week, Jake."

Jake Dillon then looked at the Producer very carefully.

"No strings?"

The Producer, after a moment, caught Jake's meaning. "No, Jake, no strings. I would really much rather have you as a friend than a lover."

Jake Dillon found his natural home in motion-picture public relations. He quickly became known as the only man who was ever able to get "the world's most famous actor" out of the teenaged Mexican girls on his sailboat, and then off the sailboat and back to Hollywood sober— and to get him there on time to start shooting—and in a relatively

cooperative mood. A half-dozen of his more experienced peers had
tried to do all of that, and had failed to pull him off even one of the
chiquitas.

Actresses trusted him. If Jake showed up at some party and told you
there was an early call tomorrow and it was time to drink up and tuck
it in, you knew he had your interests at heart and not just the fucking
studio's. So you went home. Sometimes with Jake.

And the Producer, who found that Jake offered a comforting shoulder to weep on when his romances went sour, made it known among
those of similar persuasion, a powerful group in Hollywood, that Jake
was his best "straight" friend.

And he gradually came to be known as a man with a rare insight
into how a motion picture or an actor should be publicized. In other
words, his nerve endings told him what he could get printed in newspapers, or broadcast over the radio, and what would be thrown away.

Within two years, his pay tripled. And he began to run around not
only with stuntmen and grips but also with a small group of the big-time
actors. He fished with Duke Wayne, hunted with Clark Gable, played
poker with David Niven, and with all three of them he drank and
jumped on the bones of an astonishing number of ladies.

And he could often be found—puffing on his cigar and sipping at
a cool beer—in screening rooms when daily rushes and rough cuts were
screened. The stars of these opera invited him there. And they solicited
his opinions, and he gave them. Sometimes his judgments were not
flattering.

But, as the head of the studio said, "Jake is a walking public-opinion
poll. He knows what the ticket buyers will like, and what they won't."

Jake Dillon's opinions of a story, a treatment, a screenplay, rushes,
rough cuts, and final cuts were solicited and respected.

The only thing he failed to do, because he refused to do it, was talk
some sense to David Niven. Niven was clearly on the way to superstar-
dom. Which meant that very few people in Hollywood could understand why he was about to throw his career down the toilet. He was
returning to England and again putting on the uniform of an officer of
His Britannic Majesty's Royal Army.

"You guys don't understand," Dillon told the head of Niven's studio. "David went to Sandhurst—that's like our West Point. He's an old
soldier, and somebody blew the fucking bugle. He had to go."

With Europe at war, Hollywood's attention turned to making war
movies. One of them dealt with the United States Marine Corps,
specifically with Marine fighter pilots. Headquarters USMC sent a full
colonel to Los Angeles to serve as technical adviser. Ex-Marine Dillon
was charged with keeping the Colonel happy.

Their relationship was a little awkward at first, for both of them were aware that the last time they'd met, Jake Dillon had been in Shanghai wearing sergeant's stripes and standing at attention for the Colonel's inspection. But the relationship quickly grew into a genuine friendship. This was based in large part on the Colonel's realization that Jake was as determined as he was that the motion picture would reflect well on the Corps.

There was an element of masculine camaraderie in it, too. The Colonel took aboard a load one night at Jake's house in Malibu and confessed that he couldn't get it up anymore—not after his wife of twenty-two years had left him for a doctor at Johns Hopkins. Dillon was more than sympathetic; he arranged for the Colonel to meet a lady the Colonel had previously seen only on the Silver Screen. The lady owed Jake Dillon a great big favor, and she was more than happy to discharge it the way Dillon had in mind. She did wonders vis-à-vis restoring the Colonel's lost virility.

And Jake took a load aboard and confessed to the Colonel that he'd felt like a feather merchant when he'd put David Niven on the Broadway Limited on his way to England. He was as much a Marine as Niven was a soldier. And Niven had gone back in. And here he was, sitting with his thumb up his ass in Malibu, with the country about to go to war.

When the Colonel returned to Washington, he wrote a Memorandum for the Record to the Director of Personnel, stating his belief that in the event of war, the Corps was going to require the services of highly qualified public-relations officers; that he had recently, in the course of his duties, encountered a man who more than met the highest criteria for such service; that he could be induced to accept a reserve commission as a captain; and that he believed a commission as a reserve captain should be offered to him, notwithstanding the fact that the man did not meet the standard educational and other criteria for such a commission.

The Colonel was two weeks later summoned to the office of the Deputy Commandant, USMC, who tossed his Memorandum for the Record at him.

"I know you and Colonel Limell don't get along," the Deputy Commandant said. "I think that's why he sent this to me—to make you look like a fool. Can you really justify giving this ex-sergeant a captain's commission, or did you lose your marbles out in Hollywood?"

The Colonel made his points. Though he wasn't sure how well they were being received, he did see the Deputy Commandant's eyes widen when he told him how much money Jake Dillon was paid (it was more than twice as much as the Major General Commandant got); and he took some small comfort that he was neither interrupted nor dismissed.

When he was finished, the Deputy Commandant looked at the

Colonel thoughtfully for a very long thirty seconds. Then he grunted and reached for his telephone.

"Colonel Limell, about this Hollywood press agent, the one who was a sergeant with the 4th Marines? Offer him a majority."

Then, surprising the Colonel yet again, Jake Dillon was not overwhelmed with gratitude when he was offered a Marine Majority.

"I'm not qualified to be a major. Jesus Christ! I was thinking about maybe a staff sergeant. Maybe even a gunnery sergeant. But a major? No way."

The Colonel argued unsuccessfully for thirty minutes that the greatest contribution Jake Dillon could make to the Corps was as a public-relations officer, and that to do that well, he had to carry the rank of a field-grade officer on his collar points. The best he was able to do was to get Jake to agree to come to Washington and talk it over.

"I'll put you up, Jake."

"That's nice, but we keep a suite in the Willard," Jake said. "I'll stay there. I'll catch a plane this afternoon, and call you when I get there."

Jake called two days later, at three in the afternoon, as soon as he got into the studio's suite in the Willard. The Colonel, who had a certain sense of public relations himself, immediately called the Deputy Commandant.

"Sir, Mr. Dillon is in Washington."

"That's the press-agent sergeant?"

"Yes, Sir."

"I want to talk to him."

"Yes, Sir, I thought you might want to. Sir, I understand you're taking the retreat ceremony at Eighth and Eye today?"

"Splendid," the Deputy Commandant said, taking the Colonel's meaning. "I'll have my aide arrange two seats for you in the reviewing stand."

The Formal Retreat Ceremony (the lowering of the colors at sunset) is held at the Marine Barracks at Eighth and Eye Streets, Southeast, in the District of Columbia. The Marine Band, in dress blues, plays the Marine Hymn, while impeccably uniformed Marines march with incredible precision past the reviewing stand. The ceremony has brought tears to the eyes of thousands of pacifists and cynics.

Its effect on a former 4th Marines sergeant was predictable: When the Color Guard marched past, Jake Dillon was standing at attention with his hand on his heart. And tears formed in his eyes.

When the ceremony was over, and the Marine Band was marching off the field to the tic-tic of drum sticks on drum rims, a first lieutenant in dress blues walked up to him.

"Sir, the Deputy Commandant would like a word with you."

"Dillon?" the Deputy Commandant of the U.S. Marine Corps, in his dress blues, said to former Sergeant Dillon, offering him his hand.

"Yes, Sir."

"Once a Marine, always a Marine. Welcome back aboard, Major."

"Thank you, Sir."

"When you get settled, call my aide. I want a long talk with you."

"Aye, aye, Sir."

Jake Dillon never again raised the question of his lack of qualifications to be a major. If the Deputy Commandant of the Corps thought he could hack it, who was he to ask questions?

In the Corps, you say, "Aye, aye, Sir," and do what you're told to the best of your ability.

When Major Dillon reported two weeks later for duty at Headquarters USMC, he was assigned as Officer-in-Charge, Special Projects, Public Affairs Office.

The visit of the team of *Life* photojournalists to the Parachute School at Lakehurst Naval Air Station was a Special Project. And from the moment Major Jake Dillon met Lieutenant Colonel Franklin G. Neville, he knew in his bones that something or someone was going to fuck it up.

He couldn't understand the feeling, but he trusted it. He anticipated no trouble with the people from *Life*. He knew a couple of them; and more important, he knew their bosses. And the story itself looked like a natural. Marines were always good copy, and parachutists were always good copy, and here he had both. The confirmation of that came when he called a guy he knew at *Life* and learned that unless something else came along of greater importance, and providing that the pictures worked out, they were scheduling the Para-Marines as the cover story, two issues down the pike.

"Bill, do me a favor, forget you ever heard the phrase 'Para-Marines.' I don't know why, but it pisses off a lot of the important brass."

The Managing Editor of *Life* chuckled.

"OK. So what do I call them?"

"Marine Parachutists, please."

"Marine Parachutists it is. You going to be at Lakehurst?"

"Sure."

"What I sort of have in mind, Jake, is a nice clean-cut kid hanging from a parachute. For the cover, I mean."

"You got him. I'll have a dozen for you to choose from."

"Excuse me, Major," Lieutenant R. B. Macklin said to Major Homer J. Dillon, "may I have a word with you, Sir?"

Jake Dillon gave Lieutenant Macklin an impatient look, shrugged his shoulders, and jerked his thumb toward the door.

God only knows what this horse's ass wants.

"This is far enough," Major Jake Dillon said to Lieutenant R. B. Macklin, once they were out of earshot of the people from *Life*. "What's on your mind?"

"Sir, I thought I had best bring you up to date on PFC Koffler."

"OK. What about him?"

"I have confined him to barracks. My adjutant is drawing up the court-martial charges. He believes that 'conduct prejudicial to good order and discipline' is the appropriate charge."

"What the *hell* are you talking about?"

"The Major is aware that Koffler . . . that Koffler said 'Fuck you' to the gentleman from *Life* when he asked him what his name was?"

"I wasn't, but so what?"

"Right there on the Landing Zone, as he stood over Colonel Neville's body. I was there, Sir."

"I repeat, so what?"

"Well, Sir, we just can't let something like that pass."

"Jesus H. Christ!" Jake Dillon flared. "Now listen to me, Macklin. What you're going to do, Lieutenant, is tell your adjutant to take his goddamned court-martial charges out of his goddamned typewriter and put in a fresh sheet of paper. And on that sheet of paper, backdated to day before yesterday, he will type out an order promoting PFC Koffler to corporal."

"Sir, I don't understand."

"That doesn't surprise me at all, Lieutenant. Just do it. I want to see that kid here in thirty minutes. Showered and shaved, in a fresh uniform, with his parachute wings on his chest and corporal's stripes on his sleeves. Those parachutists' boots, too. I just talked to AP. They saw the picture of him that *Life* took, and they're coming down here to interview him. And that Flying Sergeant who was flying the airplane. If AP's coming, UP and INS won't be far behind. Get the picture?"

"Sir, technically," Macklin said, uneasily but doggedly, "he's not entitled to wear either boots or wings. We haven't had the graduation ceremony. Colonel Neville delayed it for the *Life* people, and after . . . what happened . . . I postponed it indefinitely."

"Parachute boots, wings, and corporal's stripes, Lieutenant," Jake Dillon said icily. "Here. In thirty minutes."

"Aye, aye, Sir," Lieutenant Macklin said.

(FIVE)

"I think that's about enough, fellas," Major Jake Dillon said, rising to his feet. "Sergeant Galloway and Corporal Koffler have had a rough day. I think we ought to let them go."

There were the expected mumbles of discontent from the press, but they started to fold up their notebooks and get to their feet. The interview was over.

Jake Dillon was pleased that he had thought about putting Sergeant Galloway in the press conference. Galloway had handled himself well, even better than Dillon had hoped for. And Corporal Koffler, bless his little heart, was dumber than dog shit; if Galloway hadn't been there, that would have come out.

And the press seemed to have bought the story line that it was a tragic accident, something that just happened to a fine officer who was undergoing training with his men.

But Jake Dillon knew that when two or three are gathered together in the name of honest journalism, one of them will be a sonofabitch determined to find the maggots under the rock, even if he has to put them there himself. In this case, he wouldn't have to look far.

Jake Dillon had formed his own unvarnished version of the truth vis-à-vis the tragic death of Lieutenant Colonel Franklin G. Neville, USMC, based on what he had heard from the jumpmaster, from Corporal Steve Koffler, and on his own previous observations of Lieutenant Colonel Franklin G. Neville.

Neville had been bitten by the publicity bug. When the guys from *Life* had shown very little interest in Neville himself, preferring instead to devote their attention to young enlisted men, it had really gotten to him. The whole thing was his idea, and nobody gave a damn.

And so he flipped. He was determined to have his picture in *Life*, and that meant he had to put himself in a position where the photographers could not ignore him. And he figured out that would be when they were shooting the parachutists exiting the aircraft. If he was first man out the door, they would have to take his picture, and they couldn't edit him out.

So he pushed out of the way the kid Koffler, who was supposed to be first man out, and jumped. And something went wrong. Instead of being in center frame, he found himself wrapped around the horizontal stabilizer. That either killed him straight off, or it left him unconscious. Either way, he couldn't pull the D-ring on his emergency 'chute.

Jake Dillon didn't want that story to come out. It would hurt the widow, and would hurt the Corps.

"I would like a word with you, Sergeant, please," Jake Dillon called after Galloway as Galloway and Koffler left the room. "You and Corporal Koffler."

When he had them alone and out of earshot, he said, "OK. Where are you two headed?"

"Sir," Sergeant Galloway said, "I understand that General McInerney's coming up here in the morning. I've been told to make myself available to him for that."

"I mean now, tonight. I know about the General."

"Well, Sir, I thought I would like to get off the base. Find a room somewhere."

"Good. Go now, and take Corporal Koffler with you. The one thing I don't want you to do is talk to the press. Period. Under any circumstances. Consider that an order."

"Aye, aye, Sir," Charley Galloway said. A split second later, Steve parroted him.

"I've talked to General McInerney," Major Dillon went on. "Here's what's happening. Colonel Neville's body is to be taken to the Brooklyn Navy Yard for an autopsy. Then it will be put in a casket and brought back here. After the inquiry tomorrow morning, you and Koffler will take it to Washington. You will travel with General McInerney and an honor guard of the parachutists. Colonel Neville will be buried in Arlington. You and Koffler will be pallbearers."

"Yes, Sir," Sergeant Galloway said.

Jake Dillon thought he could bleed the story for a little more, with pictures of the honor guard and the flag-draped casket. And if they were still burying people in Arlington with the horse-drawn artillery caisson, maybe a shot of that and the firing squad, too. With a little bit of luck, he could get a two-, three-minute film sequence tied together for the newsreels. But that was none of Galloway's or Koffler's business, so he didn't mention it.

"I don't care where you guys go, or what you do. But I will have your ass if you either talk to the press or get shit-faced and make asses of yourselves. Do I have to make it plainer than that?"

"No, Sir," they said, together.

Jake Dillon put his hand in his pocket.

"You need some money, either of you?"

"No, Sir," they replied.

"OK. I want you back here at seven in the morning."

"Get in the backseat," Technical Sergeant Charles Galloway ordered Corporal Stephen Koffler as they approached the Mercury station wagon.

Galloway got in the front beside Mrs. Caroline Ward McNamara.

"Now what?" Aunt Caroline said, touching Charley's hand.

"I'm sorry you had to wait like this," Charley said. "Caroline, this is Corporal Steve Koffler. Koffler, this is Mrs. McNamara."

"Hello," Aunt Caroline said, looking at Steve. "I repeat, now what?"

"I have been ordered to keep an eye on Corporal Koffler overnight, and to bring him back here at 0700 in the morning."

"Oh," Aunt Caroline said.

"We are going to find a hotel room—rooms—someplace," Charley said. "I wondered how that would fit in with your plans."

"Well, it's already dark, and I hate to drive at night, with the snow and all. Maybe I should think about getting a hotel room myself. Where's Jim and the other lieutenant?"

"I understand Major Dillon sent for them. Maybe it would be better if we got off the base before he's finished with them. I'm a little afraid that Major Dillon will tell one of them to keep an eye on me and Koffler."

"Oh, I see what you mean," Aunt Caroline said. She started the engine and headed for the gate.

"Just how close an eye do you have to keep on the corporal?" Aunt Caroline asked.

"I think an adjacent room would be close enough."

"Adjacent but not adjoining, you mean?" Aunt Caroline said.

"Exactly."

"Excuse me, Sergeant?" Corporal Koffler said.

"What, Koffler?"

"Sergeant, I live in East Orange. Do you suppose it would be all right if I went home?"

"You live where?"

"East Orange. It's right next to Newark."

"Oh, really?" Aunt Caroline said. "Maybe you could find a hotel in Newark for yourself, and Corporal Koffler could spend the night with his family."

"The Essex House Hotel's in Newark," Steve offered helpfully. "I never stayed there, but I hear it's real nice. You both probably could get rooms there."

"Now there's a thought," Aunt Caroline said innocently.

"But I'm supposed to keep an eye on him," Charley Galloway said. "If he went home alone, and Major Dillon or Lieutenant Ward or Lieutenant Schneider ever heard about it, we'd all be in trouble."

"Well, we don't have to tell them, do we?" Steve asked shrewdly.

"No, I guess we wouldn't really have to," Charley Galloway said. "Could I trust you to stay out of trouble, Koffler, and be waiting for me at, say, 0530, outside your house in the morning?"

"It's an apartment house," Steve said. "Sure, you could trust me, Sergeant. I'd really like to see my girl, Sergeant."

"You'd better be careful about that, Koffler. Women have been known to suffer uncontrollable sexual frenzies at the mere sight of a Marine in uniform. That could lead to trouble."

Aunt Caroline giggled, and Charley Galloway yelped in pain, as if someone had dug fingernails into the soft flesh of his upper thigh.

"My girl won't get me in trouble, Sergeant," Steve said.

"OK. Then we'll do it. You give Mrs. McNamara directions to your house."

On the outskirts of Newark, Aunt Caroline pulled into a gasoline station. As the attendant filled the tank and she visited the rest room, Charley Galloway saw a rack of newspapers.

"I'll be damned," he said, and went to the rack and bought two copies of the *Newark Evening News*.

He walked back to the station wagon and handed one to Steve Koffler.

"You're a famous man now, Koffler," he said. "Try not to let it go to your head."

There was a three-column picture in the center of the front page. It showed Steve Koffler holding the risers and shroud lines of his parachute against his chest; he was looking down at the body of Lieutenant Colonel Franklin G. Neville. Tears were visible on his cheeks.

Over the picture was a headline, EVEN THE TOUGH CAN WEEP, and below it was a caption: "Cpl. Stephen Koffler, of East Orange, a member of the elite U.S. Marine Corps Parachute Force, weeps as he looks at the body of his commanding officer, Lt. Col. F. G. Neville, who fell to his death moments before when his parachute failed to open during training exercises at the Lakehurst Naval Air Station this morning. Koffler was second man in the 'stick' jumping from the Marine airplane, behind Col. Neville. [Associated Press Photograph from *Life*]"

On the way from the gasoline station to 121 Park Avenue, East Orange, Corporal Stephen Koffler of the "elite U.S. Marine Corps Parachute Force" (*Jesus Christ, that sounds great!*) ran over several times in his mind the sequence of events that would occur once he got home.

Dianne would have seen the *Newark Evening News*. Everybody read it. She would see his picture. She would wonder, naturally, when she would see him again. And she would more than likely realize that the reason he had been unable to come to see her was that he was busy with his duties with the Elite Marine Corps Parachute Force.

He would appear at her door. She would answer it. Her family would be gone somewhere. She would look into his eyes. They would embrace. Her tongue would slip into his mouth. She would break away.

"I saw your picture in the paper," she would say. "Was it just awful?"

And he would say, "No. Not really. You have to expect that sort of thing."

And they would kiss again, and she would slip her tongue in his mouth again. And this time he would put his hand up under her sweater, or maybe down the back of her skirt.

And she would say, "Not here," but she wouldn't mean it, and he would take her into her living room and do it to her on the couch. Or maybe even into her bedroom—and do it to her in her own bed.

Just by way of saying hello.

"Let's get out of here," he would say. "Where we can really be alone."

"But where could we go?" she would ask.

"How about the Essex House?"

And she would say, "The Essex House? Could we get a room in the *Essex House*?"

And he would say, "Sure, we can. I'm a corporal on jump pay."

He wasn't born yesterday. Sergeant Galloway and the blond lady in the station wagon were going to shack up in the Essex House. That was just so much bullshit about getting two rooms. And if Sergeant Galloway was going to screw this blond lady in the Essex House, why shouldn't he screw Dianne there?

And Dianne would say, "But what about Leonard?"

And he would say "Fuck Leonard. You're through with that candy-ass civilian."

No. He didn't want to talk like that around Dianne. He would say, "To hell with Leonard. You're through with that civilian."

And once he got her into the Essex House and they'd done it a couple of times more, he would tell her that it didn't matter that she was a couple of years older than he was, he was psychologically older than the age on his birth certificate. He was a Marine, for Christ's sake, a member of the Elite Marine Corps Parachute Force. What he had done, and what he had seen, made him at least as old as Leonard, psychologically speaking.

It did not work out quite the way Steve envisioned it.

The first thing that went wrong was that his mother was not only home but looking out the window when Sergeant Galloway stopped to let him out of the blond lady's station wagon.

By the time he got to the foyer, she had run downstairs and was waiting for him. She threw her arms around him and started crying, for Christ's sake.

Steve hadn't even thought of his mother. As she gave him the weepy bear hug, he was conscious that if she hadn't been looking out the window, he could have gone straight to Dianne's and started things off the way he planned.

But he was caught now. He was only too aware that he would have to spend a little time with her before going to see Dianne.

His mother's husband appeared and shook his hand and, for the first time ever, seemed glad to see him. The sonofabitch even worked up a smile and said, "Come on up, I'll make us a little Seven-and-Seven."

As they were going up the stairs, Dianne came down them. Dianne and Leonard.

"Hi!" Steve said.

"Hey, kid," Leonard said. "I saw your picture in the paper."

"Hello, Steve," Dianne said. "Nice to see you."

"Great to see you."

That was it. The next second, Dianne and Leonard were down the stairs and gone.

The phone was ringing when they got in the apartment. It was Mrs. Danielli. She had probably seen his picture in the *Newark Evening News,* because his mother said to her, "Yeah, sure, we seen it. He's *here,* Anna, he just this minute walked in the door."

And then Mrs. Danielli must have told Vinny that he was home, because his mother handed him the telephone and said, "Say hello to Vinny, Stevie."

"Ask them if they want to go out with us and get some spaghetti or something, why don't you?" Steve's mother's husband chimed in. Steve pretended not to hear him. If he got involved with the Daniellis, he would never get loose to go look for Dianne.

His mother jerked the phone out of his hand.

"Vinny, tell your mother Stanley asked do you and your mother and father want to go out with us and get some spaghetti."

It was agreed they would meet the Daniellis at the Naples Restaurant on Orange Street by Branch Brook Park in half an hour.

His mother hung up the telephone and turned to him.

"What were you so nice to that tramp about?"

"What are you talking about?"

"I'm talking about Dianne Marshall whatever-her-married-name-is, is what tramp I'm talking about—the one whose husband threw her out because she was fooling around."

"You don't know what you're talking about!"

"Don't you ever dare talk to me like that!"

"You don't know what the hell you're talking about, Ma!"

She slapped him.

"Don't think you're a big shot, Mr. Big Shot, who can swear at his mother!"

"What the hell is going on out there?" his mother's husband called from the kitchen.

"Nothing, dear."

They had to wait for a table at the Naples Restaurant. The Daniellis—Mr. and Mrs., and Maria and Beryl, Vinny's little sisters, and Vinny—showed up just before they finally got one.

When they got inside, Dianne and Leonard were there, sitting at a table for two with a candle in a Chianti bottle. The table was over against the wall-sized mural of what was supposed to be, Steve guessed, Naples and some volcano with smoke coming out of it.

They were just finishing up their meal. Leonard hadn't seen them, and Steve wasn't sure whether Dianne had or not. She wasn't looking in their direction, anyhow. And then she got up to go to the john.

She saw me. She pretended she didn't see me. She must know what my mother thinks about her, so she wanted to avoid trouble. And she doesn't really have to go to the toilet; she knows I'll see her go in there and will meet her outside, in that little corridor or whatever the hell it is.

"Excuse me, please, I have to visit the little boys' room."

"Again?" his mother said. "You just went before we left the apartment!"

He prayed his mother had not seen Dianne.

He had to wait a long time in the little corridor between the door that said REST ROOMS and the doors to the men's and ladies' johns, but finally Dianne came out.

"Hi!"

"What the hell are doing here?"

"Waiting for you."

"You crazy, or what? Christ!"

Steve tried to kiss her. She averted her face. When he tried harder, and started putting his arms around her, she kneed him in the balls.

"Jesus Christ," Dianne said, as he leaned against the wall, faint and in agony. "Can't you take the hint? Stay the hell away from me. You come near me again, I'll tell my father, and he'll beat the shit out of you!"

VIII

(ONE)
THE FOSTER LAFAYETTE HOTEL
WASHINGTON, D.C.
17 FEBRUARY 1942

Captain Fleming Pickering, USNR, got out from behind the wheel of the black Buick Roadmaster two-door sedan and tiptoed through the slush to the marquee. He had purchased the Buick, used, three days before, from a classified advertisement in the *Washington Post*.

"You should have slid out the driver's side, Captain Pickering," the doorman said, chuckling.

"But that would have been the intelligent thing to do," Pickering said. "I won't need it anymore today. But presuming you can make it run, can you have it out here at half past seven in the morning?"

"It'll start. The garage told me all it needed was a battery."

"We'll see," Pickering said. "I would be very surprised."

"Senator Fowler came in a couple of minutes ago, Captain," the doorman said. "Asked if I'd seen you."

"As soon as I thaw my frozen feet, I'll call him," Pickering said. "Thank you."

He checked at the desk for mail, but his slot was empty. Then he remembered that it would of course be empty. If they hadn't sent it up with a bellboy, the ever-efficient Mrs. Ellen Feller would have picked it up when she came to the apartment.

Pickering and Mrs. Feller had been assigned office space in the Navy Department. He thought of it as "the closet," but it was just outside Secretary Knox's suite. Since there was really no reason for him to spend much time there, he had had Max Telford, the hotel manager, install a desk and a typewriter in his suite for Mrs. Feller. She brought whatever papers needed his attention to the hotel, and he went to his official office as seldom as possible.

Am I getting old? Or am I just tired?

The junior United States Senator from California, the Hon. Richardson S. Fowler, was in the sitting room of Pickering's suite when Pickering let himself in.

"Senator, finding a politician sitting in my chair tossing down my booze is not an entirely unexpected cap to an all-around lousy day," Pickering greeted him.

Fowler swung his feet off the footstool of a high-backed leather overstuffed chair, and started to get up.

"Oh, for Christ's sake, stay there. I was only kidding."

"I never know with you."

"Whenever I call you 'Senator,' I'm kidding," Pickering said. "OK?"

He took off his uniform overcoat, tossed it on the back of one of the two couches facing a coffee table before the fireplace, laid his gold-encrusted uniform cap on top, sat down on the left couch, and started taking off his shoes and socks.

"My God," Ellen Feller said, coming into the room from the small bedroom that was now more or less converted into an office for her, "you're all wet!"

She wore a dark green silk dress with an unbuttoned cardigan over it. Her hair was combed upward from the base of her neck.

"I've noticed," he said.

"You look frozen. Can I get you a cup of coffee?" she asked. "Or a drink?"

"I don't suppose that's in your official job description, Ellen, but yes, thank you, both."

"Sir?"

"Put a generous hooker of cognac in a cup of black coffee, please."

"Where the hell have you been?" Senator Fowler asked.

"At Arlington. At a funeral. Standing in a snowdrift."

"You'd better change your trousers, too," Ellen said, as she poured coffee into a cup.

"A funeral? Anybody I know?" Senator Fowler asked.

"The last time I counted, I owned three pairs of trousers. I refuse to believe that the other two are already back from the cleaners."

"Count again," Ellen chuckled. "There was an enormous package from Brooks Brothers. *I* counted three blue jackets and *six* pairs of blue trousers when I hung it all up."

"Thank God! Finally!" Pickering said, and picked up his shoes and socks and went into the master bedroom.

Senator Fowler went to Mrs. Feller, took the brandy-laced coffee from her with a smile, and carried it into the bedroom. Pickering was in his shorts, buttoning braces to a pair of uniform trousers.

He took the coffee, nodded his thanks, and took a sip.

"Thank you," he said.

"Who were you burying?"

"A Marine lieutenant colonel. Fellow named Neville. His parachute didn't open."

"I saw that in the paper," Fowler said. "You knew him?"

"I was there representing Frank Knox. Frank knew him. He said he would have preferred to go himself, but if he did, it would be setting a precedent; he would be expected to show up every time they buried a lieutenant colonel or a commander."

"You didn't seem grief-stricken," Fowler said dryly.

"From what I hear, he did it to himself," Pickering said.

"Suicide?"

"Jake Dillon told me 'he got so carried away with his role that he got run over by the camera,' Pickering said, chuckling.

"Jake Dillon? The press agent?"

"Yeah. He's a major in the Corps."

"I didn't know, and I didn't know you knew him."

"Oh, sure. Jake shoots skeet with Bob Stack. That's how I met him. Interesting man. He stayed at the house in '39, he and the Stacks, when we had the state championships in San Francisco. Anyway, Jake was sort of running the burial ceremony. Newsreel cameras, three buglers, an honor guard of Marine parachutists, a firing squad, and a cast of thousands. Look for me at your local movie. I will be the handsome Naval person saluting solemnly as I stand there up to my ass in snow."

"I thought you said this man committed suicide?"

"No. Not the way that sounded. What Jake said was that when he found out *Life* wasn't going to take his picture, he flipped. He figured if he was the first man out of the airplane when they jumped, they'd have to take his picture. So he pushed the kid who was supposed to be first out of the way, and jumped himself. The wind, or the prop blast, caught him the wrong way and threw him into the horizontal stabilizer. The autopsy showed that hitting the horizontal stabilizer killed him. Not the sudden stop when he hit the ground."

"You sound pretty goddamned coldblooded, Flem, do you realize that?" Senator Fowler said.

Pickering, who was pulling on his trousers, didn't reply until he had the braces in place, the shirttail tucked in, and the zipper closed.

"Before I went out to Arlington," he said in an even voice, "I was reading a pretty reliable report that the Japs just executed two-hundred-dred-odd American civilians—the labor force we took out to Wake Island to fortify it and then permitted to get captured when we didn't reinforce Wake. They shot them out of hand. I find it a trifle difficult to get worked up over a light colonel here who did it to himself."

"Jesus Christ!" Fowler said, shocked.

"And an hour before that," Pickering went on dryly, "I had a telephone call from my wife, who is finding it difficult to understand why I didn't telephone her when I was on the West Coast. I was seen having lunch at the Coronado Beach Hotel, but I didn't have time for her. . . ."

"Tell me about the civilians on Wake."

"No. I shouldn't have said that much."

"Why not?"

"Senator, you just don't have the right to know," Pickering said.

"The operative word in that sentence, Flem, is 'Senator,' " Fowler said flatly.

Pickering looked at him with his eyebrows raised.

"As in 'United States Senator, representing the people," Fowler went on. "If a United States Senator doesn't have 'the right to know,' who does?"

"Interesting point," Pickering said. "Fortunately, I am not at what is known as the policy-making level, and don't have to make judgments like that. I just do what I'm told."

"How much do you know that I don't?" Fowler asked.

"Probably a hell of a lot," Pickering said.

"I want to know about the civilians on Wake Island," Fowler said. "I won't let anyone know where I got it, if that's bothering you."

"About ten people, including the cryptographers, know about it. If Frank Knox finds out you know about it, he'll know damned well where you got it."

"You wouldn't be a captain in the Navy, Flem, working for Knox, if I hadn't brought him here," Fowler said. "And it seems to me that the American people have a right to know if the Japanese are committing atrocities against civilian prisoners."

"They do, but they can't be told," Pickering said.

"Why not?"

"Because . . . do you realize what a goddamned spot you're putting me on, you sonofabitch?"

"Yes, I do," Fowler said.

"Oh, goddamn it!"

"I am rapidly getting the idea that you don't think I can be trusted with something like this," Senator Fowler said. "I can tolerate your contempt for Congress, generally. But this is getting personal. I don't think you question my patriotism, so it has to be my judgment you question."

"Shit!" Pickering said in frustration. He picked up and drained the brandy-laced cup of coffee, then turned to face Fowler. "We have broken the Japanese naval code. The information about the Japs shooting the civilians came from what they call an 'intercept.' If the Japanese find out we know about them shooting the civilians, they'll know we broke their code. And I can't tell you how valuable reading their radio traffic is to us."

"Thank you," Fowler said, seriously. "That will, of course, go no further than these walls."

Pickering nodded.

"Unless, of course, Mrs. Feller, in her role as oh-so-efficient secretary, has been eavesdropping at the door," Fowler added.

"I don't think she has," Pickering said. "But she knows."

"They really shot two hundred civilians?"

"Made them dig their graves, twenty at a time, and then shot them. Too much trouble to feed, you understand."

"God*damn* them!"

"I wonder what Frank'll do with me now?" Pickering said, as he pulled fresh stockings on his feet. "Let me out of the Navy, in which case I could go back to running Pacific & Far East, or send me to Iceland, someplace like that, as an example?"

"What are you talking about?"

"Obviously, I'm going to have to tell Knox that I told you about what happened on Wake. And about our having broken the Japanese code."

"Why?" Fowler asked.

"I realize the concept is seldom mentioned around Washington, but, ethically, I have to. He made me privy to this—"

"Flem," Fowler interrupted him. "Christ, you're naïve!"

"I haven't been accused of that in a long time."

"I know Frank Knox pretty well, too, you know," Fowler said. "Much better than you do, as a matter of fact. And he knows that we're very good friends. It hasn't occurred to you that he told you about Wake, and probably about some other things, pretty sure that you would tell me? *Hoping* you would?"

Pickering raised his eyes to Fowler. After a moment he said, "I am having trouble following that convoluted line of reasoning."

"I think Frank Knox wants me to know about Wake Island. And about a lot of other things the Secretary of the Navy cannot conveniently—or maybe even legally—tell the Junior Senator from California. And now I do, and Frank can lay his hand on a Bible and swear he didn't tell me."

"You really believe that?" Pickering asked doubtfully.

"Yeah, Flem, I do. And if you rush over there crying, 'Father, I cannot tell a lie. I chopped down the cherry tree,' you'll put the system out of kilter. It would not, Flem, be in the best interests of the country."

"My God!"

"Welcome to the real world, Captain Fleming," Fowler said dryly.

"You're suggesting that's the reason he got me this commission," Pickering said.

"It's certainly one of them. I'm on his side, Flem. He knows that. I really should know what the hell is really going on."

"Then why doesn't he just call you in and tell you? Brief you, as they say?"

"The Senate is full of monstrous egos. If he briefed me, he would have to brief a dozen other people. Two dozen. Some of whom, I'm sorry to say, should not be trusted with this kind of information."

"You're right, I'm naïve. Until just now, I thought what I was doing was lending my shipping expertise."

"That too," Fowler said. "But think about it. What does this Wake Island atrocity have to do with that? You don't really have that 'need to know' you threw in my face."

Pickering put on a fresh pair of shoes, tied them, and stood up, holding the wet pair in his hand.

"I think I'm going to have a stiff drink," he said. "Interested?"

"Fascinated," Fowler said, touching his arm. "But one final comment, Flem. Knox has paid you one hell of a compliment. Since he can't tell anyone what material should be passed to me, he had to have someone in whose intelligence and judgment he felt safe. He picked you."

"You didn't get into that?"

"No. For obvious reasons."

"I feel like Alice must have felt when she walked through the looking glass," Pickering said.

He went back into the sitting room, opened the door to the corridor, and put the wet shoes outside. Then he went to the bar and poured an inch of Scotch into a large-mouthed glass.

"I would have made that for you," Ellen Feller said.

"Ellen, would you get Secretary Knox on the phone for me?" Pickering said.

"What are you doing, Flem?" Fowler asked, concern in his voice.

"Why don't you just listen? And see if everybody has guessed right about my judgment and intelligence?"

He walked to where Ellen was dialing a telephone on a small, narrow table against the wall.

"Captain Pickering for Secretary Knox," she said when someone answered the phone. Pickering wondered how she knew where Knox would be at this time of day.

Knox came on the line. "Yes, Pickering?"

"I thought I had best report on the funeral of Colonel Neville, Sir."

"Well, thank you. But it wasn't really necessary. I trust you."

"It went well, Sir."

"Good."

"If you have nothing more for me tonight, Sir, I think I'm going to just get in bed. I got chilled out at Arlington."

"Well, we can't have you coming down with a cold. I need you. But why don't you put off actually going to bed for a while? I ran into Senator Fowler, and he said he was going to drop in on you for a drink. We can't afford to disappoint him. We have very few Republican friends on the Hill, you know."

"I understand, Sir."

"Yes," Knox said. "Good night, Captain."

Pickering hung the telephone up and turned to look at Fowler, who met his eyes.

"Ellen," Pickering said, "you might as well run along. Senator Fowler and I are going to sit here and communicate with John Barleycorn. I'll see you in the morning."

"There are some things in here you should read, Captain," she said.

"Leave them. I'll read them when I get up in the morning."

"There's a couple of 'eyes only' in there," she said, nodding toward a leather briefcase, "which should go back in the vault. I could either wait, or arrange for a courier."

"I'll call for a courier when I'm through with them," Pickering said. "Thank you, Ellen."

"Yes, Sir."

When she had gone, Fowler said, "Very nice. Speaking of naïve, does Patricia know about her?"

"What the hell do you mean by that?"

"Now I know that Patricia has the understanding of a saint, but there are some women whose active imaginations would jump into high gear if they learned their husbands were spending a lot of time in a hotel suite with an attractive—very attractive—female like that."

"Dick . . . Jesus! *A,* I don't run around on Patricia, never have, and you know it. *B,* she's some kind of a missionary."

"Oh, a *missionary!* I *forgot.* Missionaries are neutered when they take their vows. They don't have whoopee urges. The reason your missionary lady looks at you the way she does is because she sees in you a saint who would *never* even *think* of slipping it to her."

"You're a dirty old man, Dick," Pickering said. He walked to the briefcase, picked it up, worked the combination lock, and opened it. He spent a full minute looking at the folders it contained without removing them, and then he handed the briefcase to Senator Fowler.

"In for a penny, in for a pound," he said. "Read what's in there, and then I'll answer any questions."

Fowler handed the briefcase back to him.

"You still don't understand the rules of the game, do you?" he said.

"I guess not."

"Right now I can put my hand on the Bible and swear that you never showed me one classified document, and you can swear that you never showed me one. I want to keep it that way."

"So what do you want?"

"I want a briefing," Fowler said. "I want *your opinion* of what's going on."

"With a map and a pointer?" Pickering asked sarcastically.

"A map would be nice," Senator Fowler said. "You probably won't need a pointer. Have you got a map?"

Pickering saw that Fowler was serious.

"Yeah," he said. "I've got a map. It's in the safe. I had a safe installed in here to make sure people who don't have the need to know don't get to look at my map."

"Why don't you get it, Flem?" Senator Fowler said, ignoring the sarcasm. "Maybe thumbtack it to the wall?"

Fleming went into his bedroom, and returned a moment later with several maps.

"I don't have any thumbtacks," he said seriously. "I'll lay these on the floor."

"Fine."

"OK, what do you want to know?"

"I know a little bit about what's going on in Europe," Fowler said. "And your area of expertise is the Pacific. So let's start with that."

I have a counterpart, maybe in the Army, who's doing this for him for Europe. I'll be damned!

"Where should I start?"

"December seventh," Fowler said. "I know you're not prepared for this, Flem. Would it help if you went on the premise that I know nothing about it?"

"OK," Pickering said, getting on his knees beside the large map. "Here's the way the pieces were on the board on December seventh. The U.S. Pacific Fleet was here, at Oahu, in the Hawaiian Islands. That's about three thousand nautical miles from San Francisco, and four thousand from Tokyo. It's as far from San Francisco to Hawaii as it is to New York. And it's about as far from San Francisco to Hawaii as it is from New York to London.

"Wake Island is here, 2,200 miles from Tokyo and 2,500 from Pearl Harbor. Guam, here, is two thousand miles from Tokyo, and four thousand from Pearl, and it's about two thousand miles from Tokyo to Luzon, in the Philippines, and 8,500 from the West Coast to Luzon."

Pickering sat back and rested on his heels.

"So, Factor One is that distances in the Pacific favor the Japanese."

"Obviously," Fowler said.

"Factor Two is protection of the sea lanes. We lost most of our battleships at Pearl Harbor. How *well* they could have protected the sea lanes is a moot point, but they're gone. And, obviously, their loss had a large part to do with the decision to pull back Task Force 14 to Pearl, and not to reinforce Wake Island."

"Should we have taken the chance with the aircraft carriers and reinforced Wake?" Fowler asked.

"I think so. We could, in any event, have made taking it far more costly. The Japanese do not have a really good capability to land on a hostile beach. They managed it at Wake because there was not an effective array of artillery on Wake. They only had one working range-finder, for one thing. And not much ammunition. And no planes. All were aboard Task Force 14. I think they should have been put ashore."

Fowler grunted.

"Again, now a moot point, Wake is gone. So is Guam. On December tenth, the Japanese landed two divisions on Luzon. Three weeks later they were in Manila. We are now being pushed down the Bataan Penin-sula. It will fall, and eventually so will Corregidor."

"It can't be reinforced?"

"There is a shortage of materiel to load on ships; a shortage of ships; and the Japanese have been doing a very creditable job of interdicting our shipping."

"And how much damage are we doing to them?"

"MacArthur has slowed down their advance. From our intercepts, we know that the Japanese General—Homma is his name; interesting guy, went to school in California, speaks fluent English, and did not, *did not,* want to start this war—anyway, Homma is under a lot of pressure to end resistance in the Philippines. It's a tough nut to crack. After they finally get rid of Luzon and Corregidor, they have to take Mindanao, the island to the south. We have about thirty thousand troops there, and supplies, under a general named Sharp."

"Why don't they use his forces to reinforce Luzon?"

"Transportation. If they put out to sea, the Japanese have superior-ity: submarines, other vessels. It would be a slaughter."

"And what are we doing to the Japanese?"

"Very little. They're naturally husbanding what's left of the fleet: aircraft carriers, cruisers. . . ."

"What about our submarines?"

"Our torpedoes don't work," Pickering said simply.

"What do you mean, they don't work?"

"They don't work. They either don't reach the target, or they do and don't explode."

"I'd never heard that," Fowler said, shocked. "Not *all* of them?"

"No, of course, not all of them. But apparently many. A hell of a lot, maybe half, maybe even more. The submarine brass, obviously, are not talking about it much. The story goes that submarine captains returning to Pearl Harbor who complained have been ordered to keep their mouths shut. I'm going out there to see for myself."

"I can't understand that," Fowler said. "Didn't they have any idea they wouldn't work?"

"I don't know. I understand it has something to do with the detonators. And since the detonators are the brainchildren of some highly placed admirals, obviously the submarine captains, not the detonators, are at fault."

"How can you hide something like that? In training, I mean. A torpedo that doesn't explode?"

"They didn't fire many of them in training, apparently. I asked that question. It cost too much," Pickering said. "The admiral I asked also made it rather clear that he objected to a civilian, even one wearing a captain's uniform, asking questions like that of a professional sailor."

"How did that go down?" Fowler asked.

"I told him I had been master of a ship when he was still a midshipman."

"You didn't!"

"No, I didn't. I was tempted, Christ, how I was tempted. But I kept my mouth shut."

"I'm impressed, Flem," Senator Fowler said.

"OK. Let's get on with this. The Japanese were already in French Indochina. The French—I don't suppose they had much choice, with the Germans occupying France—permitted them to station troops and aircraft in Hanoi, Saigon, and other places, and there was a naval presence as well. From French Indochina, the Japs moved into Thailand. The Japanese have been in Korea for years.

"They landed in Malaya and conquered Singapore, our British allies having cleverly installed their artillery pointing in the wrong direction. The British surrendered seventy thousand men. That's the largest Allied surrender so far—Frank Knox told me it was the worst defeat the English had suffered since Burgoyne surrendered at Saratoga—but it will lose its place in the history books when the Philippines fall."

"There's no way we can hang on to the Philippines? Not even Mindanao? What about General Sharp and his thirty thousand men?"

"We probably could—hang on to Mindanao, I mean. But Roosevelt has decided the first stage of the war has to concentrate on Europe. That means no reinforcement for the Philippines."

"You sound as if you disagree."

"So far as I'm concerned, we should let the Germans and the Russians bleed each other to death," Pickering said. "But my theories of how the war should be fought have so far not been solicited."

"So what happens now?" Fowler asked.

"Well, we try to keep the Japanese from taking both Australia and New Zealand, which are obviously on their schedule. And we try to establish bases in Australia and New Zealand from which we can eventually start taking things back. It's six thousand five hundred miles from San Francisco to Brisbane. At the moment that sea lane is open. MacArthur has already been asked, politely, to leave the Philippines and go to Australia."

"What do you mean, 'asked'?"

"I mean *asked*. If he doesn't go, I suppose Roosevelt will eventually make it an order. General Marshall's been urging him to do it right away. MacArthur and Marshall hate each other, did you know that?"

"I'd heard rumors."

"When George Marshall was a colonel at Fort Benning, MacArthur was Army Chief of Staff. He wrote an efficiency report on Marshall, saying he should never be given command of anything larger than a regiment. MacArthur thinks Marshall—who's now in MacArthur's former position, of course—was returning the compliment when he recalled MacArthur as a lieutenant general."

"I don't understand."

"MacArthur retired as a general, a full four-star general, when he was Chief of Staff. Then he got himself appointed Marshal of the Philippine Armed Forces. When Roosevelt called MacArthur back from retirement to assume command in the Philippines, he called him back as a lieutenant general, with three stars—junior to a full general, in other words. MacArthur thinks Marshall was behind that. I frankly wouldn't be surprised if he was. Anyway, their relationship is pretty delicate.

"So the idea is that MacArthur will go to Australia. And that we will stage out of Australia and New Zealand. That's presuming we can hang on to New Zealand and Australia. There are no troops there to speak of. They're all off in Africa and England defending the Empire.

"And the Japanese know they can take it unless we can maintain a reasonably safe sea route to Australia and New Zealand, and they have already made their first move. On January twenty-third—which is what, three weeks ago?—they occupied Rabaul. Here."

He pointed at the map, at the Bismarck Archipelago, east of New Guinea.

"They've already established forces on New Guinea, and if they can build an air base at Rabaul, they can bomb our ships en route to Australia and New Zealand. And, of course, they can bomb New Zealand and Australia."

"And we're doing nothing about that, either?"

"In that briefcase you won't look at—"

"I told you why."

"—there is just about the final draft of an operations order from Admiral King. Unless somebody finds something seriously wrong with it, and I don't think they will, he'll make it official in the next couple of days. It orders the soonest possible recapture of Rabaul. To do that, we'll have to set up a base on Éfaté Island, in the New Hebrides."

"Where the hell is that?"

Pickering pointed to the map. Fowler saw that Éfaté was a tiny speck in the South Pacific, northwest of New Caledonia, which itself was an only slightly larger speck of land east of the Australian continent.

"Why there?"

"It's on the shipping lanes. Once they get an airfield built, they can bomb Rabaul from it. And again, once the airfield is built, they can use it to protect the shipping lanes."

"Have we got any troops to send there? And ships to send them in?"

"Army Task Force 6814, which isn't much—it's much less than a division—is already on the high seas, bound for Éfaté," Pickering said.

"Not even a division? That's not much."

"It's all we've got, and it's something."

"What about the Marines?"

"What about them?"

"Where are they? What are they doing?"

"The day the Japanese landed at Rabaul, the 2nd Marine Brigade landed on Samoa, reinforcing the 7th Defense Battalion. The 4th Marines, who used to be in China, are on Bataan. They're forming Marine divisions on both coasts, but they won't be ready for combat until early 1943."

"This is all worse than I thought. Or are you being pessimistic?"

"I don't think so. I think . . . if we can keep them from taking Australia, or rendering it impotent, we may even have bottomed out. But right now, our ass is in a crack."

"I heard . . . I can't tell you where . . ."

"Can't, or won't?"

"Won't. I heard that Roosevelt has authorized the launching of B-26 bombers from an aircraft carrier to bomb Japan."

"B-twenty-*fives*," Pickering corrected him. "The ones they named after General Billy Mitchell. They're training right now on the Florida Panhandle."

"What do you think about that?"

"I think it's a good idea. It may not do much real damage, but it will hurt the Japanese ego, and probably make them keep a much larger home defense force than they have at home; and it's probably going to do wonders for civilian morale here. That's probably worth the cost."

"What cost?"

"I talked to Jimmy Doolittle. He used to be vice-president of Shell. Very good guy. He left me with the impression he doesn't really expect to come back."

"Jesus!"

"There are lieutenant colonels and then there are lieutenant colonels," Pickering said.

"You're talking about the one you buried?"

"You accused me of being cold-blooded."

"OK. I apologize."

"I wish I was," Pickering said. "Cold-blooded, I mean."

"I was going to use my knowledge of Jimmy Doolittle and the B-25s to dazzle you, and get you to tell me about the Marine Raiders."

"Same sort of thing, I think. Roosevelt is dazzled by all things British, and thinks we should have our own commandos. We have to have some kind of military triumph or the public's morale will go to hell."

"You think that's all it is? A public-relations stunt, for public morale?"

"I think there's more, but I don't find anything wrong with doing something to buttress public morale. And Roosevelt's at least putting his money where his mouth his. His son Jimmy is executive officer of one of the Raider battalions, the 2nd, now forming at San Diego."

"Tell me about it," Senator Fowler said. "You say you were out in San Diego?"

"After dinner. I didn't have any lunch."

"You buying?"

"Why not?"

They ate in the hotel's Grill Room, lamb chops and oven-roast potatoes and a tomato salad, with two bottles of Cabernet Sauvignon.

"Did I tell you," Pickering said, as he selected a Wisconsin Camembert from the display of cheeses, "that the 26th Cavalry in the Philippines just shot their horses? They needed them for food."

"Jesus Christ, Flem!" the Senator protested.

"Why don't I feel guilty about eating all this? Maybe you're right, Dick. Maybe I really am cold-blooded."

"I don't know whether you are or not, but that's the last you get to drink. I know you well enough to know there are times when you should not be drinking, and this is one of those times."

After dinner, Captain Fleming Pickering, USNR, returned to his suite, took a shower, had a nightcap—a large brandy—and went to bed.

Something happened to him that had not happened to him in years. He had an erotic dream; it was so vivid that he remembered it in the morning. He blamed it then on everything that had happened the day before, plus the Camembert, the wine, and the cognac.

He dreamed that Mrs. Ellen Feller, the missionary's wife, had come into his bedroom wearing nothing but the black lace underwear she had been wearing the day he met her, and then she had taken that off, and then he had done what men do in such circumstances.

(TWO)

OFFICE OF THE CHIEF OF STAFF
HEADQUARTERS, 2ND JOINT TRAINING FORCE
SAN DIEGO, CALIFORNIA
21 FEBRUARY 1942

Captain Jack NMI Stecker, USMCR, knocked at the open door of Colonel Lewis T. "Lucky Lew" Harris's office and waited for permission to enter.

"Come," Colonel Harris said, throwing a pencil down with disgust on his desk. "Why the hell is it, Jack, that whenever you tell somebody to put some simple idea on paper, he uses every big word he ever heard of? And uses them wrong?"

"I don't know, Sir," Stecker smiled. "Am I the guilty party?"

"No. This piece of crap comes from our beloved adjutant. They're worse than anybody, which I suppose is why we make them adjutants." He raised his voice: "Sergeant Major!"

The Sergeant Major, a very thin, very tall, leather-skinned man in his late thirties, quickly appeared at the office door.

"Sir?"

"Sergeant Major, would you please give this to the Adjutant? Tell him I don't understand half of it and that it needs rewriting. Tell him I said he is forbidden to use words of more than two syllables."

"Aye, aye, Sir," the Sergeant Major said, chuckling, winking at Stecker, and taking the clipped-together sheaf of papers from Colonel Harris's desk. "Sir, I presume the Colonel knows he's about to break the Adjutant's heart? He really is proud of this."

"Good," Harris said. "Better than good. Splendid! Tell him I want it in the morning. Anybody who writes crap like that doesn't deserve any sleep."

"Aye, aye, Sir," the Sergeant Major said, smiling broadly, and left the office.

"Close the door, Jack," Colonel Harris said. Stecker did so. When he turned around, there was a bottle of Jack Daniel's bourbon and two glasses on Harris's desk. "A little something to cut the dust of the trail, Jack?"

"It's a little early for me, Sir."

"We're wetting down a promotion," Harris said. "And now that I am about to be a general officer, I will decide whether or not it's a little early for you."

"In that case, General, I would be honored," Stecker said.

"I said 'about to be a general.' Not 'am.' You listen about as closely as that goddamned Adjutant. You're going to have to watch that, Jack, now that you're a field-grade officer."

"Sir?"

"Now I've got your attention, don't I?" Harris said, pleased with himself. He handed Stecker an ex–Kraft Cheese glass, half-full of whiskey.

"Yes, Sir."

"Mud in your eye, Major Stecker," Colonel Harris said.

"I'm a little confused, Sir," Stecker said, as he raised the glass to his mouth and tossed the whiskey down.

"General Riley was on the horn just now," Harris said. He drained his glass and returned the bottle to the drawer before going on. "He said that my name has gone to the Senate for B.G., and presumably, as soon as they can—*if* they can—gather enough of them, sober enough to vote, for a quorum, the orders will be cut."

"It's well deserved," Stecker said sincerely.

"I'm glad you think so," Harris said softly. "Thank you, Jack."

Harris touched Stecker's arm in what was, for him, a gesture of deep affection.

Then the tone of his voice changed.

"But we were talking about *your* promotion, weren't we, *Major* Stecker? You owe me a big one for this, Major."

"I didn't realize that I was even being considered," Stecker said.

"Let me tell you what happened," Harris said. "You ever know a guy named Neville? Franklin G. Neville?"

"Yeah. The last I heard, he was on a tailgate assignment as a Naval attaché somewhere."

"In Finland. Well, he came back, got involved with parachute troops of all things, and made lieutenant colonel. A couple of days ago, he jumped out of an airplane at Lakehurst without a parachute, or at least with one that didn't work, and killed himself."

"I'm sorry to hear that."

"Well, they need a replacement for him. I remain to be convinced that paratroops have any place in the Corps, but we have them. I think if the Army came up with an archery corps, some wild-eyed sonofabitch in Headquarters would start buying bows and arrows and claiming it was our idea in the first place."

He looked at Stecker for a little appreciation of his wit, and found instead concern—perhaps even alarm—in his eyes.

"No, Major Stecker," he said, chuckling. "You are not going to the Para-Marines, or whatever the hell they call them. You are going to the 1st Division at New River, North Carolina, to replace the guy who is going to jump into—pun intended—the shoes of the late Colonel Neville."

"You had me worried for a moment," Stecker confessed.

"I could see that," Harris said. "Here's what happened: General Riley asked me if I had a major I could recommend to take this guy's place in the 5th Marines. He's the Exec of Second Battalion. I told him no, but that I did have a captain I knew for a fact could find his ass with either hand . . ."

"Battalion Exec? Christ, I don't know . . ."

"Come on, Jack. When I was a battalion commander, I had a master gunnery sergeant who made it pretty clear that he thought he could run the battalion at least as well as I could. His name was Jack Stecker."

"That attitude goes with being a gunny," Stecker said. "I'm not sure how it really works."

"Well, you're about to find out," Harris said. "The original idea . . . Riley is one of your admirers, Jack, did you know that?"

Stecker shook his head.

"Well, he is. The original idea was to send you there as a captain. But then, genius that I am, it occurred to me that, *A,* you're junior as hell, and that, *B,* if I had the battalion, I would assign an ex–master gunnery sergeant, now a captain, as a company commander."

"I'd like to have a company," Stecker said. "You know that."

"Yeah, well, we have nice young first lieutenants who can be trained to do that. By a battalion exec who knows what it's like in a battalion. So I told this to the General, and he said, 'Well, I guess we'll have to make him a major before we cut the orders sending him to New River.'"

"How's the Battalion Commander, and, for that matter, the Regimental Commander, going to like having somebody shoving Jack Stecker down their throats? They're bound to have somebody in mind."

"Well, they'll probably hate it at first, to tell you the truth. But after they are *counseled* by the Assistant Division Commander, I'm sure they will come to understand the wisdom of the decision."

"Why should he do that? I don't even know, off the top of my head, who the 1st Division ADC is."

"As soon as they can sober up enough senators for a quorum, his name will be Brigadier General Lewis T. Harris," Harris said.

Stecker, smiling, shook his head.

(THREE)

OFFICE OF THE CHIEF OF NURSING SERVICES
UNITED STATES NAVAL HOSPITAL
SAN DIEGO, CALIFORNIA
27 FEBRUARY 1942

"You wanted to see me, Commander?" Ensign Barbara Cotter, NC, USNR, asked, sticking her head into the office of Lieutenant Commander Jane P. Marwood, NC, USN.

"Come in, Cotter," Commander Marwood said. Commander Marwood, whom Barbara Cotter thought of as "that skinny old bitch," was in blues. She was a very small woman, and thin. With the three and a half gold stripes of a lieutenant commander on her jacket cuffs, and several ribbons over her breast, Barbara Cotter thought she looked like a caricature of a Naval officer, almost like a woman dressed up for a costume party.

Barbara saw that Lieutenant Commander Hazel Gower, NC, USN, her newly promoted immediate supervisor, was also in the office, standing up and looking out the window.

I'm in some kind of trouble, otherwise good ol' Hazel wouldn't be here. I wonder what I'm supposed to have done?

And then she had an even more discomfiting thought: *I wonder how long this is going to take?*

She was supposed to meet Joe Howard in forty-five minutes. She would be pressed for time as it was, going through the controlled-drug inventory with the nurse who would come on duty, and then getting out of her whites, grabbing a quick shower, dressing, and then meeting him at the main entrance.

She had been thinking about Joe—and about herself and Joe—when she'd been summoned to Commander Marwood's office. She had come to the conclusion that she was in love with him. *In love,* as opposed to *infatuated with,* sexually or otherwise. The emotion was new to her. She had been infatuated before. This was different.

Viewed clinically, of course, Barbara Cotter knew it was probably just sex alone, and nothing more than that. He was a healthy young male, and she was a healthy young female. There was nothing Mother

Nature liked better than to turn on the chemical transmitters and receptors of a well-matched pair. She had a way of convincing both parties that the other was a perfect specimen, in all respects, of the opposite sex, and of turning off that portion of the brain that might question the notion that the two of them were experiencing an emotion never felt by anyone before.

What Mother Nature was after was propagation of the species, and Mother was totally unconcerned with the problems that might cause. Such as her family's reaction to someone like Joe, and that there was a war on, and that she was in the United States Naval Service.

But none of that really mattered to Barbara. The only thing that mattered was that when she was with Joe, in bed or out of it, she felt complete and content, and that when they were separated, she felt incomplete and miserable.

She had felt incomplete and miserable all week. Joe had gone somewhere in northern California with an officer and a sergeant from the 2nd Raider Battalion at Camp Elliott. They'd gone to some Army depot to get weapons for the Raiders.

She had been unpatriotically overjoyed with the realization that Joe was what he called an "armchair commando," a Marine officer who commanded only a desk, and was not about to be sent off to fight the Japanese. And that when he was in San Diego, he was free just about every night and every weekend, and not running around in the boon-docks day and night, practicing war.

And in forty minutes he would meet her at the main entrance, and they would get in her car and drive over to the Coronado Beach Hotel, and because the bar looked so crowded, they would go upstairs and have a drink before dinner in the Pacific & Far Eastern Suite, which translated to mean that half an hour after she met Joe, forty-five min-utes from now, they would be in one of the wide and comfortable beds in their birthday suits.

And now this, whatever the hell this is all about!

Barbara walked over and stood before Commander Marwood's desk.

I don't care what she thinks I've done, what good ol' Hazel has told her I've done. I will plead guilty, swear I will never do it again, and beg forgiveness. Just so I can meet Joe!

"Yes, Ma'am?"

"Apparently, Cotter," Commander Marwood said, "the Navy has decided there is a slot where you may practice your special skills."

What the hell is she talking about?

"Ma'am?"

"There has been a TWX from the Surgeon General's office," Marwood said. "Actually, two of them. The first of them requested a list of the nurses in San Diego with experience, or special training, in psychiatric service. I provided your name. The second TWX put you on orders."

"Excuse me?"

"This is your formal notification, Miss Cotter, of your selection for overseas service. Do you understand what I'm telling you?"

"No, Ma'am."

"I didn't think you would," Marwood said. "When a member of the Naval Service is officially notified that he, or she, is about to be sent to sea, or overseas, as I have just notified you, the officer making the notification is required to advise the person being sent overseas that failure to make the shipment—missing the ship or the airplane, or failing to report to the departure point as scheduled—is a more serious offense than simple absence without leave. Specifically, that offense is called 'absence without leave for the purpose of avoiding hazardous service.' Severe court-martial penalties are provided."

Barbara felt rage flow through her; Joe Howard was immediately forgotten.

"Are you implying that I would go AWOL?" she flared.

"Not at all," Commander Marwood replied.

"It sounded like it!"

"I don't like your tone of voice, Ensign Cotter," Commander Marwood said, angrily.

Barbara glared at Commander Marwood, but said nothing. Commander Marwood glared back.

Finally, Commander Marwood said, "Cotter, there was nothing personal in this. Regulations require that an individual being sent overseas be informed of the penalties provided for AWOL with the intent of avoiding hazardous service."

"Then I'm sorry," Barbara said.

"I'm really getting sick and tired of telling you, Cotter," Lieutenant Commander Hazel Gower said, "that a junior appends 'Ma'am' to whatever she says to a superior officer."

"I'm sorry, Ma'am," Barbara said.

Commander Marwood waved her hand in a sign that meant, *OK, forget it.*

"Where am I going?" Barbara asked, remembering just in time to append "Ma'am."

"I don't know," Commander Marwood said. "Possibly to Hawaii. Possibly elsewhere. If they were going to station you aboard one of the hospital ships, I think your orders would have spelled that out. All your orders say is that you are to report to the Personnel Center, San Diego Navy Yard, for overseas service."

"When?" Barbara asked.

"There's some processing to go through. A physical. Shots, that sort of thing. Getting your pay up to date. Getting your personal affairs in order. Making sure you have the necessary uniforms and equipment. That'll take a couple of days. Then you will be given a delay en route leave, up to fourteen days, which should give you time to go home. So, as a specific answer to your question, you will report to the Navy Yard two weeks from the day your processing is over and you begin your leave. When you will leave there depends on the availability of shipping."

"I see."

"Now, regulations also require that I ask you if there is any reason you wish to apply for relief from your orders on humanitarian grounds."

Joe Howard reappeared in Barbara's thinking.

"Sick parents, that sort of thing?" Commander Marwood pursued.

"No, Ma'am," Barbara said. "Nothing like that."

"I've scheduled your last day of duty for Sunday," Lieutenant Commander Gower said. "You can start your out-processing on Monday morning."

"I'd sort of planned on having the weekend off," Barbara said, adding, again, just in time, "Ma'am."

"Your shipping out has left me short of people," Commander Gower said. "I had to rearrange the shifts. That requires that you pull a shift on Sunday. Sorry."

Barbara nodded her understanding.

"That will be all then, Cotter," Commander Marwood said. "Good luck. I'll try to see you before you ship out."

"Thank you," Barbara said.

She had not appended "Ma'am" to her reply, but neither Commander Gower nor Commander Marwood called her on it.

When she was gone, Commander Gower said, "Well, there goes the romance of the century, down the toilet."

"That's a pretty goddamned bitchy thing to say, Hazel!" Commander Marwood snapped.

Ensign Barbara Cotter was twenty-five minutes late meeting First Lieutenant Joseph L. Howard. Her replacement was late, and taking the goddamned drug inventory took longer than it usually did, and then she caught herself just standing in the shower, washing the same shoulder over and over again, lost in thought, and with no idea whatever how long she'd been doing that.

And then when she finally got to the main entrance, he wasn't there.

He was here, and left.

Or he couldn't get off, and won't be here.

Oh, Jesus, now what?

A LaSalle convertible pulled up before the main entrance and tapped its horn. She saw a Marine officer in it.

No, goddamn you, I don't want a goddamned ride!

Where the hell can he be?

The Marine officer in the shiny LaSalle convertible blew the horn again. Barbara glowered at him, working up what she hoped was a magnificent look of contempt. The Marine officer waved at her.

Oh, my God, it's Joe!

She ran to the car as he opened the door.

"Hi!" he said, as she got in.

She kissed him. Hard. On the lips.

"They frown on public displays of affection," Joe said.

"Fuck 'em," Barbara said.

"Ooooh! I'll have to wash out your mouth with soap."

She slid next to him on the seat.

I'll have to tell him. But not just yet.

"Where did you get this?"

"Nice, huh?" he said.

"Where'd you get it?"

"It belongs to the guy from the 2nd Raiders," Joe said. "We're going to have dinner with him and his girlfriend."

"Do we have to?"

"I told him we would," he said. "Any reason you don't want to?"

"I wanted to be alone."

"He's a nice guy. A Mustang, like me. Out of the 4th Marines. But he went through officer candidate school. Killer McCoy."

"*Killer* McCoy?"

"Yeah. They call him that because he killed a bunch of Chinese and a couple of Italian Marines in China," Joe said admiringly. "He carries a knife in his sleeve."

He pointed to his left sleeve to demonstrate.

"You're kidding, right?"

"No, I'm not. Everybody in the Corps knows about Killer McCoy."

"I know," she said, aware that she was acting the bitch, "you and your friend the Killer and me, we're going to go down to the waterfront and see if we can pick a fight, right?"

"Hey!" he said. "What's the matter with you?"

"Sorry," Barbara said.

"Actually, we're going to the San Diego Yacht Club," Joe said. "How's that for class?"

"Where?"

"The Yacht Club. Killer lives there. On a yacht."

"I don't believe any of this conversation," she said.

"You'll see."

Twenty minutes later, they passed through the gates of the San Diego Yacht Club. And five minutes after that, they stepped from a floating pier onto the aft deck of a fifty-three-foot, twin-diesel-powered Mitchell yacht named *Last Time*.

"Hi!" a very good-looking young woman greeted Barbara. She wore her black hair in a pageboy, and was wearing shorts and a T-shirt. "Welcome aboard! I'm Ernie Sage."

"Hello," Barbara said.

A trim, brown-haired young man in shorts and a Hawaiian shirt appeared at the door to the interior. He was even younger than Joe.

"I was getting a little worried," he said. "And you're right, she's gorgeous!"

"I'm very glad to meet you," Barbara said. "I'm Barbara."

"I'm Ken McCoy," he said. "Romeo here has been bending my ear all week about you."

"He was just pulling your leg. He does that," Barbara replied. "He told me on the way over here that we were going to meet somebody who carries a knife in his sleeve, and is called 'Killer' because he kills people. Chinese and Italians, Joe said."

"Thanks a lot, asshole," Ken McCoy said furiously, and went back inside the cabin of the boat.

"Ken!" the girl called Ernie Sage said, and, after giving Joe a withering look, went into the cabin after him.

"What did I say?"

"I'm the asshole, not you. I should have warned you, getting called 'Killer' pisses him off."

"You mean it's true? He *has* killed people?"

Joe nodded.

Ernie Sage reappeared, holding Second Lieutenant Kenneth R. McCoy, USMCR, by the ear.

"Ken has something to say," she said.

"Ouch!" he said, as she twisted the ear. He looked at Barbara. "I apologize for my language." Ernie Sage let go of his ear, whereupon McCoy added, "I'm sorry I called your asshole of a boyfriend an asshole."

"You *bastard!*" Ernie Sage said, and jabbed him in the ribs.

"Hey, Ken," Joe said. "I'm sorry."

"Ah, forget it," McCoy said. "I never thought you were very bright."

"What we're going to do," Ernie Sage said brightly, "is do this all over again. Hello, my name is Ernestine Sage. This gentlemen is Lieutenant Kenneth R. McCoy. I know that you're Lieutenant Howard, but I don't believe I know this young lady."

"How do you do," Barbara said, going along, and deciding she liked both this young woman and her boyfriend. "I'm Barbara Cotter."

"How do you do," Ernie Sage said. "Welcome aboard the *Last Time.*"

"Miss Cotter?" Ken McCoy asked politely. "May I call you Barbara?"

"Yes, of course."

"Anybody ever tell you, Barbara, that your boyfriend is an asshole?"

"That did it," Ernie Sage said, and struck McCoy with both hands, palms open, on the chest—which action caused him to stagger backward, encounter the low rail of the aft cockpit, and do a backward flip into the water.

Joe Howard laughed deep in his stomach, went to the rail, looked over the side, and waved.

Whereupon Ensign Barbara Cotter struck Lieutenant Howard in the small of his back with both hands, palms open, which caused Lieutenant Howard to go over the side and into the water, face first.

Ernie Sage looked at Barbara Cotter.

"Why do I have this feeling that what we're witnessing here is the beginning of a long, close, rewarding friendship?"

"Oh, God!" Barbara wailed, and tears formed in her eyes.

"Did I say something wrong?" Ernie asked.

Barbara did not trust her voice to speak; she shook her head.

"I'm sorry, really sorry, if this upset you," Ernie said.

Barbara shook her head and made a gesture with her hand meaning that it didn't matter.

"Can I get you a drink?" Ernie asked.

"I got my orders today," Barbara blurted. "I haven't told him yet."

Ken McCoy's head appeared at the rail.

"If you're wearing anything that will melt in water, I respectfully suggest you have ten seconds to take it off."

"Barbara got her orders today," Ernie said evenly. "Joe doesn't know."

"Oh, Christ!" McCoy said. He hoisted himself into the boat. Then he turned and gave his hand to Joe Howard and hauled him aboard.

Joe stood there, dripping water onto the deck.

"Which of these two goes in first?" he asked.

"Barbara got her orders today," Ernie said.

"Oh, Jesus!" Joe said. "When?"

"I start processing Monday," Barbara said softly.

"When did you find out?"

"Just before I met you."

He took a couple of steps toward her, and then, remembering he was soaking wet, stopped.

And then she took several steps to him and threw herself in his arms.

(FOUR)

PENSACOLA NAVAL AIR STATION

PENSACOLA, FLORIDA

1525 HOURS 28 FEBRUARY 1942

The pilot of the Army Air Corps twin-engine "Mitchell" bomber was slight and balding. There were the silver leaves of a lieutenant colonel on his collar points. He picked up his microphone, then put it back in its hanger, adjusted the frequency of his transceiver, and then picked up the microphone again.

"Pensacola, Army Six-Four-Two, a B-25 aircraft, twenty miles east of your station, for approach and landing."

"Army Six-Four-Two, Pensacola, say again?"

"Six-Four-Two, a B-25 aircraft, twenty miles east of your station, for approach and landing."

"Army Six-Four-Two, be advised that Pensacola is closed to transient traffic without prior approval. Suggest you try Eglin Army Air Corps Field."

"Pensacola, Six-Four-Two has a Navy captain aboard who wishes to deplane at Pensacola. We will require no ground services."

"Army Six-Four-Two, advise Naval officer's name and purpose of his visit to Pensacola."

"Pensacola, the Navy Captain's Pickering. I spell: Peter Item Charley King Easy Roger Item Nan George. Be advised that any questions regarding him are to be directed to the Office of the Secretary of the Navy."

"Army Six-Four-Two, stand by."

There was a ninety-second pause.

"Army Six-Four-Two, Pensacola. You are cleared for a straight-in approach to runway two-seven. The winds are from the west at fifteen. The altimeter is two-nine-niner-eight. The time is two-five past the hour. Report over Pensacola Bay."

"Army Six-Four-Two, Pensacola. Thank you very much."

As the B-25 Mitchell, a light bomber, dropped low over Pensacola Bay, a telephone call was placed from the office of Base Commander, Pensacola Naval Air Station, to the office of the Secretary of the Navy:

"Office of the Secretary, Captain Haughton."

"Captain, this is Captain Summers. At Pensacola. I'm calling for the Admiral."

"What can I do for you?"

"Does the name Pickering mean anything to you, Captain?"

"Is Captain Pickering at Pensacola?"

"He's about to land here."

"Great! The Secretary's been wondering where he was. Would you ask him to call me just as soon as he can, please, Captain?"

"Yes, of course. Be glad to. Captain, we could probably be of greater usefulness to Captain Pickering if we knew what it is he's after at Pensacola."

Captain Haughton chuckled.

"I have no idea, I'm afraid, but I'm sure he'll tell you when he lands. When did you say that will be?"

"He should be landing right now. I'll relay the message."

Captain Summers first called the Officer of the Day.

"I don't know who this captain the B-25 wants to drop off—Pickering—is, Jack," Captain Summers said, "or what he wants. But pass the word to him to call Captain Haughton in the Secretary of the Navy's office, as soon as he can. And then ask what we can do for him."

He then called Rear Admiral Richard B. Sayre, who stood third in the chain of command at Pensacola, and was, at the moment, the senior officer aboard. He reported what little he knew about Captain Pickering, and what steps he had taken. Admiral Sayre grunted, and then told Summers to keep him posted.

Less than a minute later, Admiral Sayre called back.

"Pickering, you said? The VIP from Washington?"

"Yes, Sir."

"Present my compliments to Captain Pickering, please, and inform him I would be pleased to receive him at my office at his earliest convenience."

"Aye, aye, Sir."

Captain Fleming Pickering was driven directly to Admiral Sayre's office from the airfield. The Admiral's aide was waiting on the sidewalk when the staff car pulled up, and escorted him directly to the Admiral's office.

"Welcome to Pensacola, Captain," Admiral Sayre said. "May I offer you a cup of coffee, or something a little stronger?"

"Admiral, I feel like a kid caught with his hand in the cookie jar," Fleming Pickering said. "I'm not here officially . . ."

"You did get the message to call Captain Haughton?"

"Yes, Sir. I did. Thank you. Sir, I was about to say that I'm not here officially, and that what I hoped to do was get off and back on the base with no one noticing."

"Oh?"

"Sir, I've been over at Eglin Field on duty. I've got a seat on the courier plane to Washington from here tomorrow morning. I have some personal business in Pensacola."

"I thought that might be it," Admiral Sayre said.

"Sir?" Pickering asked, surprised.

"He's a nice boy, according to both my wife and Doc McInerney," the Admiral said. "And actually, he's the reason I asked you to come to see me."

Pickering's surprise was evident on his face.

"Doc and I went through flight school here together," Admiral Sayre said. "We're still pretty close. When your boy was sent here, Doc called me and told me about him. And you. I frankly found it comforting."

"Sir?"

"He spoke highly of your boy—Pick, they call him, don't they?"

"Yes, Sir."

"And he said that the only favor you asked of him was that the Marine Corps didn't make him a club officer. I thought that spoke well of you, Captain. And, as I said, I found that rather comforting."

"Comforting, Sir?"

"Your son is in hot pursuit of my daughter," Admiral Sayre said. "I'm not supposed to know that, but I do."

Pickering didn't reply.

"You don't seem surprised to hear that," the Admiral said.

Pickering knew more than his son thought he knew about the boy's romantic affairs. There had been an astonishing number of them, and they could more accurately be described as "carnal" than "romantic."

"Pick is attracted to the ladies, Admiral," Pickering replied. "And vice versa. Actually, from what I've seen, more the latter than the former. I can only presume your daughter is not only extraordinarily good looking, but something special. Pick is seldom reported 'in pursuit'; usually the phrase is 'in flight from.'"

The Admiral chuckled.

"I have *seen* him," he said. "Good-looking young Marine officers driving Cadillac convertible automobiles do seem to attract the ladies, don't they?"

"I've noticed," Pickering said, chuckling.

"Once Martha told him, rather forcefully, that she's not interested, I would have thought that he would have looked elsewhere."

What is this? Did he call me in here to tell me to keep my son away from his precious daughter?

"Pick's not her type? Has he been making an ass of himself?"

"No. He's been a perfect gentleman," Admiral Sayre said. "And I have the feeling that Martha is more attracted to him than she's willing to admit to herself or anyone else."

"Admiral—"

"My daughter's a widow," Admiral Sayre interrupted. "Her husband, Admiral Culhane's boy, an aviator, was killed at Wake Island."

"Oh," Fleming Pickering said, and then added, "I'm sorry to hear that."

"He was a really nice kid," Admiral Sayre said. "It's a damned shame."

"Are you saying this . . . relationship . . . between Pick and your daughter is serious?" Pickering asked.

Hell, of course it's serious. Chasing after a widow, especially a widow whose husband has been dead only a couple of months, and especially after she told him to get lost, is simply not Pick's style.

"I don't know," Admiral Sayre said. "But since Colonel Doolittle was kind enough to drop you in my lap, I thought I should introduce myself and mention it."

"Colonel Doolittle?" Pickering asked, trying to sound confused.

"Oh, come on, Pickering. Doc and Jimmy and I used to race airplanes together. And I thought that, doing what you're doing, you would have learned by now that whenever two people know something, it's no longer a secret. I know what's going on at Eglin, and my Officer of the Day recognizes Jimmy Doolittle when he sees him in a cockpit window."

"I think, Admiral, if that invitation is still open, I will have a drink."

(FIVE)

THE SAN CARLOS HOTEL
PENSACOLA, FLORIDA
1725 HOURS 28 FEBRUARY 1942

"Good afternoon, Sir," Second Lieutenant Richard J. Stecker, USMC, said to the Navy Captain. "May I help you, Sir?" The Captain was in the act of hanging up the telephone in the penthouse suite of the San Carlos Hotel.

Dick Stecker, a good-looking, trim young man wearing a fur-collared leather jacket over a flight suit, was torn between surprise, anger, and alarm at finding a fucking four-striper nosing around the suite. But he was a graduate of the United States Military Academy at West Point and a regular officer of the United States Marine Corps, and West Pointers and regular Marine officers do not demand of U.S. Navy captains, *Who the fuck are you, and what are you doing in my hotel room?*

"You must be Lieutenant Stecker," Captain Pickering said.

"Yes, Sir."

"It has been reported to me that these quarters are not only infested with females of notorious reputation, but awash, as well, in cheap whiskey," Pickering said sternly.

Lieutenant Stecker looked stunned.

Another Marine second lieutenant, similarly dressed, stepped around Lieutenant Stecker to see what the hell was going on, and then yelped in delight:

"Dad! God, am I glad to see you! What are you doing here?"

He ran across the room and wrapped his father in a bear hug.

"I'm catching a plane out of here in the morning," Pickering said.

"You've been on the base?" Pick asked uneasily.

He does not want anyone to know that his father is a Navy captain. Good boy!

"Just to get off an airplane," Pickering said. "I was hoping I could bunk with you tonight."

"Hell, yes! But what are you doing down here?"

"I was over with the Army Air Corps at Eglin Air Force Base," Pickering said. "It's right down the coast."

"Doing what?"

"None of your business, Lieutenant."

"You're involved with the B-25s," Pick Pickering challenged.

"What B-25s?" Pickering asked innocently.

"As if you didn't know," Pick said. "They've got an airfield over there with the dimensions of an aircraft-carrier deck painted on it. And they're trying to get B-25s off it."

"I have no idea what you're talking about," Pickering said. "But if I were you, I'd watch my mouth. You haven't seen those posters, 'Loose Lips Sink Ships'?"

Pick's look was both hurt and wary.

"That sounded pretty official," he said after a moment. "You're my *father,* for Christ's sake!"

"Pick, you and I are officers," Pickering said.

"See, wiseass?" Dick Stecker said. "Learn to keep your mouth shut."

"I'd still like to know what the hell they think they're doing over there," Pick Pickering said.

"You keep wondering out loud about it, you can read all about it in the newspapers. In your cell at Portsmouth. I'm serious, Pick."

Their eyes met.

"I didn't mean to put you on the spot, Dad," he said. "Sorry."

"Forget it," Pickering said.

"*Don't* forget it," Dick Stecker said. "Write it on your goddamned forehead."

"Well, the both of you can go to hell," Pick said cheerfully. "You can stand here and feel self-righteous. I need a shower."

"Can I make you a drink, Captain Pickering?" Dick Stecker asked. "You name it, we've got it."

"At least one of the occupants of this rooftop brothel is an officer and a gentleman," Pickering said. "Scotch, please. With soda, if you have it."

"Yes, Sir. Coming right up."

"I saw your dad a while back. In San Diego."

"Yes, Sir. Dad wrote me that he'd seen you; that you were in the Corps in War One together."

"Is that what you call it now? 'War One'?"

"Yes, Sir. Isn't that what it was, the First World War?"

"At the time, it was called 'the war to end all wars,' " Pickering said.

Dick Stecker handed him a drink.

"Thank you," Pickering said. "Is my being here going to interfere with any serious romantic plans you two had for tonight?"

"No, Sir. Not at all."

"When I had them let me in here, I was a little surprised not to find an assortment of local lovelies," Pickering said.

"Yes, Sir," Stecker said uncomfortably, then blurted, "You're asking about Martha Culhane, aren't you, Captain?"

"I am. But I would rather Pick didn't know I knew about her. Something about her. If this puts you on a spot, the subject never came up."

Dick Stecker made a circling motion with his index finger at his temple.

"He's nuts about her," he said. "She's a widow. Did you know?"

Pickering nodded.

"He's really got it bad for her. And she won't give him the time of day."

"You think that's maybe what it is? That she's not interested? That his Don Juan ego is involved?"

"No. I wish it was."

"What do you think of her?"

"I don't know what to think," Stecker said. "Maybe it'll pass when we graduate and get the hell out of here. But I don't know."

"OK. Thank you. Subject closed."

They ate in the hotel dining room, which was crowded with men in Navy and Marine Corps uniforms.

Over their shrimp cocktail, Fleming Pickering told them he was headed, via Washington and the West Coast, for Hawaii.

"When are you coming back?"

"I don't know," Pickering said. "Captains, like second lieutenants, go when and where they're told to go."

That was not true. Although he was still traveling on the vague orders that Captain Jack NMI Stecker had described as "awesome," permitting him to go where and when he pleased, no questions asked, he now had specific orders from the Secretary of the Navy:

Stay at Pearl Harbor as long as you want, Flem; learn what you can. But the President is going to order MacArthur out of the Philippines and to Australia. I want you there when he gets there. I want to know what he's up to. Haughton will message you wherever you are when Roosevelt orders him to leave, if you're not already in Australia by then.

Lieutenants Pickering and Stecker laughed dutifully.

There was a stir in the room while they were eating their broiled flounder. Pickering followed the point of attention to the door. Rear Admiral Richard Sayre, a woman almost certainly his wife, and a beautiful young blond woman almost certainly the widowed daughter, followed the headwaiter to a table across the room. Moments later, a Marine captain, a Naval Aviator, walked quickly to join them.

"That's Admiral Sayre, Captain," Dick Stecker said. "He's number three at Pensacola. And his wife and daughter."

Fleming Pickering was aware that his son was looking intently, perhaps angrily, at Stecker.

"And Captain Mustache," Stecker added.

"Captain 'Mustache'?" Pickering asked.

"He's one of our IPs . . . Instructor Pilots," Pick said.

"Oh," Pickering said.

"And like a lot of people around here, he's got a crush on the Admiral's daughter," Stecker said.

"She's a beautiful young woman," Pickering said.

"Yeah," Pick said. "She is."

That was all he had to say about Martha Sayre Culhane. But he kept looking over at her. And when Fleming Pickering looked in that direction, more often than not, Martha Sayre Culhane was surreptitiously looking in their direction.

IX

(ONE)
ABOARD THE MOTOR YACHT *LAST TIME*
THE SAN DIEGO YACHT CLUB
SAN DIEGO, CALIFORNIA
7 MARCH 1942

Ensign Barbara Cotter, USNR, and Miss Ernestine Sage were alone aboard the *Last Time*. Ensign Cotter was barefoot; she wore the briefest of white shorts, and her bosom was only barely concealed beneath a thin, orange kerchief bandeau. Miss Sage was wearing the briefest of pale blue shorts and a T-shirt, beneath which it was obvious she wore nothing else.

Although it was nearly noon, they were just finishing the breakfast dishes. They had been up pretty late the night before; there had been a certain amount of physical activity once they had gone to bed. After breakfast, they'd waved bye-bye to Lieutenants Joseph L. Howard, USMCR, and Kenneth R. McCoy, USMCR, as they departed for duty. Then Miss Sage had suggested to Ensign Cotter, "To hell with the dishes, let's go back to bed," and they had done just that, rising again only a few moments ago.

Barbara Cotter did not go home to Philadelphia on her overseas leave. She had called her parents and told them she was being shipped out; and no, she didn't know where she was going, and no, she wouldn't be able to get home before she left.

It was the first time she had ever lied to her parents about anything important, and it bothered her. But the choice had been between going home, alone, and staying in San Diego with Joe for the period of her leave. She was perfectly willing to admit that she was being a real shit for not going home, and then lying about it, but she wasn't sorry.

And in Ernie Sage she had found both a friend and a kindred soul; it was no time before Ernie offered Barbara and Joe the starboard stateroom for as long as they wanted it—just because they felt so close so quickly. Both of them were nice, Protestant, middle-class (in Ernie's

245

case, maybe upper-class) girls who had gone to college and had bright futures. And both of them were shacked up with a couple of Marines.

And were completely unashamed about it.

In no time they were both sharing deep, mutual confidences:

The first time they had laid eyes on Joe and Ken, they had known in their hearts that if they wanted to do *that*, and they hoped they would want to do *that*, they were going to let them.

It was the first time either of them had *really* felt that way, although in Ernie's case there had been a poet from Dartmouth, and in Barbara's case a gastroenterologist, who had made them feel *almost* that way.

And they talked, seriously, about why those things were going on. Barbara's theory was that Mother Nature caused the transmitters and receptors to be turned on in the interests of propagation. And Ernie's tangential theory was that Nature wanted to increase pregnancies in time of war.

And they talked of getting pregnant, and/or of getting married. They both reached the same conclusion: they weren't going to get married, not right away, anyhow. Because Joe and Ken thought they were probably going to get killed—or worse, crippled—in battle, both men refused to consider marriage. Yet Barbara and Ernie both agreed that what they really wanted, maybe most in the world, was to make babies with Joe and Ken. If they did, Joe and Ken would be furious—for the same reason they didn't want to get married. And further, since it was really better to have a baby when the baby was wanted, it was probably really better to wait until The Boys Came Home.

And in the meantime, they played housewife, and they loved it. They either prepared elaborate meals in the *Last Time*'s galley, or they went out for dinner to the Coronado Beach Hotel dining room, or to some hole-in-the-wall Mexican or Chinese restaurant. They carried their men's uniforms to the laundry, sewed their buttons on, and bought them razor blades and boxer shorts and Vitalis For The Hair. And loved them at night. And refused to think that it couldn't last forever—or, in Barbara and Joe's case, not later than the time her orders gave her, 2300 hours 16 March 1942. She was supposed to report to the Overseas Movement Officer, San Diego Naval Yard; and for her the *Last Time* would turn into a pumpkin.

Ernie told Barbara that after she was gone, and after Ken McCoy had shipped out, she was going back to New York City and back to work. She promised to visit Barbara's family in Philadelphia then, and tell them about Joe. She would confirm what Barbara was going to write them about him once she was on the ship headed nobody would tell her where.

The telephone rang, and Ernie Page answered it, then held up the phone to Barbara.

"It's somebody from the Navy Yard," she said.

Lieutenant Joe Howard, ever the dedicated officer, had advised her that if she wasn't going home, she was required to let "the receiving station" (by which he meant the Navy Yard) know where she was and how she could be reached.

"Ensign Cotter," Barbara said to the telephone.

"Ma'am, this is Chief Venwell, of Officer Movement, at the Navy Yard."

"What can I do for you, Chief?"

"Ma'am, you're to report here, with all your gear, for outshipment by 0630 tomorrow."

"What are you talking about? I'm on leave until the sixteenth."

"No, Ma'am. That's why I'm calling. Your orders have been changed. You're to report in by 0630 tomorrow."

"Why?"

"Ma'am, I guess they found a space for you to outship."

"But what if I was in Philadelphia?"

"Ma'am?"

"I was authorized a leave to Philadelphia. You couldn't do this to me if I was in Philadelphia," Barbara said. "I couldn't get from Philadelphia to San Diego by six o'clock tomorrow morning."

"Ma'am, you're in San Diego," Chief Venwell said. "Ma'am, I'm sorry about this, but I can't do a thing for you."

(TWO)

THE CORONADO BEACH HOTEL
SAN DIEGO, CALIFORNIA
8 MARCH 1942

"It's been a long time since I came here with a man in uniform," Patricia Foster Pickering said to her husband as they approached the hotel entrance.

Fleming Pickering was at the wheel of a 1939 Cadillac Sixty-Two Special he had borrowed from J. Charles Ansley, General Manager, San Diego Operations, Pacific & Far Eastern Shipping. He looked at his wife in some confusion until he took her meaning.

"Oh," he said wickedly, "that stuck in your mind, did it?"

It was a reference to their rendezvous in San Diego in 1919. Corporal Fleming Pickering, USMC, was going through the separation process at the San Diego Marine Barracks when, unannounced, Miss Patricia Foster of San Francisco had shown up at the gate to announce that she just happened to be in the neighborhood and thought she would just drop by.

She had had a suite in the Coronado Beach, a complimentary courtesy rendered by the management to the only daughter of Andrew Foster, Chairman of the Board of the Foster Hotel Corporation. There she had presented him with a welcome-home present of a nature he had not really expected to receive until after their relationship was officially sanctioned by the Protestant Episcopal Church.

"From time to time, I think of it," she admitted.

Throughout their marriage, Patricia had often surprised him. She had surprised him at two-fifteen that morning by slipping, naked, into his bed at Charley Ansley's house on a bluff overlooking the Pacific.

He had called her from Oklahoma City to tell her that he was en route in a Navy plane to San Diego, where he had some business with the Navy. He also intended to see his secretary—soon his ex-secretary—aboard the U.S. Navy transport *President Millard G. Fillmore*, ex–*Pacific Princess*. He would then, he told her, see about catching a plane home.

She could expect him late that night, or early the following morning. They would have four or five days home before he had to take the San Francisco–Pearl Harbor courier plane. She should think of something interesting for them to do.

He had wrapped his arms around her in Charley Ansley's bedroom and somewhat sleepily asked, "What brings you here, honey?"

"You said I should think of something interesting for us to do," Patricia had said, gently touching a sensitive part of his anatomy. "How does this strike you?"

She had come to join him by plane to Los Angeles, and then on the damned Greyhound bus to San Diego. Over breakfast, she told him she thought it would be fun to borrow a car from Charley Ansley, drive to Los Angeles, have dinner with friends there, and then drive leisurely on to San Francisco, perhaps spending another night on the way.

He told her he had to make a quick call on the Admiral commanding the San Diego Naval Yard, prepare a quick memorandum for Frank Knox reporting what the Admiral had told him, and then find an officer courier to take it to Washington. He also told her that Ellen Feller had arrived a couple of days before and was in the Pacific & Far East suite at the Coronado Beach.

"She's going to work at CINCPAC," Pickering said. There was an implication that she was going to become secretary to someone else. That was not actually the case. Officially, Ellen was going to work with the highly secret cryptographic unit at Pearl Harbor, putting her knowledge of Japanese and Chinese to work. And she had a second mission, to serve as a conduit for Fleming Pickering's confidential reports to the Secretary of the Navy. He would prepare the reports himself and send them to her at Pearl Harbor, sealed, via an officer courier. At Pearl Harbor, Ellen Feller would encrypt them with a special code and send them to Washington, either by cable or radio, classified TOP SECRET, EYES ONLY, THE SECRETARY OF THE NAVY.

That way, only Pickering, Ellen Feller, a cryptographer who worked solely for Captain Dave Haughton, Haughton himself, and the Secretary of the Navy would ever see Pickering's reports. Knox knew that if more people were brought into the link, or if standard Navy encryption-decryption procedures were followed, the Navy brass would be reading Pickering's reports before they got to him. Since the reports made considerable reference to the Navy brass, including, for instance, Pickering's opinion of their ability and performance, it would not have been clever to offer them to the brass on a silver platter, as it were.

None of that, obviously, was any of Patricia's business.

"Aren't you going to miss her?" Patricia asked, poker-faced. He wasn't sure whether she was serious or teasing, or even if there was a touch of jealousy in the question.

"There's a war on, Madam. We must all make what sacrifices are necessary in the common good," Pickering replied sonorously.

After Pickering stopped the Cadillac in front of the door, he opened the car door and started to get out. As he did that, the doorman rushed over and said, "I'm sorry, Sir, we no longer offer valet parking . . ." And then he recognized Pickering. "I'll take care of it, Mr. Pickering. You going to be long?"

"We're going to have lunch."

"Then I'll leave it right over there, Sir. Nice to see you, Mrs. Pickering. It's been some time."

"Hello, Dick. How are you?" Patricia said.

Pickering called the Pacific & Far East suite from a house phone in the lobby.

"I'm not quite packed," Ellen Feller said. "Could you come up for a minute?"

"Sure," Pickering said. "The ship sails at two-forty-five, so I've been told."

"Then we have plenty of time."

Pickering put the phone down.

"She's not quite ready," he said.

"I thought she was Miss Efficiency of 1942?" Patricia said.

"We're not running late," Pickering said loyally.

"You go up," Patricia said. "I'll get her a box of candy or a basket of fruit. For Bon Voyage."

"I'll go with you."

"No, you won't. You know how I hate it when you breathe impatiently over my shoulder in a shop. And I know where the suite is."

(THREE)

Ellen Feller spent a good deal of time considering very carefully the pluses and minuses of her new assignment. Some of the pluses were inarguable. She'd been promoted from Oriental Languages Linguist to Intelligence Analyst. And after her name on her travel orders now appeared the parenthesized phrase "(Assimilated Grade of Lt. Commander)." That meant she was entitled to the privileges the armed forces gave to an officer of that rank; and that she was earning just about as much money as a Lieutenant Commander made.

Back in Washington, Commander Kramer had informed her that when she reached Hawaii, she would be provided with bachelor women officer's quarters on the Navy Base at Pearl Harbor. ("The last time I was there, lieutenant commander nurses had nice little bungalows; they'll probably assign you one of those.") And she would be entitled to membership in the officers' club, where she would take her meals, and have access to everything else—the base exchange and the golf course, that sort of thing—that a lieutenant commander would have.

A remarkably short time after starting as a temporary civilian employee brought in to help with foreign-language translation (really a sort of multilingual clerk), she had risen to the upper echelons of Navy intelligence. The proof was that she was privy to, and would be working with, the Big Secret: that the Navy had cracked the Imperial Japanese Navy code. And she would continue to work—though remotely—with Captain Fleming Pickering, who answered to nobody but the Secretary of the Navy.

It now seemed very unlikely that there would be any difficulty about the crates shipped home from China. And since she was going to Hawaii, it would no longer be necessary for her to make the weekly trips to the nursing home in Baltimore to see her father. Or to endure the hour-long sermon he always delivered.

There were just a few minuses to her promotion and transfer; and they were all spelled Captain Fleming Pickering, USNR.

She had been attracted to him from the very first moment she had met him in his suite in the Foster Lafayette Hotel. The expensively furnished suite itself represented a style of living that she had previously believed existed only in the movies. And as she had learned more about him, her fascination with him grew: He *owned* steamships, a *fleet* of them! His wife's father *owned* a chain of hotels, including the Foster Lafayette! He personally knew a large number of *very important* people, people like Senator Fowler and Henry Ford, and even the President of the United States!

There was a physical attraction, too. From that first day, she had wondered what it would be like to be in bed with him. He was tall, good looking, and in splendid physical shape. She loved the deep timbre of his voice. But just about as immediately, she also recognized that any notions of getting him into her bed were dangerous.

Since a rich and handsome man like Fleming Pickering must have had any number of women to choose from, she was convinced that he must have grown very selective. It was entirely possible that he would not be interested in her at all, and that any overtures from her would see her returned to her old job. It didn't especially surprise her to learn that he was faithful to his wife, and that they apparently had had a long and successful marriage . . . but it disappointed her, all the same.

After a while, as he grew to rely on her faithful services, she realized that he was taking her under his wing. She was protected by his authority and influence. If questions about the crates from China now came up, she was sure that she could convince him of her innocence, and that he would defend her—with all of his influence—against any accusations.

Of course, with her in Hawaii and Fleming Pickering in Australia— or God knew where else—that would no longer be the case. She would be an ex-employee, no longer his faithful right hand. She could probably call on him for help, but the situation would be changed. She might be an "assimilated lieutenant commander" in Hawaii, but she would no longer be Captain Fleming Pickering's assistant.

On the train to California, she wondered whether she had made a mistake in playing out her perfectly platonic half of their entirely platonic relationship. More than once she had seen him looking at her as a man looks at a desirable woman.

But it would now be in her interest for Fleming Pickering to remember her as a woman he had bedded, and who had asked for nothing from him. There had been several occasions in the Foster Layfayette suite when he might well have responded to an overture. More than once he had been at his Old Grouse beyond the point where his judgment was affected.

But she had let those opportunities pass, and there was nothing that would bring them back. That was really a pity, she thought ruefully. It almost certainly would have been a very pleasant experience to have Fleming Pickering in her bed. Or, for that matter, on the floor. Anywhere.

And then he had sent word that he would come to the hotel and see her aboard the ship.

(FOUR)

When Ellen Feller answered Pickering's knock at the door, she was wearing a dressing gown. It was flowing—and translucent. Not missionary-lady style, he thought, recalling the black lace underwear she had worn the day he met her. And in that grossly embarrassing erotic dream.

"Hi!" she said. "Come in. I'm almost ready. I just stopped to make myself a drink. Nerves."

"I didn't know you drank," Pickering said.

"There's a lot about me you don't know," Ellen said. She walked across the room to the bar. The light behind her revealed the outline of her body beneath the thin dressing gown. And certain anatomical details.

"Old Grouse," she said, reaching for a bottle. "I know how you like it."

She made a drink, and then held it out to him. Her upper leg parted the dressing gown as he, uncomfortably, walked to her to take the drink.

"I don't mind if you look," Ellen said.

"I beg your pardon?"

"I said, I don't mind if you look," she repeated. "I was beginning to think there was something wrong with me. The most fascinating man I've ever met, and he appears totally immune."

"Ellen . . ."

"Have a good look," she said. She tugged at the dressing-gown cord and it fell open. "Do I pass inspection?"

"My wife is on her way up here," Pickering said.

Oh, Goddamn it! What have I done now?

"I'm sorry," she said evenly, after a moment.

"You'd better get your clothes on."

"Pity," she said, then put his glass of Scotch down and walked into one of the bedrooms. She stopped at the door and looked at him. The dressing gown was still open.

"Fleming," she said, using his first name for the first time ever, "the last thing in the world I want is to cause you trouble with your wife."

He nodded.

"Thank you."

She walked into the bedroom, took the dressing gown off, and tossed it toward the bed. Then she walked, naked, to the door and closed it.

Jesus Christ! She must be drunk. I wonder if we can get through the next couple of hours without a major disaster.

Fantastic teats!

(FIVE)

UNITED STATES NAVY YARD
SAN DIEGO, CALIFORNIA
8 MARCH 1942

"Sir, I can pass you in, but not with these ladies," the Marine sergeant at the gate said, handing the identification card back to Captain Fleming Pickering, USNR.

"Sergeant, this lady is on orders," Pickering said. "Ellen, show him your damned orders."

Mrs. Ellen Feller took from her purse a thin stack of mimeographed orders and her identification card and handed them over the seatback to Pickering, who then passed them to the sergeant. The sergeant read the orders, looked at the ID card, compared the photograph on it with her face, and then handed it all back.

"Sir, this lady can pass. But the other one—"

"'The other one' is my wife!" Pickering flared.

"Sir, she doesn't have any ID."

"Flem," Patricia Foster Pickering said, aware that her husband was about to lose his temper, "I'll just wait here. You put Ellen on the ship and come back and pick me up."

"Patricia, please butt out of this," Pickering said sharply.

They had managed to get through lunch without a disaster. When Ellen came out of the bedroom to meet Patricia, she was modestly dressed, her hair was done up in a simple bun, and she wore no makeup. She thanked Patricia for the basket of fruit, apologized for not having been ready, and never again called him Fleming. She was a perfect lady at lunch. But he didn't want to set the stage for something happening aboard the ship by being alone with her there.

"Sergeant, please call the Officer of the Guard," Captain Pickering ordered.

"Aye, aye, Sir."

It took the Officer of the Guard three minutes to reach the gate in a Navy-gray Ford pickup. He found a Navy captain at the wheel of a glistening 1939 Cadillac Sixty-Two Special sedan, which did *not* have San Diego Navy Base identification. A civilian woman was next to him, a nice-looking lady wearing a diamond engagement ring that looked like it weighed a pound. Another woman was sitting in the back of the Cadillac. She was a little younger than the other one, but somewhat plain—not at all bad-looking, though. She had a Navy Department ID card and a set of orders giving her AAA travel priority to CINCPAC Headquarters in Hawaii.

The Officer of the Guard was a first lieutenant; Pickering thought he looked like a regular. The Officer of the Guard saluted.

"Good afternoon, Sir. May I help you?"

"My name is Pickering, Lieutenant. This lady is my wife. The other lady is Mrs. Feller, who is to board the . . . the *President Fillmore.* I don't want to leave my wife here at the gate while I take Mrs. Feller aboard."

"No problem at all, Sir," the Lieutenant said. "If you'll just follow me in the pickup."

Pickering looked at the sergeant who had denied him access.

"Sergeant, when I was a Marine corporal, there was a saying that 'a Marine on guard duty has no friends.' Do they still say that?"

"Yes, Sir, they do."

"Your sergeant, Lieutenant, was the soul of tact," Pickering said.

"I'm glad to hear that, Sir. If you'll just follow me, Sir?"

The little convoy moved out.

In the Cadillac, Patricia Foster Pickering said, "What was that all about?"

"That sergeant was just doing his duty. I didn't want to get him in trouble."

"Why should he?"

"The Lieutenant obviously knows who I am," Pickering said.

"Who you are? What a monumental ego! Am I missing something? Who *are* you?"

"I mean that I work for Frank Knox. We're in, aren't we? And what does ego have to do with it?"

In the cab of the pickup, the Marine Lieutenant said to the driver, "Take us down to the *Millard Fillmore.*"

"That's that great big civilian liner, Sir?"

"Yeah. They used to call it the *Pacific Princess.* As soon as I take that Captain up the gangplank, you find a telephone, call the Officer of the Day, and tell him that Captain Pickering just came into the yard, and that I'm escorting him aboard the *Millard Fillmore.* You get that name?"

"Yes, Sir. Pickering. Who is he?"

"He works for the Secretary of the Navy. He's got the brass scared shitless. He showed up here yesterday for a private conference with the Admiral, after which the Admiral thought Pickering was going back to Washington. But he didn't. He wasn't on the courier plane. They passed the word that the Admiral was to be notified the moment anybody saw him anywhere."

The pickup truck driver drove as close as he could to the great ship, and then stopped. The Lieutenant got out and walked to the Cadillac.

"This is as close as we can get, Sir. If you'll wait a moment, I'll get someone to carry the lady's luggage."

"I'm not too old to carry a couple of suitcases," Pickering said.

"Sir, they frown on officers, particular senior ones, carrying luggage."

"Oh, hell. OK. Go get someone, then."

"Aye, aye, Sir."

Pickering got out from behind the wheel, walked to the edge of the wharf, and looked up at the stern of the ship. Her once-glistening white hull was now a flat Navy gray. PRESIDENT MILLARD G. FILLMORE was painted in enormous letters across her stern. But if you looked closely, you could see where the raised lettering PACIFIC PRINCESS SAN FRANCISCO had been painted over.

Her superstructure was still mostly white, although her funnels were also in Navy gray, probably so that the Pacific & Far Eastern logo on them could be obliterated. Pickering had learned from the Admiral the day before that they were carrying a work crew aboard in order to finish the painting and to make other modifications under way. Shipping space was so tight they could not afford to take her out of service for modifications any longer than was absolutely necessary.

What I should be doing is standing on her bridge, preparing to take her to sea, not functioning as a make-believe Naval officer and high-class errand boy for Frank Knox.

"It's sad, seeing her in gray," Patricia said softly, at his elbow.

"It has to be done, I suppose," he said. "Anyway, she's now the Navy's. Not ours."

(SIX)

One by one, the umbilicals that tied the *President Millard G. Fillmore* to the dock were cut. Finally, only one gangplank remained, and there seemed to be no activity on that.

From the boat deck, Ensign Barbara Cotter, NC, USNR, looked down at the small crowd of people on the dock. Ernie Sage was there, and her Ken McCoy, and Joe. They had waved excitedly at each other when Barbara had found a place for herself at the rail. But that was forty-five minutes ago; now they just forced smiles and made little waves at each other.

Finally, three people appeared on the single remaining gangway, a Marine officer, a Navy captain, and a civilian woman.

"Oh, my God!" Ernie Sage said. "Ken, that's Pick's father and mother."

"Where?" McCoy asked.

"The Navy guy and the woman coming down the gangway."

"You want me to get their attention, or what?"

"No!"

"I know them. I met them when we graduated from Quantico."

"If they see me here, Aunt Pat would feel obliged to tell my mother," Ernie said.

"Just where do you think your mother thinks you are? She doesn't know what you're doing?" McCoy said.

"Will you just leave it, please?"

Right in front of them, two sailors pulled an enormous hawser free of a hawser stand, and it began to rise up along the steep side of the ship.

Joe Howard looked down the dock. Nothing now held the *President Millard G. Fillmore* to the shore.

"It's moving," Ernie said.

A rather small Navy band began to play "Anchors Aweigh."

The *President Millard G. Fillmore* was an enormous ship and difficult to get into motion. When the band finished "Anchors Aweigh" and segued into "The Marine Hymn" there were only a few feet of water between the ship and the dock. Then, in deference to a battalion of U.S. Army Engineers aboard, the band played "The Caissons Go Rolling Along." By the time that was finished, twenty feet of water separated the shore and the ship.

Then the ship added the power of her engines to that of the tugs; there was a swirl of water at her stern, and her stern moved farther away from the dock.

The band began to play "Auld Lang Syne."

Barbara Cotter and Joe Howard waved bravely at each other.

"You OK, Joe?" Ken McCoy asked.

"This is not the way it's supposed to be," Joe Howard said. "I'm the goddamned Marine, and here I am on the goddamned shore, waving good-bye as my girlfriend goes overseas."

The band stopped playing; and to the ticking of drumsticks on drum rims, they marched off toward a Navy-gray bus.

First Lieutenant Joe Howard walked to the end of the dock and stood there watching until the *President Millard G. Fillmore* sailed out of sight.

(SEVEN)

```
┌─ ═ ═ ═ ═ ═ ─┐
║ TOP SECRET ║
└─ ═ ═ ═ ═ ═ ─┘
```

Eyes Only—The Secretary of the Navy

  DUPLICATION FORBIDDEN
  ORIGINAL TO BE DESTROYED AFTER ENCRYPTION AND TRANSMITTAL
TO SECNAVY

Melbourne, Australia
Saturday, 21 March 1942

Dear Frank:

  Despite a nearly overwhelming feeling that this should be
addressed "Dear Mr. Secretary," I am complying with your orders to write this in the form of a personal letter; to include
my opinions as well as the facts as I understand them; and to
presume that I am your sole source of information regarding
what is going on in this area of the world.
  This is written in my apartment in the Menzies Hotel, Melbourne, which I was able to get through the good offices of our
(Pacific & Far East) agent here. It is my intention to deliver
it, triply sealed, into the hands of the Captain of the USS John
B. Lester, a destroyer which put in here for emergency repairs
(now just about completed), and that is bound directly for
Pearl Harbor. Using my letter of authority from you, I will direct Captain (Lt. Commander) K. L. White to deliver it into the
hands of Mrs. Feller, or, if for some reason that is impossible,
to burn it.
  His willingness to comply with those orders, it seems to me,
depends on whether he accepts your letter of authority at face
value. The whipping we have taken so far seems to me to have
produced a lack of confidence here—perhaps even an aura of defeatism. What I'm suggesting is that he may decide either to
throw this whole thing away or to open it, or to do something
other than what I am ordering him to do. Ellen Feller—if she

gets this—will be able to determine whether or not it has been opened. I would very much appreciate your advising me of the receipt of this, including when, and to tell me if this is the sort of thing you would like to have me continue to do.

Obviously, I did not get into the Philippines. Haughton's message that MacArthur had been ordered to leave Corregidor was waiting for me when I arrived in San Francisco from San Diego on March 10. I left the next morning for Hawaii aboard a Navy Martin Mariner. At CINCPAC, I was told that the only way into the Philippines, either Corregidor or Mindanao, would be by submarine. I had just missed the <u>Permit,</u> which was scheduled to be at Corregidor on the 13th, and another "courier" submarine was not scheduled.

I could not have reached Corregidor, in other words, until after MacArthur was gone. And it was made clear to me that it would be very difficult to leave the Philippines once I got there. Under those circumstances, I decided not to go. I visited the Special Detachment and told the commanding officer of your special orders to Mrs. Feller. He was very cooperative, and I feel there will be no problems with him.

The next morning, I left Hickam Field, TH, aboard an Army Air Corps B-17, one of a flight of four en route from Seattle to Vice Admiral Herbert F. Leary's command in Australia. We arrived without incident early on March 13.

I presented myself to Admiral Leary and showed him my letter of authority from you. He was obviously torn between annoyance at having someone from Washington looking over his shoulder and a hope that perhaps I could convince "those people in Washington" of the terrible shape things are in here.

The only bright light in the whole area, he said, was that elements of Task Force 6814, including some Engineer troops, had the day before landed on Efate Island. If Admiral King's order to recapture Rabaul as soon as possible can be carried out at all, it is essential for them to construct an air base on the island. I sensed that Leary is not overly confident that the Army can build such a field in a short time.

Leary also told me that a radio message had come from Cor-

TOP SECRET

regidor reporting that MacArthur, his wife, and small son, together with President Quezon and some others, had left Corregidor at sunset, March 11, bound for Mindanao. They were aboard four PT boats; and there had been no report on them since then. Leary said he was not yet concerned; the boats were under the command of a Lieutenant Buckley, whom he knows, and considers an extraordinarily competent officer.

He was far more concerned to learn that the Japanese have occupied the island of Buka, 170 miles southeast of Rabaul, and that aerial reconnaissance has shown them unloading the engineer equipment for building an airfield.

While I was in his office, he and I learned that MacArthur and his people had turned up safe. A radio came from General Sharp's headquarters on Mindanao reporting that "the shipment was received" but that it would "require some maintenance." Leary and I decided (correctly, it turned out) that this meant the trip had been rough on MacArthur and/or Quezon and/or the others. MacArthur is, after all, sixty-two, Quezon is even older, and they had just completed a long voyage in small boats across rough seas.

At this point Major General George S. Brett, the senior Army Air Corps officer here, entered the picture. Brett wanted Leary to dispatch four B-17s to Mindanao to pick up the MacArthur party and bring them here. Leary refused, citing as his reasons that the four planes had just flown from the United States and required maintenance; and that in any event, he needed them for operational use. He had just learned that the 20,000-odd Dutch troops on Java had surrendered, and in his opinion that had removed the last obstacle the Japanese had to overcome before invading Australia. He could not spare heavy bombers to carry passengers, no matter how important the passengers.

I was privy to this conversation. I think Leary knew what Brett wanted of him, and wanted me to hear it so that it would be reported to you.

Brett was highly upset. Part of it, I think, was that he placed more importance on getting the MacArthur party out of

Mindanao than Leary does; and part of it was the humiliation an Air Corps officer felt about asking a Navy officer for Army Air Corps airplanes, and then getting refused. Anyway, Brett stormed out, promising that the President would hear about this and make it right. Leary said he did not see the need for immediate action; Sharp has 30,000 effective troops, and Mindanao is not in immediate danger of being overrun. The MacArthur party, he feels, can be safely taken off by submarine. I was prone to agree with Leary.

Brett came back shortly afterward, saying that he had learned of a B-17 that was available. Leary was already aware of it; it was an early model, old and worn, and he could not guarantee how safe it was. Brett insisted, and Leary gave in.

The plan was for MacArthur and party to be flown in the B-17 from Mindanao to Darwin, which is on the northern coast of Australia. There they would transfer to two civilian DC-3s Brett chartered from the Australian airlines and fly across the continent to Melbourne. General Brett graciously allowed me to fly to Darwin on one of the civilian airplanes.

We expected to find the MacArthur party waiting for us at Darwin. But on landing we learned that MacArthur had inspected the B-17 sent to pick him up, and had refused to fly in it. The airplane then returned to Australia without passengers.

Brett shortly afterward learned that Leary had changed his mind about the newer B-17s, and three of the four took off to get MacArthur. One of them had to turn back when it developed engine trouble over the Australian desert; the other two made it to Mindanao just before midnight on Monday (March 16). (These details from Lt. Frank Bostrom, Army Air Corps, who was the senior pilot, and who flew MacA's airplane.)

An engine supercharger on one of Bostrom's engines went out en route. He could have made it back without having it repaired, but it would have lowered his weight-carrying ability and caused other problems I don't really understand. He managed to get it repaired, however, which meant that he and the other B-17 could carry all of the MacArthur party (but none of their luggage).

But then another of Bostrom's engines acted up during take-off, and he was really afraid he couldn't get the airplane off the ground. In the end, though, he managed it. After that, it was a five-hour flight to Darwin—about the same distance as from New Orleans to Boston—and there was violent turbulence en route. Nothing had been done to convert the airplanes from their bombing role. Mrs. MacArthur and the boy had the only "upholstery," a mattress laid on the cabin floor. MacArthur rode in the radio operator's seat.

Along with his immediate family, the general brought his staff out with him, none of whom, frankly, I care for—although MacArthur feels they are to a man superb officers. To me they're more like the dukes who used to surround a king.

As soon as they were able to establish radio contact with Darwin, they were informed that Darwin was under Japanese air attack and that they should divert to Batchelor Field, which is about fifty miles away. I was already there with the two Air Australia DC-3s, when they landed about nine in the morning (Tues., Mar 17). A good deal of what follows may well be unimportant—certainly, some of it is petty—but you wanted my opinion of MacArthur, his thinking, and the people around him.

He seemed very disturbed to find on hand to greet him only Brigadier Royce (who had been on the Air Australia plane with me), representing General Brett. For good cause, certainly, he looked exhausted.

I told his aide, a man named Huff, that I was your personal representative, and that I wished to pay my respects to MacArthur and ask him for his evaluation of the situation so that I could pass it on to you. Huff made it plain that MacArthur was entitled to a far more senior Navy officer than a lowly captain. He also felt that I had seriously violated military protocol by not presenting myself to Admiral Rockwell before daring to approach the throne of King Douglas. Rockwell was the former senior Navy officer in the Philippines, and he came in on the second B-17.

Admiral Rockwell was displeased with me, too, and you may hear about that. There was a scene that in other circumstances

would have been humorous, during which he kept demanding to know who was my immediate superior, to which I kept answering "Secretary Knox," to which he kept replying, ad infinitum, "You're not listening to me. I mean your *immediate* superior." During all this, he simply refused to look at my letter of authority from you until I answered the simple question of who was my immediate superior.

This little farce came to an end when Mrs. MacArthur recognized me. Not as a Naval officer, but as my wife's husband. Apparently, they had met in Manila, and Mrs. MacA. regards Patricia as a friend. Or at least a social peer. She told her husband of my connection with Pacific & Far East, and I was permitted to approach the throne.

I had met MacArthur only briefly once or twice before, and I am sure he did not remember those occasions; but he greeted me warmly and told me he was anxious to learn (these are his words as closely as I can remember them) "details of the buildup in Australia; troop and naval dispositions; and the tentative timetable for the recapture of Luzon."

I explained to him that there was no buildup; that there were only about 34,000 troops of any description in Australia; that the only unit of any size was the understrength 1st Brigade of the 6th Australian Division; and that the strategic problem as I understood it was to attempt to keep the Japanese from taking Australia which might not be possible and that, consequently, nothing whatever had yet been done about attempting to take Luzon back from the Japanese.

His eyes glazed over. He turned to another of his aides, a brigadier general named Sutherland, and said, "Surely he is mistaken." Then he marched off to a small shack where breakfast (baked beans and canned peaches) was served.

Brigadier Royce, who is a nice fellow, followed him into the shack. And later he emerged from it looking dazed. Mrs. MacArthur did not wish to fly anymore, perhaps ever again, and General MacArthur had therefore ordered Royce to immediately form a motorcade to transport the party to the nearest railhead. Royce had informed MacArthur that the nearest

TOP SECRET

railhead was in Alice Springs, about as far away across the desert (1,000 miles or so) as Chicago is from New Orleans, and that, among other things, there were no vehicles available to form a motorcade.

MacArthur's response was, "You have your orders; put them into execution."

This apparently impossible situation was resolved by Major Charles H. Morehouse, an Army doctor who had come out of the Philippines with them. He told Royce that such a trip would probably kill the MacArthur boy, Arthur, who is five or six, and who was ill. Morehouse was feeding him intravenously. Morehouse also said that he could not guarantee whether MacArthur himself would live through a 1,000-mile automobile trip across the desert.

Royce somewhat forcefully suggested to Dr. Morehouse that he make this point emphatically to MacArthur. So Morehouse went into the shack. After several minutes MacArthur came out and announced, "We are prepared to board the aircraft." It was the royal "we," Frank.

We got on the airplanes. As the engines were being started, the air-raid sirens went off; several of the Japanese bombers attacking Darwin had broken off their attack and were headed for Batchelor Field. Whether or not they knew the MacArthur party was there, I don't know.

All the same, we got off safely, and made the trip to Alice Springs without incident. Alice Springs looks like a town in a cowboy movie, and it's the northern terminus of the Central Australian Railway . . . and it lies a good deal beyond the range of the Japanese Mitsubishi bombers.

Alice Springs, MacArthur announced, was as far as he intended to fly. He could not be moved from this position even after he was told that the next train would not come for six days. And then Ambassador Hurley[1] flew in to tell MacArthur

---

[1] Patrick Jay Hurley, formerly Secretary of War and then Ambassador to New Zealand.

TOP SECRET

that MacA. had been named Supreme Commander, Allied Forces, Southwest Pacific, by Prime Minister Curtin and President Roosevelt. He also tried to get MacA. to take a plane to Melbourne, but he had no more luck than anybody else.

So a special train was ordered up. We still had the Air Australia DC-3s. So Hurley and most of MacA.'s staff—except Huff, Sutherland, and Dr. Morehouse, the intimate guardians of the throne—flew off to Melbourne. I was sorely tempted to fly with them, and I might have gone—until General Sutherland imperiously ordered me to do it.

I guess I'm learning the Machiavellian rules of the game: I did not think the Personal Representative of the Secretary of the Navy should place himself under the orders of an Army officer.

The train arrived the next morning. It too looked like something from a cowboy movie: a tiny locomotive, two third-class coaches, and a caboose. The tracks there—between Alice Springs and Adelaide, a thousand-odd miles—are three feet between the rails. Should the Japanese invade Australia, this single-track, narrow-gauge railroad, with rolling stock to match, will simply not be adequate to supply, much less to transport, anything close to an infantry division. Which doesn't matter, I guess: we don't have an infantry division to transport; and if we did, one division would obviously not be adequate to repel a Japanese invasion.

The first coach of the train had wooden seats; and the second held an Australian Army nurse, a couple of Australian Army sergeants, an army field stove, and a supply of food. It was a three-day trip. For the first twenty-four hours, no one spoke to me but the sergeants.

Then MacArthur sent for me. He ran Sutherland and Huff off and began a nonstop lecture that lasted several hours. Obviously, he was playing to you, vicariously, through me. He began with Japanese economics and politics and how these made the war in the Pacific inevitable. Then he discussed Japanese strategy generally and in the Philippines specifi-

cally. He had at his fingertips a literally incredible ency-
clopedia of dates, names, and figures (tonnages, distances,
etcetera).

By the time it was over, I was dazed. Using the word very
carefully, the man is clearly a genius. I shall never think of
him again as just one more general. It seems to me now that he
fits in the same category as Roosevelt and Churchill. I also
believe that, like Roosevelt and Churchill, he sees himself as
a latter-day Moses, divinely inspired to lead his people out of
the desert. In this connection, he feels a personal obligation
to the Filipinos.

MacA. seems to understand that Roosevelt's decision to aid
Britain (and the Russians) first is irrevocable and that, as a
good soldier, he will of course support it. But he also makes it
plain that he believes the decision was the wrong one, made because (a) Churchill can play Roosevelt like a violin (and I
rather agree with that), and (b) George Marshall, who has
Roosevelt's ear, is determined that MacArthur shall not be allowed to demonstrate his military genius (which, of course, is
absurd).

General Marshall (MacA.'s Deputy C/S; not the other one,
obviously) boarded the train at a small station several hours
before we got to Adelaide the next afternoon. I started to
leave, but MacA. motioned for me to stay. Marshall then confirmed what I had told MacA. in Darwin; that there were no
troops to speak of in all of Australia; and that there was doubt
that Australia itself could be held.

Marshall said something to MacA. about creating a "Brisbane
Line"; the Australian General Staff was planning to abandon
the northern ports, including Darwin, to the Japanese, and attempt to hold the population centers along the southern and
eastern coasts.

"They can just forget that," MacArthur said. "We shall hold
Australia."

Logic told me, Frank, that that was highly improbable. But
my heart told me that we would indeed hold Australia. MacArthur
had just said so.

Marshall also reported that two companies of the 182nd Infantry and a company of Army Engineers had landed on Efate with orders to build an airfield, "whatever the hell that means."

Without reference to a map, and more important, without my having told him that Admiral King had ordered the recapture of Rabaul—and if I hadn't told him, who else had this knowledge and could have?—MacArthur explained that Efate was an island in the New Hebrides, about 700 miles southeast of Tulagi, and that "someone with a knowledge of strategy" had seen the establishment of an air base there as essential to the recapture of Rabaul, which was itself essential to deny the Japanese a chance to make a successful landing on the Australian continent.

Marshall also told him that there would be reporters waiting for him in Adelaide, and that some sort of a statement would be expected.

The two of them started to work on that, and were still working on it when he arrived at Adelaide. This is, essentially verbatim, what he said there:

"The President of the United States ordered me to break through the Japanese lines for the purpose, as I understand it, of organizing the American offensive against Japan, a primary object of which is the relief of the Philippines. I came through, and I shall return."

If you want to know what he's thinking, Frank, I suggest you study that short speech carefully. It was not off the cuff.

The Commissioner of Railroads had sent his own private car to Adelaide, where it was attached to the Melbourne Express. From Adelaide to Melbourne, the track is standard width. I scurried around getting a sleeper on the train, and had just succeeded when Huff found me. I was, so I was informed, to have one of the staterooms in the private car. I don't know who was more surprised, Huff or me.

We got to Spencer Street Station, Melbourne, just before ten a.m. the next day. We backed in, with MacA. standing like a

politician on the rear platform of the private car. There were half a hundred reporters in the station, and even an honor guard.

MacA. delivered another speech, which I am sure was as carefully prepared as the "I shall return" speech in Adelaide. In it, again just about verbatim, he said, "success in modern war means the furnishing of sufficient troops and materiel to meet the known strength of the enemy. No general can make something out of nothing. My success or failure will depend primarily upon the resources which the respective governments place at my disposal."

He cold-shouldered General Brett and General Royce at the station, rather cruelly I thought; and I think he's going to hold a grudge about the B-17s. There is no excuse for it that I can see. Nor—as I just learned from Huff—is there any excuse for recommending the award of a Presidential Unit Citation to every unit on Corregidor except the 4th Marines. His reason for not giving it to the Marines, again quoting Huff, is that "they have enough publicity as it is."

He also, politely, refused the offer of several mansions and moved into the Menzies. I can only wonder what will happen when he finds out that lowly Captain Pickering, USNR, occupies an identical apartment directly above him.

I don't think he has made up his mind what to do about me, and for the moment, at least, I am considered a member pro tem of the palace guard.

One final thing: I learned from the Australians that they have left behind, on various islands now (or about to be) occupied by the Japs, former colonial officers, planters, missionaries, etcetera. They are calling these people "Coastwatchers," and they feel they will be able to provide very valuable intelligence. They have commissioned them into the Royal Australian Navy Reserve, so they'll be under the Geneva Convention. I suspect that they are just whistling in the wind about that.

Admiral Leary does not seem to be impressed with their potential. I am. If we have anybody who speaks Japanese, and who

TOP SECRET

can be spared, I suggest you send them over here now to establish a relationship with the Coastwatchers.

I really hope this is what you were hoping to get from me.

Respectfully,
Fleming Pickering, Capt., USNR.

TOP SECRET

(EIGHT)

WALKER HASSLINGER'S RESTAURANT
BALTIMORE, MARYLAND
1 APRIL 1942

The basic principles of both leadership and organization have evolved over many centuries. Among the most important of these principles is the chain of command. The military services, and for that matter any organization, may be thought of as a pyramid. Authority and responsibility flow downward from the pinnacle, passing through progressively junior levels of command. Simplistically, if the first sergeant of an infantry company, for example, wants a PFC to load a truck with sandbags, he does not stop the first PFC he encounters and tell him to do so. Instead, he tells a platoon sergeant, who tells a section leader, who tells a corporal, and the corporal selects the PFC who gets the sandbags loaded.

To do otherwise would create chaos. The corporal would wonder where his PFC had gone without orders. The man in charge of the sandbags would question the PFC's right to take them away. The truckdriver would not know why sandbags were being loaded on his truck.

The chain of command is even more important at the highest echelons of military and naval service. Although in law the Secretary of the Navy has the authority, he does not issue direct orders to captains of ships, or even to commanders-in-chief of the various fleets.

He tells the Chief of Naval Operations what he wants done, in general terms: "I think we should reinforce the Pacific Fleet." The Chief of Naval Operations decides how the Pacific Fleet should be reinforced, again in rather general terms: "Add a battleship, two cruisers, and a half-dozen destroyers." As the order moves down through the pyramid, other officers make more specific decisions and issue more specific orders: which battleship, which cruisers, and which destroyers; in other words, which commands will lose assets to reinforce the Pacific Fleet, and when.

Only six or seven levels down in the chain of command will the captain of a destroyer finally order the officer of the deck to make all preparations to get under way, and then to set course for the Hawaiian Islands. And he will not associate the movement of his vessel with a vague suggestion given to the Chief of Naval Operations by the Secretary of the Navy.

The chain of command is so important that it is almost never violated. People at the top, civilian or military, very rarely issue orders to anyone not in the level of command immediately subordinate to them.

But there are exceptions to every rule.

Captain David Haughton, USN, Administrative Assistant to the Secretary of the Navy, got off the Congressional Limited of the Pennsylvania Railroad and climbed the stairs to the Baltimore Pennsylvania Station. He walked across the waiting room, left the station, and turned right. He was in uniform, and he was carrying a black briefcase.

A block away, he entered the bar of Walker Hasslinger's Restaurant, a Baltimore landmark that justly enjoyed the reputation of serving the finest seafood in town. Captain Haughton had been coming to Walker Hasslinger's since he was a midshipman at Annapolis. He looked up and down the bar for the man he was here to meet, but didn't find him.

He took a stool at the bar, and reached for a bowl of oyster crackers.

"The free lunch went out when the New Deal came in," a large, red-faced man in chef's whites said, sliding the bowl out of his reach. "Now it's cash on the bar."

But Eckley Walker, the proprietor, was smiling and extending his hand.

"How are you, Dave?" he said. "It's been some time."

"You still serving those condemned oysters?" Haughton said.

"Only to sailors who can't tell the difference," Walker said. He snapped his fingers and a bartender appeared. He said only one word, "Rye," but made certain gestures with his head and hand that conveyed to the waiter that he wanted a dozen oysters and two drinks, the latter from his private bottle of rye whiskey, which was kept out of sight.

The bartender poured stiff drinks, added a dash of ginger ale, and slid them across the bar.

"Mud in your eye," Walker Hasslinger said. "Good to see you, Dave."

"Bottoms up," Haughton said.

They smiled at each other.

A slight, tall, balding man in civilian clothing, holding a beer glass, slipped onto the stool next to Haughton.

"Amazing, the strange people you run into in obscure, out-of-the-way restaurants," he said.

"Eckley," Haughton said, "have you got a little room someplace where this guy can make his life-insurance pitch without disturbing the paying guests?"

"We've already got one," the slight man said.

"I'll have them take the oysters there, if you like," Eckley Walker said.

"Please," Haughton said.

Walker nodded. "Enjoy your lunch."

As they walked to the rear of the bar, the slight man turned and said, "I suppose I should warn you. I've got my boss with me."

"Is there a reason for that?"

"He asked me where I was going, and when I told him, he said he thought he would come along. If you don't like that, tell him."

There was a door at the end of the barroom, opening on a flight of stairs. At the top of stairs was a corridor. The tall, slight man opened a door and gestured for Haughton to precede him.

A trim man, his gray hair shorn in a crewcut, sat at the table. A napkin was tucked into his collar to protect his pin-striped, double-breasted blue suit from dripping butter as he attacked a steaming pile of crab and shrimp.

"You look unhappy to see me, Haughton," he said. "Now I'm glad I came."

"Good afternoon, General," Haughton said. "I am a little surprised, Sir."

"Consider your hand shaken, Captain," said Brigadier General Horace W. T. Forrest, Assistant Chief of Staff G-2 (Intelligence), USMC. "My fingers are dirty."

"Thank you, Sir," Haughton said.

"I could tell you I came here because this is the best seafood on the East Coast, but that would be a lie. What the hell are you up to, Haughton?"

"I'm acting for the Secretary, Sir," Haughton said.

"Clever fellow that I am, I already had that figured out," General Forrest said, "but the question was, 'What the hell are you up to?' "

There was a knock at the door, and the waiter appeared with a battered oblong tray holding what looked like two dozen oysters.

"Why don't you order while he's here?" General Forrest said. "Then we can talk without being disturbed every two minutes."

"Can I get a lobster?" Haughton asked. The waiter nodded. "A cup of clam chowder and a lobster, then, please," Haughton said.

"Twice," the slight man said. He was Lieutenant Colonel F. L. Rickabee, USMC. Rickabee was carried on the organizational chart of Headquarters USMC as being assigned to the Office of Congressional Liaison. That had absolutely nothing to do with what he really did.

"And to drink? A bottle of wine?" the waiter asked.

"I don't want a whole bottle," Haughton said.

"We'll help you, Haughton," General Forrest said. "Yes, please. A dry white."

"And a lobster for you, too, Sir?"

General Forrest looked at the shrimp and oysters before him.

"What the hell, why not? I just won't eat again for the next couple of weeks. But hold the clam chowder."

The waiter left.

"You were saying, Haughton?" General Forrest said, the moment the door closed.

Haughton hesitated just perceptibly. He had decided that Rickabee had told him the truth, which was that General Forrest had asked where he was going, and Rickabee had told him. He knew Rickabee well enough to know that while he often would do a great many things without telling General Forrest, he would not evade a question from him. And Forrest was naturally curious as to why the Secretary of the Navy's alter ego wanted to meet Rickabee in a restaurant in Baltimore, rather than somewhere in Washington. That implied an unusual degree of secrecy, and that had fired his curiosity.

"I have a project for Colonel Rickabee, General," Haughton said. "One which we will fund from the Secretary's Confidential Fund."

General Forrest, who had just popped a large shrimp in his mouth, gestured for Haughton to continue.

"Do you know Captain Fleming Pickering, Sir?" Haughton asked.

"I don't *know* him. I know who he is. I *don't* know what he's doing."

"He's in Australia, Sir, as the Secretary's personal liaison officer to General MacArthur."

"The admirals must love that," Forrest said dryly.

"Captain Pickering has learned from the Australians of a special force they have. Coastwatchers. They have arranged for people who lived on the islands in that area—plantation managers, civil servants, even some missionaries—to remain behind when the islands were lost to the Japanese—"

"I've heard about that," Forrest cut him off.

"Captain Pickering feels that these people have an enormous intelligence potential," Haughton went on. "His opinion is apparently not shared by senior Navy officers in the area."

"I can understand that," Forrest said. "I mean, hell, everybody knows that if you didn't go to Annapolis, you're stupid, right?"

Haughton smiled at General Forrest, but did not rise to the challenge. "The Secretary feels that Captain Pickering is right, and that these people could be of great use to us," he said. "He is, however, understandably reluctant to intervene personally and override the officers in question."

Forrest grunted.

"What I wanted to discuss with Colonel Rickabee was the formation of a special Marine unit to establish contact with the Coastwatcher organization, see what, if anything, we can do to assist them, and ensure that their intelligence is readily available to us when we commence operations in that area. In the interests of efficiency, and considering the time element, the Secretary feels that setting up such an organization under Colonel Rickabee is the way to go."

"And with a little bit of luck, maybe the admirals won't find out what's going on, right, until it's too late to do anything about it?"

"That's just about it, Sir."

"Now drop the other shoe, Haughton," Forrest said. "You couldn't hide an operation like that from the admirals, and both you and I know it."

Did I handle that badly? Or is he that clever? You don't get to be head of Marine Corps intelligence by being dull, and it's a sure thing he and Rickabee played "What's Haughton up to?" for an hour, as they drove over here from Washington.

"In addition to his liaison duties with General MacArthur's headquarters, Captain Fleming is performing other, classified, duties for the Secretary," Haughton said.

"Spying on the admirals, you mean," Forrest said. "And, of course, MacArthur."

"I don't think I'd use those words, Sir."

"I'll bet those are the words the admirals are using."

"If they are, Sir, they're wrong," Haughton said.

Forrest met his eyes. "They are?" he asked softly.

"The Secretary feels that he needs a set of eyes on the scene. Expert eyes. Dispassionate. Perhaps *nonparochial* would be a better word. Captain Pickering has been charged with reporting to the Secretary on matters he feels will be of interest to the Secretary. If the Secretary feels that's necessary, I don't think it appropriate for me to categorize it as 'spying.'"

"You don't?"

"I think Captain Pickering's role is analogous to that of an aide-de-camp in the nineteenth century. Or the eighteenth. He has no command function. All he is, as aides on horseback were, is an extra set of eyes for the commander."

Captain David Haughton had originally been offended both by the way Fleming Pickering had entered the Navy—commissioned from civilian life as a captain, a rank Haughton had taken eighteen years to reach—and by the role intended for him. It had taken him a long time and a lot of thought to come up with the aide-de-camp analogy. But once he had reached it, he knew it to be the truth.

"You dropped the other shoe, Haughton," General Forrest said, "but so far I haven't heard it."

"The Secretary feels that Captain Pickering can better perform his duties if he has some help," Haughton said carefully. "What I had hoped to get from Colonel Rickabee is an officer who could, covertly, provide that help, in addition to his intelligence duties. With the Coastwatchers, I mean."

"A *junior* aide-de-camp on a horse, huh?" Forrest said dryly. He looked at Colonel Rickabee.

"Banning," Rickabee said.

Forrest grunted.

"Excuse me?" Haughton asked.

"We have an officer," Forrest said, "who just might fit the ticket. He used to be the 4th Marines' intelligence officer in Shanghai. In the Philippines, too. He went blind over there—temporarily, apparently some sort of concussion from a Japanese artillery round—and they evacuated him by submarine. He regained his sight. Just made major. Bright, tough officer. His name is Ed Banning."

"There would be few raised eyebrows in the Corps," Rickabee said, "or in the Navy, if Banning was sent to Australia with an intelligence detachment."

"You seem pretty willing to go along with Haughton," Forrest said.

"I want to get in with the Coastwatchers," Rickabee said. "I think that's important. And this way, we get the Confidential Fund to pay for it."

"And, just incidentally, you'd like to know what Pickering is reporting to the Secretary, right?" Haughton said.

"You're a pretty bright fellow, Haughton," General Rickabee said. "Why aren't you a Marine?"

Haughton laughed.

"You seem rather unconcerned about the possibility that Banning would report to me what your man Pickering is up to, and that I would promptly tell the Navy," General Forrest said.

"I've always thought you were a pretty bright fellow yourself, General," Haughton said. "Certainly bright enough to know that would not be in your best interests."

General Forrest glared icily at Haughton for a long moment. Finally he looked at Rickabee. "You're right, Rickabee," he said. "He *is* a Machiavellian sonofabitch. I like him."

The door banged open, and the waiter returned with an enormous tray heaped high with steaming lobsters.

X

(ONE)

HEADQUARTERS
U.S. MARINE CORPS PARACHUTE SCHOOL
LAKEHURST NAVAL AIR STATION
LAKEHURST, NEW JERSEY
8 APRIL 1942

First Lieutenant R. B. Macklin, USMC, (Acting) Commanding Officer, USMC Parachute School, had a problem. He had been directed by TWX from Headquarters USMC to furnish by TWX the names of volunteers for a special mission. The volunteers must be enlisted men of his command who met certain criteria. He was to furnish these names within twenty-four hours.

That special mission was officially described as "immediate foreign service of undetermined length; of a classified nature; and involving extraordinary hazards. Volunteers will be advised that the risk of loss of life will be high."

The criteria set forth in the TWX directed that "volunteers should be at least corporals but not higher in rank than staff sergeants; and have no physical limitations whatever.

"The ideal volunteer for this mission will be an unmarried sergeant with at least three years of service who has, in addition to demonstrated small-arms and other infantry skills, experience in a special skill such as radio communications, demolitions, rubber-boat handling, and parachuting.

"Especially desirable are volunteers with French and Japanese language fluency, oral or written. Individuals who are now performing, or in the past have performed, cryptographic duties are not eligible."

In compliance with his orders, Lieutenant Macklin had his First Sergeant gather together all the corporals, sergeants, and staff sergeants of his command in the brand-new service club, where, after warning them that the subject of the meeting was classified and was not to be discussed outside the room where they had gathered, he read them the pertinent portions of the TWX.

There were twenty-one men present. Nineteen of them lined up before the First Sergeant, and he wrote their names down on a lined pad on his clipboard.

Viewed in one way, nineteen of twenty-one eligibles volunteering for an undefined mission where "the risk of loss of life will be high," could be interpreted as one more proof that young Marine noncoms were courageous, red-blooded American patriots, eager for an opportunity to serve their country, regardless of the risk to their very lives.

Viewed in another, more realistic, way, Lieutenant Macklin was very much afraid that if he forwarded the names of all nineteen, as he had been directed, questions would be asked as to why ninety percent of his junior noncoms were willing to take such a chance. It suggested, at the very least, that they didn't like their present assignment and would take a hell of a chance to get out of it.

And that would tend to reflect adversely on the professional reputation of First Lieutenant R. B. Macklin, USMC.

And of course, if he sent the names forward and only half of them wound up on orders, that would play havoc with the parachute training program. And if the program collapsed, that too would reflect adversely on his professional reputation.

Lieutenant Macklin was very concerned with his professional reputation, especially since Colonel Neville had jumped to his death before there had been time for him to write an efficiency report on Macklin. Macklin didn't even know who was going to write his efficiency report, now that Neville was dead.

But he did know that unless he handled this volunteer business the right way, he was in trouble.

He flipped through the stack of service records on his desk.

Every one but two of those ungrateful, disloyal sonsofbitches volunteered! Goddamn them! Willing to leave me in a lurch like this, making me look like some Captain Bligh with a mutiny on his hands! The ungrateful bastards, after all I've done for them!

He wondered who the two loyal Marines were. He compared the names of the volunteers against the roster.

Staff Sergeant James P. Cumings, the mess sergeant, was one of those who had not volunteered. Cumings was in his middle thirties, a career Marine, married and with a flock of kids.

Nor had Corporal Stephen M. Koffler. He was the little sonofabitch who went AWOL and then turned out to be the first one to reach Colonel Neville's body on The Day That It Happened.

And then he had been painted as some sort of hero and given an unjustified promotion to corporal—just because he happened to be next out of the airplane when the Colonel jumped to his death.

He was practically useless around here, too. The first sergeant had him driving a truck.

Christ, you'd just know that the one sonofabitch you would like to get rid of would be the only one that doesn't want to go!

Lieutenant R. B. Macklin, USMC, tapped his pencil absently against his white china coffee cup as he thought the problem through.

The basic question, he thought, is what is *best for the Corps?*

While it's probably true that whatever these volunteers are needed for is important, I don't know *that. What I* do *know is that parachutists are the wave of the future, and ergo, that the parachute school is very important, perhaps even critical, for future Marine operations in the Pacific and elsewhere. It follows logically from that that if I lose all, many, or even* any *of my middle-ranking noncommissioned officers to whatever it is they have volunteered for, I am setting parachute training back for however long it would take to train their replacements. I don't think I have the right to do that to the Marine Corps.*

I do know *that Corporal Stephen M. Koffler is* not *needed around here. Truckdrivers are a dime a dozen.*

First Lieutenant R. B. Macklin made his decision.

"First Sergeant!" he called.

(TWO)

First Sergeant George J. Hammersmith, having determined that Corporal Koffler had not been given a pass and that he was not in his barracks, looked for him first in the slop chute, and finally located him in the service club.

The service club was a new building that had been put up in a remarkably short time not far from the huge dirigible hangar. It was a large building, two stories tall in the center, and with one-floor wings on either side. It had been furnished with upholstered chairs and couches, tables, magazine racks, and pool and Ping-Pong tables. Somewhere down the pike there was supposed to be a snack bar and a small stage for USO shows and for a band, for dances.

With the exception of Corporal Koffler and two hostesses in gray uniforms, it was now empty. Lieutenant Macklin thought that parachutist trainees had more important things to do in their off-duty hours than loll around on their asses, and had placed the service club off limits to trainees except on weekends.

The permanent party did not patronize the club very much. There was a club, with hard liquor, for noncommissioned officers, and a slop chute, beer only, for corporals and down. Furthermore, the permanent party was well aware that the First Sergeant and other senior noncoms held the belief that only candy-asses would go someplace where you couldn't get anything to drink or do anything more than smile at the hostesses.

Corporal Koffler was sitting in an upholstered armchair, a can of peanuts at his side, reading the *Newark Evening News,* on which there was a banner headline:BATAAN FALLS; WAINWRIGHT'S FORCES WITH-DRAW TO FORTRESS CORREGIDOR.

That news had been on the radio all day, and it had bothered George Hammersmith. He had a lot of buddies with the 4th Marines, and the last he'd heard, they'd taken a real whipping. And he'd done his time in the Far East. There was no way that Corregidor could hold out for long. The fortress had been built on an island in Manila Bay to protect Manila; and Manila was already in the hands of the Japanese.

That little shit probably doesn't have the faintest fucking idea where the Philippines are, much less Corregidor. Sonofabitch probably never even looked at the front page, just turned right to "Blondie and Dagwood" in the comic section.

First Sergeant Hammersmith restrained a surprisingly strong urge to knock the paper out of Koffler's hands, but at the last moment he just put his fingers on it and jerked it, to get Koffler's attention.

"Jesus!" Koffler said. He was, Hammersmith saw, surprised but not afraid. So far as he knew, there was nothing wrong with Koffler except that Macklin had a hard-on for him. He had never explained why, and Hammersmith had never asked.

"Got a minute, Koffler?"

"Sure."

"You was at the formation when they asked for volunteers, wasn't you?"

"I was there."

"I was sort of wondering why you didn't volunteer."

Because I'm not a fucking fool, that's why. "Volunteers will be advised that the risk of loss of life will be high." I learned my lesson about volunteering when I volunteered for jump duty. So I didn't volunteer for whatever the fuck this new thing is.

"I didn't think I was qualified," Steve said.

"Why not?"

"They want people with special skills. I don't have any. I don't speak Japanese or French, or anything."

"You're a Marine parachutist," Hammersmith said.

"I just made corporal," Steve said. "I ain't been in the Corps a year."

"You're yellow, is that it?"

"I'm not yellow."

"You didn't volunteer."

"That don't mean I'm yellow; that just means I don't want to volunteer."

"What's Lieutenant Macklin got on you?"

"I don't know."

"He doesn't like you."

"Maybe because they promoted me."

"Maybe. But I do know he doesn't like you. He thinks you're a worthless shit."

"I didn't know that."

"I don't like you, either," Hammersmith said. "You're supposed to be a Marine, and you're yellow."

"I'm not yellow."

"You were given a chance to volunteer for an important assignment, and you didn't. In my book that makes you yellow."

"They said 'volunteer.' "

"And you didn't."

"What do you want from me, Sergeant?"

"I don't want anything from you."

"Then I don't understand what this is all about."

"Just a little chat between Marines," First Sergeant Hammersmith said, "is all."

"You want me to volunteer, that's what this is all about."

"If I made you volunteer, then you wouldn't be a volunteer, would you?" Hammersmith asked. "Don't do nothing you don't want to do. But you know what I would do if I was you?"

"No."

"If *I* was in an outfit where *my* company commander thought *I* was a worthless shit, and *my* first sergeant thought I was yellow, *I* would start thinking about finding myself a new home."

(THREE)

SAN DIEGO, CALIFORNIA

17 APRIL 1942

Major Edward J. Banning, USMC, arrived in San Diego carrying all of his worldly possessions in two canvas Valv-Paks.

That fact—that he had with him all he owned—had occurred to him on the Lark, the train on which he had made the last leg of his trip from Los Angeles. He had flown from Washington to Los Angeles.

He had once had a good many personal possessions, ranging from books and phonograph records to furniture, dress uniforms, civilian clothing, a brand-new Pontiac automobile, and a wife.

Of all the things he'd owned in Shanghai six months before, only one was left, a Model 1911A1 Colt .45 pistol; and that, technically, was the property of the U.S. Government. The 4th Marines were now on Corregidor. Banning sometimes mused wryly that in one of the lateral tunnels off the Main Malinta tunnel under the rock, there was probably, in some filing cabinet, an official record that the pistol had been issued to him and never turned in. The record—if not Major Ed Banning or the 4th Marines—would more than likely survive the war. And his estate would receive a form letter from the Marine Corps demanding payment.

His household goods had been stored in a godown in Shanghai "for later shipment." It was entirely credible to think that some Japanese officer was now occupying his apartment, sitting on his chairs, eating supper off his plates on his carved teak table, listening to his Benny Goodman records on his phonograph, and riding around Shanghai in his Pontiac.

He did not like to think about Mrs. Edward J. (Ludmilla) Banning. Milla was a White Russian, a refugee from the Bolshevik Revolution. He had gone to Milla for Japanese and Russian language instruction, taken her as his mistress, and fallen in love with her. He had married her just before he flew out of Shanghai with the advance party when the 4th Marines were ordered to the Philippines.

There were a number of scenarios about what had happened to Milla after the Japanese came to Shanghai, and none of them were pleasant. They ranged from her being shot out of hand to being placed in a brothel for Japanese enlisted men.

It was also possible that Milla, who was a truly beautiful woman, might have elected to survive the Japanese occupation by becoming the mistress of a Japanese officer. Practically speaking, that would be a better thing for Milla than getting herself shot, or becoming a seminal sewer in a Japanese Army comfort house.

Ed Banning believed in God, but he rarely prayed to Him. Yet he prayed often and passionately that God would take mercy on Milla.

He was profoundly ashamed that he could no longer remember the details of Milla's face, the color of her eyes, the softness of her skin; she was fading away in his mind's eye. Very likely this was because he had taken another woman into his bed and, for as long as the affair had lasted, into his life. He was profoundly ashamed about that, too. No matter how hard he tried to rationalize it away, in the end it was a betrayal of the vow he had made in the Anglican Cathedral in Shanghai to cleave himself only to Milla until death should them part.

He had met Carolyn Spencer Howell in the New York Public Library. He had been sent to the Navy Hospital in Brooklyn, ostensibly for a detailed medical examination relating to his lost and then recovered sight. But he was actually there for a psychiatric examination. During his time in Brooklyn he was free—indeed, encouraged—to get off the base and go into Manhattan. (There'd also been strong hints that female companionship wouldn't hurt, either.)

Carolyn was a librarian at the big public library on 42nd Street in Manhattan. He went to her to ask for copies of the *Shanghai Post* covering the months between the time he had left Milla in Shanghai and the start of the war. He also wanted whatever she had on Nansen Passports. As a stateless person, Milla had been issued what was known as a Nansen Passport. He had a faint, desperate hope that perhaps the Japanese would recognize it, and that she could leave Shanghai somehow for a neutral country. Because Banning had given her all the cash he could lay his hands on, just over three thousand dollars, Milla didn't lack for the resources she'd need to get away. Would that do her any good? Probably not, he realized in his darkest moments.

He did not set out to pursue Carolyn as a romantic conquest. It just happened. Carolyn was a tall, graceful divorcee. Her husband of fifteen years, whom Banning now thought of as a colossal fool, had, as she put it, "turned her in for a later model, without wrinkles."

They met outside the library in a small restaurant on 43rd Street, where he'd gone for lunch. And they wound up in her bed in her apartment. Banning and Carolyn were very good in bed together, and not only because being there ended long periods of celibacy for each of them. They both had a lot of important things they needed to share with someone who was sensitive enough to listen and understand. He told her about Milla, for instance, and she told him about her fool of a husband.

It was nice while it lasted, but now it was over. He could see in her eyes that she knew he was lying when he said good-bye to her and told her he would write. And she actually seemed to understand, which made him feel even more like a miserable sonofabitch.

Since Carolyn knew about Milla from the beginning, they managed to convince themselves for a while that they were nothing more than two sophisticated adults who enjoyed companionship with the other, in bed and out of it. They both told themselves that it was a temporary arrangement, with no possibility of a lasting emotional involvement—much less some kind of future with a vine-covered cottage by the side of the road. They thought of themselves as friends with bed privileges, and nothing more.

But it became more than that. Otherwise, why would a sophisticated, mature woman be unable to keep from hugging her friend so tightly, not quite able to hold back her sobs, while a Marine major tried, not successfully, to keep his eyes from watering?

The bottom line seemed to be that he was in love with two women, and he was in no position to do anything for either of them.

Major Jack NMI Stecker, USMC, was waiting on the platform when Major Ed Banning threw his Valv-Paks down from the club car. There was nothing fragile in the bags except a small framed photograph of Carolyn Howell she had slipped into his luggage. He had found it while rooting for clean socks when the plane had been grounded for the night in St. Louis.

They shook hands.

"How'd you know I'd be on the train?" Banning asked.

"Colonel Rickabee called and told me what plane you were on. And I knew you couldn't get a plane further than L.A. And I didn't think you would take the bus."

"Well, I'm grateful. When did you put the leaf on, Major?"

"Day before yesterday. I just cleared the post. *You* can put *me* on the train in the morning."

"You didn't stick around because of me, I hope?"

"Well, sort of. I got you an office, sort of, in a Quonset hut at Camp Elliott, and I thought I should show you where it is. You've already got eight people who reported in. I put the senior sergeant in charge and told him you would be out there in the morning."

"Thank you," Banning said, simply.

They walked to Stecker's Ford coupe. When Stecker opened the trunk, there were two identical Valv-Paks in it. There was not enough room for two more, so one of Banning's was put in the backseat.

Stecker got behind the wheel and then handed Banning a sheet of teletype paper.

HEADQUARTERS US MARINE CORPS
WASHINGTON DC 1345 9APR42

COMMANDING GENERAL
2ND JOINT TRAINING FORCE
SAN DIEGO, CAL

1. SPECIAL DETACHMENT 14 USMC IS ACTIVATED 9APR42 AT CAMP ELLIOTT CAL. DETACHMENT IS SUBORDINATE TO ASSISTANT CHIEF OF STAFF FOR INTELLIGENCE, HEADQUARTERS USMC.

2. INTERIM TABLE OF ORGANIZATION & EQUIPMENT ESTABLISHED MANNING TABLE OF ONE (1) MAJOR; TWO (2) CAPTAINS (OR LIEUTENANTS); AND SIXTEEN (16) ENLISTED MEN.

3. COMMANDING GENERAL 2ND JOINT TRAINING FORCE IS DIRECTED TO PROVIDE LOGISTICAL AND ADMINISTRATIVE SUPPORT AS REQUIRED.

BY DIRECTION OF THE COMMANDANT:

HORACE W. T. FORREST, BRIG GEN USMC

Stecker started the car. After Banning had read the teletype message, he said, "That came in day before yesterday. The G-2 here is very curious."

"I'll bet he is," Banning said. "Do I get to keep this?"

"Yeah, sure."

Banning looked out the window and saw they were not headed toward Camp Elliott.

"Where are we going?"

"Coronado Beach Hotel," Stecker said. "I figured before you begin your rigorous training program, you're entitled to one night on a soft mattress."

"What training program? My orders are to collect these people and get them on a plane to Australia."

"You just can't do that," Stecker said. "There's a program to follow. You have to draw your equipment—typewriters, field equipment, a guidon, field stoves, organizational weapons, training films and a projector to show them—all that sort of thing. Then you start the training program. If there's no already published training program, you have to write one and submit it for approval."

Banning looked at Stecker with shock in his eyes, and then saw the mischief in Stecker's eyes.

"Jack?"

"Well, that's what I'm going to have to do the minute I get to New River and start to organize a battalion," he said. "And I figured that if I have to do it, you should."

"You had me worried."

"You *are* going to have to do some of that stuff. You're going to have to turn in a morning report every day, which means you will need a typewriter and somebody who knows how to use it. There's all kinds of paperwork, Ed, that you just won't be able to avoid—payrolls, allotments, requisitions."

"That never entered my mind."

"That's why I brought it up," Stecker said. "Maybe one of the people you've recruited can handle the paperwork, but just in case, I had a word with the G-1 about getting you a volunteer who can do it for you."

"Jesus!" Banning said.

"The Marine Corps, Major," Jack Stecker said solemnly, "floats upon a sea of paper."

"I'd forgotten."

"Your manning chart calls for two company-grade officers," Stecker said. "You got them?"

"No. I asked for McCoy—and not only because he speaks Japanese. But I got turned down flat."

"You know what McCoy is up to. That didn't surprise you, did it?"

"I guess not."

"I know a guy—Mustang first lieutenant—named Howard. He doesn't speak Japanese. Before the war, he was on the rifle team. He's been seeing that the 2nd Raider Battalion got all the weapons they thought they wanted. That's about over. Good man."

"How come you don't want him for your battalion?"

"I do. I offered him a company."

"And?"

"He told me he wasn't sure he could handle it. He was at Pearl on December seventh. He panicked. He found himself a hole—actually a basement arms room—and stayed there. *After* he saw that the arms were passed out."

"That doesn't sound so terrible."

"He thinks it makes him unfit to take a command."

"You don't, I gather?"

"No. And I told him so. I think he would be useful to you, Ed."

"Would he volunteer?"

"I don't know. All you could do is ask him, I suppose."

"Where would I find him?"

"You'll see him tomorrow. I told him to keep an eye on your people."

"All this and the Coronado Beach Hotel, too? Or are you pulling my leg about that, too?"

"No," Stecker chuckled. "That's where we're going. Truth being stranger than fiction, I've got the keys to the Pacific & Far Eastern Shipping Company suite there. They keep it year round for the officers of their ships who are in port."

"How the hell did you work that?"

"The guy that owns the company and I were in France together."

"His name is Fleming Pickering, and he's a captain in the Navy reserve."

"How'd you know?"

"He's the man I'm to report to in Melbourne," Banning said. "I didn't know about you and him. Or that he'd been a Marine."

"Somehow, I don't think you were supposed to tell me that."

"I'm sure I wasn't."

"Then I won't ask why you did. But at least that solves the problem of where you sleep while you're out here."

"You mean in the hotel?"

"Sure. Why not? I'm sure Pickering would want me to give you the keys. And speaking of keys, I'm going to leave you the Ford, too."

"I don't understand that."

"Well, cars are getting harder and harder to come by. They've stopped making them, you know, and people are buying up all the good used cars. I figure that I'll be out here again, or my boy will, or else friends who need wheels. So why sell it? I've got two cars on the East Coast."

"Jesus, Jack, I don't know . . ."

"I've already arranged to park it in the hotel garage. Just leave the keys with the manager when you're through with it."

"Things are going too smoothly. A lot of that, obviously, is thanks to you. But I always worry when that happens."

"You know what the distilled essence of my Marine Corps experience is?" Stecker said.

"No," Banning chuckled.

"You don't have to practice being uncomfortable; when it's time for you to be uncomfortable, the Corps will arrange for it in spades. In the meantime, live as well as you can. I'm surprised you didn't learn that from McCoy."

Stecker pulled up in front of the Coronado Beach Hotel.

"Here we are," he said. "Of course, if you'd rather, I can still drive you out to Elliott, and the Corps will give you an iron bunk and a thin mattress in a Quonset hut."

"This will do very nicely, Major Stecker, thank you very much."

"My pleasure, Major Banning."

(FOUR)

HEADQUARTERS MOTOR POOL
2ND JOINT TRAINING FORCE
CAMP ELLIOTT, CALIFORNIA
18 APRIL 1942

When First Lieutenant Joseph L. Howard, USMCR, walked up to the small shack that housed the motor pool dispatcher, he gave in to the temptation to add a little excitement to the lives of the dispatcher and the motor sergeant. Both of them, he saw, were engrossed in the *San Diego Times.*

He squatted and carefully tugged loose from the ground a large weed and its dirt-encrusted root structure. Then he spun it around several times to pick up speed, and let it fly. It rose high in the air.

"Good morning," Lieutenant Howard said loudly, marching up to the dispatch shack.

The weed reached the apogee of its trajectory, and then began its descent.

The motor sergeant looked up from his newspaper and got to his feet.

"Good morning, Sir," he said, a second before the weed struck somewhere near the center of the tin roof of the dispatch shack. There was a booming noise, as if an out-of-tune bass drum had been struck.

"Holy fucking Christ!" the motor sergeant said, "what the fuck was that?"

"Excuse me?" Lieutenant Howard said. "Were you speaking to me, Sergeant?"

The motor sergeant, still wholly confused, looked at Lieutenant Howard suspiciously.

"If the chaplain," Joe Howard said, still straight-faced, "heard a fine noncommissioned officer such as yourself using such language, Sergeant, he would be very disappointed."

The sergeant's wits returned.

"What the fuck did you do, Lieutenant?" he asked. "You scared the shit out of me."

"You're not really suggesting that an officer and gentleman, such as myself, would do anything to disturb your peace and quiet, are you, Sergeant?"

"No, Sir, I'm sure the Lieutenant wouldn't do nothing like that," the motor sergeant said, "but I used to know a wiseass armorer corporal at Quantico who had a sick sense of humor."

Howard laughed. "Les, you looked like you were coming out of your skin."

"You shouldn't do things like that to an old man like me."

"I'm trying to keep you young, Les."

"Christ, you got a letter," the motor sergeant said.

"Huh?"

"Mail clerk brought it over," the motor sergeant said. "He called over here yesterday, looking for you. Said the letter had been there three days. I told him you would be here this morning. Wait till I get it."

He rooted in a drawer and came out with a small envelope and handed it to Howard. There was no stamp on the envelope, just a signature. As a member of the armed forces of the United States serving overseas, the sender was given the franking privilege.

Howard's heart jumped when he saw the return address. He tore the envelope open and resisted the temptation to sniff the stationery; he thought he detected a faint odor of perfume.

He was afraid to read the letter. He hadn't heard from Barbara since she'd sailed, and was beginning to wonder if he ever would. His fear grew when he saw how short the letter was, and how it began:

Special Naval Medical Unit
Fleet Post Office 8203
San Francisco, California

My Dearest Joe,
Well, here I am. I can't tell you where.
We have been told that, because we are officers and can be trusted not to write home things that would interest the enemy, our mail will not be censored. It will be, however, subject to "random scrutiny." What that means, I think, is that the senior nurses here will open outgoing letters they think will be interesting, in terms of intimacy. Consequently, I will not write the things I would like to write. I don't consider what we have to be a spectator sport, and I don't want a bunch of dried-up old maids giggling over my correspondence.
On the way over here, I had a lot of time to think about us, and you are constantly in my thoughts here "somewhere in the South Pacific." There is not much for us to do, except prepare for what we all know is going to happen.
I have carefully considered what happened between us, and I've given a lot of thought to our different backgrounds. I am fully aware that the both of us behaved very foolishly, and that any marriage counselor worthy of hanging out his shingle would have to conclude that the odds against us getting married in the first place, much less making a success of it, are very long indeed.
Having said that, I have concluded that meeting you was the best thing that's happened to me in my life. Until you, I really had no idea what being a woman really meant. I will not be alive until I feel your arms around me again.
I love you. Today. Tomorrow. Forever.

May God protect you,
Barbara

PS: Picture enclosed, so you don't forget what I look like.

Joe Howard had trouble focusing his eyes on Barbara's picture; they seemed to be full of tears.
He put the letter back into its envelope and carefully put it into his pocket.
"Thanks very much, Les," he said.

"Ah, hell, Lieutenant," the motor sergeant said. Then he raised his voice, and the tenor changed. "Well, get off your ass, asshole," he said to the dispatcher, "and go get the Lieutenant's truck."

(FIVE)

HEADQUARTERS
SPECIAL DETACHMENT 14
CAMP ELLIOTT, CALIFORNIA
18 APRIL 1942

The Quonset hut was so called because it had been invented at the Quonset Point Naval Station. It was originally envisioned as an easy-to-erect shelter—sort of a portable warehouse—not as barracks. The huts were built out of curved sheets of corrugated steel, which formed the sides and roof in a half-circle. And there was a wooden floor, the framework of which visibly traced its design to forklift pallets.

When they were to be transported, the curved sheets of corrugated steel could be nestled together. Then they, and the framework which supported them, could be steel-banded together on top of the plywood floor and its underpinning. So packed, they took up little cubic footage, and could be erected quickly at their destination by unskilled labor using simple tools.

Quonset huts had sprouted like mushrooms over the rolling hills of Camp Elliott. Many of these had been put to use as barracks in lieu of tents, "until adequate barracks could be erected."

Major Edward J. Banning followed Major Jack NMI Stecker up to one of them and stepped through the door behind him in time to hear someone call "Ten-*hut.*"

The hut was furnished with two folding metal chairs, two small folding wooden tables, on one of which sat a U.S. Army field desk, and a telephone. There were eight Marines in the forty-foot-long room. They were now all standing erect, at attention; but most of them, obviously, had a moment earlier been sprawled on mattresses on the floor. Their duffle bags, some of them open, were scattered around the floor. Their stacked '03 Springfield rifles were at the far end of the room.

Banning wondered idly why Jack Stecker didn't put them at rest, and then he belatedly realized that Jack was deferring to him, as the commanding officer.

"At ease," Banning said. He smiled. "My name is Banning. I have the honor to command this splendid, if brand-new, military organization."

There were a couple of chuckles, but most of them looked at him warily. That was understandable. Reporting aboard an ordinary rifle company was bad enough. The unknown is always frightening; and you naturally wonder what the new company commander and first sergeant will be like, how you will be treated, where you will be going, and what you will be doing. Reporting in here posed all those questions, plus those raised by the words "classified"; "involving extraordinary hazards"; and "the risk of loss of life will be high."

And there wasn't much he could do to put their minds at rest. This was one of those (in Banning's judgment, rare) situations where the necessity for secrecy was quite clear. It was even possible that the Japanese didn't know of the very existence of the Coastwatchers. Sometimes, not often, the Japanese were quite stupid about things like that; this might be one of them. If the Japanese did not yet know about the Coastwatchers, then every effort, clearly, should be made to keep them from finding out, as long as possible. They inevitably would, of course. When that happened, the less they learned the better.

All I can do is try to get these people to trust me. I can't even tell them where we're going, much less what we're going to be doing, until we're on the ship. Or maybe not even then. Not until we get to Australia. If we go over there on a troopship, I can't afford to have everybody else on the ship talking, and talk they would, about that strange little detachment with the strange mission.

Banning had long ago learned that enlisted Marines trust their officers on a few occasions only: first, when the officer knows more about what's expected of them than they do; second, when he will not ask them to do something he will not do himself; and, third, perhaps most important, when he is genuinely concerned with their welfare.

There were two staff sergeants, five buck sergeants, and a corporal. Banning went to each man in turn and shook his hand. He asked each man his name, what he had been doing up to now in the Corps, and where he was from.

"Who's senior?" Banning asked, after he'd met them all.

One of the staff sergeants took a step forward.

"Richardson, right?"

"Yes, Sir."

"Well, for the time being, Sergeant, you'll act as First Sergeant. Your first orders are to get some bunks and bedding to go with those mattresses."

Staff Sergeant Richardson looked uncomfortable.

"Problem with that, Sergeant?"

"Sir, the warehouse is a hell of a ways from here, and we don't have any motor transport."

"You seem to have managed to draw mattresses and get them here without transport," Banning said.

That made Sergeant Richardson look even more uncomfortable. Banning glanced at Major Stecker, whose eyes looked mischievous again. And then Banning understood: somewhere on the post, much closer than the issue point for bedding, another Marine Corps unit was dealing with the problem of eight missing mattresses.

That was clearly theft, or at least unauthorized diversion of government property—in either case a manifestation of a lack of discipline. On the other hand, getting mattresses to sleep on when the Corps didn't provide any could be considered a manifestation of initiative, which was a desirable military quality.

"Well, I'll look into the problem of transportation, Sergeant. What I would like to do, right now, is have a look at everybody's service record, and then I'd like to talk to you one at a time."

"Yes, Sir," Staff Sergeant Richardson said, visibly relieved that the subject of the source of the mattresses seemed to have been passed over.

"Sergeant, has Lieutenant Howard been over here today?" Jack Stecker asked.

"Yes, Sir. He was here about oh-six-hundred to make sure we were going to get breakfast. He said he would be back"—he raised his wrist to look at his watch—"about now, Sir. He said he would be back before you got here, Sir."

As if on cue, there came the sound of tires crunching and an engine dying. A moment later, Lieutenant Joe Howard came through the door.

"Good morning, Sir," he said to Stecker. "Sorry to be late. I had a little trouble getting wheels from the motor officer."

"Major Banning," Stecker said. "This is Lieutenant Joe Howard."

"How do you do, Sir?" Howard said.

Banning liked what he saw. Like others before him, he thought that Joe Howard looked like everything a clean-cut, red-blooded, physically fit young Marine officer should look like. And then he remembered what Jack Stecker had said about Howard having found, and stayed in, a safe hole during the attack at Pearl Harbor.

I'm in no position to be self-righteous about that. When the Jap barrages began, I would have swapped my soul for a safe hole to hide in.

"I'm happy to meet you, Howard," Banning said, putting out his hand and raising his voice just enough to make sure everyone in the hut heard him. "Major Stecker speaks very highly of you. I've known him a long time, and he doesn't often do that."

Lieutenant Howard looked as uncomfortable as Staff Sergeant Richardson had a moment before.

"I've got to get out of here," Stecker said. "I can't miss that plane. Howard can drive me."

He put out his hand to Banning. "Good luck, Ed. Send a postcard."

"Take care of yourself," Banning said. "Say hello to Elly."

"I will," Stecker said, and then turned to the men watching curiously. "Listen up," he said. "You guys have fallen in the you-know-what and come up smelling like roses. Major Banning is one hell of Marine. He probably wouldn't tell you, so I will: He's already been in this war, wounded and evacuated from the 4th Marines in the Philippines. Before that, he was with the 4th Marines in China. When he tells you something, it's not coming out of a book, it's from experience. So pay attention and do what he says, and you'll probably come out of what you're going to do alive. Good luck. Semper Fi."

And then, without looking at Banning again, Stecker quickly walked out of the Quonset hut. Banning found himself alone with his new command; they were now looking at him almost with fascination.

That was a hell of a nice thing for Jack Stecker to do, Banning thought.

"Well, Sergeant Richardson," he said, "now that we have wheels, we can get bedding. Take half the men and the truck and go get it."

"Aye, aye, Sir."

"And when you've finished, take the mattresses here back where you got them."

"Aye, aye, Sir."

"Try not to get caught," Banning said.

"Yes, Sir."

"I want to talk to each of you alone," Banning said, after Richardson and the men he took were gone. "I'll start with you, Sergeant. The rest of you wait outside."

The first man, the other staff sergeant, a thirty-year-old named Hazleton, was a disappointment. By the time he finished talking with him, Banning was sure he had volunteered for a mission "where the risk of loss of life will be high" because he was unwelcome where he was. That he had, in other words, been "volunteered" by his first sergeant or company commander. For all of his last hitch before the war, he had been the assistant NCO club manager at Quantico. Rather obviously, he had been swept out of that soft berth when the brass was desperately looking for noncoms to train the swelling Corps.

And at 2nd Joint Training Force, where the broom had swept him, Hazleton had been found unable to cut the mustard. When the TWX soliciting volunteers had arrived, his company commander had decided it was a good, and easy, way to get rid of him.

Banning was not surprised. That was the way things went. No company commander wanted to lose his best men. Lieutenant Colonel

Rickabee had warned Banning that was going to happen, and he had made provision to deal with it. The staff sergeant's name would be TWXed to Rickabee, and shortly afterward there would be a TWX from Headquarters USMC, transferring the staff sergeant out of Special Detachment 14.

Banning wondered how many of the others would be like the staff sergeant. With one exception, however, none were. To Banning's surprise, the others were just what he had hoped to get. They were bright—in some cases, very bright—young noncoms who were either looking for excitement or a chance for rapid promotion, or both.

Unfortunately, none of them spoke Japanese, although four of them had apparently managed to utter enough Japanese-sounding noises to convince their first sergeants that they did. That wasn't surprising either. Japanese linguists were in very short supply. Officers who had them would fight losing them as hard as possible. Nevertheless, Rickabee had promised to pry loose as many as he could (maybe four), and send them directly to Melbourne.

The last man Banning interviewed, the only corporal who had so far arrived, was the second disappointment. Corporal Stephen Koffler had come to Special Detachment 14 from the Marine Corps Parachute School at Lakehurst Naval Air Station. It didn't take more than a couple of minutes for Banning to extract from him the admission that he had "been volunteered." The kid's first sergeant had made what could kindly be called a pointed suggestion that he volunteer.

"Why do you think he did that, Koffler?"

"I don't know, Sir. So far as I know, I didn't do nothing wrong. But right from the first, Lieutenant Macklin seemed to have it in for me."

"What was that name? Who 'had it in' for you?"

"Lieutenant Macklin, Sir."

"Tall, thin officer? An Annapolis graduate?"

"Yes, Sir. Lieutenant R. B. Macklin. He told us he went to Annapolis. And he said that he had learned about the Japs from when he was in China."

I'll be damned. So that's where that sonofabitch wound up! Doesn't sound like him. You could hurt yourself jumping out of airplanes. But maybe that pimple on the ass of the Corps was "volunteered" for parachute duty by somebody else who found out what a despicable prick he is, and hoped his parachute wouldn't open.

"I believe I know the gentleman," Banning said. "Tell me, Koffler, what were you doing at the Parachute School? Some kind of an instructor?"

Even if this kid is no Corporal Killer McCoy, if he's rubbed Macklin the wrong way, he probably has a number of splendid traits of character I just haven't noticed so far. "The enemies of my enemies are my friends."

"No, Sir. They had me driving a truck."

"I don't suppose you can type, can you, Koffler?"

There was a discernible pause before Corporal Koffler reluctantly said, "Yes, Sir. I can type."

"You sound like you're ashamed of it."

"Sir, I don't want to be a fucking clerk-typist."

"Corporal Koffler," Banning said sternly, suppressing a smile, "in case you haven't heard this before, the Marine Corps is not at all interested in what you would like, or not like, to do. Where did you learn to type?"

That question obviously made Corporal Koffler just as uncomfortable as he'd been when he was asked if he could type at all.

"Where did you learn to type, Corporal? More important, how fast a typist are you?"

"About forty words a minute, Sir," Koffler said. "I got a book out of the library."

"A typing book, you mean? You taught yourself how to type?"

"Yes, Sir."

"Why?"

"I needed to know how to type to pass the FCC exam. You have to copy twenty words a minute to get your ticket, and I couldn't write that fast."

"You're a radio operator?" Banning asked, pleased.

"No, Sir. I'm a draftsman."

"A draftsman?" Banning asked, confused.

"Yes, Sir. That's why I volunteered for parachuting."

"Excuse me?"

"Sir, they wanted to keep me at Parris Island as a draftsman, painting signs. The only way I could get out of it was to volunteer for parachute training."

"In other words, Corporal Koffler," Banning said, now keeping a straight face only with a massive effort, "it could be fairly said that you concealed your skill as a radio operator from the personnel people . . ."

"I didn't *conceal* it, Sir," Koffler said. "They didn't ask me, and I didn't tell them."

"And then, since the personnel people were unaware of your very valuable skill as a radio operator, they elected to classify you as a draftsman?"

"That's about it, Sir."

"And then you volunteered for the Para-Marines because you

didn't want to be a draftsman, and then you volunteered for the 14th Special Detachment because you didn't want to be a Para-Marine?"

Koffler looked stricken.

"It wasn't exactly that way, Sir."

"Then you tell me exactly how it was."

There was a knock at the door of the Quonset hut.

"Come!" Banning said, and Lieutenant Joe Howard entered the hut.

"Major Stecker got off all right, Sir. I've got the keys to his car for you."

"Stick around, Lieutenant. I'll be with you in a minute," Banning said. "Corporal Koffler and I are just about finished. Go on, Corporal."

"I don't know what to say, Sir," Steve Koffler said unhappily.

Banning glowered at him for a moment.

"I will spell it out for you, Koffler. This is the end of the line for you. There's no place else you can volunteer for so you can get out of doing things you don't like to do. From here on in, you are going to do what the Marine Corps wants you to do. You are herewith appointed the detachment clerk of the 14th Special Detachment, U.S. Marine Corps. And if there are any signs to be painted around here, you will paint them. Am I getting through to you?"

"Yes, Sir."

"Any questions?"

"No, Sir."

"Then report to Sergeant Richardson, tell him I have appointed you detachment clerk, and tell him I said he should see about getting you a typewriter. Do you understand all that?"

"Yes, Sir."

"I don't want to hear that you are even thinking of volunteering for anything else, Koffler!"

"No, Sir."

"That will be all, Corporal," Banning said solemnly.

"Aye, aye, Sir. Thank you, Sir," Steve Koffler said, did an about-face, and marched to the door of the hut. When the door had closed, Banning pushed himself back on the legs of his folding chair and laughed.

"Oh, God," he said, finally.

"What was that all about, Sir?" Howard asked, smiling.

"I'd forgotten what fun it is sometimes to be a unit commander," Banning said. "That's a good kid; but, my God, how wet behind the ears! Anyway, I need a clerk, and he can type. He can also paint signs. The square peg in the square hole."

"He really isn't what you think of when somebody says, 'Para-Marine Corporal,' is he?"

"Until I started talking to him and somebody said, 'Corporal,' I usually thought of one I had in the 4th. I used to send him snooping around the Japanese for weeks at a time and never thought a thing about it. I'm not sure that kid could be trusted to go downtown in 'Diego and get back by himself."

"He might surprise you, Sir. He *is* wearing parachutist's wings. He had the balls to jump out of an airplane. I'm not sure I would."

Banning's smile vanished as he looked at Howard.

"Talking about balls, Lieutenant. The 14th Special Detachment is accepting company-grade volunteers."

"Are you asking me to volunteer, Sir?"

"No. I'm just telling you I need a couple of lieutenants. Whether you would care to volunteer is up to you."

"Sir, there's something about me I don't think you know," Joe Howard said.

"Major Stecker told me all about that. We're old friends, and we both think you're wrong about what happened at Pearl Harbor."

"Sir, with respect, you weren't there."

"For Christ's sake, Howard, anybody with the brains to pour piss out of his boots gets scared when shells start falling. Or sick to his stomach when he sees somebody blown up, torn up, whatever. What the hell made you think you would be different?"

"Sir—"

"You have two options, Lieutenant. Of your own free will, you volunteer for this outfit, or a week from now you'll report to New River, North Carolina, where you'll be given a company in the 2nd Battalion, 5th Marines."

Howard's face worked for a moment. He did not need Banning to remind him of his options. He had been thinking of them carefully. And since getting Barbara's letter this morning, he had been thinking of little else.

"Actually, Sir, there's a third option. Colonel Carlson said he would like to have me in the 2nd Raider Battalion."

"That's right, you've been working with them, haven't you? You tell Colonel Carlson about this low opinion you have of yourself?"

"Yes, Sir. I mean, I told him about what happened to me at Pearl."

"And he still wants you?"

"Yes, Sir. He said . . . just about the same thing that you and Major Stecker said, Sir."

"Well, make up your mind, Howard. If you don't want in here, I've got to find somebody else."

"Sir, I'd like to go with you, if that would be all right. But I've already told Colonel Carlson I'd volunteer for the Raiders."

"Don't worry about that. I'll handle Colonel Carlson. You're in. Your first job is to teach our new detachment clerk to fill out the appropriate forms to send a TWX to Washington. As soon as he knows how, send one. Here's the address. The message is to transfer Staff Sergeant Hazleton out and you in."

"Aye, aye, Sir."

"You may first have to get Corporal Koffler a typewriter," Banning said.

"Yes, Sir. I thought about that. I know where I can get one. Actually, two, an office Underwood and a Royal portable. And some other stuff we're going to need."

"Aren't they going to miss you where you're working?"

"No, Sir. Major Stecker arranged with 2nd Training Force for me to work for you for a week. By the time the week is over, I suppose I'll have orders transferring me here."

"Did Major Stecker tell you what they're going to have us doing?"

"No, Sir. I don't think he knows."

"I'd like to tell you, but I don't think I'd better until we get you officially transferred."

"I understand, Sir."

"We won't be able to tell the men what we're going to do, or even where we're going, until we get there. That may be a problem."

There was no question in Howard's mind where they were going. They were going to the Pacific. Anywhere in the Pacific would be closer to Barbara than New River, N.C.

"I understand, Sir."

"OK, Howard. Go get our new detachment clerk a typewriter. As a wise old Marine once told me, the Marine Corps floats on a sea of paper."

"Aye, aye, Sir."

(SIX)

Eyes Only—The Secretary of the Navy

   DUPLICATION FORBIDDEN
   ORIGINAL TO BE DESTROYED AFTER ENCRYPTION AND TRANSMITTAL
TO SECNAVY

Melbourne, Australia
Tuesday, 21 April 1942

Dear Frank:

   I suspect that you have been expecting more frequent reports than you have been getting. This is my second, and it was
exactly a month ago that I sent the first. So, feeling much like
a boy at boarding school explaining why his essay has not been
turned in when expected, let me offer the following in extenua-
tion:
   Your radio of 1 April, in addition to relieving me of my enormous concern that I was not providing what you hoped to get,
also told me that it is going to take 7-9 days for these reports
to reach you, if they have to travel from here to Hawaii by sea
for encryption and radio transmission from there. I see no solution to shortening this time frame, other than hoping that
some sort of scheduled air courier service between here and
Pearl Harbor will be established. Encryption here, for radio
transmission via either Navy or MacA.'s facilities, would mean
using their codes and cryptographers, and the problems with
that are self-evident.
   The only way I see to do it is the way I am preparing this
report, all at once, to be turned over to an officer bound for
Pearl. This one is being given to Lt. Col. H. B. Newcombe, U.S.
Army Air Corps, who has been here visiting General Brett, and is
returning to the United States. He is flying as far as Pearl on

TOP SECRET

a converted B-17A Brett has placed into service as a long-range transport.

Let me go off tangentially on that: The service range of the newer B-17s is 925 miles. That is to say, they can strike a target 925 miles from their base and return to their takeoff field. That limitation is going to have a serious effect on their employment here, where there are few targets within a 925-mile range of our bases.

The B-17A on which this will travel has had auxiliary fuel tanks installed; these significantly add to its range, but eliminate its bomb-carrying capacity. This one, which everyone calls the "Swoose," never even had a tail turret; and it was built up from parts salvaged off the B-17s lost in the early assaults on the Philippines. The Air Corps phrase for this is "cannibalization," and it applies to much that we are doing here.

In addition to the difficulty of transmission, the week-to-nine-day transmission time seems to me to render useless any "early warning" value my reports might have. By the time my reports reach Washington, you will have already learned through other channels most of what I have to say.

So what these letters are going to be, essentially, are after-action reports, narrating what has happened here from my perspective, together with what few thoughts I feel comfortable offering about the future.

MacA. and his wife and son are still occupying the suite immediately below this one in the Menzies Hotel. That I am upstairs doesn't seem to bother the Generalissimo, in fact quite the contrary seems true; but it does greatly annoy what has become known as "The Bataan Gang," that is, those people who were with him in the Philippines.

I have resisted pointed suggestions from Sutherland, Huff, and several others that I vacate these premises in order to make them available to the more deserving (and, of course, senior) members of the MacA. entourage. I have been difficult about this, for two major reasons. First, being where I am, close to MacA., permits me to do what I believe you want me to do. Second,

giving in to the suggestion (in the case of Huff, an order: "I have arranged other quarters for you, Captain Pickering.") that I move out would grant the point that I am subject to their orders. I don't think that the Special Representative of the Secretary of the Navy should make himself subordinate even to MacA. himself, and certainly not to members of his staff.

I do actually believe the above, but I must in candor tell you that I took great pleasure in telling them, especially Huff, to go to hell. I know I probably should not have taken pleasure in that, but I don't like them. And they don't like me. I'm convinced that their hostility mostly arises from MacA.'s growing tendency to have me around, often alone with him. And I'm sure it is constantly exacerbated by that. Huff, in particular, sees himself as Saint Peter, guarding access to the throne of God. He simply cannot understand MacA. waiving the rules of protocol for anyone, and especially for a civilian/sailor.

I have spent a good deal of time wondering why MacA. does want me around, and have come up with some possible reasons, listed below, not in order of importance.

It began shortly after he was given office space for his headquarters. The Australians turned over to him a bank building at 401 Collins Street. He now occupies what was the Managing Director's office. The old board room is now the map room.

There was—is—a critical shortage of maps. I was able to help somewhat here when I learned about it.

Going off tangentially again: I learned about the map shortage at dinner, shortly after we arrived in Melbourne. My telephone rang, and in the Best British Manner, one of the Australian sergeants they gave him as orderlies announced to me, "General MacArthur's compliments, Sir. The General and Mrs. MacArthur would be pleased to have you join them for dinner in half an hour."

I went downstairs to the restaurant half an hour later and found the Bataan Gang and an assortment of Australians having their dinner. But not MacA. I asked one of the entourage where MacA. was, and was informed that the General dines alone. When I went to the MacA. apartment, I was perfectly prepared to find

myself the butt of a practical joke. But I was expected. We
dined en famille; in addition to MacA. and his wife, there were
little Arthur and his Chinese nurse/governess.

Dinner was small talk—about people Mrs. MacA. knew in Manila, Honolulu, and San Francisco. The war wasn't mentioned
until after dinner. Brandy and a cigar were produced for me, and
Mrs. MacA. left us alone. I had the feeling (I realize how absurd this sounds; and please believe me, I gave it a lot of
thought before putting it down on paper) that MacA. regards me
as a fellow nobleman, the visiting Duke of Pickering, so to
speak—with himself, of course, as the Emperor. The rules that
apply to common folk—everybody around here but us—naturally
do not apply to the nobility. The common folk don't get to eat,
for example, with the Emperor, en famille.

Some of this, I am quite sure, is because I think I am one of
the few really well-off individuals he has been close to. I
think Mrs. MacA. told him that Pacific & Far East is privately
held, and that Patricia is Andrew Foster's only child, and this
has made an extraordinary impression on him. In support of that
thesis, I offer this: On 6 April, the Pacific Duchess was part
of the convoy that brought the 41st Infantry Division into Adelaide. MacA. informed me of this by saying, "Your ship, the PD,
has arrived in Adelaide." I responded that she was no longer
mine, that she now belonged to the Navy. He asked me how much I
had been paid for it, and what the taxes were on a transaction
like that. I told him. The numbers obviously fascinated him.

On the other hand, most of the special treatment I am getting, I'm sure, is because I am your special representative.
MacA.'s clever. More than clever, brilliant. He knows how useful a direct line to your ear will be.

In any event, over my cigar and his cigarette, he discussed
his intention to immediately return to the Philippines, and
how he planned to do so. In the course of the conversation, he
explained how very much aware he is of the vast distances involved, and of the problems that is going to pose. In that connection, he bitterly complained about the lack of maps. He is
convinced that the Navy has better maps than he has, and that

for petty reasons they are refusing to make them available to him.

I volunteered to look into that. The next day I spoke with Admiral Leary, and then with his intelligence and planning people. And it turned out that MacA. was wrong about the reason he didn't have decent maps. The Navy was not being petty. The Navy doesn't have decent maps either. I was astonished to see the poor quality of the charts they had, and equally astonished to see how few charts are available, period.

I don't pretend to have solved the problem, only to have made a dent in it: but I did manage to gather together charts from the various ship chandlers around (a thought that apparently did not occur to the Navy). The charts I picked up, anyhow, were superior to any the Navy had. I then went to the P&FE agent here and borrowed, on a semipermanent basis, several of his people. They are going to all the masters of ships plying the Southwest Pacific trade, down to the smallest coaster, as they make port; and they'll get them to update charts, especially for the small islands, based on the mariners' own observations.

The P&FE agent here has arranged to have the updated charts printed. I offered to make them available to Admiral Leary, but he made it clear that (a) he is not interested: not having come from the appropriate Navy bureaucracy, they cannot be considered reliable; and that (b) therefore it is an effrontery on my part to ask that I be reimbursed for expenses incurred.

MacA., on the other hand, was really grateful for the maps. I think that was the reason I was invited to go with him on March 25, when he was invested with the Medal of Honor. His acceptance speech was brilliant; my eyes watered.

And the next day, for the first time, MacA. met John Curtin, the Prime Minister. Now, in case you don't know it, Curtin is so far left that he makes Roosevelt look like Louis XIV. All the same, he and MacA. immediately began to act like long-lost brothers. I know for a fact (the P&FE agent here sits in the Australian parliament) that Curtin was flatly opposed to (a) abolishing the Australian Military Board and (b) transferring all of its powers to MacA.

Apparently, neither Willoughby (his G-2) nor our State Department explained to MacA. just who Curtin is or what he'd done. Indeed, MacA. seems to believe exactly the opposite, i.e., that Curtin was responsible for his being named commander-in-chief and given all the powers of the former Military Board. Or else MacA. was told, and regally decided to ignore the implications. With a massive effort, I have obeyed your orders not to involve myself in something like this.

Or—an equally credible scenario—he knows all about Curtin and his politics, and his publicly professed camaraderie and admiration for Curtin is a sham intended for public consumption to bolster the very much sagging Australian morale. The people believe, with good reason, that they are next on the Japanese schedule. Curtin has complained bitterly that Australian (and New Zealand) troops are off in Africa fighting for England when they are needed to defend their homeland. He consequently stands high in the public esteem, even of those who think he is a dangerous socialist.

Into this situation comes MacArthur, promising to defend the Australian continent. The words he used in his Medal of Honor acceptance speech "we shall win or we shall die; I pledge the full resources of all the mighty power of my country, and all the blood of my countrymen" were reported in every newspaper, and over the radio . . . again and again. There was hope once more.

And right on top of that came word of Colonel Doolittle's raid on Tokyo. From my perspective here, I think it's impossible to overestimate the importance of that raid. Militarily, MacA. told me, it will require the Japanese to pull back naval and aerial forces, as well as antiaircraft artillery forces, to protect the homeland. Politically, it is certain to have caused havoc within the Japanese Imperial Staff. Their senior officers are humiliated. And it will inevitably have an effect on Japanese civilian morale.

Since MacArthur, not surprising me at all, immediately concluded that the attack had been launched from an aircraft carrier, I decided that the Commander-in-Chief SWPAC was entitled

TOP SECRET

to hear other information the Japanese probably already knew. I therefore provided him with the specific details of the attack as I knew them. An hour or so later, when Willoughby came to the office and provided MacA. with what few details he had about the raid, MacA. delivered a concise lecture to him and to several others, based on what I had told him. It was of course obvious where he'd gotten his facts. The unfortunate result is I am now regarded as a more formidable adversary than before.

But Doolittle's bombing of Tokyo, added to MacArthur's presence here and his being named Commander-in-Chief, and his (apparently) roaring friendship with Curtin, gave Australian morale a really big boost just when one was needed. And that surge of confidence would have been destroyed if MacA. had started fighting with Curtin—or even if there was any suggestion that they were not great mutual admirers or were not in complete agreement.

The more I think about it, I think this latter is the case. MacArthur understands things like this.

Turning to the important question "Can we hold Australia?" MacArthur believes, supported to some degree by the intelligence (not much) available to us, that the following is the grand Japanese strategy: While Admiral Yamamoto is taking Midway away from us, as a steppingstone to taking the Hawaiian Islands, the forces under Admiral Takeo Takagi will occupy Australia's perimeter islands, north and west of the continent.

We have some pretty good intelligence that Takagi intends to put "Operation Mo" into execution as soon as he can. That is the capture of Port Moresby, on New Guinea. Moresby is currently manned, I should say undermanned, by Australian militiamen with little artillery, etcetera. They could not resist a large-scale Japanese assault. Once Moresby falls, all the Japanese have to do is build it up somewhat and then use it as the base for an invasion across the Coral Sea to Australia. It's about 300 miles across the Coral Sea from Port Moresby to Australia.

Both to repel an invasion and to prevent the Japanese from

marching across Australia, MacA. has two divisions (the U.S. 32nd Infantry, arrived at Adelaide April 15); one brigade of the 6th Australian Division; and one (or two, depending on whom one chooses to believe) Australian divisions being returned "soon" from Africa. He has sixty-two B-17 bombers, six of which (including the "Swoose," which carries no bombs) are airworthy. Some fighter planes have begun to arrive, but these are generally acknowledged to be inferior to the Japanese Zero.

MacA. believes further that the Japanese intend to install fighter airplane bases in the Solomon Islands. We have some unconfirmed (and probably unconfirmable) intelligence that major fighter bases are planned for Guadalkennel (sp?) and Bougainville. Fighters on such strips could escort Japanese Betty and Zeke bombers to interdict our ships bound for Australia, cutting the pipeline. We don't have the men or materiel to go after them at either place.

On top of this, we have had what MacA. feels is an unconscionable delay in reaching an interservice agreement about who is in charge of what. I found myself wondering too, frankly, just who the hell was in charge in Washington. MacA. was not named CIC SWPA until April 18. And even when that happened, it violated a rule of warfare even Fleming Pickering understands: that it is idiocy to split a command. Which is exactly what appointing Admiral Nimitz as CIC Pacific Ocean Areas does.

It means that from this point on, we have started another war. In addition to fighting the Japanese, the Army and the Navy are going to be at each other's throats. A sailor, or a soldier, MacArthur or Nimitz, should have been put in charge. Somebody has to be in charge.

Under these circumstances, I was not at all surprised, the day Bataan fell, when MacA. radioed Marshall asking for permission to return to the Philippines to fight as a guerrilla. I could hear the snickers when that radio arrived in Sodom-on-Potomac.

He showed me the cable before he sent it. I told him what I thought the reaction would be. He said he understood that, but thought there was a slight chance his "enemies" (George Mar-

shall, Ernie King, and the U.S. Navy) would see that he was given permission as a way to get rid of him.

I think I should confess, Frank, that if he had been given permission, I think I would have gone with him.

Colonel Newcombe just called from the lobby. I have to seal this up and give it to him.

Respectfully,
Fleming Pickering, Captain, USNR

XI

(ONE)
THE WILLARD HOTEL
WASHINGTON, D.C.
30 APRIL 1942

"**G**eneral," Congressman Emilio L. DiFranco (D., 8th N.J. Congressional District) said to Brigadier General D. G. McInerney, USMC, "I so very much appreciate your finding time for me in your busy schedule."

The Congressman waited expectantly for the General to notice him; but General McInerney was listening to Congressman DiFranco with only half an ear. The rest of his attention was smitten by a hard rush of curiosity. It was the group sitting three tables away from him in the upstairs cocktail lounge of the Willard Hotel that had caught his eye, indeed his fascination. He had not in fact seen the Congressman making his way across the room to him.

"The Marine Corps always has time for you, Congressman," General McInerney said, rising to his feet and with some effort working up a small smile. He cordially detested Congressman DiFranco, whom he had met a half-dozen times before.

Doc McInerney wasn't *sure* that the tall, remarkably thin blond woman at the table was *really* Monique Pond, the motion-picture actress, but she sure as hell looked like her. A photograph of the actress wearing a silver lamé dress open damned near to her navel hung on every other vertical surface in the military establishment.

Two other people were at the table with Miss Pond, if indeed it was Miss Pond. One was another long-legged, long-haired blond female. McInerney wouldn't have been surprised if that one was also a star of stage, screen, and radio. She was pretty enough. He didn't recognize her, but he wasn't all that familiar with movie stars.

Nor, for that matter, was he all that familiar with the upstairs cocktail lounge of the Willard Hotel. The Willard was an expensive hostelry, catering to high government officials and members of Congress—and, more important, to those individuals who wished to influence government policy and Congressional votes, and who did their drinking on an expense account.

The word *lobbyist* was coined around the time of the Civil War to describe those who hung around the lobby of the Willard Hotel, waiting for Congressmen whose vote they hoped to influence. Not much had changed since then.

The prices in the Willard were of such magnitude that few members of the military establishment, including general officers, could afford them. McInerney came here rarely—only when, as today, there was no way he could get out of it. He had been invited for a drink by the Hon. Mr. DiFranco; it does not behoove officers of the regular Marine Corps to turn down such invitations.

McInerney knew what the Congressman wanted. When the invitation had come, he had checked with the Congressional Liaison Office and learned that Congressman DiFranco had been in touch with them regarding the son of one of his more important constituents. After an initial burst of patriotic fervor that had led to his enlisting in the Marine Corps, this splendid young gentleman now found that he didn't like the life of a Marine rifleman. He wanted instead to be assigned to duties that were more to his liking; specifically, he wanted to be an aircraft mechanic. He had apparently communicated this desire to his daddy, and his father had gotten in touch with Mr. DiFranco.

With all the courtesy due a Congressman, the Congressional Liaison Office had in effect told the Congressman to go fuck himself. At that point, Congressman DiFranco had apparently remembered meeting Brigadier General McInerney a number of times. He decided then to take his constituent's problem directly to the second senior man in Marine Aviation, unofficially, socially, over a drink at the Willard.

It was not the first time this sort of thing had happened to Doc McInerney, nor even the first time with the Hon. Mr. DiFranco. Getting someone special treatment in the Corps because his father happened to know a Congressman rubbed McInerney the wrong way.

Congressman DiFranco sat down and started looking for a waiter. General McInerney looked again at the table where maybe Monique Pond sat with another good-looking blonde who might also be a movie star. Both ladies were with a young man about whose identity Doc McInerney had no doubts at all. His name was Charles M. Galloway, and he was a technical sergeant in the United States Marine Corps.

"I'll have a dry martini with an onion," Congressman DiFranco said to a waiter. "And you, General?"

"The same," McInerney said, raising his glass. He was about through with his second Jack Daniel's and water.

Congressman DiFranco handed General McInerney a slip of paper. On it was written the name of PFC Joseph J. Bianello, his serial number, and his unit, Company A, Fifth Marines, New River, North Carolina.

"What's this?" McInerney asked, innocently.

"He's the young man I want to talk to you about."

McInerney saw that the waiter was busy at the other table. He delivered three fresh drinks and a small silver platter of hors d'oeuvres.

I hope you're having a good time, Galloway. When the bill comes, you'll probably faint.

"Oh?" McInerney said to Congressman DiFranco.

"I've known him all his life. He's a really fine young man. His father owns a trucking firm, Bianello Brothers."

"Is that so?"

The other blonde, the one who was not (maybe) Monique Pond, lovingly fed Technical Sergeant Galloway a bacon-wrapped oyster on a toothpick. He chewed, looked thoughtful, and then nodded his head approvingly, which obviously thrilled the blonde.

"What he did was act impetuously," Congressman DiFranco said. "He's young."

"How do you mean, impetuously?"

"Without thinking before he leaped, so to speak."

"You mean he now regrets having joined the Marine Corps?"

"No, not at all," the Congressman said firmly.

The blonde who was maybe Monique Pond now fed Technical Sergeant Galloway something on a toothpick that Doc McInerney couldn't identify. Galloway chewed, made a face, and valiantly swallowed. The blonde who was maybe Monique Pond leaned over and kissed him on the cheek. Galloway drank deeply from his glass.

"I'm afraid I don't understand," Doc McInerney said.

Squirm, you bastard.

"His father wants to get him out of the infantry," Congressman DiFranco said.

The Congressman's unexpected candor surprised McInerney. He met DiFranco's eyes.

"The kid complained to Daddy, and Daddy came to you. Is that it?"

"The boy knows nothing about this," DiFranco said.

McInerney decided he was being told the truth.

"I'm glad to hear that," he said.

"The boy is eighteen years old, General."

"I saw some statistics last week that said the average age of enlisted men in the First Marine Division—the Fifth Marines are part of the First Division—is eighteen-point-six years," McInerney said. "He won't be lonely."

"Well, I asked," DiFranco said.

"His father is important to you, huh?"

DiFranco shrugged, acknowledging that.

"OK. I'll tell you what I'll do—" McInerney said, and then stopped abruptly. Another Marine had entered the cocktail lounge and was making his way to the table where Technical Sergeant Galloway sat with maybe Monique Pond. This one was a major. He looked familiar, but Doc McInerney could not put a name to the face.

The Major shook Galloway's hand, kissed maybe Monique Pond, then looked around for the waiter. When he had caught his eye, he mimed signing the check.

"General?" Congressman DiFranco said, puzzled by McInerney's pause.

"You can tell this kid's father that you talked to me; that I was difficult about special treatment, but in the end, as a special favor to you, I told you I would arrange to have him transferred into a battalion in the Fifth Marines which is commanded by a friend of mine, who happens to be one of the finest officers in the Marine Corps. That much is for the father. For you, I will add that I will do it in such a way that my friend will not learn why he is getting this boy, and will see that his records don't get flagged as someone who has Congressional influence."

Congressman DiFranco looked at General McInerney carefully.

"I really can't ask for more than that, can I?" he said, finally.

"No, I don't think you can," Doc McInerney replied. "This way, everybody stays honest."

"Then I'm grateful to you, General," Congressman DiFranco said, putting out his hand.

"Any time, Congressman," McInerney said, shaking it.

The waiter delivered a check to the Marine major, who scrawled his name on it, and then walked out of the cocktail lounge.

What the hell is that all about?

"Would you be offended if I cut this short?" DiFranco said. "I really have a busy schedule."

"Not at all," McInerney said. "So do I."

DiFranco fished money from his pocket and dropped a ten-dollar bill on the table.

"Thank you again, General," he said, and walked out of the room.

McInerney drained his glass and then stood up. He started to leave, but as he did, the waiter delivered the drinks Congressman DiFranco had ordered.

"Let me settle up now," he said to the waiter. The four drinks and a ten-percent tip ate up most of the Congressman's ten dollars; McInerney waved the rest of the change away, thinking, *This has to be the most expensive booze in town!*

Then he picked up the fresh drink and walked to Galloway's table.

"Hello, Sergeant Galloway," he said. "How are you?"

Galloway stood up.

"Good evening, Sir."

"Keep your seat. What brings you to town?"

"I've got a VIP flight back and forth to New River in the morning, Sir. Miss Pond and some other people. Oh, excuse me, Sir. General McInerney, this is Miss Pond and Mrs. McNamara."

So it is her. Of course! Now I know who that major is! Jake Dillon, the ex-Hollywood press agent. I met him when Colonel Whatsisname's parachute didn't open.

"I thought I recognized you, Miss Pond. And of course, you too, Mrs. McNamara. I'm very pleased to meet you."

"You recognized me?" Mrs. Caroline Ward McNamara asked, surprised. "Have we met?"

"Well, aren't you an actress, too? Or should I say 'the actress'?"

"No," Caroline McNamara said, laughing throatily. "But thank you. I love your mistake. I'm just a friend of Charley's." She patted Charley's hand fondly, possessively.

McInerney saw on her hand several thousand dollars' worth of rubies set in gold.

Galloway didn't meet this woman in the staff NCO mess at Quantico.

"Well, I just wanted to say hello," McInerney said. "It's nice to meet you."

He walked back to his table and sat down.

Less than a minute later, Galloway and the two women got up and left the lounge. McInerney followed them. They walked across the lobby and got into an elevator.

This is really none of my business, McInerney decided, only to amend that decision a moment later: *Fuck it! Watching out for the welfare of his Marines is always an officer's responsibility.*

He went to the desk and inquired whether Miss Monique Pond was registered in the Willard. The desk clerk took a moment to decide that a man in the uniform of a brigadier general of the United States Marine Corps was probably not a fan intent on bothering a movie star.

"I believe that Miss Pond is part of the party staying with Mr. Dillon, Sir."

"You mean *Major* Dillon? And the rest of the party being the other Marine and the other lady?"

"Yes, Sir. They're in the Abraham Lincoln suite."

"Thank you," McInerney said, and walked to the house phones and asked the operator to connect him with the Abraham Lincoln suite.

"Hello?"

"Major Dillon, please."

"This is Jake Dillon."

"Major, this is General McInerney. I'm in the lobby, and I'd like a moment of your time."

There was a perceptible pause before Dillon asked, "Would you like to come up, General?"

"I think it would better if you came down. I'll wait for you in the bar. The one on the second floor."

"I'll be right there, Sir."

A waiter did not appear to serve General McInerney until after Major Dillon walked in the room. Then one appeared almost immedi-ately, carrying on a tray a drink McInerney knew Dillon hadn't had time to order.

"They do that," Dillon said. "They know what I like. Should I just let it sit there?"

He had used neither of the words "Sir" nor "General," McInerney noticed.

"This is not official," McInerney said. "Bring me a Jack Daniel's and water, please."

Dillon pushed his glass across the table to him.

"Please," he said. "Help yourself."

"I'll wait."

"Please take it. I'm trying to be ingratiating."

"Why would you want to do that?"

"Because I think this has to do with Charley Galloway, not with me. He told me you'd come up to him in here."

"It has to do with both of you," McInerney said.

"What's the problem, General?"

"I don't know if there is one. I am curious what one of my sergeants is doing in here, sharing an expensive suite with a movie star, a field-grade officer, and a woman with rubies on her hand worth more money than he makes in a year."

"She's good for him. I wouldn't be surprised if she's in love with him. She keeps him on the straight and narrow."

"What about the field-grade officer?" McInerney said.

"I thought that's what this was about," Dillon said. "I didn't just come into the Corps, General. I just *came back* in the Corps. I know all about not crossing the line between officers and enlisted men."

"Then why are you crossing it?"

"You did say, General, that this conversation isn't official?"

"Not yet. I'm trying to keep Charley Galloway out of trouble. You too, if that can be arranged."

"Well, if there's going to be trouble about this, dump it on me. I invited Charley here, and when he said that might cause trouble, I told him we'd be careful, and that if something—like this—happened, I'd take the rap."

"What's your interest in Galloway?"

"I like him. We're pals."

"He's a sergeant and you're an officer."

"I'm not really a major, I'm a flack wearing a Marine uniform."

"A what?"

"A press agent. My contribution to the war effort is getting people like Monique Pond to go to New River so she can flash her boobs at the cameramen and get the Marine Corps in the newsreels. Charley, on the other hand, is one hell of a Marine. He told me about flying the Wildcat out to the carrier off Pearl Harbor. But instead of commanding a fighter squadron, the Corps has him flying a bunch of brass hats and feather merchants around in a VIP transport airplane. So what we have here is an officer who should be an enlisted man, and a sergeant who should be an officer. So we hang around together. My idea, not his."

"What you're doing, both of you," General McInerney said, "is important."

Why did I say that? I don't believe it.

"General, I told Charley I would take the heat if something like this came up. I really would be grateful if you let me do that."

"Major Dillon," General McInerney said, after a long moment during which a few connections went *click* in his mind, "I really have no idea what you're talking about. The reason I asked to have a word with you, when I saw you come in here alone, was that I know you are in charge of the public-relations activities marking the bringing of the 1st Marine Division to wartime strength at New River tomorrow. I want to know if there is anything, anything at all, that Marine Corps Aviation can do to insure that the ceremonies are a rousing public-relations success."

Dillon's eyebrows rose thoughtfully.

"I can't think of a thing, Sir," he said.

"And to make sure there is absolutely no problem at all flying the VIPs back and forth to New River, I wanted to tell you that I have personally assigned one of our finest enlisted pilots, Technical Sergeant Galloway, to the mission. If he has not reported to you yet, I am sure he will do so momentarily. I remind you that, as an officer, you are responsible for seeing that the Sergeant is properly quartered and rationed. If there are questions regarding how and where, in the necessarily extraordinary circumstances, you elect to do that, refer whoever raises them to me."

"Aye, aye, Sir."

"That will be all, Major Dillon. Thank you."

"Yes, Sir."

Dillon stood up and started to leave. He had taken three steps when McInerney called his name.

"Yes, Sir?"

"Just between a couple of old Marines, Dillon, I don't like flying my goddamned desk, either."

(TWO)

THE COMMANDANT'S HOUSE
UNITED STATES MARINE CORPS BARRACKS
EIGHTH AND "I" STREETS, S.E.
WASHINGTON, D.C.
2230 HOURS 9 MAY 1942

A glistening black 1939 Packard 180 automobile pulled into the driveway and stopped before the Victorian mansion. Mounted above its front and rear bumpers it had the three silver stars on a red plate identifying the occupant as a lieutenant general of the United States Marine Corps.

The driver, a lean, impeccably turned-out Marine staff sergeant, got quickly out from behind the wheel, but he was not quick enough to open the rear door before Thomas Holcomb, the first Marine ever promoted to lieutenant general, opened it himself. The Commandant was home.

"*Early* tomorrow, Chet," General Holcomb said to his driver. "Five o'clock."

"Aye, aye, Sir."

The general's senior aide-de-camp, a very thin lieutenant colonel, slid across the seat and got out.

"Goodnight, Chet," General Holcomb said.

"Goodnight, Sir."

"I don't see any need for you to come in, Bob," General Holcomb said to his aide. "I'm for bed."

The porch lights came on. General Holcomb's orderlies had seen the headlights.

"General," the aide said, "I took the liberty of telling Captain Steward to be prepared to brief you on the Coral Sea battle. He's probably inside, Sir."

"OK," Holcomb said wearily. He was tired. It had been a long day, ending with a long and tiring automobile ride back to Washington from

Norfolk, where there had been an interservice conference at Fortress
Monroe. Whatever had happened in the Coral Sea had already happened; he didn't have to learn all the details tonight. But young Captain
Steward had apparently worked long and hard preparing the briefing,
and it would not do right now to tell him it wasn't considered important.

*Besides, I'll have to take the briefing sooner or later anyway, why
not now and get it over with?*

The Commandant raised his eyes to the porch, intending to order,
as cheerfully as he could manage, that the orderly put on the coffeepot.
There was someone on the porch he didn't expect to see, and really
would rather not have seen.

"Hello, Doc," he called to Brigadier General D. G. McInerney.
"Did I send for you?"

"No, Sir. I took the chance that you might have a minute to spare
for me."

*Good God, a long day of the problems of Navy Ordnance and the
Army's Coast Artillery Corps is enough. And here comes Marine Aviation wanting something!*

"Sure. Come on in the house. I was about to order up some coffee,
but now that you're here, I expect Tommy had better break out the
bourbon."

"Coffee would be fine, Sir."

"Don't be noble, Doc. God hates a hypocrite."

"A little bourbon would go down very nicely, Sir."

"I'm about to be briefed on a battle in the Coral Sea. You familiar
with it?"

"Only that we lost the *Lexington,* Sir."

"Yeah. Well, you can sit in on the briefing," Holcomb said. He led
the small procession into the house, handed his uniform cap to an
orderly, and then went into the parlor.

"Good evening, Sir," Captain Steward said. Holcomb saw that
Steward had come with all the trappings: an easel, covered now with
a sheet of oilcloth bearing the Marine Corps insignia; a large round
leather map case containing a detailed map; and a dozen folders covered with TOP SECRET cover sheets—probably the immediate, radioed
after-action reports themselves.

"Hello, Stew," he said. "Sorry to keep you up this late. You know
General McInerney."

"Yes, Sir. Good evening, General."

"Is there anything in there General McInerney is not supposed to
hear?"

"No, Sir. General McInerney is on the Albatross list."

The Albatross list was a short list of those officers who were privy to the fact that the Navy codebreakers at Pearl had broken several of the most important Japanese naval codes.

That's a pretty short list, General Holcomb remembered now, *a* goddamned *short list, and for very good reason. If the Japanese don't find out we're reading their mail, it's hard to overestimate the importance of the broken codes. But the more people who know a secret, the greater the risk it won't stay a secret long.*

"How is that, Doc?" Holcomb asked evenly. "Why are you cleared for Albatross?"

"General Forrest brought me in on that, Sir."

The Commandant considered that for a moment, and decided to give Brigadier General Horace W. T. Forrest, Assistant Chief of Staff for Intelligence, the benefit of the doubt.

If Forrest told Doc, he must have had his reasons.

The Commandant turned to one of the orderlies. "Coffee ready?"

"Yes, Sir."

"Well, bring it in, please. And a bottle of bourbon. And then see that we're not disturbed."

"Aye, aye, Sir."

"While we're waiting, Stew, why don't you pass around those after-actions. That's what they are, right?"

"Yes, Sir."

Captain Steward divided the half-dozen documents with the TOP SECRET cover sheets between Generals Holcomb and McInerney. Before they had a chance to read more than a few lines, the orderly pushed in a cart with a coffee service, a bottle of bourbon, glasses, and a silver ice bucket. It had obviously been set up beforehand.

"Tommy must have been a Boy Scout," Holcomb said. "He's always prepared. We'll take care of ourselves, Tommy. Thank you."

The orderly left the room, closing the sliding doors from outside. Holcomb closed his folder.

"Let's have it, Stew. I can probably get by without reading all that."

"Yes, Sir."

Captain Steward went to the easel and raised the oilskin cover. Beneath it was a simple map of the Coral Sea area. A slim strip of northern Australia was visible, as was the southern tip of New Guinea. Above New Guinea lay the southern tip of New Ireland and all of New Britain. Rabaul, which was situated at the northern tip of New Britain, was prominently labeled; it had fallen to the Japanese and was being rapidly built up as a major port for them.

To the east were the Solomon Islands. The major ones were labeled: Bougainville was the most northerly; then they went south through Choiseul, New Georgia, Santa Isabel, Tulagi, Guadalcanal, Florida, and Malaita, to San Cristobal, the most southerly.

"Keep it simple, Stew, but start at the beginning," the Commandant ordered.

"Aye, aye, Sir," Captain Steward said. "In late April, Sir, we learned, from Albatross intercepts, details of Japanese plans to take Midway Island, and from there to threaten Hawaii, with the ultimate ambition of taking Hawaii, which would both deny us that forward port and logistic facility and permit them to threaten the West Coast of the United States and the Aleutian Islands.

"Secondly, they planned to invest Port Moresby, on the tip of Eastern New Guinea. From Port Moresby they could threaten the Australian continent and extend their area of influence into the Solomon Islands. If they succeed in this intention, land-based aircraft in the Solomons could effectively interdict our supply lines to Australia and New Zealand."

I've heard all this before, and I'm tired. But I'm not going to jump on this hardworking kid because I'm grouchy when I'm tired.

"Via Albatross intercepts we learned that there would be two Japanese naval forces. Vice-Admiral Takeo Takagi sailed from the Japanese naval base at Truk in command of the carrier striking force, the carriers *Zuikaku* and *Shokaku,* which represented a total of 125 aircraft, and its screening force.

"The second Japanese force, under the overall command of Vice-Admiral Shigeyoshi Inouye, and sailing from their base at Rabaul on New Britain, included the carrier *Shoho* and several cruisers, transports, and oilers.

"On 3 May, elements of this second force, which had apparently sailed from Rabaul several days earlier, landed on Tulagi, a small island here in the Solomons"—Steward pointed with what looked like an orchestra leader's baton—"approximately equidistant between the three larger islands of Santa Isabela, Malaita, and Guadalcanal. They immediately began to construct a seaplane base.

"Based on the Albatross intercepts, Admiral Nimitz ordered Task Force 17, with Admiral Fletcher flying his flag aboard the carrier *Yorktown,* into the area. At the same time, Admiral Nimitz ordered Task Force 11, with Admiral Fitch flying his flag aboard the carrier *Lexington,* and Task Force 44, a mixed force of U.S. and Australian cruisers, under Admiral Crace, to join up with Task Force 11.

"Admiral Fletcher ordered a strike on the Japanese invasion force on Tulagi, which was carried out at 0630 hours 6 May. The after-action reports on the success of that attack, which are in the folder marked 'Tulagi,' have had to be revised."

"What the hell does that mean?" the Commandant asked sharply.

"Sir, there are Australian Coastwatchers on Tulagi. Their radioed reports of the damage inflicted differed from that of the personnel

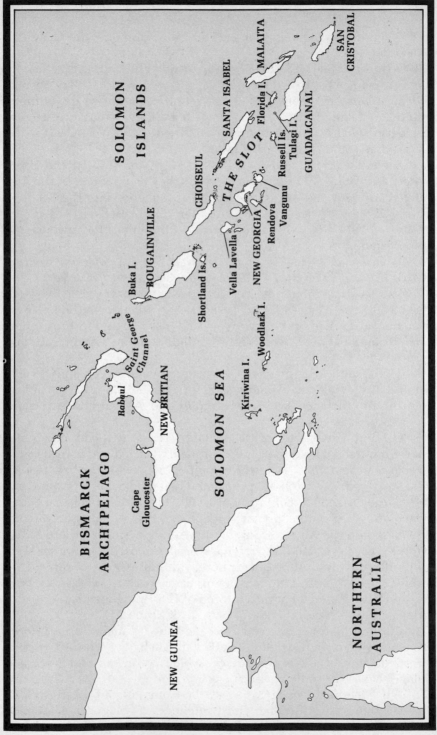

involved in the attack. Admiral Nimitz feels that inasmuch as the Coast-watchers are on Tulagi, theirs are the more credible reports."

"In other words," the Commandant said angrily, "the flyboys let their imaginations run wild again, but the Coastwatchers produced the facts."

"Yes, Sir," Captain Steward said uncomfortably.

"Nothing personal, Doc," the Commandant said.

"I know why it happens, Sir," McInerney said evenly. "But that doesn't excuse it."

"Why does it happen? I'm really curious, Doc."

"I think it has to do with movement, Sir. Perspective. Two, or three, or four pilots report, honestly, what they have seen. But because they are looking at what they all see from different places, both in terms of altitude and direction, no two descriptions match. For example, one aircraft shot down, or one seaplane destroyed in the water, becomes three airplanes shot down, or four seaplanes destroyed, because there are four different reports from people who are, in fact, reporting honestly what they saw. You need a pretty good G-2 debriefing team to separate the facts. Or consolidate them."

The Commandant grunted. "Bad intelligence is worse than no intelligence."

"I agree, Sir," McInerney said.

"We sent a special unit over there to work with the Coastwatchers," the Commandant said. "Did you know about that?"

"Yes, Sir."

"Is that going to help this, do you think?"

"Sir, I don't think it's possible to overstate the value of the Coastwatchers. They will get us, quickly, valid intelligence from the islands, particularly about Japanese air activity, but also of course about ship movement. If we know as soon as it happens what the Japanese are launching against us, what type of aircraft, and how many, we can launch our own aircraft in time to have them in the air when and where it is to our advantage. As opposed to detecting the enemy with patrolling aircraft, or worse, learning about the attack only when it begins, which catches us on the ground. Or when we're in the air almost out of fuel."

The Commandant grunted.

"I recommended to General Forrest," McInerney went on, "that he—we—should do whatever it takes, whatever it costs, to get our people tied in to the Coastwatchers. And I want some of our own people as quickly as possible to get onto the islands as Coastwatchers. I think I was preaching to the convinced, but he said he intended to do just that. But if you were asking, Sir, whether it will do anything about the confusing reports we get from pilots, I don't think so. We're just going to have to work on that. It's inexperience, Sir, rather than dishonesty."

"I didn't mean to insult your people, Doc. You know that."

"Yes, Sir."

"OK, Stew. Pardon the interruption."

"After the attack on Tulagi, Sir, Task Force 17 moved south to join up with Task Forces 11 and 14. They did so at 0930 6 May, and together steamed westward to intercept the Port Moresby invasion force.

"At 1030 hours, 6 May, Army Air Force B-17 aircraft from Australia bombed the carrier *Shoho* and her covering force, apparently without effect.

"The next day, 7 May, at 1135 hours, aircraft from the *Lexington* spotted the *Shoho* again. They attacked and sank her. Three of Lady Lex's aircraft were lost in the attack."

"But they got the Jap carrier? That wasn't one of these perception problems General McInerney is talking about?"

"No, Sir. In addition to the pilot's after-action reports, there has been confirmation of the loss via Albatross intercepts."

"OK. Go on."

"At noon, 7 May, Japanese bombers and torpedo bombers flying off Admiral Takagi's carriers, the Zuikaku and Shokaku, found the fleet oiler *Neosho*, escorted by the destroyer *Sims*. The *Sims* was sunk and the *Neosho* damaged. The last word on that is that she will probably have to be scuttled.

"Just before noon the next day, Japanese aircraft from Admiral Tagaki's carriers attacked the combined Task Force. Both *Yorktown* and *Lexington* were damaged. Yorktown's damage was minimal, but Lexington was badly damaged, and she was scuttled at 1956 hours 8 May."

"Damn!" the Commandant said.

"At that point, Admiral Nimitz ordered Task Forces 11 and 17 to withdraw to the south. Task Force 44, the cruiser force, steamed westward to intercept the Port Moresby invasion force.

"By that time, Albatross intercepts indicated that Admiral Inouye had called off 'Operation Mo,' which was the Port Moresby invasion, but inasmuch as this information could not be made available to Admiral Crace, his Task Force patrolled the Coral Sea South of New Guinea until word from the Coastwatchers confirmed the withdrawal of the Japanese invasion force."

"That's it, then, Stew?" the Commandant asked.

"Sir, the radio messages are in the folders, and I have precise maps—"

"No, thank you. That was first-class, Stew. I know how hard you had to work to get that up in the time you had. I appreciate it."

Captain Steward beamed.

"My pleasure, Sir," he said.

"Now go get some sleep," the Commandant said. "And you too, Bob," he added to his aide. "I'm going to have a quick drink with General McInerney and then hit the sheets myself."

The Commandant waited until Captain Steward and his aide had gathered up all the briefing material before speaking.

"Was it worth it, Doc? One of our carriers for one of theirs?"

"Probably not," McInerney said, after a moment's thought. "They have more carriers to lose than we do. But if it—and it looks like it did—if it called off, or even delayed for any appreciable time, their invasion of Port Moresby, then it was. If they had taken Moresby, I don't think we could have held Australia."

"You don't think they'll be back?"

"I think they will. But we've bought some time. What worries me is that seaplane base on that island—what was it?—Tulagi. If they get a decent air base going in that area, we're in deep trouble as far as our shipping lanes are concerned. We're going to have to do something about that."

"Such as?"

"Maybe take one of the other islands and put a dirt-strip fighter base on it."

"With what? We don't have anything over there. My God, we couldn't even hang on to Corregidor."

Three days earlier, on May 6, Lieutenant General Jonathan M. Wainwright, USA, had surrendered the fortress of Corregidor, in Manila Bay, to the Japanese.

"I know."

"That's the first time a Marine regiment ever had to surrender," the Commandant said. *"Ever!"*

"They were ordered to surrender, Sir, by the Army."

"That's a lot of consolation, isn't it?"

The Commandant walked to the whiskey tray and poured himself a drink. He held up the bottle to McInerney, who shook his head no and said, "No, thank you, Sir."

"What's on your mind, Doc?" the Commandant asked.

"General, I'm really desperate for qualified fighter squadron commanders."

"I'll bet if Al Vandergrift was here, he would say, 'I'm really desperate for qualified company commanders.' "

Major General Alexander Vandergrift commanded the 1st Marine

Division, which consisted of the 1st and 5th Marines, plus the 11th
Marines, Artillery, and which had just been brought up to war strength
on May 1 at New River, North Carolina.

"Sir, I have one Naval Aviation Pilot, Technical Sergeant Galloway,
who is qualified by both experience and temperament to command a
fighter squadron. I would like to commission him and give him one."

The Commandant flashed him an icy stare.

"Galloway? That's the young buck who flew the Wildcat onto the
carrier off Pearl and enraged the Navy? I'm still hearing about that.
Whenever the Navy wants an example of irrational Marine behavior,
they bring up Sergeant Galloway's flight onto the *Saratoga.*"

"Yes, Sir."

"You ever hear the story, Doc, of General Jubal T. Early in the Civil
War? Somebody sent him a plan he turned down. So this staff officer
sent it back, respectfully requesting that the commanding general re-
consider his previous decision. Early sent that back, too, after he wrote
on it, 'Goddammit, I already told you "no." I ain't gonna tell you
again.' "

"Yes, Sir."

The Commandant looked at him thoughtfully, even disbelievingly.

"That's the *only* reason you came here tonight? You sat out there
on the porch for hours, waiting for me to come home just to ask me to
do something you knew damned well I wouldn't do?"

"Sergeant Galloway got a raw deal, Sir. And I need squadron commanders."

"Loyalty to your men is commendable, General," the Commandant said, "but there is a point beyond which it becomes counterpro-
ductive."

"Yes, Sir."

"And goddammit, Doc," the Commandant said, warming to his
subject, "I'm disappointed that you don't know what that point is."

Well, I tried, McInerney thought. *And really pissed him off. I
wonder what that's going to cost Marine Aviation somewhere down the
pike?*

He set his glass on the table.

"With your permission, Sir, I'll take my leave."

The Commandant glowered at him.

"Keep your seat, and finish your drink, you hard-headed Scotch-
man," he said. "I can't afford to lose any more old friends."

(THREE)

HEADQUARTERS, U.S. MARINE CORPS PARACHUTE SCHOOL
LAKEHURST NAVAL AIR STATION
LAKEHURST, NEW JERSEY
15 MAY 1942

First Lieutenant Richard B. Macklin, USMC, heard the knock at the jamb of his open office door, and then his peripheral vision picked up First Sergeant George J. Hammersmith standing there with a sheet of teletype paper in his hand.

Macklin did not raise his eyes from the papers on his desk. First Things First made sense. If you interrupted your work every time someone appeared at your door, you never got anything done. And he certainly didn't want Sergeant Hammersmith to form the opinion, as so many old Marines did, that a commanding officer had nothing to do but sit behind a desk and wait for payday while the sergeants ran the Corps.

He finished what he was doing, which was to consider a request from the Navy Commander of Lakehurst that he permanently detail two enlisted men a day to work with the Base Engineer on roads and grounds. He decided against it; Para-Marines had more important things to do than pick up trash and cut weeds. Then he raised his head.

"You wish something, First Sergeant?"

"Got a TWX here, Sir, I thought you'd want to see right away."

Macklin made an impatient gesture for Hammersmith to give him the sheet of teletype paper. He judged in advance that the message would probably be of little genuine importance and could just as easily have been sent by mail. In his view, ninety-five percent of TWXs were a waste of time.

He was wrong.

HEADQUARTERS USMC
WASHDC 0755 15MAY42
ROUTINE

COMMANDING OFFICER
USMC PARACHUTE SCHOOL
LAKEHURST NAVAL AIR STATION
LAKEHURST NJ

1. ON RECEIPT, ISSUE NECESSARY ORDERS DETACHING 1ST LT RICHARD B. MACKLIN, USMC, FROM HEADQUARTERS AND HEADQUARTERS COMPANY USMC PARASCHOOL LAKEHURST NAS NJ FOR TRANSFER TO HQ & HQ COMPANY 1ST USMC PARA BN, FLEET MARINE FORCE PACIFIC.

2. LT MACKLIN WILL REPORT TO US NAVAL BASE SAN DIEGO CAL NOT LATER THAN 2400 HOURS 30 MAY 1942 FOR FURTHER SHIPMENT TO FINAL DESTINATION. TRAVEL BY FIRST AVAILABLE MIL AND/OR CIV RAIL, AIR, OR MOTOR TRANSPORTATION TO SAN DIEGO IS AUTHORIZED. TRAVEL BEYOND SAN DIEGO WILL BE BY US GOVT SEA OR AIR TRANSPORT, PRIORITY BBBB2B.

3. TIME PERMITTING LT MACKLIN IS AUTHORIZED NO MORE THAN SEVEN (7) DAYS DELAY EN ROUTE OVERSEAS LEAVE.

4. LT MACKLIN WILL COMPLY WITH ALL APPLICABLE REGULATIONS CONCERNING OVERSEAS TRANSFER BEFORE DEPARTING LAKEHURST. STORAGE OF PERSONAL AND HOUSEHOLD GOODS AND ONE (1) PRIVATELY OWNED AUTOMOBILE AT GOVT EXPENSE IS AUTHORIZED.

5. HEADQUARTERS USMC (ATTN: PERS/23/A/11) WILL BE NOTIFIED BY TWX OF DATE OF LT MACKLIN'S DEPARTURE.

BY DIRECTION:

FRANK J. BOEHM, CAPT, USMCR

The first thing that occurred to Lieutenant Macklin was that it was sort of funny that as the Commanding Officer of the Parachute School, he would be ordering himself overseas.

Then it no longer seemed amusing at all.

His promotion had not come through.

He was supposed to be in San Diego two weeks from tomorrow, and from there he was going to the Pacific—in other words, to war.

It didn't seem fair. Just as he was getting the Parachute School shipshape, they were taking it away from him.

It seemed to him that he could make a far greater contribution to the Marine Corps where he was—as an expert in place, so to speak— than in a routine assignment in the 1st Parachute Battalion.

After some thought, he picked up the telephone and called Captain Boehm, who had signed the TWX and had presumably made the decision to send him overseas. He outlined to Boehm the reasons it would be to the greater benefit of the Marine Corps if the TWX was rescinded.

Captain Boehm was not at all receptive. He was, in fact, downright insulting:

"I heard you were a scumbag, Macklin. But I never thought I would personally hear a Marine officer trying to weasel out of going overseas."

(FOUR)

THE OFFICERS' CLUB
U.S. MARINE CORPS BASE
QUANTICO, VIRGINIA
1730 HOURS 17 MAY 1942

When he entered the club, First Lieutenant David F. Schneider, USMC, was not exactly *pleased* to bump into First Lieutenant James G. Ward, USMCR, and Lieutenant Ward's aunt, Mrs. Caroline Ward McNamara. But neither was he exactly unhappy. He reacted like a man for whom fate has made a decision he would rather not have made himself.

Now that he had accidentally bumped into them, so to speak, as opposed to having gone looking for them, he could now begin to rectify an unpleasant situation that it was his duty, as a regular Marine officer, to rectify for the good of the Corps.

Schneider had learned of Mrs. McNamara's presence on the base the day before: He was looking for Lieutenant Ward; so he walked into the squadron office and asked the sergeant on duty if he had seen him.

"He took the lady over to the Officers' Guest House, Lieutenant."

The Guest House was a facility provided to temporarily house (there was a seventy-two-hour limit) dependents and friends of Quantico officers.

"What lady?"

"Didn't get her name. Nice looking. First, she asked for Sergeant Galloway; and when I told her he wasn't back yet, she asked for Lieutenant Ward, so I got him on the phone, and he came over and fetched her and told me he was taking her over to the Guest House." There was a perceptible pause before the sergeant added, "Sir."

There was little question that the lady was Mrs. Caroline Ward McNamara, but Schneider was a careful, methodical man. He called the Guest House later that day to inquire if there was a Mrs. McNamara registered. And, of course, there was.

Technical Sergeant Charles M. Galloway had gone to Washington in response to a telephone call from General McInerney's office. But Washington was to be only his first stop. Schneider suspected that Major Jake Dillon, the Public Affairs Officer, was behind the mysterious call from General McInerney's office. If that was the case, there was no telling where Galloway had gone after he left Washington.

"Hey, Dave," Ward called to him. "I thought you would show up here."

"Good evening," Schneider said.

"You remember my Aunt Caroline, don't you?"

"Of course. How nice to see you again, Mrs. McNamara."

"Oh, call me Caroline!"

Dave Schneider smiled at her, but did not respond.

"Let's go in the bar," Jim Ward suggested. Schneider smiled again, and again did not reply.

The bar was crowded with young officers. With varying degrees of discretion, they all made it clear that they considered Mrs. Caroline Ward McNamara one of the better specimens of the gentle gender.

Dave Schneider wondered if they would register so much approval of the "lady" if they were aware that Mrs. McNamara was not only shacked up with an enlisted man but apparently didn't much care who knew about it.

They found a small table across from the bar.

"Dave, do you have any idea where Charley Galloway is?" Jim Ward asked, as soon as the waiter had taken their order.

"I believe he's in Washington," Schneider said. "Specifically, with Major Dillon."

"No, he's not," Caroline said. "We just called Jake. Jake said he hadn't heard from him since Tuesday morning, when he left the Willard. He spent Monday night there with Jake."

Reserve officer or not, Mustang or not, Lieutenant Schneider thought angrily, *Major Jake Dillon should know better than to offer an enlisted man the freedom of his hotel suite.*

"He called Caroline from Pensacola—" Jim Ward said.

"Pensacola?" Schneider interrupted.

"Pensacola. He called on Wednesday. He told Caroline he was going to the West Coast," Jim Ward said.

"Actually, he said he had a week to get out there," Caroline McNamara said, "and suggested we could drive out there together."

Jim Ward looked a little uncomfortable when she said that, Schneider noticed.

And well he should. There is absolutely no suggestion that his aunt finds anything wrong with the idea that she has been asked to drive cross-country alone with a man to whom she's not married. Having a shameless aunt like that should embarrass anybody.

"That sounds like he's on orders," Jim Ward said. "But when Caroline showed up here, and no Charley Galloway, I checked. No orders have come down on him that anyone knows about."

"I can't imagine what's going on," Schneider said. "Did anyone in the squadron office know he was in Pensacola?"

"All the squadron knows is that he went to Washington on the verbal orders of Colonel Hershberger. That was eight, nine days ago," Jim Ward said.

"Is there a Lieutenant Jim Ward in here?" the bartender called, holding up a telephone.

Jim Ward got up and walked to the bar and took the telephone. Less than a minute later he was back at the table, smiling.

"Our wandering boy has been heard from," he said. "That was Jerry O'Malloy. He's the duty officer. I asked him to let me know the minute he heard anything about Galloway."

"And?" Caroline McNamara asked excitedly.

"Charley just called the tower. He's twenty minutes out," Ward said, then turned to look at Schneider and added, "In an F4F."

"In a what?" Caroline asked.

"A Wildcat," Jim Ward said. "A fighter plane. I wonder where he got that, and what he's doing with it?"

"Well, I intend to find out," Lieutenant David Schneider said, and started to get up.

"Sit down, Dave. I told O'Malloy to have Charley call me here the minute he gets in."

"I'm going to be at Base Operations when he lands," Schneider said.

"What the hell is the matter with you?"

"You know damned well what's the matter with me. For one thing, and you know it as well as I do, he is absolutely forbidden to fly fighters."

"And for another?" Ward asked coldly.

"I would prefer to discuss that privately with you, if you don't mind."

"Sit down, Dave," Jim Ward said.

Schneider looked at him in surprise.

"You heard me, sit down," Jim Ward repeated firmly. "I don't know what Charley is doing with an F4F, but I do know that it's none of your business or mine. That's between him and the squadron commander."

Schneider sat down.

"When he calls, I'll ask him what's going on," Jim Ward said. "In the meantime, we'll pursue the legal principle that you're innocent until proven guilty."

"I don't like the way this sounds," Caroline said. "What's going on? What's wrong?"

"Never worry about things you can't control," Jim Ward said. "So far as we *know*, nothing is wrong."

Charley Galloway did not telephone. Half an hour later, he walked up to the table, leaned down, said, "Hi, baby," to Mrs. McNamara, and kissed her on the lips.

He was wearing his fur-collared leather flight jacket over tropical worsteds. He had jammed a fore-and-aft cap in one pocket of the flight jacket, and thin leather flying gloves in the other. He almost needed a shave, and there was a light band around his eyes where his flying goggles had protected the skin from the oily mist that often filled a Wildcat cockpit. It was obvious that he had come to the club directly from the flight line.

"Where have you been, honey?" Caroline asked. "I was getting really worried."

"That's a long story," he said.

"Charley," Jim Ward asked uncomfortably, "should you be in here?"

"He knows damn well he shouldn't," Dave Schneider flared. "What the *hell* do you think you're doing, Galloway?"

"Are you talking to me, Lieutenant?" Charley asked pleasantly. He shrugged out of the leather jacket and dropped it on the floor.

"Yes, I am."

"Then please use the words 'Captain,' and 'Sir,' Charley said. He faced Dave Schneider, smiled broadly, and pointed to the twin silver bars on each of his collar points.

"Jesus!" Jim Ward said. "Are they for real?"

"I got them from the Commandant himself, believe it or not," Charley said. "Together with a brief, but memorable, lecture on the conduct expected of me now that I was going to be an officer and a gentleman."

"What about the West Coast?" Caroline asked softly.

"I'm going to be given a fighter squadron, baby," Charley Galloway said. "As soon as I can get out to the Pacific and organize one. They're going to fly me at least as far as Pearl. I've got six days to get to San Diego."

"Oh, God!"

"Can I go with you?" Jim Ward asked softly.

"With Aunt Caroline and me? Hell, no," Charley Galloway said indignantly. "Didn't you ever hear that three's a crowd?"

"That's not what I meant, Captain, Sir."

"If, in the next three weeks or a month, you can scare up an IP here who is willing to check you out in that Wildcat I just brought up here, you can come along later. I've got authorization to steal five pilots from here," Galloway said. Then he faced Dave Schneider. "That's an invitation to you too, Dave. You're a real horse's ass sometimes, but you're not too bad an airplane driver."

(FIVE)

MELBOURNE, AUSTRALIA
19 MAY 1942

The Martin PBM-3R Mariner made landfall on the Australian continent near Moruya, in New South Wales, seventy-five miles southeast of
the Australian capital at Canberra. The PBM-3R Mariner was the unarmed transport version of the standard PBM Mariner, a deep-hulled,
twin-engined gull-winged monoplane.

Aboard were a crew of six, nineteen passengers, and eight hundred
pounds of priority cargo, including a half-dozen mail bags.

When the excitement of finally making landfall had died down—for
most aboard, it was their first view of Australia—Captain D. B. Toller,
Civil Engineer Corps, USN, permitted his curiosity to take charge. He
walked to the forward part of the cabin, just below the ladder leading
to the cockpit, and sat down beside a Marine Corps major.

"All right if I sit here?"

"Certainly, Sir."

"I'm Captain Dick Toller, Major," he said, offering his hand.

"Ed Banning, Sir."

"Well, we're finally here. Or almost. This has been a long flight."

"Yes, Sir, it has. I'll be glad to get off this thing and stretch my legs."

"Now, if I'm asking something I shouldn't, just tell me to mind my
own business," Captain Toller said. "But I'm really curious about something."

"Yes, Sir?"

"Him," Captain Toller said, nodding his head to a small area to the
left of the ladder of the cockpit, where Corporal Stephen M. Koffler was
curled up asleep, under blankets he had removed from his duffel bag.
Koffler had rolled around in his sleep and wound up with his arm
around his Springfield 1903 rifle. It looked as if he was holding it protec-
tively, affectionately, as a child holds a teddy bear.

Banning chuckled.

"Corporal Koffler. He's got the right idea. He slept from 'Diego to
Hawaii; and except to eat, he's been asleep most of the way here."

"I saw you get on the plane at Pearl," Captain Toller said. "I mean
to say, I saw a very annoyed lieutenant commander and an even more
annoyed captain being told to give up their seats in favor of passengers
with higher priorities. And then you two came aboard."

Banning didn't reply. He was not particularly surprised by the
question. The bumped-from-the-flight captain and lieutenant commander had glowered at him with barely contained indignation when

they climbed down from the airplane into the launch and he and Koffler climbed aboard. Getting bumped by a Marine major was bad enough; but to be bumped by a Marine corporal with a higher priority was a little too much of a blow to a senior officer's dignity.

It *was* a question of priorities. Lieutenant Colonel F. L. Rickabee had set up their travel; and he apparently had easy—and probably unquestioned—access to the higher priorities. Special Detachment 14 had occupied most of the seats on the Mariner from San Diego to Pearl. The Air Shipment Officer at Pearl had been almost apologetic when he explained that seats were in even shorter supply from Pearl onward, and that all he could provide on this flight were two seats. The others in Special Detachment 14 would have to follow later. A lot of people with high priorities had to get to Australia.

Banning had decided to take one of the two available seats himself, not as a privilege of rank, but because he was hand-carrying a letter from the Secretary of the Navy himself to Captain Fleming Pickering, and because he thought that, as commanding officer, he should get there as soon as possible. He had taken Koffler with him because he suspected that his most important personnel requirement immediately on reaching Australia would be for a typist. Koffler had boarded the Mariner carrying his portable typewriter as well as his rifle.

Banning had no intention of satisfying Captain Toller's curiosity about Corporal Koffler's presence on the Mariner. For one thing, it was none of Captain Toller's business why Koffler was aboard the Mariner. And for another, it would only exacerbate the Captain's annoyance if he told him the unvarnished truth.

"It's a strange war, isn't it?" Captain Toller went on, "when getting a major and his corporal to the theater of operations is of more importance to the war effort than getting a lieutenant commander and a captain there."

Banning resisted the temptation to, politely of course, tell the Captain to go fuck himself.

"Our orders are classified, Sir," Banning said. "But out of school, apropos of nothing at all, may I observe that there are very few people in the Naval Service, commissioned or enlisted, who were raised in Yokohama and speak Japanese fluently?"

Captain Toller nodded solemmly.

"I thought it might be something like that," he said. "I wasn't trying to pry, Major, you understand. Just curious."

"Your curiosity is certainly understandable, Sir. But I think I've said more than I should already."

Captain Toller put his finger in front of his lips in the gesture of silence, and winked.

"Thank you, Sir," Banning said politely.

There was now a range of mountains off the right wing tip. When there was a break in their tops, Banning could see what was obviously a near-desert area on the far side. Below them, the terrain was either green or showed signs of fall cultivation.

I should have remembered that the seasons here are the reverse of those in America.

The plane began to let down an hour or so later. When the pilot corrected his course, Banning for a moment could see they were approaching a populated area. And then an enclosed body of water appeared.

Port Phillip Bay, Banning decided, pleased that he had taken the trouble to look at some maps.

He went to Koffler and pushed at him with the toe of his shoe. And then pushed twice more, harder, before Koffler sat up.

"Yes, Sir?"

"We're here," Banning said.

"Already?" Koffler asked.

The Mariner touched down several minutes later with an enormous splash, bounced airborne again; and then, with an even larger splash, it made final contact with the waters of Port Phillip Bay and slowed abruptly.

A launch carried them from the Mariner to a wharf. U.S. NAVY was stenciled on the wharf's sides. There was a bus, an English bus, now painted Navy gray. But when Banning started toward it, someone called his name.

"Major Banning?"

A tall, handsome, distinguished-looking man in a Navy captain's uniform was smiling at him.

"Yes, Sir."

"I'm Fleming Pickering," the Captain said, offering his hand. "Welcome to Australia."

Steve Koffler came up to them, staggering under the weight of his duffel bag, rifle, and typewriter.

"I'll get your bags, Sir," he said, and walked back toward the launch.

"He's with you?"

"Yes, Sir. I thought I was probably going to need a typist."

"Good thinking," Pickering chuckled. "But I didn't know you would have him with you, so that's one problem I hadn't thought of."

"Sir?"

"Putting him up," Pickering said. "You'll be staying with me. But having a corporal there would be a little awkward."

"I understand, Sir."

"Don't misunderstand me, Major," Pickering said. "I have nothing whatever against Marine corporals. In fact, I used to *be* a Marine corporal; and therefore I am well acquainted with what splendid all-around fellows they are. But you and I are in the Menzies Hotel, in an apartment directly over MacArthur and his family. We'll have to get him into another hotel for the time being."

"Sir, I have a letter for you from Secretary Knox."

"Wait till we get in the car," Pickering said, and gestured toward a 1939 Jaguar drop-head coupe.

"Nice car."

"Yes, it is. I hate like hell having to give it back. It belongs to a friend of mine here. It annoys the hell out of MacArthur's palace guard."

Major Ed Banning decided he was going to like Captain Fleming Pickering, and his snap judgment was immediately confirmed when Pickering picked up Steve Koffler's duffel bag and Springfield and started toward the Jaguar.

"It's been a long time since I had a duffel bag in one hand and a Springfield in the other," Pickering said, smiling. "You go help the Corporal with your bags, while I put these in the car."

"Your tax dollars at work," Captain Pickering said, chuckling, to Major Banning, when Banning came out of the bathroom in a bathrobe. He handed Banning a green slip of paper.

It was a check drawn on the Treasurer of the United States. It was payable to the bearer, and was in the amount of $250,000.

They were in Pickering's suite in the Menzies Hotel. First they'd installed Corporal Koffler in a businessmen's hotel (Pickering had handed him some money and told him to get something to eat, and to try to stay out of trouble). Then they'd come to the Menzies, where Pickering had made him a drink, then called the valet to have Banning's uniforms pressed.

"The Commander-in-Chief dresses in worn thin khakis, no tie, and wears a cap I think he brought home from World War I. Naturally, if you know MacArthur, he consequently expects everyone else around him to look like a page from *The Officer's Guide.*"

"Sir, what is this?" Banning asked, pointing to the check.

"Your expense money. Or *our* expense money. It's from the Secretary's Confidential Fund. It was in the letter you brought. Knox says that it's unaccountable, but I think it would be wise for us to keep some sort of a record of where we spend it. Koffler's hotel bill, for example. In the morning we'll go around to the Bank of Victoria, deposit it, and arrange for you to be able to write checks against it. And you'd better take some cash, too. Six thousand–odd dollars of that is mine."

"Sir?"

"I bought some maps that neither the Army nor the Navy could come up with on their own. I was happy to do it, but I want my money back. Whiskey all right?"

"I'm overwhelmed by your hospitality, Sir."

"I'm delighted that you're here. I sometimes feel very much the lonely soul. At least I won't have to watch what I say to you after I've had a couple of drinks."

"I'm carrying a message for you from Mrs. Feller, Sir, too."

"Oh. She was my secretary in Washington when I first came in the Navy. And, of course, you know what she's doing in Hawaii."

"Yes, Sir. When I saw her there, she said to give you her best regards, and to tell you that she hopes you'll soon have a chance to resume your interrupted conversation."

"What?"

"She sends her regards and says she hopes you'll soon have a chance to resume your interrupted conversation."

"Oh. Yes, of course. Private joke."

My God, she's not only not embarrassed about what happened in the Coronado Beach Hotel, but wants me to know she meant what she said. Thank Christ she's in Hawaii!

A bellman delivered a crisply pressed uniform and a pair of highly polished shoes.

Pickering followed Banning into the bedroom as Banning started to get dressed.

"Tomorrow, I'm going to take you around to meet Admiral Brewer," he said. "Australian. Deputy chief of their naval intelligence. I want you to meet him and see if we can't get a letter of introduction for you to the man who runs the Coastwatcher operation. They're working out of a little town called Townesville, on the northeastern coast. The man in charge is a guy named Eric Feldt, Lieutenant Commander, Australian Navy. Nice guy. Until I met you, I was a little worried. He is not overly fond of the U.S. Navy officers he's met. But I think he'll get along with you."

"That's flattering, Sir, but why?"

"Just a feeling. I think you're two of a kind."

"Captain, I don't know how soon, but probably within the next couple of days, the rest of my people will be coming in from Hawaii, probably in dribs and drabs. Should I make arrangements to put them into that hotel with Koffler?"

"How many?"

"One officer, a first lieutenant, and fifteen enlisted men."

"I'm not trying to tell you how to run your operation, but presumably you'll be moving them, or at least most of them, to Townesville?"

"If that's where the Coastwatchers are, yes, Sir."

"Open to suggestion?"

"Yes, Sir, of course."

"I think you'd better go up there alone at first. If things work out, you can rent a house for them up there."

"'If things work out,' Sir?"

"Commander Feldt can be difficult," Pickering said. "Both the Army and the Navy have sent people up there. He told both groups to 'sod off.' Can you guess what that means?"

"I think so, Sir," Banning said, smiling.

"I'm hoping that he will see you as someone who has come to be of help, not take charge. If he does, then you can rent a house for your people up there. In the meantime, it might get a little crowded, so we'll put them up in my house, here."

"Your house, Sir?"

"Against what I suppose is the inevitable—my being told to vacate these quarters—I rented a house." He saw the confusion on Banning's face. "A number, a large number, of MacArthur's Palace Guard want me out of here; I am too close to the Divine Throne."

"I understand, Sir," Banning said, turning from the mirror where he was tying his field scarf to smile at Pickering.

"I'll call. Right now, as a matter of fact, and have the house activated. If I had known you would have that kid with you, I would already have done it."

"Activated, Sir?"

"It comes with a small staff. Housekeeper, maids, a cook. Since I'm not in it, I put them on vacation."

"That sounds fine, but who pays for it? I'm not sure I'm authorized to put my people on per diem."

"Frank Knox's Confidential Fund will pay for it," Pickering said, "but let me make it clear to you, Banning, that you're authorized to do about anything you damned well please. You answer only to me."

He went to a telephone and gave the operator a number.

"Mrs. Mannshow, this is Fleming Pickering. I'm glad I caught you in. Do you think you could get those people to come off Ninety Mile Beach and start running the house starting tomorrow?"

He looked at Banning and smiled, and gestured for Banning to make himself another drink.

(SIX)

TOP SECRET

Eyes Only—The Secretary of the Navy

   DUPLICATION FORBIDDEN
   ORIGINAL TO BE DESTROYED AFTER ENCRYPTION AND TRANSMITTAL
TO SECNAVY

Menzies Hotel
Melbourne, Australia
Wednesday, 20 May 1942

Dear Frank:

   I thought it appropriate to report on the status quo here,
especially the thinking of the General, insofar as the Battle
of the Coral Sea and other events seem to have affected it.

   But before I get to that, let me report the arrival of my own
reinforcements. Major Ed Banning arrived yesterday, together
with his advance party, one ferocious Marine paratrooper who
must be all of seventeen. The balance of his command is still in
Hawaii, trying to get on an airplane for the trip here. If it
could be arranged to get them a higher priority without causing
undue attention, I suggest that it be provided to them. In my
judgment, it is more important to get Banning's people here and
integrated with the Australian Coastwatchers than it is to
send more Army and Marine colonels and Navy captains here so
they can start setting up their empires.

   Banning, of course, carried your letter, for which I thank
you (and the check, for which I thank you even more; if Banning
has to start chartering fishing boats, etc., his operation can
become very expensive, very soon). And he brought me up to date
on Albatross operations in Hawaii, in particular their effec-
tiveness vis-a-vis what happened in the Coral Sea.

   I am very impressed with Banning, but fear that he is less

TOP SECRET

than pleased with me. He made it clear that he considers himself to be under my orders, which I immediately made use of by forbidding him even to think about going behind Japanese lines himself. Because of his Japanese language skills and understanding of their minds, for one thing, and for another, because I think he knows too much about Albatross, he is too valuable to risk being captured.

Now to the General:

Until he learned that the Japanese had occupied Tulagi, I really didn't think he paid much attention to the fact that the border between his area and Nimitz's had been moved from 160 degrees east longitude, where the Joint Chiefs originally established it, to where it is now. But after the Japs took Tulagi, he became painfully aware that Nimitz now had responsibility for both Tulagi and Guadalcanal, the much larger island to the south.

He is now convinced that the new division of responsibility was established—the line changed—by his cabal of enemies, Marshall and King again, to deny him authority over territory he considers essential to his mission of defending Australia. I am finding it harder and harder to fault his logic and support that of the JCS.

The argument, I know, is that it is the Navy's responsibility to maintain the sea lanes, and that was the argument for putting the border at 160 EL. MacArthur counters that this would hold water only if the Navy were occupying the land in question and using it for that purpose. And, of course, they are not, and have shown no indication that they intend to.

All of this was exacerbated when he learned that the day after he had surrendered Corregidor, General Wainwright went on the radio in Manila and ordered all forces in the Philippines to lay down their arms. This enraged him for several reasons, not necessarily in proportion to their importance to the war.

He seemed most enraged (and found it another proof that George Marshall stays awake nights thinking up new evil things to do to him) by the fact that Wainwright, apparently encouraged by Washington, no longer considered himself subordinate

to MacArthur, and thus surrendered Corregidor on his own—without, in other words, MacA.'s authority to do so.

Second, he is absolutely convinced that Wainwright, again encouraged by Washington, went even further than that, by assuming authority for all U.S./Filipino Forces in the Philippines, an authority MacA., with reason, believed he still retained, having never been formally relieved of it.

General Sharp, on Mindanao, was specifically ordered to surrender by Wainwright. According to MacA., Sharp had 30,000 U.S./Filipino troops, armed, and in far better shape insofar as ammunition, rations, etcetera, than any others in the islands. It is hard to understand why they were ordered to surrender. As it turns out, MacA. has learned that Sharp paid only lip service to Wainwright's orders and encouraged his men to go to the hills and organize as guerrillas. He himself and most of his immediate staff felt obliged to follow orders, and they surrendered.

MacArthur feels a sense of shame (wholly unjustified, I think) for the loss of the Philippines. And he has an at least partially justified feeling that he is being treated unfairly by Washington in his present command.

Two days after Corregidor fell, he cabled General Marshall (ignoring the implication that Marshall couldn't figure this out himself) that the Japanese victory in the Philippines will free two infantry divisions and a large number of aircraft that they will probably use to take New Guinea, and then the Solomons. They will then cut his supply routes to the United States, which would mean the loss of Australia.

MacA. proposed to go on the counterattack, starting with the recapture of Tulagi, and then establishing our own presence on Guadalcanal. In his mind (and in mine) he tried to be a good soldier and to "coordinate" this with South Pacific Area Headquarters. But he was (a) reminded that Guadalcanal and Tulagi are not "within his sphere of influence" and that (b) under those circumstances it was really rather presumptuous of him to ask for Navy aircraft carriers, etcetera, to conduct an operation in their sphere of influence, but that (c) he was not

to worry, because Admiral Nimitz was already making plans to recapture Tulagi with a Marine Raider battalion.

There is no way that one small battalion can take Tulagi; but even if they could, they cannot hold it long—if the Japanese establish bases, which seems a given, on either Guadalcanal or Malaita.

What MacArthur wants to do makes more sense to me than what the Navy proposes to do, unless, as MacA. believes, the Navy's primary purpose is to render him impotent and humiliated, so that the war here will be a Navy war.

I fight against accepting this latter theory. But what I saw at—and especially after—Pearl Harbor, with the admirals pulling their wagons into a circle to avoid accepting the blame, keeps popping into my head.

Respectfully,
Fleming Pickering, Captain, USNR

XII

(ONE)

THE ELMS

DANDENONG, VICTORIA, AUSTRALIA

22 MAY 1942

"Oh, good morning! We didn't expect you to be up so early," Mrs. Hortense Cavendish said, with a smile, to Corporal Stephen M. Koffler, USMC, when she saw him coming down the stairway. "Why don't you just go into the breakfast room, and I'll get you a nice hot cup of tea?"

"Good morning, thank you," Steve said, smiling, but not really comfortable.

Mrs. Cavendish was as old as his mother, and looked something like her, too. She was the housekeeper at The Elms, a three-story, twelve-room, red brick house set in what looked to Steve like its own private park fifteen miles or so outside Melbourne. It was called The Elms, Major Banning had told him, because of the century-old elm trees which lined the driveway from the "motorway" to the house.

He also told him *(You've come up smelling like a rose again, Koffler.)* that the whole place had been rented by Captain Pickering, and, for the time being at least, he and the other members of Special Detachment 14 would be living there. He explained that the housekeeper was something like the manager of a hotel, in charge of the whole place, and was to be treated with the appropriate respect.

At the moment, Corporal Koffler was the only member of Special Detachment 14 in residence. The day before, Major Banning had driven him out here in a brand-new Studebaker President, then had him installed in a huge room with a private bathroom. After that, Captain Pickering had come out and taken Major Banning to the railroad station in Melbourne. Banning was going "up north" to some place called Townesville, Queensland, where the Coastwatchers had their headquarters. He told Steve he had no idea when he would be back, but that he would keep in touch.

Steve now understood that Queensland, New South Wales, and Victoria were something like the states in America, but that was really about all he understood about Australia.

From what Major Banning had told him, and from what he'd heard from the other guys, the Japs were probably going to take Australia. He had heard Major Banning talking to Lieutenant Howard back in 'Diego about it. Steve had long ago decided that if *anybody* would have the straight poop about *anything*, Major Banning would. Major Banning had told Lieutenant Howard that he didn't see how anything could keep the Japs from taking Australia, as long as they took some island named New Guinea first. And he really didn't see how the Japs could be kept from taking New Guinea.

To tell the truth, the closer they got to Australia, the more nervous Koffler had become. More than nervous. Scared. He tried hard not to let it show, of course, in front of all the Army and Navy officers on the airplane (he was, after all, not only a Marine, but a Marine parachutist, and Marines aren't supposed to be nervous or scared). But when the airplane landed, he would not really have been surprised if the Japs had been shelling or maybe bombing the place. That would have meant they'd have started fighting right away. He had cleaned and oiled his Springfield before they left Hawaii, just to be double sure.

But it hadn't been that way at all. There was no more sign of war, or Japs, in Melbourne than there was in Newark. Melbourne was like Newark, maybe as big, and certainly a hell of a lot cleaner. Except for the funny-looking trucks and cars, which the Australians drove on the wrong side of the road, and the funny way the Australians talked, sort of through their noses, you'd never even know you were *in* Australia.

He'd spent his first night in a real nice hotel, and Captain Pickering had given him money, and he had had a real nice meal in a real nice restaurant. The steak was a little tough, but he had no call to bitch about the size of it—it just about covered the plate—and he had trouble getting it all down. Then he went to the movies, and they were playing an American movie. It starred Betty Grable, and he remembered seeing it in the Ampere Theatre in East Orange just before he joined the Corps. And that started him off remembering Dianne Marshall and what had happened between them. And between the movie and the memories, he got a little homesick . . . until he talked himself out of that by reminding himself that he was a Marine *parachutist,* for Christ's sake, and not supposed to start crying in his goddamned beer because he was away from his mommy or because some old whore had made a goddamned fool out of him.

The table in the breakfast room was big, and the wood sort of glowed. There was a bowl of flowers in the middle of it. When he sat down at it, he looked out through windows running from the ceiling to the floor; outside he could see a man raking leaves out of a flower garden. There was a concrete statue of a nearly naked woman in the garden, in the middle of a what looked like a little pond, except there wasn't any water in the pond.

Mrs. Cavendish followed him in in a moment, and laid a newspaper on the table. Right behind her was a maid, a plain woman maybe thirty years old, wearing a black dress with a little white apron in front. She smiled at Steve, then went to one of the cabinets in the room, and took out a woven place mat and silver and set it up in front of him.

"What would you like for breakfast?" Mrs. Cavendish asked. "Ham and eggs? There's kippers."

Steve had no idea what a kipper was.

"Ham and eggs would be fine," he said. "Over easy."

"We have tomato and pineapple juice."

"Tomato juice would be fine," Steve said.

"The tea's brewing," Mrs. Cavendish said. "It'll just be a moment."

She and the maid left the room. Steve unfolded the newspaper. It was *The Times of Victoria*. The pages were bigger than those of the *Newark Evening News,* but there weren't very many of them. He flipped through it, looking in vain for comics, and then returned to the first page.

There were two big headlines: ROMMEL NEARS TOBRUK and NAZI TANKS APPROACH LENINGRAD. There was a picture of a burning German tank, and a map of North Africa with wide, curving arrows drawn on it.

Steve wondered why there wasn't anything in the newspaper about the Japs being about to invade Australia.

He went through the newspaper, mostly reading the advertisements for strange brands of toothpaste, used motorcars, and something called Bovril. He wondered what Bovril was, whether you ate it, or drank it, or washed your mouth out with it, or what.

The maid delivered his ham and eggs, cold toast in a little rack, tomato juice, and a tub of sour orange marmalade. He had just about finished eating when the maid came in the breakfast room.

"Telephone for you, Sir," she said, and pointed to a telephone sitting on a sideboard.

The telephone was strange. There was sort of a cup over the mouthpiece, and the wire that ran from the base to the handset was much thinner than the one on American phones; it looked more like a couple of pieces of string twisted together than like a regular wire.

"Corporal Koffler, Sir," Steve said.

"Good morning, Corporal," a cheerful voice said. "Lieutenant

Donnelly here." He pronounced it "leftenant," so Steve knew he was an Australian.

"Yes, Sir?"

"I'm the Air Transport Officer, Naval Station, Melbourne. We have two things for you. Actually, I mean to say, two shipments. There's several crates, priority air shipment, and we've been alerted that several of your people are scheduled to arrive about noon."

"Yes, Sir."

"Your Captain Pickering said to send the crates out there by lorry, and that you'll meet the aircraft. Any problems with that?"

"No, Sir," Steve said, an automatic reflex. Then he blurted, "Sir, I'm not sure if I can find . . . where the plane will be. Or how to get back out here."

Lieutenant Donnelly chuckled. "Well, you'll be able to able to find your way about soon enough, I'm sure. In the meantime, I'll just send a map, with the route marked, out there with the lorry driver. Do you think that will handle it?"

"Yes, Sir. Thank you."

"The lorry should be there within the hour. Thank you, Corporal."

"Thank you, Sir."

Steve hung up and went looking for Mrs. Cavendish. He was going to need some place to store the crates, whatever they contained. She showed him a three-car garage behind the house, now empty, that was just what he was looking for. There were sturdy metal doors which could be locked, and there were no windows.

The truck arrived forty-five minutes later. Steve, who had been looking out his bedroom window for it, saw that it said "Ford" on the radiator, but it was unlike any Ford Steve had ever seen. There were three people in the cab, all in uniform, and all female.

They all wore the same kind of caps, something like a Marine cap, except the visor wasn't leather. They wore the caps perched straight on top of their hair, and Steve thought they all looked kind of cute, like girls dressed up in men's uniforms. Two of them wore gray coveralls. The third, who looked like she was in charge, wore a tunic and a shirt and tie and a skirt, with really ugly stockings.

"Corporal Koffler?" she said, smiling at him and offering her hand. "I'm Petty Officer Farnsworth."

"Hi," Steve said. She was, he guessed, in her early twenties. He couldn't really tell what the rest of her looked like in the nearly shapeless uniform and those ugly cotton stockings, but her face was fine. She had light hazel eyes and freckles.

"Good day," the other two women said. In Australia that came out something like "G'die," which took some getting used to. One of them looked like she was about seventeen, and the other one looked old enough to be the first one's mother. Neither of them, Steve immediately decided, had the class of Petty Officer Farnsworth.

"How are you?" Steve said, and walked over and shook hands with them.

"After we unload your crates," Petty Officer Farnsworth said, "Lieutenant Donnelly said I was to ask if you would like me to wait around and drive into Melbourne with you, to show you the way."

"Great!" Steve said.

"Where would you like the crates?"

"Let's see what they are," Steve said, and walked to the back of the truck. He saw three wooden crates, none of them as large as a footlocker. He couldn't tell what they contained, and there was nothing stenciled on them to identify them.

Petty Officer Farnsworth, who had followed him, handed him a manila envelope. "The shipping documents," she said.

He tore the envelope open. The U.S. Army Signal Center, Fort Monmouth, New Jersey, had shipped, on AAAA Air Priority, by authority of the Chief Signal Officer, U.S. Army, to the Commanding Officer, USMC Special Detachment 14, Melbourne, Australia:

1 EA SET, TRANSCEIVER, RADIO, HALLICRAFTERS MODEL 23C, W/48 CRYSTALS

1 EA ANTENNA SET, RADIO TRANSMISSION, PORTABLE, 55-FOOT W/ CABLES & GUY WIRES

1 EA GENERATOR, ELECTRICAL, FOOT AND HAND POWERED, 6 AND 12 VOLT DC

"Wow!" Steve said. He knew all about the Hallicrafters 23C, had studied carefully all of its specifications in the American Amateur Radio Relay League magazine, but he'd never seen one before.

"Am I permitted to ask what they are?" Petty Officer Farnsworth asked.

"Just about the best shortwave radio there is," Steve said.

"Lieutenant Donnelly said that I wasn't to ask questions," Petty Officer Farnsworth said, "about what you're doing out here."

"You didn't. You just asked what was in the boxes. There's nothing secret about that."

She smiled at him.

Nice teeth. Nice smile.

"Where would you like them?"

"Around in back," Steve said. "I'll show you."

When the crates had been unloaded, Petty Officer Farnsworth sent the truck back into Melbourne.

"It will take us no more than forty-five minutes to get to the quay," she said. "Which means we should leave here at eleven-fifteen. It's now quarter past nine. Where can I pass two hours out of your way, where I will see nothing I'm not supposed to see?"

"I don't have anything to do. And there's nothing out here for you to see. Would you like a cup of coffee?"

"Tea?"

"Oh, sure."

"That would be very nice, Corporal," Petty Officer Farnsworth said.

Steve took her into the breakfast room, sat her down, and then went into the kitchen and asked for tea. They waited for several minutes in an awkward silence until one of the maids delivered a tea tray, complete to toast and cookies.

"Where are you from in America?" Petty Officer Farnsworth asked.

"Where the radios come from. New Jersey. How about you?"

"I'm from Wagga Wagga, in New South Wales."

"Wagga Wagga?" he asked, smiling.

"I think that's an Aborigine name."

"That's what you call your colored people?"

"Yes, but as I understand it, they're not like yours."

"How come?"

"Well, yours were taken from Africa and sent to America, as I understand it, and the Aborigines were here when we English arrived."

"Sort of Australian Indians, in other words?"

"I suppose. New South Wales, of course, is named after South Wales, in England."

"So is New Jersey," he said. "Jersey is in England."

"I thought it was an island."

"Well, it could be. I never really paid much attention."

Petty Officer Farnsworth had an unkind thought. Corporal Koffler was a nice enough young man, and not unattractive, but obviously bloody goddamned stupid.

Petty Officer Farnsworth was twenty-three years old, and she had been married for five years to John Andrew Farnsworth, now a sergeant with the Royal Australian Signals Corps somewhere in North Africa.

Before the war, she and John had lived in a newly built house on his family's sheep ranch. When John had rushed to the sound of the British trumpet—a move that had baffled and enraged her—his family had decided that she would simply shoulder his responsibilities at the ranch in addition to her own. After all, John's father, brothers, and amazingly fecund sisters reasoned, she had no children to worry about, and One Must Do One's Part While the Family Hero Is Off Defending King and Country.

Petty Officer Farnsworth, whose Christian name was Daphne, had no intention of becoming a worn-out woman before her time, as the other women of the family either had or were about to. She used the same excuse to get off the ranch as John had: patriotism. When the advertisements for women to join the Royal Australian Navy Women's Volunteer Reserve had come out, she had announced that enlisting was her duty. Since John was already off fighting for King and Country, she could do no less, especially considering, as everyone kept pointing out, that she had no children to worry about.

The RANWVR had trained her as a typist and assigned her to the Naval Station in Melbourne. She had a job now that she liked, working for Lieutenant Donnelly. There was something different every day. And unlike some of the other officers she had worked for, Lieutenant kept his hands to himself.

Every once in a while she wondered if Donnelly's gentlemanly behavior was a mixed blessing. Lately she had been wondering about that more and more often, and it bothered her.

"Do all Marines wear boots like that?" she asked.

"No. Just parachutists."

"You're a parachutist?"

He pointed to his wings.

"Our parachutists wear berets," she said. "Red berets."

"You mean like women?"

My God, how can one young man be so stupid?

"Well, I suppose, yes. But I wouldn't say that where they could hear me, if I were you."

"I didn't mean nothing wrong by it, I just wanted to be sure we were talking about the same thing."

"Quite. So you're a wireless operator?"

"Yes and no."

"Yes and no?"

"Well, I am, but the Marine Corps doesn't know anything about it."

"Why not?"

"I didn't tell them, and then when they gave everybody the Morse code test, I made sure I flunked it."

"Why?" Now Daphne Farnsworth was fascinated. John had written a half-dozen times that the worst mistake he'd made in the Army was letting it be known that he could key forty words a minute. From the moment he'd gotten through basic training, the Army had him putting in long days, day after day, as a high-speed wireless telegrapher. He hated it.

"Well, I figured out if they was so short of guys who could copy fifty, sixty words a minute—you don't learn to do that overnight—they would be working the ass off those who could. Ooops. Sorry about the language."

"That's all right," Daphne said.

Well, Daphne, you bitchy little lady, you were wrong about this boy. Not only is he smart enough to take Morse faster than John, but he's smart enough not to let the service hear about it.

"My husband's a wireless operator," Daphne said. "With the British Eighth Army in Africa. He's a sergeant, but he hates being a wireless operator."

"I figured somebody as pretty as you would be married," Steve Koffler replied.

Is that the distilled essence of your observations of life, or are you making a pass at me, Corporal Koffler?

"For five years."

"You don't look that old."

"Thank you."

"You know what I'd really like to do before we go into town?"

Rip my clothes off, and throw me on the floor?

"No."

"I'd like to unpack that Hallicrafters. I've never really seen one. Could you read the newspaper, or something?"

"I think I'd rather go with you and see the radio. Or is it classified?"

"What we're doing is classified. Not the radio."

And now I am curious. What the bloody hell is going on around here? Marine parachutists? Villas in the country? "World's best wireless" shipped by priority air?

(TWO)

TOWNESVILLE STATION
ROYAL AUSTRALIAN NAVY
TOWNESVILLE, QUEENSLAND
24 MAY 1942

The office of the Commanding Officer, Coastwatcher Service, Royal Australian Navy (code name FERDINAND) was simple, even spartan. The small room with whitewashed block walls in a tin-roofed building was furnished with a battered desk, several well-worn upholstered chairs, and some battered filing cabinets. A prewar recruiting poster for the Royal Australian Navy was stapled to one wall. On the wall behind the desk was an unpainted sheet of plywood, crudely hinged on top, that Major Ed Banning, USMC, immediately decided covered a map, or maps.

The Officer Commanding, Lieutenant Commander Eric A. Feldt, Royal Australian Navy, was a tall, thin, dark-eyed, and dark-haired man. He was not at all glad to see Banning, or the letter he'd brought from Admiral Brewer; and he was making absolutely no attempt to conceal this.

"Nothing personal, Major," he said finally, looking up at Banning from behind the desk. "I should have bloody well known this would be the next step."

"Sir?" Banning replied. He was standing with his hands locked behind him, more or less in the at-ease position.

"This," Feldt said, waving Admiral Brewer's letter. "You're not the first American to show up here. I ran the others off. I should have known somebody would sooner or later go over my head."

"Sir," Banning said, "let me make it clear that all I want to do here is help you in any way I can."

"Help me? How the hell could you possibly help me?"

"You would have to tell me that, Sir."

"What do you know about this area of the world?"

Banning took a chance: "I noticed you drive on the wrong side of the road, Sir."

It was not the reply Commander Feldt expected. He looked carefully at Banning; and after a very long moment, there was the hint of a smile.

"I was making reference, Major, to the waters in the area of the Bismarck Archipelago."

"Absolutely nothing, Sir."

"Well, that's an improvement over the last one. He told me with a straight face that he had studied the charts."

"Sir, my lack of knowledge is so overwhelming that I don't even know what's wrong with studying the charts."

"Well, for your general information, Major, there are very few charts, and the ones that do exist are notoriously inaccurate."

"Thank you, Sir."

"I don't suppose that you're any kind of an expert concerning shortwave wireless, either, are you, Major?"

"No, Sir. I know a little less about shortwave radios than I do about the Bismarck Archipelago."

There was again a vague hint of a smile.

"I know about your game baseball, Major. I know that the rule is three strikes and you're out. You now have two strikes against you."

"I'm sorry to hear that, Sir."

"Here's the final throw—"

"I believe the correct phrase is 'pitch,' Sir."

"The final *pitch*, then. What do you know of our enemy, the Jap?"

In Japanese, Banning said, "I read and write the language, Sir, and I learned enough about them in China to come to believe that no Westerner can ever know them well."

"I will be damned," Commander Feldt said. "That was Japanese? I don't speak a bloody word of it myself."

"That was Japanese, Sir," Banning said, and then translated what he had said a moment before.

"What were you doing in China?"

"I was the Intelligence Officer of the 4th Marines, Sir."

"And you went home to America before they were sent to the Philippines?"

"No, Sir, afterward."

"Are we splitting a hair here, Major? You went home before the war started?"

"No, Sir. After."

"You were considered too valuable, as an intelligence officer who speaks Japanese, to be captured?"

"No, Sir. I was medically evacuated. I was blinded by concussion."

"How?"

"They think probably concussion from artillery, Sir. My sight returned on the submarine that took me off Corregidor."

"Are you a married man, Major?"

"Yes, Sir."

"How would your wife react to the news—actually, there wouldn't be any news, she just wouldn't hear from you—that you were behind the Japanese lines?"

"That's a moot point, Sir. The one thing I have been forbidden to do is serve as a Coastwatcher myself."

Feldt grunted. "Me too," he said.

"My wife is still in China, Commander," Banning said.

Feldt met his eyes.

"I'm sorry," he said.

Feldt grunted as he heaved himself to his feet. He raised the sheet of plywood with another grunt, and shoved a heavy bolt through an eyebolt so that it would stay up. A map, covered with a sheet of celluloid, was exposed.

"This is our area of operation, Major," Commander Feldt said. "From the Admiralty Islands here, across the Pacific to the other side of New Ireland, and down to Vitiaz Strait between New Guinea and New Britain, and then down into the Solomon Sea in this area. The little marks are where we have people. The ones that are crossed out are places we haven't heard from in some time, or know for sure that the Japs have taken out."

Banning walked around the desk and studied the map for several minutes without speaking. He saw there were a number of Xs marking locations which were no longer operational.

"The people manning these stations," Feldt explained, "have been commissioned as junior officers, or warrant officers, in the Royal Australian Navy Volunteer Reserve. The idea is to try to have the Japs treat them as prisoners of war if they are captured. There's sort of a fuzzy area there. On one hand, if someone is in uniform, he is supposed to be treated as a POW if captured. On the other hand, what these people are doing, quite simply, is spying. One may shoot spies. The Japanese do. Or actually, they either torture our people to death; or, if they're paying attention to the code of Bushido, they have a formal little ceremony, the culmination of which is the beheading of our people by an officer of suitable rank."

Banning now grunted.

"My people," Feldt went on, "are primarily former civil servants or plantation managers and, in a few cases, missionaries. Most of them have spent years in their area. They speak the native languages and dialects, and in some cases—not all—are protected by the natives. They are undisciplined, irreverent, and contemptuous of military and naval organizations—and in particular of officers of the regular establishment. They are people of incredible courage and, for the obvious reasons, of infinite value to military or naval operations in this area."

"I heard something about this," Banning said. "I didn't realize how many of them there are."

"Supporting them logistically is very difficult," Feldt went on, as if he had not heard Banning, "for several reasons. For one thing, the distances. For another, the nonavailability, except in the most extreme circumstances, of submarines and aircraft. And when aircraft and submarines are available, they are of course limited to operation on the shorelines; and my people are most often in the mountains and jungle, some distance from the shore. Landing aircraft in the interior of the islands is ninety percent of the time impossible, and in any case it would give the Japs a pretty good idea where my people are. The result is that my people are eating the food they carried with them into the jungle (if any remains), and native food, which will not support health under the circumstances they have to live under. If illness strikes, or if they accidentally break an ankle, their chances of survival are minimal."

"Christ!" Banning said.

"In addition, the humidity and other conditions tend to render wireless equipment inoperable unless it is properly and constantly cared for. And these people are not technicians."

Banning shook his head.

"And now, Major, be good enough to tell me how you intend to help me."

"In addition to what you tell me to do," Banning said, after a moment, "money, parachutists, and radios. I might also be able to do something about aircraft priorities."

"Do you Americans really believe that money can solve any problem? I noticed you mentioned that first."

"I'm not sure about *any*," Banning replied. "But *many*? Yes, Sir, I believe that. I've got a quarter of a million dollars in a bank in Melbourne that can be used to support you, and I can get more if I need more."

"That sounds very generous."

"The Marine Corps wants access to your intelligence," Banning said.

"You would have it anyway, wouldn't you, via your Navy?"

"We would like it direct," Banning said.

Feldt grunted.

"You said 'parachutists'? Have you got parachutists?"

"I have one, Sir, already in Australia," Banning replied. He did not say, of course, *The notion of sending Koffler off on a mission like these is absurd on its face.* Then he added, "I can get more in a short period of time."

"What about wireless sets? I thought you said you didn't know anything about that."

"Sir, I don't," Banning said. "But some are on the way."

"What kind?"

"Sir, I don't know. I was told 'the best there is.' "

"I would like to know what kind."

"I'll find out for you," Banning said. "Just as soon as they show up. So far, the only asset I have in Australia is the money."

"And, of course, you."

"Yes, Sir. And my clerk," Banning said, and added, "He's the parachutist I mentioned. He's eighteen years old. I can't imagine sending him off to parachute onto some island. But, Sir, he knows about parachuting. He could tell us what we need, and probably what's available in the States."

Feldt either grunted or snorted, Banning wasn't sure which. Then he turned and pulled the bolt out of the eyebolt and lowered the sheet of raw plywood so that it again covered the map.

"Tell me, Major Banning," he said, "do you have a Christian name?"

"Yes, Sir. Edward."

"And your friends call you that? Or 'Ed'?"

"Ed, Sir."

"And do you drink, Ed? Wine, beer, spirits?"

"Yes, Sir. Wine, beer and spirits."

"Good. Having a Yank around here will be bad enough without him being a sodding teetotaler."

"May I interpret that to mean, Sir, that I may stay?"

"On condition that you break yourself of the habit of using the word 'Sir.' Are you aware, Ed, that you use 'Sir' in place of a comma?"

"I suppose I do."

"My Christian name is Eric," Feldt said. "But to keep things in their proper perspective around here, Ed, I think you had better call me 'Commander.' "

They smiled at each other.

"Let's go drink our lunch," Feldt said. "When we've done that, we'll see what can be done about getting you and your savages a place to live."

(THREE)

TOWNESVILLE STATION
TOWNESVILLE, QUEENSLAND
31 MAY 1942

Major Edward Banning, USMC, was on hand when his command, less the rear echelon (Corporal Koffler), disembarked from the Melbourne train. USMC Special Detachment 14 debarked after the last of the civilian and a half-dozen Australian military passengers had come down from the train to the platform.

The first Marine off the train was Staff Sergeant Richardson, the senior NCO, who either didn't see Major Banning or pretended not to. He took up a position on the platform facing the sleeper car. Then, one by one, quickly, the others filed off and formed two ranks facing Staff Sergeant Richardson. They were carrying their weapons at sling arms. Most of them had Springfields, but here and there was a Thompson submachine gun.

They were not, however, wearing any of their web field equipment, Major Banning noticed. They were freshly turned out, in sharply creased greens, their fore-and-aft caps at a proper salty angle. Two or three of them seemed a bit flushed, as if, for example, they had recently imbibed some sort of alcoholic beverage.

Staff Sergeant Richardson fell them in, put them through the dress-right-dress maneuver, and did a snappy, precise, about-face. At that point, First Lieutenant Joseph L. Howard descended the sleeping-car steps.

He too either did not see Major Banning or pretended not to. He marched before Staff Sergeant Richardson, who saluted him crisply.

"Sir," Staff Sergeant Richardson barked, "the detachment is formed and all present or accounted for."

Lieutenant Howard returned the salute crisply.

"Take your post, Sergeant," he ordered.

Salutes were again exchanged. Then Staff Sergeant Richardson did a precise right-face movement, followed by several others that ultimately placed him in line with, and to the right of, the troop formation. At the same time, Lieutenant Howard did an equally precise about-face movement and stood erectly at attention.

Major Banning understood his role in the ceremony. He dropped his cigarette to the ground, ground his toe on it, and then marched erectly until he faced Lieutenant Howard.

Howard saluted.

"Sir," he barked, "Special Detachment 14, less the rear echelon, reporting for duty, Sir."

Banning returned the salute.

He looked at his men, who stood there stone-faced, even the two or three who he suspected had been at the sauce.

"At ease!"

The detachmen' ssumed the position.

"Welcome to Townesville," Banning said. "And let me say the good news: your drill sergeants would be proud of you. You would be a credit to any parade ground."

There were smiles and chuckles.

"The bad news is that it's about a mile and a half from here to our billets, and there are no wheels."

Now there were grins on all their faces.

"May I respectfully suggest that the Major underestimates his command, Sir?" Joe Howard said.

"What's that supposed to mean?" Banning asked.

"If the Major would be good enough to accompany me, Sir?" Howard asked.

"Where?"

"To the rear of the train, Sir," Howard said.

"All right," Banning said.

"First Sergeant," Lieutenant Howard ordered formally, "take the detachment."

Staff Sergeant Richardson marched up in front again, and a final salute was exchanged.

Banning and Howard walked to the end of the train, where he

stopped at a flatcar. Whatever it carried was covered with a canvas tarpaulin.

"They call these things 'open goods wagons' over here, Sir," he said. "That caused a little confusion for a while. We kept asking for flatcars, and they didn't know what the hell we were talking about."

"What's in here? The radios?"

"I think the radios are in the last car, Sir," Howard said.

He put his fingers in his mouth and whistled shrilly, then gestured. Half a dozen Marines handed their weapons to the others and came trotting down the platform.

An officer and a gentleman is not supposed to whistle like that, Banning thought, *so it's a good thing there's nobody here but me to see it.*

The Marines clambered up on the flatcar and started to remove the tarpaulin. Large wheels were revealed.

"You stole a truck," Banning accused Howard.

"No, Sir. That truck was issued to us. It's perfectly legal."

The tarpaulin was now almost off, revealing a Studebaker stake-bodied truck. In the bed of the truck was a 1941 Studebaker automobile. On the doors of both the truck and the car were neatly stenciled the Marine Corps emblem and the letters USMC.

"Is that the car from The Elms?" Banning asked, and then, without giving Howard a chance to reply, continued, "You sure that's not stolen, Joe?"

"I checked on it myself, Sir, when Richardson showed up with them."

"Them?"

"We have two trucks and three cars, Sir. I mean, counting the one you already had. I left that in Melbourne with Koffler. I figured you'd need it when you went back there."

Banning saw that the automobile was stuffed with duffel bags.

Well, that explains why they weren't carrying them over their shoulders when they got off the train.

"How do you propose to get that truck off the flatcar?" Banning asked.

"No problem, Sir," Lieutenant Howard said.

The Marines now pulled thick planks from under the truck and placed them against the flatcar, forming a ramp. As two of the Marines loosened chains holding the truck chassis to the railroad car, a third got behind the wheel and started the engine.

Moments later, the truck was on the platform. The planks were now moved to form a ramp so that the car could be driven off the truck. The duffel bags were taken from the car and thrown onto the truck.

As the entire process was being repeated for the second flatcar,

Major Banning said to Lieutenant Howard, "why do I have this uncomfortable feeling that I am going to end my career in Portsmouth?"

"This is all perfectly legal, Sir," Howard said. "Trust me."

"God, it better be!"

When the tarpaulin covering a third flatcar was removed, Banning walked down to see what it held. There were wooden crates, containing Hallicrafters radios, portable antennas, and generators.

Well, they're here. I hope to hell they work. I'm going to look like a fool in front of Eric Feldt if they don't.

"Let's hope at least one of them works," Banning said to Howard.

"They all work, Sir," Howard said. "Sergeant Haley and Corporal Koffler checked them out."

Sergeant Haley, Banning remembered, was a pudgy-faced buck sergeant, one of his three radio operators. But he also remembered that Haley had told him he was an operator, not a technician. And *Koffler?*

"Haley and Koffler?"

"Yes, Sir. When I got to The Elms, I saw Koffler had set up one of the radios and an antenna and some batteries and was listening to KYW in Honolulu. I had them check out the others as they came in to make sure they worked. I figured if they didn't, it would be easier to get them fixed in Melbourne than here. A couple of them needed a little work, but they're all working now."

"Haley fixed them?"

"No. Koffler. Haley had never seen one of them before."

"And Koffler had?"

"No. But . . . it took me a while to figure this out, Major. Haley went to Radio School. He knows about Marine and Navy radios. Koffler was a radio amateur, what they call a ham."

"He told me," Banning interrupted. "So what?"

"So he can apparently make a radio from parts. He understands what makes them work. Even Haley was impressed. There's more to Koffler than meets the eye."

"That wouldn't be hard," Banning said dryly, then asked, "How many radio sets are there?"

"Eight, Sir. I brought seven of them up here. Koffler rigged one of them so we can talk to Melbourne as soon as we get one set up here."

Another sergeant, whose name, after a moment, Banning remembered was Solinski, marched happily up and saluted.

"Sir, the convoy is formed. If the Major would care to enter his staff car?"

"Thank you, Sergeant," Banning said. "Nice work, getting this all organized so quickly."

"Thank you, Sir," Sergeant Solinski said, pleased.

Lieutenant Commander Feldt had arranged for USMC Special Detachment 14 to take over a two-story, tin-roofed frame building that had belonged to the now-defunct Townesville Young Men's Christian Association. In addition to a small suite of offices, there was a room with a billiards table, as well as six small bedrooms, a small gymnasium with a rusty collection of weightlifting machines, and a reception room with a soft-drink bar that Banning suspected was about to be converted to a saloon.

Banning had prepared notes for the little speech he intended to deliver to his men, but he decided that would have to wait until he got the full story of the cars and trucks. The speech mostly dealt with the importance of getting along with the Aussies, and included the details of their rationing (with the Aussies) and other housekeeping information. The story of the cars and trucks was obviously more important.

He called Lieutenant Howard and Staff Sergeant Richardson into what would serve as the detachment office and told Howard to close the door.

"I want to know about the trucks and cars," he said. "And I want the truth, the whole truth, and nothing but the truth."

"Yes, Sir," Staff Sergeant Richardson said. "Well, Sir, Lieutenant Howard sent me and Sergeant Jenkins on the next plane. After yours and Koffler's. Koffler met us on the dock, with the Studebaker, and drove us out to The Elms. I asked him where he got the car. He said he didn't know where it had come from."

"Captain Pickering arranged for it. He got it from a Navy depot."

"Yes, Sir. But Koffler didn't know that. So I told him to ask somebody. He asked an Aussie lady sailor he'd met, and she told him there was a Navy depot. A U.S. Navy depot. So I went down there. It's not a regular depot. What I found out is that it's a place they store stuff that was supposed to go China, but didn't make it."

"Go over that again?"

"Well, Sir. There was a lot of stuff being shipped to China. What they call Lend-Lease. When they couldn't get in there, they went on to Australia and just unloaded the stuff. The only Americans around was a small Corps of Civil Engineers depot, and they suddenly had all this stuffed dumped in their laps. They didn't know what the hell to do with it all. One of the ships was full of Studebakers, cars and trucks."

"I see. And you stole the ones you brought with you?"

"No, Sir. I didn't have to. I just had Koffler drive me down there, and I told an officer I found that I had come for the rest of our vehicles. He said he couldn't issue any of what he had without authority, and I told him we had the authority, and there was our Studebaker, to prove it. He asked me who we worked for, and since you weren't in Melbourne, I told him this Captain Pickering. Lieutenant Howard gave me his name in Hawaii, in case we needed it."

"And this officer called Captain Pickering?"

"Yes, Sir. And Captain Pickering, I guess, told him it was all right. He asked me how many trucks I wanted, and how many cars, and I said two, and he said, 'All right, but you're going to have to get them running yourself, I don't have anybody to help you.' I think I could have gotten a dozen of each, if I had been smart enough to ask for them."

"I think you've done very well, Sergeant Richardson," Banning said. "Thank you."

(FOUR)

AIR TRANSPORT OFFICE
ROYAL NAVAL STATION, MELBOURNE
1 JUNE 1942

Lieutenant Vincent F. Donnelly, RAN, said, "Yes, Sir. Right away," and put the telephone handset back in its cradle.

He looked across the crowded office to where Yeoman Third Class Daphne Farnsworth, her lower lip clipped under her teeth in concentration, was filling out one more sodding form on her typewriter.

"Daphne!" he called. He had to call again before he broke through her concentration.

"Yes, Sir?"

"We've been summoned to the Captain's office," Donnelly said.

"I don't suppose we could ask him to wait thirty minutes, could we?" Daphne asked, smiling. "I'm finally *almost* finished with this."

"He wants us right away."

"Should I bring my pad?"

"No, I don't think so."

Lieutenant Junior Grade Eleanor McKee, Royal Australian Navy Women's Volunteer Reserve, commanding officer of all the women aboard RA Naval Station, Melbourne, was in the Captain's office when they got there.

She looks as if she's been sucking a lemon again, Daphne thought. *I wonder what the hell this is all about. I haven't done a damned thing, so far as I know.*

The Captain stood up.

"Yeoman Farnsworth," he said, "it is my sad duty to inform you that your husband, Sergeant John Andrew Farnsworth, Royal Australian Signals, has been killed in action in North Africa."

"Oh, God!"

"You will, I am sure, be able to find some solace in knowing he died for king and country," the Captain said.

"Oh, shit!" Daphne said.

"I'm very sorry, my dear," the Captain said.

(FIVE)

TOWNESVILLE, QUEENSLAND

5 JUNE 1942

"I'm only saying this, you two must understand, because I have been drinking," Lieutenant Commander Eric A. Feldt, RAN, said to Major Edward J. Banning, USMC, and Lieutenant Joe Howard, USMCR, "but I am far more impressed with your band of innocents than I ever thought would be the case."

They were in Commander Feldt's quarters, sitting on folding steel chairs, facing one other across a rickety wooden table on which sat a half-filled bottle of Dewar's Scotch and the empty hulk of another. A rusting bucket on the floor held a half-dozen bottles of beer and a soda siphon in a pool of melting ice.

"You're only saying that," Major Banning responded, "because you found out I outrank you."

"That's beneath you, Banning," Feldt said, "bringing up a sodding six days' difference in the dates of our promotions."

"And we gave you a truck," Joe Howard said, somewhat thickly. "We have a saying in America, 'Never look a gift truck in the mouth.' "

"You didn't *give* me the truck, you only *loaned* it to me. And anyway, the steering wheel is on the wrong side."

"The steering wheel is in the right place," Howard said. "You people insist on driving on the wrong side of the road."

Feldt stood up and walked, not too steadily, to a chest of drawers. He returned with a box of cigars, which he displayed with an elaborate gesture.

"I mean it," he said. "Have a cigar."

"Thank you, I don't mind if I do," Banning said. He took one and passed the box to Howard.

"I got them from a Dutchman, master of an inter-island tramp," Feldt said, sitting down again, and helping himself to a little more of the Dewar's. "He swore they were rolled between the thighs of fourteen-year-old Cuban virgins."

Banning raised his glass. "Here's to fourteen-year-old Cuban virgins."

"Here, here," Banning said.

"And here's to Captain Vandenhooven," Feldt said. "He gave me those cigars just in time."

"Just in time?" Banning asked.

"The next time he went out for me, the Japs got him. One of their sodding destroyers. They caught him off Wuvulu Island."

"Shit," Howard said.

Banning raised his glass again. "To the Captain," he said.

He lit the cigar and exhaled slowly through pursed lips.

"That's all right," he said approvingly.

"Virginal thighs'll do it every time," Feldt pronounced solemnly.

There was a polite knock at the door.

"Come," Feldt called.

A young, thick-spectacled young man in the uniform of a Leading Aircraftsman, Royal Australian Air Force, came into the room and, in the British manner, quick-marched to the rickety table and saluted with the palm outward as he stamped his foot.

"Sir!" he barked.

Feldt made a vague gesture with his right hand in the direction of his forehead; it could only charitably be called a salute.

"What have you there, son?"

"Group Captain Deane's compliments, Sir. He said he thought you should see these straight off."

He handed Feldt a large manila envelope. Feldt tore it open. It contained a slightly smaller envelope, this one stamped MOST SECRET. Feldt opened this one and took out a half-dozen eight-inch-square photographs. Banning guessed they were aerials.

"These are from where?" Feldt asked after a moment. Banning heard no suggestion in his voice now that Feldt had been drinking.

"Buka Island, Sir," the RAAF man said.

"That will be all, thank you. Please convey to Group Captain Deane my deep appreciation."

"Sir!" the RAAF man barked again, saluted and stamped his foot, and quick-marched out of the room.

Feldt shoved the thin stack of photographs across the table to Banning and then stood up.

Banning saw a man in a field, holding his arms above his head. There were three views of this, each differing slightly, as if they had been taken within seconds of each other. Matching each view were blow-ups, showing just the man and a small area around him.

Feldt reappeared with a large magnifying glass with a handle. He dropped to his knees and examined each of the photographs with great care.

"Well, at least he was still alive when these were taken," Feldt said.

"What am I looking at?" Banning asked. He enunciated the words very carefully; for he now very much regretted helping himself so liberally to the Scotch, and he wanted at least to sound as sober as possible.

"Can I look?" Joe Howard asked.

"Sure," Feldt said, and then went on, "Sub-Lieutenant Jacob Reeves. From whom we haven't heard in the last ten days or so. He's on Buka. Important spot. I was afraid the Nips had nipped him. But it's just that his wireless is out."

Banning looked at him. There had been no intent on Feldt's part, he saw, to play with words. Feldt was perfectly serious when he said nipped by the Nips. He was now icily serious.

"How do you know his radio is out?" Howard asked.

"What the bloody hell else do you think 'RA' could mean?" Feldt asked impatiently, almost contemptuously. He pointed, and Banning saw what he had missed. The tall grass, or whatever the hell it was, in the field had been cut down so it spelled out, in letters twenty-five or thirty feet tall, the letters *RA*.

More gently now, as if he regretted his abruptness, Feldt said, "Interesting man, Jacob Reeves. He's the far side of forty. Been in the islands since he was a boy. Been on Buka for fifteen years. Never married. Has a harem of native girls. I don't think he's been off the island more than three times since he's been there. We had a hell of a time teaching him Morse code, at first. And of course, he doesn't know a sodding thing about how a wireless works."

Banning raised his eyebrows at that.

"It could be anything from a loose wire," Feldt explained, "through a complete failure. Or his generator has gone out—he has a small gasoline-powered generator . . . God only knows."

"Where does he get gas for the generator?" Howard asked.

"There were supplies of it on Buka," Feldt said. "He took a truckload of supplies, presumably including fuel, when he went up into the hills. If he was out of petrol, I think he would have cut PET in the grass."

"Where did the pictures come from?" Banning asked.

"I asked Group Captain Deane to send an aircraft over there. He has a couple of Lockheed Hudsons."

Banning nodded. The twin-engine, low-winged monoplane with a twin tail obviously traced its heritage to the famous airplane in which Amelia Earhart had been lost trying to set an around-the-world speed record.

"I think we had better send Sub-Lieutenant Reeves one of your Hallicrafters sets, Major Banning," Feldt said. "I'm glad you mentioned the petrol. I have no idea how much he has left. If any. That bicycle generator is what he needs."

"They're yours," Banning said immediately.

"That poses several questions. First, how we get it to him. He's in the hills, so that eliminates either a submarine—even if I could get the use of one—or a ship."

"By parachute, then," Banning said. "Would your Group Captain Deane be able to do that?"

Feldt nodded, meaning that he could get an aircraft. "The question then becomes, can a Hallicrafters set be dropped by parachute?"

"I'm sure our Corporal Koffler could answer that," Banning said. "Off the top of my head, I can't think of a reason why not."

"The question then becomes, would your Corporal Koffler be willing to go in with it?"

"Why would that be necessary?" Banning asked.

He immediately saw on Feldt's face that his simple question had been misinterpreted; Feldt suspected that Banning was reluctant to send one of his men behind the Japanese lines.

"I'm afraid it really would be necessary, Banning," Feldt said. "Otherwise dropping the Hallicrafters would be useless; Reeves would have no idea how to operate it. And I don't think he could work from a set of directions; his mind doesn't work that way."

"How soon would you like Koffler to jump in?" Banning asked.

"Today's Friday. How long would it take your man to prepare the Hallicrafters to be rigged for a parachute drop?"

"Again, I'll have to ask him. But again, off the top of my head, I can't imagine why it would take more than a couple of hours. I presume we can get parachutes from the RAAF?"

Feldt nodded. "I'll ring Deane and ask him to arrange for your man to be flown up here tomorrow."

"Am I allowed to say something?" Howard asked.

Banning looked at him curiously, even impatiently.

"Sure," Feldt said.

"If I understand this correctly," Howard said, "what we have here is a very important Coastwatcher station—"

"Arguably, *the* most important station," Feldt agreed. "Certainly one of the most important."

"Staffed by one man who apparently knows very little or nothing about radios."

"That's why we're going to jump Koffler in to join him."

"Koffler doesn't know a Zero from a Packard," Howard said. "If something happens to your man Reeves, Commander, what you're going to have is a perfectly functioning radio station from which we'll get no intelligence because Koffler won't know what to send."

"Granted," Feldt said. "So what?"

"So what you need is a team. Send two people in. The other one should be someone who can identify Japanese aircraft and ships as well as your man Reeves. If something should happen to Reeves, that man could possibly keep the station operating. At least better than someone who was in high school this time last year."

"I don't have anybody to spare at the moment," Feldt said. "I grant your point. Reeves should have a replacement. I'll work on it."

"The time to send him in is now," Howard argued. "You said that getting planes is difficult. You might not be able to get another; and even if you could, it seems to me the Japanese would sense that something important was going on in that area."

"Commander Feldt says he doesn't have anyone to send," Banning said curtly.

"I was in the First Defense Battalion at Pearl," Howard said. "In addition to my other duties, I taught Japanese aircraft and vessel recognition."

"Fascinating," Commander Feldt said, softly.

"You're not a parachutist," Banning said.

"Neither was Steve Koffler, this time last year," Howard argued.

"Ed," Feldt said softly, "I was given a briefing on agent infiltration by an insufferably smug British Special Operations Executive officer. He told me, among other things, that their experience parachuting people into France has been that they lost more people training them to use parachutes than they did jumping virtually untrained people on actual operations. Consequently, as a rule of thumb, they no longer subject agents going in to the risks of injury parachute training raises."

Banning looked between the two of them, but said nothing.

"What worries me about this is why Joe wants to go," Feldt said. He looked directly at Howard. "Why do you want to do this?"

"I *don't* want to do it," Howard said after a moment. "I think somebody has to do it. Of the people available to us, I seem to have the best qualifications."

"Are you married? Children?" Feldt asked.

"I have a . . . fiancée," Joe said. It was, he realized, the first time he had ever used the word.

"The decision, of course, is Major Banning's," Commander Feldt said formally.

Banning met Howard's eyes for a moment.

"I think it might be better if Joe and I went to Melbourne," Banning said finally, evenly. "I don't know, but maybe Joe and Koffler will need some equipment I don't know about. If there is, it would more likely be available in Melbourne to a major than to a lieutenant."

"Your other ranks seem to do remarkably well getting things from depots," Feldt said. "But of course you're right. I'll arrange with Deane to have you two flown down there in the morning."

He reached for the Scotch bottle and topped off everyone's glass. "And of course, Melbourne's the best place to get the shots."

"Shots?"

"Immunizations."

"The Marine Corps has given me shots against every disease known to Western man," Howard said.

"I don't really think, Joe, that your medical people have a hell of a lot of experience with the sort of thing you're going to find on Buka," Feldt said. "And since Major Banning and I have decided to indulge you in this little escapade, it behooves you to take your shots like a good little boy."

"Aye, aye, Sir," Howard said.

"Cheers," Feldt said, raising his glass.

(SIX)

TWO CREEKS STATION
WAGGA WAGGA, NEW SOUTH WALES
6 JUNE 1942

It had been called a memorial service, but what it really had been, Daphne Farnsworth realized, was a regular funeral missing only the body. There had even been an empty, flag-covered casket in the aisle of St. Paul's Church. The Reverend Mr. Bartholomew Frederick, his World War I Australian–New Zealand Army Corps ribbons pinned to his vestments, had delivered a eulogy that had been at least as much a recitation of the virtues of Australian military prowess and courage generally as it had been a recounting of the virtues of the late Sergeant John Andrew Farnsworth.

And before and after, before even she had gotten home, the neighbors had gone through the ritual of visiting the bereaved. In the event, Daphne Farnsworth only barely counted as one of the bereaved. The visitors had "called on" John's parents at the big house, instead of at John's and her house. Their house had been more or less closed up, of course, and his parents' house was larger; but she suspected that the roasts and the casseroles and the clove-studded hams and potato salad would have been delivered to the big house even if she hadn't joined the Navy.

She was both shamed and confused by her reaction to the offerings of sympathy. They annoyed her. And she resented all the people, too. She was either being a genuine bitch, she decided, or—as she had heard at least a half-dozen people whisper softly to her in-laws—she was still in shock and had not really accepted her loss. That would come later.

She had been annoyed at that, too. They didn't know what the hell they were talking about. She had accepted her loss. She knew that John was never coming back, even, for Christ's sake, in a casket when the war was over. She knew, with a horrible empty feeling in her heart and belly, that she would never again feel John's muscular arms around her, or have him inside her.

She was angry with him, too—the decisive proof that she was a cold-hearted bitch. He didn't have to go. He had gotten himself killed over there for the sole reason that he had *wanted* to go over there, answering some obscene and ludicrous male hunger to go off and kill something . . . without considering at all the price she was going to have to pay.

And their childlessness—a question John had decided for all time by enlisting and getting himself killed—had been a subject of some conversation by those who had come to call to express their sympathy. The males, gathered in the sitting room, drinking, and the women in the kitchen, fussing with all the food, seemed to be divided more or less equally into two groups: those who thought it a pity there wasn't a baby, preferably a male baby, to carry on the name; and those who considered it a manifestation of God's wise compassion that he had not left poor Daphne with a fatherless child to add to her burden.

Daphne had started drinking early in the morning, when she awoke in their bed and cried with the knowledge that John would never again share it with her. She had tossed down a shot of straight gin before she'd left their bed for her bath.

And she'd had another little taste just before they'd gotten in the cars to go to St. Paul's for the service. And she had had three since they had returned from church, timing them carefully. John had once told her that if you took only one drink an hour, you could never get drunk; the body burned off spirits at the rate of a drink an hour. She believed that.

As if she needed another one! There was one more proof that she was a bitch, because she knew that what she really wanted to do was get really drunk. She had been really drunk only three times in her life, the last time the day after she had returned here after watching John's ship move away from the pier in Melbourne.

She could not do that today, of course. It would disgrace her—not that that seemed important. But it would hurt her family, especially her mother and John's mother, if she let the side down by doing something like that, when she was expected to be the grieving, virtuous young widow.

She left the crowd of people in the big house to walk to her own house. She did that because she had to visit the loo, and there was actually a line before the loo in the big house.

She just happened to notice the car coming across the bridge over the Murrumbidgee River. It made the sharp right onto their property.

Still somebody else coming? I really *don't want one more expression of sympathy, one more man to tell me, "Steady on, girl," or one more woman to tell me, "The Lord works in mysterious ways. You must now put your trust in the Lord."*

There's no one behind the wheel.

Of course not. It's an American car, a Studebaker like the Americans at The Elms have.

What is an American car doing coming here?

Oh, my God, it's him. It can't be. But it is.

What in the name of God is Steve Koffler doing here?

She cut across the field and got to the Studebaker a moment after Steve Koffler had parked it at the end of a long row of cars, got out, and opened the rear door.

The first thought she had was unkind. When she saw his glistening paratrooper boots, sharply creased trousers, and the tightly woven fabric of his tunic and compared it with the rough, blanketlike material John's uniform had been cut from, and his rough, hobnailed boots, she was annoyed: *Bloody American Marines, they all look like officers.*

He got whatever he was looking for from the backseat of the Studebaker, then stood erect and turned around and saw her.

"Hello," he said, startled, and somewhat shy.

"What are you doing here?"

"Lieutenant Donnelly told me about your husband," Steve said, holding out what he had taken from the backseat: a bouquet of flowers, a tissue-wrapped square box, and a brown sack, obviously containing a bottle.

"What are you doing here?" Daphne repeated.

"I didn't know what you're supposed to do in Australia," he said, "to show you're sorry."

"What is all that?"

"Flowers, candy, and whiskey," Steve said. "Is that all right?"

"It's unnecessary," Daphne snapped, and was sorry. *"What* are you *doing* here?"

"I came to tell you how sorry I am about your husband getting killed," Steve said.

"And you drove all the way out here to do that?"

"It's only two hundred and eighty-six miles," he said. "I just checked. And that includes me getting lost twice."

It never even entered his stupid American mind that he might be intruding here; he wanted to come, so he just got in his sodding car and came!

"I really don't know what to say to you," she said.

"You don't have to say anything," he said. "I just wanted you to know I'm sorry."

Is that it? Or did you maybe think that now that I'm a widow, you could just jump into my bed?

What the hell is the matter with me? He's just stupid and sweet. Except that I know he's not really as stupid as I first thought. Naïve and sweet, rather than stupid.

"That's very kind of you, Steve, I'm sure. Thank you very much."

Steve Koffler relaxed visibly.

"It's OK. I wanted to do it."

But my mother is not going to understand this. Or John's mother. Or anybody. They're going to suspect that this boy and I are . . . what? Something we shouldn't be. That that is absurd won't matter. That's what they're going to think.

And I can't just send him packing, either. Not only would that be cruel of me, but by now everyone has seen the car and will be wondering who it is. What the hell am I going to do?

"I suppose you must think I'm terrible," Daphne Farnsworth said to Steve Koffler as the Studebaker turned onto the bridge over the Murrumbidgee River, "lying to my family like that."

"No. I understand," he replied, turning his head to look at her.

"Well, I feel rotten about it," she said. "But I just couldn't take any more. I was going to scream."

After quickly but carefully coaching Steve in the story, she had led him up to the big house and introduced him to her family. She had told them that her officer, Lieutenant Donnelly, had learned that the American Marines were sending a car to the Wagga Wagga airfield. The lieutenant had arranged with a Marine officer to have Steve, the driver, whom she referred to as "Corporal Koffler," stop by the station and offer her a ride back to Melbourne. Her "death leave" was up the next day anyway. It would save her catching a very early train, and a long and uncomfortable ride.

It sounded credible, and she was reasonably sure that no one had questioned the story. They had been effusive in their thanks to Steve for doing her a good turn. All of which, of course, had made her feel even worse.

"I'm just glad I decided to come," Steve Koffler said.

They rode in silence for a long time, while Daphne wallowed in her new perception of herself as someone with a previously unsuspected capacity for lying and all-around deceit, the proof of which was that she felt an enormous sense of relief at being able to get away from people who shared her grief and would, quite literally, do anything in the world for her.

Steve Koffler broke the silence as they reached the outskirts of Wangaratta, fifty miles back into Victoria.

"Would it be all right if I looked for someplace I could get something to eat? I could eat a horse."

"You mean you haven't eaten?"

He nodded.

"You should have said something at the station," she said. "There was all kinds of food . . ."

He shrugged.

"On condition that you let me pay," Daphne said. "I really do appreciate the ride."

"I've got money," he said.

"I pay, or you go hungry."

He smiled at her shyly.

As he wolfed down an enormous meal of steak and eggs, Daphne asked, "Tell me about your family, Steve. And your girl."

"There's not much to tell about my family. My mother and father are divorced. I live with her and her husband. And I don't have a girl."

"I thought Marines were supposed to have a girl in every port."

"That's what they say," he said. "I know a *bunch* of girls, of course, but there's no one special. I've been too busy, I suppose, to have a steady girl."

He's lying. That was bravado. He's afraid of women. Then why did he drive all the way out to Wagga Wagga? For the reason he gave. He felt really sorry for me. Whatever this boy is, he is no Don Juan. He's just a sweet kid.

When they were back on the road, she found herself pursuing the subject, wondering why it was important.

"There must have been one girl that . . . stood out . . . from all the others?"

From his reaction to the question, she sensed that there had not only been a girl in Steve Koffler's life, but that it had not been a satisfactory relationship.

"Who was she, Steve?"

Why am I doing this? What do I really care?

Over the next hour and a half, Daphne drew from Steve, one small detail after another, the story of Dianne Marshall Norman. By the time she was sure she had separated fact from fantasy and had assembled what she felt was probably the true sequence of events, she had worked up what she told herself was a big-sister-like dislike for Diane Marshall Norman and a genuine feeling of sympathy for Steve.

Women can be such bitches, she thought, *getting what they want and not caring a whit how much they hurt a nice kid like Steve Koffler.*

(SEVEN)

U.S. NAVY ELEMENT
U.S. ARMY GENERAL HOSPITAL
MELBOURNE, AUSTRALIA
1705 HOURS 6 JUNE 1942

Soon after they met, Commander Charles E. Whaley, M.D., USNR, told Ensign Barbara T. Cotter, NC, USNR, that he had given up a lucrative practice of psychiatry in Grosse Point Hills, Michigan, and entered the Naval Service in order to treat the mental disorders of servicemen who had been unable to cope with the stress of the battle-field. He was happy to do so.

But he had not entered the Naval Service, he went on to tell Ensign Cotter, to administer to the minor aches and pains of the Naval brass gathered around the headquarters of the Commander-in-Chief, South-west Pacific, General Douglas MacArthur, and especially not to cater to their grossly overdeveloped sense of medical self-protection. And he had absolutely no intention of doing so.

He specifically told Ensign Cotter, who was in his eyes an unusually nice and bright kid, that he had no intention of making a goddamned house call to the "residence" of some Navy brass hat named Pickering. This guy had apparently heard somewhere of a battery of rare tropical diseases. Since, for some half-assed reason, he felt threatened by those diseases, he wanted himself immunized against them. At his quarters.

"I think I know where this goddamn thing started, Barbara," Dr. Whaley said. "I have never even *seen* a case of any of these things—and I interned and did my residency in Los Angeles, where you see all sorts of strange things—but this morning there was a Marine officer in here, armed with a buck slip from an admiral on MacArthur's staff, ordering that he be immediately immunized against them. They had to get the stuff from the Australians to give it to him.

"Then I get a message—if I'd been here to take the call, I would have told him what I thought—from this Captain Pickering, ordering me to come to his residence prepared to give the same series of shots to at least one other person. What I think happened is that this sonofa-bitch Pickering heard about the Marine and decided he wasn't going to take the risk of coming down with something like this himself, No, Sir. I mean, why should he? I mean, after all, here he is, far from the Army-Navy Club in Washington, risking his life as a member of MacArthur's palace guard."

Barbara chuckled.

"What would you like me to do, Doctor?"

"If I go over there, Barbara, I'm liable to forget that I'm an officer and a gentleman and tell this Pickering character what I think of him specifically and the Naval Service generally. So, by the power vested in me by the Naval Service, Ensign Cotter, I order you to proceed forthwith to"—he handed her an interoffice memorandum—"the address hereon, and immunize this officer by injection. See if you can find a dull needle. A large one. And it is my professional medical judgment that you should inject the patient in his gluteus maximus."

"Aye, aye, Sir," Ensign Cotter replied.

"And go by ambulance," Commander Charles E. Whaley, M.D., USNR, added.

"Ambulance?"

"With a little bit of luck, Captain Pickering will inquire about the ambulance. Then you will tell him that the immunizations sometimes produce terrible side effects," Dr. Whaley said, pleased with himself. "And that the ambulance is just a precaution."

"You're serious?" Barbara chuckled.

"You bet your ass I am," Commander Whaley said.

(EIGHT)

THE ELMS
DANDENONG, VICTORIA, AUSTRALIA
1755 HOURS 6 JUNE 1942

When Barbara Cotter saw The Elms, she was glad that Dr. Whaley had sent her and not come himself. This Captain Pickering, whoever he was, seemed one more proof that Karl Marx might have been on to something when he denounced the overaccumulation of capital in the hands of the privileged few. Navy captains, for rank hath its privileges, lived well. But not this well. Dr. Whaley could have gotten himself in deep trouble, letting his Irish temper loose at this Navy brass hat.

A middle-aged woman opened the door.

"Hello," Mrs. Hortense Cavendish said with a smile. "May I help you?"

"I'm Ensign Cotter, to see Captain Pickering. I'm from the hospital."

"Are you a doctor?"

"I'm a nurse," Barbara said.

"I think he was expecting a doctor," Mrs. Cavendish said. "But please come in, I'll tell him you're here."

She left Barbara waiting in the foyer and disappeared down a corridor. A moment later a man appeared and walked up to her. He was in his shirtsleeves and wearing suspenders. And his collar was open and his tie pulled down. He held a drink in his hand.

Barbara was prepared to despise him as a palace-guard brass hat with an exaggerated opinion of his own importance—and with what Dr. Whaley had so cleverly described as "an overdeveloped sense of medical self-protection."

"Hello," Pickering said. "I'm Fleming Pickering. I was rather expecting Commander Whaley, but you're much prettier."

"Sir, I'm Ensign Cotter."

"I'm very pleased to meet you," he said. "We saw the ambulance. What's that all about? Is the Navy again suffering from crossed signals?"

"Sir, I'm here to administer certain injections," Barbara said. "There is a chance of a reaction to them. The ambulance is a precaution."

"Well, the first stickee seems to be doing fine," Pickering said. "We're hoping that your intended target will show up momentarily. I'm afraid you're going to have to wait until he does."

"Sir?"

"You're here to immunize Corporal Koffler," Pickering said. "At the moment, we don't know where he is. You'll have to wait until he shows up. If that's going to pose a problem for you at the hospital, I'll call and explain the situation. This is rather important."

"I was under the impression the immunizations were intended for you, Captain."

"Oh, no," Pickering said, and smiled. "I suspected crossed signals. Shall I call the hospital and straighten things out?"

"If I'm going to have to stay, I'd better call, Sir," Barbara said.

"The phone's right over there," Pickering said, pointing to a narrow table against the foyer wall. "If you run into any trouble, let me know. Sometimes the Regular Navy is a bit dense between the ears."

She looked at him in shock.

"Between us amateurs, of course," Pickering smiled. "I presume you're a fellow amateur?"

"I'm a reservist, Sir, if that's what you mean."

"I was sure of it," Pickering said. "When you're through on the phone, please come in the sitting room." He pointed to it.

"Yes, Sir," Barbara said.

*   *   *

"Oh, Barbara," Dr. Whaley said when she called him at his quarters. "I hope you're calling because you're lost."

"Excuse me?"

"You found The Elms without any trouble?"

"Yes, Sir. I'm here now. I've just met Captain Pickering."

"How did that go?"

"It's not what you thought, Doctor."

"I already found that out. The men to be immunized, the Marine officer who was here at the hospital, and the one you're there to see, are about to go on some hush-hush mission behind the lines. High-level stuff. And I learned five minutes after you left that Pickering is not what I led you to believe he was."

"He's really nice," Barbara said.

"He's also General MacArthur's personal pal," Dr. Whaley said. *And* Frank Knox's personal representative over here. *Not* the sort of man to jab with a dull needle."

"No, Sir," Barbara chuckled. "The other man to be immunized isn't here yet. Captain Pickering said I'll have to stay here until he shows up. That's why I'm calling."

"You stay as long as you're needed," Dr. Whaley said, "and be as charming as possible, knowing that you have our Naval careers in your hands."

"Yes, Sir."

"You better send the ambulance back, Barbara. When you're finished, I'll send a staff car for you."

"Yes, Sir."

Barbara hung up, walked out of The Elms, sent the ambulance back to the hospital, and then reentered the house.

"Everything go all right?" Captain Pickering asked her when she reached the room he'd directed her to. "Come in."

"Everything's fine, Sir," Barbara said.

"Gentlemen, this is Ensign Cotter," Pickering said. "Ensign Cotter, this is Major Ed Banning, Lieutenant Vince Donnelly, and Lieutenant Joe Howard."

Lieutenant Joe Howard, who had been mixing a drink at the bar, turned, looked at Barbara, dropped the glass, and said, "Oh, my God!"

"Joe!" Barbara wailed.

"Why do I suspect that these two splendid young junior officers have met?" Banning asked dryly.

"Lieutenant Howard," Captain Pickering said, "Ensign Cotter was just telling me that sometimes these shots have adverse effects. Why don't you take her someplace where she can examine you?"

He hardly had time to congratulate himself on having produced—

snatching it from out of the blue—a Solomon-like solution to the problem of how to handle two young lovers who were embarrassed to manifest a display of affection before senior officers. For, unfortunately, his brilliance was wasted; Ensign Cotter, forgetting that she was an officer and a gentlewoman, ran to Howard and threw herself in his arms, and cried, "Oh, my darling!"

After a moment, Captain Pickering spoke again.

"Joe, why don't you take your girl and show her the grounds?"

Howard, not trusting his voice, nodded his thanks and, with his arms around Barbara, led her out of the sitting room and started down the corridor.

All of a sudden, she stopped, spun out of his arms, and faced him.

"You're on this mission, aren't you?" she challenged.

He nodded.

"Oh, my God!"

"It'll be all right," he said.

"They don't send people on missions like that unless they volunteer," she said, adding angrily, "You volunteered, didn't you?"

He nodded.

"Goddamn you!"

He didn't reply.

"Why? Can you tell me why?"

"It's important," he said.

"When do you go?"

"Tomorrow."

"Tomorrow?" she wailed. He nodded.

"What are we going to do now?" she asked.

He shrugged helplessly.

"We could go to my room," Joe blurted.

She met his eyes.

"They'd know," she said.

"Do you care?" he asked.

She reached out and touched his face and shook her head.

He took her hand from his face and held it as he led her the rest of the way down the stairs and then up the broad staircase to his room.

XIII

(ONE)

THE ELMS

DANDENONG, VICTORIA, AUSTRALIA

2105 HOURS 6 JUNE 1942

As Corporal Stephen M. Koffler and Petty Officer Daphne Farnsworth approached Melbourne, they came up to a road sign indicating a turnoff to Dandenong. It occurred to Corporal Koffler then that he'd better check in before he took Petty Officer Farnsworth home.

"Would you mind sitting in the car for a minute while I tell Mrs. Cavendish I'm back?" Steve asked as he made the turn. "Maybe there's a message for me, or something."

"Of course not."

He drove down the long line of ancient elms that lined the driveway. When they reached the house, there were two cars parked in front of it. One was a drop-head Jaguar coupe and the other a Morris with Royal Australian Navy plates. After a moment, to her surprise, Daphne recognized it as Lieutenant Donnelly's car.

She wondered what he was doing out here, and then she wondered what he was going to think when he saw her with Corporal Steve Koffler of the United States Marines; she was supposed to be still at home, grief-stricken.

"Oh, shit!" Steve Koffler said, when he saw the cars.

When Major Edward J. Banning, USMC, noticed the glow of the headlights flash across the front of The Elms, he rose to his feet and went to one of the French windows in the library. As he pushed the curtain aside, the Studebaker pulled up beside the Jaguar and the Morris.

It has to be Corporal Steven Koffler, goddamn the horny little AWOL sonofabitch!

I am not going to eat his ass out. It is not in keeping with the

373

principles of good leadership to eat the ass out of an enlisted man just before you ask him to parachute onto an enemy-held island. If he doesn't kill himself in the jump, there is a very good chance he will be killed by the Japanese, probably in some very imaginative way.

If I were a corporal, and they left me all alone with the keys to a car, would I take the car and go out and try to get laid? Never having been a corporal, I can't really say. But probably.

Banning couldn't help recalling Kenneth R. "Killer" McCoy, late Corporal, 4th Marines, Shanghai.

If I had set up the Killer in a house like this in China, and told him he would be left alone for a week or ten days minimum, he would have had a nonstop poker game going here in the library, a craps table operating in the foyer, half a dozen ladies of the evening plying their trade upstairs; and he'd be using the Studebaker to ferry customers back and forth to town.

It was not the first time Banning had thought of Corporal Killer McCoy during the past twenty-four hours. He started remembering McCoy just after he and Captain Pickering arrived at The Elms; they were informed then by Mrs. Cavendish that Corporal Koffler had taken the Studebaker at five the previous afternoon, and that he hadn't been seen since. And no, she had no idea where he might have gone. That sounded like something McCoy would have done.

Which did not mean that Corporals McCoy and Koffler were not stamped out of the same mold—far from it. Banning would have been nervous about sending Killer McCoy to jump on Buka, but he wouldn't have had this sick feeling in his stomach. Killer was probably capable of carrying off something like this with a good chance of coming through it alive. Banning did not think that would be the case with Joe Howard and Steve Koffler. The words had come into his mind a half-dozen times: *I am about to send two of my men to their deaths.*

It was not a pleasant feeling, and his rationalizations, although inarguably true, sounded hollow and irrelevant: *I am asking him to risk, and perhaps even give, his life so that other men may live.* And: *He's a volunteer, nobody pushed him into this at the point of a bayonet.* And even: *He's a Marine, and Marines do what they are ordered to do.*

There was really no point whatever in wishing that the Killer was here. For one thing, Killer was no longer a corporal. He was now an officer and a gentleman and would soon find himself ordering some enlisted Marine to do something that would probably get him killed.

And there was no other enlisted man in Special Detachment 14 who could be sent. No one else, not even the Commanding Officer, knew how to jump out of an airplane without getting killed. And *that,* as applied to Joe Howard, violated a principle of leadership that Banning devoutly believed, that an officer should not order—or ask—someone to do something he would not do himself.

"I think that's him," Banning said, turning from the window to Captain Pickering and Lieutenant Donnelly. He kept his voice as close to a conversational tone as he could muster as he continued, "Maybe I'd better go find Howard and his nurse." They had not been seen, which surprised no one, since they had left the sitting room.

"I'll get him, Major," Lieutenant Donnelly said.

"Good evening, Sir," Corporal Koffler said, coming into the library. Nervously, he looked at Pickering and Banning in turn, and said, "Sir," to each of them.

"Welcome home," Banning said.

"Sir, I didn't expect to see you."

"Well, you're here. Have you been drinking?"

"No, Sir."

Lieutenant Donnelly came into the room.

"They'll be here in a minute," he said.

"You know Captain Pickering," Banning said to Koffler, "and I understand you've met Lieutenant Donnelly."

"No, Sir. I talked to him a couple of times on the phone."

"How are you, Corporal?" Donnelly said.

"How do you do, Sir?"

Banning saw in Donnelly's eyes that he had expected Corporal Koffler to be somewhat older. Say, old enough to vote.

"Something pretty important has come up," Banning said.

"Yes, Sir?"

"There's several *if*s," Banning continued. "Let me ask a couple of questions. First, would it be possible to drop one of the Hallicrafters sets by parachute? Or would it get smashed up?"

"I thought about that, Sir."

"You did?" Banning replied, surprised.

The door opened again, and Ensign Barbara Cotter and Lieutenant Joe Howard came into the room.

Barbara Cotter averted her eyes and looked embarrassed, confirming Fleming Pickering's early judgment of her as a nice girl. Then he had a thought that made him feel like a dirty old man: *Christ, I could use a little sex myself.*

"How goes it, Steve?" Joe Howard asked. "We were getting a little worried about you."

"Hello, Sir."

"The lady is Ensign Cotter, Koffler," Banning said. "Lieutenant Howard's fiancée."

"Hello," Barbara said.

"Ma'am," Koffler replied uneasily.

"Should I be in here?" Barbara asked.

"You don't look like a Japanese spy to me," Pickering said. "And it seems to me you have an interest in what's going on."

"Sir . . ." Banning started to protest. Ensign Barbara Cotter, whatever her relationship with Joe Howard, had no "need to know."

"Ensign Cotter is a Naval officer," Pickering said formally, "who is well aware of the need to keep her mouth shut about this operation."

Banning had called Pickering as soon as he arrived at the airport in Melbourne. He thought he should know that USMC Special Detachment 14 was about to drop two of its men behind Japanese lines. Pickering had been more than idly interested. In fact, he promptly announced that if he "wouldn't be in the way," he would pick Banning up and drive him out to The Elms while the operation was being set up. Banning had wondered then if Pickering was in fact going to get in the way, and now it looked as if he was.

For a moment, Banning looked as if he was on the edge of protesting further, but then reminded himself that Special Detachment 14 wouldn't even exist if it weren't for Pickering.

"Yes, Sir," Banning said finally.

"Corporal Koffler was telling us how he would drop one of the Hallicrafters by parachute," Pickering said. "Go on, please, Koffler."

"You'd need a parachute," Koffler said. "I mean," he went on quickly, having detected the inanity of his own words, "I mean, I think you'd have to modify a regular C-3 'chute. All the cargo 'chutes I've ever seen would be too big."

"I don't understand," Fleming Pickering confessed.

"Sir, the whole set, when you get it out of the crates," Steve Koffler explained, "doesn't weigh more than maybe a hundred and fifty pounds. Cargo 'chutes, the ones I've seen, are designed to drop a lot more weight—"

"The question is moot," Lieutenant Donnelly said. "There are no cargo 'chutes available. Period. You're talking about modifying a standard Switlick C-3 'chute, Corporal?" Steve nodded. "How?" Donnelly pursued.

"Do you think I might be able to get you the parachute, parachutes, you need, Banning?" Pickering asked.

"Sir," Donnelly replied for Banning, "I don't think there's a cargo parachute in Australia."

"OK," Pickering said. "You were saying, Corporal Koffler?"

"Sir, I think you could make up some special rigging to replace the harness. Make straps to go around the mattresses."

"Mattress?" Banning asked.

"Mattress*es*," Steve said. "What I would do is make one package of the antenna and the generator. I think you could just roll them up in a mattress and strap it tight. And then add sandbags, or something, so that it weighed about a hundred seventy-five pounds. Where do you want to drop the radio, Sir?

"Why sandbags? Why a hundred seventy-five pounds?"

"That's the best weight for a standard 'chute. Any more and you hit too hard. Any lighter and it floats forever. You couldn't count on hitting the drop zone," Koffler said, explaining what he evidently thought should be self-evident to someone who was not too bright.

He obviously knows what he's talking about. Why does that surprise me?

"And then do the same thing with the transceiver itself," Koffler went on. "Wrap it in mattresses, and then weight it up to a hundred seventy-five pounds. It would probably make sense to wrap some radio tubes—I mean spare tubes—in cotton or something, and put them with the transceiver. They're pretty fragile."

"I have some parachute riggers, Corporal," Lieutenant Donnelly said. "Civilian women. They have some heavy sewing machines. Could you show them, do you think, how to make such a replacement for the harness?"

"Yes, Sir," Koffler said. "I think so."

He looked uncomfortable.

"Speaking of civilian women, Sir, I've got a lady outside in the car. Could I take a minute to talk to her? I was about to take her home."

"Sure," Banning said. "Go ahead."

When he was gone, Fleming Pickering said, "Well, what do you think, Ed?"

"I don't know what to think, Sir. He doesn't seem to think there will be much of a problem. More important, he seems to know what he's talking about."

"I was thinking, for a moment, that he seems so young for something like this. But then I remembered that I was a Corporal of Marines when I was his age; it's probably not that he's so young, but that I'm so old."

Steve Koffler didn't have to go out to the Studebaker to find Yeoman Daphne Farnsworth; she was standing in the foyer, just outside the corridor to the library.

"I had to go to the ladies'," she said.

"You found it all right, I hope?"

"Yes, thank you."

"Something's come up," Steve said.

"I heard, I went looking for you."

"I don't know how long this will take," Steve said. "I'm sorry, I should have taken you home first."

"Are you in some kind of trouble? About taking the car, maybe?"

"No, I don't think so. I thought I would be when I saw that Captain Pickering was here, but I think they want me to jump in with the radio. Otherwise, I think my ass would have been in a crack."

"You're sure?"

He nodded. "I'm sorry you have to wait. I was going to tell you to wait in there," he said, pointing toward the sitting room. "There's couches and chairs and a radio."

"All right," Daphne said. "You're sure you didn't get in trouble coming out to see me?"

"I'm fine," he said, smiling. "No trouble. Things couldn't be better."

He turned and went back down the corridor. Daphne walked into the sitting room. She sat down on a couch and picked up a magazine, and then threw it down angrily.

That American Navy captain and Steve's major and lieutenant and Donnelly didn't come here on a Saturday evening to discuss a training mission. I know what the Marines are doing here with the Coastwatchers. If they're going to parachute him anywhere, it will be onto some island in Japanese hands. And the only reason they would do that is because there's some sort of trouble with the Australian already there.

She looked impatiently around the room. Her eyes fell on several bottles, one of them of Gilbey's gin. She walked over to it, looked over her shoulder nervously, and then took a healthy pull at the neck of the bottle.

" '*Otherwise,*' " she quoted bitterly, " 'I think my ass would have been in a crack! Oh, Steve, you bloody ass!"

Then she capped the Gilbey's bottle and walked down the corridor to the library door, where she could hear what was being said.

"I'll try to get to the airfield to see you off, Steve," Captain Fleming Pickering said, "but if something comes up . . . good luck, son."

"Thank you, Sir," Steve said.

They were standing on the porch of The Elms. All that could be done tonight had been done. The officers, except Lieutenant Howard and his girlfriend, were leaving.

"You've been taking some kidding, I'm sure, about being a corporal, as young as you are," Pickering went on.

"Yes, Sir. Some."

"Well, it's going to get worse," Pickering said. "As of this moment, you're a sergeant."

"Sir?"

"I think, Ed," Pickering said to Banning, "that between us we should have the authority to make that promotion, shouldn't we? I'm not going to have to trouble the Secretary of the Navy with an administrative problem like that, am I?"

"No, Sir," Banning chuckled. "I don't see any problem with that."

"Then good luck again, Sergeant Koffler," Pickering said, and patted Steve, a paternal gesture, on the arm. He went down the stairs and got in the Drop-Head Jaguar.

"I will see you and Lieutenant Howard at half past six, *Sergeant*, right?" Lieutenant Donnelly said. "At the airfield."

"Aye, aye, Sir."

"Don't get carried away with your girlfriend tonight, *Sergeant*," Banning said softly. "Have fun, but be at the airport at 0630."

"She's not my girlfriend, Sir," Steve said.

"Oh?"

"I wish she was, but all she is . . . is a very nice lady."

"I see."

"I'll be at the airport on time, Sir."

"Goodnight, Steve," Banning said.

He got in Pickering's Jaguar. Steve stood on the porch until both cars had disappeared down the driveway, then went looking for Daphne. He suspected that she would probably be sort of hiding in the sitting room. It would have been very embarrassing for her if Lieutenant Donnelly had seen her. He would have gotten the wrong idea.

Daphne Farnsworth was not in the sitting room. Nor in the toilet off the corridor. Nor in the kitchen, Nor anyplace.

Jesus! What she did was walk all the way to the goddamned road, so that she can try to catch a ride!

He ran to the Studebaker. Daphne's bag was not in the backseat.

She's even carrying her goddamned suitcase!

He got behind the wheel, squealed the tires backing out and turning around, and raced down the drive between the ancient elms. She was not in sight when he reached the highway. He swore, and then drove toward Melbourne. Once he thought he saw her, but when he got close it was not Daphne sitting on her suitcase, but a pile of paving stones, neatly stacked by the side of the road.

Finally, swearing, he gave up, and drove back to The Elms.

At least she didn't have to carry that heavy goddamned suitcase; I would have carried it to her in the morning.

And that would have at least given me the chance to say "so long."

When he got back to The Elms, he saw there was only one light on, on the second floor. That meant Lieutenant Howard and his girlfriend had gone to bed. Together.

Jesus, talk about good luck! Having your girlfriend right here. But then he considered that. *Maybe it would be better if she wasn't here, especially since she knows what's going to happen tomorrow. The minute they were alone, she probably started crying or something, and that would be hard to deal with.* And then he considered that again. *At least they could put their arms around each other and not feel so fucking alone.*

Steve went into the library. He thought he would write his mother. But when he was sitting at the little writing table with a sheet of paper in front of him, he realized that was a lousy idea.

What the hell can I write? "Dear Mom, I'm fine. How are you? I've been wondering when I'm going to get a letter from you. Nothing much is happening here, except that I'm living in a mansion outside Melbourne; and tomorrow or the next day they're going to jump me onto an island called Buka. I don't even know where it is."

I can't even write that. This whole thing is a military secret.

He thought about going into the kitchen and maybe making himself an egg sandwich, but decided against it; the last time he'd done that, he'd awakened Mrs. Cavendish, and he didn't want to do that tonight.

He went up the broad staircase to the second floor, and down the corridor to his room.

Tomorrow night, or maybe the night after that, I'll be sleeping in the goddamned jungle with bugs and snakes and Christ knows what else. I should have known a good deal like this couldn't last—a room of my own, with a great big bed all for myself.

He pushed open the door to his room and turned on the light.

Yeoman Daphne Farnsworth was in his bed, with the sheet pulled up around her chin.

"Jesus Christ!" Steve said.

"I saw you drive off in the car," Daphne said. "I didn't know when, or if, you would be back, so I decided to go to bed and worry about getting into Melbourne in the morning."

"I was looking for you," he said. "When I couldn't find you downstairs, I thought you had probably tried to hitch a ride into Melbourne."

"Oh," she said.

"I'm going to jump onto some island called Buka."

"I know. I heard."

"How come you took your bag out of the car?" Steve blurted. "I mean, you must have—"

"I know what you mean," she said, very softly.

"Jesus!"

"I didn't want you to be alone tonight," Daphne said. "If that makes you think I'm some kind of a wh—"

"Shut up!" he said sharply. "Don't talk like that!"

"And I didn't want to be alone, either," she said.

"Once, in the car," Steve said, "we were talking about something, and you leaned close to me and put your hand on my leg, and I could smell your breath and feel it on my face, and I thought my heart was going to stop. . . ."

They looked into each other's eyes for a long moment.

Finally, softly, reasonably, Daphne said, "Steve, since you have to be at the airfield at half past six, don't you think you should come to bed?"

(TWO)

PORT MORESBY, NEW GUINEA
0405 HOURS 8 JUNE 1942

When Flight Sergeant Michael Keyes, RAAF, went to the tin-roofed Transient Other Ranks hut to wake him, Sergeant Steve Koffler, USMC, was awake and nearly dressed, in greens that still carried the stripes of a corporal.

Lieutenant Howard had tried to fix it so they could be together overnight, but the Aussies hadn't let them. Steve had told Howard not to worry about it. He thought Howard had enough to worry about, like making his first jump, without having to worry about him having to sleep by himself.

"Briefing time, lad," Sergeant Keyes said.

"OK."

"First, breakfast, of course. The food here is ordinarily bloody awful, which explains the stuff we brought with us."

"I'm not really very hungry."

"Well, have a go at it anyway. It's likely to be some time before steak and eggs will be on your ration again."

"Some time," shit. By tonight I'm probably going to be dead.

"I guess I better put this on now, huh?" Steve said, holding up an RAAF flight suit, a quilted cotton coverall.

"Yes, I think you might as well," Keyes said.

Steve put his legs into the garment and shrugged into it. There were the chevrons of a sergeant of the United States Marine Corps on the sleeves, and the metal lapel insignia of the Corps on the collar points. Staff Sergeant Richardson had taken care of that yesterday in Townesville, when Steve and the crew of the Lockheed Hudson were packing the Hallicrafters set and loading it into the airplane.

He had also given Steve a Colt Model 1911A1 .45 pistol. Steve suspected that Staff Sergeant Richardson had given him his own pistol; only the officers and a couple of the staff sergeants had been authorized pistols. He thought that had been a very nice thing for Staff Sergeant Richardson to do.

Steve had decided the best—really the only—way to take his Springfield along was to drop it with the antenna set; it and his web cartridge belt and two extra bandoliers of .30-06 ammunition and a half-dozen fragmentation grenades had been wrapped in cotton padding, and then that bundle had been strapped to the antenna parts.

Now that Richardson had given him the pistol, at least when he got on the ground he would have a weapon right away. There was no telling how quickly he could get the Springfield out of the antenna bundle. If he could find it at all.

Steve took a couple of foil-wrapped Trojans from a knee pocket in the flight suit, ripped one of them open with his teeth, unrolled it, and then tied it around the top of his boots. Then he bloused the left leg of the flight suit under it.

As he repeated the process for the right leg, Flight Sergeant Keyes said rather admiringly, "I wondered how the hell you did that to your trousers."

"They call it 'blousing,' " Steve said.

He strapped Staff Sergeant Richardson's pistol belt around his waist, and then tied the thong lace around his leg through an eyelet at the bottom of the holster.

"Ready," he said.

"Good lad," Keyes said. "We have to get hopping."

They left the tin-roofed hut and walked across the airfield to the mess. Based on his previous experience—in the movies—with what war should look like, Port Moresby was what Steve had expected to find when he got off the Martin Mariner in Melbourne. The people here went around armed, and they wore steel helmets. There were sandbags all over the place, at the entrances to bomb shelters, and around buildings, and to protect machine-gun positions. This place had been bombed.

Their airplane, the Lockheed, had been pushed into a revetment with sandbag walls. There were other airplanes, none of which was very impressive. There were three bi-wing English fighter planes, for instance, that looked as if they were left over from the First World War.

In the mess hut, Sergeant Keyes took his arm and guided him into an anteroom under a sign that said, OFFICERS. Lieutenant Howard and the rest of the airplane crew were there: the pilot, who was a "flying officer," and the navigator, who was a sergeant, and the gunner, who was a corporal. Steve decided that in the RAAF, if you were a flyer, you got to eat with the officers.

But he quickly learned that wasn't the reason Sergeant Keyes had taken him in the Officers' Room.

"Good morning, Sergeant," a voice said behind him. "About ready to get this show started?"

Startled, Steve looked over his shoulder. There was another RAAF officer, an older one, with a bunch of stripes on his sleeve, standing by the door.

He's at least a major, or whatever the hell they call a major in the RAAF.

"Yes, Sir," Steve said.

"We're running a bit behind schedule, so I'll just run through this while you eat, all right?"

"That'll be fine, Sir," Lieutenant Howard said.

The officer gestured to the navigator, who picked up a four-by-four sheet of plywood and set it down on the table.

"Sit here, Sergeant," the navigator said, indicating a chair at the table beside Howard. Steve saw that Howard had already been served his breakfast, but hadn't eaten much of it.

Steve sat down. The old RAAF officer went to the map.

"Here we are, in Port Moresby," the RAAF officer said, pointing. "And here's where you're going.

"Buka is an island approximately thirty miles long and no greater than five or six miles wide. It is the northernmost island in the Solomons chain, just north of Bougainville, which is much larger. Where you are going, here, is 146 nautical miles from the Japanese base at Rabaul on New Britain. There is a Japanese fighter base on Buka, another on Bougainville, and of course there are fighters based at Rabaul, along with bombers, seaplanes, and other larger aircraft. From his base, Sub-Lieutenant Reeves has in the past been able to advise us of Japanese aerial movements as they have occurred. These reports have obviously been of great value both tactically and for planning purposes, and now that they have been interrupted, getting Reeves's station up and running again is obviously of great importance."

A heavy china plate was put in front of Steve. On it was a T-bone steak covered with three fried eggs, sunny side up. This was followed by a smaller plate with three pieces of toast and a tub of orange marmalade, and finally by a cup of tea.

I don't like tea, hate orange marmalade, and, anyway, I'm not hungry. But unless I start eating that crap, they're going to think I'm scared. I am, of course, but I can't let these Aussies see that I am. And maybe if I eat mine, Lieutenant Howard will eat his.

He unrolled a heavy paper napkin, took stainless-steel cutlery from it, and sawed off a piece of the steak and dipped it in the yolk of one of the eggs.

When he looked up again, he saw the RAAF officer was waiting for him to give him his attention again.

"On leaving Port Moresby, the Hudson will climb to maximum altitude, which we estimate will be about twenty thousand feet, and will maintain this altitude, passing to the west of Kiriwina Island, until it nears Buka itself. There is nothing in the Solomon Sea, except, of course, the to-be-expected Japanese Navy vessels, and possibly some Japanese naval reconnaissance aircraft. The thinking is that at high altitude our chances of being spotted—or, if spotted, identified—by Japanese surface vessels will be minimal. Further, we expect that if Japanese reconnaissance aircraft are encountered, they will be at ten thousand feet or so, and will be directing their attention downward. And again, the chances of detection are minimal. Finally, if we *are* spotted by Japanese reconnaissance aircraft, the odds are they will be seaplanes or amphibians, which will have neither the speed nor the agility to pursue the Lockheed. In the worst-case scenario, detection and/or interception by Japanese fighter aircraft, we have the twin .303 Brownings on the Lockheed to protect ourselves. Are you following me, Son?"

"Protect ourselves"? Bullshit! You're not going.

"Yes, Sir."

"As I say, I think that on the way in, our chances of detection are minimal."

"Yes, Sir."

The navigator replaced the map of the whole area with a map of Buka itself. This one was drawn on white-coated cardboard.

"You've seen the photographs, I understand, of Sub-Lieutenant Reeves, and the message he cut out in the grass?"

"Yes, Sir."

"They were taken here," the RAAF officer said, pointing. "There is a natural field, a plateau, so to the speak, in the hills. It is at 2,100 feet above sea level. It is approximately twelve hundred feet long and, at its widest, about seven hundred feet wide, narrowing to about five hundred feet near this end."

Jesus Christ! We're going to wind up in the fucking trees!

"Once the Lockheed nears the target area, it will make a rapid descent to 3,500 feet and approach the drop zone from the north. From the time the descent begins, of course, the chance of detection increases. We believe, however, that it will not be possible for the Japanese to launch fighter aircraft in time to interfere with the drop."

"What happens afterward?" Steve blurted.

"Well, you'll be gone, won't you?" the RAAF officer said.

"We'll hide in the clouds, Sergeant Koffler," Flight Sergeant Keyes said. "With a little luck, we'll have some at ten to fifteen thousand. Once we're in them, finding us will require a bit of luck on the part of the Nip."

"You will exit the aircraft at 3,300 feet, and the aircraft will have established an indicated airspeed of ninety miles per hour. If there are the expected prevailing winds, that will produce a speed over the ground of approximately seventy-five to eighty-five miles per hour."

"You can't get any lower than that? Thirty-three hundred feet will be twelve hundred feet over the drop zone. You can get yourself blown a long way if you jump at twelve hundred feet," Steve said.

"I'll put you in at any altitude you want," the pilot said.

"Eight hundred feet," Steve said.

"Done."

"Will there be enough time, if you jump at eight hundred feet, to activate your reserve parachute?" the RAAF asked.

"No," Steve said. "But I don't want us to get blown into the trees. We won't take the reserve."

The RAAF officer looked at him with his eyebrows raised for a moment.

"Is that all right with you, Lieutenant Howard?"

"Steve's the expert," Howard replied. "Whatever he says."

"Well," the RAAF officer said, after a moment's thought, "unless there are any other questions, I think that wraps it up."

Steve looked down at his steak and eggs.

He was suddenly ravenously hungry.

"Can I finish my breakfast?" he asked.

"Yes, certainly," the RAAF officer said.

(THREE)

BUKA ISLAND
0725 HOURS 8 JUNE 1942

The pitch of the Lockheed's two Pratt & Whitney 1,050-horsepower Twin Wasp radial engines suddenly changed, bringing Sergeant Steve Koffler back to the tail section of the Hudson. He had been in the neat little bungalow he was sharing with Mrs. Koffler, the former Yeo-man Daphne Farnsworth, in postwar Melbourne, Australia.

He'd seen such a bungalow, a whole section of them, on curving little streets on a hill. From the top of the hill you could see the water in Port Phillip Bay. On the way from Port Moresby, he had picked the exact house and furnished it, paying a lot of attention to the bedroom and the bathroom. In the final version of the bathroom, there was a shower—not just a tub with a shower head and a curtain, but a *pure* shower, with a door with frosty glass, so you could see somebody taking a shower inside.

When the sound of the engines changed, slowed down, he had just come home from work. He didn't know exactly what kind of job he had, but it had something to do with importing things from the States to Australia, and it was a pretty good job. He wasn't rich, but there was enough money for the bungalow and a car, and the steaks and stuff he'd brought home from the grocery store. Daphne wasn't in the kitchen or the living room. When he looked in the bedroom he heard the sound of the shower, so he stuck his head in the bathroom, and just stood there *admiring*, just that, *admiring*, nothing dirty or anything. Daphne was just standing there on the other side of the frosty glass, and she was letting the shower hit her on the face and a little lower.

Then he went to the shower and opened it just a crack and said, "I'm home, honey. I got some steaks."

And she covered her bosom and down below with her hands, be-cause she was modest, even if they were married and had done it several hundred times, not just three the way they really had.

And Daphne smiled and said, "Steaks are fine, but I'm really not hungry right now. Don't you need a shower?"

And he knew what she meant. He put the steaks down and started to get undressed so he could get in the shower with her; and then the fucking engines changed pitch, the way they do when the pilot is slowing it down and lining it up with the drop zone. And he was back in the rear of the Lockheed, wearing an oxygen mask and fifty pounds of sheepskin jackets and pants and boots and hat and still freezing his ass.

He felt like crying.

He pushed himself to his feet so he could look out the window, and at that moment the Lockheed began a steep, descending turn to the left. He slipped and fell against one of the aluminum fuselage ribs, and pulled the oxygen tube loose from the bottle.

He had a hell of a time trying to plug the damned thing in again, with the heavy gloves on, holding his breath until he did; Sergeant Keyes had told him he would lose consciousness in ninety seconds without oxygen.

He took several deep breaths when he had it back on, and then tried to look out the window again. All he could see was clouds and far below, water.

The Flight Sergeant navigator came back, carefully making his way past the bomb bay. He was wearing a walk-around oxygen bottle. When he got close to Steve, he pulled it away from his face.

"You all right?"

Steve decided if the Flight Sergeant could take his mask off, he could too.

"Fine."

"We're over Buka, making our descent."

Steve nodded.

"It won't be long now. You'd better 'chute up."

Steve looked around until he saw the parachutes, then made his way to them. Lieutenant Howard came up; and following Steve's lead, he started to take off his sheepskin flying clothes.

It was still so cold that Steve started to shiver as, with difficulty, he worked into the harness. The Flight Sergeant gave the straps a couple of good jerks, drawing them tight around his legs.

If they weren't tight, they slapped and burned the shit out of your legs when the canopy opened, and Steve had heard stories of what happened to guys who got their balls between the harness strap and their legs when the canopy opened.

If the straps were tight enough, they were too tight, and your legs started to go to sleep, like now.

Steve motioned for Lieutenant Howard to stand with his hands holding on to the fuselage frame above him, and then he checked Howard's harness, tugging the straps very tight.

He felt very sorry for Howard. Making your first jump was bad enough. Steve clearly remembered his. But when that had happened, he had had a lot of training, and a reserve parachute, and there had been medics on the ground in case something went wrong.

Lieutenant Howard must be scared shitless. Poor bastard.

It seemed like it took forever to make the descent. Steve remembered a Clark Gable movie where a test pilot had torn the wings off an airplane by making it dive too fast.

Then the plane started to level out. Steve looked out the window again, and all he could see was green. Trees. Not even a lousy little dirt road. He wondered how the hell the pilot knew where they were.

The moment the plane was level, the bomb-bay doors started to open, and there was a hell of a rush of air and the surprisingly loud sound of the slipstream.

Steve made his way to the bomb bay. The bombardier was on the far side of it, wearing a set of earphones. He had secured the two bundles on either side of the open bomb bay, their static lines already tied to a hole in one of the aluminum fuselage ribs.

The Flight Sergeant touched Steve's shoulder and, when Steve turned to look at him, gestured for Steve to get in position. Very carefully, Steve lowered himself to the aircraft floor, and then scooted forward so that his feet hung over the edge.

He looked over his shoulder again, and saw the Flight Sergeant giving a good jerk to the static line he had tied to a fuselage rib.

Steve looked across the open bomb bay, where Lieutenant Howard was getting into position. He smiled at him, to show that he wasn't scared.

I am, after all, a member of the elite of the elite, a Marine Paratrooper.

Howard smiled at him, and gave him a thumbs-up sign.

What he's doing, Steve realized with surprise and admiration, *is trying to make me feel good!*

There was immediate confirmation. Howard cupped his hands and shouted. Steve could hear him, even over the roar of the engines and the whistling slipstream.

"How you doing, Koffler?"

Steve cupped his hands over his mouth, and shouted back, "Semper-fucking-Fi, Lieutenant!"

Lieutenant Howard smiled and shook his head.

Steve smiled back, and then looked over his shoulder to smile at the Flight Sergeant.

The Flight Sergeant was doing something weird. He had his hands in holes in the fuselage ribs, and was hanging from them, with both of his feet in the air.

And, in the moment Steve understood what was going on, the Flight Sergeant really did it. Steve felt an irresistible force on his back.

That sonofabitch really kicked me out!

Arms flailing, face downward, Steve fell through the bomb bay. He felt the rush of air from the slipstream, and then a slight tug. He didn't hear, or sense, the pilot chute being pulled loose. Just all of a sudden, the canopy opened, and there came the shock, the sensation of being jerked upward.

He looked up and saw the other parachutes. Lieutenant Howard's canopy filled with air as he watched, and then, almost together, the canopies of the cargo chutes opened. The load in one of them began to swing wildly back and forth. The second load was hanging just about straight down. Both were going to land on the field.

Steve looked down between his legs. He had three or four seconds to realize that he was going into the fucking trees, and to realize that there was not one fucking thing he could do about it.

"Oh, shit!" he said.

He pulled his elbows against his side and covered his face with his hands and waited to hit.

There was a brief sensation of his feet touching something, and then of passing through something, and then something was lashing against his legs and body and the hands he had against his face. And then he felt another jerk, even harder than the opening shock, and he stopped.

He opened his eyes. Everything was fuzzy at first, but then came into focus. It was dark, and he wondered if something had happened to his eyes, but then he saw bright spots, with rays of light coming through them, and understood that the reason it was dark was because the branches and leaves of the trees came together, forming a roof.

He was swinging gently back and forth, forty or fifty feet in the air. When he looked up, he could see the canopy, torn and collapsed, with tree branches holding it. Above the canopy, the branches of the trees had closed up again.

I've got to get the fuck out of here before the canopy starts ripping and lets me fall the rest of the way.

He started to make himself swing, by jerking his legs, with ever increasing force. Twice the canopy ripped and he felt himself falling, once about six feet. But both times other branches caught part of the canopy and stopped his fall.

Eventually he was able to reach a branch with his hand, and then, carefully, to pull himself onto a substantial limb. He straddled it, holding it tightly between his legs, pulled the safety from the quick-release, and shoved on it. The harness came free and moved upward with surprising and frightening speed, propelled by the elasticity of the branches on which the canopy was caught. One of the metal ends slashed across his forehead, hurting him like getting hit in the head with a rock. When he put his hand to it, it came away covered with blood.

He probed his face with his fingers and they all came away bloody.

"Shit!" he said softly.

After a moment his heart stopped pounding so quickly, so he moved his extremities and limbs enough to know that while he was sore all over, nothing was broken. Then he started, very carefully, to climb down the tree.

Twenty feet off the ground, he ran out of branches to stand or hang from. He wrapped his arms around the trunk, putting his fingers in ridges in the bark. They were more like ribs in the tree than bark.

Like handles! I can even wedge my toes in them!

He started to very carefully climb the rest of the way down. He had gone perhaps two feet when, at the same moment, the bark his left hand was holding and the bark his left toe was jammed into gave way.

He fell to the right, on his back. He felt himself hit something squishy and then everything went black.

Someone was slapping his face. He opened his eyes.

A man was looking at him, so close that Steve could smell garlic on his breath. He was sharp-featured and had a bushy black mustache. Steve started to try to get up.

He felt strong hands pushing him back.

"See if you can move your legs," the man ordered. Steve moved his legs. "And your arms." Steve moved his arms.

The hands that had been pushing him down now pulled him into a sitting position.

"I'm Jacob Reeves," he said. "Who are you?"

"I'm Corp—*Sergeant* Koffler, United States Marine Corps."

"*United States* Marine Corps? Well, I *will* be goddamned. A sodding American!"

"Yes, Sir," Steve said.

Steve felt a sting, and slapped at his face, and then looked at his hand. It was the largest mosquito he had ever seen, if it was a mosquito. He also became aware of a stench, something rotten.

"What smells?" he asked.

"At the moment, old boy, I'd say that's you. The jungle stinks, but not quite that much."

Oh, my God, I shit my pants! he thought in horror. And then he had another horrifying thought: *Lieutenant Howard! Where the fuck is he? Did he go into the trees, too?*

"Sir, there's somebody else. And two cargo parachutes . . ."

"We have the mattresses," Reeves said. "Your other man landed in the trees."

"Is he all right?"

"I don't know. We're still looking for him. The girls are already carrying the packages to the village. Are you all right to walk?"

"I think so," Steve said.

"Good," Reeves said. "The sodding Jap chose to send another of his sodding patrols looking for us. We're going to have to do something about that."

"You think they're going to find us?"

"*We* have to find *them*," Reeves said. "They must have seen the aircraft and the sodding parachutes, so they know there's something going on up here except some unfriendly natives."

"I don't understand, Sir."

"The Japs are now headed down the hill," Reeves explained, "to report what they saw. We have to make sure they don't make it. Otherwise, the Jap will send troops up here and keep them here until they do find us."

Steve got to his feet. He had to steady himself for a moment against a tree trunk, but then he was all right.

He slapped at another mosquito.

"What about Lieutenant Howard?" he asked.

"I told my head boy he has five minutes to find him," Reeves said.

"And if he doesn't find him in five minutes, then what?"

"Then we'll have to stop looking, I'm afraid. What has to be done is stop the sodding Japs from reporting what they saw."

"Fuck you," Steve said. "I'm not going anywhere without Lieutenant Howard."

"I've explained the situation, lad," Reeves said evenly.

"So have I," Steve said. "I'm a fucking Marine. We just don't take off and leave our people behind."

"That's a very commendable philosophy, I'm sure, but—"

"I don't give a shit what you think of it," Steve interrupted. "That's the way it's going to be."

The discussion proved to be moot.

A brown-skinned, fuzzy-haired man appeared out of nowhere. He was wearing a loincloth, a bone in his nose, and a web cartridge belt around his neck, and he was carrying a British Lee-Enfield MK III .303 rifle. He announced, in understandable English, "We have the other bloke, Mr. Reeves. He was hanging from the trees. He has broken his arm."

At least he's alive, Steve thought. *Thank God!* Then he thought, *What's he going to think when he finds out I shit my pants? My God, I can't believe I really did that!*

A moment later, there was the sound of something moving through the muck on the forest floor. And then Lieutenant Howard appeared. His left arm was folded and strapped across his chest with his cartridge belt; his right arm was around the shoulder of a short, plump, brown-skinned, fuzzy-headed, bare-breasted woman. She was wearing what looked like a dirty towel, and carrying Howard's Thompson .45-caliber submachine gun.

"Jesus, I was worried about you," he said to Koffler.

"I'm Jacob Reeves," Reeves said.

"Lieutenant Howard, U.S. Marine Corps," Howard said.

"Cecilia," Reeves said to the bare-breasted woman, "I want you to take this gentleman to the village. You think you can do that?"

Cecilia smiled, revealing that her teeth were stained almost black.

"Of course," she said. "I think one or two of the other girls are about to help, if need be."

Christ, she sounds just like Daphne!

"Make him as comfortable as you can. Give him some of the whiskey. When we get there, we'll tend to his arm."

"You better take that tommy gun, Sergeant," Reeves said to Steve Koffler, adding to Howard, "We'll see you a bit later, then."

"Where are you going?" Howard asked.

Reeves didn't answer. He started trotting off into the jungle. Steve Koffler took the Thompson and two extra twenty-round magazines from Howard's pocket, and ran after him.

(FOUR)

Steve became aware as they moved through the forest that others were with them besides Jacob Reeves and the guy with the bone through his nose, although he had trouble getting a clear look at any of them.

They were going downhill. Although it wasn't like the sticky muck where they had landed, the ground was still wet and slippery. He had to watch his footing and to keep his eye on Reeves. His chest hurt from the exertion. There seemed to be a cloud of insects around his face, crawling into his ears and nostrils and mouth.

What seemed like hours later, they stopped. According to his watch, it was only thirty-five minutes. Steve stood there, sweat-soaked, breathing hard, looking with mingled amazement and horror at his hands and arms, which were covered with insect stings.

Reeves came up to him.

"Do you know how to use that tommy gun?"

"I fired it in boot camp," Steve said.

"In other words, you don't."

"I qualified," Steve said sharply.

"The way we're going to do this," Reeves said, "the Japs will be coming down a path this way. What I would like you to do is make sure that none of them gets past you. This will be successful only if we take all of them. If one of them gets away . . . You understand?"

Steve nodded.

"We'll have our go at them about fifty yards up the footpath," Reeves said. "It then passes just a few yards from here. You go have a look at it, and then find yourself a place. Clear?"

"OK," Steve said.

"It shouldn't take them long to get down here, so be quick," Reeves ordered.

"OK," Steve repeated. He swung the Thompson off his shoulder. When he looked up again, Reeves was nowhere in sight.

Steve made his way through the thick undergrowth until he found the path. He walked ten yards up it, and then ten yards in the other direction, and then backed off into the underbrush again and leaned against a tree.

After a moment, he allowed himself to slip to the ground. This action reminded him that his shorts, and now his trouser legs, were full of shit.

He started to think about his and Daphne's bungalow in postwar Melbourne again.

Shit, if I do that, I'm liable to doze off and get my fucking throat cut!

All he could hear was the buzzing of the insects.

And then there was noise.

He worked the action of the Thompson and then looked down inside at the shiny brass cartridge. When he pulled the trigger, the cartridge would be stripped from the magazine by the bolt, driven into the chamber, and fired. Then, so long as he held the trigger and the magazine held cartridges, the bolt would be driven backward by recoil, hit a spring, and then fly forward again, stripping another cartridge from the magazine.

He heard something on the trail.

What the fuck is that? It can't be a Jap. If it was a Jap, Reeves and the others would have been shooting by now.

But, curious, he slowly pulled himself to his feet.

It was a Jap. He was wearing a silly little brimmed cap on his head; and he was carrying a rifle slung over his shoulder that looked much too big for him. He was coming down the trail as if he were taking a walk through the fucking woods.

Shit!

The one thing he had learned at Parris Island was that you couldn't hit a fucking thing with a Thompson the way Alan Ladd shot one in the movies, from the hip. You had to put it to your shoulder like a rifle, get a sight picture, and just *caress* the trigger.

He did so.

Nothing happened. He really pulled hard on the trigger. Nothing happened.

The safety! The fucking safety!

He snapped it off, pulled on the trigger, and the Thompson jumped in his hands.

The Jap dropped right there.

There was no other sound for a moment, and that too was scary.

And then there was fire. Different weapons. A burp-burp noise, probably from that funny-looking little submachine gun Reeves had; and booming cracks like from a Springfield, and sharper cracks. Probably from the Japs' rifles.

Now he could see figures moving through the trees. Not well. Not enough to tell if they were Reeves's Fuzzy-Wuzzies, or whatever the fuck they were, or Japs.

Jesus Christ!

There's a Jap!

The Thompson burped again and suddenly stopped.

Oh, shit! Twenty rounds already?

He slammed another magazine in and saw another Jap and fired again, and seemed to be missing.

Another figure appeared.

One of the fucking Fuzzy-Wuzzies.

And then Jacob Reeves.

"I think that's all of them," Reeves said. "We counted. There were eight. They usually run eight-man patrols."

Steve came out of the underbrush onto the trail.

"You all right, son?" Reeves asked.

"I'm all right," Steve said.

There was a body on the trail. Steve walked up to look at it. It was the first one he'd shot.

He looked at the face of the first man he had killed.

The first man he had killed looked back at him with terror in his eyes.

"This one's still alive!" Steve said.

"We can't have that, I'm afraid," Reeves said, walking up.

Steve pointed the Thompson muzzle at the Jap's forehead and pulled the trigger.

I already shit my pants and now I think I'm going to throw up.

The village looked like something out of *National Geographic* magazine. It was much larger, too, than Steve had expected, although when he thought about that, he couldn't understand why he thought it would be any particular size at all.

Brown-skinned, flat-nosed people watched as he marched after Reeves into the village. Some of them had teeth that looked like they had been dyed blue and then filed to a point. Most of the women weren't going around in nothing but dirty towels with their boobs hanging out, like Cecilia. They were wearing dirty cotton skirts and loose blouses, some of which opened in the front to expose breasts that were anything but lust inciting.

There were chickens running loose, and pigs with one leg tied to a stake. There were fires burning. And he saw women beating something with a rock against another rock.

A clear stream, about five feet wide and two feet deep, meandered through the center of the collection of grass-walled huts.

"I'll go see about your lieutenant's arm," Reeves said.

"What can you do about it?" Steve asked.

"Set it, of course," Reeves said.

"Can you do that? I mean, really do it right?"

"I'm not a sodding doctor, if that's what you mean," Reeves snapped.

"No offense," Steve said lamely.

"I'll have them put up a hut for you, while you're having your bath," Jacob Reeves said after a moment. "Just leave your clothing there. The girls will take care of it for you. And I'll send you down a shirt and some shorts to wear."

He pointed to a muddy area by the stream, at the end of the village. It was apparently the community bath and wash house.

I think he actually expects me to just take off my clothes in front of everybody and sit in that stream and take a bath.

"That water's safe for bathing," Reeves said, as if reading Steve's mind. "But don't drink it. I've been here since Christ was a babe, and I still haven't built up an immunity to the sodding water. There's boiled water and beer."

Steve looked at him in surprise.

"Well, it's not really beer," Reeves admitted. "We make it out of rice and coconuts. But it's not all that bad."

Reeves walked off. And after a moment, Steve Koffler walked to the edge of the stream and started to take his clothing off.

(FIVE)

Eyes Only—The Secretary of the Navy

DUPLICATION FORBIDDEN
ORIGINAL TO BE DESTROYED AFTER ENCRYPTION AND TRANSMITTAL
TO SECNAVY

Melbourne, Australia
Monday, 8 June 1942

Dear Frank:

This will deal with the Battle of Midway, from MacArthur's perception of it here, and the implications of it for the conduct of the war, short- and long-term, as he sees them.

But before I get into that: Willoughby somehow found out, I have no idea how, that I am on the Albatross list; and he promptly ran to tell MacA. MacA., of course, knew; like everyone else on it, he had been furnished with the list itself. I am quite sure that MacA. brings Willoughby in on anything that would remotely interest him whenever he (MacA.) receives Magic intelligence. But Willoughby is not on the Albatross list himself, and as a matter of personal prestige (he is, after all, a major general and MacA.'s G-2), he found this grossly humiliating even before he learned that lowly Captain Pickering was on it.

The result of this is that MacA. fired off a cable demanding that Willoughby be added to the Albatross list. Then he made a point of mentioning to me that he understands how critical it is that Magic not be compromised, and the necessity for keeping the Albatross list as short as possible. The implication I took was that he really would be happier if Willoughby were kept off the list and rather hoped that I would pass this on to you.

I'm not sure what his motive is (motives are), but I don't

think they have anything to do with making sure Magic isn't compromised. Quite possibly, MacA. regards the Albatross list as
a prerogative of the emperor, not to be shared with the lesser
nobility. He may also be hoping that if you ("Those bastards in
Washington") refuse to add Willoughby to the Albatross list,
it will ensure that Willoughby hates you as much as the emperor
himself does.

Personally, I <u>hope</u> that Willoughby is added to the list. It
would certainly improve my relationship with him and make my
life here in the palace a little easier. But that's <u>not</u> a recommendation. Magic is so important that I refuse to recommend
anything that might pose any risk whatever that would compro-
mise it.

Tangentially, I do <u>not</u> receive copies of Magic messages
reaching here. I don't have any place to store them, for one
thing. I don't even have an office, much less a secretary with
the appropriate security clearances to log classified material in and out. There are four people here (in addition to
MacA. and me) on the Albatross list. They are all Army Signal
Corps people: the Chief of Cryptographic Services, a captain;
and two cryptographers, both sergeants. There is also a Lieutenant Hon, a Korean (U.S. citizen, MIT '38) who speaks fluent
Japanese. He is often able to make subtle changes in interpretation of the translations made at Pearl.

When a Magic comes in, the captain calls me. I go to the
crypto room and read it there. Lieutenant Hon hand-carries the
Magics to MacA., together with his interpretation of any portion of them that differs from what we get from Pearl. MacA.
stops whatever else he is doing and reads them—or, I should
say, commits them to his really incredible memory. The paper
itself is then returned to the crypto safe. Only twice to my
knowledge has MacA. ever sent for one of them to look at again.

On the subject of the Albatross/Magic list: I would like
permission to make Major Ed Banning privy to Magic messages. He
has managed to establish himself with the Australian Coastwatchers. He speaks Japanese, and has, I think, an insight into
the way the Japanese military think. I have the feeling that

with input both from the Australians and the Magic intercepts,
he could come up with analyses that might elude other people—
of whom I'm certainly one. He already knows a good deal about
Albatross/Magic, and I can't see where my giving him access to
the intercepts themselves increases the risk of compromising
Magic much—if at all. I would appreciate a radio reply to this:
"yes" or "no" would suffice.

Finally, turning to the Battle of Midway: We had been getting some rather strong indications of the Japanese intentions
throughout May—not only from Magic—and MacA. had decided that
it was the Japanese plan to attack Midway, as a steppingstone to
Hawaii.

I asked MacA. what he thought the American reaction to the
loss of Hawaii would be. He said that it might wake the American
people up to the idea that basic American interests are in the
Pacific, not in Europe; but that if it fell, which he couldn't
imagine, American influence in the Pacific would be lost in our
lifetimes, perhaps forever. Then he added that a year ago he
would have been unable to accept the thought that the American
people would stand for the reinforcement of England, knowing
that it would mean the loss of the Philippines.

MacA. expected that Admiral Yamamoto, for whom he has great
professional admiration, would launch either a two-pronged
attack, with one element attacking Midway, or a diversionary
feint coinciding with an attack on Midway. He would not have
been surprised if there had been a second attack (or a feint) at
Port Moresby.

MacA. reasoned that the Japanese loss of the carrier *Shoho*
and the turning of the Port Moresby invasion force in early May
had been the first time we'd actually been able to give the Japanese a bloody nose. For the first time, they had been kept from
doing what they had started out to do. Their admirals had lost
face. But now they'd had a month to regroup, lick their wounds,
and prepare to strike again. They could regain face by taking
Port Moresby, and that would have put their Isolate Australia
plan back on track.

He was surprised when the Magic messages began to suggest an

TOP SECRET

attack on the Aleutians. He grilled me at length about the Aleutians, whether there was something there he hadn't heard about. He simply cannot believe the Japanese want to invade Alaska. What could they get out of Alaska that would be worth the logistical cost of landing there? MacA. asks. Their supply lines would not only be painfully long, but would be set up like a shooting gallery for interdiction from the United States and Canada.

He therefore concluded that the attack on the Aleutians, which came on June 3, was a feint intended to draw our Naval forces off; that the Japs believe that the Americans would place a greater emotional value on the Aleutians than was the case; and that we would rise to the bait. MacA. predicted this would be a miscalculation on their part.

"Nimitz is no fool," he said. "He doesn't care about the Aleutians."

Events, of course, proved him right. We learned from Magic intercepts that Admiral Nagumo (and thus the entire Japanese fleet) was very surprised on 4 June, when his reconnaissance aircraft reported seeing a large American Naval force to the northeast of Midway.

We later learned—from Magic!—that these were the aircraft carriers <u>Yorktown, Enterprise,</u> and <u>Hornet,</u> under Admirals Spruance and Fletcher. We were getting our information about the movements of our own fleet from Japanese intercepts, via Hawaii, before we were getting reports from the Navy. MacA. is convinced, in the absence of any other reason to the contrary, that the Navy believes that the war in the Pacific is a Navy war, and consequently they have no obligation to tell him what's happening.

I have a recommendation here: I strongly recommend that you direct Nimitz (or have King direct Nimitz) to assign one commander or captain the sole duty of keeping MacA. posted on what's going on while it's happening—not just when the Navy finds it convenient to tell him.

We learned (again via Magic intercepts) that the Japanese came under attack by torpedo bombers at 0930 4 June. The air-

TOP SECRET

craft carriers Hiryu, Kaga, Soryu, and Akagi all reported to
Yamamoto that they were relatively unhurt, and that the American losses were severe. Then came a report from Hiryu, saying
she had been severely damaged by American dive bombers. Nothing was intercepted from any of the others.

Then there were Magic intercepts of Yamamoto's orders to
the fleet to withdraw.

And then, many hours later, we heard from the Navy, and
learned that the carriers Soryu, Kaga, and Akagi had been sunk,
and that we had lost the carrier Yorktown. It was a day later
that we learned that the Hiryu was sunk that next morning, and
about the terrible losses and incredible courage of the Navy
torpedo bomber pilots who had attacked the Japanese carriers.
And that Marine Fighter Squadron VMF-211, land-based on Midway, had lost fifteen of its twenty-five pilots; in effect it
had been wiped out.

The Japanese seem to have suffered more than just their
first beating; it was also a very bad mauling. And MacA. sent
what I thought were rather touching messages to Nimitz, Spruance, and Fletcher, expressing his admiration and congratulations.

And today he sent a long cable to Marshall, asking permission to attack New Britain and New Ireland (in other words, to
take out the Japanese base at Rabaul) with the U.S. 32nd and
41st Divisions and the Australian 7th Division. To do so would
mean that the Navy would have to provide him both with vessels
capable of making and supporting an amphibious invasion, and
with aircraft carriers. I don't think he really expects the
Navy to give him what he asks for. But not to ask for the operation—indeed fight for it, and the necessary support for it from
the Navy—would be tantamount to giving in to the notion that
the Navy owns the war over here.

I won't presume to suggest who is right, but I frankly think
it is a tragedy that the Army and the Navy should be at each
other's throats like this.

I mentioned earlier on in this report that Banning has developed a good relationship with the Australian Coastwatch-

ers. Early this morning, the RAAF parachuted two Marines, a
lieutenant and a sergeant, and a replacement radio, onto Buka
Island, north of Bougainville, where the Coastwatcher's radio
had gone out. Loss of reports from the observation post was so
critical that great risks to get it up and running again were
considered justified. The only qualified (radio operator,
parachutist) Marine was eighteen years old. And that is all he
can do. He can't tell one Japanese aircraft from another, or a
destroyer from a battleship. So one of Banning's lieutenants,
Joe Howard, a Mustang, who had taught aircraft/ship recognition, volunteered to parachute in, too, although he had never
jumped before. Banning confided to me that he thought he had one
chance in four or five of making a successful landing.

The Lockheed Hudson that was to drop them was never heard
from. We took the worst-possible-case scenario, and decided it
had been shot down by Japanese fighters on the way in and that
everyone was lost. Banning immediately asked for volunteers to
try it again. All of his men volunteered.

As I was writing this, Banning came in with the news that Buka
was back on the air. The Lockheed had been shot down on the way
home. With contact reestablished, the RAN people here had routinely asked for "traffic." This is what they got, verbatim:
"Please pass Ensign Barbara Cotter, USNR, and Yeoman Daphne
Farnsworth, RAN. We love you and hope to see you soon. Joe and
Steve."

Those boys obviously think we're going to win the war.
Maybe, Frank, if we can get the admirals and the generals to
stop acting like adolescents, we can.

Respectfully,
Fleming Pickering, Captain USNR

(SIX)

Lieutenant Hon Song Do, Signal Corps, Army of the United States, was sitting in one of the chairs lining the hotel corridor when Captain Fleming Pickering, USNR, stepped off the elevator. Captain Pickering had just finished dining, *en famille,* with the Commander-in-Chief and Mrs. Douglas MacArthur. Over cognac afterward, General MacArthur had talked at some length about the German campaign in Russia. The dissertation had again impressed Captain Pickering with the incredible scope of MacArthur's mind; and the four snifters of Remy Martin had left him feeling just a little bit tight.

"Well, hello, Lieutenant," Pickering said when he saw Lieutenant Hon. Hon sometimes made him feel slightly ill at ease. For one thing, he didn't know what to call him. Something in his mind told him that "Hon" was, in the American sense, his last name. He could not, in other words, do what he had long ago learned how to do with other junior officers; he couldn't put him at ease by calling him by his first name, or even better, by his nickname. He simply didn't know what it was.

And Lieutenant Hon was not what ordinarily came to Pickering's mind when "Asian-American" or "Korean-American" was mentioned. For one thing, he was a very large man, nearly as tall and heavy as Pickering; and for another, he had a deep voice with a thick Boston accent. And on top of this, he was what Pickering thought of as an egghead. He was a theoretical mathematician. He had been commissioned as a mathematician, and he'd originally been assigned to Signal Intelligence as a mathematician. Only afterward had the Army learned that he was a Japanese linguist.

"Good evening, Sir," Lieutenant Hon said, rising to his feet. "I have a rather interesting decrypt for you, Sir."

"Why didn't you bring it downstairs?"

"I didn't think it was quite important enough for me to have to intrude on the Commander-in-Chief's dinner."

Pickering looked at him. There was a smile in Lieutenant Hon's eyes.

"Well, come on in, and I'll buy you a drink," Pickering said, then added, "Lieutenant, I think I know you well enough to call you by your first name."

"I wouldn't do that, Sir," Lieutenant Hon said dryly. "Do' doesn't lend itself to English as a first name. Why don't you call me Pluto?"

"Pluto?"

"Yes, Sir. That's what I've been called for years. After Mickey Mouse's friend, the dog with the sad face?"

"OK," Pickering chuckled. "Pluto it is."

He snapped the lights on.

"What will you have to drink, Pluto?"

"Is there any of that Old Grouse Scotch, Sir?"

"Should be several bottles of it. Why don't you give me the decrypt and make us both one? I think there's a can of peanuts in the drawer under the bar, too. Why don't you open that?"

"Thank you, Sir," Pluto Hon said, and handed Pickering a sealed manila envelope.

Pickering tore it open. Inside was a TOP SECRET cover sheet, and below that a sheet of typewriter paper.

```
NOT LOGGED
ONE COPY ONLY
DUPLICATION FORBIDDEN
FOLLOWING IS DECRYPTION OF MSG 234545 RECEIVED 061742
OFFICE SECNAVY WASHDC 061642 1300 GREENWICH
COMMANDER-IN-CHIEF SOUTHWEST PACIFIC
EYES ONLY CAPTAIN FLEMING PICKERING USNR
REF YOUR 8 JUNE 1942 REPORT
SECNAVY REPLIES QUOTE
PART ONE YES
PART TWO YOUR FRIEND BEING INVITED HAWAIIAN PARTY
PART THREE BEST PERSONAL REGARDS SIGNATURE FRANK
END QUOTE
HAUGHTON CAPT USN ADMIN OFF TO SECNAVY
```

TOP SECRET

Pickering walked to the bar. Pluto was just about finished making the drinks.

"A little cryptic, even decrypted, isn't it?" he said to Pluto, taking the extended drink.

Pluto chuckled. "I don't think it's likely, but even if the Japs have broken the Blue Code, their analysts are going to have a hell of a time making anything out of that."

"Would you care to guess, Pluto?"

"There was a message from the JCS adding General Willoughby to the Albatross list. Am I getting warm?" Banning smiled and nodded. "I have no idea what 'Yes' means," Pluto Hon said.

"I asked for permission to give Major Banning access to Magic intercepts," Pickering said. "What I decide to show him. I didn't ask that he be put on the Albatross list."

Pluto nodded. "Are you going to want that logged, Sir?"

Pickering shook his head, then took out his cigarette lighter and burned the sheet of typewriter paper, holding it over a wastebasket until it was consumed.

Lieutenant Pluto Hon refused a second drink and left. Pickering went to bed.

In the morning, at breakfast, Major General Willoughby walked over to Captain Pickering's table in the Menzies Hotel dining room and sat down with him. A large smile was on his face.

"Have you had a chance to read the overnight Magics yet, Pickering?"

"No, Sir," Captain Pickering said.

"You should have a look. Very interesting."

General Willoughby looked very pleased with himself.

(SEVEN)

THE ELMS
DANDENONG, VICTORIA, AUSTRALIA
1825 HOURS 1 JULY 1942

It was windy; and there was a cold and unpleasant rain. As Captain Fleming Pickering drove the drop-head Jaguar coupe under the arch of winter-denuded elms toward the house, he was thinking unkind thoughts about the British.

As cold as it gets in England, and as much as this car must have cost, it would seem reasonable to expect that the windshield wipers would work, and the heater, and that the goddamned top wouldn't leak.

As he neared the house and saw Banning's Studebaker, his mind turned to unkind thoughts about Major Ed Banning, USMC.

He didn't know what he was doing here, except that he would be meeting "a friend" and somebody else Banning wanted to introduce him to. Banning, on the telephone, acted as if he was sure the line was tapped by the Japanese, even if all he was discussing was goddamned dinner. No details. Just cryptic euphemisms.

And I will bet ten dollars to a doughnut that both "a friend" and "somebody else" are going to be people I would rather not see.

He got out of the car and ran through the drizzle up onto the porch.

Mrs. Cavendish answered his ring with a warm smile.

"Oh, good evening, Captain," she said. "How are you tonight?"

"Wet and miserable, Mrs. Cavendish, how about you?"

She laughed. "A little nip will fix you right up," she said. "The other gentlemen are in the library."

I had no right to snap at her, and no reason to be annoyed with Banning. For all I know the goddamned phone is tapped. Maybe by Willoughby. And it is absurd to fault an intelligence officer for having a closed mouth. You are acting like a curmudgeonly old man. Or perhaps a younger man, suffering from sexual deprivation.

The latter thought, he realized, had been triggered by the perversity of his recent erotic dreams. He had had four of them over not too many more nights than that. Only one had involved the female he was joined with in holy matrimony. A second had involved a complete stranger who had, in his dream, exposed her breasts to him in a Menzies Hotel elevator, then made her desires known with a lewd wink. The other two had been nearly identical: Ellen Feller had stood at the side of his bed, undressed slowly, and then mounted him.

"I didn't mean to snap at you, Mrs. Cavendish," Pickering said.

"I didn't know that you had," she said, smiling, as she took his coat.

He walked down the corridor to the library and pushed the door open.

"I will be damned," he said, smiling. It really was a friend. "How are you, Jake?"

Major Jake Dillon, USMC, crossed the room to him, smiling, shook his hand, and then hugged him.

"You should be ashamed of yourself," Dillon said. "Patricia's sitting at home knitting scarfs and gloves for you, imagining you living in some leaking tent; and here you are, living like the landed gentry—even including a Jaguar."

"If I detect a broad suggestion of jealousy, I'm glad," Pickering said. "I see you're already into my booze."

"Banning took care of that, after I told him how dry it was all the way from the States to Wellington, New Zealand."

"That was probably good for you. I'm sure you hadn't been sober that long in years. You came with the 1st Division?" Headquarters, 1st Marine Division, and the entire 5th Marines had debarked at Wellington, New Zealand, on June 14, 1942.

"All the way. And it was a *very* long way. The ship was *not* the *Pacific Princess.* The cuisine and accommodations left a good deal to be desired."

"What are you doing here? And where did you meet Ed Banning?"

"Here. Tonight. He's a friend of Colonel Goettge."

"Who's Colonel Goettge?"

"I am, Sir," a voice said, and Pickering turned. Banning and a tall, muscular Marine colonel had come into the library from the kitchen. "I suspect that I may be imposing."

"Nonsense," Pickering said, crossing to him and offering his hand. "Any friend of Banning's, etcetera etcetera."

"Very kind of you, Captain," Goettge said.

"Also of Jack Stecker's," Jake Dillon said. "It was Jack's idea that I come along. He sends his regards."

"So far, Colonel," Pickering said, "that's two good guys out of three. But how did you get hung up with this character?"

"Watch it, Flem. I'll arrange to have you photographed being wetly kissed by a bare-breasted aborigine maiden, and send eight-by-ten glossies to Patricia."

"He would, too," Pickering said, laughing. "Colonel, you're in dangerous company."

"Colonel Goettge is the 1st Division G-2, Captain Pickering," Banning said. "He was sent here to gather intelligence on certain islands in the Solomons."

Pickering met Banning's eye for a moment. They both knew more about pending operations in the Solomon Islands than Colonel Goettge was supposed to know, even though he was G-2 of the 1st Marine Division.

Pickering was worried, however, about how much Goettge actually knew.

On Friday, June 19, twelve days before, Vice-Admiral Robert L. Ghormley, USN, had activated his headquarters at Auckland, New Zealand, and become Commander, South Pacific, subordinate to Admiral Nimitz at Pearl Harbor.

Pickering immediately flew down to meet him, not sure in his own mind if he was doing so in his official role as observer for Frank Knox, or as a member (if unofficial) of MacArthur's palace guard.

Once he saw Pickering's orders, Admiral Ghormley had no choice but to brief him on his concept of the war, and on his planning. But he went further than paying appropriate respect to an officer wrapped in the aura of a personal representative of the Secretary of the Navy required.

There were several reasons for this. For one, they immediately liked each other. Over lunch, Ghormley drew out of Pickering the story of how he had worked his way up from apprentice seaman in the deck department to his "Any Ocean, Any Tonnage" master's ticket. And it quickly became clear that the two of them were not an admiral and a civilian in a captain's uniform, but that they were two men who had known the responsibility of the bridge in a storm.

And, too, Ghormley had come to the South Pacific almost directly from London. Thus he had not spent enough time in either Washington or Pearl Harbor to become infected with the parochial virus that caused others of his rank to feel that the war in the Pacific had to be fought and won by the Navy alone—perhaps as the only way to overcome the shame of Pearl Harbor.

And to Pickering's pleased surprise, Ghormley had independently come up with a strategy that was very much like MacArthur's. He saw the Japanese base at Rabaul on New Britain as a likely and logical target for the immediate future. He thought it would be a very reasonable expenditure of assets to assault New Britain amphibiously with the 1st Marine Division, and, once the beachhead was secure, to turn the battle over to the Army's 32nd and 41st Infantry Divisions.

Pickering then informed Admiral Ghormley that he was privy to General MacArthur's thinking, and that the two of them were in essential agreement. He made this admission after briefly considering that not only was it none of Ghormley's business, but that telling Ghormley such things would enrage both Frank Knox and Douglas MacArthur if they learned of it, as they almost certainly would.

Which was to say, of course, that MacArthur and Ghormley both disagreed with Admiral Ernest King's proposed plans for immediate action: These called for a Navy attack under Admiral Nimitz on both the Santa Cruz and Solomon Islands, while MacArthur launched a diversionary attack on the East Indies.

When Pickering returned to Brisbane, he dropped the other shoe (after one of MacArthur's private dinners) and informed MacArthur of Ghormley's ideas for the most efficient prosecution of the war. Lengthy "independent" cables then went from Ghormley (to Admiral King, Chief of Naval Operations) and MacArthur (to General Marshall, Chief of Staff of the Army). These strenuously urged an attack to retake Rabaul as the first major counterattack of the war.

General Marshall cabled MacArthur that he fully agreed Rabaul should be the first target, and that he would make the case for that before the Joint Chiefs of Staff.

Admiral King, however, not only flatly disagreed with that, but was so sure that his position would prevail when the final decision was made by the Joint Chiefs of Staff that he "unofficially" alerted Nimitz, who in turn "unofficially" alerted Ghormley, that a Navy force, with or without MacArthur's support, would attack the Solomons as soon as possible— probably within a month or six weeks.

"Presuming" that Nimitz certainly would have told MacArthur of the Navy's plans, Ghormley discussed (by memoranda, hand-carried by officer courier) Nimitz's alert with MacArthur. This, of course, resulted in more emphatic cables from MacArthur to Marshall. It was still possible that the Joint Chiefs of Staff would decide against King and in favor of striking at Rabaul first.

The decision of the Joint Chiefs of Staff was not yet made, although it was clear that it would have to be made in the next few days.

Pickering had briefed Banning on his meetings with Ghormley and all that had happened after that. He now wondered if that had been a serious mistake. Had Banning told his old friend, Goettge, the First Division G-2, any—or all—of what Pickering had told him in confidence?

"Captain Pickering," Colonel Goettge said, "it's been my experience that when you have something delicate to say, you almost always get yourself in deeper trouble when you pussyfoot around it."

"Mine, too," Pickering replied. "What's on your mind?"

"I can only hope this won't leave this room—"

"You're pussyfooting," Pickering interrupted.

"The word in the 1st Division is that General MacArthur's attitude toward the Navy generally, and the Marine Corps in particular, is 'Fuck you,'" Goettge said.

"That's unfortunate," Pickering said.

"There's a story going around that he wouldn't give the 4th Marines a Presidential Unit Citation in the Philippines because 'the Marines already get enough publicity,'" Goettge said.

"I'm afraid that's true," Pickering said. "But I'm also sure that he made that decision under a hell of a strain, and that he now regrets it. MacArthur is a very complex character."

"General Vandergrift thinks we will invade the Solomons. Or at least two of the Solomon Islands, Tulagi and Guadalcanal," Goettge said.

"Where did he get that?" Pickering said.

"I don't know, Sir."

Pickering looked at Banning. Banning just perceptibly shook his head, meaning *I didn't tell him.*

I should have known that, Pickering thought. *Why the hell did I question Banning's integrity?*

"My job, therefore," Colonel Goettge said, "is to gather as much intelligence about Guadalcanal and Tulagi as I possibly can. Phrased as delicately as I can, there is some doubt in General Vandergrift's mind—and in mine—that, without a friend in court, so to speak, I won't be able to get much from General Willoughby when I go to see him tomorrow."

My God, Pickering thought, sad and disgusted, *has it gone that far?*

"And you think I could be your 'friend at court'?"

"Yes, Sir, that's about it."

"It's all over Washington, Flem," Jake Dillon said, "that you and Dugout Dough have become asshole buddies."

A wave of rage swept through Fleming Pickering. It was a long moment before he trusted himself to speak.

"Jake, old friends or not," he said finally, calmly, "if you ever refer to MacArthur in those terms again, I'll bring you up on charges myself." But then his tone turned furious as anger overwhelmed him: "God-*damn* you, you ignorant sonofabitch! General Willoughby—who is a fine officer despite the contempt in which you, Goettge, and others seem to hold him—told me that on Bataan, MacArthur was often so close to the lines that there was genuine concern that he would be captured by Japanese infantry patrols. And on Corregidor they couldn't get him to go into the goddamned tunnel when the Japs were shelling! Who the *fuck* do you think *you* are to call *him* 'Dugout Doug'?"

"Sorry," Dillon said.

"You fucking well should be sorry!" Pickering flared. "Stick to being a goddamned press agent, you miserable pimple on a Marine's ass, and keep your fucking mouth shut when you don't know what the fuck you're talking about!"

There was silence in the room.

Pickering looked at them, the rage finally subsiding. Jake Dillon looked crushed. Colonel Goettge looked painfully uncomfortable. Ed Banning was . . .

The sonofabitch is smiling!

"You are amused, Major Banning?" Pickering asked icily.

"Sir, I think Major Dillon was way out of line," Banning said. "But, Sir, I was amused. I was thinking, 'You can take the boy out of the Marines, but you can't take the Marines out of the boy.' I was thinking, Sir, that you sounded much more like a Marine corporal than like the personal representative of the Secretary of the Navy. You did that splendidly, Sir."

"Christ, Flem," Jake Dillon said. "I just didn't know . . . If I knew what you thought of him . . ."

"Jake," Pickering said. "Just shut up."

"Yes, Sir," Dillon said.

"Do something useful. Make us a drink."

"Would it be better if I just left, Sir?" Colonel Goettge asked.

"No. Of course not. I'm going to get on the phone and ask General Willoughby out here for dinner. I'm going to tell him that you're an old friend of mine. If he comes, fine. If he doesn't, at least he'll know who you are when I take you in tomorrow morning to see him."

"Sir," Banning said, "I thought it would be a good idea to put Colonel Goettge in touch with the Coastwatchers—"

"Absolutely!"

"To that end, Sir, I asked Commander Feldt—he's in town—"

"I know," Pickering interrupted.

"—and Lieutenant Donnelly to dinner."

"Good."

"He's bringing Yeoman Farnsworth with him," Banning said.

"Why?"

"It was my idea, Sir. I thought it would be nice to radio Lieutenant Howard and Sergeant Koffler that we had dinner with their girls. I asked Ensign Cotter, too."

"If General Willoughby is free to have dinner with us, Ed, I can't imagine that he would object to sharing the table with two pretty girls. God knows, there's none around the mess in the Menzies."

XIV

(ONE)

Eyes Only The Secretary of the Navy

    DUPLICATION FORBIDDEN
    ORIGINAL TO BE DESTROYED AFTER ENCRYPTION AND TRANSMITTAL
TO SECNAVY

Water Lily Cottage
Manchester Avenue
Brisbane, Australia
Tuesday, 21 July 1942

Dear Frank:

    I'm not sure if it was really necessary, but the emperor decided to move the court; and so here, after an enormous logistical effort, we are. It is (MacA.'s stated reason for the move) "1,185 miles closer to the front lines."

El Supremo's Headquarters are in a modern office building, formerly occupied by an insurance company. MacA. has a rather elegant office on the eighth floor (of nine). I am down the corridor, and was surprised to learn that General Sutherland himself assigned me my office. I would have wagered he would put me in the basement, or left me in Melbourne.

MacA. and family, and the senior officers, are living in Lennon's Hotel, which is a rambling, graceful old Victorian hostelry that reminds me of the place the Southern Pacific railroad used to operate in Yellowstone Park. This time I was assigned quarters appropriate to my rank: that is to say, sharing a two-room suite with an Army Ordnance Corps colonel. Because the Colonel is portly, mustached, and almost certainly snores, and because I wanted a place affording some privacy, and because I didn't think I should permit anyone in Supreme Headquarters to tell me to do anything, I have taken a small cottage near the (unfortunately closed for the duration) Doomben Race Track, where this is written.

It should go without saying that I think the JCS decision of 2 July to invade the Solomons was wrong. I have the somewhat nasty suspicion that it was based on Roosevelt's awe of King, and his dislike of MacA., rather than for any strategic purpose.

The night before (1 July) I had dinner with a colonel named Goettge, who is the First Marine Division G-2. There was no question in his mind how the JCS was going to decide the issue. I found that rather disturbing, as theoretically it was still under consideration. He was in with MacA.'s intelligence people, getting what they had on Tulagi and Guadalcanal when the JCS cable ordering Operation PESTILENCE came in.

He tells me—and I believe—that it is going to be one hell of a job getting the 1st Marines ready to make an amphibious landing in five weeks, including, of course, the rehearsal operation in the Fiji Islands.

Ghormley has requested that the 2nd Marines, of the 2nd Marine Division, be combat-loaded at San Diego. The 5th Marines were <u>not</u> combat-loaded, which means that they had to unload

everything onto the docks, Aotea Quay, at Wellington, sort it out, and then reload it, so that it meets the needs of an amphibious landing force. That's what they are now doing; and according to a friend of mine in the 5th Marines, it is an indescribable mess, with cans spilling out of ordinary cardboard boxes, and so on.

The problem is compounded by the dock workers, a surly socialist bunch who, I suspect, would rather see the Japs in New Zealand than work overtime or over a weekend. I'm sure that the Marines and Navy people here have been raising hell about it with port people in America, but if you could add your weight to getting something <u>done</u> about it, your effort would be worthwhile.

On the Fourth of July, we learned from Coastwatchers that the Japanese have started construction of an airfield on Guadalcanal. That's frightening. Both MacA. and Ghormley are fully aware of the implications of an air base there, but they both, separately, insist that the Guadalcanal operation should not be launched until we are prepared to do it properly. It is not pleasant to consider the ramifications of a failed amphibious invasion.

That opinion is obviously not shared by the JCS. I don't know how Ghormley took it in Auckland, but I was with MacA. when a copy of the JCS cable of 10 July ordering Ghormley to "seize Guadalcanal and Tulagi at once" reached here. He thinks, to put it kindly, it was a serious error in judgment.

It wasn't until the next day (11 July) that the other infantry regiment (the 1st Marines) and the artillery (11th) of the 1st Marine Division reached Wellington, N.Z. Now they are expected to unload, sort, and combat-load their equipment and otherwise get set for an amphibious landing in twenty days.

The same day, as you know, we learned that Imperial Japanese Headquarters has called off its plans to seize Midway, New Caledonia, and Samoa. Under those circumstances, no one here can see the need for "immediately" landing at Guadalcanal.

Last Thursday (16 July), a courier brought a copy of Ghormley's operation plan (OPPLAN 1-42). There are three phases: a

rehearsal in the Fiji Islands; the invasion of Guadalcanal and Tulagi; and the occupation of Ndeni Island in the Santa Cruz Islands. MacA.'s reaction to it was that it is as good as it could be expected to be, given the circumstances.

MacA. made B-17 aircraft available to the 1st Marine Division for reconnaissance, and they flew over both Guadalcanal and Tulagi on Friday. On Saturday we learned that the aerial photographs taken differ greatly from the maps already issued —and there is simply no time to print and issue corrected ones.

I'm going to leave here first thing in the morning for New Zealand, and from there will join the rehearsal in the Fijis. I don't know what good, if any at all, I can do anyone. But obviously I am doing no one any good here.

Respectfully,
Fleming Pickering, Captain, USNR

(TWO)

SUPREME HEADQUARTERS
SOUTHWEST PACIFIC AREA
BRISBANE, AUSTRALIA
1705 HOURS 21 JULY 1942

It was the first time Pickering had been to the Cryptology Room in Brisbane. He found it in the basement, installed in a vault that had held the important records of the evicted insurance company. There was a new security system, too, now run by military policemen wearing white puttees, pistol belts, and shiny steel helmets. The security in Melbourne had been a couple of noncoms armed with Thompson submachine guns, slouched on chairs. They had come to know Captain Fleming Pickering and had habitually waved him inside. But the MPs here not only didn't know who he was, but somewhat smugly told him that he was not on the "authorized-access list."

Finally, reluctantly, they summoned Lieutenant Pluto Hon to the steel door, and he arranged, not easily, to have Pickering passed inside.

Hon waved Pickering into a chair, and then typed Pickering's letter to Navy Secretary Frank Knox onto a machine that looked much like (and was a derivative of) a teletype machine. It produced a narrow tape, like a stock-market ticker tape, spitting it out of the left side of the machine. Hon ripped it off, and then fed the end of the tape into the cryptographic machine itself. Wheels began to whir and click, and there was the sound of keys hitting paper. Finally, out of the other end of the machine came another long strip of tape.

When that process was done, Lieutenant Hon took that strip of paper and fed it into the first machine. There was the sound of more typewriter keys, and the now-encrypted message appeared at the top of the machine, the way a teletype message would. But there were no words there, only a series of five-character blocks.

Hon gave his original letter and both strips of tape to Pickering; then, carrying the encrypted message, he left the vault for the radio room across the basement. Pickering followed him.

"Urgent," Hon said to the sergeant in charge. "For Navy Hawaii. Log it as my number"—he paused to consult the encrypted message—"six-six-oh-six."

Pickering and Hon watched as a radio operator, using a telegrapher's key, sent the message to Hawaii. A few moments later there came an acknowledgment of receipt. Then Hon took the encoded message from the radio operator and handed it to Pickering.

In a couple of minutes, Pickering thought, that will be in the hands of Ellen Feller. He wondered if her receiving a message from him triggered any erotic thoughts in her.

He followed Hon back to the Cryptology Room. Hon turned a switch, and there was the sound of a fan. Pickering dropped his letter, the two tapes, and the encrypted printout into a galvanized bucket, and then stopped and set it all afire with his cigarette lighter. He waited until it had been consumed, and then reached in the bucket and broke up the ashes with a pencil.

It wasn't that he distrusted Hon, or any of the others who encrypted his letters to the Secretary of the Navy. It was just that if he personally saw to it that all traces of it had been burned, there was no way it could wind up on Willoughby's, MacArthur's, or anyone else's desk.

"I wish I was going with you," Pluto Hon said.

Pickering was surprised. It was the first time Pluto had even suggested he was familiar with the contents of one of Pickering's messages. He was, of course—you read what you type—but the rules of the little game were that everyone pretended the cryptographer didn't know. "Why?"

"It's liable to be as dull here as it was in Melbourne," Pluto said.

"I could probably arrange to have you dropped onto some island behind Japanese lines," Pickering joked. "They're short of people, I know."

"I already asked Major Banning," Pluto replied, seriously. "He said I could go the day after you let him go. 'We also serve who sit in dark basements shuffling paper.'"

"It's more than that, Pluto, and you know it," Pickering said, and touched his shoulder.

"Good night, Sir," Lieutenant Hon said.

Pickering walked back through the basement, then up to the lobby and to the security desk, where, after duty hours, it was necessary to produce identification and sign in and out.

"There he is," a female voice said as he scrawled his name on the register.

I am losing my mind. That sounded exactly like Ellen Feller.

He straightened and turned around.

"Good evening, Captain Pickering," Ellen Feller said.

"I hope you have some influence around here, Captain," Captain David Haughton said, as he offered Pickering his hand, smiling at his surprise. "We have just been told there is absolutely no room in the inn."

"Haughton, what the hell are you doing here?" Pickering asked. He looked at Ellen Feller. "And you, Ellen?"

"I'm on my way to Admiral Ghormley in Auckland. They're servicing the plane. Ellen's for duty."

"For duty?" Pickering asked her. "What do you mean?"

"I was asked if I would be willing to come here," Ellen Feller said. "I was."

Jesus Christ, what the hell is this all about?

"The boss arranged it," Haughton said. "In one of your letters you said something about not having a secretary. So he sent you one. Yours."

"You don't seem very pleased to see me, Captain Pickering," Ellen said.

"Don't be silly. Of course I am," Pickering said.

"Your billeting people are being difficult," Haughton said. "I tried to get Ellen a room in the hotel . . . Lennon's?"

"Lennon's," Pickering confirmed.

"And they say she's not on their staff, and no room."

"I can take care of that," Pickering said.

"I tried to invoke your name, and they gave me a room number. But the door was opened by a fat Army officer who said he hadn't seen you since Melbourne."

"I've got a cottage just outside of town. We can stay there tonight, and I'll get this all sorted out in the morning. Christ, no I won't either. I'm leaving first thing in the morning. But I'll make some phone calls tonight."

"Where are you going?"

"To the rehearsal," Pickering said. "I just sent Knox a letter . . ."

Ellen Feller read his mind.

"I've taken care of everything in Hawaii. If it's in Hawaii now, it will be on his desk, decrypted, in three hours."

"Have you got a car?" Haughton asked.

Pickering nodded. "Why?"

"Well, Ellen's luggage is still at the airfield. If you've got a car, you could pick that up; and at the same time, I can check in about the plane."

Pickering pointed out the door, where the drop-head Jaguar was parked in front of a sign reading GENERAL AND FLAG OFFICERS ONLY.

"That's beautiful," Ellen said. "What is it?"

"It's an old Jaguar. The roof leaks."

Haughton chuckled. "I see you are still scrupulously refusing to obey the Customs of the Service."

Pickering was surprised at how furious the remark made him, but he forced a smile.

"Shall we go?"

Ellen Feller sat between them on the way to the airport. Whether by intent or accident, her thigh pressed against his. That warm softness and the smell of her perfume produced the physiological manifestation of sexual excitement in the male animal.

An inspection of the aircraft had revealed nothing seriously wrong, Haughton was told. They would be leaving in an hour.

There was a small officers' club. They had three drinks, during which time Ellen Feller's leg brushed, accidentally or otherwise, against Pickering's. Then they called Haughton's flight. They watched him board the Mariner for New Zealand.

Fleming Pickering would not have been surprised at anything Ellen did now that they were alone. She did nothing, sitting ladylike against the far door, all the way out to the cottage.

"What's this?" she asked.

"It's a cottage I rented. I told you—"

"I would have bet you were taking me to an officers' hotel!" she said.

Why the hell didn't I? I could have gotten her a room if I had to call General Sutherland himself.

"No."

"Fleming, don't look so guilt-stricken," Ellen said. "We both know you wouldn't do this if Mrs. Pickering were around."

He didn't reply for a moment. Then he pulled up on the parking brake, took the key from the ignition, got out of the car, and walked up to the house and unlocked the door.

The telephone rang. He walked across the living room to it.

"Pickering."

"*Captain* Pickering?"

"Yes."

"Sir, this is Major Tourtillott, Billeting Officer at the Lennon."

"Yes, Major."

"Sir, there was a Naval officer, a Captain Haughton, looking for you."

"Yes, I know, he found me."

"Sir, he was trying to arrange quarters for a Navy Department civilian, a lady, an assimilated Oh-Four."

"A what?"

"An assimilated Oh-Four, Sir. Someone entitled to the privileges of an Oh-Four, Sir."

"What the hell is an Oh-Four?"

"An Army or Marine Corps major, Sir, or a Navy Lieutenant Commander."

"The lady has made other arrangements for tonight, Major. I'll get this all sorted out in the morning. She is a member of my staff, and quarters will be required."

"Yes, Sir. I'll take care of it. Thank you, Sir."

Pickering hung the telephone up and turned to see what had happened to Ellen Feller.

She wasn't in the small living room. He found her in the bedroom, in bed.

"I've been flying for eighteen hours," she said. "I'm probably a little gamey. Will that bother you? Should I shower?"

Fleming Pickering shook his head.

(THREE)

ABOARD USS *LOWELL HUTCHINS*

TRANSPORT GROUP Y

17 DEGREES 48 MINUTES SOUTH LATITUDE, 150 DEGREES WEST

LONGITUDE

4 AUGUST 1942

Just about everyone on board knew that five months ago the USS *Lowell Hutchins* had been the Pacific & Far East passenger liner *Pacific Enchantress;* no one had any idea who Lowell Hutchins was, or, since Naval ships were customarily named only after the dead, who he had been.

She had been rapidly pressed into service, but the conversion from a plush civilian passenger liner to a Naval transport was by no means complete. Before she had sailed from the States with elements of the 1st Marine Division aboard, she had been given a coat of Navy gray paint. It had been hastily applied, and here and there it had already begun to flake off, revealing the pristine white for which Pacific & Far East vessels were well known.

The furniture and carpeting from the first-class and tourist dining rooms had been removed. Narrow, linoleum-covered, chest-high steel tables had been welded in place in the former tourist dining room. Enlisted men and junior officers now took their meals from steel trays, and they ate standing up.

Not-much-more-elegant steel tables, with attached steel benches, had been installed in the ex-first-class dining room. Generally, captains and above got to eat there, sitting down, from plates bearing the P&FE insignia.

Most of the former first-class suites and cabins, plus the former first- and tourist-class bars, libraries, lounges, and exercise rooms, had been converted to troop berthing areas. It had been relatively easy to remove their beds, cabinets, tables, and other furniture and equipment and replace them with bunks. The bunks were sheets of canvas, suspended between iron pipe, stacked four high.

The bathrooms were still identified by porcelain BATH plates over their doors, although they had now become, of course, Navy "heads." It would have taken too much time to remove the plates. And it would also have taken too much time to expand them. So a "bath" designed for the use of a couple en route to Hawaii now served as many as thirty-two men en route to a place none of them had ever heard of a month before, islands in the Solomon chain called Guadalcanal, Tulagi, and Florida.

There was not, of course, sufficient water-distilling capability aboard to permit showers at will. Showers, and indeed drinking water, were stringently rationed.

The former tourist-class cabins had proved even more of a problem for conversion. To efficiently utilize space, the beds there had usually been mattresses laid upon steel frameworks, with shelves built under them. These could not be readily moved. These rooms had become officers' staterooms for captains and above, sometimes with the addition of several other bunks. Because they afforded that most rare privilege of military service, privacy, the few single staterooms now became the private staterooms of senior majors, lieutenant colonels, and even a few junior full colonels.

The most luxurious accommodations on the upper deck had been left virtually unchanged. Even the carpets were still there, and the oil paintings on the paneled bulkheads, and the inlaid tables, and the soft, comfortable couches and armchairs. These became the accommodations of the most senior of the Marine officers aboard, the one general officer and the senior full colonels. These men took their meals with the ship's officers on tables set with snowy linen, glistening crystal, and sterling tableware.

It was almost taken as gospel by those on the lower decks that this was one more case of the brass, those sonsofbitches, taking care of themselves. But the decision to leave the upper-deck cabins unchanged had actually been based less on the principle that rank hath its privileges than on the practical consideration that to convert them to troop berthing would have required two hundred or so men to make their way at least twice a day from the upper deck to the mess deck through narrow passageways. That many men on that deck might actually interfere with the efficient running of the ship.

Brigadier General Lewis T. Harris, Deputy Commander, 1st Marine Division, and the senior Marine embarked, actually had a strong feeling of uneasiness every time he took his seat in the ship's officers' mess.

Because he often went twice a day to see it, he knew what was being served in the troop messes. The troop mess—jammed full of men, some of them seasick, standing at tables with food slopped around steel mess trays—offered a vivid contrast to the neatly set table at the officers' mess, with its baskets of freshly baked rolls and bread, and white-jacketed stewards hovering at his shoulder to make sure the levels in his delicate china coffee cup and crystal water glass never dropped more than an inch, or to inquire How the General Would Like His Lamb Chop.

General Harris tried to live the old adage that an officer's first duty was the welfare of the men placed under his command. If it had been within his power, Marines on the way to battle would all be seated at a linen-covered table, eating steaks to order. That was obviously out of the question, a fantasy. He had done the next best thing, however. He told his officers that he expected the men to be fed as well as humanly possible under the circumstances, and then he repeatedly went to see for himself how well that order was being carried out. He was convinced that the mess officers and sergeants were indeed doing the best they could.

He could, he knew, take his meals with the troops in that foul-smelling mess; and if he did, his officers would follow his example. But the only thing he would accomplish—aside from being seen there, implying that he was concerned about the chow—would be to strain the facilities that much more.

The ship's officers—and why not?—would go on eating well, no matter where he and his officers ate. The officers' mess cooks and stewards were not being strained by feeding the Marine senior officers. And every meal they fed to a senior Marine officer was one less to be prepared down below.

So, in the end, after making sure the senior officers knew he expected them to check on the troop mess regularly and personally, General Harris continued to eat off bone china and a linen tablecloth; and he continued to feel uneasy about it.

There was a table by the door to the ship's officers' mess, on which sat a coffee machine and three or four insulated coffee pitchers and a stack of mugs. Between mealtimes, it was used by the stewards to take coffee to the bridge and to the cabins on the upper deck.

When General Harris left the mess, he stopped by the table, filled a pitcher a little more than half-full of coffee, and picked up two of the china mugs.

"General," one of the stewards said, "can I carry that somewhere for you?"

"I can manage, thank you," Harris said with a smile. He left the mess and went to his cabin.

In one of the drawers of a mahogany chest, there were a dozen small, olive-drab cans. Each was neatly labeled BORE CLEANER, 8 OZ. They looked like tiny paint cans, and there was a neat line of red candle wax sealing the line where the top had been forced tight on the body of the can. Anyone seeing the cans would understand that General Harris did not want the bore cleaner to leak.

He took a penknife from his pocket and carefully scraped the wax seal from one of the cans, and then switched to the screwdriver blade. He pried the lid carefully off, then poured the brown fluid the can held into the coffee pitcher.

After that, he left his cabin, headed aft, and passed through a door opening onto the open deck. This deck had previously been a promenade where the affluent could take a constitutional or sit on deck chairs in an environment denied to the less affluent down below. Now he had trouble making his way past the bulky life rafts that had been lashed on the deck to provide at least a shot at survival, should the USS *Lowell Hutchins* be torpedoed.

There was still enough light to see several of the ships of the Amphibious Force. There were eighty-two ships in all, sailing in three concentric circles. The twelve transports, including the USS *Lowell Hutchins,* formed the inner circle. Next came a circle of cruisers and, outside that, the screening force of destroyers.

General Harris stared at the ships long enough to reflect (again) that although it appeared to be a considerable armada, it was not large enough to accomplish their mission with a reasonable chance of success. He then made his way down three ladders to what had once been the second of the tourist decks, and through a passageway to cabin D-123, where he knocked at the door.

When there was no response, he put his mouth to the slats in the door and called, "Stecker!"

"Come!"

He pushed the door open. Major Jack NMI Stecker, Commanding Officer, 2nd Battalion, 5th Marines, wearing only his skivvies, was sitting on the deck of the tiny cabin beside the narrow single bunk that formed part of the bulkhead.

"Jack, what the hell are you doing?" Harris asked.

Stecker turned and, seeing the General, jumped to his feet.

"At ease, Major," Harris said, just a trifle sarcastically. "What the hell were you doing down there?"

"I was cleaning my piece, Sir," Stecker said, gesturing at the bunk.

Harris went to look. There was a rifle, in pieces, spread out on the bunk.

Harris snorted, and then extended the coffee pitcher.

"I thought you might like some coffee, Jack," he said.

"I'm pretty well coffeed out, Sir."

"Jack. Trust me. You need a cup of coffee."

"Yes, Sir," Stecker said.

Harris set the cups down on a steel shelf, filled each half-full of the mixture of "bore cleaner" and coffee, and handed one to Stecker.

Stecker sipped his suspiciously, smiled, and said, "Yes, Sir, the General is right. This is just what I needed."

Harris smiled back. "We generals are always right, Jack. You should try to remember that. What are you doing with the Garand? And now that I think about it, where the hell did you get it?"

"I found it on post at Quantico, General," Stecker said. "And just as soon as I can find time, I will turn it in to the proper authorities."

Harris snorted. He walked to the bunk and picked up the stripped receiver. His expert eye picked out the signs of accurizing.

"I forgot," he said. "You think this a pretty good weapon, don't you?"

"It's a superb weapon," Stecker said. "I've shot inch-and-a-half groups at two hundred yards with that one."

"Bullshit."

"No bullshit. And the kid—I shouldn't call him a kid—Joe Howard. He took a commission, and is now off doing something hush-hush for G-2—the *man* who did the accuracy job on that one had one that was more accurate than this one."

"You realize that ninety-five percent of the people in the Corps think the Garand is a piece of shit that can never compare to the Springfield?"

"Then ninety-five percent of the people in the Corps are wrong."

"Ninety-five percent of the people in this Amphibious Force think that Guadalcanal is going to be a cakewalk, a live-fire exercise with a secondary benefit of taking some Japanese territory."

"Ninety-five percent of the people in this Amphibious Force have never heard a shot fired in anger," Stecker said.

"Is that the same thing as saying they're wrong, too?" Harris asked.

"You're putting me on the spot," Stecker said uncomfortably.

"That's why I'm sharing my bore cleaner with you," Harris said. "I want to get you drunk, so you'll give me a straight answer."

Stecker looked at him without replying.

"Come on, Jack," Harris said. "We go back a long way. I want to know what you're thinking."

Stecker shrugged, and then asked, "You ever give any thought to why the brass are going ahead with this, when they damned well know we're not ready?"

"You're talking about the drill?" Harris asked.

The "drill," the practice landings in the Fiji Islands that the convoy carrying the Amphibious Force had just come from, had been an unqualified disaster. Nothing had gone as it was supposed to.

"That's part of it, but that's not what I meant," Stecker said. "The brass knew before the Fiji drill that the LCP(L)s were no fucking good."

There were 408 landing craft in the Amphibious Force. Of these, 308 were designated LCP(L), a thirty-six-foot landing craft with a fixed bow. In other words, when the craft touched shore, personnel aboard would have to exit *over* the bow and sides, rather than across a droppable ramp. Similarly, supplies would have to be manhandled over the sides. And, of course, LCP(L)s could not discharge vehicles or other heavy cargo onto the beach.

"They're all we have, Jack. We can't wait to re-equip with LCP(R)s or LCMs."

Both the thirty-six-foot LCP(R) and the forty-five-foot LCM had droppable ramps. The LCP(R) could discharge over its ramp 75mm and 105mm howitzers and one-ton trucks. The LCM could handle 90mm and five-inch guns and heavier trucks.

"Ever wonder why we can't?" Stecker asked softly.

"Because the Japanese are almost finished with their air base on Guadalcanal. We can't afford to let them do that. We have to grab that air base before they make it operational."

"That's what I mean. The Japanese know how important that air base is. To them. And to us—if we take it away from them and start operating out of it ourselves. So they're going to fight like hell to keep us from taking it; and if we do, they're going to fight like hell to take it back."

"That's what we're paid to do."

"No cakewalk. No live-fire exercise. An important objective. If it's important to them, they're going to be prepared to defend it. We're going to have three-fourths of our landing barges exposed as the troops try to get over the sides and onto the beach. And once we start manhandling cargo out of those damned boats . . . Jesus, if they have any artillery at all, or decent mortar men, or, for that matter, just some well-emplaced machine guns, we're going to lose those boats! No boats, no reinforcements, no ammunition, no rations."

"You don't sound as if you're sure we can carry it off," Harris said. "Is that what you think?"

"I wouldn't say this to anyone but you, but I don't know. I've got some awful good kids, and they'll try, but balls—courage, if you like— sometimes isn't enough."

Brigadier General Lewis T. Harris and Major Jack NMI Stecker had known each other for most of their adult lives. They had been in combat all over the Caribbean basin together. Harris didn't have to recall Stecker's Medal of Honor for proof of his personal courage. Stecker was no coward. He was calling the upcoming battle for Guadalcanal as he saw it.

Harris was afraid Stecker's analysis was in the X-ring.

"Have some more coffee, Jack," Harris said.

"No, thank you, Sir."

" 'No, thank you'? You getting old, Jack? Taken up religion?"

"Yes, Sir, I'm getting old," Stecker replied. He pulled a canvas rucksack from under the mattress of his bunk, and took from it a large pink bottle which bore a label from the Pharmacy, Naval Dispensary, Quantico, Virginia. Under a skull and crossbones, it read, CAUTION!! HIGHLY TOXIC!! FOR TREATMENT OF ATHLETE'S FOOT ONLY. IF FLUID TOUCHES EYES OR MOUTH, FLOOD COPIOUSLY WITH WATER AND SEEK IMMEDIATE MEDICAL ATTENTION!!

He put the bottle to his mouth and took a healthy pull, then exhaled in appreciation.

Harris chuckled.

"I'm giving some serious thought to religion, General, but I haven't said anything to the chaplain yet," Stecker said. "Do you have to go, or can we sit around and drink coffee, cure my athlete's feet, and tell sea stories?"

"I'm not going anywhere, Jack," Harris chuckled. "But you better put that Garand back together before you take another pull at that pink bottle and forget how."

(FOUR)

OFF CAPE ESPERANCE
GUADALCANAL, SOLOMON ISLANDS
0240 HOURS 7 AUGUST 1942

At 0200, Transport Groups X and Y, the Amphibious Force of Operation PESTILENCE, reached Savo Island, which lay between the islands of Guadalcanal and Florida. The skies were clear, and there was some light from a quarter moon, enough to make out the land masses and the other ships.

The fifteen transports of Transport Group X turned and entered Sealark Channel, between Savo and Guadalcanal. They carried aboard the major elements of the 1st Marine Division and were headed for the beaches of Guadalcanal.

Transport Group Y sailed on the other side of Savo Island, between it and Florida Island, and headed toward their destination, Florida, Tulagi, and Gavutu islands. Group Y consisted of four transports carrying 2nd Battalion, 5th Marines, and other troops, and four destroyer transports. These were World War I destroyers that had been converted for use by Marine Raiders by removing two of their four engines and converting the reclaimed space to troop berthing. These carried the 1st Raider Battalion.

The Guadalcanal Invasion Force was headed for what the Operations Plan called "Beach Red." This was about six thousand yards east of Lunga Point, more or less directly across Sealark Channel from where the Tulagi/Gavutu landings were to take place. The distance across Sealark Channel was approximately twenty-five miles.

The Guadalcanal Fire Support Group (three cruisers and four destroyers) began to bombard assigned targets on Guadalcanal at 0614, adding their destructive power to the aerial bombing by U.S. Army Air Corps B-17s which had been going on for a week. At 0616, the Tulagi Fire Support Group (one cruiser and two destroyers) opened fire on Tulagi and Gavutu.

By 0651 the transports of both groups dropped anchor nine thousand yards off their respective landing beaches. Landing boats were put over the side into the calm water, and nets woven of heavy rope were put in place along the sides of the transports. Marines began to climb down the ropes into the landing boats.

Minesweepers began to sweep the water between the ships of both transport groups and their landing beaches. No mines were found.

The only enemy vessel encountered was a small gasoline-carrying schooner in Sealark Channel. It burned and then exploded under both Naval gunfire and machine-gun fire from Navy fighter aircraft and dive bombers. These were operating from carriers maneuvering seventy-five miles from the invasion beaches.

The Navy sent forty-three carrier aircraft to attack Guadalcanal, and nearly as many—forty-one—to attack Tulagi and Gavutu. The aircraft attacking Tulagi either sank or set on fire eighteen Japanese seaplanes.

Zero-Hour for Operation PESTILENCE, when Marines were to hit Beach Red on Guadalcanal, was 0910. H-Hour, when Marines would go ashore on Tulagi, was an hour and ten minutes earlier, at 0800. But the first Marine landing in the Solomons took place across the beaches of Florida Island. That operation, however, did not rate having its own Hour in the Operations Order.

At 0740, B Company, 1st Battalion, 2nd Marines, went ashore near the small village of Haleta, on Florida Island. Their mission was to secure an elevated area from which the Japanese could bring Beach

Blue on Tulagi under fire. They encountered no resistance; there were no Japanese in the area.

At 0800, the first wave of the Tulagi force—landing craft carrying Baker and Dog Companies of the 1st Raider Battalion—touched ashore on Blue Beach. There was one casualty. A Marine was instantly killed by a single rifle shot. But there was no other resistance; the enemy had not elected to defend Tulagi on the beach, but from caves and earthen bunkers in the hills inland and to the south.

The landing craft returned to the transports and loaded the second wave (Able and Charley Companies, 1st Raiders) and put them ashore. Then a steady stream of landing craft made their way between the transports and the beach and put the 2nd Battalion, 5th Marines, on shore.

Once on Tulagi, the 2nd Battalion, 5th Marines, crossed the narrow island to their left (northwest) to clear out the enemy, while the Raiders turned to their right (southeast) and headed toward the southern tip of the island. About 3,500 yards separates the southern tip of Tulagi from the tiny island of Gavutu (515 by 255 yards) and the even smaller (290 by 310 yards) island of Tanambogo, which was connected to Gavutu by a concrete causeway.

Operation PESTILENCE called for the invasion of Gavutu by the 1st Parachute Battalion at 1200 hours. The parachutists, once they had secured Gavutu, were to cross the causeway and secure Tanambogo.

The Raiders encountered no serious opposition until after noon. And 2nd Battalion, 5th Marines, encountered no serious opposition moving in the opposite direction until about the same time.

Off Guadalcanal, at 0840, the destroyers of the Guadalcanal Fire Support Group took up positions to mark the line of departure for the landing craft, five thousand yards north of Beach Red.

Almost immediately, small liaison aircraft appeared over Beach Red and marked its 3,200 yard width with smoke grenades.

Immediately after that, at exactly 0900, all the cruisers and destroyers of the Guadalcanal Fire Support Group began to bombard Beach Red and the area extending two hundred yards inshore.

The landing craft carrying the first wave of the Beach Red invasion force (the 5th Marines, less their 2nd Battalion, which was on Tulagi) left the departure line on schedule. When the Landing Craft were 1,300 yards off Beach Red, the covering bombardment was lifted.

At 0910, on a 1,600-yard front, the 5th Marines began to land on the beach, the 1st Battalion on the right (west), and the 3rd Battalion on the left (east). Regimental Headquarters came ashore at 0938. Minutes later they were joined by the Heavy Weapons elements of the regiment.

Again, there was virtually no resistance on the beach.

As the landing craft returned to the transports to bring the 1st Marines ashore, the 5th Marines moved inland, setting up a defense perimeter six hundred yards off Beach Red, along the Tenaru River on the west, the Tenavatu River on the east, and a branch of the Tenaru on the south.

Once it had become apparent that they would not be in danger from Japanese artillery on or near the beach, the transports began to move closer to the beach, dropping anchor again seven thousand yards away.

At about this point, serious problems began with the offloading process on the beach. In many ways these duplicated the disastrous trial run in the Fiji Islands.

The small and relatively easy-to-manhandle 75mm pack howitzers (originally designed to be carried by mules) of the 11th Marines (the artillery regiment) had come ashore with the assault elements of the 5th Marines.

The 105mm howitzers now came ashore. But because there were not enough drop-ramp landing craft to handle them, they did not bring their "prime movers." The prime mover intended to tow the 105mm howitzer was the "Truck, 2½ Ton, 6×6," commonly called the "six-by-six." Six-by-six refers to the number of driving wheels. The standard six-by-six actually had eight wheels in the rear, for a total of ten powered wheels. So equipped, the six-by-six became legendary in its ability to carry or tow enormous loads anywhere.

But the 11th Marines were not equipped with six-by-sixes. Instead, they had been issued a truck commonly referred to as a "one-ton." It was rated as having a cargo capacity of one ton (as opposed to the two-and-a-half-ton capacity of the six-by-six), and it had only four powered wheels with which to move itself through mud, sand, or slippery terrain.

Since there were insufficient drop-bow landing craft to move this "prime mover" immediately onto Beach Red, when the 105mm howitzers arrived on the beach, there was no vehicle capable of towing them inland to firing positions—except for a few overworked amphibious tractors, which had a tanklike track and could negotiate sand and mud.

These were pressed into service to move the 105mm howitzers. But in so doing, their metal tracks chewed up the primitive roads—as well as whatever field telephone wires they crossed. That effectively cut communication between the advanced positions and the beach and the several headquarters.

Within an hour or so of landing on the beach, moreover, the Marines were physically exhausted. For one thing, the long periods of time they'd spent aboard the troop transports had caused them to lose much of the physical toughness they'd acquired in training.

For another, Guadalcanal's temperature and high humidity quickly sapped what strength they had. And the effects of the temperature and humidity were magnified because they were slogging through sand and jungle and up hills carrying heavy loads of rifles, machine guns, mortars, and the ammunition for them.

And there was not enough water. Although medical officers had strongly insisted that each man be provided with two canteens (two quarts) of drinking water, there were not enough canteens in the Pacific to issue a second canteen to each man.

The Navy had been asked, and had refused, to provide beach labor details of sailors to assist with the unloading of freight coming ashore from the landing craft, and then to move the freight off the beach to make room for more supplies.

It was presumed by Naval planners that the Marines could provide their own labor details to offload supplies from landing craft, and that trucks would be available to move the offloaded supplies from the beach inland.

Marines exhausted by the very act of getting ashore managed slowly to unload supplies from landing craft, further exhausting themselves in the process. But then, at first, there were no trucks to move the supplies off the beach; and when the one-ton trucks finally began to come ashore, they proved incapable of negotiating the sand and roads chewed up by amphibious tractors.

The result was a mess. Landing craft loaded with supplies were stacked up three rows deep off the beach. They were unable even to reach the beach, much less rapidly discharge their cargoes.

(FIVE)

ABOARD LCP(L) 36
OFF GAVUTU ISLAND
1225 HOURS 7 AUGUST 1942

First Lieutenant Richard B. Macklin, USMC, was unhappy with Operation PESTILENCE for a number of reasons, and specifically with his role in the operation.

He had arrived at the 1st Parachute Battalion three weeks earlier after long and uncomfortable voyages, first aboard a destroyer from San Diego, and then a mine sweeper from Pearl Harbor. When he had finally reached the 1st Parachute Batallion, the commanding officer,

Major Robert Williams, had promptly told him that he hadn't expected him and frankly didn't know what the hell to do with him.

"I had rather hoped, Sir, that in view of my experience, I might be given a company."

Macklin felt sure service as a company commander would get him his long-overdue promotion.

"Company commanders are captains, Macklin," Williams replied.

"Company 'C' is commanded by a lieutenant," Macklin politely argued, "one who is junior in rank to me."

"I'm not going to turn over a company to you at this late date. They're a team now, and I don't intend to screw that up by throwing in a new quarterback just before the kickoff," Williams said. "Sorry."

Not only was what they were about to do not a football game, Macklin fumed privately, but refusing to give him the command was a clear violation of regulations, which clearly stated that the senior officer present for duty was entitled to command.

Williams seemed to be one of those officers who obeyed only those orders it was convenient to obey. In this regard he had obviously been influenced by the Army paratroopers with whom he had trained. Macklin had seen enough of that collection of clowns to know that any resemblance between Army paratroop officers and professional officers was purely coincidental.

They thought the war *was* a football game, and acted like it. Macklin had actually witnessed Army paratroop officers drinking, and probably whoring, if the truth were known, with their enlisted men in Phoenix City, Alabama, across the river from Fort Benning. If the Army's 82nd Airborne Division was ever sent into combat, there was no question in Macklin's mind that it would fail, miserably, to accomplish its mission. Discipline was the key to military success, and Army paratroop discipline was a disgrace.

But insisting on his legal rights would not have been wise, Macklin concluded. There was no doubt in his mind that if he appealed to the proper authorities, Williams would be ordered to place him in command of "C" Company. But if he did that, Major Williams would from that moment just be looking for an excuse to relieve him. And being relieved of command was worse than not being given a command at all.

So here he was, in a landing craft, about to assault an enemy-held beach, having been officially designated a "supernumerary officer." *Supernumerary* was a euphemism for "replacement"—an officer with no duties, waiting to replace someone wounded or killed.

Meanwhile, the First Parachute Battalion, the "Chutes," was obviously being improperly employed, that is to say as regular infantry. The rationale for that was that there were no aircraft to drop them.

Macklin personally doubted that. He had seen ships in San Diego loaded with partially disassembled R4Ds, for instance. Perhaps they were Air Corps C-47s, destined for China or Australia, as he had been told; but the planes were identical, only the nomenclature was different. If the senior officers had wanted to use Para-Marines, they could have gotten the aircraft somewhere.

And if aircraft were truly not available, then the obvious thing to do was not commit the Para-Marines. It made no military sense to waste superbly trained men, the elite of the elite, as common infantry, sacrificing them in assaulting a beach on an island that had no real military importance that Macklin could see. It was only five hundred yards long and half that wide!

What they should have done, if they really thought the island was a threat, was to shell or bomb it level. Not send Marines to throw away their lives and all their superb training to occupy it. All the Japanese were using it for was a seaplane base. By definition, seaplanes could be used anywhere there was enough water for them to land and take off.

Probably the whole thing was regarded by the brass as a live-fire exercise, to give the Para-Marines a blooding and Naval Aviation some practice. Navy SBD dive-bombers had attacked Gavutu for forty minutes, starting at 1145.

Ten minutes after the dive-bombers started their attack, the Navy started shelling the island, a barrage that lasted five minutes, causing huge clouds of smoke and dust to rise from Gavutu.

Macklin reminded himself of what he knew of the explosive force of one-hundred-pound bombs and Naval artillery. It was awesome. It was reasonable to assume that, on an island only five hundred yards long, very few Japanese soldiers, much less their armament, could survive forty minutes of dive-bombing and an intense five-minute Naval barrage.

Macklin was close enough in the landing barge to hear the Coxswain when he muttered, with concern and resignation, "Oh, shit!"

"What's the matter?"

The Coxswain took his hand from his wheel long enough to point ahead, at the beach. Macklin was reluctant to raise his head high enough over the bow to look—doing so would make his head a target—but curiosity, after a moment, got the best of him. He raised his head, kept it up long enough to look around, and then ducked again.

Either bombs from the dive-bombers or shells from the Naval artillery, or maybe some of each, had struck the concrete landing ramps used by the Japanese to get their seaplanes in and out of the water. Huge blocks of concrete had been displaced.

The Operations Order called for this landing craft and the landing craft to each side to run aground on the concrete ramps. But that would not be possible.

Aware that his heart was beating rapidly and that his mouth was dry, Macklin considered the alternatives. The Coxswain could continue on his prescribed course until the landing craft ran into one of the huge blocks of concrete and had to stop. There was no telling how deep the water would be at that point; it was even possible they would be in water over their heads when they went over the side of the landing craft. If he had to jump into water over his head with all the equipment he was carrying, he would drown.

There was a concrete pier extending maybe two hundred yards from shore. The Coxswain could run the landing craft against that, and the Marines could then climb onto the pier and run down the pier to shore.

But, he realized with alarm, if the Naval artillery had hit the concrete ramps, it probably had hit the concrete pier as well. There was a good possibility that at least a portion of the pier was destroyed, and that it would be impossible to run all the way ashore.

And in the moment it occurred to him that even if the pier was intact, anyone running down its length would be like a target in a shooting gallery for riflemen and machine-gunners defending the beach, the Coxswain throttled back his engine. A moment later, the landing craft grated against the concrete pier.

Now it was quiet enough for the Coxswain to shout to the senior officer in the boat, the Captain commanding Able Company, "There's debris in the water by the landing ramps; this is as close as I can take you!"

Macklin could tell by the look on the Captain's face what he thought of this news.

"Everybody out of the boat!" the Captain shouted. "Follow me! Let's go! Get the lead out!"

He clambered up onto the side of the landing craft and from there onto the concrete pier, and vanished from sight.

Lieutenant Macklin decided that in the absence of orders to do something specific (his orders had been, "Macklin, you go in with Boat Nine.") it behooved him to remain aboard the landing craft to make sure that everyone else got off.

He did so.

Then he climbed onto the pier, on his stomach, with his Thompson submachine gun at the ready. He heard the engine of the landing craft rev, and knew that the boat was backing away from the pier to return to the transport for the second wave.

When he looked down the pier, the last of the Marines reached the end of it, turned to the left, and disappeared.

There was the sound of small-arms fire, but it was, as far as Macklin could tell, the familiar crack of .30-06 rifles and the deeper-pitched boom of .45-caliber submachine-gun and pistol ammo. He had been told that the sound of the smaller-caliber Japanese small arms would be different.

That means we're not under fire!

He got to his feet and began to trot down the pier toward the shore. Once erect, he could see Marines on the beach, moving inland through the vegetation and around the burned and shattered buildings of the Japanese seaplane base.

He started to run, to catch up.

Near the shore, he saw that his initial assessment of probable damage from the bombing and shellfire had been correct. A bomb, or a shell, had struck the pier about fifteen yards from shore, taking out all but a narrow strip of concrete no more than three feet wide.

As he made his way carefully across this narrow strip, he felt as if, in the same moment, someone had struck his leg with a baseball bat and slapped him, very hard, in the face.

And then he felt himself flying through the air. There was a splash, and he went under water. There was a moment of abject terror, and then his flailing hand encountered a barnacle-encrusted piling. He clung to it desperately, to keep himself from slipping off and drowning.

Then he became aware that his foot was touching bottom. He straightened his bent leg, and found that he was in water about chest-deep.

Where the hell is my weapon?

I dropped it. It's in the water. I'll never be able to find it. Now what the hell am I going to do?

What the hell did I fall over? I must have slipped. No. I was struck by something!

He put his hand to his face. His fingers came away sticky with blood.

My God, I've been shot in the face! I'll be disfigured for life!

And then he remembered the blow to his leg. He felt faint and nauseous, but finally gathered the courage to try to find some damage to his leg. He became aware of a stinging sensation. Salt water, he realized, was making an open sore—a *wound!*—sting.

He couldn't bend far enough over to reach the sting without putting his face into the water. Gingerly, he raised the stinging leg. He couldn't feel anything at first, and only after a moment detected a swelling in the calf.

But then he saw a faint cloud of red oozing out of his trouser leg.

I've been shot in the leg! But why doesn't it hurt?

Shock! It doesn't hurt because I'm in shock!

I'm going to pass out and then drown!

A glob of blood dropped off his cheek into the water and began to dissolve as it sank.

I'm going to bleed to death!

Our Father which art in heaven, hallowed by Thy Name . . .

What the hell is the rest of it?

Dear God, please don't let me die!

Yea, though I walk through the valley of the shadow of death . . .

"Move your ass! Run!Run!Run!Run!Run!Run!"

It's the second wave!

Now there was small-arms fire, single shots and automatic, and it didn't sound like .30-06s or Thompsons, and then there was a whistling sound followed by a *crump* and then a dull explosion, and he felt a shock wave and then another and another in the water.

"Get your dumb ass up and off the pier, or die here, you dumb sonofabitch!"

He saw, vaguely, figures running across the pier above him.

He found his voice.

"Medic! Medic! Medic!"

There was no response, and there didn't seem to be any more movement on the pier above him. The strange-sounding—the *Japanese*—smalls-arms fire continued, and there were more mortar rounds landing in the water.

"Medic! Medic! For Christ's sake, somebody help me!"

Now the leg started to ache, and his cheek. He put his hand to his face again, and the fingers came away this time with a clot of blood.

"For the love of Christ, will somebody help me? Medic! Medic!"

There was splashing in the water from the direction of the shore.

It's a Jap! It has to be a Jap! The invasion failed, and now I'm going to die here under this fucking pier!

"What happened to you, Mac?"

"I've been wounded, you ignorant sonofabitch! And it's 'Lieutenant'!"

Fingers probed his face.

"That's not bad," the medic said, professionally. "Another half an inch and you would have lost your teeth, maybe worse. But you just got grazed. Is that all that's wrong with you?"

"My leg, I've been wounded in the leg."

Fingers probed his leg.

"That hurts, goddamn you!"

"I'll tell you what I'm going to do. I'm going to get you ashore. Let go of that piling and wrap your arms around my neck."

"Ashore?"

"Lieutenant, I've got badly wounded people ashore. Please don't give me any trouble."

"*I'm* badly wounded," Macklin said indignantly.

"No, you're not. Your leg ain't broke. You got one of them half-million-dollar wounds. Some muscle damage. Keep you out of the war for maybe three months. In ten days you'll be in the hospital in Melbourne, looking up nurses' dresses. Now come on, put your arms around me and I'll get you ashore, and somebody will be along in a while to take you back to the ship."

Lieutenant Macklin did as he was told. The medic carried him on his back to the shore, and a few yards inland. Then he lowered him gently onto the sand, cut his trouser leg open, and applied a compress bandage.

"My leg," Macklin said, with as much dignity as he could muster, "is beginning to cause me a great deal of pain."

"Well, we have just the thing for that," the medic said, taking out a morphine hypodermic. "Next stop, Cloud Nine."

Macklin felt a prick in his buttocks, and then a sensation of cold.

"I gotta go," the medic said, patting him comfortably on the shoulder. "You're going to be all right, Lieutenant. Believe me."

A warm sensation began to ooze through Macklin's body.

I'm going to be all right, he thought. *I'm going to live. They're going to send me to the hospital in Melbourne. It will probably take longer than three months for my leg to heal. I will receive the Purple Heart.* Two *Purple Hearts, one for the leg and one for the face. There will probably be a small scar on my face. People will ask about that. "Lieutenant Macklin was wounded while attacking Gavutu*—twice *wounded when assaulting the beach at Gavutu with the first wave of the Para-Marines."*

I'll be a captain for sure, now. And for the rest of my Marine Corps career, the scar on my face will be there to remind people of my combat service.

(SIX)

COMMAND POST, TULAGI FORCE
1530 HOURS 8 AUGUST 1942

The headquarters of Brigadier General Lewis T. Harris, Commanding General of the Tulagi/Gavutu/Tanambogo Force, were now in the somewhat seedy white frame building that had before the war housed the Colonial Administrator of Tulagi, and was somewhat grandly known as "the Residence."

Thirty minutes before, the building had been the forward command post of Lieutenant Colonel "Red Mike" Edson, commanding the 1st Raider Battalion. When the Commanding Officer, 2nd Battalion, 5th Marines, drove up to attend a commanders' conference called by General Harris, the small detachment of Raiders charged with protecting the Raider command post were still in place, close to but not actually manning their weapons (rifles, BARs, and light .30-caliber machine guns).

Thirty minutes before, the island of Tulagi had been officially reported "secure."

There was a moment's hesitation before a sergeant called, "Atten-*hut!*" and saluted the 2nd Battalion Commander. For one thing, he was hatless, riding a captured Japanese motorcycle, and was carrying a rifle slung over his back, which was not the sort of thing the Raiders expected of a Marine major.

But the salute was enthusiastic and respectful. The reputation of the 2nd Battalion Commander had preceded him. It had been reliably reported that during the mopping-up phase of the invasion, the 2nd Battalion Commander had been seen standing in the open, shooting a particularly determined Japanese sniper who had until then been firing with impunity through a one-foot-square hole in his coral bunker. The Commanding Officer of the 2nd Battalion had fired at him twice; and when they pulled his body from the cave, they learned the sniper had taken two hits in the head.

The story had been of particular interest, and thus had quickly spread, both because that wasn't usually the sort of thing majors and battalion commanders did personally, and also because he had done it with an M-1 Garand rifle. The Garand was supposed to be the new standard rifle, although none had yet been issued to the Marine Corps; and it was supposed to be a piece of shit, incapable of hitting a barn door at fifty yards.

But there was no denying the story. A dozen people had seen Major Jack NMI Stecker stand up, as calmly as if had been on the rifle range at Parris Island or 'Diego, and let off two shots and put both of them, so to speak, in the X-ring.

There was also scuttlebutt going around that Major Stecker had won the Big One, the Medal of Honor, as a buck sergeant in the First World War in France. No one could remember ever having seen a real, honest-to-Christ hero like that. And as Major Stecker walked up the shallow steps to the Residence, two dozen sets of eyes watched him with something close to awe.

General Harris was in his office, the Sergeant Major told Major Stecker, and he was to go right in.

There were no enlisted men in General Harris's office, but only the other two commanding officers he had summoned to the commanders' conference, Major Robert Williams of the 1st Parachute Battalion and Lieutenant Colonels Red Mike Edson and Sam Griffith, CO and Exec of the 1st Raider Battalion.

They were all holding canteens, presumably full of coffee. There were two cans of bore cleaner on the shelf of the field desk.

"Forgive me for saying so, Major," General Harris greeted Major Stecker, "but aren't you a little long in the tooth for a motorcycle?"

"With respect, General," Major Stecker said, "I am not too old for a motorcycle. I *am* too old, and much too tired, to walk up here."

"May I then offer you coffee, to restore your vitality? Or did you bring your own athlete's-foot lotion?"

"I gave that to my company commanders," Stecker said.

General Harris handed him a canteen cup.

"That's the good news," he said.

"Thank you, Sir," Stecker said. "What's the bad?"

"You're about to go report to General Vandergrift," Harris said.

"Why me?"

"You're junior to these three," Harris said.

"I couldn't plead old age?" Stecker asked.

"No," Harris said simply.

"Aye, aye, Sir," Stecker said. "Sir, before I go, I want to put in one of my officers for a Silver Star. I'd like to be able to tell General Vandergrift that you approve."

"Who?"

"Captain Sutton, Sir."

"What did he do?"

"We were having a hell of a time getting pockets of Nips out of their caves," Lieutenant Colonel Griffith answered for him. "We couldn't shoot them out, and when we threw grenades and explosives in, they just threw it right back out. Sutton—I saw this, and agree with Jack that he should be decorated—Sutton tied explosives to a piece of timber—"

"Where'd he get the timber?" Harris asked curiously.

"From the blown-up buildings on the beach," Griffith went on. "As I was saying, he tied explosives to a plank, a board, and then under covering fire ran to the mouth of the cave—*caves;* I saw him do it half a dozen times—and put it inside."

"Why didn't the Japs just throw it back out?" Harris asked. "Am I missing something?"

"He hung on to the board, General," Griffith said. "Wedged it against the inside of the cave until it blew."

"Oh," Harris said.

"If any of the Japs had figured out what was going on, they'd have come a little further toward the mouth of the cave and shot him. He was really exposed, doing what he was doing, and he saved a lot of lives."

"OK," Harris said. "You can tell the General that I approve of the award of the Silver Star to your Captain Sutton, Jack."

"Thank you, Sir."

"Now that that's decided," Red Mike Edson said, laughing, "I will tell you something else Captain Sutton did."

"Something funny?" Harris said, as he poured more bore cleaner in their canteen cups.

"He got carried away. He found some gasoline somewhere, and added a can of that to the explosives."

"That didn't work?"

"It worked. It blew his clothes off and damn near fried him."

"Was he hurt?" Harris asked.

"No, not seriously. But he was down to his skivvy shorts, and they were singed, and there's not a hair on his body."

There were chuckles all around.

"And speaking of people who really exposed themselves," Edson said, "I heard of an officer—and I think Sam saw this, too—who stood out in the open, really exposed, with a Mickey Mouse rifle he got somewhere, and put two rounds into the head of a Jap sniper at a hundred, maybe a hundred and fifty yards. How about a medal for him?"

"No," Jack Stecker said firmly. "Absolutely not."

"The motorcycle kid here?" General Harris asked.

"Sir, I did what any Marine private is supposed to do. Engage the enemy with accurate rifle fire. That's all. Nobody should get a medal for doing his duty."

"I'm not sure I can disagree with that," Harris said, after a moment. "And what the hell, Red, Jack's already got enough medals."

"He sure inspired a lot of kids out there," Edson said.

"I'm sure he did, but that's something else we have to expect from a Marine officer," Harris said, his tone of voice making it clear that he did not wish to entertain any further discussion of the matter. "Before Jack goes over there, I want from each of you, starting with Jack as the junior commander, a one-word description of the Japanese we just fought."

"What for?"

"I want it, and I want Jack to give it to General Vandergrift, something we're thinking before the adrenaline goes away. Jack?"

" 'Courageous.' Maybe 'tenacious.' "

"One word."

"Then 'courageous,' " Stecker said.

General Harris wrote that down, then said, "Williams?"

"I'll agree with 'tenacious,' " Major Williams said after a moment's thought.

"Griffith?"

"Fanatical," Lieutenant Colonel Griffith said.

"Red?"

"I was going to say 'fanatical,' " Edson said.

"Say something else, anything but 'zealous,' " Harris said.

"OK. How about 'suicidal'?" Edson said.

"If that's what you think, fine," Harris said, as he wrote it down.

"Just out of idle curiosity, why couldn't I have said 'zealous'?"

"Because that's my word," Harris said.

" 'Zealous'?" Edson asked incredulously. "As in 'He was zealous in his pursuit of the busty virgin'?"

"The word comes from *zealot*," Harris explained. "They were a band of Jews in biblical times who jumped off a mountain rather than surrender—after a hell of a fight—to the Romans."

"I wonder how well versed General Vandergrift is in biblical lore?" Edson replied dryly.

"They're not really small, bucktoothed people needing thick glasses, that we can whip with one hand tied behind us, are they?" Major Stecker asked softly.

"It doesn't look that way does it, Jack?" Harris replied, then added, "But so far things seem to be going pretty well on Guadalcanal."

"I've been on the radio to the 5th Marines," Stecker said. "That's not the case. So far, all we have is a beach. We're about to lose the equipment that's still aboard the transports, including rations and ammunition; and we're going to lose the Marines that are there, too. The Japanese have not yet counterattacked. They will, and I think they will in force. If not today or tomorrow, then soon. They want that airfield as much as we do, maybe more. And they're in a much better position to reinforce than we are. That's going to be a long and bloody fight, and I wouldn't give odds who's ultimately going to win it."

"Jesus Christ, Jack," Griffith protested. "When I was in England I heard the Germans shoot their officers out of hand for talking like that. They call it 'defeatism.' You're a goddamned Marine. I don't like hearing something like that from a Marine."

"That's enough, Sam!" General Harris flared. "I think Jack put the situation very succinctly." He raised his voice, "Sergeant Major!"

When the Sergeant Major appeared at the door, General Harris said, "Find some wheels to drive Major Stecker to the beach. I don't want him having an accident on his motorcycle between here and there."

(SEVEN)

Eyes Only—The Secretary of the Navy

   DUPLICATION FORBIDDEN
   ORIGINAL TO BE DESTROYED AFTER ENCRYPTION AND TRANSMITTAL
TO SECNAVY

Aboard USS McCawley
Off Guadalcanal
1430 Hours 9 August 1942

Dear Frank:

   This is written rather in haste; and it will be brief because I know of the volume of radio traffic that's being sent, most of it unnecessarily.
   As far as I am concerned, the battle of Guadalcanal began on 31 July, when the first Army Air Corps B-17 raid was conducted. They have bombed steadily for a week. I mention this because I suspect the Navy might forget the bombing in their reports. They were MacA.'s B-17s, and he supplied them willingly. That might be forgotten, too.
   The same day, 31 July, the Amphibious Force left Koro in the Fijis, after the rehearsal. On 2 August, the long-awaited and desperately needed Marine Observation Squadron (VMO-251, sixteen F4F3 photo-recon versions of the Wildcat) landed on the new airbase at Espiritu Santo. Without the required wing tanks. They are essentially useless until they get wing tanks. A head should roll over that one.

TOP SECRET

The day before yesterday, Friday, 7 Aug., the invasion began. The Amphibious Force was off Savo Island on schedule at 0200.

The 1st Marine Raider Bn under Lt. Col. Red Mike Edson landed on Tulagi and have done well.

The 1st Parachute Bn (fighting as infantrymen) landed on Gavutu, a tiny island two miles away. So far they have been decimated and will almost certainly suffer worse losses than this before it's over for them.

The 1st and 3rd Bns, 5th Marines, landed on the northern coast of Guadalcanal, west of Lunga Point, to not very much initial resistance. They were attacked at half past eleven by Japanese bombers from Rabaul, twenty-five to thirty twin-engine ones.

I can't really tell you what happened the first afternoon and through the first night, except to say the Marines were on the beach and more were landing.

Just before eleven in the morning yesterday (8 Aug.), we were alerted (by the Coastwatcher on Buka, where Banning sent the radio) to a 45-bomber force launched from Kavieng, New Ireland (across the channel from Rabaul). They arrived just before noon and caused some damage. Our carriers of course sent fighters aloft to attack them, and some of our fighters were shot down.

At six o'clock last night, Admiral Fletcher radioed Ghormley that he had lost 21 of 99 planes, was low on fuel, and wants to leave.

I am so angry I don't dare write what I would like to write. Let me say that in my humble opinion the Admiral's estimates of his losses are overgenerous, and his estimates of his fuel supply rather miserly.

Ghormley, not knowing of this departure from the facts, gave him the necessary permission. General Vandergrift came aboard the McCawley a little before midnight last night and was informed by Admiral Fletcher that the Navy is turning chicken and pulling out.

This is before—I want you to understand, in case this

becomes a bit obfuscated in the official Navy reports—before we took such a whipping this morning at Savo Island. As I understand it, we lost two U.S. cruisers (Vincennes and Quincy) within an hour, and the Australian cruiser Canberra was set on fire. The Astoria was sunk about two hours ago, just after noon.

In thirty minutes, most of the invasion fleet is pulling out. Ten transports, four destroyers, and a cruiser are going to run first, and what's left will be gone by 1830.

The ships are taking with them rations, food, ammunition, and Marines desperately needed on the beach at Guadalcanal. There is no telling what the Marines will use to fight with. And there's not even a promise from Fletcher about a date when he will feel safe to resupply the Marines. If the decision to return is left up to Admiral Fletcher, I suppose that we can expect resupply by sometime in 1945 or 1950.

I say "we" because I find it impossible to sail off into the sunset on a Navy ship, leaving Marines stranded on the beach.

I remember what I said to you about the admirals when we first met. I was right, Frank.

Best Personal Regards,
Fleming Pickering, Captain, USNR

(EIGHT)

HEADQUARTERS, 1ST
U.S. MARINE DIVISION
GUADALCANAL, SOLOMON ISLANDS
1705 HOURS 9 AUGUST 1942

"I don't believe I know you, Colonel, do I?" Major General A. M. Vandergrift, Commanding, said to the tall man in Marine utilities with silver eagles pinned to his collar. The Colonel was sitting on a sandbag in the command post.

"No, Sir," the man said, rising to his feet and coming to attention. "I don't have the privilege. And it's 'Captain,' Sir. I borrowed the utilities."

"Are you waiting to see me, Captain?"

"I'd hoped to, Sir. I'd hoped to make myself useful somehow."

"You have about fifteen minutes to get to the beach in time to board your ship before they pull out, Captain."

"With your permission, Sir, I'm staying."

"We don't really need the services of a Naval captain right now, Captain, but I appreciate the thought."

"How about those of a Marine corporal, Sir?"

"What?"

"Once a Marine, always a Marine, Sir. I served in France."

"Oh, now I know who you are. You're Jack NMI Stecker's friend, right? Pickleberry? Something like that. Frank Knox's spy?"

"Pickering, Sir," he corrected.

"Isn't Admiral Fletcher going to wonder why you're not on the *McCawley?*"

"Fuck Admiral Fletcher, General."

Vandergrift flashed him an icy look.

"My hearing goes out from to time, Captain," he said. "I didn't hear that. But I rather liked the sound of it." He raised his voice. "Sergeant Major!"

That luminary appeared at just about the same moment that Major Jack NMI Stecker came into the command post.

"Get Captain Pickering some sort of a weapon," Vandergrift said. "And then take him down to Colonel Goettge."

"Get him an '03, Sergeant Major," Major Stecker said.

The Sergeant Major, who had been told that a Navy captain was outside waiting to see General Vandergrift, looked at this senior Naval personage and then back at Major Stecker, whom he knew and admired, and asked, dubiously, "A *rifle*, Sir?"

"It's all right, Sergeant Major. Captain Pickering is a Marine; he knows what a rifle is for," Major Stecker said.

"You heard the Major, Sergeant Major," General Vandergrift said. "Get him a Springfield."

"Aye, aye, Sir."